# DAUGHTER
## OF DUSK

*Also by Livia Blackburne*
Midnight Thief

# DAUGHTER OF DUSK

LIVIA BLACKBURNE

HYPERION
LOS ANGELES   NEW YORK

All rights reserved. Published by Hyperion, an imprint of Disney Book
Group. No part of this book may be reproduced or transmitted in any
form or by any means, electronic or mechanical, including photocopying,
recording, or by any information storage and retrieval system, without
written permission from the publisher. For information address Hyperion,
125 West End Avenue, New York, New York 10023.

First Edition, August 2015
10 9 8 7 6 5 4 3 2 1
G475-5664-5-15135
Printed in the United States of America

Library of Congress Cataloging-in-Publication Data
Blackburne, Livia.
    Daughter of dusk / Livia Blackburne.—First edition.
        pages cm
    Sequel to: Midnight thief.
    Summary: "As tensions rise within Forge's Council, and vicious Demon
Rider attacks continue in surrounding villages, Kyra knows she must
do something to save her city. But she walks a dangerous line between
opposing armies: will she be able to use her link to the Demon Riders for
good, or will her Makvani blood prove to be deadly? Kyra and Tristam
face their biggest battle yet as they grapple with changing allegiances,
shocking deceit, and vengeful opponents"—Provided by publisher.
    ISBN 978-1-4847-2208-4 (hardback)—ISBN 1-4847-2208-6
    [1. Fantasy.   2. Identity—Fiction.   3. Love—Fiction.]   I. Title.
    PZ7.B532235Dau 2015
    [Fic]—dc23                                    2015006755

Reinforced binding

Visit www.hyperionteens.com

SUSTAINABLE   Certified Sourcing
FORESTRY
INITIATIVE     www.sfiprogram.org
               SFI-00993

THIS LABEL APPLIES TO TEXT STOCK

To my favorite astronomer and literary snob

The snow was a problem, the way it crunched beneath Kyra's shoes and bore marks of her passing. Though her Makvani blood made her light-footed, it wasn't enough to keep her from leaving a trail of footprints between the trees. The previous four times Kyra had come into the forest, she'd told herself it would be her last. If she were wise, she'd stay away. But apparently, she wasn't wise, not where her past was concerned.

The moon was almost full tonight. Its light passed through the leafless canopy, making the ground shine silver. Though the snow muffled the forest's sounds, there was still plenty to be heard. Wind blew through the trees. Occasionally an owl hooted. A shadow moved nearby, and Kyra trained her eyes on it, focusing on the shades of darkness that teased themselves apart if she looked hard enough. She sampled the odors of bark, new snow, and frozen leaves, and she listened. There was the snuffling of a raccoon, a scratching of tiny paws. Her Makvani blood sharpened her senses, and her brief time with the clan had taught her to use them to their fullest. It had been exhilarating to see the world like this, and Kyra had reveled in these new discoveries.

But they were no longer enough.

Even now, as she stood awash in the forest's sights, sounds, and smells, Kyra was thinking about something else. *A crisp fall morning. A circle of witnesses. Her life hanging in the balance.* She'd been a captive of the Makvani, fighting the assassin James in Challenge, and he'd beaten her. He'd had her at his mercy, and she'd been sure she was going to die.

But then she'd changed. Kyra could feel it still, the warmth that started in her core and expanded out until her body melted and her bones stretched into the frame of a giant wildcat. The world had come to her in stark clarity—sights, sounds, and smells overwhelming her with their strength.

And with it had come the bloodlust. Kyra shrank back from that detail, but it was there, as clear in her mind as the taste of the forest on her tongue. She'd wanted nothing more than to tear James limb from limb, to savage his body beyond recognition. Though Kyra had resisted the urge, the memory stayed with her, as did her horror at what she might have done. She'd sworn she would never take her cat form again.

And yet, here she was, back in the forest. Still in her skin but teetering on the edge, far too tempted for her own good.

Kyra placed her hand on a nearby tree. Its rough bark felt solid enough to keep her from being swept away. Kyra closed her eyes and sent her senses inward, daring herself to find the spark that would bring out her other form. But what would happen afterward? How long would she remain in her fur? What atrocities would she commit before she turned back?

2

She opened her eyes and stopped reaching. Maybe someday she would go through with it, but not tonight. Kyra glanced up at the constellations and noted the time, a habit formed years ago from her early days as a thief. She suspected she'd be checking the sky for the rest of her life.

That was when she heard something move, something that didn't have the small scurrying steps of prey. Though the footsteps weren't loud, she could sense a bulk to them—a difference in the feel of the ground and the way the air moved. A bear would have that kind of weight, but it would be louder. That left one other possibility....

Kyra backed against a tree, her heartbeat suddenly twice as fast as before. If it really was a demon cat coming toward her, climbing the tree would do her no good. She balanced her weight on the balls of her feet, muscles taut, as the beast came into view. Sleek muscle, long tail, pointed ears—a wildcat the size of a horse. Kyra didn't recognize this particular demon cat. Its eyes fixed on her, and its tail swished dangerously. There was no friendliness in its gaze. Kyra hadn't exactly left the Makvani on good terms.

"I mean no harm," Kyra said. "I don't come on Palace business." Her voice quavered. As if the beast would believe her. As if the beast would care.

It continued advancing, and though it would do no good, Kyra turned to run. The forest had gone silent around her, and all she could hear were her own quick breaths and the crunch of snow underfoot. She managed a few steps before powerful paws knocked her down. Kyra skidded along the ground. Icy snow spilled into her sleeves and melted against her skin. Kyra rolled onto her side and scrambled for the knife in her boot, only to drop it as the beast knocked her again to the ground. Hot breath bore down on her, and Kyra crossed her arms in front of her face to ward off teeth and claws. Could she change now? The beast gave her no quarter, not even a chance to breathe.

There was a roar. A creature—another demon cat—collided with the beast on top of her. The two cats tumbled along the ground, growling and snapping, a blur that was impossible to follow. Kyra had only just made sense of the scene when the two cats broke apart and faced each other. The second cat let out a low growl. After a long moment, the first beast turned and retreated into the forest, leaving Kyra alone with her rescuer.

Kyra's heart still beat wildly in her chest, and she couldn't quite believe that the threat was gone. She didn't recognize this new beast. She'd hoped it was Pashla, the clanswoman who had been her advocate during her time with the Makvani, but this tawny-yellow creature was much bigger, with muscular shoulders and haunches that were formidable even for a demon cat. As Kyra climbed to her feet, the beast's shape began to blur. A moment later, Leyus stood before her. Leyus, the leader of the Makvani, who had only grudgingly spared her life the last time she'd seen him. In his human form, Leyus was tall with long hair that matched the tawny yellow of his fur, and the same muscular shoulders he carried as a beast. Kyra kept her eyes on his face because, like all Makvani who had just changed into his skin, he was naked.

"You tread a dangerous line, coming back to this forest," said Leyus. He turned to leave without waiting for a response.

Kyra stood dumbfounded. "Thank you," she called.

Leyus looked over his shoulder. "You have chosen your loyalties," he said without stopping. "Do not expect to be safe out here. If you come into our territory, you alone bear the risks and the consequences."

And then he was gone.

Kyra's younger friends Idalee and Lettie were sound asleep by the time she returned to the small room the three of them rented from a wealthy jeweler's widow. The two sisters lay curled together on the straw pallet they all shared. Idalee's dark hair was spread wild around her on the pillow, while Lettie had burrowed completely under the covers and was only visible as a small mound at her sister's back. They didn't stir when Kyra climbed in next to them.

Though the bedding was blissfully warm compared to the icy forest, Kyra stayed awake long after she lay down, staring into the darkness as the attack and rescue played in her mind. It was a foolish thing, going back into the forest time after time with no reason. The Demon Riders had made it very clear that she was no longer welcome in their midst, and Leyus could very well have let her die. Kyra didn't know if it was residual gratitude for saving his clan, a desire to avoid trouble with the Palace, or Kyra's own mixed blood that had led Leyus to intervene, but she wasn't naïve enough to expect her good fortune to hold if she continued going. Trouble was, she couldn't seem to stay away.

She'd spent her entire life wondering who her parents were and where she'd come from. Just as she'd learned more about her history, however horrifying it was, it had been taken away from her. The draw of her past was strong, as was that tantalizing memory of those few moments she'd had in her second form.

But maybe there was a better way to go after her past—one that wouldn't get her killed. Pashla had once mentioned that Far Ranger trade caravans had long memories and might be able to give Kyra clues about her origins. Perhaps it was time to seek them out.

*She was running through the forest on four legs, dodging trees and leaping over rocks. It was a joy to use her limbs this way, to stretch her back legs behind her and reach with her front paws for the next push. The trees were a blur around her, and she ran until she arrived, breathless, in front of Forge's walls. Kyra sat back on her haunches, tongue lolling, but something wasn't right. The walls were lined with Red Shields, and even as she climbed back to her feet, they streamed down from the walls and surrounded her. The last man to close the circle was Malikel, stern in his official's robes and looking much taller than Kyra remembered.*

*"It brings me no joy to do this," he said, "but you're a threat to the city. We can't let you live."*

*Kyra's fur stood on end, and she arched her back as the Red Shields raised sharp spears and pointed them toward her in silent unison. A growl stirred in her throat. If this was how it would be, then she would go down fighting....*

"Kyra, wake up."

Kyra's eyes flew open and she reached under her pillow for

her dagger. She'd drawn the blade and was pushing herself to her feet when she finally regained her bearings. It was morning. She'd been dreaming.

The single room she shared with Idalee and Lettie was still. The muted noises of the street one story below filtered in through the window. The girls were nowhere to be seen, but her good friend Flick sat at the table across the room, looking as carefree as ever with his feet propped up on the table and his brown curls slightly mussed atop his head.

Kyra sank back into the bedding. "Fiery cities, Flick. Are you trying to scare me to death?" Flick lived with friends several streets away, but he spent so much time here that he might as well have been a fourth resident, especially since he'd stopped courting the wool merchant's daughter.

"What was it this time? Assassins? Demon cats? Old ladies wielding poisoned knitting needles?"

She sheathed her dagger and threw it at her pillow. "Red Shields. Malikel."

"Ah." Flick dipped a chunk of bread into a tumbler of watered wine and stared at it pensively before popping it into his mouth. "Hunting you down because they learned what you were?"

"Aye."

"At this rate, you're likely to worry yourself to death before they find out."

Given the way her heart was beating wild rhythms in her rib cage, Kyra couldn't argue with his reasoning. But neither could she stop worrying.

When the Demon Riders first started raiding farms around

Forge, everyone had assumed that the enormous wildcats they rode were simply well-trained pets. It was only after the barbarians captured Kyra that she learned they were shape-shifters, the mythical felbeasts of legend. Kyra told the Palace upon her return, but she'd kept one detail to herself: that she shared their shape-shifter blood.

Only five humans knew Kyra's secret. Tristam and James had seen her change shape in the forest, and Kyra had told her adopted family—Flick, Idalee, and Lettie—after she returned to Forge. While Tristam and her family could be counted on to keep her secret, James most definitely could not. After Kyra captured James and turned him over to the Palace, she'd gone to sleep every night expecting to be woken by soldiers at her door. But it hadn't yet happened, and though it was the best possible outcome, Kyra couldn't shake the feeling that something wasn't right.

"If you want, we could still go to Edlan. Play it safe," said Flick.

She rubbed the back of her neck. Flick's offer was generous, but he didn't really want to leave Forge. None of them did—Forge was all they'd ever known. "I don't know. Mayhap if I can earn Malikel's trust, he won't think me a threat to the city when he finally finds out."

Flick gave a noncommittal shrug. "I didn't wake you up just to get you out of that nightmare. Tristam's waiting for you outside."

"Tristam?" It was only then that Kyra noticed the angle of light coming in the room's small window. She'd slept past noon. "We're to report to duty today. I've found a member of

9

the Assassins Guild." She threw a tunic over the shift and trousers she'd slept in, splashed her face at the washbasin by the door, then grabbed a hairbrush and tugged at her hair until she could tie it back with a leather thong. She tried a few times to smooth down the wrinkles in her tunic, but they just popped back up.

Flick tipped backward in his chair, eyeing her with amusement. "Why don't you go to such efforts to look presentable for *us*?"

Kyra gave up on the wrinkles. "All right if I let him in?"

"Fine by me. *My* hair's been combed all morning."

The door to their quarters opened into a plain wooden corridor that ended in a narrow staircase. When Kyra came out, she found Tristam at the top of the stairs, his tall form bent slightly as he peered over the low railing. She walked quietly up behind him and placed a hand on his back.

"Looking at anything interesting?"

His muscles tensed under her hand, and he whipped around, reaching for the dagger at his waist. But then his eyes landed on her, and his face relaxed into an embarrassed smile.

A warmth spread around her ribs as she looked up at him and returned his grin. He must have just washed this morning, because she could smell the soap on him, layered over the familiar scent of his skin.

"Latrine duty for you," she admonished. It was an old joke between them, a remark he'd made the first time she'd snuck up on him. "I'm sorry to keep you waiting."

"Late night?" asked Tristam. He straightened to his full height, and Kyra craned her neck to keep eye contact.

"Aye." She was thankful when Tristam didn't ask where she'd been. He was dressed in Palace livery—not that of a knight, Kyra noticed again with a pang, but the plainer tunic of a Red Shield, with an embroidered *F* on the left breast, over plain black breeches. He'd been stripped of his knighthood for a year because he'd rescued Kyra from the Demon Riders against direct orders from the Council. While Tristam had never complained about his punishment, Kyra couldn't help wondering if he regretted his decision. Though she noticed he wore this livery well. He held himself like a soldier, and his movements were precise and confident.

They returned to the room. Flick gave Tristam a sideways glance then and grunted a half greeting, not bothering to take his feet off the table. Flick was the illegitimate son of a minor nobleman and had decided long ago that wallhuggers could not be trusted. Kyra glared at him, but he'd already turned his attention back to his breakfast.

"Let me fetch my daggers," said Kyra. "And then I'll be ready to go."

She'd picked up the one on her bed and was rummaging through her chest for others when the door opened and Lettie stepped in, followed by Idalee carrying a basket of bread. The two sisters were bundled against the cold with matching wool dresses, scarves wrapped around their hair, and warm boots. Months of shelter and good food seemed to be paying off. Lettie now stood as high as Kyra's waist, and Idalee's dress was stretching tight around her chest and hips. The girl hadn't even started her monthly blood and she already had more curves than Kyra. They'd have to get her cloth to make a new dress soon.

Both girls stopped short when they saw Tristam.

"Ho, Tristam," said Lettie, breaking into a dimpled grin.

Tristam bowed. "Hello, Lady Lettie."

Lettie giggled, her dark brown curls bouncing beneath her headscarf.

Idalee gave Tristam a halfhearted curtsy and took her basket to the hearth without saying a word. Then she turned her back to the room, removed a loaf from the basket, and started vigorously brushing it off.

Kyra frowned and walked closer. "What are you doing?" She'd always had problems with Flick and Tristam getting along, but this was the first time she'd seen rudeness from Idalee.

"Nothing," Idalee said. A strand of black hair stuck to her forehead as she bent protectively over the bread. The girl was standing so close to the fireplace that her skirt almost brushed the embers.

Kyra saw now that Idalee's bread was covered with dirt. "What happened?" She put her hand on Idalee's shoulder, but the girl shook it off.

"I dropped the basket," said Idalee.

Kyra and Flick exchanged a worried glance over Idalee's head. Flick turned to Lettie. "Is that what truly happened?" he asked.

Lettie had climbed up onto one of the chairs. "A fatpurse pushed me in the market," she said, cringing at Idalee's warning glance. "Idalee yelled at him, and he knocked the basket out of her hand."

Kyra looked to Flick in alarm. His mouth tightened in a grim line, and he shook his head. Idalee had always been fiercely protective of her sister.

"Lettie, did the fatpurse hurt you?" said Flick. He used the low, steady tone he always did when trying to stay calm.

Lettie shook her head, and Flick looked her up and down, silently verifying her answer. Then he leaned against the fireplace mantel so Idalee would have to look at him, even if it was only out of the corner of her eye. "You're lucky it was only the bread that came to harm," he said.

Idalee put down one clean loaf and picked up the next. "It in't fair," she said to the bread.

Of course it wasn't fair. Kyra's own pulse was rising at the thought of any wallhuggers laying hands on either Idalee or Lettie. But acknowledging the injustice wouldn't keep Idalee safe the next time some nobleman offended her. "Idalee, you can't go testing your luck with the wallhuggers," she said. "If they do something you don't like, you walk away. They're dangerous and unpredictable."

The words had barely left her mouth when Kyra remembered that Tristam was standing quietly at the edge of the room. She shot a mortified glance in his direction. "I mean, not all—"

"No offense taken," Tristam said before she could finish. He pushed away from the wall, his gaze keen. "Idalee, do you know the name of the man who pushed Lettie?"

Idalee finally stopped attacking the bread, and her eyes were slightly hopeful when she raised them to Tristam. "No. Could you do something, if I did?"

"There are no laws against pushing, I'm afraid," he said gently. "But I would have liked to know." He glanced out the window. "It's about time we go. Kyra, are you ready?"

"Almost." Kyra ran back to her trunk and finally fished out her daggers. "Everything all right over here?" she asked as she tucked them into her boots.

"We'll be fine," said Flick.

She supposed they would have to be. "Take care, then," she said, and followed Tristam out the door.

Forge was laid out in rough concentric circles with the Palace at its center. The nobility lived in the ring just outside the Palace wall, hence their nickname "wallhuggers." Wealthy merchants, including Kyra's new landlady, lived in the ring outside that. As Kyra and Tristam set out from her quarters, they headed farther away from the Palace, toward the beggars' circle.

Kyra tried again to apologize for her comment about dangerous wallhuggers, but Tristam waved her words aside.

"It just means that you're comfortable enough around me to speak freely. I'm glad of it."

He'd thrown a cloak over his livery to disguise his affiliation with the Palace, and the two of them strolled down the street like any other couple. A silk vendor waved a gold scarf to get Kyra's attention. "It will bring out the warm tones of your skin, lovely lady." When she ignored him, the silk vendor turned his efforts to Tristam. "Young Lord, get your lady a scarf to match her beauty."

Kyra chuckled. The merchant's honeyed words would have

been more convincing if he hadn't said the same thing to every other person walking down the street.

The silk merchant's voice echoed after them. "You're a feisty pair of young lovers. I can tell that you adore each other."

Kyra's laugh trailed off, and she took an involuntary glance at Tristam. The street vendor's words rattled in her mind. Feisty? She supposed she'd been called that before. Young? That was certainly true. But lovers?

Six weeks ago, after they'd been released by the Makvani, the two of them had shared a kiss. It didn't take much effort at all to conjure the memory of his arms around her that night, or the tingle on her skin as they'd leaned their faces close. But that had been one moment in the forest, when they didn't know what the future held. Now they were back in the city, and things felt less clear. Tristam was the son of a noble house, and she was a pardoned criminal. How could a stolen kiss in the forest stand against that? After weeks of working together under Malikel, they were comfortable with each other, even flirted on occasion. But things remained . . . uncertain.

As they continued walking, the lively trappings of the merchant circle gave way to the blackened walls of the fire-burned district, the part of the city that had been destroyed in the Demon Rider raid orchestrated by James. The streets were lined with charred frames. A few of the ruins had been torn down, and some of the poor had set up tents and lean-tos in the burnt-out buildings. The air still smelled faintly of charcoal, and though the ash was gone, Kyra couldn't shake the impression that breathing too deeply would clog her nose with blackened dust.

"It doesn't look much different from before, does it?" said Kyra. "There's been some rebuilding near the merchant sector, but not down here."

"The landlords are likely waiting for the city to clean it up," said Tristam. "The first person to rebuild has to also clean the wells and unclog the gutters. Nobody wants to do that."

"It would only take a crew of Red Shields a couple weeks to clean everything," said Kyra.

"That sounds about right," said Tristam. Neither mentioned the obvious, that the Council hadn't seen fit to use its soldiers this way.

Their path didn't take them directly by the ruins of The Drunken Dog, for which Kyra was grateful. Her friend Bella, who had been like a mother to her, had died after the fire overtook the tavern, and Kyra didn't want to dwell on the loss today. She sped up her steps as they neared the vicinity of her old home and didn't stop until it was far behind her. Tristam kept pace with her and didn't comment.

Finally, they came to a place where the houses stood intact, though they were still marked by smoke. The beggars along the street became more numerous, and soon Kyra and Tristam neared a corner where she recognized other Palace men. All of them, like Tristam, wore plain cloaks to hide their Palace livery. In addition to Kyra and Tristam, there were three Red Shields and Sir Rollan, a knight new to Malikel's command. He'd been transferred after Malikel dismissed another knight for taking bribes while on gate duty. The Defense Minister was one of the few who actually enforced honesty in his men—most other commanders simply overlooked such infractions.

Rollan nodded a greeting as they approached. He was a big man with messy yellow hair, about ten years older than Tristam. "That's all of us. Kyra, give us an update."

The men gathered around. "Ashley's a low-ranking member of the Guild," said Kyra. "If he keeps his patterns from earlier this week, he should be home. He's a good fighter, so be careful."

It had taken Kyra considerable time to track him down. After the Palace pardoned Kyra's crimes, she'd agreed to help Malikel track down the rest of the Guild and bring them to justice. The first assassin, a taciturn man named Jason, had been easy to capture. But as word of Jason's imprisonment had spread, the rest of the Guild went underground. Kyra found nothing for weeks, until finally she'd run across rumors of Ashley hiding in an old house in the beggars' sector.

"Kyra, scout the house," said Rollan. "Brancel, go help her."

Kyra kept her head low as she and Tristam set off down the street. The streets here were narrow and dirty, with the upper stories hanging over the lower ones and blocking the light. She could sense the handful of loiterers and beggars on the street giving them suspicious looks. The Palace folk stood out here despite their efforts to blend in. Their clothes were too nice, and they carried themselves too straight. Well, it was too late to do anything about that. She quickened her steps and turned into an empty alleyway.

"You'll be climbing up here?" Tristam asked quietly.

Kyra nodded, pleased that Tristam knew her habits well enough to anticipate her movements. "Give me a boost?"

He checked over his shoulder to make sure no one was watching, then joined his hands to form a step for her.

She pushed off him and pulled herself over the edge of the roof. The old wooden shingles felt as if they'd come apart if she bent them hard enough, and she was glad she had gloves to protect her from splinters. "Thank you. You're a decent stepladder."

"You know," came his voice from below, "in some circles I'm known for my combat skills and quick strategic mind."

"And here I thought it was your pretty face," she said under her breath.

Kyra looked down from the roof to find Tristam's mouth quirked in a mischievous smile. "You think so?"

Their gazes met for a moment, and the flutter in Kyra's stomach was not at all convenient for running a mission. She scowled and traced the line of the rooftop with her gaze. "I'm off, then."

This entire street was lined with cheaply constructed boardinghouses, favored by landlords who often rented out each room to a different family. Kyra had to use a soft step and watch her way carefully so she wouldn't tread on any rotten tiles. There was far more creaking and shifting underneath her feet than she would have liked.

The assassin, Ashley, lived in an attic apartment. These rooms had windows that protruded out of the roof under slanted eaves, and Kyra counted them as she climbed over each one, finally stopping at the fifth. Though the shutters were closed, there was a thin gap where they met. When Kyra put her eye to the crack, she could make out a man sitting on the floor, doing some work with his hands. She had only seen Ashley once or twice during her time at the Guild, but it was definitely him.

Her target found, Kyra crept to the very edge of the roof. About ten people walked the streets below. Though they all could have seen Kyra easily in the afternoon sun, Tristam was the only one looking up. His eyes met hers, and then he walked casually away.

Her message delivered, Kyra went back to the window and waited, straining her ears for any sound from within—hard to do because the street noise below was louder. She thought she heard a faint knock—not loud enough to be someone at Ashley's door, though it could have been Rollan's men knocking on the building's main entrance. She risked another peek inside and saw Ashley pause in his work and inch his way toward the door. He held a dagger in his hand. Kyra drew her own blade but stayed put. Her orders were to wait by this window in case he tried to escape.

The door to Ashley's room crashed open and Rollan's men rushed in. The clashing of blades scraped Kyra's ears. A man screamed in pain, and Ashley pushed past the Red Shields out the door as Rollan yelled a command to follow him. Kyra squinted through the crack, trying to see who'd been hurt, but there was too much going on. She jostled the latch. When it wouldn't budge, she stepped back and aimed a kick at the window. The flimsy shutters gave way, and she swung herself into the room.

It was empty. The door was flung open. A Red Shield named Daly sat in the corridor outside while his comrade, a skinny young Red Shield named Fitz, bound a bandage around his thigh. Judging from the amount of blood, the wound looked deep.

"He needs a healer," said Fitz as Kyra came closer. Kyra crouched next to them, relieved that the injured man hadn't been Tristam, then feeling guilty for thinking it. Together, she and Fitz helped Daly to his feet. They had just started hobbling toward the staircase when Tristam and Rollan came running back up.

Rollan shook his head when Kyra caught his eye. "Gone. He went out a trapdoor."

Kyra sagged under Daly's weight. All that time tracking the assassin down, and he was out of reach again.

Rollan's brows knitted together as he took in Daly's condition, and he motioned for Tristam to take Kyra's place. "Back to the Palace. Everyone."

Rollan made the decision to continue hiding their livery as they helped Daly back to the Palace. There was no need to broadcast weakness on the Palace's part. The party did get its share of curious looks as it marched, but nobody stopped the group, and nobody asked any questions. Rollan dismissed Kyra when they reached the Palace gate.

"We'll have to consult with Malikel about the next step," the knight said. "But he'll be busy entertaining the Edlan and Parna delegations for the next week. He may not be ready to deal with the Guild until after they're gone."

As the others entered the Palace, Kyra gratefully headed back home. Idalee was probably cooking dinner by now, and

Kyra wanted to be in a place where she didn't have to hide her frustration. The merchant sector was starting to empty out for the evening. A wide avenue lined with shops had only a handful of people walking through. Kyra had just turned down a smaller street toward home when a wire looped around her neck.

A garrote.

Kyra almost didn't react in time. Another moment of hesitation, and the noose would have closed. As it was, she fell back into her attacker and managed to snake her arm between the wire and her neck so the metal dug into the wool of her tunic instead of the exposed skin of her throat. She ducked and grabbed the knife from her boot with her free hand, twisting around so her blade touched her opponent's stomach just as his grazed her throat.

Bacchus, James's second in command, wore a frightening grin as their eyes met. His wire was still tight around her arm, and his knife held steady at her neck. But he didn't press his attack.

"You've gotten quicker," he said. There was no trace of fear in his expression. Now that James was imprisoned, he was probably the highest-ranking man in the Assassins Guild. Kyra wondered what the Guild had been doing under his leadership.

"Put your blade away, Bacchus. It'd be a pity if we both died tonight," said Kyra. While Bacchus looked calm enough to have been taking an evening walk, every muscle in Kyra's body was taut. Her arm was going numb.

He snorted. "Why don't you withdraw yours?"

"Because my word means something, and yours doesn't," she said through gritted teeth. What would happen if she changed shape now? It had worked with James, but Bacchus could just as easily stab her while she was distracted.

To her surprise, Bacchus laughed and stepped back. He loosened his grip on her arm, and she flung the garrote to the ground. Kyra kept a firm grip on her blade and scanned the street around her. The few people who had been around before had all fled.

"If you're trying to scare me into stopping my work with the Palace, it won't work."

Bacchus spat on the ground. "You snagged one of our lowest-ranking men and failed at snagging another. I in't losing any sleep." Kyra couldn't tell if he was bluffing. "I didn't come to kill you," he added. "I bring a message." Kyra eyed the garrote on the ground, and he shrugged. "James said to leave you alive. He didn't say how alive."

James? Kyra couldn't help looking around. "Where is he?"

"Where you left him," he said. "But he's got a message for you."

"How did he get word to you if he's still in the dungeon?"

The assassin gave Kyra a look that conveyed just how stupid it was for Kyra to expect an answer to that question.

"He tells you to think carefully about what you're doing against the Guild. You think you're helping the city by cooperating with the Palace, but the wallhuggers aren't your friends. They never will be."

The last time Kyra and James had talked at length, he'd warned her that the Palace would betray her. Was he still trying to sway her to his side? Was he confident enough of her capitulation that he would show his hand like this?

"And James claims to be my friend?" she asked.

Bacchus's eyes glittered over his ebony beard. "Trust me, lass. He doesn't want you for a friend. But he wants you to go talk to him when you finally see clearly."

"I've no interest in seeing him," said Kyra. "He's in the dungeon, where he belongs. I won't fall prey to his schemes again."

Bacchus didn't seem surprised by her answer. He spun his blade in his hand and contemplated her thoughtfully. "You still living with the two girls?"

Idalee and Lettie. If he wasn't threatening them outright, he was smugly reminding her of the time James had blackmailed Kyra by threatening her friends. Hot rage ran through her. "I swear, Bacchus," she said. "If you ever so much as hint a threat toward my family again, I will kill James and track you down. You can't keep me out of your hideaways if I want to get to you." It was surprising how easily those words came out.

He laughed at that. "You've changed, lass, and I see I touched a sore spot. Don't worry. Your friends are safe for now. James's message is simply a request. The rest is up to you." He looked her over. "You don't look like one of them demon beasts."

Kyra went cold. James had told Bacchus. Why hadn't he told the Palace?

"Get away from me," Kyra said.

Bacchus gave a mocking bow and walked away.

## THREE

Tristam let out a groan as he eased the helmet off his head. At least it wasn't summer, when the leather trapped the sun's heat in a miasma of oil and sweat. But even in the winter, he hated how the helmet pinched his temples. The icy breeze blew through his damp hair as he stood outside the guard armory after his morning shift, standing in line behind his fellow Red Shields to hang up his gear. Each Red Shield had his own armor and basic uniform, but the overcoat that marked on-duty guards was shared, as were the ceremonial shields and helmet covers.

"I could use a flagon right now," said a man from inside.

"Aye, me too," said another. "Though I've a craving for a good fine wine. My cousin gifted me a bottle last fall, and I still taste it in my dreams."

"You're turning into a right proper fatpurse." The man raised his voice in a snooty imitation of the other. "'I'd prefer me a fine wine.'" He cut off abruptly amidst muttered warnings to hush, and a few men in front of Tristam looked nervously in his direction. He ignored their stares and entered to put away his own equipment.

"Good day, all," he said after he finished, and left. The room remained silent behind him as he walked out the door.

A month in the Red Shield ranks hadn't yet inured him to the scrutiny of his comrades. His fellow Red Shields were too intimidated by his bloodlines to give him trouble outright, but there were constant whispers about "the disgraced knight," and nervous glances when someone forgot his presence and spoke too freely about the Palace's noblemen. Every morning, Tristam breathed a sigh of relief when his daily rounds ended. He rubbed heat into his arms as he made his way back to his quarters.

He'd gone about halfway when someone called his name.

"Brancel!" Tristam turned at the voice. Sir Rollan was coming toward him with long, rolling strides. "Malikel requires everyone's presence in his study."

"Do I have time to get changed?"

"No. He wants everyone now."

Whatever had happened must have been urgent, if everyone was being summoned on such short notice. "What is it?" Tristam asked.

"James managed to send a message out of the dungeon. To Kyra."

"*What?*"

Rollan smiled fiercely. "You're not the first to react this way."

Malikel's study was already filled with people when they

arrived. Tristam spotted Kyra right away, standing next to Malikel's desk and looking unusually subdued. He caught her eye, and she managed a wan smile in greeting. Was she all right? Had James threatened her? The room was too crowded and too quiet for Tristam to get a word with her. In addition to Kyra, there were the twenty knights and Red Shields under Malikel's direct command. The Defense Minister himself paced in front of his desk, his dark eyes cutting through anyone who matched gazes with him. They waited in tense silence for a few more people to arrive. Then Malikel spoke.

"This is unacceptable," he said, his voice hard as granite. "Our holding cells are not summer homes for criminals to lounge in and send missives from at their pleasure. I want the names of every man, woman, child, and dog who has come within a stone's throw of the prison building. And I want them all questioned today."

No one in the study dared respond or even move. After sweeping his gaze one more time around the room, Malikel started dividing the men into groups. "Tristam," he said. "Take Fitz and Cecil, and round up the guards who were on duty two nights ago."

Sir Rollan and another knight exchanged a glance at Malikel's words. Tristam noticed, and stared straight ahead to disguise his annoyance. The other knights under Malikel's command were still trying to figure out what Tristam's demotion really meant. Here, he'd been given command of Red Shields again, a role that should not have fallen to him.

"Is there a problem, gentlemen?" Malikel asked.

"No, sir," said Rollan.

"At your tasks, then," Malikel said. "Make this quick."

Tristam caught Fitz's and Cecil's eyes and led them out the door. He recognized Fitz as the wiry blond Red Shield who had helped the wounded Daly back to the Palace yesterday. Cecil, he didn't know as well.

"Are the two of you willing to take orders from me?" he asked as they left the building.

"Aye," said Cecil. "If Martin thought you were worth following, that's good enough for me." The look Tristam turned on Cecil must have been intimidating because the Red Shield immediately added, "I hope I've not spoken out of turn."

"No...no...of course not," Tristam said, pausing midstride to clear his head. "I just didn't expect you to bring him up." Martin had been a Red Shield and a subordinate, but he and Tristam had genuinely liked each other. He'd gone with Tristam in search of Kyra after she was captured by the Makvani, and he'd died at their hands. Tristam still couldn't quite forgive himself.

"I'm glad you feel that way," said Tristam. "Many think I led him to his death."

"You forget we actually knew Martin," said Fitz. "He wouldn't blindly follow anyone without good reason."

"Thank you." That, at least, was a weight off his chest.

Tristam took a wagon from the Palace stables so they could move about the city faster, and they started down the list of guards. Most of the guards they fetched were alarmed by the summons but came into the cart willingly. When Tristam arrived at the boardinghouse where the fourth guard lived, however, no one answered the door.

Tristam tried knocking again. "Open up. This is official Palace business."

Still silence. Fitz, waiting next to him, gave a nervous shrug. Tristam circled to a side window and peered through a gap in the shutters. It was hard to see much of anything, but something seemed off. He looked around the boardinghouse again. The landlord likely lived in another part of the city entirely, and it would take hours to track him down. Kyra would have been really useful right about now. He made a mental note to ask her to teach him lock picking next time he saw her.

Tristam picked up a large stone and returned to the front door. "Give me a hand, will you?" he asked Fitz.

Fitz's eyes widened, but he helped Tristam support the weight of the stone.

"On the count of three," said Tristam. "One, two . . ."

They swung the rock, and the latch gave way with a crash. The door opened, and Fitz whistled.

The living quarters were empty. The bed was in disarray, and several chests along the walls looked like they had been hurriedly emptied. Their lids had been left open, and discarded objects were strewn all around the floor.

"Looks like whoever was here made a quick escape," said Fitz.

The missing guard and his family could not be found anywhere in the city. Based on the testimonies of those who'd last seen them, the entire family had probably fled the night before. Had it been bribery? Blackmail? There was no way to know.

The rest of the guard force made it through questioning without raising suspicions. Though it seemed this man had worked alone, Malikel personally reviewed the prison guard roster to narrow the list to the most loyal and least vulnerable to persuasion.

Much later that day, Malikel summoned Tristam to his study. The Defense Minister's door was closed when Tristam arrived, so he waited in the corridor. After a while, Kyra stepped out, her jaw set and her eyes flinty. Tristam stepped back, surprised at her demeanor, and she walked past him without a word.

"Tristam, come in," came Malikel's voice.

Tristam threw one last concerned glance in Kyra's direction before stepping inside. The Defense Minister was seated at his desk. Now that the mystery of James's message had been partially solved, Malikel's gaze no longer carried the same murderous intensity. Tristam sat cautiously in a chair opposite him.

"I just informed Kyra that the Council has forbidden her from entering the prison or having any contact with James," said Malikel.

That would explain her ire. A command like this from the Council was an empty one and only served to underscore their mistrust. If Kyra wanted to see James, she'd find a way. Did the Council really think they could control her like this, or did they simply feel better having delivered a command?

"I tell you this because you wouldn't otherwise be able to concentrate on anything I say. But I didn't summon you to discuss Kyra," said Malikel. Tristam shifted in his chair, chagrined at being so transparent. "I realized today that it's time I speak with you about your future. I'm afraid I've not been the best mentor to you in the time you've spent under my command."

Tristam started to object, but Malikel raised his hand to stop him.

"I come from a different background than the rest of the Council members, and I sometimes make decisions that make me unpopular amongst certain of my colleagues."

That was an understatement. Malikel's rise to power was the stuff of legend. The idea of a mercenary from the southern kingdom of Minadel becoming Defense Minister of Forge would have been unthinkable thirty years ago. But a series of heroic acts—most notably, saving the life of the former Defense Minister in a skirmish—had moved him into positions of command. And from there, Malikel had flouted tradition and followed his own judgment on everything from the way he trained his troops to the way he structured their hierarchy underneath him. There had been disapproving glances and clucking of tongues for the entirety of his career, but no one could deny that Malikel was very, very good at what he did. And eventually, that had been enough. Tristam knew all this by heart, but what did it have to do with him?

Malikel's eyes crinkled, as if he could read the thoughts going through Tristam's mind. "Going against convention, disapproval from the court—these are waves I'm willing to make. But in a sense, the consequences for me are not severe. When I made my entry into court, I had very little social capital to risk. Being from Minadel, I had no family to which I was responsible." Malikel spoke matter-of-factly, and nothing in his manner invited pity. "That's not the case, however, with you."

"Sir?"

"I worry I've been a bad influence on you. You've already been demoted once. And though it's a temporary censure, that kind of mark will affect both your future and that of your family's."

"I don't regret any of the decisions I've made," said Tristam. Actually, it was more complicated than that. His entire attempt to rescue Kyra had been a disaster. Martin had died, and it turned out that Kyra hadn't actually needed rescuing. So in that sense, he had many regrets. But given what he'd known at the time, going after Kyra had been the right thing to do. The disgrace that he suffered now at the hands of his peers was a small price to pay.

"And that's admirable," said Malikel. "Just be aware of the choices you make, and make your decisions with your eyes open. It would be remiss of me as your commander not to mention it."

"Thank you, sir." Tristam didn't quite know what else to say.

"You will be at the diplomatic ball tomorrow night, correct?" said Malikel.

"Yes, sir." Every three years, the leaders of the three cities gathered for a summit that started with a diplomatic ball. All under Malikel's direct command were required to attend.

"Good. Take some time with Kyra there. She'll need some help learning the protocols of court. And think on what I've said. It's a lot to process but ultimately not something you can afford to ignore."

Tristam struggled to unravel his thoughts as he made his way out the door. Malikel's advice unsettled him. He might have expected such words from Willem or one of the more active members of court, but Malikel, he couldn't dismiss so readily. He looked down at his livery, contemplating the *F* that marked his rank. Somehow, he had the feeling that things weren't going to get any simpler.

FOUR

Flick had an excruciatingly loud wolf whistle. Kyra heard it often enough when he flirted with his favorite serving girls, but until this evening, she had never appreciated just how obnoxious it could be. That was probably because, until tonight, he had never directed it at her.

She scowled again, squinting at her reflection as she angled the bottom of a polished copper pot to see her entire body. She wore a gown that Malikel commanded she have made for diplomatic occasions. It was made of soft emerald silk and gathered with a velvet ribbon just below her bust. The same ribbon, a darker shade of green than the fabric, trimmed her sleeves, neckline, and hem. The cost of the dress would have covered her lodging for a month, but it was hard to maintain a proper sense of guilt at the extravagance when the silk fell so lightly around her feet.

Idalee, who had tied Kyra's hair into a simple twist, stood to the side with her arms crossed and a smug grin on her face. She'd recently started washing dishes at a nearby tavern and had clearly picked up some tricks from the more fashionable serving girls. Lettie sat at the table, legs dangling and mouth open in a small O as she stared at Kyra.

And Flick, of course, was whistling.

"Will you stop that?" Kyra said. "You'll annoy the landlady."

"And besides," said Idalee, "Kyra looks too fine tonight to be whistled at."

"That's right," Kyra said. "Another whistle from you and I'll have one of my manservants toss you in the gutter."

Flick snorted. "Watch yourself, lass. I can still hang you upside down by your ankles."

Kyra stifled a giggle. It had been a while since Flick had tried that particular trick, but she imagined he'd be able to if he put his mind to it.

"You do look very pretty, Kyra," piped up Lettie. "I wish I could see the ball."

"Me too," said Flick. "Seems it'd be quite the spectacle."

"You, Flick?" said Idalee. "I thought you wanted nothing to do with the wallhuggers."

Flick shrugged. "Just because I don't like shoveling peacock manure doesn't mean I don't appreciate their plumage."

Her friends might have been intrigued by the ball, but Kyra herself was terrified. Perhaps her friends thought her glamorous, but she knew she wouldn't be able to keep up the act once she went into the ballroom. What did she know about nobles and foreign visitors? The night would end in humiliation. She'd bet money on it.

She slipped on her shoes, velvet as well, and wiggled her toes at their softness. "I just hope I don't get kicked out of the

Palace for some breach of manners," she said, heading out the door.

Kyra dodged the usual assortment of street vendors, servants, and beggars on her way to the Palace. She got a few curious looks, but nobody gave her any trouble. The Palace gate was ornamented with winterberries and candles for the occasion. When the guard challenged her, Kyra reached inside her collar and brought out a medallion that bore Malikel's emblem.

"Malikel's command?" He waved her in.

Kyra fingered the medallion, running her fingers over the coat of arms before letting it drop. She respected Malikel and believed he respected her in return. The rest of the Council though, was another matter altogether. That was clear enough in their hurry to ban her from seeing James or even entering the Palace prison. The Council wanted her as a trained dog, a thief on a leash. They wouldn't say no to her skills, but they were quick to cut her off if they sensed her becoming a threat.

The outer compound looked finer tonight than Kyra had ever seen it. Extra torches and lamps had been brought out to light the pathway, and the gray-white granite walls of the buildings had been scrubbed until they shone. Even the snow, which had started to turn into muddy slush the past few days, had been cleared out and the ground underneath covered with fine rugs. Fire pits had been set up at regular distances so that guests could move about comfortably without heavy cloaks or furs.

A whole host of horses and carriages filled the main courtyard. Porters and servants took bags and led horses away, while foreign dignitaries stood mingling with Forge's nobility. Kyra recognized the Edlan dignitaries by their waxed beards and mustaches. Delicately waxed facial hair was the current fashion in Edlan and the butt of many a joke in Forge and Parna. Many of the Edlan men had women with them, some wearing sturdy travel gowns, others in their evening finery. The Parnans were harder to recognize, but Kyra suspected that many of the unfamiliar wallhugger faces belonged to that contingent.

The entire scene was intimidating. Kyra walked the perimeter of the courtyard, scanning the crowd for people she knew. She saw Malikel, his black, curly hair and beard freshly cropped against his dark brown skin, wearing a maroon tunic and breeches instead of his usual official's robes. The Defense Minister stood talking to a tall, stout man with a well-curled auburn mustache. Close by, Forge's Head Councilman, Willem, held court amongst a whole circle of nobles.

Kyra finally caught sight of Tristam next to one of the carriages, looking very handsome in a midnight-blue tunic and black breeches. He was talking to an older gentleman from Edlan, and his eyes swept over Kyra without seeing her at first. But a moment later, he snapped his gaze abruptly back toward her, a startled expression on his face. She waved a few fingers in greeting. To her surprise, Tristam immediately bowed to his conversational companion and took his leave. Kyra's arms felt awkward at her sides as he crossed the courtyard toward her. Her fingers itched to start fidgeting with her dress, but she forced them still.

When he came close, Tristam reached his arm toward her, palm up. After a moment's confusion, Kyra gave him her hand, and he bowed low, pressing his lips to her skin. It was hard not to shiver at the tingle that went up her arm. Tristam straightened, and his eyes swept over her. "You look beautiful."

She smiled, a pleasant warmth spreading through her chest. Until she'd seen Tristam's reaction, she hadn't admitted to herself that she'd been hoping for one. "You look very nice yourself," she said. "Care to introduce me to all this court fanciness?"

"My pleasure." He offered her an arm. "The crowd is moving to the ballroom. Shall we follow?"

Uniformed servants directed the guests through a massive set of double doors into the Palace's main ballroom. The sparkle of countless candle flames greeted them as they drifted in with the crowd, and Kyra couldn't help but gasp at the sight. The walls and ceilings were lined with mirrors, and they caught the light from crystal chandeliers overhead. The glass also reflected swirls of color from the hall—silk finery, feathered headdresses, rouged lips, and kohl-rimmed eyes. A group of ten musicians played at one end of the dance floor, while tables at the other end of the hall bore mouthwatering displays of delicacies, desserts, and wine. Servants weaved through the crowd, carrying platters that left tantalizing scent trails behind them. Uniformed guards in both Forge red, Edlan blue, and Parnan silver stood at attention along the walls, their stillness even more apparent against the constantly shuffling crowd.

"There's more soldiers here than I expected," said Kyra.

Tristam chuckled. "Well, yes. That's the uncomfortable truth about the three cities. We're not at war, but we're never completely at peace either. Don't let the pomp and ceremony fool you. We come together to 'enhance cooperation between our three peoples.' We'll smile at each other, even help one another as a gesture of goodwill. But behind the honeyed words, we're still trying to get an advantage on the others."

Kyra thought she could sense some of this tension in the careful smiles and polite conversations around her. "What do I need to know about Edlan and Parna?"

Tristam led her to a table, where a bowing servant handed him two glasses of sparkling wine. "Think of our three city-states as three brothers," he said, passing her a glass and lowering his voice. "Forge is the eldest, with a respectable inheritance of rich farmland and plentiful forests. We have the most people, the most fealty from families who live outside the city proper, and access to the best trade routes. Edlan is the second brother, living at the base of the Aerins in a harsher clime. They're a hearty city and a tough people, but they're always feeling second-best."

Kyra wondered if the Edlanese folk would agree with that assessment. "And Parna?"

"Parna is the young upstart who, while the two elder siblings were squabbling, stumbled upon a fortune of his own."

Kyra sipped her wine, savoring the feel of the bubbles against her tongue. "Your comparisons are getting unwieldy, Tristam."

His eyes twinkled. "Fair enough. Parna lies at the fork of the Vera River. She's the smallest and youngest city-state out of the three, but she's also extremely fortunate in her location and resources. The Parnans discovered some lucrative mines about two hundred years ago that have served them well. The river also provides an excellent defense for them, so the Parnan government spends its money on arts and learning instead of large armies. I visited their Palace once. They have poets and bards in residence, philosophers holding court every evening. It's really quite impressive."

"Are the Councils of Edlan and Parna similar to ours?"

"Edlan doesn't have a Council, actually. It's ruled by Duke Symon. He has his advisers, but they have very little power to overrule his decisions, whereas every decision made in Forge has to pass a majority vote. Parna has two Councils: one like ours and another that's chosen by the people every—"

Tristam stopped short as someone clapped him on the shoulder. Kyra turned to see a young nobleman even taller than Tristam, looking them over with a broad smile on his face.

"Enjoying the festivities?" said the newcomer.

Tristam leaned back, eyes wide, before his face also split into a grin. "Henril! I didn't know you would be here." He clasped Henril's arm with his free hand and turned to Kyra. "This is my eldest brother. I've not seen him in two years. Henril, this is Kyra, also under Malikel's command."

*Brother.* Henril had wider shoulders than Tristam, a heavier frame, and lighter hair, but the two men shared the same long face and tall nose. Henril took Kyra's hand and bowed low over it. "A pleasure to meet you, Kyra. Word of your deeds reaches even into the countryside."

Kyra wondered briefly just exactly what those deeds entailed. "Are you the brother who stole sweets from the kitchen and blamed it on Tristam?"

Henril laughed. "I'm wounded you would think such a thing, Lady Kyra. I would never betray my sibling for something as trivial as sweets."

"It's true," said Tristam. "He preferred to steal meat pies."

The two brothers were still grinning at each other, clearly looking forward to catching up. Henril looked friendly enough, but Kyra didn't want to be the one holding back the conversation. "I'm sure you have much to talk about," she said. "I should go check if Malikel needs me for anything."

"Are you sure?" asked Tristam, looking hesitantly between her and Henril.

She gave what she hoped was a reassuring smile. "If I can survive in a forest of demon cats, I'll survive some time by myself in the ballroom. I'll be back soon."

⬭ ⬭ ⬭

Tristam gazed after Kyra's retreating form. He couldn't seem to stop looking at her tonight, and he wondered if she'd noticed him gawking earlier. Compared with the fashionable noblewomen around them, Kyra was underadorned. Her dress had no embroidery, and she wore no jewelry or face paint. But she had a way of bringing elegance to anything she wore. The silk of her dress skimmed her subtle curves and swirled in response to her movements in a way that was simply captivating.

But Henril was here, and Tristam had already let the conversation lag too long. He turned back to his brother. "She's not usually quite so scared. Diplomatic balls aren't exactly her element."

Henril crossed muscled arms over his broad chest. "I can imagine, if all I've heard is true. Did she really try to assassinate Malikel?"

"That she did. I found her on the ledge outside his bedroom

wall. She almost got away." He saw her as she'd been that night, how well she'd faded into the shadows, how impossibly fleet she'd been once she started running.

"I hear you tackled her. Kind of an unfair advantage, I'd say," Henril said.

Tristam laughed at that one. "Don't judge her by her size. She's better with a dagger than I, and I was fighting for my life. I'm glad she's on our side now."

"Is there anything more to that?" asked Henril, his expression carefully neutral. "Other than being on the same side?"

"No. We're comrades-in-arms. Nothing more." Tristam wasn't sure why he'd told that lie, and he despised himself as soon as it came out. Tonight, of all nights, it was clear to him that they were not simply "comrades-in-arms." But he found that he couldn't take the words back either. To answer any other way would have raised questions that Tristam didn't yet know how to answer. Especially since nothing between him and Kyra had actually been said.

Henril tilted his head in a gesture that didn't convey much confidence at all in Tristam's words, and Tristam decided to change the subject. "How have things been at home?"

At this, Henril's expression darkened and he hunched his shoulders as if huddling against a cold wind. "Not good. Demon Rider attacks have been increasing these past few weeks. Father and I have been riding the grounds every day, and we sent for Lorne to return as well."

Lorne was Tristam's second brother. "That bad?" said Tristam.

Henril lifted the sleeve of his tunic to reveal a bandage

around his forearm. "Got that from a demon cat two weeks ago."

Tristam's chest tightened at the sight. Demon Rider attacks on Forge itself had all but stopped since James's capture, but they still happened in the countryside. He'd known this, but it was a very different thing to see his wounded brother in front of him. And here he'd been, enjoying the respite. "It's strange the attacks have increased so much in the countryside, even taking into account that the barbarians avoid the city proper. If things are this bad, perhaps I should return home too."

His brother shook his head. "No, it's good to have someone within earshot of the Council. Father, Lorne, and I can handle the manor for now. Just keep an eye out for messages from us. We might need your help on short notice."

Kyra had no sooner stepped into Malikel's field of vision than the Defense Minister waved her over. "Kyra, we've need of you."

She hesitated. Though she'd told Tristam she was going to see Malikel, Kyra realized now that she hadn't actually meant to follow through. Well, Malikel had seen her. She steeled herself and approached.

Kyra didn't recognize the majority of officials standing around Malikel, and the one face she did recognize, Kyra was not at all happy to see. Head Councilman Willem had no special love for Kyra, and he made no secret of it.

"You already know Councilman Willem," said Malikel.

"This is Duke Symon of Edlan and Lord Alvred, the Edlan defense minister."

Perhaps this was the day for noticing family resemblances, because Kyra was struck by the similarity between Duke Symon's and Willem's features—something about the thin line of their lips and the way their well-trimmed eyebrows angled in on their foreheads. Kyra seemed to remember hearing that the two were distant cousins and that this relation was why Forge had been able to maintain peace with Edlan in recent years. She shifted her gaze to Lord Alvred, whom she now recognized as the large man she'd seen with Malikel earlier. He towered over her, and Kyra imagined that his hefty limbs might have been solid with muscle in his youth. Even now that he had a softer physique, Kyra got the impression he could crush her with very little effort. This was the man who would be Malikel's archenemy should war arise. Kyra wondered how they got along in times of peace.

"Lord Alvred had some questions about the Demon Riders," said Malikel. "They've had a few attacks in Edlan as well."

Alvred leaned over Kyra, absently smoothing down his mustache. "Is it true that they and their cats are the same type of creature?"

That was an easy enough question. "It's true," she said. "I saw them change shape many times."

He raised his eyebrows in keen interest. "And what have you found to be the best way of fighting them?"

"Spears, sir." Military strategy was Tristam's domain, but Kyra had been around long enough to answer at the simplest level. "That and telling folk to stay out of their way. They're usually going for livestock, though they're ruthless if you attack them."

Alvred had a few follow-up questions, and Kyra found she could answer them to his satisfaction. Other officials came to their circle as she spoke, and the air around her grew warmer with the crowd. Apparently, the Demon Riders were high in everybody's interest. As she spoke, Kyra became self-conscious about her lowborn speech. She was tempted to try to match the wallhuggers' smoother consonants and intonation, but she suspected she'd only come across as foolish.

Alvred downed his wine in one swig. "This is all very interesting," he said. "We've not found the Demon Riders to be much of a threat in Edlan. We did have a few attacks, which we fought off. After that, the barbarians have left us alone. Perhaps they've found easier marks elsewhere."

The insult didn't go unnoticed. All eyes went to Malikel, who looked to be suppressing a smile. "I congratulate you, Alvred, on the success of your excellent army."

"It's colder and rockier near Edlan, in't it?" said Kyra. "Mayhap the Demon Riders just prefer warmer weather."

Alvred peered down his nose at her. "And you would presume to know the minds of the barbarians? What kind of training does a girl like you have in warfare?"

Kyra flushed and squared her stance. "No formal learning, sir, but you'll remember I was their prisoner for a month."

Head Councilman Willem cleared his throat. His presence was commanding enough that everyone looked to him, though he didn't start talking until the pretty serving girl attending him had finished refilling his glass. "You raise a good question, Alvred, and one that we at Forge might do well to remember. Kyra *of Forge*"—he emphasized the city name, subtly underscoring Kyra's lack of affiliation with a noble house—"is a former assassin who was convicted of high treason, a member of the very group who first brought the Demon Riders against Forge. Certainly an unconventional choice to ask for counsel when the city's safety is at stake. But Malikel's choice in subordinates has always been unique."

Kyra choked at Willem's words. *Willem* had been the one to recruit Kyra into the Palace service after the pardon. How dare he reframe things now to cast suspicion on Malikel?

She might eventually have found her voice, but Malikel spoke first. "Thank you, Willem," he said mildly. "Kyra is valuable to us precisely because of her history with the Assassins Guild. Her experience with them and as a prisoner of the Demon Riders gives her a perspective that we lack. Any tome on strategy will fall short upon meeting an unfamiliar enemy. Sometimes firsthand experience is the best." He turned to Kyra. "I believe we've heard all we need from you. You are dismissed."

Tristam intercepted her before she could go very far, looping his arm into hers as if they were any one of the elegant couples in the ballroom.

"Don't leave." He spoke conversationally and looked out over the crowd, though there was a layer of compassion in his tone. "If you let him know he's upset you, then he's won. It's all part of the game."

Kyra let him guide her through the revelers, frustrated that he'd read her intentions so easily and wondering how much he'd overheard. "Can we go somewhere quieter at least? I can't stomach much more of this."

"How about here, by the wall?" He guided her to a space far enough from any posted guards to give them a semblance of privacy. "We can watch the dancing."

She nodded gratefully. Kyra started to lean against the mirrored walls but stopped when she saw Tristam standing straight. He gave her a faint smile. "Lean against me. I'm plenty sturdy, and the servants don't have to polish me at the end of the evening."

Kyra had to laugh at that, and she took his offered arm. They made quite a pair, the two of them in their finery, behaving in what must have been an incredibly unsociable way.

"Are you all right?" Tristam asked after a while.

Kyra nodded and found that she was indeed feeling better. "I'm used to Willem's barbs by now."

"Willem shouldn't have spoken like that, undermining our own people to Edlan officials. It's not even a matter of decorum. As Head Councilman, what he did was unacceptable."

"I suppose he just really dislikes me." Kyra tried to make her voice light, but Tristam just shook his head.

"No. Willem is too much of a politician to let his own feuds leak through to his official duties. He had a reason for saying what he did."

"And what was that?"

"I can't know for sure," said Tristam. "But Malikel's been gaining favor in the Council. He's been pushing an initiative against corruption in the Palace, and he's been convincing the other Council members. Perhaps Willem is trying to push back."

Across the room, Willem was enjoying a brief moment of solitude, attended by the same unusually pretty serving girl who'd refilled his cup before. The girl smiled at Willem, tilting her head as she refilled his glass, though it was clear to anyone with eyes in his head that her true function involved more than simply pouring wine. She wore the usual undyed linen dress of Palace serving women, but she'd cut it to a tighter fit, and the collar was much lower than the usual modest cut. The girl had accentuated her already striking features with a hint of kohl and berry stain, and she had the kind of figure that made men stop in the streets. Willem didn't even try to hide his glances at her cleavage as he leaned over to speak in her ear.

"Doesn't he care about word getting back to his wife?" Kyra snapped. She scanned the ballroom. Kyra didn't know what Willem's wife looked like, but she must have been present at such an important event.

It took Tristam a moment to discern whom she was talking about. "From what I hear, his wife has her own line of companions. Theirs was an arranged marriage."

"Is that how it's done with nobles? A marriage for politics' sake and a plaything on the side?" Kyra didn't bother to remove the distaste from her voice. Flick had come from such a union. His father had enjoyed his mistress's company and then abandoned her when illness took her beauty.

Tristam's gaze went to her face and lingered there a moment before he carefully replied, "It's commonly done but it's . . . frowned upon. Many couples do try to make it work. My

47

parents had a political marriage, but they now love and respect each other deeply."

Willem's serving girl sidled up closer to him, and the Head Councilman put a possessive arm around her waist. Kyra turned away. "I can't watch them carrying on like this. How can any serving girl stand to be that close to him? It turns my stomach."

Tristam looked at her in bemusement. "I've never seen you react this strongly to Willem, and he's done some pretty despicable things."

Kyra didn't want to think about why the sight of Willem with his mistress upset her so much. The answer was there. She just didn't like it. "Why's Malikel unmarried?" she asked. "All the other Council members have wives, don't they?"

"You know, I've never considered that. I suppose I always saw Malikel as a solitary entity." Tristam tilted his head thoughtfully. "To be honest, I think it would be difficult for him to find a family open to an alliance with him."

"Because he's Minadan? Even though he's a Council member?"

Tristam hesitated, then gave an uncomfortable nod. "Allowing a foreigner into the workings of one's city is hard enough. Allowing him into one's family…I can't see it happening."

Kyra chewed on his words. She supposed she wasn't all that surprised. Though Malikel had power and influence, he'd never completely lost the aura of an outsider. The children of Forge stared openly at Malikel when he toured the city, and Kyra remembered at least one serving girl new to the Palace who had been afraid to wait on the Defense Minister. In a sense, Malikel's situation was the opposite of hers. He was a good man and dedicated to the city, yet people feared him because of his dark skin and foreign ways. Whereas people who saw Kyra tended to underestimate her, seeing only a young girl of low birth.

"To be honest, Willem had a good point," she said. "I still wonder why Malikel trusts me. I did try to kill him."

"You were ordered to assassinate him," Tristam corrected. "And you didn't carry out that order. Furthermore, you captured James and turned him over to the Palace. That, if anything, should prove you're no longer loyal to him."

James. Kyra shivered as the assassin's face appeared in her mind. He'd changed her life the day he'd walked into The Drunken Dog to hire her. "There was a time when I believed in his cause. He really did think he was fighting for justice."

The problem was, he'd taken the fight further than Kyra had been willing to go. Things had gone sour when Kyra refused to kill innocent bystanders. And though she'd once been his most promising recruit, he'd eventually counted her his enemy.

Tristam spoke again. "And now you're working for the very people you once thought to bring down."

Kyra glanced sideways at him. "Are *you* doubting my loyalties now?"

He gave a faint smile. "Do I think you'll do anything to harm the city? No. Nor would I hesitate to entrust you with my life. But I do wonder sometimes if you regret joining the Palace."

Tristam owed her his life several times over, and she him. So she believed Tristam when he said he trusted her, and she took her time thinking his question over. When Kyra had been in the Assassins Guild, she'd feared that she was slowly becoming something she hated, that the horror of taking someone's life would fade into normalcy. What about now? She was glad she no longer had to follow James's orders, but was the Palace changing her in subtle ways as well?

"You do look lovely, you know." Tristam's words startled her out of her reverie. "I'm so used to seeing you in trousers."

She knew instinctively that he'd changed the subject on purpose, to give her permission not to answer right away. Kyra was grateful. "I prefer trousers. Certainly can't run anywhere in this dress," she said. "But you don't have to stand by the wall with me all night. Feel free to go charm the Edlan ladies."

Tristam pantomimed taking a lady's hand. "Good evening, fair lady. I'm Tristam, recently stripped of my rank. Would you like to dance?"

"They might find the idea of a disgraced knight romantic, if you frame it right."

Tristam nodded slowly in mock consideration. "You might have a point. But I'm too tired for courtly conversation." He paused. "Actually, the reaction to my disgrace has been much more complex than I expected. The richer and more influential families, the ones that used to view me as a promising match— they stay far away from me. But the slightly less respectable houses, their daughters seem to be paying me *more* attention. It's as if they think an alliance with Brancel is now within reach."

*An alliance with Brancel.* Kyra hadn't meant to steer the conversation to Tristam's marital prospects, and she regretted it now. Thankfully, a servant came by just then to offer them some lamb meatballs. Tristam took one, but Kyra declined.

"They'll be at this all night," said Tristam after the servants bore the tray away.

"What?"

He gestured toward the ballroom. Dancers twirled in pairs in front of the musicians, weaving patterns between and around each other that were hypnotizing to watch. "The dancers. It's amazing how they can keep it up for so long. Hours and hours of this, with only champagne and delicately frosted cakes to fuel their exertions."

"It all looks unnecessarily complicated," said Kyra. "How does anyone remember all the steps?"

"I would have thought you'd like dancing."

"Why's that?"

"You're not exactly someone who trips over her feet."

She turned her head to hide a smile. "I do like some dancing." There had been a few dancing girls at The Drunken Dog. Kyra had never bothered to learn what they did, mostly because she hated how the tavern's men leered at them. But once in a while on a festival day, someone would start up a circle dance in the dining room. Kyra had loved those. The steps were simple, and there was plenty of laughing and clapping and cheering. This Palace dancing was completely different though. The elegance of it intimidated Kyra, the feeling that everything had to be done exactly right.

"It looks complicated," said Tristam. "But really, the patterns make sense after a while." He nodded toward the dance floor. "This one, the valsa, you don't even have to learn any patterns—the gentleman chooses the steps and guides the lady through it. They say a good leader should be able to teach his partner to dance without speaking."

"Are you a good leader?" Kyra supposed Tristam must have been trained in these social graces at some point in his upbringing.

A smile touched his lips. "I'm decent."

Before Kyra could react, Tristam moved toward her, ringing her waist with one hand and taking her hand in the other. Without warning, he lifted her onto her toes and pivoted them both around until they stood at the edge of the dance floor. Kyra was speechless for a moment, then, seeing the sparkle in his eye, punched him in the chest.

"I could have stabbed you for that."

"Words, words, words. Don't worry. I'll be sure to catch you if you trip."

Maybe it was the pure absurdity of the situation, but the misgivings that had been weighing Kyra down all night dissipated. Kyra laughed and let him guide her through the steps. He kept them on the edge of the ballroom, out of the crowds. This was a stately dance, with tambour and bells keeping the rhythm as a trio of cornets trumpeted a dignified melody. Though Tristam had downplayed the dance's complexity, Kyra still found it a great challenge to keep up. It was only after the first few repetitions, after she started getting the hang of when she was to twirl and when she was to curtsy, that Kyra became more aware of his hand on her waist, the confident strength with which he led her. The frame of the dance was firm, and their bodies were separated by a good distance. But there was an energy between them, and Kyra wasn't sure whether she wanted to be farther from him or closer.

"I must be making a mess of things," she said.

"Not at all. You're doing great." He spoke calmly, his eyes intent on her face. In the strict confines of the dance, Kyra had no choice but to look back at him. Kyra found her mouth suddenly dry. It was hard sometimes to tell the difference between happiness and dread.

The dance floor was getting more crowded, and though Tristam kept them to the edges, more couples twirled around them. The occasional whiff of perfume wafted by, layered over the mustier backdrop of bodies in motion. Kyra stumbled just slightly when she noticed Tristam's brother Henril looking at them, his brow furrowed. But it was the sight of Willem dancing nearby that brought her to a complete stop. He was partnered with an older Edlan noblewoman, well coiffed and tastefully adorned with a headdress of three peacock feathers, and he paused as well to address them.

"By all means, keep dancing," said Willem. "It's not often done to bring one's mistress onto the dance floor, but given your situation, I'll let it pass." With that, Willem led his partner away.

Kyra stood rooted to the floor. She knew that the Councilman's words shouldn't bother her. Her opinion of him was as low as his opinion of her, but she still found herself flushing hot with shame.

"Kyra," Tristam began.

She shouldn't react to this. It was exactly what would bring Willem satisfaction. But then she noticed Willem's mistress standing on the side, one delicate hand to her throat as she watched them with interest. And Kyra finally admitted to herself why the girl upset her so much. She was a living reminder of a future that could very well be Kyra's, if she allowed things to continue with Tristam.

"I think that's enough for tonight," Kyra said. "This was a mistake." She didn't just mean the dance, and she could see that Tristam understood.

She ran for the ballroom door, and Tristam chased after her. "Kyra, wait. Talk to me, at least."

Perhaps that was one thing to be thankful for. Now that Willem had laid it on the table, Kyra was finally able to say the words. She ducked into a side corridor, where the ballroom's music faded enough to ease her frazzled mind. "Willem is right. I could never be more than a mistress to you."

He drew back as if she'd slapped him. "Is that what you think I'm doing? Using you as a diversion to throw away?"

Kyra started to speak and then stopped. "No. I mean, I don't think you're like—" She'd almost mentioned Flick's father, but that secret wasn't Kyra's to share. "But I know how things work. You're the son of a noble house. You have your duties to your family, and they don't involve anyone like me. Thing is, Willem doesn't even know the whole truth. He thinks I'm just a commoner and a pardoned criminal. He doesn't even know"—she looked around, then lowered her voice—"the rest." That she was a monster, bound by blood to the barbarians who were terrorizing their city.

Tristam opened his mouth again, and she knew from the set of his shoulders that he was going to argue.

"Please, Tristam," she interrupted. "Just be honest with me. You were just talking about the lesser noble houses of Forge as if they were a step down from Brancel. I come from the *gutter*, Tristam. If an alliance with Brancel is a reach for them, how could you think anything possible between you and me?"

His shoulders fell at her words, and regret washed over his features. "I'm sorry. I shouldn't have spoken so flippantly," he said.

Kyra gave a sad smile. "Whether or not you spoke flippantly, you spoke the truth. We both know that."

He fell silent. A few times, his mouth worked as if he were going to say something but decided against it. From the ballroom, a flute started trilling a quick tune over an accompaniment of viols. "So is this it, then? We're just going to be comrades-in-arms?"

Kyra swallowed hard. Part of her had still hoped he would disagree. "It's better to stop this now before anyone gets hurt, in't it?"

He chuckled wryly and looked to the mirrored ceiling. "Of course. Before anyone gets hurt. Shall I escort you back to the ballroom?"

Kyra backed away. "No, I'll leave now. Malikel's got no more need for me this evening."

Tristam studied her expression, his eyes scanning over her

features like so many times before, but this time without his usual warmth. He bowed, his face the perfect mask of courtly politeness. "Have a pleasant evening."

Kyra watched him return to the ballroom. Then she fled, walking as quickly as her dress would allow as the viols and flutes slowly faded into the distance.

## FIVE

It took Idalee and Lettie about five seconds to realize that things at the Palace had gone poorly, and only a few more to understand that Kyra wouldn't be talking about it. They asked questions, and when Kyra refused to answer, the questions changed into significant glances behind her back. This continued for a few days, but after a while, even Kyra had to admit she was being difficult. She couldn't mope over Tristam forever.

She needed a distraction, and once again, the question of her origins came to mind. Now would be a good time to track down her past. Malikel was busy entertaining the foreign guests, and she had the leisure time to find Far Rangers who might know more about the Demon Riders.

Kyra had seen traders around before, though they were an insular bunch. There was a large market not far from the beggars' sector, and it seemed as good a place as any to find one. So when Flick suggested the four of them visit the city's gutter rats with a trip to the market afterward, Kyra agreed.

She should have suspected something when Idalee made a vague exclamation about a street juggler and pulled Lettie to walk ahead. But Kyra was too distracted by her own thoughts and thus was caught unawares when Flick cleared his throat.

"So," he said. "We couldn't help but notice you've been a mite morose lately."

Kyra almost laughed at how easily they'd maneuvered her in. "They decided you're the best person to get me talking?"

Flick flashed his most disarming smile. "I'm the most persuasive."

Kyra kicked a pebble. It rolled forward a few paces and bounced off the skirts of a serving woman in front of her. "Sorry," she mumbled when the woman shot a glare over her shoulder.

Flick tried again. "I've not seen Tristam around since the ball."

Actually, Tristam's absence was nothing out of the ordinary. It wasn't as if the nobleman came by all that often. But as much as she hated to admit it, Flick was right that this *was* about Tristam. She really was predictable. But then, so was Flick.

"It in't what you think, Flick."

"And what's it that I think?"

She threw up her hands. "Tristam's not thrown me aside. I'm not quietly mourning my broken heart."

Both Flick and Kyra stopped to make way for a passing cart. He had the grace to look slightly sheepish as they continued. "You know me well, I'll give you that. But I refuse to believe that there's nothing wrong. You've been acting strange for days."

Kyra glanced in the direction of the Palace. From this distance, she could see the Forge flag, a rearing horse on a red background. Flick was going to keep badgering her until she told him.

"I cut things off with Tristam. Or rather, I stopped anything before it started." It was easiest to get the words out quickly.

"That's . . . a surprise," said Flick after a moment.

"So you've no need to worry," said Kyra. "I know how the world works. I'm not a fool."

"Are you all right?" asked Flick.

"I'll be fine." And she would be. After a few more days.

Flick stuffed his hands into his pockets and cleared his throat, choosing his words carefully. "I've nothing to say against Tristam as far as wallhuggers go. It's just that—"

"I know, Flick," said Kyra. "Can we talk about something else?"

They were getting close to the beggars' sector, and Flick fell silent. Much of this neighborhood had burned down in the recent fire, though some of Kyra's old haunts had survived. The courtyard where Kyra had met Idalee and Lettie was untouched, the same dusty dirt square surrounded by run-down buildings, though it was crowded with more beggars since residents of the burned-out southwest quadrant had moved in. The entire area felt more dangerous these days, but Kyra still spied children climbing out of makeshift lean-tos, preparing themselves for a day of wandering the market. Idalee and Lettie were already talking with a street girl who'd been a friend of theirs.

It was a strange feeling, coming back these days. Kyra used to fret constantly over food and money—those worries had made up the bulk of her early existence. Now her material needs were no issue at all, thanks to the Palace. And though she had no desire to go back to the way things were, she couldn't help feeling a bit of guilt.

One of the boys spotted Kyra and ran to her.

"Ho, Kyra. Ho, Flick." Ollie was a few years older than Idalee and growing a little taller each time Kyra saw him. He'd been on the streets for years now, ever since his parents were thrown in prison for unpaid debts.

"Ollie, where'd you get that hat?" asked Kyra. It was a floppy, round style that Kyra often saw at the Palace, bright blue silk with a tassel hanging off the edge.

The boy grinned. "I found it."

"Found it?" asked Flick, one eyebrow raised.

Ollie's smile faded slightly.

"Nipped it off a fatpurse, did you?" Kyra asked.

Ollie shifted uncomfortably. "It was just in fun," he said.

Kyra couldn't believe the boy's stupidity. "You know better than that," she said. The lecture would have been more impressive if she'd been able to talk down at him, but Ollie was as tall as she was these days. "You want to nip something, you go for coin, food, or something you can sell. Fetching a useless trinket like that and parading it around will get you nothing but a beating."

The boy avoided her eyes. A crowd of children had gathered to watch, and he glared at them, daring anyone to make a comment.

Ollie straightened. "I see your clothes are mighty nice these days, Kyra. How do *you* get them? By kissing the wallhuggers' feet?"

There were a couple of gasps from around the circle, and Kyra herself drew back. She hadn't expected that. Out of the corner of her eye, Kyra saw Idalee stop talking and glance in her direction.

"What did you say?" Kyra said.

"It's what you're good at now, in't it?" said the boy. "Must be nice to eat off the Palace tables."

She had an urge to box the boy's ears. Except, again, he weighed more than she did, and his words rang a little too close to the truth. Flick squeezed her shoulder, the usual voice of restraint. She took a deep breath and told herself that the boy was just trying to salvage his pride. She stepped back from him and addressed the crowd.

"I brought coin this morning for folk who need it. If any of you want my help, you look me in the eye and you take the coin from my hand. If you don't like what I do with the Palace, you're free to stay back." She opened her bag. "Anyone?"

It didn't take them long to start coming. One by one, the children stepped around Ollie and took a copper from her. When almost all the children had received a coin, Kyra looked at Ollie again. He approached her grudgingly—not too proud to refuse money, though he'd stubbornly refused to take off his hat.

"Just be careful," she said as she pressed a coin into his hand. He mumbled something and left.

Kyra rubbed the bridge of her nose as Idalee and Lettie rejoined them. Idalee folded her coin pouch with studied care, and Lettie looked back and forth at everyone's faces, eyes wide.

"He didn't mean what he said," said Flick as they made their way to the market.

"Aye, he did," said Kyra. To be honest, she should have expected it sooner. Kyra had noticed a change in the children the past few times she'd come. The newer ones especially, the ones who didn't know her as well, looked upon her with suspicion. They took her money, but they kept their distance. It couldn't be helped, she supposed. She was there passing out bags of Palace coin. And as far as they knew, everything from the Palace was suspect.

"Do they say the same things to you, Idalee?" she asked.

"A few, but it in't so bad," said Idalee. "I'm not always spending time with the wallhuggers like—" She stopped.

"It's fine. You can say it. I'm the only one who spends all my time with wallhuggers," said Kyra. Ollie's comment still rankled. "Everybody thinks that's a problem. Either I've sold my self-respect for money, or I'm a love-struck victim waiting to be chewed up and spat out. Does everyone really think that badly of my judgment?"

Flick winced at her words. "It's not a matter of judgment, Kyra," he said. "My ma was a woman of good judgment." He broke off abruptly. "Sorry. We're done with that topic now. I promise." Flick squeezed her shoulder apologetically. "I'm going to go track down a locksmith for some tools. Good luck with your traders." He disappeared into the crowd.

"You should marry Flick, Kyra," Lettie said as they looked after him.

Coming from anyone else, that comment would have rubbed Kyra's already raw nerves, but Lettie looked so earnest that Kyra had to chuckle. She and Flick had been getting those types of comments since before he could grow a full beard, but Flick was too much like a brother to her. It would have been strange.

She bent down to Lettie's level. "He's far too good-looking for me, Lettie," she said, her face a mask of perfect seriousness. "Everyone would stare at us and say, 'What's that handsome lad doing with a girl in trousers?'"

Lettie's face scrunched up. "But you're pretty, Kyra, even if your bosom in't very big."

Idalee had a sudden and very violent coughing fit.

"Thanks, Lettie," Kyra said drily. Maybe next time she should just say that Flick belched too loudly. "Idalee, do you two have somewhere to be?"

"We need more wool for our dresses," said Idalee.

"Off you go, then. I'll see you back home."

The marketplace was still getting set up. Vendors pushed their carts into place and raised awnings to block the sun. None of the actual sellers at the stalls were traders, but they were the first step to finding the caravans that supplied them.

Kyra sweetened a fishmonger's opinion of her by buying a bag of smoked mussels, then asked if he knew where the caravanners stayed. He pocketed her coin and pointed her toward a large, boxlike storehouse a few streets away. It was not unlike the building that the Assassins Guild had once used for its headquarters. There were a few wagons hitched out front with rough-looking, travel-worn men and women walking amongst them. Kyra approached cautiously.

A tall man stood near the front gate, directing wagons in and out. He looked at her. "You with a caravan?"

Kyra shook her head. "No. But I've need of a Far Ranger to talk to. Are there any here?"

"Depends on what you mean by Far Ranger."

"Someone who's crossed the Aerins."

The man squinted at her. "You looking to cause trouble?"

Kyra pressed a coin into his hand. "I'm just looking to chat. The Far Rangers have got their ear to the ground more than most."

He fingered her coin and looked her over. Then he jerked his head at a wagon toward the back. "Jacobo's caravan travels the Aerins."

There were wagons of all types in this courtyard, ranging from flat carts for hauling lumber to covered wagons that could serve as semi-permanent homes. The people who came out of them were equally eclectic in their look and dress. There were brown-skinned Minadans who wore heavy furs over their native tunics and tucked their bright pantaloons into winter-friendly northern boots. Plenty of traders from the three cities were here too, clad in sturdy neutral-colored clothing. The trader women wore trousers like Kyra, so she actually looked less out of place here than she did in the rest of Forge.

Jacobo's wagon had seen its share of repairs. The awning was patched in several places, and not all the wood of the wagon's body matched the rest. Kyra slowed as she came closer, unsure what to expect. A trader stepped out from behind the wagon and fixated on her immediately. His skin was tanned, tough, and wrinkled, and there was more than one scar across his face. He looked like someone who had weathered storms, ice, and hunger, and thought little enough of it that he did it over and over again.

"Are you Jacobo?" said Kyra.

He gave a careful nod. "I'm Jacobo. And you are?"

Kyra extended her hand. "My name is Kyra. Of Forge."

The trader glanced at the tall man at the gate. "Gregor let you in here?"

"I made a convincing case," Kyra said, indicating her coin purse. She wasn't quite sure if admitting to a bribe was the best idea, but this trader didn't seem the type who appreciated being lied to.

Jacobo chuckled. "I reckon he wasn't too hard to convince. Well, maidy, why take the trouble of searching out my company?"

"I'm looking for a Far Ranger," said Kyra, hoping she was projecting at least some confidence. "Your people have a reputation for a long memory."

"Depends on what you mean by long."

"Have you heard any stories of Demon Riders crossing the mountains before this year? Mayhap in the past twenty years?"

Jacobo gave her a curious look. "That's an odd question. Why do you want to know?"

"I work under the Palace defense minister. We're trying to learn more about the barbarians." All true, except that Malikel had no idea she was here.

"The Palace has never come to us for information before. And you don't look like the usual fatpurse's crony." Kyra was wondering how to persuade Jacobo to talk when he continued.

"About fifteen years ago, a trade caravan was attacked near Forge, in the forest right above the upper waterfall. The wagons were destroyed and the crew was scattered, some killed. One survivor said they were attacked by felbeasts—that's what they're called across the mountains."

Fifteen years? Kyra didn't know her exact age, but she'd guessed she was about seventeen or eighteen years old. If there had been a clan around the three cities about that long ago... She tried not to let her excitement show. "You said there were survivors?"

"You say you're from Forge?" asked Jacobo abruptly. "You don't look it. Your skin's a shade darker than most, and the slant of your cheekbones..."

"Not everyone from Forge looks the same," said Kyra, scrambling to make sense of his words. Did he know something?

"How old are you?"

"I don't know."

Jacobo kept studying her. "I've met one of the survivors from that caravan," he said. "I could send word to him, see if he has anything to add, if that suits you."

Kyra rummaged around in her belt pouch and pulled out a piece of parchment. She scribbled Flick's address, thinking it better not to leave anything that would lead directly back to her. "You can find me here if you learn of any news. I'd be grateful."

Jacobo tucked the parchment away. "I'm in Forge for the winter. We're camped a quarter day's walk to the west, along the main road. If I hear from the survivor, I'll find you."

She thanked him and went on her way. The market was filling with people, but Kyra barely saw them as she mulled over

Jacobo's words. A clan had come to Forge over a decade ago. Could she be descended from them? It was still morning, and Kyra had no plans for the rest of the day. The upper waterfall where the attack had happened wasn't far. Everything would be gone after so long, but she was still tempted to take a look. Kyra turned toward the city outskirts. She could probably get there in an hour.

She was just making her way out of the market when she heard a scream.

The cry came from someone young, and it came from close by. Now that Kyra was listening for it, she heard other shouts as well. She sped up toward the commotion.

A courtyard next to the market was crowded with people, all watching something in the center. There was a sickness to the air. As Kyra came closer, several people broke away from the crowd and hurried away.

"You'll learn to respect your betters," came a man's voice. "Tell me why we shouldn't cut that tongue of yours clean out."

Kyra thought she heard a whimper in response. She nudged a beggar woman next to her. "What happened?" she whispered.

"Some kind of row between fatpurses and a gutter rat. Gutter rat's getting the worst of it now."

Kyra redoubled her efforts to break through the crowd, her thoughts immediately going to Ollie. Had a nobleman taken exception to his hat? A few people protested when she pushed past them, but most were too distracted by the spectacle in the square.

There was a sickening thud and a low moan as Kyra pushed

in front of the people blocking her view. Now that she was through, she saw that the crowd pressed against the outer perimeter of the courtyard, leaving the middle empty. Folk were afraid to get too close to the scene in the center, and Kyra couldn't blame them.

Three young noblemen, peacocks in their colorful silk tunics, stood over a muddied body in the courtyard. The victim wore a dress—it wasn't Ollie, then, though the girl looked to be in bad shape. Then the victim rolled over, and Kyra's heart stopped beating.

It wasn't Ollie. It was Idalee.

The girl was hunched over in the mud, her face twisted in pain as a nobleman waved a dagger in front of her eyes. Even as Kyra watched, the wallhugger, a skinny young man in a purple tunic, grabbed Idalee's hair and pushed her face into the mud. His friend pulled his leg back for another kick. Kyra drew her dagger and made a mad rush into the circle. "Stop!"

Her momentum was enough that the noblemen jumped back, and Kyra threw herself in front of Idalee. The wallhuggers stared. If a squirrel had jumped off a roof and started talking to them, they couldn't have been more surprised.

"Kyra?" Idalee seemed to have trouble focusing her eyes on her.

Kyra crouched and placed her hand on Idalee's shoulder. The girl's nose was bleeding, and her lip was torn. "I don't know what imaginary offense this girl committed," said Kyra. "But this is far beyond anything she could possibly deserve. Leave her be."

The one in the purple tunic looked her over, still more confused than angry. "Who *are* you?"

He took a step toward her. Kyra raised her dagger.

"You'll answer to the magistrate," said Kyra. "There's a courtyard full of witnesses."

That was apparently the wrong thing to say. Purple Tunic's expression changed from confusion to annoyance, and he advanced on her.

"The lesson we were teaching the girl could just as easily be extended to you," the nobleman said, drawing his sword. All three of the wallhuggers had swords, she saw now. They were probably good with them too, and there was no way she could fight them all with a dagger. Kyra scanned the crowd, looking for anyone who might help her. Faces stared back at her, but no one stepped forward. There were even two Red Shields in the crowd, simply watching. Lettie was nowhere in sight, though Kyra supposed that was a good thing at the moment.

Well, there was one way she could defeat three swordsmen. Kyra felt inward for the sense of her fur. But she was surrounded by people. What would she do to them if she changed? She snuck another glance at Idalee behind her. The girl lay with her temple against the ground, too tired even to lift her head.

There was a flash of motion in her periphery as Purple Tunic chose that moment to attack. Kyra jumped to the side to dodge his blade, remembering at the last moment not to impale herself on her dagger. The slick mud cushioned her fall, but it was also ice-cold and sucked at her clothes when she tried to stand. The nobleman advanced on her. As Kyra regained her feet, he stopped and stared at her neck. Kyra looked down to see that Malikel's medallion had come out of her tunic.

"Where did you get that? Did you steal it?"

Kyra gripped the medallion in her hand. "My name is Kyra of Forge. I'm under the Defense Minister's direct command."

"Liar."

But then one of Purple Tunic's companions stepped forward. "Santon, Malikel did take on the girl criminal recently."

Santon looked at Kyra again, his eyes narrowing. Kyra dropped into a defensive crouch, but the nobleman spat on the ground and backed away. "I don't know who you are, wench, but be careful. Not even Malikel's protection goes very far."

The three wallhuggers turned, and the crowd parted for them as they left.

Kyra rushed to Idalee's side, choking back a sob as she tried to discern the extent of Idalee's injuries. There were cuts and bruises on the girl's face, and the way she lay there without propping herself up made Kyra wonder about her arm. Idalee's breathing was pained and shallow, and her skin was deathly pale.

"I'm sorry," Idalee whispered. Her voice was devoid of emotion.

"Shush." Kyra wiped the blood from Idalee's nose. "It wasn't your fault." Then Kyra sat up in panic. "Where's Lettie?"

"She's here." The crowd parted to reveal Ollie holding Lettie's hand, and Kyra squeezed the girl to her chest. "Are you all right?"

"Aye." The child was trembling, but she was otherwise composed. It wasn't the first beating she'd witnessed.

The gutter rats crowded around now, a tangle of rags and bony limbs. A girl with mousy features wiped the mud off Idalee's face, while a pale boy poured water over her cuts. It suddenly struck Kyra how efficiently they went about their tasks, how everybody seemed to already know what to do when one of their own was gravely hurt.

"Tell me what happened," Kyra said to Lettie.

Lettie wiped her nose with the back of her hand. "It was the same wallhuggers who overturned her bread basket. Idalee called him a sniveling purple-headed worm."

*Oh, Idalee.*

"We need to get her to a healer," said Kyra. She looked down at Idalee. "Can you walk?"

Idalee nodded, her face lined with pain, and Kyra took her good arm to help her up. But after a few steps, Idalee started to whimper and her legs folded underneath her. There was a layer of sweat on the girl's brow as Kyra eased her back to the ground, and she was so very pale.

"Stay with her," Kyra said to the children. "I'll be back."

Kyra wasn't aware of much as she sprinted to the Palace, just the next corner to turn and the next person or obstacle to dodge. If anyone complained about her passing so carelessly, she didn't hear it. After the Red Shield at the Palace gate waved her in, she made straight for the Palace healer named Ilona, who had tended to Kyra's wounds before. Though she was in the Palace's employ, she wouldn't hesitate to help an injured child of low birth.

Ilona was a slender woman with ebony hair and a heart-shaped, freckled face. She took a half step back when she saw

Kyra's wild expression, and listened intently as Kyra related her story. Once Kyra finished, Ilona gathered two apprentices and took a wagon down to the beggars' sector. Her lips pressed into a thin line when she saw Idalee. In a commanding voice that belied her small frame, Ilona ordered the gutter rats away and commanded her apprentices to help Idalee up.

As the wagon rolled out of the courtyard, the beggar woman Kyra spoke to earlier called after them.

"The noblemen who beat your friend were the three sons of Lord Agan," the woman said. "If anyone at the Palace cares to know who did this, or cares at all."

*Or cares at all.* That was the question.

Idalee was listless by the time they arrived at the Palace, her head lolling side to side whenever the wagon hit a bump in the road. They brought the girl into Ilona's patient room, and the healer set to work right away. She wasted no breath in explaining anything, and Kyra relegated herself and Lettie to the corner of the room, huddling next to shelves of dried spices and staying as much out of her way as possible. Lettie's eyes never left her sister. The girl stared at Idalee as if she couldn't see the healer or apprentices circling her bed at all. It broke Kyra's heart, and she wrapped her arms around Lettie, wishing she could tell her that Idalee would be just fine. But she couldn't bring herself to lie.

Footsteps sounded in the hall, and Malikel swept through the door. "Kyra, what is this?"

Kyra hadn't expected to see Malikel so soon. Ilona must have dispatched some servants. "Sir, my sister was beaten by Lord Agan's three sons."

Malikel came to a stop at the head of Idalee's bed, looking far too much like Death's messenger looming over Idalee in his flowing red robes. "How is she, Ilona?"

"Not good, sir," Ilona answered quietly.

Malikel turned to Kyra again. "Tell me what happened."

The Councilman didn't interrupt Kyra as she told him what she'd pieced together. "They could have killed her," she said. "The magistrate should know about this."

"You say there were witnesses?" Malikel asked.

"A crowd had gathered to watch, but nobody interfered. Two of them were Red Shields," Kyra said. *And they'd stood by while Idalee choked on mud.*

Idalee whimpered again, and Ilona apologized, though Kyra wasn't sure if Ilona was speaking to Idalee, Malikel, or Kyra.

Malikel took one last look at the girl. "I'll speak to the magistrate on her behalf. We'll see what we can do."

Kyra was afraid to hope for justice, not with everything she'd seen on the streets. But if Malikel were behind Idalee... "Thank you, sir."

"Don't thank me yet."

After Malikel left, Lettie started to nod with fatigue. Kyra took a blanket from a shelf next to Idalee's bed and coaxed Lettie to lie down. Lettie resisted at first, but she finally gave in, and Kyra rubbed her back. The floor was hard stone, and the blanket was a closely woven wool that didn't offer much padding, but the girl nonetheless fell quickly asleep. Kyra left her there and found a servant boy to carry a message to Flick. Then she sat in the corridor outside Ilona's door and sifted through the guilt-laden questions whirling through her head.

Should she have tried harder to get Idalee to listen to her warnings? Anger flared through her at the thought. A child shouldn't have to fear for her life every time she misspoke, no matter whom she was talking to.

She'd been there a while when Tristam came hurrying around the corner, still in uniform. Though their argument was still fresh in her mind, Kyra's spirits lifted to see him. She began to stand, but he motioned for her to sit back down.

"I heard," he said softly, those two words heavy with concern. He peered carefully into Ilona's room. "How is she?" Under these circumstances, their fight seemed sadly trivial.

"Ilona's been working on her a long time," said Kyra. Her voice sounded hollow.

Tristam's face grew shadowed as he watched Ilona's movements. Finally, he backed away and sank down onto the floor opposite her. "Is there anything I can do to help?"

"Malikel's reporting to the magistrate. Ilona's doing what she can."

"Ilona's one of our best," Tristam said.

Kyra nodded, staring at the empty space in front of her. The cold of the walls and floor seeped through her tunic, and she hugged her knees closer to keep warm.

"Lord Agan has three sons," said Tristam. "Santon's the oldest, then Douglass. Dalton, the youngest, was in my cohort when we were squires. They've always had a reputation for causing trouble, getting into fights when the commanders weren't looking."

"Ever been punished?" asked Kyra.

"A few times."

*Not enough to dissuade them from beating a child to near death.*

"I've been beaten before," said Kyra. "Once a couple Red Shields wanted to take my coin for a fake bridge toll. I tried to run away, but I wasn't fast enough. Things like that aren't uncommon in the city."

Tristam shook his head in disgust. "Now that I spend more time in the Red Shield ranks, I see things. Soldiers abusing their power, extorting money from the citizens. There are a few commanders who almost certainly take bribes to look the other way. And the Council turns a blind eye. Rumors say that Willem is one of the worst offenders."

"Must be nice to have the city's forces do your bidding."

Tristam didn't reply. Kyra could hear Ilona's soft footsteps in the patient room, the clank of mortar and pestle, the swish of pouring water.

"I'm sorry about the ball," Tristam suddenly said. "I reacted badly to what you said."

It took a moment for Kyra to follow Tristam's words, but once she did, she met his eyes gratefully. His apology released a ball of tension inside her that she'd forgotten she was carrying.

"I didn't exactly bring it up in the best way," she said.

He met her gaze from across the hallway, eyes relaxing a little. "You're just trying to think ahead, and really, it shouldn't have fallen to you to bring it up. Though I hope you know that I've never seen you as . . . I mean, I would never see you as just a potential mistress."

"I know."

Ilona came out then, and both Kyra and Tristam stood to meet her. The healer moved as if her entire body were weighed down by stones.

"Two broken ribs, a broken arm, a knock on the head, and many bruises. She's bleeding in her abdomen as well," she said. "I've given her herbs to sleep, and that will be the best for her right now. You and the little one should go home and rest. I'll send word if anything changes."

Kyra rubbed her dry eyes and thanked Ilona. There was nothing more she could do.

Idalee seemed better early the next morning. She still slept, thanks to one of Ilona's concoctions, but Kyra imagined that some of her color had returned. The healer was already there when Kyra arrived, and Kyra wondered if Ilona had slept at all. Though perhaps Ilona was indeed tiring, because she finally allowed Kyra to help change the girl's bandages. They had just finished when Tristam came through the door.

"I thought I might find you here," he said. "Malikel says to go see him when Idalee no longer requires your attention." Tristam might have caught the hopeful cast of Kyra's face, because he spoke again. "Don't expect too much. I'm not sure how much even Malikel can do."

When Tristam and Kyra arrived at Malikel's study, the Defense Minister motioned for them to sit down in front of his desk. He wore an expression that Kyra had only seen on him after the most frustrating of Council meetings, and Kyra's heart sank.

"I spoke with the magistrate," he said. "He's adamant that the evidence does not warrant a trial."

"Evidence? There were well over fifty witnesses," said Kyra.

"I did inform him of that. Regardless, the magistrate is not convinced." Malikel's eyes conveyed far more meaning than his words.

"What can we do, then?" said Kyra. A knot of panic was forming in Kyra's stomach, a looming inevitability that she refused to accept.

"Willem is a powerful man. This particular magistrate is one of his favorites, as is Lord Agan. There may not be much we can do."

It was an expression of powerlessness that Kyra heard every day in the beggars' sector, but she had never expected to hear it in the Defense Minister's study. She glanced over at Tristam and, in growing disbelief, saw the resigned expression on his face as well.

"You're a member of the Council, Malikel," she said. "Idalee was beaten in broad daylight."

"By some very well-connected young men," said Tristam. He was speaking gently now, as if she were some madwoman who might go into fits. "It's crazy and wrong, Kyra, but there's a reason why they thought they could get away with it."

Kyra stared at Tristam, unable to wrap her mind around the fact that he agreed with Malikel. "There's a lass on the brink of death and more people who could testify to this than could fit in the magistrate's study. I don't understand the difficulty."

Malikel and Tristam exchanged a glance, and the look of

understanding that passed between them was the final straw. Kyra stood up so quickly that her chair toppled backward and clattered on the stone behind her. "Are we finished here?" She needed to leave before she did something she would regret. When Malikel didn't respond, she stormed out.

It was all she could do not to scream her frustration as she ran out into the courtyard below. She'd known it would be hard to get justice for Idalee, but somehow she'd allowed herself to hope that Malikel, at least, could help her. *Are you really so surprised? Did you really think you could go up against three noblemen and bring them down in the courts?* She'd been a fool to think anything would be different now that she was in the Palace. A gutter rat in fancy clothes was still a gutter rat. The sons of Lord Agan would go on with their lives as if this had never happened, while Idalee struggled to draw breath in Ilona's patient room.

Kyra headed for the Palace gate, unable even to look at the fatpurses she passed. Who were these people who lorded over the city and did what they wished? *The wallhuggers are not your friends, and they never will be.*

She'd walked only a short distance when she noticed Tristam trailing her. She didn't slow, but he caught up.

"Are you content to let this go too?" she snapped.

He took a while to answer. "I'm sorry," he said, his voice subdued. "I hate this as well. Malikel tried everything in his power."

"Tried what?" Kyra asked. "He's a member of the Council. He's not some beggar off the streets." A servant coming down the pathway toward them stopped short at Kyra's murderous gaze and stepped off the pathway to go around them.

"Malikel is bound by the law," said Tristam. "He cannot simply ignore the magistrate's ruling and do as he wishes. But he's been making changes. He's been gathering support from other Council members who also hate the corruption, and together they're starting to form a block of votes."

"I don't want a lesson in politics. I want the men who did this to hang from the city walls."

Kyra froze. Standing near the pathway were Willem, Lord Agan's three sons, and a man in black magistrate's robes. They looked to be finishing a conversation. The magistrate left in the opposite direction, but Willem came toward them.

"Kyra of Forge." Willem's voice was sharp as a raptor's, and there was a hardness in his gaze. "Be careful you do not overstep your bounds." He left without waiting for a reply. Kyra clenched her jaw until it hurt.

Tristam opened his mouth to say something but stopped as Lord Agan's sons approached. Santon's smile didn't reach his eyes, and Kyra's fingers curled for her knife. Next to her, Tristam moved his hand closer to his scabbard.

"Kyra of Forge, is it?" said Santon. "So you weren't lying about being in Malikel's service. Though I suppose it makes sense. More convenient for him than going to a brothel."

Kyra felt Tristam's hand clamp around her wrist, and none too quickly. "Watch your words, Santon," he said. "You're not untouchable."

"Perhaps you should follow your own advice, Red Shield." Santon's voice dripped with contempt. Tristam's grip on Kyra remained firm as Santon and his brothers walked away.

*I could kill you in your sleep,* Kyra thought to their retreating forms. *I could slip right past your bodyguards and have you begging for mercy. Let's see how cocky you can be when you don't have Willem's skirts to hide under.*

"Kyra." Tristam still hadn't let go of her. She tried to pull her arm away, but he didn't budge. "Kyra, it's not worth it."

"What's not worth it? Idalee's life?"

"Doing something stupid because you're angry," he said. "Promise me you won't go after them. Ending up under another death sentence will do you no good at all."

She stared at Santon and his brothers. They were still talking and laughing, their voices fading as they walked away. Kyra wrenched her arm from Tristam's grip. "Funny that you say Malikel can't walk in and do what he wishes," she said. "Seems to me that if you know the right people and have enough coin, you can do exactly as you wish."

Kyra lay awake that night and combed through her memories of James—not the most recent ones, where he'd betrayed her and tried to kill her, but their interactions from earlier. There had been a time when she and James had been in accord, surprisingly so. He'd been the one to show her that she could be more than a petty thief, that she could use her skills to correct wrongs done by the wallhuggers. Discovering her own power had been exhilarating, and James had shown real pride in her progress. They both took pleasure in bringing the fatpurses down a notch, in hitting the nobles where they thought themselves invulnerable. Kyra had admired James once, and—if she was honest with herself—had been attracted to him as well. Which had made it all the more devastating when he'd turned against her.

In the end, they'd disagreed not on their goals but the means by which to accomplish them. She'd refused to shed innocent blood, and he'd called her naïve. *We're dealing with the Palace and the Council, the most powerful men in the three cities, and the swords they control,* he'd told her. *You don't win this war with petty raids on their storehouses. You draw blood.* That had been his philosophy, that it simply wasn't possible to end the abuses by the wallhuggers without a costly fight. If someone had asked Kyra a week ago whether she agreed with James, she would have said no.

Kyra hadn't seen James since his capture. Even before the Council's explicit prohibition, she'd kept her distance. James knew too much about Kyra, and he still embodied too many painful memories. It had made sense to stay away. But now . . .

She started preparations the next day. When Flick took Lettie for a walk, Kyra locked the door behind them. She tore a few strips of cloth from an old tunic, placed them on the table, and drew her dagger. Then she hesitated. The Makvani thought nothing of spilling a few drops of their own blood, but Kyra still found it difficult. After a few false starts, she sliced a shallow cut across the top of her arm. It wasn't deep, but it stung, and Kyra drew a sharp breath through her teeth as the blood welled out. She sopped up her blood with the cloth strips, rolled them into balls, and tucked them into her belt pouch.

The next day, she dutifully reported to the Palace to discuss the rash of new Demon Rider attacks in the countryside. The Defense Minister had no further news on Lord Agan's sons, and Kyra didn't press him. Instead of leaving the Palace afterward, she took a back path that led to the prison building. She was somewhat familiar with the layout. The building itself was built solidly of stone, with barred windows in the aboveground floors. Since her series of break-ins to the Palace, Malikel had gone through and made sure that none of the windows were vulnerable. Not that it mattered much. The most dangerous and valuable criminals were imprisoned in holding cells two floors belowground.

The building was thoroughly guarded, with Red Shields patrolling the corridors at all hours. The locks were well crafted and impossible to pick—she'd tried a few times out of curiosity. The only keys were kept by the head warden in the guardhouse in front of the building. He knew Kyra—had guarded her when she was a prisoner there—and probably wasn't keen to trust her. The warden was supposed to keep his keys on his person at all times, but Kyra, who still paid attention to things like guards and keys, knew that he often removed his key ring from his belt and placed it on his desk while he worked.

Now she approached the guardhouse from the back, out of view from passersby. The window was open. The warden was at his desk, and his keys were next to him. *Perfect.*

The holding cells also had dog patrols—usually a deterrent to intruders, but in this case, Kyra would make them work for her. She pulled out the strips of cloth, stiff with her blood. Looking around one more time to make sure nobody was watching, she tied the cloth pieces to some bushes in front of the guardhouse, low enough so they wouldn't be easily seen. Then she backed some distance away and waited.

The dog patrol came by half an hour later, a Red Shield with a mean-looking wolfhound on a leash. Kyra watched the dog carefully as its handler brought him closer. A low growl came from its throat as he neared the place where Kyra had secured the cloth strips. The Red Shield pulled on the dog's leash and looked around, but urged the animal forward when he found nothing awry. The dog's growling continued, and as it came closer to Kyra's dried blood, the growls turned into full-on panic. The Red Shield cursed and struggled to get the animal under control as it tried to bolt.

"What's going on?" The prison warden came out of the guardhouse, voice sharp.

Kyra made her move, creeping closer to the guardhouse as quickly as she could. There was a slight wind, and she could hear the dog's panic increase as it caught a whiff of Kyra herself. She needed to be fast. The back window to the guardhouse was open, thankfully, and she lifted herself easily through it. She could still hear the warden yelling at the Red Shield outside as the dog continued to bark and growl. His keys were still on the table.

She made a mental note of the key ring's position before she lifted it up, holding it carefully to keep the keys from clanging. They were arranged by floor, and she wanted the farthest cell in the lowest level. When she found it, she took a piece of clay from her belt and pressed the key into it—once on each side. She also copied the key to the main prison itself. The dog was still barking madly when she climbed back out.

It took her four nights to file keys that would work, using one of Flick's files that she'd borrowed and neglected to return. Kyra might have finished sooner, but these keys were complicated, and she wanted to be absolutely sure they were done right. Plus she had to do it when neither Flick nor Lettie was around. They wouldn't have understood.

On the fifth night, she dressed in dark clothes and snuck out of her quarters as Lettie slept. Kyra had an odd feeling of nostalgia as she crept back into the Palace. She hadn't scaled these walls since her capture. She supposed she could have come in through the gates, but she didn't want any record of her having entered the compound that night. Her muscles remembered the routine well—the angle at which to cast her grappling hook, the familiar scramble up the side of the wall, the slight slipperiness of the granite against her leather shoes. The guard schedules were different now, changed in part thanks to her, so she had to be careful not to let old routines lower her guard. She kept her eyes alert and her ears open. Her blood flowed faster as she sped up her pace. It was exhilarating.

Kyra made her way from building to building, finally slowing as the prison's shadow loomed above her. The entrance was lit by two torches, and two guards stood on either side of the arched entryway. They never left their post, and they kept their eyes sharply trained on the path in front of them. They were attentive guards, for sure. But they hardly ever glanced upward.

Kyra checked the sky, estimating that she had about a quarter hour before the Palace clock rang out the time. She skirted to the back of the building, keeping her steps soft. She didn't hear any guards coming, so she ran straight for the wall and clambered skyward, wrapping her fingers around bars, ledges, and outcroppings in the stonework. Four stories up, then she pulled herself onto the roof and crossed to the front.

The next step was more delicate. Carefully, Kyra worked her way back down. If she peered over her shoulder, she could see the guards standing sentry on either side of the entry archway below her. If she dislodged anything and it fell between the Red Shields, she'd have to run.

She crept her way down until she neared the circle of light created by the torches on the wall. Kyra wrapped her fingers around some solid outcroppings and thrust her toes into secure niches. Then she pressed herself flat and waited.

It wasn't fun. The wind was freezing, and Kyra wondered whether her muscles would cramp up before the turn of the hour. Three hundred and twenty breaths later, the clock finally chimed, and Kyra sprang into action, her limbs cold but thankfully functional. She checked quickly over her shoulder to see if there were any people around besides the guards, breathing a quick word of thanks for her halfblood vision. Then, she climbed down into the circle of torchlight. As the clock finished up its hourly melody, she lowered her legs into the entryway and swung her entire body into the archway behind the guards. The chimes masked the sound of her landing. The clock started to mark the time—it was three in the morning. Kyra slipped her key into the door.

*First chime.*

Kyra turned the key. It rotated halfway and then caught.

*Second chime.*

She jiggled the key. The tumblers gave way.

*Third chime.*

The lock clicked open. Kyra slipped in and closed the door behind her. As the clock's chimes faded from her ears, she let out a slow breath. She was in.

Kyra stood in a dark and mercifully empty entryway. A stone corridor stretched out ahead, with solid wooden doors lining each side. The first floor consisted of interrogation cells and a few holding cells. Though there were no guards in her immediate line of sight, she could hear boots echoing not far away. She hurried for the stairway down.

As Kyra moved into the lower levels, the smell of mold and human waste became stronger, and the silence was broken by the occasional shout or moan. Progress was slow. Several times, she had to dive into a niche or perch atop a doorframe to evade a passing Red Shield. But she did work her way little by little until she stood in front of James's cell. She doubted that he would be unbound, but she readied her dagger just in case. Her key worked on the first try.

Her first glimpse of James knocked her back several steps. Kyra had expected to hate him. She'd steeled herself for memories of Bella and of her own near death at his hands. Those images did come back, but she also saw James as he was now, and it left her speechless.

He was shackled to the wall by short chains that connected to rings around his wrists. He wore the same tunic and trousers that he had been captured in, though now they were soiled and torn. James's face was covered with bruises and cuts, as was what exposed skin Kyra could see. His white-blond hair was matted with what looked like blood.

He hung from his chains with his face cast down, and at first Kyra thought he was asleep. But then he slowly raised his head. His eyes were still the same cold, clear blue as they had always been.

"I wondered when you'd come," he said.

She had nothing to say. James watched her, and there was a hint of an amused smile on his lips. "Surprised at the sight of me? The Council spares no expense in welcoming its guests."

Kyra didn't know why the marks of torture on James affected her so much. She had certainly known what the Palace did to criminals, though her own treatment while imprisoned had been nothing compared to this. Was it because she had cooperated early on? Or was it because the knights of Forge still held too much to their chivalrous notions to torture a young woman?

Kyra took a few steps closer to James, though not within his reach. He was still a dangerous man, and she had the scars to prove it. But she wanted a better look at him. Now that she had gotten over the shock of his appearance, she could see that James's imprisonment hadn't taken the glint of intelligence out of his eyes—nor had it broken him, she suspected. Kyra felt her old wariness return.

"Did they torture you for information about the Guild?" she asked.

"Did you come down simply to check on my well-being?" he asked. His eyes flickered over her dark clothing. "Why do I get the feeling that Malikel doesn't know you came to see me?"

Yes, James was still definitely all there.

"I don't have to answer to you anymore," Kyra said.

James actually laughed, though the laugh ended in a cough. "And yet, you're here. No, Kyra. If you've gone to this much trouble to speak to me, you want something from me. And unless you plan to add your own cuts to those your masters have decorated me with, then I'll have something from you in return. Starting with the real reason why you came."

Funny. Kyra had planned this break-in perfectly, from fashioning the keys to getting past the door guards. But here in this cell, her plans came up short. As she'd lain awake plotting, she'd known that she wanted to talk to James. But now she didn't have the words.

"You've not given me away," she said.

"Of course." James's eyes refocused on her face. "Your... surprising identity. Did you know what you were before the Demon Riders took you?"

Kyra didn't answer.

"I'll wager you didn't. You didn't have their bloodlust. And you still don't."

"You tried once to tell Malikel about me." She had only barely convinced Malikel that James was lying.

"And you want to know why I didn't continue to try," he finished for her. "It was a mistake on my part even to attempt the first time, and I should thank you for not letting me succeed. It might have turned them against you, but it would have gained me nothing more than short-lived satisfaction. Information is power in my trade, Kyra. I hold on to it until it gains me something."

"If you think you can blackmail me into letting you go," said Kyra, "you're wrong. I knew when I turned you in that I'd risk getting found out."

"And I believe you," he said calmly. "Is that the only reason you're here? To satisfy your curiosity about your good luck?"

It wasn't. Yet Kyra was reluctant to give the reason James was waiting for, to admit that there might have been some truth to his words all along. *The wallhuggers aren't your friends.* James wasn't either, but she would hear him out.

She rubbed her forearms, trying to scrub the dungeon's stink from her skin. "A lass was beaten by three noblemen." She couldn't bring herself to say Idalee. "Lord Agan's sons."

James leaned his head against the wall and stretched his arms within the confines of his chains. "They've been a problem for a while now." Kyra supposed she shouldn't be surprised that he knew their reputation. James had long maintained informants in the Palace, and she suspected she only knew a tiny fraction of what he had done as leader of the Assassins Guild. "And then what happened?" he asked.

"The magistrate pardoned them," she said, her fury returning as she spoke. "There was a courtyard full of witnesses, yet the magistrate said there wasn't enough evidence for a trial." She paused. "It's wrong."

"Are you surprised?"

Kyra didn't answer, and there was clear understanding in James's eyes at her silence.

"You think I'm evil," James finally said. "You cringe at the fact that I'd spill the blood of innocents to take down my enemies. But what you've refused to understand, and what you're resisting even now, is that there's no other way. The powerful do not let go of their positions so easily. Change doesn't occur without blood."

Blood. James had made sure there was plenty of that. "I won't become like you," said Kyra. "Burning down half the city to save it marks you just as guilty as the wallhuggers."

"Then why are you still here?"

To that, she had no answer.

James shifted his position. Pain flashed across his face, and it was a few more moments before he could speak again. "I didn't start out trying to destroy the city," he said. "I don't take pleasure in the pain of others."

In that, at least, Kyra believed him. There were some in the Guild who enjoyed violence—Bacchus, for one. Kyra had seen it on the few jobs they'd taken together. He'd smiled as he beat his victims, and it had frightened Kyra to the core. James was different. He was ruthless, and he tolerated people like Bacchus, but everything he did, he did for a reason.

"After Thalia died," he said, "I took possession of the Guild. It took me a year to weed out those who weren't loyal to me. I solidified my control, and then I considered what I wanted to do. For a long time, the Guild had become another tool of the wallhuggers. I put an end to that and thought, *Why not go further?* Who was it, after all, who decreed that the fatpurses should keep their positions? Why should they dictate how we live and how we die?"

"And that was when you started infiltrating the Palace," said Kyra.

"The wallhuggers don't pay attention to their servants nearly as well as they should. I learned much about the upper levels of Forge simply with careful bribes."

He'd learned much, but there had still been things he couldn't get to, like secret documents, trade schedules, and guard assignments. For that, he'd needed a thief who could get deep into the compound. He'd needed Kyra.

James continued. "At first I thought I would only go after the bad ones. The first wallhugger I targeted was named Hamel. He was the lowest kind of worm, and few people considered his death a loss to Forge. Yet folk suffered nonetheless when I killed him. Those who'd been in his employ went hungry that winter, and the political gaps left by Hamel's death were soon filled by another."

"Willem," Kyra guessed.

"He was already Head Councilman at the time, but he gained allies as those who'd looked to Hamel were cast afloat." James's gaze swept across the cell, as if he were viewing the myriad connections that held Forge together. "My point is, corruption in the city's not like a scab to be torn away. It's a tumor, spread throughout the body, and it grows back when you excise it. You can't remove a cancer without digging out healthy flesh."

"But what's the cost?" said Kyra. "What's the point of destroying the cancer if the body dies as well?"

"What's the point of having a body if it's riddled with disease?"

Kyra shook her head to dispel the headache that was starting to take root. "You can't mean that. You don't really want to raze the city to the ground."

"And you don't really believe me capable of obliterating the city." He locked his eyes on hers. "It's pointless to talk in extremes, because none of it will actually happen. But no matter how far we range with our philosophical fancies, the hard truth remains. You hold a blade now, Kyra, as does everyone who possesses power in this city. And every time you wield this blade, you must decide how deeply you wish to cut."

## SEVEN

Tristam was in his quarters, getting changed after his morning rounds when someone knocked on his door. A servant of Malikel's bowed when Tristam answered.

"Sir Willem has called an emergency Council meeting at the tenth hour to discuss several Demon Rider attacks that occurred this morning. Your presence is required."

Demon Rider attacks? He immediately feared the worst. "Were the attacks at Brancel?" *Henril. Lorne.*

"No, milord. Sir Malikel requires your presence because of your expertise with the Demon Riders, not because of any connection to Brancel. You are to observe the meeting and be prepared to answer questions if called on."

For a moment, he was selfishly relieved, though the attacks in question must have been bad if they warranted an emergency Council meeting. "I'll be there."

The clock had chimed half past nine a short while ago, so he didn't have long. Tristam changed out of his plain tunic into more appropriate court finery—an embroidered silk tunic with breeches and soft leather boots—and headed out the door.

The Council Room antechamber was a large room in its own right, lined with smooth black marble decorated with gold accents. A crowd had already gathered in anticipation of the meeting. Tristam saw no sign of Malikel, but Kyra came through the door soon after he arrived. She wore a gown of wine-colored linen to accommodate the Council's dress expectations, though she no doubt still had at least one dagger strapped to her leg underneath. He knew she chose her dresses based on their sturdiness and how easily she could climb in them if needed. Her gaze drifted around the room, not quite focusing on anything, and Tristam had to call her name twice to get her attention. That was almost unheard of. Kyra was nothing if not alert.

She raised tired eyes to him as he approached. "Ho, Tristam."

"Are you all right?"

There was the slightest pause before she answered. "I'm fine. Just didn't sleep well last night."

He might have questioned her further, but a herald announced the beginning of the meeting, and the crowd filed through the double doors. On the far side of the main room was a raised platform where the full Council sat in two semicircular rows of tables. Observing benches lined the floor between the door and the Council seats, and Kyra and Tristam settled near the back with other observers of low rank.

Willem called the meeting to order, and a scribe took the stage. "Two farms and the guesthouse of one manor were attacked in the predawn hours. Two deaths have been reported thus far, and several more were injured."

Concerned murmurs spread throughout the crowd. Three

attacks in one morning was alarming indeed. Tristam thought back to the day he and his friend Jack had stumbled upon a farm in the midst of a raid. He still remembered the chaos, the fleeing people, the panicked bleats and bays of livestock. Jack had died that day at the hands of the Demon Rider Pashla and her companion.

The scribe finished speaking, and Willem took the stage. "This is the biggest threat that has faced the city since our war with Edlan twenty years ago." Willem was a convincing speaker when he wanted to be. He spoke with authority, punctuating his points with bold sweeps of his hand. "And our Defense Minister does nothing. The Demon Riders sleep safely in our forest and pillage our fields at their pleasure. What can possibly be your justification for this, Malikel?"

"The Demon Rider threat must be met with caution," said Malikel from his seat. His voice was level, though Tristam could sense anger just beneath. "I've explained this to the Council many times. The Demon Riders are not a threat like Parna or Edlan that we should simply throw our soldiers at them. They refuse to face us in open battle. They know the forest better than we do, and they're better at disappearing into its depths. Without a sound strategy, sending our soldiers to meet them would result in far more casualties than we currently suffer."

"You argue for a good strategy," said Willem. "Let's hear it, then."

"Our best course of action is to focus on defending our vulnerable farms and manors while we prepare our soldiers with new weapons and tactics. The Palace smithies are forging new spears as we speak, and our soldiers are learning new formations for forest combat. We secure our farms first. Then we start driving the Demon Riders back and establishing larger and larger defensible boundaries."

"And how long before we'd be rid of the barbarians?"

"We're already training private guard forces around Forge. The majority of our farms could be much better defended within a year."

"The majority, you say. But the barbarians would still plague our people."

"If you have a counter proposal," said Malikel, his voice tight with impatience, "let's hear it."

Willem straightened and slowly swept his eyes across the Council. "As Head Councilman, I'm not usually involved in directly planning the city defense, but in trying times, when demands outweigh what our Defense Minister is able to handle, I'm forced to take a more direct approach. I propose a systematic sweep of the forest with our soldiers."

Tristam frowned. That was a horrible idea. Willem should have known better.

"That's preposterous," said Malikel, rising to his feet. "We do not have nearly enough men to do this. It would be sending them to their deaths, one battalion at a time."

"You're right, Malikel, that as it stands we do not have enough troops to mount such an attack. But the laws of Forge give the Council authority to expand our defense forces from within the city during times of need."

Tristam's head snapped up at these words. Willem couldn't possibly mean ...

"Are you suggesting conscripting soldiers from the city population?" said Malikel.

"Indeed, I am," said Willem. "Circumstances are dire enough."

"Dire enough to send untrained citizens to their deaths? Willem, the current raids are alarming, but even with the uptick in attacks, we still count the weekly casualties with one hand. If we take your strategy and go on an offensive with untrained and underarmed peasants, we could lose hundreds, if not more."

"What kind of city are we?" Willem's voice rang through the hall. "Did Forge become the great city it is by shrinking into the corner at the first sign of an enemy? By hiding like a mouse? Last month, our Defense Minister assured us the Demon Riders were a diminishing threat. Last night, we were called out of our beds by reports of not one, not two, but three attacks. What will next month bring? The only way to protect ourselves is to remove the threat now. Our neighboring cities have already taken steps to fight the barbarians. Edlan's people do not suffer the shame of sitting by while their farms are ravaged. Do we of Forge continue to be meek, or do we step up and show our strength?"

Kyra shifted uncomfortably. Tristam gave her hand a quick squeeze and received a grateful smile in response. Kyra hated the farm raids as much as anyone, but it was hard for her to hear people talk of Demon Riders as monsters and barbarians, to be reminded what kind of reaction she'd get if her secret was revealed.

Back on the platform, Willem raised his voice. "Answer me one question, Malikel. If we sweep the forest with the numbers I propose, given what you know about these clans, will we succeed in driving them out?"

There was a long silence as all eyes settled on Malikel. The Defense Minister stood with one hand on his table, staring down at it as if he meant to crush it by thought alone. "We have a reasonable chance at success," he said slowly. "But our casualties will be many times theirs, and the citizens of Forge would be bearing a burden that should rightly fall to the military."

"Let the Council decide where the burden should fall," said Willem. "I call for a vote."

Tristam leaned forward, his eyes fixated on the Council as Willem called each Councilman in turn to speak his vote. As the numbers fell evenly on each side, the air in the room became increasingly tense. When the last Council member gave his choice, Willem nodded. "The final tally is eleven for, eight against, and one abstain," he said. "The measure is passed."

Tristam stayed motionless as the scope of what had just happened sank in. When Willem formally ended the meeting, the room filled with the sounds of a hundred different conversations. He glanced at the stage to see Malikel in forceful dialogue with one of the Councilmen who had voted in support of Willem.

The crowd filed out, and Tristam waited with Kyra in the courtyard for Malikel. Servants were already running from the Council building, foregoing the pathways and running directly over the snow in their haste to carry their masters' messages. Councilmen and courtiers split off into groups, some huddled in quiet conversation, others shouting. When Malikel finally appeared, he was angrier than Tristam had ever seen him. Tristam got the impression that anyone in his way would have simply been knocked down.

"Follow me," he said.

Once they were in Malikel's study with the door closed, the Councilman turned to address them.

"Were you able to hear the proceedings?" he asked. When Kyra and Tristam indicated that they had, he continued. "Willem knew I wouldn't support a conscription of the citizenry. A similar thing was done in Minadel. It's how I became a soldier, and I've seen what happens when you throw peasants into battle with no training," said Malikel. "But the Council is scared, as is the nobility, and I'm bound by the oaths I've taken to uphold the will of the Council."

"Is there any way to overturn this?" asked Kyra.

"A vote this close can be brought up before the Council for reconsideration. But it can only be done once, and we cannot count on any of the other members changing their vote."

"What now, then?" asked Tristam.

Malikel pushed back the sleeves of his official's robes, though they fell right back to his wrists. "I will continue trying to sway my colleagues who voted with Willem. In the meantime, we do our best to prepare those who will be sent in. I'll have the smithies work as fast as they can. Tristam, I want you to help me develop training drills and formations for unskilled soldiers against these beasts."

"Yes, sir." He was already sifting through the possibilities. Basic spear work was essential. Any complex maneuvers would be too difficult, but perhaps some simple formations...

"Kyra," said Malikel.

She straightened. "Aye?"

"I need your help with the Demon Riders. I realize they've warned you to stay away, but your history with them still makes you better suited to approach them than anyone else in the city." There was something unnerving about the way Malikel looked at Kyra, and Tristam wasn't sure if he detected another layer of meaning behind his words. He wondered again how much the Defense Minister knew and felt a stab of guilt at deceiving him.

Malikel continued. "I need to make one more effort to negotiate peace. They've not been willing to talk to us before, but perhaps, if we impress on them what lies ahead, we can avoid mutual destruction."

Slowly, it dawned on Tristam what Malikel was asking. "You want to send Kyra as an emissary for peace? Sir, if I may speak freely, we have no reason to think we can trust any promises made by the Demon Riders." If Malikel had seen firsthand how the Makvani looked at humans, he would understand how naïve it was to try for peace.

A flicker of something passed over Kyra's face, but Malikel spoke before Tristam could give it more thought.

"In affairs of the city," Malikel said, "I will decide who is trustworthy."

Tristam bowed his head, and the Defense Minister turned again to Kyra. "Kyra, you're not sworn to me as a soldier or an emissary. I can't command you into the forest, given the risks. But if you are willing to go back to the forest once more, the city would be grateful."

Kyra met Malikel's gaze for a moment before she looked down again. "I'll have to think about it."

The Defense Minister dismissed them after that. Kyra left the compound, and Tristam worked his way through the still-buzzing courtyards back to his own quarters. To his surprise, an old courier of his father's waited outside his building. The man bowed as Tristam approached, and Tristam's fear for his family returned.

"Stanley," said Tristam. "Is all well at Brancel?"

"Your father and brothers are well, milord, though they fight hard. I carry a message from your father." The servant bowed again as he handed a parchment to Tristam. It was addressed in his father's unmistakable bold script.

"Thank you," Tristam said, breaking the seal. The letter inside was long, and he began to read.

Despite Kyra's show of reluctance, she knew she'd go back to the forest. She'd been feeling the need to return, the same itch that had driven her out there the night the demon cat attacked her. Malikel's request was just the excuse she needed.

The city was abuzz with activity when she left the next morning. Word of the Council's new measure had gone out. Heralds made rousing speeches against the Demon Riders in the city squares, and many citizens declared they would volunteer to fight the menace. Kyra wondered how long this excitement would last once folk started dying. Word was that a few units would be recruited and deployed immediately to test new strategies and start securing the forest, with the main offensive to happen in a month.

Once Kyra left the city, she wasn't quite sure what to do. There was no point in trying to find the Demon Riders herself. She couldn't sneak up on a full-blooded demon cat. But she *could* go into the forest and make herself available to be found, and there was that caravan attack Jacobo the trader had mentioned, the one that had happened just above the upper waterfall. Kyra had wanted to see the place for herself before Idalee's beating drove it from her mind.

It took her a few hours to walk to the waterfall, and the sound of crashing waters guided her the last few steps of the way. Big blocks of ice were piled at the bottom, though water still flowed underneath. Kyra scrambled up a boulder-strewn track. There was a clearing at the top scattered with young trees, as one would expect from a campsite that had been abandoned a few years ago. Kyra's imagination kept her jumping as she wandered. Perhaps this scrap of wood sticking out of the snow had been a wagon wheel. Or maybe that glint of metal came from a wheel sprocket. But whenever she looked closer, it turned out to be a trick of the eye.

There were wildflowers here, tall stalks that came up to her waist with cone-shaped clusters of blue, pink, and purple blossoms. They were called forever sprays because they bloomed all year round. Their perfume evoked a memory in which she stumbled through a field of these flowers. In her memory, the flowers grew as high as her head.

"What are you looking for?" a low woman's voice asked from behind her.

Kyra suppressed a shudder, and she slowly turned around. A middle-aged Demon Rider woman stood ten paces away, scrutinizing Kyra with a stare that could have sliced glass. She was beautiful, with large dark eyes and an arched nose, an angular face, and long black hair with the slightest hints of gray. She wore the familiar wraparound tunic and leggings of the Demon Riders, though the leather was tanned a darker color than the ones Kyra had seen. Behind her stood a Makvani man about Leyus's age. His features were milder and less stern compared with the woman's, and his gaze held more interest than suspicion.

"You're the halfblood, are you not?" demanded the woman in heavily accented speech. "The one who lets Leyus fight her battles."

Kyra backed away, unable to make sense of the woman's words. The Makvani man laid a hand on the woman's arm.

"She doesn't recognize you, Zora. You were in your fur."

The woman was the one who'd attacked her, then. The one Leyus had stopped from killing her. Kyra backed up, ready to reach for her dagger. If they tried to change, she would have an opening.

"Why are you here?" asked Zora.

Kyra did her best to stand tall. "I've got a message from the city for Leyus."

"I don't mean why you are in the forest. I want to know why you are in this clearing."

This clearing? Why would they care why she was in this clearing?

The man cut in. "We bear you no ill will." Given the glare Zora shot at him, Kyra thought he should amend that to "no ill will, for now."

Just then, a new voice spoke from behind her. Kyra couldn't understand the words, but she recognized the speaker, and she felt a sliver of cautious hope. She turned around.

Pashla looked exactly the same as Kyra remembered: tawny-yellow hair spilling over her shoulders, proud bearing, and a way of looking at Kyra that made her wonder, always, what the clanswoman was thinking. Their eyes met for a moment, and Kyra breathed easier when she saw no animosity in Pashla's gaze.

"Zora, Havel," Pashla said, nodding to each in turn. Then, to Kyra's surprise, Pashla ran one finger down the front of her neck in the Makvani bow of respect that Kyra had only ever seen Pashla give to Leyus. Zora asked Pashla a question in the Makvani tongue, which Pashla answered respectfully. Zora took another look at Kyra, then turned abruptly and left. Havel's gaze lingered on Kyra for a moment longer before he followed Zora.

Kyra stared after them, wondering what had happened. Pashla stood next to her, calmly watching the two Demon Riders disappear, and Kyra found she didn't know what to say. Pashla had nursed her back to health after James almost killed her, and she'd been deeply hurt when Kyra turned her back on the clan to return to Forge. Over the past weeks, Kyra had often wished to see Pashla again, to somehow make amends, but she didn't know where to begin.

"Be careful with Zora and Havel. They are new to this side of the Aerins, and they do not look as kindly on humans as Leyus does." She spoke with the same patient inflection she'd used when teaching Kyra the ways of the forest.

Kyra fought a perverse urge to laugh. If Leyus was a shining example of human–Makvani relations, then Forge was in deep trouble indeed. But Pashla's other words concerned her more. "What do you mean, they are new to this side of the mountains?"

"Have you not noticed? A second clan has crossed the mountains. Zora and Havel are their leaders."

Pashla was looking at her as if she had missed something patently obvious, and Kyra couldn't help but wonder if she had. Did Havel and Zora look any different from the others? Of course, a new clan would explain the recent increase in attacks. "They are in contact with your clan?"

"They used to be clan mates with Leyus. Leyus and Havel are like brothers."

Kyra took a moment to ponder Pashla's words. Things had been bad enough with one clan. With two . . . She had to try to make peace.

"Pashla, I'm here on behalf of the Palace," she said.

The effect on Pashla was immediate. Her expression closed off, and her voice when she spoke again was cool. "What errand do they send you on?"

Pashla's reaction stung, but there were more important things at stake. "I need to speak with Leyus. The clan is in danger. The city means to mount an attack, but our Defense Minister wishes to negotiate peace."

"Leyus will not speak with you. He has no desire to negotiate with humans."

"Even if they outnumber his people by a hundred-fold? It would cost the city greatly to destroy you, but they could do it."

"That's enough," said Pashla, a hint of anger in her voice. "I didn't think you'd be so foolish as to deliver threats while in our midst."

Kyra fell silent. She had gone about this all wrong. "I'm sorry. I don't mean to deliver threats. And I wish I wasn't here on Palace business. I wish we didn't have to be enemies." Truth was, Kyra had missed Pashla—the long walks they'd taken in the forest, the clanswoman's patience and gentle touch. Was it too much to hope for forgiveness? "You taught me so much, and I owe you more than I could ever repay." Immediately, she felt embarrassed and very small, but it was too late to unsay her words.

The clanswoman studied her again, her gaze gliding over Kyra with the serenity of falling snow. "Your wounds have healed well."

Kyra put a hand to her stomach. "I just have a light scar. I don't feel it at all."

Pashla motioned for Kyra to lift the edge of her tunic so she could see. The clanswoman ran a finger over the scar. It was an odd sensation, Pashla's touch on her toughened scar tissue.

"Time forms bonds," Pashla finally said. "Those we grow up with, those we live with, we become connected to them, even if they're different from us."

Pashla's words were an olive branch, the clanswoman's way of saying that she somewhat understood Kyra's choice to return to Forge, if not completely. "Thank you," Kyra said. When Pashla didn't respond right away, Kyra found her courage and kept going. "Does it have to be one or the other? Why must I choose a side? I've been coming back into the forest by myself. I know it's foolish, but I can't stay away."

"I know you've been coming," said Pashla.

Kyra stopped. "You know?"

"Of course we watch those who come from the city." The clanswoman broke a forever spray off its stalk and rolled it between her fingers. "Your blood calls to you, does it?"

Calls to her? She hadn't thought of it that way, but it seemed apt.

"I can't stop thinking about what it was like to change shape," said Kyra. "Though I've not been brave enough to do it."

The wind blew snow off the trees around them, and Pashla dusted off her sleeves. "I suppose it can't be avoided. The temptation is too great. You cannot silence something that is yours by right."

Was Pashla just expressing sympathy? Or was she actually... Kyra was afraid to breathe for fear that her hope would be extinguished. Just the thought that she might experience her other form again...

The clanswoman tossed the wildflower to the ground. "If you must change, then better to do it with my help."

Kyra's breath rushed out of her.

It was late enough in the morning that the sunlight shone straight into the clearing. Pashla turned her face to its rays for a moment, eyes closed, before turning again to Kyra. "The sun is warm today. Take off your tunic, your trousers, and anything else that will tear. You can keep your cloak to block the wind. Once you are in your fur, you won't feel the cold at all."

"Right now?" This was exactly what she'd been hoping for, but somehow she hadn't expected the lesson to start immediately.

"Do you have somewhere to be? I do not know when we will cross paths again."

She was right, of course. Kyra gathered her courage. "I don't have anywhere to be," she said. And she reached to untie her belt.

The first few tries, she couldn't go through with it. As she stood there, eyes closed with a cloak wrapped around her and the cold breeze whipping at her bare feet and ankles, Kyra concentrated and found the sense of her other form. She nudged it, coaxing it like a small flame, feeling it burn stronger. But when she sensed it reaching the point of overflow, Kyra drew back and opened her eyes again.

Pashla watched her. After the third time, she simply said, "Do not be afraid."

Kyra nodded and closed her eyes again. This time she didn't stop.

It was just as she remembered. The spreading warmth in her limbs, the sense of melting and growing, her fur forcing itself through her skin and making her arms tingle. She threw off her cloak as her limbs stretched and her muscles thickened. Her vision darkened for a moment, and when it returned, everything was clear. So very clear.

Pashla stood in front of her, still in her skin. The clanswoman held herself with her muscles relaxed and her hands down by her sides. While Kyra's previous transformation had been in the heat of battle, this time her feral instinct was muted. She could still feel its presence, a constant readiness for a fight that hovered in the back of her mind. But she was far more interested in the world around her. The wind, so bitingly cold a few moments before, now blew ripples in her fur and raised a tickling sensation along her back. She bent down to smell the wildflowers. The scents were heady, almost too strong. And such vivid colors. Kyra sneezed, then stepped around Pashla. The snow's coolness seeped through the tough pads of her feet.

Behind her, Pashla spoke. Kyra ignored her, but Pashla persisted, and Kyra finally took the effort to pay more attention. She found she could make sense of her words if she tried hard enough. Pashla was telling her that she'd done well.

A new scent reached her nostrils. Unlike Pashla's words, the meaning of this new smell was immediately clear. There was a deer upwind, just a short sprint away.

"Kyra, stay here."

Kyra shook off the command like water from her fur and started off toward the scent.

"No, Kyra." A hand on her flank, and a firmer command this time. Kyra spun around and slashed at Pashla, who jumped back, stumbling. As Pashla regained her balance, Kyra whipped around and sprinted toward her prey. She dove into the trees at the edge of the meadow, jumping over rocks and dodging branches. The scent was as clear to her as a path she could follow. Ahead of her, she caught a glimpse of the deer and smelled its alarm. Birds took flight at her approach, wing beats like drums against the air, their warning calls sharp and bold. Kyra ran faster.

Something heavy landed on her back and knocked her paws out from under her. The weight was so strong, so sudden, that Kyra realized it must have fallen from a tree. Kyra writhed and twisted to face this new attacker, striking out with her claws. Her opponent kept out of her way and opened cuts on Kyra's forelimbs with her teeth. It stung, and the pain infuriated her.

The deer was getting away. She could hear its light hoof-beats fading, and she roared with frustration. Her attacker—Pashla, it was Pashla, Kyra realized—was strong, and Kyra couldn't get the best of her. She tired, and it gradually became clear to Kyra that they shouldn't be fighting at all. She stopped moving and let Pashla pin her to the ground.

As Kyra's breath slowed and her blood cooled, she felt the sense of her fur waning. She let herself melt back into her skin.

Pashla, her own form still shifting, pulled Kyra to her feet. "Get dressed before you freeze."

It was a cold run back to her clothes. Kyra wrapped her cloak around herself to block the wind, then reached with stiff fingers for her trousers and tunic.

Pashla joined her. "You need control. But it was not too bad."

"I'm sorry I slashed at you."

"If I'm slow enough to let some young cub touch me, then I deserve it."

Kyra finished dressing and rubbed the heat back into her limbs.

"I almost envy you," said Pashla after a while.

"Me?"

"You know the ways of the humans, and now you're learning ours."

Her hands were starting to regain some warmth. "I'm surprised you'd want to learn about the humans."

"I've no interest in being human. But it would be useful to know how to move in their world. With your mixed blood, you're able to blend in anywhere."

Kyra remembered that Pashla had been the liaison between James and the Makvani, back when the clan had been allied with the Guild. It made sense that Pashla would value advantages like this. Though Kyra didn't exactly see herself as being able to blend in anywhere. On the contrary, half the Palace thought her a criminal, the Demon Riders didn't want her in the forest, and even the gutter rats didn't trust her anymore. It was a fine line, she thought, between being able to blend in everywhere and nowhere.

Kyra left the forest a short while later. And though she had failed in her mission, Kyra felt hopeful. She'd spoken to Pashla again, and the clanswoman had forgiven her. Perhaps it was selfish of her to be relieved when the city was still under threat, but Kyra couldn't help feeling that a weight had come off her shoulders.

There remained plenty of energy in the city when she returned. Kyra skirted past the busy streets and squares toward home, avoiding the crowds that still loitered in the public spaces.

Lettie was not home yet—Tristam had taken her to see Idalee that morning—but Flick sat waiting at their table. Kyra hadn't bothered to give him an extra key; he just picked the lock when he so desired. But it was rare to see him waiting at their place when no one was there.

"Flick," said Kyra. "You're here early."

He wasn't smiling as he tossed a sheet of parchment on the table. Kyra slid it closer and picked it up. Her stomach dropped.

"A notice of conscription already?" she asked.

"Looks like I'm a lucky member of the early units," said Flick.

Kyra took the parchment and turned it over, as if she could find something in the back that would mark it false. Her stomach churned. Suddenly, her inability to speak to Leyus today seemed a much graver failure. "Of all the folk in the city, what are the chances they would pick you?"

Flick's voice was humorless when he responded. "That's what I wondered myself. I don't suppose you've offended anyone in the Palace recently?"

Kyra was tempted to crumple the parchment in her hands. "I can't believe Willem would do this."

"You've got enemies in high places, Kyra."

Kyra had seen soldiers die at the hands of the Makvani before. The thought of Flick—jovial, charming Flick—facing off with the barbarians was unbearable. Kyra racked her mind for any way to change this. "Your father. Can he do anything?"

"He wouldn't even acknowledge my dying ma's existence, much less mine. He won't do anything on my behalf."

"I'm so sorry, Flick," Kyra said. She meant every word. "I'll speak with Malikel as soon as I can."

It was becoming an all-too-familiar routine, sitting in Malikel's study and filtering through the truth for what she could reveal. Kyra wasn't a natural liar. Flick could spin fifteen different tales to twenty different people and keep the details straight, all the while maintaining a face that convinced the most skeptical of listeners that he was the soul of earnestness. It was different for Kyra. She found it hard to keep track of the lies as they piled on top of each other. Plus Malikel wasn't exactly the best audience for someone engaging in selective truth-telling. The Defense Minister listened carefully—very carefully—to anyone who spoke to him, from fellow Councilmen to lowly serving maids.

"Pashla found me after I was in the forest awhile," she said. "She wouldn't let me speak to Leyus, but I did learn that a new clan's crossed the mountains and that the leaders of the clan are very close with Leyus."

Malikel leaned forward. "A new clan? Did you get any sense of their numbers?"

"I saw only the two leaders."

"Judging from the uptick in attacks though, we can assume they are numerous. Did you speak with Pashla about anything else?"

"No," she lied. Then Kyra gathered her courage. "Sir, there was one other thing I wanted to talk to you about. I understand that a few early units have been conscripted already for Willem's forest sweep."

Malikel indicated his desk. It was covered with maps and diagrams of Forge and its surrounding forest, some with symbols representing soldiers in battle formations. "I will be training the new units myself. Hopefully, these early groups will give us a better overall strategy when we bring in the rest of the new conscripts."

"Were the new units chosen at random?" Kyra asked.

"Yes. Why do you ask?"

"Flick, my good friend, was conscripted yesterday."

Malikel had reached out to take hold of a map, but upon hearing Kyra's words, he drew his hand back again and fixed a keen gaze on Kyra. "And you suspect that it wasn't an accident."

"Aye, sir."

Malikel folded his hands in front of him. He didn't speak for a while, and his face darkened with every passing moment of silence. Just when Kyra was wondering if he'd ever speak again, he did. "I'll be honest. There are many ways an official could influence who was chosen. And many ways an official could then cover his tracks."

"Is there anything that can be done? I'm not asking for special treatment for Flick," she hurriedly added. "It's just that, if someone had picked him on purpose to get at me..."

"Willem, you mean," said Malikel. "We can speak plainly in this study."

"After what happened with the Agan brothers, he warned me not to overstep my bounds. He might be sending me a warning."

The Defense Minister raised his hand. "Or it could be chance—I'm not saying it is, but you don't have any proof. If it was indeed Willem, it was a clever move on his part. I've built my entire career on fighting corruption. If I were to specially excuse one of the conscripted soldiers, it would undermine my entire position." He raised a hand again before Kyra could object. "That's not to say I cannot help you at all. But I would need proof that Willem had something to do with Faxon's original conscription." Malikel used Flick's real name, which he had learned when the Palace had sheltered him from the Assassins Guild.

"Proof?" Kyra echoed. How could she get proof?

"I'll have some of my men investigate," said Malikel. "And you would do well to avoid attracting any more of Willem's attention in the meantime. I know you might be tempted to take this matter into your own hands, but any misstep on your part could make things worse for your friend."

"Yes, sir," she said. She wasn't sure if Malikel really believed she'd sit back while Flick's life was at risk, but she saw no use in arguing.

It took her a moment to realize that Malikel was looking intently at her. "Kyra," he said, and there was something in his voice that demanded attention.

Kyra snapped to attention. Had her previous response been too flippant?

"There are several skills that a good Defense Minister needs on a regular basis. One is an ability to judge the truth and see through anything that obfuscates it. When facts have been kept from me, it's almost always better if the one who's been hiding these things reveals them first." Kyra had the distinct impression that they were no longer talking about Flick.

"I'm charged with upholding the law, but I also don't consider the law a rigid thing. Character comes into account, as do the specific circumstances. We can't always control our past."

"I don't understand, sir." Who knew what the expression on her face was right now?

"I cannot have someone under me who only entrusts me with partial information. I understand it is hard to throw your fate in with the Palace when there are so many people, like Willem, who may not look on you as their equal. But those people will always exist. In the end, you must make a decision. Either you decide that you can accomplish something for this city and you commit fully to the job. Or you leave."

"Leave the Palace?"

"Leave the city," Malikel said.

Her mouth had gone completely dry. He knew about her bloodlines, or at least suspected. Kyra licked her lips in a failed attempt to get some moisture on them. "Can I ask a question, sir?" she said.

"You may."

"Why don't you return to Minadel? You could be respected there, live a normal life without folk looking at you sideways because you're a foreigner."

Another man might have thought her question a deflection, but Malikel seemed to take it in stride.

"I was a common mercenary in Minadel. I would have amounted to nothing there. It was here in Forge where fate smiled on me. That was why I stayed at first, though you are correct that if I were to leave now, the Minadan court would welcome my expertise and experience." He turned to look at a map on the wall, his gaze lingering on his old homeland. "But I have unfinished work in Forge. There are times when I want to wring the necks of my colleagues at the Council, but minds are slowly changing."

"If I may speak plainly, sir, hundreds of folk might lose their lives in the forest before minds in the Palace are finished changing."

"If one wants to live under the rule of law, one must accept both the good and the bad. I don't pretend to have perfect solutions, but think on what I've said. About everything." Malikel turned his attention back to the parchment on his desk. "You may go."

It took a moment for Kyra to realize that she'd been dismissed. She managed a stately walk down the rest of the corridor, but once she got to the staircase, her nerves won out and she bolted down.

Outside, the Palace staff went about their business as usual. A contingent of Red Shields marched past on their way to replace the gate guards. A nobleman strolled behind them, dictating thoughts to a courtier who scribbled them down on a slate. Kyra slowed and pushed back a strand of hair that had fallen from her ponytail. Maybe she should tell Malikel the truth of what she was. He was a fair man, and she trusted him to look beyond her bloodlines to what she'd done for Forge. But the thing was, her actions hadn't exactly been impeccable. Would they be enough to deem her not a threat? And even if Malikel himself decided he trusted her, the Council was something different altogether. There was no way they would be able to look past what she was.

It was with immense relief that Kyra spotted Tristam crossing the courtyard. She ran to him, desperately needing to talk this over. Kyra started to say his name, but the expression on his face gave her pause. Tristam stopped in his tracks, and Kyra would have sworn that he looked guilty. Belatedly, Kyra noticed the strange path he took. He hadn't been heading to the building that housed Malikel's study. Instead, he'd been walking toward one of the smaller administrative structures. And he wasn't in uniform. Instead, he was once again in full court finery.

"I've not seen much of you these few days," Kyra said. "Have you been busy?"

He paused for just a moment, looking very tired. "I've been performing some duties for my father."

"Oh," Kyra said. "Everything is all right, I hope?"

"They're fine. I mean—" He wasn't exactly avoiding her eyes, but he wasn't looking straight at her either. "They're not fine, but that's to be expected. We've been having some troubles at our manor with Demon Riders. My father asked me to spend some time here negotiating on the family's behalf."

Tristam rarely mentioned his duties to his family. As far as Kyra knew, his older brothers bore the majority of the responsibility. "Do the negotiations have something to do with the Demon Rider attacks?"

"There's a family from Parna offering to help us with our defenses." He rubbed his temples. "How have you been? How is Idalee?"

"Idalee's doing much better. Ilona says she might be able

to come home in a few…" Kyra trailed off. Tristam's thoughts were clearly elsewhere. "Tristam?"

"I'm sorry, Kyra. I'm a bit distracted." He paused again. "I should go. There's a courtier expecting me."

He continued on his way before Kyra finished saying good-bye.

EIGHT

"How much do you hate me, James?" Kyra stood at the opposite side of his cell, shifting her weight from one foot to the other when she tired. She had no desire to lean against the damp moldy walls.

James looked slightly better this time. None of his wounds looked fresh. Perhaps everyone was too busy dealing with the Demon Rider threat to spend much time on him. "Were I free right now, I would slit your throat, though I'd regret having to do so."

"That's sentimental of you."

"You let your talents go to waste. I've always thought that, even before I found out what you really are."

She shifted uncomfortably. Insults and threats, she was prepared for. Praise, though, felt wrong. "There's to be a war," she said. "Willem wants to launch an all-out attack against the Demon Riders, and he's conscripting soldiers from the city to do it."

"Why tell me this?"

"It will be a bloodbath. Hundreds will die, most of them

from the poor. And meanwhile, Willem will be marked a hero."
*More people will die than perished in James's Demon Rider raids.*
That thought disturbed her in more ways than one.

A guard's footsteps came through the door of the cell. James looked on in amusement as Kyra froze, then relaxed as the guard walked away. "There's more," he said. "You'd not come to me again simply out of concern for your city. They've conscripted someone important to you, haven't they?"

She didn't answer, but Kyra guessed that her thoughts were plain on her face. James gave a satisfied nod. "It's always personal. You can handle the abuse when it happens to others, or at least you don't care enough to make an extra effort to stop it. But when they take someone you care about, that's when you're willing to put yourself on the line."

It was frightening sometimes how right he could be. First Idalee, then Flick. And each time, Kyra became willing to do just a little bit more. Was this what had happened with James? Kyra thought about Thalia, the mysterious girl whom James had fallen in love with, and who had died at a nobleman's hand. How much of what James had done was because of her?

"Do you still think about Thalia?" The anonymity of the dungeon made it easier to ask such questions.

For a long moment, he didn't respond, and Kyra wondered if she'd inadvertently ended the conversation. The only sound in the room was the occasional drip of water somewhere in the darkness.

"Every day," James finally said. As he spoke, Kyra caught a hint of fatigue in his voice, true exhaustion that for a moment was written all over the lines of his body.

"What would she think of everything you've done?"

James lifted his head, his eyes regaining their steely focus. "We'll never know, will we?"

That answer hung between them, heavy with its implications. There was an entire lost lifetime in those words. Decades in which a woman Kyra had never met might have loved, fought, and grown old. Kyra realized that this was one story she would never know.

Finally James shifted. "I tire of this conversation. Tell me what you came for."

"You've got spies in the Palace," said Kyra. "I know you do. If I knew more about what Willem was doing, if I could find something against him, I might stop this."

"If you wanted my help, mayhap you shouldn't have handed me over to the Palace."

"We're not allies, James, but we have a common enemy. I'm offering you another chance to bring Willem down. You said you didn't give me up to the Palace because you might still get something from me. This could be it. Mayhap I can do something with that information to serve both of us."

His eyes were shrewd as he considered her offer. "Everything about my spies stays with you. No word of this goes to Malikel or any wallhugger."

Kyra thought for a moment. "I can do that."

"Make no mistake, Kyra. You'll owe me for this. Someday I'll call in a favor from you, and I'll hold you to it."

Kyra stepped back, widening the space between them. "There are some things I won't do. You know that."

"I know your limits," said James. The way he said it made

it sound like a weakness. "I won't push you to break them. But you'll be indebted to me. I want your word."

Dealing with James was never straightforward. He was so quick, so deadly most of the time that it was easy to think violence his only weapon. But you couldn't discount his subtler skills. He understood people, knew how to assess their strengths and manipulate their motivations. On the surface, he was asking for a promise he couldn't enforce, but Kyra knew better than to make such a vow lightly. She didn't know his whole game. She never did, but that was a risk she would take.

"I won't help you escape," said Kyra. "But you have my word that I will repay you within the limits of my conscience."

James scrutinized Kyra, and she stared right back at him. Finally he nodded. "I've an informant in Willem's household. He's a servant named Orvin, and he's good at overhearing things. I pay in silver for each useful piece of information. He's a tall man with dark brown hair that's thinning at the front. About forty years of age, and he wears a tunic with Willem's family crest when he's on the Palace grounds. Go talk to him."

## NINE

Kyra asked one of Malikel's servants about a man named Orvin in Willem's household. The man did, in fact, exist. After a couple of days discreetly watching the pathways leading to Willem's quarters, Kyra spotted him. When she tailed him home, she saw that he lived on the first floor of a boardinghouse in the merchant district. Kyra counted at least six children when she peeked in the windows.

Now that she had him, the question was when and how to approach him. The Palace was too dangerous, and surprising him in his house seemed too threatening. Kyra watched his door that night and followed him as he left the next morning. Luckily, he didn't head straight for the Palace but instead went to the markets. That would be as good a place as any. Kyra pulled her cloak over her head and sped up until she fell in step with him. The man was deep in thought, and it took a while for him to notice her. He stopped in his tracks.

"James told me he paid you in silver. That right?" Kyra said. Stark fear crossed his face.

"I in't planning on turning you in," she said quickly, worried that she would have to grab him to keep him from bolting. "Otherwise you'd already be in the dungeons. But I'd like your help, and I can pay for it."

The man squinted at her, trying to see beneath her cloak. "Who are you?"

Kyra supposed she didn't look or sound like anyone from the Palace or the Guild. Marketplace shoppers brushed past them, and the shouts of vendors made it hard to hear. She jerked her head toward a nearby alleyway. "Best for both of us to be out of sight." He hesitated to follow her, and Kyra sighed. "You and I can have this chat out here or in the alley. Your choice." The look he gave her wasn't kind, but he followed her to the back street. It was empty and darker than the thoroughfare. The smell of rot that always plagued alleyways near the markets was dampened by the cold. Kyra glanced around, checking to make sure there were no windows. She dropped her hood.

Fear crossed Orvin's face again. "You're Malikel's woman."

It looked like her days of anonymity were over. "I've sworn no oaths to Malikel, and he doesn't know I'm here. I just want some information."

"And if you don't get it, will you turn me in?"

She had to think before she answered. Blackmail would have been easy, and certainly tempting, but she shook her head. "I won't betray a city man to the wallhuggers without good reason. But I'm guessing that you've no love for Willem, if you've sold information to James before."

His stance lost a bit of its defensive tilt. "I'll have you know that I didn't choose this path lightly," he finally said. "I have seven mouths to feed, and His Grace is stingy with his wealth.

You're common-born like me. You know what it's like to be under them. If it comes out that I've betrayed the Palace, my family will starve."

"I know," said Kyra.

He let out a resigned breath. "What do you want to know?"

"Willem's pushing a strategy against the Demon Riders that's almost certain to end in many deaths. I'm looking for any weakness on his part that I might be able to use against him."

Orvin's eyes showed clear understanding as he took in her words. "Willem's ambitious, I'll give him that. He has a vision of Forge as a bastion of greatness—what Parna has done, but bolstered with our greater numbers." He indicated Kyra. "You yourself have benefited from Willem's ambition. The Palace healers are some of the best in this part of the world, and it was Willem who invested in their training. Of course, gains made by the more refined layers of society are paid for by the masses. This Demon Rider offensive is just the latest. Glory for the city, paid for by the blood of soldiers on the ground." He threw a quick glance over his shoulder and lowered his voice. "I can tell you this. Willem has been receiving private messengers late at night, about once a week. They come into the Palace past midnight, when the main gates are closed."

"What messages do they bear?" asked Kyra.

He shook his head. "The meetings are closed, with only Willem and the messengers. I wouldn't even have known about them had I not been paying extra attention to His Grace's movements. But he would not receive the messengers in such secrecy if he had nothing to hide."

She made note of his words. "One other thing. I suspect Willem might be making changes in the conscription lists. A good friend of mine was in the first conscripted unit, and it seems too much a coincidence. Do you know anything about that?"

"It wouldn't surprise me," said Orvin. "But I've heard nothing of it, though that kind of evidence would be hard to find. You'd have to track down whichever scribe he persuaded to change the lists."

That was disappointing, but Kyra was marginally familiar with the Palace's roster of scribes from all the time she'd spent stealing Palace records. She could look into some of the more likely suspects. "And what about at court? Does Willem have any new allies or enemies?"

"He's never been a friend of the Defense Minister, as you surely know. The rivalry seems more pronounced lately after Malikel was voted Second to the Head Councilman last month."

"That's right," said Kyra. It had happened shortly after Kyra started working for Malikel, and it meant that Malikel would become Head Councilman if something were to happen to Willem. "But Willem couldn't possibly think that Malikel would consider foul play, would he?" said Kyra.

"No, I don't think Willem worries about assassination. But Malikel's been pushing a good number of controversial measures—a law was passed last week requiring landlords to wait two months before evicting a tenant. Changes like these tend to be unpopular amongst the nobility who form the core of Willem's support. So Willem's been attempting to undermine

Malikel's competence. He might hope, for example, that your friend's early conscription into the army would distract you from Malikel's assignments."

"By making me chase scribes instead of pursuing peace with the Demon Riders?" Kyra asked, chagrined.

"Aye. And the Brancel marriage negotiations are another example. Willem's voiced his support, and the only reason he'd do so would be to hinder Malikel."

Brancel marriage negotiations? Orvin had brought it up in such an offhand way, as if he expected her to already know about it. She grasped for something to say that would get more details out of him. "But would Willem really undermine Forge's war efforts just to hurt Malikel?"

Orvin shrugged. "It'll be a bloodbath either way. A few more deaths won't matter. And Malikel's plenty competent. If your friend Tristam were to marry, it would take him away from Forge for the duration of the nuptial preparations. Malikel would lose Tristam's help, but it probably wouldn't change the overall outcome."

Orvin kept talking, but his words became like buzzing in her ears. *Marriage negotiations. For Tristam.* Kyra was vaguely aware that she needed to say something, to pretend that what she'd heard was nothing new to her.

Orvin trailed off and squinted at her, and Kyra wondered if her attempt at a calm expression had worked at all. "That's useful information," she said. Before Orvin could speak again, she took out a bag of coins and pressed them into his hand. "I can't pay as well as James, but I hope this will help."

The pouch disappeared under his cloak with a smoothness

that spoke of experience. "I'll keep watching, and I'll send word if I learn anything else," he said.

"Thank you," said Kyra. Somehow, she maintained her composure until Orvin had disappeared from view.

It was ironic how the conversation with Orvin had turned out. Kyra had expected to surprise him, had in fact worried that the shock would scare him away. But instead, Orvin had quickly adjusted to his circumstances, and Kyra was the one left in the alleyway, reeling at his words.

It made sense now, when she thought back to her past few days with Tristam. The endless meetings, the courtiers, his evasiveness at her questions.

Why hadn't he told her? The reasonable part of her recognized that she had no right to be upset. She was the one who had cut things off in the first place. And yet...

Kyra dug her fingernails into her palm. Perhaps Orvin was wrong. How well could a turncoat servant be trusted? And regardless of whether the news was true or false, she couldn't stay here and flounder. Ilona had sent word this morning that Idalee was ready to return home, and Kyra had promised to come get her.

She saw no sign of Tristam on her way to Ilona's patient room, for which she was grateful. Idalee was already dressed and waiting for her, looking subdued but ready to go. The girl's arm was in a sling. She was thinner than she'd been before, and her coloring was still pale, but Idalee was in far better shape than she'd been when she came in. Kyra gave the girl a careful hug.

"I'm glad you're better," she whispered.

"Idalee should be fine to walk home," said Ilona. "Just make sure she doesn't push her body past her limits."

Idalee's grip on Kyra's hand tightened as they left the herb-scented safety of Ilona's room and made their way down the stairs. The girl faltered at the building's main entrance.

"Are they here?" Idalee asked.

It took Kyra a moment to realize whom Idalee was talking about, and when she did, she felt like the worst friend in the world. Here she'd been preoccupied about whether she'd run into Tristam, when she really should have been making sure that Santon and his brothers were nowhere in sight for Idalee's departure. "I didn't notice them on the way in," she said. "We'll go quickly."

The girl's features strengthened into resolve, but her eyes remained haunted, and it tugged at Kyra's heart. This was the girl who'd thought nothing of attacking boys twice her size in order to protect Lettie, and now she was frightened even to cross a Palace courtyard. Kyra did her best to dispel the hopeless anger building in her chest. It would do Idalee no good.

There was no sign of Lord Agan's sons as they stepped out onto the path. "All right so far?" Kyra asked.

Idalee nodded. Since they couldn't walk quickly, Kyra pulled Idalee to the side to let two noblewomen bundled in furs go past. When they stepped back onto the path, Idalee said, "Look there!"

Kyra's eyes snapped to follow Idalee's gaze, her nerves keying up as she scanned the grounds for Santon. She didn't know whether to laugh or cry when she saw that it was Tristam whom Idalee had seen, coming out of the same administrative structure he'd been hurrying to a few days before. By now, he'd turned to walk toward them, taking away Kyra's initial hope that they might have passed unseen. Funny how a simple piece of information could change everything. The fine tunic that Kyra had admired before now seemed ostentatious. And the hint of guilt she thought she'd detected a few days ago now permeated every single movement he made.

"Idalee," said Tristam. "I'm glad to see you on your feet."

Idalee curtsied. "Ilona says I'm out of danger's way now."

"Are the two of you going home?" he asked.

"Malikel gave me the day to see Idalee settled," Kyra said. "And how are you, Tristam? Still negotiating with the family in Parna?" *Who is she? How much money does her family have?* She wasn't sure how good a job she did of keeping her voice neutral, but Tristam seemed too distracted to notice.

"Yes, and it's taking a while. They're an old family. Old money, lots of influence. They control a large private guard force." He spoke the last part as if it pained him.

It was falling into place far more easily than Kyra wanted. The family from Parna had offered to help defend Brancel Manor. Of course they'd want something in return, like a permanent alliance with the family. Kyra felt a pang in her gut. If what Orvin said was true, then Tristam was lying to her, or at the very least deliberately hiding the truth.

She didn't know what to do. Kyra couldn't confront him with Idalee right there. Even if she and Tristam had been alone,

Kyra didn't know if she was ready. She gave Tristam her best attempt at a smile. "We should be getting home. I wish you progress on your negotiations."

Unexpectedly, Tristam took her hand. "It's good to see you, Kyra," he said, with more fervency than those words usually warranted. "Both of you."

Kyra stood stock-still, unable to react at first. Then she carefully extricated her hand from his. "Have a good day," she said, and left, pulling Idalee after her.

## TEN

Kyra wondered if James ever got used to the dungeon's smell. The stink faded after the first few minutes, but it never quite disappeared. Though, as she looked at the fresh bruises on James's face, she realized that the smell would be the least of his worries.

"Did you make contact with Orvin?" he asked.

"He told me Willem's taking private messengers in the middle of the night. I'm going to try and find out what they're for." She deliberated a bit before asking her next question. "How reliable is Orvin? Had he ever jumped to false conclusions?"

"Everything from Orvin's always been accurate," said James. "He's very keen on the affairs of noblemen."

That was good for her mission, though not for the selfish part of her that still hoped Orvin was wrong about Tristam.

A guard's footfalls sounded in the corridor, and Kyra wondered if she should go. There was nothing more that she needed from James tonight. Actually, she hadn't needed to come see him at all, but she found herself reluctant to leave. Somehow, over the past weeks, the prison cell of her enemy had become the one place where she could speak freely. Kyra wouldn't say she enjoyed visiting James—he still set her off balance far too easily. But James had a keen mind and an incisive tongue, and she could discuss things with him that she couldn't discuss with anyone else.

"What do you think makes Willem the way he is?" she finally asked. "Or any of the wallhuggers who trample on the rest of the city. Are they really that different from us?"

"Power is seductive. Once you have a little, it's easy to go after more."

"To the point of sending hundreds of people to their deaths for political power?" *Or negotiating a loveless marriage.* She told herself that this wasn't about Tristam, but thoughts of him kept intruding into her mind.

"Is it really that hard to believe? Can you honestly say you've not used your new position at the Palace for personal gain?"

James always had a way of stripping away her excuses. She saw herself in Malikel's study just a few days prior, pleading with the Defense Minister to get Flick out of the early units. Of course, if Flick had been excused, someone else would have been conscripted in his stead, but that hadn't stopped Kyra.

"What's the point, then?" Kyra wasn't sure if the disgust in her voice was aimed more at the wallhuggers or at herself. "What's the point of fighting against the ones in power if others'll just take their place? Mayhap it's better just to live my own life and let things fall as they will."

"That was the life you were living before I took you into the Guild. But I don't believe you can just turn a blind eye, once you've seen what the world is like. I couldn't."

"What do you want for Forge?" Kyra asked. "Would you see the whole Palace razed to the ground?"

"Does the city truly need to make its decisions in marble-lined halls? Would we really forget how to live our lives if the Council were not there to dictate it?"

"You can't possibly want anarchy," said Kyra.

"There are ways to rule that don't require the rich to step on the weak. The city's trade guilds rule themselves adequately without wallhuggers. Parna's people elect representatives that rule in concert with the nobles."

"So my efforts to discredit Willem—is that goal too small for you?" she asked.

"It's a step. Willem must go, but he cannot simply be dispatched. He's a good enough politician that his death would make him a martyr and cement his cause. No. Willem must be disgraced before he's brought low."

Kyra wondered again about what kind of man James had been before. For a moment, she imagined what might have happened if she'd stayed in the Guild, if she hadn't killed that manservant so early on, or if she hadn't had Bella or Flick to keep her grounded. Would she have followed in James's footsteps, becoming just slightly more ruthless, year after year? Would she have become his lover and protégé, taken up his cause?

James looked at her again, perhaps sensing the direction of her thoughts. "You and I are not very different," he said. "Not very different at all."

"You keep saying that," she said. The dankness of the dungeon settled on her skin.

"I say it because it's true."

## ELEVEN

If it hadn't been for the whole "being sent out to fight demon cats" thing, Flick might well have enjoyed being conscripted into the early patrol units. His fellow recruits were friendly folk—men ranging from Kyra's age to those with young grandchildren. The Palace fed them well enough (some of the merchants complained about the food's quality, but Flick wasn't picky), and he learned quite a few new skills. And while Sir Malikel and his men exhibited some wallhugger snobbishness from time to time, Flick had encountered far worse.

Since his conscription, Flick reported to the Palace every day for training. Today, he and his unit congregated on the training fields. The large, flat fields were supposedly covered with grass during the summer, though the surface was now well-packed straw and dirt. While the grounds were large enough to run horses, the only people currently on it were on foot.

Malikel's crew took turns training the new recruits. This morning, Tristam arranged them in concentric circles: Flick stood with four men in the outer circle with their spears pointed diagonally up, while three more stood in the middle with spears angled closer to vertical. Sixteen men formed two of these formations, while the remaining four members of their unit stood to the side, holding sticks with bags of straw tied to the end— stand-ins for demon cat heads.

"This is a variation of the formation our infantrymen use against cavalry charges," Tristam said. It was interesting to finally see the wallhugger in his element. Tristam was comfortable here and competent (at least, to Flick's untrained eye), and he seemed to genuinely want this ragtag group of soldiers to do well. "The difference, of course, between cavalry and demon cats is that cavalry don't come at you from above. That's why we have three men in the middle whose job is to watch the trees. You'll have an easier time holding ranks if you brace your spears against the ground. Remember, these beasts pack a lot of force."

"So the demon cats will oblige us by attacking only while we're in this formation?" piped a young baker named Tommy.

Tristam ignored the sniggers that followed the question. "You take this formation when you are able, whether it's because you've had advance warning of an attack or because your enemy has given you enough quarter to re-form. If they give you no space, then you will have to use another strategy."

He gestured toward the four men of Flick's unit who held cat head targets. "All right, demon cats. See what you can do."

Shouts rose up from the trainees as they fell into mock battle. Funny enough, these exercises reminded Flick of the games he used to play as a street child. The level of chaos was certainly comparable, though the participants were a little less nimble. Flick raised his spear as a demon cat charged in, digging his feet into the mud to get a more stable stance. He got a good thrust into the center of the sack as it came at him, though he was momentarily distracted by an image of Kyra's face as he pulled his spear back out. It was an odd duality, the thought of Kyra as both the young street urchin he knew so well and a different sort of creature altogether. Over the last few months, she'd experienced things that were far beyond his ken. Flick couldn't keep up with her anymore, and he worried how she'd fare by herself in uncharted waters.

Loud guffaws came from the next circle over. Apparently, one of the target holders had tripped and fallen on his face. The fallen man regained his feet, covered in mud, and joined in the laughter. Tristam's lips tightened with impatience as the ranks dissolved, but Flick understood the compulsion to laugh. The wallhuggers might have been raised with the expectation of riding out to battle, but this type of danger was new to the men in this unit. They needed to laugh, if only to dispel their fear.

"Hold it together," said Tristam. "You could be facing live ones tomorrow."

That quieted them down. Orders had come in the morning that their unit was to start trial sweeps of the forest the next day. It was much earlier than anyone had anticipated. Even Malikel, usually so stoic, had failed to hide his surprise.

They drilled like this a while longer, then Tristam called out a break. "Get some water. Sir Rollan will take up your spear training in a quarter hour."

The recruits laid down their weapons and gratefully made their way to the edge of the field. Malikel was there, handing out ladles of water. Flick had to give the Defense Minister credit. Malikel had been at the training fields almost every day, and not just ordering his subordinates around. He'd been in the thick of things and had spoken to every man in the unit at least once.

There was a rustle behind Flick. He turned to see Tristam wipe his brow, pick up a demon cat head, and stuff the protruding straw back into the sack. He paid Flick no mind.

"They still get to you, don't they?" said Flick.

"They're not trained military. I need to remember that," said Tristam, his voice gruff. He moved on to the next target and retied the knot securing the bag to its stick.

"I don't mean the recruits. I mean the demon cats."

At that, Tristam stopped what he was doing.

"I see it in your eyes when you tell us about them," Flick said. "Sometimes your hands shake. What do they call it? Battle ghosts?" Flick didn't know much about it firsthand, but he'd heard enough stories from former soldiers. Sometimes a battle stayed with a soldier, haunting his dreams and never quite letting him move on.

Tristam's expression closed off. "I fight the battles my commander orders me to. Whatever ghosts they create are irrelevant." He put the target on the ground and turned toward the water barrels.

"What do you see when you're with Kyra?" Flick asked. "Given what she is, I'm surprised that the two of you, uh . . ." He stopped, remembering that Kyra had cut things off.

Tristam's jaw tightened. "Kyra's a fellow soldier. Nothing

more." He took a few steps toward the water barrels, then looked back again. "Her bloodlines do scare me, but they frighten her much more. That's the difference between her and the others."

As Tristam joined Malikel by the sidelines, Flick picked up the fake demon cat head and looked it in its nonexistent eyes. "I'm beginning to think I've been too hard on that wallhugger."

The hemp bag swayed back and forth on its stick. If it had any insights, it kept them to itself.

Kyra arrived at the training fields just in time to see Flick charge a straw demon cat with a spear. It went cleanly through, and he pulled it out again. He caught sight of Kyra watching from the sidelines and waved. A knight, Sir Rollan, barked an order, and Flick continued his exercises.

"How do they look?" Kyra asked Malikel. Tristam was also there, along with several knights. It was a slightly overcast day, and the sun blinked in and out of the clouds.

"Decently against straw," said Malikel. "Against live cats, on the other hand, there is more work to do."

She watched their progress for the next hour. Kyra was supposed to give suggestions based on what she knew of the cats, but military strategy was beyond her. While Tristam could comment on formations and tactics, Kyra could only think that these men needed to move much faster if they wanted to stay alive. It gave her a modicum of comfort that Flick seemed one of the more competent with a spear.

"When will they be sent out against live cats?" asked Kyra.

"They're to do a training round in the forest tomorrow."

"Tomorrow?" The knights standing around her turned at her exclamation, and Kyra lowered her voice. "You must see they're not ready."

"It is the wish of the Council," said Malikel. His tone warned her not to object again.

"The Council is—"

"That's enough, Kyra. You are dismissed."

Kyra stood immobile for a moment, wanting to argue more, but there was a dangerous set to Malikel's jaw, and she could see that it was hopeless. She turned and stormed from the practice fields. She'd gone maybe a hundred paces when Tristam called after her.

"Kyra, wait!"

"Don't you have some courtiers to talk to?" she snapped. Tristam flinched at her words, but Kyra wasn't feeling inclined to pity.

"You can't question a commander like that in front of his men. He won't have it."

Kyra wondered why Flick hadn't told her he was being sent into the forest the next day. Had he been trying not to worry her, or had he not known either? She'd spent several nights trying to track down the scribe responsible for Flick's conscription, but the search had proved difficult. That, along with Orvin's insight into Willem's true reasons for conscripting Flick, had forced her to halt her efforts. Though now she wondered if she should have tried harder.

"Do you have some time?" said Tristam. "I'm off for the afternoon, and I'd like to talk a bit."

Kyra lowered her head so he wouldn't see her irritation. Now he wanted to talk? After Malikel had proved himself impotent and Tristam had shown himself to be untrustworthy? "Where would you like to go?" she asked.

"To my quarters?"

She nodded and turned in that direction without making eye contact. Tristam's living quarters had been a subject of some controversy after he was demoted and could no longer stay in the officials' dormitories. He could have lodged in the barracks, but the thought of the son of a noble house, even a disgraced one, rubbing shoulders with common soldiers had been offensive enough to influential people at the Palace that the option was ruled out. Instead, he'd moved into a small but comfortable room in a building that housed visiting noblemen.

They walked there together now, and Tristam held the door open for her. His neatly made bed sat next to the window across from a writing desk and a dresser. His sword and armor hung on racks against the wall. Tristam also had a small table, where he pulled out a chair for Kyra before sitting down himself.

"Is there anything in particular you wanted to talk about?" she asked.

"Yes, there is." Tristam stared at his hands and appeared to collect himself. It suddenly occurred to Kyra that he might tell her about the marriage negotiations after all, and she had no idea how to respond. She wiped her palms on her trousers. *Don't say it, Tristam. I don't want to have that conversation right now.*

"I'm sorry about Flick," said Tristam. "I've been doing my very best to prepare them. We all have."

Kyra took a moment to swallow the ball of disappointment

and annoyance that was quickly replacing the panic in her chest. She was being silly, she knew, wanting one thing and then the other. "How long will the rounds in the forest be? How dangerous?" she asked.

"The first round will just be a few hours in the morning, basic maneuvers in more realistic terrain. It could very well be uneventful. But even if something does happen, the new recruits are already much better than they were when they started. I honestly think that many of them, Flick included, have a fair chance of killing a demon cat if they run across one."

*Killing a demon cat.* Of course, if Kyra had to choose between Flick and any one of the Makvani, she would pick Flick in a heartbeat. But Tristam's words still left a bad taste in her mouth.

"I wish there was some other way," she said.

"What do you mean?"

"Why does it have to be a slaughter? If only I'd convinced Pashla to take me to Leyus."

Tristam drummed his fingers on the table, his nostrils flaring slightly. "I hold Malikel in high esteem, but in this endeavor I think he's misguided. I don't trust the Makvani to keep any promises they make."

"I trust Pashla," Kyra said. "And there might be others like her."

"Pashla killed Jack. If she's the best of the lot, then I see no reason to trust them."

If Kyra had been in a better frame of mind, she might have acknowledged that he had a fair point. It was actually Pashla's companion who'd killed Jack, but Pashla had allowed it to happen. Though Kyra's own experiences with Pashla had been good, she wasn't naïve enough to forget the disdain with which the Makvani viewed humans.

But it had been a long week with many unwelcome revelations, and there was a layer of disgust in Tristam's voice that Kyra couldn't ignore.

"If you don't trust them, then why trust me?" she asked.

Tristam looked up at her, uncertain. "Kyra?"

"I share their blood. I could hunt someone down as easily as they. Why trust me if you can't trust them?" She didn't bother to hide the hardness in her voice.

He pushed off the table, backing away from the unexpected attack. "Kyra, I would think we know each other well enough now that—"

That was too much.

"Know each other?" she snapped. "How well do I actually know you? Do you want to tell me what you've actually been talking to those courtiers about all week? What that family from Parna really wants from you?" Her last word rang in the air, and then there was absolute silence in the room. The shock in Tristam's expression slowly turned to guilt, and any last hope of a misunderstanding slowly faded away.

"How did you find out?" Tristam had the look of a criminal who'd just been handed his judgment.

"When were you planning to tell me?"

He stared at her, and several times his jaw worked as if he were about to start speaking. "You may or may not believe me, but that was the real reason I wanted to talk to you today. I knew I couldn't keep putting it off, but I couldn't find the courage to actually say it."

Kyra stared at him without response.

Finally he sighed and collapsed back against his chair. "Everything I've told you about that family and Parna is true. They are rich and powerful, with a great deal of resources. Our manor at Brancel has been falling more often to Demon Rider attacks. In addition to our manor, we're responsible for the protection of a small hamlet nearby, and we take those duties seriously. With our resources stretched thin, we've not been able to protect them. The family from Parna could help us . . . if we were family as well."

"What's the lass's name?" Kyra asked. She wasn't quite sure why it was important, but she wanted to know.

"Cecile," he said reluctantly. "She's the fourth daughter of Lord Salis of Routhian. They don't live far from Brancel, actually, but they swear fealty to Parna. I've never met her, but everyone says she's pleasant."

The name had sharp edges that dug into her chest. "And you have to accept this alliance?" It occurred to her that maybe she shouldn't assume Tristam opposed the marriage.

Tristam stared at the table in front of him. "It's complicated. I've already brought disgrace on my family by losing my rank as a knight. I'm unlikely to gain any position of political influence because of that, at least in the near future. The only way I can serve my family now is through a marriage, and the Routhian household cares much less about my disgrace than any house of Forge would. And we do need help."

She thought she'd been upset when she first learned the news, but it was far worse to hear Tristam talk about it, to hear him actually considering it, when two months ago, they'd held each other in the forest and kissed. He was expecting her to say something, but she couldn't. Moment by moment, the silence between them stretched longer.

"Kyra, please say something. This is not . . . something that I would choose."

He wanted her to talk to him? What could he possibly expect her to say? Kyra finally managed to clear her throat. She tried for a smile, but it didn't quite work. "I shouldn't be surprised, I suppose. That's why I broke things off in the first place, wasn't it? I guess I'd not expected to be proved right so soon."

She saw in Tristam's face the precise moment her words sank in, and felt a perverse pleasure as her jab hit home. She wanted to be alone. Kyra pushed her chair back from the table. "I should go."

She left before he could stop her.

The sun had completely set now, and Kyra was glad for it. She didn't want anyone to see the expression on her face as she rushed through the courtyard, making for the Palace gates as quickly as she could. At least the grounds had calmed now from the midday frenzy, and there were fewer people walking the torch-lit pathways. Kyra kept her head down and her steps quick. She needed to get out.

She'd just left the inner compound when someone called her name. His voice was thick with disdain, and Kyra's stomach knotted in recognition even before her mind registered who it was. She turned to see Lord Agan's son Santon walking toward her, flanked by his two brothers.

"Where are you going, Kyra of Forge?" he said. There was an unnatural loudness to his voice and just the slightest hint of unsteadiness in his step. A wind blew from their direction, and Kyra smelled wine.

Kyra cursed under her breath. Of all the times to run into these wallhuggers. The pathways around her were empty of passersby. Just her luck. Or had they waited until no one was around? *Not tonight. I don't need this tonight.* The mere sight of them disgusted her. Kyra backed away, though she didn't want to move so quickly that she'd appear frightened. The wall-huggers drew closer.

"Off to interfere with someone else's business?" said Santon.

"Girl doesn't know her place," said his younger brother. Kyra thought he was the one named Douglass.

"Just like that gutter rat she played hero for," said the third brother, Dalton.

Her eyes flicked quickly to the swords they wore at their belts. It was too bad that the unevenness in their step wasn't more pronounced. They'd still be able to handle the swords well enough to give her trouble. The wise thing to do would be to run away. There were plenty of places she could escape to. At least she wasn't boxed in by crowds as she'd been the last time, but the thought of turning tail and fleeing the cowards left a bitter taste in her mouth.

"How's your gutter rat friend, Kyra?" Santon asked. "She healing up all right?"

*Just ignore them.* These noblemen weren't worth the trouble. The building next to her had a chimney she could scale. She could be out of their reach in a few moments. Kyra did her best to push images of Idalee out of her mind, the fearful way the girl had scanned the Palace grounds as they'd left Ilona's care.

"Too bad the magistrate never found the people who beat the wench," said Santon with a savage smile. Kyra gritted her teeth. She took a firm hold on the chimney and dug her fingers into depressions in the stone. It was icy cold, but she barely felt it.

"Gutter rat wasn't worth the magistrate's time," said Dalton. "Her type's only good for cleaning chamber pots and the occasional late-night sport."

She froze.

"Better flip the order of that, Dalton. Imagine the stink otherwise," said Santon.

Kyra lowered her hand and slowly turned back toward the wallhuggers. "Shut your mouths and go home," she said, her voice dangerously quiet.

It took the noblemen a few moments to process her words. They hadn't expected her to come back toward them. They hadn't expected her to give them a command. And they were far too arrogant to heed the threat that infused every one of her words. Santon stood for a moment, and then the smile slowly returned to his face. "Girl wants to play hero again."

"If you know what's good for you," said Kyra, "you'll leave right now." There was a spark of anger in her stomach, and she nurtured it. Even as she spoke, she was hoping they wouldn't listen to her. She saw Idalee's crumpled form on the ground as the wallhuggers kicked her, heard the girl's choked cries. No, Kyra most definitely did not want Santon and his brothers to do as they were told.

"Don't be giving threats to those above your station, Kyra," said Santon, closing the distance between them. "You think you're safe because you're on Palace grounds? You're nothing but a glorified gutter rat, and you'll end up just like your friend."

He struck her across the face then, his hand moving fast and sure. She put up an arm to block him, but Santon was strong enough that the blow still connected and knocked her halfway over. Kyra stayed bent over, one hand to her aching jaw, waiting for the tears to clear from her eyes. There was a coppery taste in her mouth where she'd bitten her cheek. Her dagger was in her boot, but she didn't reach for it.

Santon grabbed her arm and shoved her to the ground. Pain lanced through Kyra's shoulder as she hit the cobblestones, and she rolled away from him. Before he could come closer, she unfastened her cloak and pulled her tunic over her head, shivering as the icy wind blew through the thin shift she wore underneath. The small voice of restraint inside her whispered one more warning, and she thrust it savagely into a far corner of her mind.

Santon slowed, staring at Kyra as she stepped out of her boots and onto the frigid ground. For a moment, he was uncertain, his wine-addled mind trying to make sense of her actions. Then his smile took on a different tone. "Well, this is new. Is this how you actually managed to rise through the ranks? Maybe Sir Malikel has better judgment than we gave him credit for." Douglas and Dalton circled behind her. Kyra's skin crawled, but still, she didn't move.

Footsteps sounded from around the corner. A Red Shield, a guard on patrol, stopped dead in his tracks, his eyes going from Kyra, huddled on the ground in her shift, to the brothers surrounding her.

"Continue on your rounds," Santon ordered. "Stay clear of this space for a while."

In an all-too-familiar routine, the guard backed away and left. Kyra couldn't keep the fury from her face as she stared after him. *Coward.*

Santon's lips curled, and he bent down to her level. "Don't be so naïve," he said. "And try to smile a little. This is better than you deserve." He grabbed a fistful of her collar, pulling her face close to his.

And Kyra let her anger explode.

## TWELVE

$S$anton didn't seem to realize what was happening at first. He was too close to see her clearly, and his mind was slow from drink. But soon enough the leer on his face turned to confusion, and Kyra could tell by the exclamations behind her that his brothers had noticed something wasn't right. Santon lost his hold on her as her bones lengthened and her limbs stretched. She pushed him away and kicked off her trousers as her shift began to tear and rip away. Santon hit the ground with a grunt. Kyra climbed to her feet and settled herself onto all fours.

In hindsight, it had been a mistake to wait until the wall-huggers were so close before changing. If they had been thinking clearly, they could have killed her right then and there. But thankfully the three of them stood paralyzed even as Kyra's vision took on that newly familiar clarity and her thoughts faded into instinct . . . and rage.

"What by the three cities . . ." Santon whispered.

Footsteps pounded behind her, growing more distant, and Kyra turned just in time to see Douglass rounding a corner. The sight of him fleeing brought an intense desire to run him down, though she hesitated—the other two were right here. Then Santon and Dalton also turned to flee, and she no longer had to choose between staying or giving chase.

Santon was laughably slow, hardly a challenge at all. She knocked him off his feet; he rolled and jumped back up with his sword drawn. The blade glinted in the moonlight. Kyra hesitated, and Santon took that opportunity to charge. His sword came down on her shoulder, but it felt like a bludgeon instead of a cut as the edge glanced off her fur. Kyra batted the weapon out of his hand.

There was a shout behind her, and Kyra turned to see Dalton running at her with his sword raised. This time, she was faster. Kyra sprang to the side as he swung, and bit down on his sword arm. He screamed, and the sound thrilled her. His blood, warm in her mouth, fueled her growing battle fury. She threw him to the ground with a quick jerk of her neck. He was a large man, but she tossed him around as easily as if he were a child.

Pain exploded in her back leg. Kyra screamed and looked back just as Santon raised his dagger again. She kicked out with her hind legs, catching him squarely in the chest. The dagger clattered to the ground, the clank of metal harsh in her ears. As Santon skidded across the dirt, Kyra felt a wave of disdain. She slashed at him with her claws, opening four ribbons of red along his torso. His cry of pain brought her some satisfaction, and she moved in for the kill. His screams broke off as her jaws closed around his throat. She held on as he struggled, but that didn't last very long at all, and soon he fell still. It had been too easy, and her blood was still hot. Kyra let go of his throat and tore at the now lifeless body, venting her frustration. Then she remembered there were two more. She raised her head and pricked her ears.

"Kyra!"

She heard the words as if from far away. She turned to the sound, teeth bared, but the speaker wasn't one of the wall-huggers who had attacked her. Kyra recognized Tristam even in the midst of her rage, and he was walking slowly toward her, speaking gently, though she couldn't quite make sense of the words. She growled deep in her throat. Even if she didn't want to fight him, he was keeping her from her prey. She turned away, but he said her name again, and his voice pulled at her, calm but insistent.

He kept talking, his hands held placatingly out in front of him. Kyra backed up as he came closer, puzzled at why he was neither fighting nor running away. Slowly, her blood cooled just enough so that Kyra understood she should change back. She gathered the heat, the feeling of her fur, and pushed it back inside, letting out a sigh as her body melted in on itself. Tristam was ready with her clothes as her skin became smooth and she started to shiver. Her nails were covered with blood.

"Kyra?" Tristam searched her eyes as if he was afraid he wouldn't find her there. "Kyra, what happened?"

She shook her head, trying to focus her eyes. It felt as if all the blood in her skull was pounding to get out. "Lord Agan's sons. They came upon me while I was leaving.... We fought... I..." She broke off as she took in the destruction around her.

Dalton was on the ground, moaning and cradling his arm. Douglass was nowhere to be seen. And on the ground behind her...

Kyra's stomach reacted instantly to the sight. She jerked away from Tristam and retched, though there wasn't much in her stomach. She could sense Tristam behind her, but he didn't touch her. As her gut stopped spasming, she wiped her mouth and forced herself to look again.

Santon's body was barely recognizable as human. The arms and legs were splayed at awkward angles. The face was covered in blood, the neck torn open. Kyra looked away, unable to reconcile her exultant memories, the bloodlust that still echoed in her veins, with the mangled corpse in front of her. She'd done that to Santon. She'd heard his screams and she'd... She couldn't think it.

Tristam grabbed her by the shoulders and shook her. The fear in his eyes was very, very real. That more than anything brought her mind back.

"Kyra, listen to me." He was looking around. Shouts echoed nearby. When he looked back at her, some of the fear was replaced by determination. "You have to go," he said. "Leave the Palace. Leave the city."

*Leave the city.* Just like that? But they'd had plans in place. When the Palace finally found out, Kyra was going to convince Malikel that she posed no threat. That even though she shared blood with the Demon Riders, she wasn't a danger.

A bloodcurdling scream rent the air. It was Dalton. He had turned over onto his side, and his eyes were fixed on Santon's remains. A dull heaviness weighed down Kyra's chest. How could she think of convincing anyone that she wasn't a danger now? Tristam was right. Fleeing was the only choice left to her.

"What about you?" she asked Tristam.

"Don't worry about me. I'll tell them you ran off."

Tristam wasn't a good liar either. He couldn't quite look her in the eye, and even with her mind muddled as it was, she knew that he was wrong. Tristam was too closely associated with her. They had to convince the Palace that he'd tried to capture Kyra, or he'd take the fall for her.

"Fight me," she said. Even as Tristam was making sense of her words, she reached for her dagger and realized it was somewhere on the ground with her boots. She thought to go back for it, but there was no time. Instead, she tackled him.

Kyra caught him off guard, and Tristam fell backward as she pummeled at his face. He grunted in pain—her blows landed harder than she intended. *Fight back, you idiot,* she thought, even as she struck him again across his cheekbone. That blow split his lip, but her blood still ran hot from the kill, and it was hard to pull back.

Finally, he started to defend himself, raising his hands to block her. A flurry of blows and stinging parries passed between them, then Tristam caught one of her wrists. When she tried to pull away, he captured the other. For a moment, they were locked together, Kyra quivering with battle rage as she leaned into him, both of them breathing in deep, painful gulps. She saw uncertainty and resolve in his eyes, and Kyra realized she didn't know when she would see him again.

"Go, Kyra. Now!"

When Kyra didn't react, Tristam set his jaw, curled his

legs between them, and kicked her off. He wasn't gentle. The kick knocked the breath out of her, and she rolled over twice before she came to a stop. Kyra coughed, then slowly pulled herself to her feet. More shouts. Three Red Shields were pointing and running toward them.

Tristam raised himself to a crouch. One of his eyes was already starting to swell. He launched himself at her again. She dodged him, grabbed her boots, and ran, pushing through the pain in her ribs and her injured leg, hearing his footsteps behind her grow fainter even though she knew he was a faster runner than she. Kyra ducked her head and bent all her energy toward getting away.

◻ ◻ ◻

Tristam watched Kyra disappear into the darkness. It wasn't hard to feign shock as Red Shields swarmed around him. His jaw ached—Kyra had hit him hard. And he was still reeling from the scene around him.

Red Shields surrounded him and pointed their swords at him. He raised his hands.

"I'm unarmed," he said.

One soldier came closer and patted him down. Tristam winced as the Red Shield hit another spot that Kyra had bruised. She'd been half-wild when she'd changed back into her human shape, more feral than he'd ever seen her. He saw her again, eyes flashing, a hint of a snarl still on her lips. She'd been out for blood, and it scared him more than he cared to admit.

The Red Shield finished his search and nodded to the others, who lowered their weapons. "You were a witness to this?" asked the soldier.

"Yes." Every limb felt heavy. His ribs complained when he drew breath to speak.

"Come with me, then," said the Red Shield, leading him back to the scene.

Santon's mauled corpse lay on the cobblestones. Dalton screamed incoherently, though Tristam could pick out the words "monster" and "girl." He slumped down and rubbed his jaw again, waiting for his mind to clear.

A crowd was gathering now, mostly nobles and guards, though a few brave servants also stopped to stare. A soldier knelt next to Dalton and called for bandages. Nobody came close to Santon's body.

"Make way." The crowd parted, and Tristam's heart skipped a beat as Malikel strode through. The Defense Minister took a long look at Santon, and then at Dalton and Tristam. "What happened?"

"A monster," croaked Dalton, his voice hoarse. "The girl changed into a demon cat." He sounded delirious in his pain, and for a moment Tristam wondered if he could still cover this up. But no, there had been a third brother who'd run.

"What's he talking about?" Malikel directed his question at Tristam.

"There was a demon cat in the Palace, sir," he said. "I was outside my quarters when I heard screams. I came running and saw it attacking these two and their brother." Actually, he hadn't simply been outside his quarters. He'd run out after Kyra, unwilling to let the conversation end the way it had, when he'd stumbled upon that scene.

"And what is he saying about the girl?"

This was it, then. Tristam sent a silent apology to Kyra. "It was Kyra, sir. She...she's a Demon Rider. I saw her change back into her human form after the attack."

Malikel's face clouded over, though he didn't look as surprised as Tristam would have expected. "You saw this with your own eyes?"

"Yes, sir," said Tristam.

"And you had no idea of this. No suspicions."

Tristam hesitated. It was bad enough to lie to any commander, but this was Malikel.

"You knew nothing of this, Tristam. It caught you by surprise," continued the Defense Minister.

Only then did he notice the way his commander looked at him, and a subtlety in Malikel's inflection, as if he was telling Tristam something rather than asking. "Yes, sir," he said hesitantly. He thought he caught a glimpse of approval in Malikel's eyes. "I tried to stop her from escaping, but I couldn't."

The crowd's energy shifted again, and a new voice spoke. "A Demon Rider attack in the Palace? Do I hear this correctly?" Tristam felt the color drain from his face as Malikel squared his shoulders. The people gathered around parted for Willem.

"You heard correctly, Willem," Malikel said.

Willem gave a passing glance to Dalton, who was only semiconscious. "What do I hear about Kyra of Forge being one of the Demon Riders?"

"That is what the witnesses claim," said Malikel. The Defense Minister stood with his feet braced and back straight. *He's preparing to take a fall,* thought Tristam. *There's no good outcome for Malikel here.*

"We had one of our enemies in our midst the entire time, working for the Ministry of Defense?" The Head Councilman spoke more loudly than he needed to, and the look in his eyes was one of a bird of prey who had spotted a rabbit. "This is grave news indeed," he said. "A very bad mistake for someone in your position, Malikel. I'm very sorry, but this will have implications."

The Head Councilman's eyes, however, glinted in a way that didn't look sorry at all.

Someone must have raised the alarm, because the air filled with shouts and the loud rhythms of booted feet. Kyra's leg throbbed where Santon had cut it. It had stopped bleeding, but her trousers kept sticking to the wound. She didn't dare slow down. It would only get harder to escape.

She ran on instinct, too shocked to think out a coherent escape route, relying only on her reflexes to find her the safest way. She kept to the ledges as much as she could to avoid the Red Shields swarming the footpaths. When she had to travel on the ground, she darted from shadow to shadow, more than once diving into a corner to avoid being seen.

Finally, she scrambled up the Palace wall and flung herself over the top. Once on the other side, she ran into a sheltered alleyway. It was as safe a place as any to catch her breath, and she took in gulp after gulp of icy air.

She'd killed again.

Kyra could still see Santon's body on the ground, the angle of his ravaged neck. The memory kept shifting. It was as if she saw the body through two sets of eyes, one that looked upon it with relish and the other with horror. The emotions didn't mix well, and she fought the sickening churn of her stomach. The first time she killed a man, when she'd slit a man's throat in a failed Assassins Guild raid, that had been an accident. But this . . .

A shadow crossed the alley's entrance, and Kyra froze. It wasn't a Red Shield. Just a man, and he continued right on down the street without stopping. But the shock reminded her of her danger. The Palace knew where she lived. There would be Red Shields at her door within a few hours—if not Red Shields, then an angry mob, and Idalee and Lettie were at home. A fresh wave of panic jolted through her. *What had she done?* The mob wouldn't differentiate between Kyra and her family. She had to warn them. Kyra set off again with renewed speed, keeping to alleyways and rooftops since she couldn't blend in with the evening crowds when her clothing was in tatters and her face smeared with blood.

Kyra burst into her quarters to find Lettie, Idalee, and Flick playing a dice game. Flick looked up with a smile, only to have the smile freeze on his face.

Kyra froze as well, staring at the three of them with wide eyes. "We have to leave," she said. "Now. Take everything."

The three of them gaped at her.

"Now!" Kyra said again, louder this time. She could hear the tinge of hysteria in her voice. Giving up on them, she ran over to her chest and started pulling things out. She threw her spare clothes onto the ground and fished out a coil of rope.

"Kyra, wait." Flick crossed the room and took her by the arm. She let him turn her around, and he bent so their eyes were level. "What's going on?"

She was shaking. Even with the pressure of Flick's hands on her shoulders, the tremors came through. She swallowed. "Santon of Agan is dead," she said finally.

"What happened?"

"He—I—" Kyra couldn't say it. "Not now, please. We have to go. The Red Shields will be here any minute." She took a deep breath. "They know what I am. I changed."

Flick's grip on her went slack. "People saw?"

She nodded.

Flick looked down at her scattered belongings with new understanding. "I need to go get my things." The readiness with which he accepted this only served to intensify her guilt. If he'd yelled at her for blowing her cover and uprooting them all, she might have found the energy to defend herself. But perhaps it was better this way. They had no time to squabble.

"Meet us at the spot by the south wall," Kyra said.

After Flick left, Kyra washed the blood off her face and changed into clean clothes. When she turned around, she saw Idalee watching her with a stricken expression.

"Idalee," Kyra said uncertainly. "We need to pack quickly."

The girl looked to be in a daze, but she moved to her own chest and started pulling out belongings with her non-splinted arm. Once Kyra was done with her own bags, she gathered Lettie's clothes. She also jumped to retrieve a stash of emergency coins that she'd hidden in a hollowed-out roof beam. Then she rushed them all out the door.

Flick stood waiting by the south wall with a bag slung over his shoulders. They'd scouted out this spot before, a stretch lined with houses that didn't have windows on their outward-facing sides. Kyra threw a grappling hook over the top—it clinked more loudly than she would have liked—then waited as Flick climbed up and hauled their bags after him. Idalee was next. Kyra tied a loop for the girl to stand on, and she held tightly with her good arm while Flick pulled her up. Lettie followed, and then Kyra came last.

A wide road circled the city wall. Beyond that were houses, not crowded as densely as the houses in the city, but there were still too many people who might see them. The main road led out from the city gates, but that was farther down the wall, and they didn't dare follow it. Instead, they took narrow footpaths that led them between houses. There were others on these roads—farmers returning home, women running errands. The four of them put their heads down and walked as if they belonged.

Flick pulled even with Kyra. "Are you going to tell me what happened?"

"The Agan brothers found me as I was leaving the compound. Started taunting me about Idalee, and then they started threatening me."

"They attacked you?"

Had they attacked her? Flick was clearly willing to believe

that it had been self-defense. And in part, it had been—once they'd laid hands on her. But she'd had a chance to flee—she'd wanted an excuse not to. Kyra shook her head. It was hard even to think back on it. Every time she did, her battle lust crept back like a slow fog. She didn't dare think about what would happen if it took over.

"I don't want to talk about it."

To her relief, Flick didn't push her. "We'll need to figure out where to go."

Kyra watched the ground pass under her feet. "I can't stay in the city. There's too many people looking for me, but it's different for you. There's no manhunt out for you, and you'll have trouble from the Palace if you disappear. You'd be labeled a deserter."

Flick considered this. "They'll likely bring me in for questioning if I stay in the city. Even if they don't, the best I have to look forward to is patrolling the forest with my unit tomorrow. I'll take my chances as a deserter."

She nodded, selfishly relieved. "Is there anyone you can take shelter with out here?"

"I have a friend who lives at the edge of the forest. We can try her."

"What do you think, Idalee? And Lettie?" said Kyra.

Bells started ringing in the city just then, and Kyra's heart nearly jumped out of her throat. She felt Flick's hand on her back. "Keep walking."

Hoofbeats sounded from the direction of the main road. A man shouted commands. Kyra looked around in panic for a place to go.

"The haystack," Idalee said.

The houses had steadily become more spaced out as they walked, changing gradually into farms and fields. The haystack Idalee mentioned was piled taller than a man and cast a significant shadow in the moonlight. They ran for it. Idalee pulled Lettie next to the pile and ducked behind her protectively as Kyra and Flick settled in next to them, crouching in the hard-packed snow. They waited there, listening to the voices until they finally faded.

They continued like this, walking when they could and taking cover when they heard any sign of the search. And though they avoided capture, it was becoming clear that they couldn't keep this up for long. Lettie started to stumble, and Idalee stared blankly ahead as she walked. Kyra found herself watching Idalee out of the corner of her eye. Ilona certainly wouldn't have approved of such exertion.

Finally Flick raised a hand and indicated a small cottage in the distance.

"Is that it?" Kyra asked.

"Aye. Wait while I see if she's there." Flick paused. "I'm going to have to tell her everything, Kyra. I'd not feel right about it otherwise."

"Tell her what you must," said Kyra. "Everybody will know soon enough."

Flick hadn't been exaggerating when he said this house was at the edge of the forest. It would have been possible to throw a stone from the back door and hit one of the trees. Kyra, Idalee, and Lettie crouched in a dip off the road. It was very dark now, and they couldn't see Flick near the house or know if he'd been let in. Lettie leaned on Kyra's shoulder, then slowly tipped into her lap. The girl had fallen asleep.

"Kyra?" Idalee's voice came timidly out of the darkness.

"I'm here," she said.

There was a silence before Idalee spoke. "Did you kill Santon because of what they did to me?"

Kyra wondered if her heart would stop beating. She was glad for the darkness just then, and grateful Idalee could not see her face. "It all happened really quickly."

"You don't have to hide it from me, Kyra. I know how angry you were."

Hearing the tremor in Idalee's voice was like seeing her get beaten all over again. Kyra reached out. It took her two tries, but she found Idalee's hand. "Idalee," she said. "What happened with Santon tonight...it was I who did it, not you. Don't ever blame yourself for what they did to you, or what I did to—" She had to stop speaking, as images of Santon's mangled corpse flashed again through her mind. "I lost my temper, and I... took things too far. I'm sorry that you have to bear the consequences." *And Tristam and Malikel as well.* She didn't know how far the ramifications would extend.

A long silence stretched between them. Idalee held tight to her hand. Lettie's weight was warm in Kyra's lap. The child's ribs expanded with every breath.

"Will you be all right?" Idalee asked.

Kyra hadn't expected that response, and she marveled at how lucky she was to have Idalee, Flick, and Lettie. She gave Idalee a grateful squeeze. "I hope so."

A small point of light appeared near the house and bobbed

toward them. It was a candlestick held by a very old woman. Her gray-white hair was loosely tied in a braid that hung over her shoulder, and she wore a luxurious night-robe of fine velvet, trimmed with fur.

Flick's voice spoke from behind her. "Kyra, this is Mercie."

The old woman looked them over. "I'll take in the four of you tonight," she said in a rich, throaty voice. "Flick and the sisters can stay until things calm down. But you"—she gave Kyra a pointed glance—"must leave tomorrow. It's too dangerous for me to keep you."

"I understand," said Kyra.

"Well, then, move quickly."

They didn't bother waking Lettie. Flick picked her up, and they all hurried behind Mercie into her house. Kyra couldn't see much by the candle flame, though the floor felt smooth and well polished under her feet. Mercie led them to a back room, where she laid out blankets and furs on the ground.

"In you go, then. We'll talk tomorrow morning."

If Flick trusted this woman, it was good enough for Kyra. She burrowed underneath the pile of blankets, not even bothering to remove her cloak. Idalee pressed her back against hers and they finally surrendered to sleep.

## THIRTEEN

There was a rush of cold air as someone pulled the blankets off her. Kyra's eyes flew open, and she reached for her dagger. Mercie took a step back, holding up empty hands.

"It's just me, lass. Red Shields are searching the houses in the area. Someone must have seen you last night. You need to get out. All of you."

That woke her up. Kyra looked around. It was early morning. Racks of shoes, dresses, and hats lined the walls of their room, and the air smelled faintly of perfume. Idalee was shaking Lettie awake, and Flick stood at the window, running his hands through his mussed-up hair.

"They're coming closer," said Flick. Idalee pulled Lettie to her feet and fastened the girl's cloak around her.

"You can go out the forest side," said Mercie. "Quickly."

They stumbled on sleep-heavy limbs through the house. Mercie opened a window and Kyra jumped through, followed by Idalee. Flick lifted Lettie over, then climbed out last. Now that Kyra was outside, she could hear voices in the distance, though the house blocked her view.

"The blankets, Mercie," said Flick. "Remember to—"

"I can handle a dozen Red Shields," Mercie snapped. She pointed to a heavy, flat stone a short distance from the window. "See that stone? When the narrow edge points toward the forest instead of the house, that will mean the soldiers are gone. You can return then."

There was already a trail of footprints from Mercie's house to the trees. They followed it, doing their best to step within the existing prints, and kept going until the road was completely out of view. There, they stopped to catch their breath. Kyra's stomach growled, and she realized she hadn't eaten anything in a long time.

"Think any of the Red Shields saw us?" she asked.

"If they had, they'd be chasing," said Idalee.

She couldn't argue with that logic. "Flick, what does Mercie do? She lives in a cottage but dresses like a wallhugger."

Flick chuckled. "Mercie was a thief, you could say. She charmed well-to-do men and made off with their coin. Doesn't do much of it anymore."

That would explain why she wasn't afraid to defy the law, and why she'd almost seemed insulted when Flick told her to hide the blankets.

"You should go back and hide with her after the search is over," said Kyra. "I'll find somewhere else to go, but there's no reason you must stay with me. There's a cave farther out in the forest where I can take shelter."

Flick shifted uncomfortably. "We can't exactly cut you loose by yourself. Mayhap we could all go to the cave."

"There's demon cats in these forests, Flick. It's not safe for you. I, at least, share their blood."

"I don't know. . . . Mayhap we can think of something else."

Kyra drew breath to respond, but her answer turned into a cry of warning as a demon cat launched itself out of the trees.

It was mind-boggling, how the cats appeared out of nowhere. There had been no sound at all. Only when the cat's shadow fell upon them did Kyra throw herself at the others, sending Lettie sprawling and landing on top of Flick. She got a knee in the ribs for her efforts, and the demon cat pounced onto the spot where they'd just stood.

"Do you know this one?" Flick yelled. He pulled his legs out from under her and hauled Kyra to her feet.

It was a sleek black felbeast. A smaller one, and Kyra guessed it was female. "No," she said. Never had a single word felt like such bad news.

The beast lunged for them. Kyra dove out of the way and rolled. When she regained her feet, she looked in panic for the others. Flick had jumped the other way. Lettie darted for the trees, and Idalee ran after her. The felbeast fixed its eyes on Flick.

"No!" Kyra shouted. Before the beast could leap, Kyra threw herself onto the creature's back and wrapped her arms around its neck. There was a rush of air across her arms as the beast snapped its teeth, and she held on for dear life while the demon cat twisted and bucked. Her grip started to fail.

The cat gave a violent shake of its head, and Kyra fell hard onto the ground. Her head spun. Now would be a good time to change shape, but she couldn't even think straight.

A streak of yellow flew above her, and a cacophony of roars drowned out Flick's yells. Kyra sat up to see a tawny-yellow cat collide with the black one. The two beasts tumbled to the ground, growling and snapping. Was the new cat Leyus? No. The beast was too small, but Kyra recognized it all the same. This was Pashla.

The two felbeasts continued to struggle, but Pashla wasn't going for blood—Kyra had seen enough fights now to know the difference. Pashla used her weight to pin her opponent. She bared her fangs and snapped, but she didn't aim for the other beast's throat. Slowly, the black cat reined in its attack, and the outlines of both cats started blurring.

As the Demon Riders changed into their skin, Kyra glanced at the others. Lettie's mouth hung open, and Idalee stared at the beasts in wonder. Flick stared as well, then raised one eyebrow when he saw Kyra watching. Kyra turned back to see Pashla crouched on the ground opposite a young woman with pale white skin and jet-black hair. The two naked women huddled against the wind as they reached into bags that had fallen at their feet. They must have been wearing the pouches around their necks when they'd been in their fur.

Kyra realized, as she looked closer, that she recognized the other woman. Her name was Adele. She and her friend Mela had once asked Kyra about her life with the humans. Adele had been friendly and curious that time. What had changed?

Pashla caught Kyra's eye and beckoned her closer. "Adele

didn't recognize you. There was fighting this morning, and she mistook you for the hostile humans."

Adele met Kyra's eyes and gave a solemn nod. "I was mistaken. Please forgive me."

Flick came up behind her, eyeing the two clanswomen warily. He looked slightly at a loss for words. At least Pashla and Adele were fully clothed now. Pashla wore a cloak over her leather wraparound tunic and leggings. Adele wore no cloak, and her tunic had no sleeves. Kyra could see goose bumps on the clanswoman's arms, but Adele didn't shiver.

"Is everything all right?" said Flick, looking from the Makvani women to Kyra.

"I think so," Kyra said, and the clanswomen didn't contradict her. Adele eyed Flick with curiosity, looking for all the world like a cat presented with a new insect. "This is Flick, my friend," Kyra said. She turned to him. "There was a misunderstanding. Adele didn't mean to attack us."

"I see," said Flick in a tone of voice that suggested he most definitely did *not* see. Kyra wondered how good the Makvani were at picking up sarcasm. But as strange as things currently were, they definitely could have ended up a lot worse. Now the question was how to proceed.

Pashla's gaze focused behind Kyra. "Those two girls, are they with you as well?"

So much for keeping them out of this. "Those are my adopted sisters. They mean no harm."

"I wish to see them," said Pashla.

Kyra hesitated but decided it was better to trust Pashla.

She nodded to Idalee, who took Lettie's hand and led her cautiously closer. Pashla looked the nervous girls over. To Kyra's surprise, Idalee and Lettie didn't cower, but instead stood taller and calmer under Pashla's gaze.

A branch cracked in the distance just then, and Pashla turned her face to the wind. "There are people coming."

"Soldiers," said Adele. Kyra heard the clank of weapons, and she remembered Pashla's earlier words about a fight and hostile humans. Had the early units out of Forge already clashed with the Makvani? Adele's eyes took on a fierce glint, and she reached to untie her belt. Pashla started to unclasp her cloak, and Kyra realized with horror that they were preparing to change shape.

She grabbed Pashla and Adele by the arm. "Don't," she said. "There's many of them. You can't face them all."

Pashla's face tightened with annoyance, and she shook off Kyra's arm.

"Who goes there?" called a voice.

Kyra's stomach plummeted. For better or worse, the soldiers were here.

Pashla gave Kyra a furious glare. A group of about twenty men picked their way toward them, and the Makvani no longer had the window of time they needed to change shape. Out of the corner of her eye, Kyra saw Flick throw his cloak around Adele's shoulders. It took Kyra a moment to realize what he was doing. Adele's wraparound tunic was the easiest way to identify her as Makvani, and Flick was covering up the evidence. Adele cast a suspicious glance toward him but kept the cloak around her shoulders.

One by one, the soldiers came into view. It wasn't Flick's unit, though like them, these soldiers lacked livery and wore the usual peasant garb of rough tunics and trousers. Despite the lack of uniforms, these men were formidable looking, much tougher than what Kyra remembered from the training fields. They were well muscled, and they carried swords and spears with confidence. A barrel-chested man stepped out to speak to them.

"Your names?"

Flick stepped out from behind her. "My name is Fyvie of Forge, good soldier," he said. "These are my sisters Marla and Isabel, Laurie, and their companions."

The soldier sized them up, and Kyra hoped desperately that Pashla and Adele wouldn't decide to attack. They wouldn't be so rash as to change shape in front of twenty soldiers, would they? Next to her, Pashla lowered her eyes just the slightest bit. Was she trying to hide the amber in them?

"Your business?" asked the soldiers.

"Winter mushrooms," said Flick. "They go for a fortune at the markets, and we used to have a good patch a little north of here. We thought we heard demon cats though, so we're cutting our losses. Best to leave here with our lives and no mushrooms than the other way around, right?" He gave the soldier a self-effacing grin.

The soldier released his hands from his scabbard. "You heard the roars too, then?"

"Aye," said Flick. "Raised the hair on the back of my neck."

The soldier jerked his head toward a man behind him. "Nyles almost got one this morning. Stuck it good in the shoulder, but the beast got away." Pashla stiffened, but the man didn't seem to notice. "Best to pick someplace to forage that doesn't put you in the path of fighting. His Grace doesn't want people in the forest these days."

*His Grace,* Kyra thought wryly. Not even *the Council.* The soldier was referring directly to Willem as if he were Duke of Forge. That didn't bode well.

The soldier waved them on their way, and Flick started walking in the direction of the main road. The rest of them followed. When the soldiers were no longer in view, Kyra let out a sigh of relief.

"Those are the soldiers you've been telling me about?" asked Pashla. She stared back in their direction, her gaze calculating.

"Aye," said Kyra. The clanswoman didn't seem as dismissive of the troops now that she'd seen them. Kyra wondered if this morning's fighting might have changed her mind. "Pashla, I know Leyus doesn't want to see me, but those soldiers could be a real threat to you. Can you please let me speak with him just once?"

In the ensuing silence, Kyra found herself wishing again that the clanswoman wasn't so hard to read. Finally Pashla gave the slightest of nods. "I'll bring you to Leyus, though he will not be happy with me."

Kyra celebrated a brief moment of triumph before she remembered Flick, Idalee, and Lettie. "I should see my friends safely out of the forest first."

"Bring them," said Pashla. "There are those in the clan who are curious to see more of the humans."

Curious? Kyra wasn't about to risk her family's life to satisfy some Makvani's curiosity.

Her hesitation must have shown, because Pashla spoke again, exasperated this time. "We are not barbarians," she said. "We do not hunt humans for sport. They will be under my protection."

"We'll come," said Idalee. When Kyra looked at her, she shrugged. "Every time we try to go somewhere safer, it just gets worse. At least Pashla says she'll protect us."

Kyra looked to Flick and then Lettie, who nodded in turn. "So be it," Kyra said.

Pashla set off without further comment, leading them through the trees. As they walked, Adele unclasped Flick's cloak and handed it wordlessly back to him.

"You don't get cold?" he asked.

"No," she said.

Kyra bit back a grin as she watched Flick waver between his usual inclination to insist she keep it and his suspicion that Adele would kill him if he argued. He took back the cloak.

After a while, Pashla asked them to wait while she and Adele changed shape. Once in her fur, Pashla threw her head skyward and roared. There was a distant roar in response. Pashla's ears perked toward the sound, and she loped off in that direction. Adele was a slender shadow next to her, almost flowing over the snow. Kyra noticed the black cat's eyes going often to Flick as they traveled, and Kyra surreptitiously inserted herself between the two of them. Pashla might have promised to watch over him, but a few extra precautions wouldn't hurt.

Eventually, Kyra spotted shapes through the trees. She recognized Leyus by his height and commanding posture. In the light of day, he was less frightening, though no more approachable. The clan leader stood talking to Havel and Zora, the Demon Riders who had come upon Kyra in the field. There were others scattered throughout the trees in their skin and their fur—fewer than twenty total, but that wasn't surprising. The Makvani came together only when necessary. Adele sniffed the air as they approached, then left them to join the others.

Kyra looked to see how her friends were holding up. Lettie held tightly to Idalee's hand, staring unabashedly at the Demon Riders. Idalee's jaw was set in a stubborn line, and Flick stayed protectively close to the two girls, one arm loosely resting on each of their shoulders. Around them, the Makvani started to notice the humans. They didn't approach, but they certainly looked, and whispered to each other.

"You'd better be right about us being under your protection," Kyra muttered to Pashla. She thought she saw Pashla's ears twitch in response.

Leyus's mouth tightened in displeasure when Kyra came closer. He turned to Pashla. "Why did you bring her here?"

"I'm here with a message from Forge," Kyra said as Pashla regained her human form. "I'm sure you've seen troops in the forest already. They're just the first step of preparation for a forest offensive meant to hunt all your people down, and it will surely result in unnecessary deaths on both sides. The Defense Minister asks you to consider negotiating peace."

"I've seen one of these so-called units in the forest," said Leyus. "We have nothing to fear from them."

Flick's group hadn't impressed Kyra either, though the unit this morning had looked more formidable. "You're right that many of them are untrained," she said. "But they outnumber you by far, and eventually they'll overwhelm you with their numbers."

Something registered in the back of her mind, and Kyra took a closer look at two demon cats lounging beneath a nearby tree. One beast was lying down, and Kyra saw that blood matted its fur. The other was licking the injured cat's shoulder, cleaning the wound as Pashla had done before for Kyra.

"How did that cat get injured?" asked Kyra.

Leyus followed her gaze. "That is none of your concern."

"He was wounded by humans, wasn't he?" said Kyra, plunging ahead. "Though the humans were weak, their spear struck true."

"Enough." The edge in Leyus's voice was sufficient to make Kyra stop. "The soldiers present no danger, and your city insults us with their quality." Leyus turned to Pashla. "Take them back to where they came from."

Pashla bowed, running three fingers down the front of her throat. Before Kyra could say anything more, Leyus and his two companions disappeared into the trees.

"Leyus has spoken," said Pashla.

"But—" Kyra began. The clanswoman silenced her with a glance. Kyra swallowed her words and followed. The others fell into step behind her.

The injured demon cat growled as they passed. Kyra thought it was growling at them but then realized that its ire was directed toward the beast tending its wound. Adele was with them. She'd changed back into her skin, and she called Pashla's name, followed by a string of words Kyra could not understand. Pashla circled back and nudged the standing demon cat aside so she could crouch next to the injured one.

"The muscle is torn, but it will heal," said Pashla. "Just keep cleaning her wound."

Flick reached into his belt pouch. "I have herbs," he said. "To help with the bleeding and the pain." He held a handful of dried moss out to the clanswomen. Adele eyed the herbs but didn't take them until Pashla nodded her reassurance. The younger clanswoman moved as if to apply the herbs to the wound but hesitated.

Flick spoke hesitantly. "I was taught to crumble some onto the wound and use the rest to press it in." He scooted closer but stopped when Adele jerked away. "Sorry," he said.

Adele handed the moss back to him. "You apply it," she said.

Flick caught Kyra's eye. She shrugged, unsure how to advise him. It seemed unwise to refuse, but tending to a wounded demon cat definitely carried its own risks. Flick drew a long breath, then did as Adele asked, crumbling the moss over the wound and then carefully, very carefully, pressing the moss to the demon cat's shoulder. Kyra slumped with relief when the creature didn't bite Flick's hand off. Flick signaled for Adele to replace his hands with hers, then sat back on his heels.

An older Demon Rider pointed to Lettie and asked Pashla a question. Kyra took a protective half step toward the girl.

"He says she looks like Libena," Pashla said, and gestured toward a very young demon cat in the shadows. Kyra recognized Libena's yellow fur and large eyes and spotted Libena's younger brother Ziben behind her. She'd met these two the last time she'd been with the Makvani.

The kittens stared at Lettie, who stared right back at them. Slowly, Libena crept closer until she stood just a few steps in front of Lettie. The kitten's head came to the same height as the girl's. Kyra watched them carefully, ready at any moment to snatch Lettie back. Libena sniffed at the air, while Lettie continued to stand completely still. Kyra found herself holding her breath. Strangely, it reminded her of the time she'd given Lettie a handful of grain and let her stand in the square for birds to land on her.

Suddenly, the demon kitten whirled around and ran back into the trees. Her brother followed quickly behind.

Pashla watched all this quietly and then signaled for Flick to stand up. "Let us go," she said. "I'll see you safely out of the forest."

## FOURTEEN

The magistrate had a way of keeping one eye on Tristam as he wrote, nailing him with a suspicious gaze even as he simultaneously made notes on his desk. It was all Tristam could do to maintain his act under this unnerving scrutiny. He was fortunate, at least, that he was being questioned in the magistrate's study rather than the interrogation rooms, and that for the past week he'd been under house arrest instead of in the Palace dungeons.

The magistrate stopped writing and lifted his parchment up to read, careful of the drying ink. This particular official wasn't one of Willem's lapdogs, though he wasn't overly sympathetic to Malikel's cause either. "I have your official statement, Tristam," he said. "You admit to working alongside Kyra of Forge, but you maintain that you had no knowledge of her identity as a Demon Rider until the night of Sir Santon's murder. Furthermore, you have no knowledge of her current whereabouts. Do you swear to this?"

"I do."

It was clear from the way the men around Tristam exchanged disgusted looks that they didn't believe him—not the magistrate, with his piercing gaze; not the Red Shields by the door, placed there "for his safety"; and certainly not Head Councilman Willem, watching the proceedings from his spot against the wall. But they had no evidence against him and more important targets to go after. The magistrate raised a questioning glance to Willem. "If Your Grace finds no problem with my report, I will declare him free to go."

Willem drummed long fingers on the table. "Your report is satisfactory, but I'll have a private word with Tristam before he's released."

"Very well, Your Grace." The magistrate addressed Tristam. "You will resume your normal Red Shield duties after your release. Any special tasks you've been undertaking for the Defense Minister are, of course, suspended until we are sure of his role in this matter."

The magistrate gathered his things and left, followed by the Red Shield guards. The door clicked shut behind them, and Tristam didn't move as he waited for Willem to speak.

Willem fixed a stern gaze on Tristam. "I won't keep you long. I know you've never been fond of me or my policies." He brushed away Tristam's clumsy attempt at contradicting him. "I simply want to suggest you keep an open mind. You must realize by now that your commander is accused of some very serious lapses in judgment."

Lapses that perhaps could have been avoided had Tristam and Kyra been more forthright about what she was. Something twisted in Tristam's stomach. Had they been wrong to keep the secret from Malikel?

"What direction do you see for Forge?" asked Willem. "Do you share Malikel's goals, giving handouts to the poor, fighting their battles for them? Your father and your brothers patrol your family manor every day at great personal risk. Why shouldn't the common people help defend the lands?"

Tristam gave grudging credit to Willem for bringing up his family. The thought of losing Henril or anyone else was hard even to consider. "We believe it our duty, Your Grace, to take those risks."

Willem gave a hard smile. "That's admirable, but have you ever considered that it might be an empty endeavor? Truth is, we could clear out the Palace treasury and sacrifice all our lives to serve the needy, yet the poor will still remain. Malikel caters to the tenderhearted, but he picks a fight he can't win. Meanwhile, he takes resources from initiatives that could make real change. Forge could be great. We could make Forge a city to be remembered in the history books, and everyone within it would prosper."

*Everyone, or simply those in a position to benefit directly?* Tristam didn't voice his thoughts.

Willem picked up the parchment from the table. "You may go, but I hope you'll think on what I said. How much will you sacrifice for those who may not deserve it?"

"Thank you, Your Grace."

Right before Tristam reached the door, Willem spoke again. "That's a nasty bruise you have on your jaw, Tristam."

Tristam paused, his hand hovering above the doorknob.

The spot on his chin where Kyra had struck him was still tender to the touch. "It's getting better," he said.

"It's a rare sort of creature who would cause such harm to a supposed friend."

Tristam left without replying. He half expected the soldiers outside the door to tackle him, but they only watched him pass.

The courtyard outside resembled a market more than the Palace grounds. Throngs of citizens lined up in front of harried scribes to enlist in Willem's new army, pushing past one another in their impatience to get through the wait. They were a far cry from the disciplined Red Shields who usually lined up within these walls. Conscripting new soldiers had caused problems in the Palace, and the difficulties didn't just stem from the recruits themselves. Word was that the record-keeping was sloppy as well. Several groups of citizens had already been called back because harried scribes had misplaced their records. The Palace simply wasn't equipped to handle an influx of so many new soldiers at one time.

Tristam hunched his shoulders and threaded through jostling bodies. The noise faded as he left the crowd behind, and he finally gathered his thoughts. He'd been cleared of suspicion. That in itself was a minor miracle. Unfortunately, that almost certainly meant that Malikel was taking most of the blame on himself. Tristam wondered again at the Defense Minister's reaction upon finding Santon's body. The more he thought about it, the more convinced he became that Malikel hadn't been surprised to learn Kyra's identity. The Defense Minister had suspected something about Kyra, but for some reason, he hadn't taken action. Now he would pay the price.

When Tristam got to his chambers, he found that the guards posted there for the past week were already gone. He closed his door, walked into the middle of his room, and surveyed the silent furniture around him. What now?

His breastplate hung on a rack against the wall, polished to Malikel's exacting standards. He could see his face reflected on its surface, and he leaned closer to examine the bruise on his chin. There was a scab on his lip where it had split from Kyra's blow. He saw her again in his mind's eye—confused, horrified, and covered in Santon's blood. Where had she gone? Was she safe? If only he had some way to contact her.

Everything had happened so fast that night. He'd known Kyra's bloodlines and what the Makvani were capable of, but Tristam never expected to find Kyra changed in the Palace courtyard, or see her standing above Santon's corpse. What had driven her to this?

Someone knocked on the door, and Tristam answered to find a servant in the corridor holding a stack of parchments. The servant was an older man whose build suggested a life spent indoors rather than in the fields. "Sir Willem has requested that your armor and equipment be inventoried, in light of the new recruits," the man said.

Now Tristam recognized him. The man was part of Willem's personal staff. "Are all the Red Shields having their equipment inventoried, or just me?" he asked, not bothering to hide the suspicion in his voice. After hearing Willem's speech about Forge and its future, Tristam had thought the Head Councilman was trying to earn Tristam's trust. This seemed a step in the opposite direction.

"Only those that His Grace has listed," the man said in a maddeningly neutral voice. "May I come in? I'm instructed not to touch or take anything at this point, just to take note of any equipment that might belong to the Palace."

Tristam didn't really have the leeway to be difficult right now. He surreptitiously checked the dagger at his belt as his unwelcome guest came to stand in front of Tristam's sword and armor.

"The weapons and equipment are my own," Tristam said, aware that he sounded like a petulant child.

The manservant nodded. "And livery. How many sets do you have?"

"I surrendered anything marking me a knight when they stripped me of my rank." His frustration was rising with every passing moment. "I have two Red Shield tunics that I wear on duty."

The manservant nodded and jotted something down on his parchment. "We may have to take one of those." Finally, he raised his head and looked around. "That will be all. Thank you. My name is Orvin of Forge, if you have further need of me."

He let himself out the door, and Tristam closed it none too lightly behind him. When he turned back around, he noticed a piece of parchment on the table. Had the servant left it there? Tristam unfolded it to find words inside.

*I have a message for Kyra,* was all it said.

Tristam read the note two or three times. A message for Kyra from Willem's household? If this was a trap, then they were woefully misled. Tristam had no idea where Kyra was, whether she'd fled to the forest or other cities, or somehow found a place to hide within the city walls.

Or could the man be sincere? Not all of Willem's servants were personally loyal to the Councilman. Tristam took two quick steps to his door and pulled it ajar, remembering at the last minute not to throw it open in his eagerness. He peered outside, hoping for another glimpse of Orvin, but the man was long gone.

## FIFTEEN

Flick hated the idea of leaving Kyra by herself, but after the near miss with Adele, it was clear that the forest wasn't safe for him and the younger girls. So when the flat stone near Mercie's window turned to signal an all clear, he took Idalee and Lettie back to the old woman's house. Kyra set up camp in a cave nearby with a small stash of food and supplies from Mercie, and Flick left her there with a promise to return soon.

Mercie ran a tight ship. Flick, Idalee, and Lettie posed as grandchildren of a friend of hers who'd come upon hard times. They had chores every day, but the workload was reasonable. After a few days, Mercie went into the city and brought back news, along with a note on a piece of parchment.

"It was left for you at your old home," she said, handing it to Flick.

The message was actually for Kyra. It looked like she'd been using Flick's address without telling him again. Flick didn't mind, though the vagueness of the wording piqued his curiosity. The next day, he packed up some bread and dried meat, and set off into the forest.

He walked quickly, not eager to spend any more time out here than he needed to. Kyra hadn't wanted him to come to the forest at all, but she was such a consummate city lass, and Flick worried about her having enough to eat. He supposed she could have hunted, but she hadn't seemed very eager to change shape.

The bare winter landscape was both a blessing and a curse. It made it easy to see people coming from far off, but also made it harder to keep oneself hidden. He found himself scanning the trees as he walked, wondering if any Demon Riders were watching him. His recent encounter with the Makvani had been one of the most frightening and fascinating experiences of his life—to be so close to death, and then to be granted entry into a world that only a handful of humans had seen. It had been terrifying, yet Flick had also come out of it feeling strangely honored. The Makvani were a brutal people. There was no doubt about that, and Flick had seen humans die at their hands. But his experience in the forest had shown him that there was more to the Makvani. Their culture, their way of being together . . . it made him wonder.

He was mulling this over when two Demon Rider women stepped out of thin air.

Flick stopped in his tracks, feeling a prickle travel down the back of his neck. He knew only one person who could move undetected like that, and that was Kyra—though he supposed he shouldn't be surprised that these women were just as silent. The first woman he recognized as Adele, the one who had tried to kill him. The second woman was a stranger, much taller than the petite Adele, statuesque with a long, graceful neck and chestnut curls. Her arm was in a sling.

As he stood frozen, Adele stepped forward. She walked with the same Makvani grace that he'd grown used to seeing in Kyra, though there was an otherworldly quality about Adele, something about her movements that was not quite human. She regarded him with her head cocked to one side, like a bird. (Flick wondered briefly if he should amend that to a cat watching a bird. But she'd been friendly enough the last time she came.)

"We mean no harm," she said. She held something sizable and grayish brown in front of her like a platter. When she came closer, Flick realized it was a dead rabbit. Newly killed, by the look of it, with blood still matted in its fur. She held it out to him.

"This is for you," she said. "In thanks for the herbs."

"Thank you." Flick took it from her, doing his best to give the impression that he received dead rabbits as presents every day. "This will ... be a welcome addition to our dinner tonight."

Adele gestured toward her friend. Even that motion seemed smoother on her. "Mela's shoulder is greatly improved."

*Mela's shoulder. Of course.* The woman standing in front of him was the injured demon cat he'd helped. As if following the direction of his thoughts, Mela met his eyes and inclined her head.

"I'm glad," said Flick. He paused again, wondering how best to proceed.

Adele looked around the forest. Her eyes darted quickly from one thing to the next, giving an impression that she didn't miss much. "You're traveling alone through the forest," she said. "This is dangerous." It wasn't immediately clear whether that was intended as a warning or a question. Flick decided to take it as the latter and hope for the best.

"Aye," he said. "But Kyra's been alone out here for a while. I worry she'll go hungry."

Adele's eyes moved over his features. "Do you share blood with Kyra?"

"Blood? Oh no," said Flick. "We met as children."

"But you are close."

"As close as brother and sister at this point, I'd say."

Adele nodded with something that looked like approval. "It's good that you are loyal to her." She exchanged a glance with Mela. "We will escort you. It will be safer for you that way."

That was unexpected, but it took a weight off his chest. "Thank you," said Flick. "I'd be grateful."

She fell in step beside him, with Mela trailing right behind. Adele asked him questions about Forge as they walked—how many people there were, how they felt about the Makvani, what kind of food they ate . . . If Flick had been the suspicious type, he might have thought she was trying to get information to use against the city. But he didn't think that was the case. Adele had an air of genuine curiosity, as did Mela, who occasionally interrupted with more fanciful inquiries about the colors that humans preferred, or why they wore tunics that required pulling over their heads to remove. Occasionally, Adele gave Mela a reproachful look, as if she thought her friend's question was too silly.

Presently, Adele slowed. "Kyra is there," she said.

It took Flick a while to spot Kyra, and by the time he did, his old friend was running toward him. Kyra's clothes were wrinkled—she'd probably slept in them for several days in a row now—but she otherwise looked healthy. She was about to throw her arms around Flick when she noticed Adele and Mela. Her expression became more guarded.

"We came with him to make sure he didn't get attacked," said Adele. She turned to Flick. "We will rejoin you when you're ready to return."

Neither Kyra nor Flick said anything until the Makvani were out of sight.

"How'd you manage to charm those two?" Kyra asked.

Flick held out the rabbit. "They liked the herbs I gave them. This was their way of thanking me. Feeling hungry?"

Kyra eyed the carcass. "Keep it. My cooking won't do it justice out here."

He handed her the bag of supplies that he'd brought. "The news from the city is bad. There's a price on your head. Malikel's been removed from Council duties and placed under house arrest while the magistrate investigates." Flick wasn't one to follow politics, but even he knew that removing Malikel from the Council would upset the balance of things greatly.

Kyra let the bag of supplies sink to the ground. "And Tristam?"

"Mercie didn't say anything about him, but my best guess is that he's also under investigation."

Her gaze went distant at his words, and Flick watched as conflicting emotions made their way across her face. Flick still wasn't completely sure what had happened between Kyra and Tristam, but he'd eat his cloak before he believed that she no longer had feelings for the wallhugger.

"This is my fault," said Kyra. "I can't just leave them there to take my punishment."

Flick sighed. He'd had a feeling she'd say that. "You won't do them any favors by going back. What could you do?"

She looked at him, her jaw set in a stubborn line.

"Be realistic, Kyra. The Palace would just kill you on sight."

He could tell she wanted to argue, but eventually her shoulders slumped. Flick relaxed slightly when he saw that she'd given up on that line of thought.

"There's one more thing," he said, pulling out the parchment Mercie had given him. "A man named Jacobo says he wants to talk to you."

Here, she perked up. Kyra looked over the parchment with interest. "I asked him about Demon Riders a while back."

"Says he's got news and he's wintering outside the city, if you want to talk to him. Is this about your family?"

She gave a careful nod, and he could tell she was afraid to hope for too much. Flick felt a twinge of compassion for her. He might not be thrilled with his own bloodlines, but at least he knew where he came from. "Will you talk to him, then?"

She hesitated a moment. "Aye," she said. "I'll go tomorrow."

"Want me to go with you?"

Kyra shook her head. "No, I'll be better able to avoid trouble if I travel alone."

As much as he hated to admit it, she was probably right. "Be careful, then, and let me know what you find out." Flick looked out toward the forest. "I should probably be getting back before my . . . escorts get tired of waiting."

Kyra gave him one last hug, coming at him from the side

to avoid the rabbit carcass he still held in his hand. "Good to see you, Flick. Go safely." She took a step back, eyed the rabbit, and then looked off in the direction Adele and Mela had gone. Suddenly, she burst out laughing.

"What?" said Flick.

Kyra shook her head. "I don't know how you do it, Flick. I really don't."

## SIXTEEN

Not much news filtered down to the dungeons, but when Kyra killed Santon of Agan and Malikel fell from grace, the Red Shields on duty talked, and James listened. The news came at a time when the assassin sorely needed something in his favor. After weeks of imprisonment, James had fallen ill, and he was running out of time.

In some ways, the illness made things easier for James. It compressed his sense of the passing hours as he hung in his cell and dulled his pain during the interrogation sessions. Over the past few days, his jailers had noticed his illness and had cut their visits short. James was thankful for it. The Palace hadn't yet gotten any useful information out of him about the Guild, but James knew his limits. He'd come close to breaking more than once. The Palace was determined, he'd give them that.

As the fever grew progressively worse, he spent less and less time awake. While before, he had done his best to exercise within the confines of his chains, he now drifted in and out of sleep. He dreamed sometimes of Thalia, her eyes aflame with purpose. She faded in and out, and it was just as well. If she'd stayed longer, he might have been tempted to give up and join her, but he wouldn't give the wallhuggers that satisfaction.

James started receiving visits from a Palace healer, who mixed foul-tasting potions and poured them down his throat. Apparently the Palace thought him too valuable to die. She brought an assistant, a scrawny young man who never quite stood up straight. James paid him no heed the first few times except to note that he stood quietly by the side and did as his mistress commanded.

Today though, James noticed that the apprentice's forehead was covered with a sheen of sweat. Several times, he dropped the herbs he was supposed to be mixing. His mistress was too caught up in examining James to notice, but James made note of it, even as he hung from his chains with his eyes half-closed. The apprentice was nervous, and that was interesting. Very interesting.

James had developed a grudging respect for the Defense Minister during his time in the dungeon. Malikel was smart. Much more competent than his predecessor, and he'd acted decisively and quickly to counter any possible attempts to break James out. The guards who watched over him had proved hard to blackmail or bribe. But with the current trouble in the Council, maybe, just maybe, there were now some holes in the Palace's precautions.

James kept his body heavy and his movements lethargic. It wasn't hard to do, with the fever pounding in his brain. The healer was finishing up now. She made notes on a piece of parchment as the apprentice packed up her jars of herbs and gathered soiled bandages. He came to stand in front of James and inspected a bandage on James's arm.

"Sloppy wrapping," the apprentice muttered. His words were tight and clipped, and his eyes darted between James and the healer. He unraveled the bandage partway and pressed something hard and flat against James's arm before rewrapping. Then he lowered his voice even more. "Two days from now. Second watch."

James wondered how Bacchus had gotten to this one. Bribery? Threats? He suspected the former. There was a glint of avarice in the young man's eyes and not enough fear for the latter. He hoped Bacchus had an adequate plan. To break someone out of the dungeons was no small task.

As the apprentice returned to his mistress's side, James flexed his forearm and felt the pressure of the blade against it. It was small. Its shape suggested that it didn't even have a hilt. But if he was careful and quick, it would be enough.

## SEVENTEEN

Kyra knew where the trade caravans wintered. There was a cluster of clearings west of the city, and she'd run across trade caravans there a few times when touring the woods with Tristam. It would take a while to get there because she'd have to avoid the main roads, and there would be some risk. Could this be a trap by Jacobo to lure her in for the reward money? She didn't think so. Jacobo hadn't seemed the type to sell people out to the Palace. And this was one circumstance under which Kyra refused to be careful. If Jacobo did have more information about her past, then she would learn what it was.

She set out early in the direction of the trader camp. It took her the better part of the morning, but eventually she noticed wagon ruts on a side path. A few more steps, and she smelled smoke. She started to hear voices through the trees after a while, and shapes around what were now clearly several campfires.

A voice called out. "Stop there, stranger. What's your business?" A man stepped out of the trees. Between his fur hat and his thick cloak, Kyra couldn't see much of his face.

"My name is Kyra," she said. "I'm looking for Jacobo. Is he wintering here?"

The sentry looked her over, then waved her past. Kyra noticed other sentries in the shadows, both men and women, warmly bundled and holding spears like they knew how to use them. She kept a mental note of where they were and the gaps in their formations.

Kyra broke through the trees and into a clearing where ten wagons circled a fire pit. When she walked through to the center, she saw Jacobo and four other men and women sitting around the campfire. The trader was much as Kyra had remembered, though he looked more at home here, reclining at the fire, than he'd been in Forge. It took him a moment to recognize her.

"Kyra of Forge," he said, extending a hand to her. "I'm glad I found you. It seems I'm not the only one looking these days."

His words gave her a jolt, and she hesitated a split second before taking his hand. If Jacobo knew there was a price on her head, then he must also know what she was. But Jacobo's handshake was firm, and his gaze didn't waver.

"I've run into some trouble lately, but I mean no harm to your camp," she said.

"I certainly hope not." He indicated the spear bearers. "We do travel the Aerins, and we have experience defending against dangers." He smiled, and his eyes crinkled. "But I didn't call you here to deliver threats, and you needn't look like we're going to knock you over the head and deliver you to the Palace. There's someone who would like to talk to you." He indicated another trader sitting by the campfire. The man's hair was mostly gray, and his face was lined with wrinkles that told of a lifetime in the sun, but he stood up with no difficulty, and his stance was sure. Kyra stopped dead in her tracks when she realized whom he must be. Jacobo had mentioned a survivor of the caravan attack fifteen years ago. . . .

Jacobo cleared his throat. "Craigson, this is Kyra of Forge."

The older trader dismissed Jacobo's introduction with a wave and swaggered over to where they stood. He then proceeded to look Kyra over from head to toe, as if evaluating a packhorse. Kyra was just about to make a rude comment when the man crossed his arms and nodded in satisfaction.

"She's not Kyra of Forge, Jacobo. She's Kyra of Mayel." Then he looked Kyra in the eye, and his gaze softened. "Your face brings up many memories, lass."

Did he recognize her? Though this was why she had come, she couldn't shake the feeling that this was impossible. She was an orphan. Her past was unknowable. To accept his words would be like putting on a glove that belonged to someone else.

Craigson took a step closer. "I've startled you. I apologize." He reached for Kyra but lowered his hand when she flinched. He spoke again, his voice thick with regret. "In fact, I must beg your forgiveness for many things. You were under my care when I lost you to the Demon Riders, and I was never able to find you."

Kyra's tongue was dry in her mouth. She felt dizzy, and she probably could not have formed words even if she'd known what to say. The most she could do was nod when Craigson suggested they go somewhere quieter to talk and follow him until they found a fallen tree some distance from the camp. As she sat and looked more closely at his face, she remembered a dream she had the first time she was in the forest with Tristam. There had been demon cats all around her, and a man had been carrying her and running away.

This man, Louis Craigson.

"I was on your caravan when it was attacked," she blurted. "You fled with me, and you smeared my face and clothes with some kind of pitch."

Craigson sat as well, holding one of the fallen log's protruding branches for support as he lowered himself down. "You remember, then," he said, eyes trained on her face. "What else do you remember?"

Kyra shook her head slowly. "I don't remember much else."

He let out a bark of a laugh. "Of course you would only remember the worst moments. You did have some good times with us, you know. You used to climb around my textile wagons and burrow under the blankets."

Kyra imagined burying her face in pungent silk as he said this, but who knew if it was a memory or just something she'd conjured?

Craigson continued. "The pitch you remember was to hide your scent from the felbeasts—demon cats, as you call them here."

"You're from across the Aerins?" Kyra asked.

"I hail from Edlan, but I was a Far Ranger much of my life, as I never had much use for dukes or cities. I crossed the Aerins often and traveled a route that went as far as your mother's village."

Her heart skipped a beat at the word "mother." The one person she'd forbidden herself from thinking about because she'd seemed so out of reach. "Who is my mother?" She was light-headed with the eagerness to know. And there was a second question, one that frightened her with its possibilities. "Is she alive?"

Craigson let out a long breath, looking down as if having a hard time picking the right words, and Kyra feared the worst.

"The answer to your second question is that I don't know," he finally said. "She was alive the last time I crossed the Aerins a decade ago, but we lost touch after I stopped traveling. But let's start from the beginning. You were born in a desert village called Mayel, about as far from here as you can get. Your mother's name was Maikana."

"Maikana," Kyra repeated, sampling the syllables. "It sounds like a different language."

"It is, but the leaders of her village speak our language too. They call it the trader tongue." Craigson paused again. "Your own name is actually Kayara," he said gently. "Though it's not hard to see why it might have turned to Kyra over the years."

She felt an irrational panic rising in her chest. For some reason, that revelation knocked her off balance more than even the mention of her mother. All these years as an orphan, she'd had at least her name. With effort, Kyra fought the panic back down.

"What was my ma like?"

"She was a strong woman. A leader of her people, and she loved her village dearly." Craigson looked at Kyra, and suddenly chuckled. "I hear you're quite a climber."

"Climber?" It was such a random thing to say. "I do climb walls when I need to. I'm a thief." She felt surprisingly ashamed at that admission, now that Craigson had just told her how respectable her mother was, but Craigson didn't react to the revelation at all.

"If you ever cross the Aerins and see your mother's village, you'll see why it amuses me. They are all well-practiced climbers. You look a great deal like her people—small, slight of form. And your face is the spitting image of your aunt." He braced a hand on his knee. "Maikana bore you and raised you for two years, but there was a drought that you couldn't weather. She put you in my care until the rains came again. I wasn't planning to take you across the Aerins, but your father somehow got word that I had you."

"My father. He was Makvani?"

"Your mother was human. Your father was a member of a Makvani slaver clan that attacked your mother's village."

Pashla had told her before about the Makvani's history as slave traders. But if her father had been a slaver who'd attacked her mother's village . . . It raised a horrifying implication. "Did he . . . force my mother . . ."

Craigson furrowed his brow. "To be honest, I don't know what happened between your parents. She never spoke of the specifics, and I never asked. I know that things were not simple between them and that it didn't end well. Maikana didn't want him to know about you, but somehow he found out. We crossed the mountains when we learned he was seeking you, but he and his companions pursued us. We managed to evade them for a while because we knew this land better, but they caught up to us near Forge. I stowed you in what I thought was a safe place and led them away." Here, Craigson paused and eyed a spot on the ground in front of him with distaste. "They left me for dead, but some travelers found me. It took me two days to get coherent, and several more until I could go search for you. And by then..." He spread his hands. "You were gone. Along with the rest of my caravan. I figured they'd taken you, or that you'd died." Kyra was surprised to hear a slight tremor in Craigson's voice. The trader seemed so gruff.

"And my da. Do you know what happened to him?"

"Aye, I kept track of his whereabouts, and I made sure to avoid him and his clan. He crossed back over the Aerins, and after a while it got too dangerous for me to travel, so I found a quiet place outside Edlan and settled down. I didn't hear of him for many years, though there was news of fighting among the Makvani and rumors that some clans were searching out new lands. So it wasn't a surprise to me when I heard he'd come back, this time with his entire clan. He must know by now that I'm here. I'm sure he keeps an eye on travelers."

It took Kyra a moment to realize the implications of Craigson's words, but when they sank in, she found it hard to breathe. Thus far, only two clans had come across the Aerins, and she'd met both their leaders. Could it be...

"Who is my father?" This time, her eagerness was mixed with dread.

Craigson hesitated then, and that space between two breaths felt like an hour. But then he met her eyes. "Your father is the leader of the first clan that came over the mountains. His name is Leyus."

## EIGHTEEN

The door to James's cell opened. He could tell from the footsteps that two Red Shields had entered, and he didn't spend any strength to look. The Palace interrogator preferred working after dark, and the guards often came for James at this hour, the second watch of the night.

"It's a dangerous line they're walking, bringing him in so often when they want to keep him alive," said one.

"Our job is to obey orders, not ask questions. He asleep?"

The first guard put a hand under James's chin and lifted. James returned his gaze with half-closed eyes.

"Naw, he's awake. But we might have to carry him." They spoke with a careless air. As the once famed leader of the Assassins Guild had sickened like any other prisoner, the guards gradually lost their caution around him. James did his best to encourage this. It made what he had to do just a little easier.

James slumped against the chains, letting his body fall heavy. He flexed his fingers just slightly, feeling for the strength in his arms, and then did the same for his torso and legs. He didn't have much left in him. It would have to be quick.

The guard's key clicked to unlock the shackles around one of his wrists, and then the other. James crumpled to the ground and landed on his knees, bending so that his body blocked his right arm from the guards' view. The faint outline of the blade was visible beneath the top layer of bandages. He coughed and used the spasms to hide his movements as he ripped those layers loose. A small blade with no handle dropped into his hand, and James gripped it, careful not to cut himself on the satisfyingly sharp edge. The guard swore and hauled James to his feet.

*Now.*

James brought the blade up, threading it between the guard's arms and slicing it across his neck. He didn't stop to check his work but turned to the other guard, who stumbled back in alarm. James closed the distance between them, thrust his elbow into the guard's ribs, and slit the man's throat as he fell forward. The whole thing happened in the span of two heartbeats. Neither guard had made a sound.

He stumbled then, and reached for the wall as a wave of nausea overtook him. That burst of speed had cost him. When he could move again, he examined the two guards on the ground. One man was much bigger than he, but the other had a similar build to James. He knelt and removed this guard's tunic. It was slick with blood, but thankfully, Red Shield livery was crimson, and it was dark. He also took the guard's sword and dagger.

He caught two other guards unawares on the ground floor of the dungeon. He'd hoped to walk right past them, but the prison guard force was small, and they knew each other by name. Another of Malikel's precautions, most likely. The first guard, he dispatched cleanly. The second called for help and opened a gash in James's thigh before James was able to drive a dagger through his stomach. As the man fell to the ground, James heard answering shouts. The door at the end of the corridor flew open, and two Red Shields appeared. James pivoted to run but stopped when another guard came up the stairs at the opposite end. They had him hemmed in.

James put his back against the wall and turned so he could see the men coming at him from either side. His initial flood of energy from the escape was ebbing away. Still, better to die fighting than wasting away under the interrogator's care. He eyed the lone guard between him and the stairs and willed one last bit of strength.

The door burst open again and two men with covered faces ran in. Two glints of metal flew through the air, and James flattened himself against the wall. There was a thud, a clink of metal on stone, and a gurgling gasp. The Red Shield closest to the door pitched forward, a knife buried in his back. His comrade pressed one hand firmly to his side as he turned to face the new threat, only to be run through as he raised his blade.

As the third Red Shield struggled to make sense of the scene, James attacked. He feinted to the left, then stepped in to close the distance. Pain lanced through his leg—he'd forgotten about that. As he collapsed, a knife flew over his head and grazed the Red Shield's arm. The soldier grunted, and James brought his knife up into the man's gut. The man fell. James heard footsteps behind him and turned just as one of the masked men came up close. A carrot-colored lock of hair had escaped the man's mask.

James smiled.

Rand peeled off his mask and offered James a hand up, which he accepted with a muffled groan. Bacchus, also unmasked now, looked James up and down. They were standing close to a torch, and its light was bright enough to illuminate James's many cuts and bruises.

Bacchus shrugged. "You were always too fond of that pretty face of yours."

Rand spat on the ground. "Never mind his face. We've got to bind that leg."

Bacchus was already cutting strips from a Red Shield's livery. As he wrapped it around James's wound, James noticed that Bacchus favored his left arm. "You're wounded," he said.

"So are you," Bacchus retorted.

James looked at Rand. "And you?"

"A few scratches and bruises," said Rand as he retrieved the daggers he and Bacchus had thrown. "We couldn't get past the guards all quiet like your thief lass, so we'd best get out soon." He wiped off his dagger and tucked it into his belt. James noticed that both Rand and Bacchus had swords as well, though they hadn't drawn them in the cramped corridor. He didn't bother to ask whether any others from the Guild had come. Loyalties didn't run very deep in an organization like his, not when the Guildleader's position seemed so close to opening up again.

Bacchus pulled back to inspect James's newly bound leg. "You able to put weight on it?"

"I'll live."

Rand pulled James's arm over his shoulder, and they made for the exit.

Once outside, they ran. Or tried to. James's time in the prison had taken its toll, and his injured leg threatened to give way. Shouts came from the direction of the prison, followed by more shouts and the ringing of bells. Bacchus gestured toward a building that was partially sheltered by bushes, and they ducked into its shadow. Rand leaned against the wall, alert but breathing heavily. Bacchus held his blade at the ready and peered around the corner, back toward the prison.

"You're trailing blood," he said to James when he turned back. "Hard to see in the dark, but someone will spot it soon enough."

Rand tore a strip from his tunic and handed it to James, who pressed it firmly to his leg. They all went still as three Red Shields ran down the path in front of them. At first it seemed they would pass without noticing what hid in the shadows, but then the last soldier slowed and squinted in their direction. "Wait," he called to his comrades. "I think there's someone—"

The soldier's words choked off as Bacchus's dagger buried itself in his stomach. Before the man hit the ground, Bacchus and Rand had drawn their swords and charged. James moved to follow and bit back a curse as he fell against the wall. When he looked up again, the two remaining Red Shields lay on the ground. Wordlessly, Rand and Bacchus dragged the bodies into the bushes. There was a fresh cut across Rand's chest.

"It in't deep," said Rand when he saw James looking at it. "Stings like a banshee's scream though."

"You shouldn't have come to break me out," said James calmly. The three ducked farther out of sight.

Bacchus snorted. "And let the wallhuggers win? Not while I draw breath." Nobody mentioned that, at this point, it wasn't very clear how much longer any of them would be drawing breath.

"What do you think?" said Rand. "West wall?"

James thought over their options for escaping. Two sets of walls stood between them and freedom. They would either have to fight their way through two guarded gates or find some way to scale the walls. But now that the alarm had been sounded, guards were lighting torches and patrolling the perimeter. He tested his injured leg again and suppressed a grunt as pain lanced through his thigh. It would take him a while to climb in this condition. Rand and Bacchus had a decent chance of getting out if luck was on their side. With James in tow though, their odds became much more dire.

"I've got news that I couldn't entrust to a messenger," Bacchus said suddenly. "I followed up on the hunch you had about that lass. You were right about her—what she knows and what she can prove."

"You mean Kyra?"

"I mean Darylene."

James went completely still. He turned his gaze to Bacchus. "Are you sure?"

"One of my crew heard her confiding to a friend. Seems she's suffering from a crisis of conscience."

Rand snapped at them to be quiet. They fell silent as more Red Shields ran past.

"This is what we've been waiting for—if she can be

convinced," said James after they'd gone. "Have we got any leverage?"

"In't that what your boyish charm is for?" said Bacchus.

James tuned out the shouts of guards around him, weighing the risks. Rand and Bacchus stood alert on either side of him. Neither interrupted his thoughts.

"Change of plan," said James. "I talk to her now."

Rand dusted off his hands. "To her quarters, then?"

"No, I go alone," said James. "Her quarters are close by. I can get there fine, but I'll need a diversion."

Rand and Bacchus exchanged a look.

"You sure you've got your wits about you?" asked Bacchus.

"Aye," he said. His tone left no room for argument.

Bacchus gave James a long, calculating look, then drew his dagger. "Well, Rand, I've always thought those ministers' houses got too chilly in the winters. What do you say?"

"I'm in," said Rand. He looked to James. "Good luck."

"I'll see you when it's done."

As Rand and Bacchus sprinted away, James crouched down behind the bushes and settled to wait. Now that he wasn't moving, the chill from the air seeped into his bones, and he hoped Rand and Bacchus wouldn't be long. Thankfully the alarm bells soon started ringing a new pattern, and new shouts arose on the grounds around him. Once the shouts moved into the distance, James gritted his teeth and made his way as quickly as he could.

James knocked on her door and claimed to be a member of the guard force. When the girl opened it a crack, he forced his way in and shut the door behind him, ensuring her silence with a hand over her mouth and a knife to her throat. She went rigid under his blade, though she didn't weep or scream.

"I mean you no harm," he said. "I wish to talk. You'll want to hear me out, if you care for this city."

Her eyes fixated on his face at the last few words, and some of the tension left her frame. He took a gamble and removed his hand, then slowly withdrew his dagger. The room they were in was not as opulent as its counterparts in the outer compound, but the furniture was well crafted, and fine blankets and silk pillows lay piled atop the bed. The girl straightened and smoothed out her gown, regathering her dignity as best she could.

"If you're here to take a hostage, you'll have to find someone the Palace actually cares about," she said.

"You undervalue yourself. But I'm not here to take a hostage."

Her eyes flickered over him, lingering on his wounded thigh, taking in the labored rhythm of his breaths and the way he leaned against the wall. He was weak enough now that she had a chance of overpowering him if she was fast. James could see her considering this, but when she moved, she backed away and sat down on a carved wooden chair.

"What do you have to say?" she asked. She spoke calmly, with her hands folded carefully in her lap.

He spoke his piece, and she listened almost without breathing, weighing every word.

"How can I be sure of you?" she asked when he was done.

"You can't be sure of anything," was his only reply.

Rand and Bacchus stood back-to-back, swords drawn, as Red Shields closed in on either side. Scattered at their feet were the bodies of men they'd already cut down. Those bodies were illuminated, as was everything else in the courtyard, by the flickering light of hungry flames. Even as soldiers regrouped around them, the flames climbed higher. Occasional cracks rent the air as roof beams buckled and walls caved in. The bleary-eyed wallhuggers who'd fled the fire had long left for a safer part of the compound.

"Think he made it?" shouted Bacchus. His voice was barely audible over the flames and shouts.

"Aye," said Rand. "He always does."

Bacchus smiled then, a dangerous smile that made the advancing Red Shields slow in their approach. "You know, he probably meant for us to do something smaller and get our hides out of here."

"Selfish bastard," said Rand. "Trying to steal all the credit for himself. But I reckon we've done enough. Time to clear out?"

"Agreed," said Bacchus. And he raised his blade to meet yet another soldier.

※ ※ ※

The girl didn't speak to James for very long, but it was enough time for him to get his point across. Nevertheless, she didn't agree to his request—it was too great a thing—though she promised him that she would consider it.

After they finished, she watched as he laboriously pushed

himself to his feet and let himself out. She remained sitting, staring at the door after it had closed behind him.

Sometime later, triumphant shouts sounded as the alarm bell rang clearly three times in a row, signaling that the escaped prisoner had been recaptured. Darylene blinked, and some sort of emotion flickered across her face. She hid it quickly behind her usual mask of calm. Then she took out her handkerchief and scrubbed away the smear of blood he'd left on the door.

## NINETEEN

Lettie was missing.

Flick was halfway through his morning chores when he noticed that the girl was nowhere to be seen in Mercie's small cottage. Between the kitchen, Mercie's bedroom, and the work-room where the three of them slept, there weren't many places a young girl could hide.

"Did she go into the city with Mercie?" Idalee asked when Flick told her.

"No," Flick said. "I saw Mercie leave alone this morning."

The two of them looked at each other, then flew into action. Flick swept the house one more time while Idalee called Lettie's name outside. It was unlike the girl to wander off by herself, and he feared the worst. But why would anyone kidnap Lettie, yet leave no word or demand?

Still no luck in the house, so Flick ran outside. Mercie's house was slightly set off from the road, between two farms on either side, with the forest at the back. He had a clear view of the neighboring farms as well as the road in the distance. He saw no one.

"Flick," called Idalee from the forest. "She's over here."

There was an odd tone to Idalee's voice. Flick found her just a few trees into the forest. Idalee pointed to the ground in front of her, and Flick looked down to see Lettie curled up... asleep... between two demon kittens.

"Lettie, what are you—" Flick strode toward them, but Idalee yanked him back.

"I don't think you want to surprise those two," she whispered.

*Fair point.* The two of them stood watching for a while, unsure what to do. Then the larger yellow kitten stirred. It sneezed, opened its eyes, and fixed them on Flick and Idalee. The next moment, it was on all fours with legs splayed out and hair standing on end. This woke the other two. The gray kitten opened its eyes and stared. And Lettie's face took on a perfect mask of guilt.

"Lettie," Flick said again, keeping his voice low lest he startle the kittens more. "What are you doing?"

Lettie shrank down and leaned a little closer to the gray kitten. "They wanted to play."

*Play?* These kittens were as big as she was, and their fangs looked sharp. "You've been *playing* with them?"

"When you and Idalee were busy around the house," Lettie said, raising her eyes to his reproachfully.

"How long has this been going on?"

"Today, yesterday, and the day before."

Flick took a step back, ran a hand through his hair, and forced himself to take a few deep breaths. Lettie was safe. She didn't look to be missing any limbs. *But what by the three cities had the girl been thinking?*

"Come here, Lettie." He took the girl's skinny wrists in his hands and rolled up her sleeves, then spun her around in front of him. She had a scraped elbow and a few bruises on her other arm. Her dress was torn at the bottom.

He opened his mouth to berate her when a familiar voice spoke from the forest. "She has been in no danger. I've been watching."

Flick supposed he was getting used to seeing Adele pop out from between the trees. The clanswoman seemed more sure of herself this time, less shy. "Flick, Idalee," she said in greeting.

"Lady Adele," said Flick, wondering briefly what the proper way to address a Makvani lass was. The day just kept getting stranger and stranger. Though he had to admit that part of him was glad to see her. The clanswoman intrigued him.

"The kittens mean no harm," said Adele. "It's play for them. That's all."

"Lettie's rather scratched up for a bit of play."

Adele cast a glance at the girl. "How do your small ones grow strong if you don't let them tumble?"

"I'll wager our small ones don't heal as quickly as yours," said Flick.

Adele held out her arm to Flick and traced a faint scar on her skin. "These marks make me a better sibling to my litter-mates, and a better fighter for my clan. But I know that your young are more delicate than ours. I made sure that Libena and Ziben were careful." She crouched next to the kittens and rubbed each of their heads in turn. "The kittens are curious about humans," she said.

"As are you," said Flick.

Adele looked at him, taken aback. Flick was beginning to notice that she startled when he stepped too close, whether physically or in conversation, though she recovered more quickly each time.

"Our elders mixed more with humans before Leyus pulled us out of the slave trade," she said. "But we younger ones have only been among our own kind."

She mentioned the slave trade without any self-consciousness, as if it were just a matter of fact, which Flick supposed it was. Kyra had mentioned something of the sort. "And what do you think now that you've spoken to us?" he asked.

"You *are* weaker, in some ways. But you are not helpless. And you solve your problems by very different means." Well, that was certainly honest. Flick got the impression that Adele rarely lied.

Adele looked up then, to some sound Flick couldn't hear. "One of my kin is close by. Stay here, and stay quiet."

She untied her tunic and let it drop to the ground as she walked to the trees. Flick caught a glimpse of her (admittedly shapely) backside before propriety prompted him to avert his gaze. Well, propriety and the fact that Idalee was smirking at him. In theory, the prospect of shape-shifting women who shed their clothes at a moment's notice had very few downsides. Of course, theory didn't include two younger sisters watching his every reaction—Idalee with noticeable amusement, and Lettie with her usual wide-eyed interest.

"Just try not to get yourselves killed, all right?" said Flick, trying his best to hold on to his dignity.

Idalee was still smirking. Flick raised an eyebrow at her,

though it warmed his heart to see Idalee's spunk returning. The girl hadn't really joked around with him since the beating.

Adele returned in her fur, and this time accompanied by a larger brown cat. They stopped a few paces away and changed back to their skin. The brown cat was a muscular young man, and this time it was Idalee's turn to blush. The only thing keeping Flick from shooting her a wide grin was the presence of the two Demon Riders. He did keep his eyes averted as they dressed themselves, and this time Adele noticed.

"We change in front of you to show our trust, but you look away," she said. "Does it frighten you?"

"I, uh . . . it's not that. We just don't customarily go without clothing." Sometimes honesty was the best approach.

Adele cocked her head, then seemed to dismiss the idea as strange. "This is Stepan, my clan mate. He wanted to meet you."

Stepan came forward and extended a hand, which was a relief because Flick didn't really know how the Makvani greeted each other. He had seen a few variants of bows, but had a feeling that there was much more complexity to them than Flick could figure out. The Demon Rider's handshake was firm.

"Idalee," said Flick, catching her eye. "Mayhap you could bring out some food to share."

Idalee tilted her head, trying to discern if Flick's request was a real one or a signal to run for her life. Flick gave her a subtle nod. If the Demon Riders were being friendly, they would be friendly as well.

As Idalee gathered her skirts and hurried back to the house, Stepan looked around and inhaled deeply. "Livestock," he said.

Flick froze. "You're not going to..."

"What would you do if we were to raid these farms?" asked Adele.

Flick swallowed and took some time to consider his response. Was Adele testing him? She was certainly watching him with interest, and he didn't think she was bluffing about raiding the farms. But neither did he think she was toying with him.

"I suppose there's not much I could do," he said. "I can't outrun you, so I wouldn't be able to warn them, and I can't fight you without any weapons. I might follow, to see if I can help get the farmhands to safety." He watched the Demon Riders' expressions carefully, alert for any sign of offense. "I wouldn't try to stop you, but it would sadden me. I've enjoyed your company, and I imagine it would drive a wedge between us, if you were to raid the nearby farms."

Adele cast her gaze down as she thought this over. "Are most humans like you, using their words to fight instead of their claws?" she finally asked.

Despite the tension, or perhaps because of it, Flick had to laugh. Kyra would have appreciated that description of him. "Can you blame me, since I don't have claws?" Flick curled his hands, with their stubby nails, into his best claw impression and showed her. He thought he saw the corners of her mouth creep up. "But no. There are many in Forge who prefer 'claws' over talk."

"We won't take anything from the farms," Adele said. She seemed to be talking as much to Stepan as to Flick.

Idalee arrived just then with a platter of bread and cheese

and a wool blanket to spread over the snow. Flick hoped that the girl didn't pick up on his residual nerves from that last exchange. Adele and Stepan took their time with the food, savoring each bite and stopping to inhale the bread's aroma. "We have not been able to cook in the past year, since we've been traveling," said Stepan.

"Czern tells me that we used to have cheese often, back when we raided more villages," said Adele.

Idalee choked on her bread, and Flick himself had a hard time keeping a calm demeanor at yet more talk of raids. Again, Adele noticed.

"It bothers you to speak of raids," said Adele. Flick would have laughed at the magnitude of the understatement, but Adele looked genuinely concerned.

He wondered how to respond. "A good friend of mine, like a mother to me, was killed in a raid. It's hard for me to think about them."

To his surprise, Adele's features softened in understanding. "I lost two brothers and a sister to raids. It saddens me still."

Idalee looked up from her bread, dropping a piece of cheese on the blanket. "Your clan was raided?"

Adele nodded, surprised at Idalee's surprise. "By another clan."

"Did this happen often?" asked Flick.

"There were many of us over the mountains," said Stepan.

"And you were constantly at war?"

"There were many of us," said Adele again, as if that were the answer to his question.

Flick chose his next words carefully. "Did anyone try to

put a stop to the fighting? I imagine it would have been taxing on your people."

Adele and Stepan looked at each other for the length of several breaths. "That is not the way we do things," said Adele.

At that moment, both the Demon Riders looked toward the road. Flick had been around Makvani enough times now to realize that they were hearing something he couldn't. He turned and saw a rider in official Palace colors coming from the city. News from the Palace, and it must have been important if a herald had come to announce it. Flick exchanged glances with Idalee. The last courier to be sent out like this had borne a description of Kyra and an announcement for the bounty on her head.

"Mercie will know the news when she comes back," said Idalee.

"It might be too late by then," said Flick. Idalee didn't argue, and Flick stood. "I'm very sorry, but I must go."

"I understand," said Adele. The two Demon Riders dusted the bread crumbs from their clothes and left with little ceremony.

Flick looked back toward the city. The heralds traveled the main roads, stopping to announce their news at crossroads, squares, and inns along the way. "There's an inn up the road," he said. "If it's important news, the people there'll be talking about it."

"Will you go by yourself?" asked Idalee.

He nodded. "I'll be careful."

The fields were quiet, and every farmhouse he passed had smoke coming out of its chimney. Folk were holed up inside, where it was warm. It was a long walk past the farms, but as he came closer to the inn, he noticed more people than usual about on the road. Flick slowed and listened for snippets of conversation.

*...A Palace building burned down....*

*... magistrate make an example of him...*

His pulse quickened, and he ducked into the inn's dining room. It was a small establishment compared with the ones in the city, but it should be busy enough to get him the news he needed.

The energy level inside was certainly high. While the dining room was usually divided into separate tables, the majority of the patrons were seated near the center, participating in one big, disorganized discussion.

"They say he single-handedly took out a dozen Red Shields," one potbellied man was saying. "And his lackeys killed even more with that fire."

Flick took a seat near the side and settled down to listen.

## TWENTY

Leyus was her father.

Even after she said good-bye to Craigson and started making her way back to her cave, the knowledge sat awkwardly in her mind. Kyra circled it warily, afraid to delve too deeply, yet unable to forget it.

*You don't choose your family.* Kyra had known this. Yet in her imaginings, she'd still conjured the warm, loving parents that every orphan wanted. This hope had taken a blow when she learned she was half Makvani, but even then, she hadn't completely given it up. She'd just re-created the picture into someone like Pashla—dangerous yet gentle.

Kyra would not have chosen Leyus. He was distant and intimidating, and he frightened her. Yet it all made more sense than she cared to admit. Leyus had always been a little too lenient with her. He'd had reason to kill her many times when she'd lived among his people, especially after he found out she worked for the Palace. But instead, he'd always sent her off with a warning.

And then there was the way the clan kept track of her

movements in the forest. Pashla had made it sound as if they watched all comers, but with Kyra it was more than that. Kyra thought back to that time Leyus rescued her from Zora's attack, and the two times Pashla had saved her, once when Zora threatened her in the clearing, and once when Adele attacked. No, Leyus wasn't just having her watched. He was having her protected.

It was that thought that spurred her into action. Even now, Kyra could sense someone watching her, and the questions became too insistent to ignore. Why would he do this, yet stay so cold and aloof? How long had he known?

"I know someone's watching me," Kyra called out into the trees. "Pashla? I need to speak to Leyus."

The forest went quiet at her voice. She cast around, alert for any response, but nothing came, and slowly the sounds of the forest returned—the fluttering of a winter bird's wings, the high bark of a fox. Kyra leaned against a tree, swallowing her disappointment and trying to make sense of everything Craigson had told her. Her mother was a woman who led a village an unfathomable distance away. And her father...

Something shifted around her. "Anyone there?" Kyra asked. She definitely sensed someone coming toward her now, someone quiet enough to keep her from zeroing in on a specific direction. It might have been Pashla, but it didn't *feel* like her. Kyra fell still, ready to run or fight if needed.

Leyus stepped out from between the trees as naturally as if Kyra had been waiting in the antechamber to his throne room. She looked at him, really looked at him this time. He was tall, larger than life, bronze-skinned, and strong despite his age. She didn't resemble him at all. His face was square and angular, his nose and eyebrows pronounced, in contrast to Kyra's heart-shaped face and softer features. But something stirred within her when she studied his eyes. They were amber, just like hers, and the arch of his lids felt familiar.

Craigson's story just seemed so unlikely. How could this imposing Makvani man possibly be her father? He certainly wasn't looking at her like she'd imagined any long-lost father would. Leyus regarded at her as he always had, with the same distant, proud gaze, and a touch of wariness or disdain.

"I met a trader," said Kyra, glad that her voice didn't shake. "Or he used to be a trader. By the name of Louis Craigson."

There was a flash of something dangerous in Leyus's eyes. "And what did he tell you?"

Kyra couldn't do it. Couldn't come right out and ask him if he was her father, like some waif in a talesinger's ballad. "Why did you protect me when Zora tried to kill me?"

Leyus gave a grunt of disgust. "The caravanner should watch his tongue. I spared his life once, but I may not do so again." He looked at Kyra. "You're Maikana's child—is that what he thinks?"

It was surreal, hearing the same name coming out of Leyus's mouth. "Aye."

He looked her over carefully, just as Craigson had, though Leyus's scrutiny was more severe. "You have the look of her people, as well as some of their . . . peculiarities. Though your face resembles her sister more than her."

That repeated detail about Kyra's aunt drove it home for her, made it clear they had moved beyond her childish daydreams to a reality that was so much bigger than two imagined parents. There was an entire world Kyra didn't know about, with implications and echoes that she was just starting to feel. Kyra realized she was trembling, and she pressed her arms to her sides in an attempt to stop. It was suddenly important to her that Leyus not see her shaken.

Leyus gazed into the distance, as if looking into the past. "Maikana trusted Craigson. When I heard rumors about a halfblood in his caravan's care, I immediately suspected."

How had this Makvani man, the same one who looked at her and other humans with such derision, ever been intimate with a human woman? "What did you do to her?" Kyra whispered.

Leyus turned furious eyes to her. "Is that what you think it was? That I ravished her like some base human bandit? Watch your words carefully, Kyra. I will not be insulted again."

The strength of his outrage caught her off guard. Had he actually cared about her mother? "I don't understand."

"It is not for you to know," he said. Under the anger in his voice, there was a layer of pain. Kyra stared at Leyus, drawn to this crack in his mask. But he looked away, and when he turned back, there was no more trace of that pain on his face. "Take care you do not put too much stock in your bloodlines, Kyra. And do not expect to hide behind your parentage. Blood relations are earned. Respect is earned. Do not expect any special treatment from me."

She widened her stance, as if somehow it would lend her strength. "Why haven't you let me die, then? You've had plenty of chances."

The smile he gave her had very little humor in it. "Misguided hope, I suppose. Maikana was a capable leader and stronger than any human I'd met or have met since. She knew who she was, and she knew what she wanted. She didn't run from her troubles." He said the last part as if it were a rebuke to Kyra. "It looks like that trait was not passed on to her daughter."

The judgment in his words was unexpected and so harsh that her uncertainty turned to anger. Heat flooded through her. "I've known my mother's name one day, and you're expecting me to live up to her example?"

"As I said, blood relations are earned. It shouldn't matter who gave birth to you, though it's a disappointment that you are so different from what you could have been. Physically, you have the strength of our people, but you shrink away from your fights, worrying about what you are and wavering between choices. Your mother would never have done that."

He was being unfair. She knew this even in the midst of her confusion, but knowing that a knife had an ill-made edge didn't make its cuts hurt any less. "You speak of my mother as if she were some heroine. But wasn't she your enemy? If you thought so highly of her, why are you on this side of the mountains?"

"She knew her duties, and I knew mine," he said. "In the end, it came between us." He looked at her again. "You're a child of mixed fates. Our blood could bring you strength, but instead it feeds your fear. That does not make you someone I would be proud to call my own."

Leyus left Kyra after their conversation, disappearing into the forest without a second glance at the daughter who stared after him, gutted by his words. When it became clear to Kyra that he wasn't coming back, she gathered herself together and headed to her cave. She wasn't aware of much of the rest of the journey, just that it was dark by the time she arrived.

She longed for Flick, Idalee, and Lettie desperately that night, but of course they were safe at Mercie's house. To make it worse, the temperature dropped and she woke up shivering violently, her limbs stiff and her toes going numb despite the layers she'd wrapped around herself. She realized that she either had to stay active all night like her Makvani kin or find a better way to keep warm. Her pouch of supplies with her flint inside lay enticingly within reach, but the cave had no good outlet for smoke. Of course, there was one other way she could keep warm, one that she had thus far been avoiding. . . .

*Our blood could bring you strength, but instead it feeds your fear. That does not make you someone I would be proud to call my own.*

Leyus's words were sharp thorns, digging themselves into the tender places of her chest. Kyra peeled off her clothes with something akin to anger, throwing them against the cave wall, hardly able to breathe as the icy air burned her skin. Soon enough though, she felt the familiar warmth of her fur forcing its way through her body. The cave around her settled into a crisper version of itself, and the air that had felt so bitterly cold a moment before no longer touched her flesh. Kyra turned a few circles on all fours before she curled back onto the ground. Sleep came more easily after that.

She was in her fur, still half-asleep, when she heard Flick approaching. She knew the cadence of his footsteps well enough to recognize him, and she hurriedly changed back before he arrived. She didn't think she would harm Flick, but she wouldn't take the risk.

"Kyra, I've got news," he said. But then he stopped when he saw her face. "Are you hurt?"

"No, I'm not hurt. I..." She fell silent, trying to get her thoughts in order. "Can we sit?"

"Of course." Flick was still looking her up and down with concern as they settled themselves at the mouth of her cave. "What is it?"

It took some time for Kyra to get her thoughts together. In bits and pieces, she related everything Craigson had told her and then recounted her conversation with Leyus. Flick let out a low whistle when she finished. "Leyus, of all people. What do you make of all this?" he asked.

Kyra took a while to answer. "I don't really know," she said. "I didn't expect my first conversation with my da to go quite like that."

Flick gave her a crooked smile. "Fathers aren't always what we wish them to be. I should know."

Flick's words triggered a loosening in her chest, and she smiled back despite herself. "I suppose we've got something new in common, then."

"High-ranking fathers who can't stand the sight of us?"

Kyra couldn't help but feel a twinge in her stomach. Leyus's words had hurt, though they shouldn't have. Why should she care what the leader of a clan of barbarian invaders had to say about her? But apparently she did, when that leader was her father. "Do you think he's right, about me living in fear of what I am?"

She was glad Flick didn't respond right away. If he had, Kyra wouldn't have believed him. "I do see you afraid of your Makvani blood," he said carefully. "But I don't think it's as bad a thing as he thinks. In fact, it gives me comfort that you're afraid. It tells me that you're still the same thief girl I met on the street years ago. You might be able to grow claws now, but I'd still trust you to watch my back."

She nodded, comforted slightly by his thoughts. "Though mayhap he has a point about running from my fights," she said. "I'm out here in the forest when things are happening in the city."

And here, Flick's expression darkened.

"What is it?" Kyra asked. "Are we found out?" She looked around her, half expecting to see soldiers in ambush.

Flick shook his head. "Nothing like that. It's about James."

"What of him? Did he escape?" She felt a shiver of fear. What would James do if he was free again?

"He did . . . almost," said Flick. "They say that he somehow got ahold of a weapon and overpowered his guards. Two of his men were there to help him."

The men were almost certainly Rand and Bacchus. But Flick had said he'd *almost* escaped. "Did they recapture him?"

"Aye, but not before they'd killed several dozen Red Shields and burned one of the Palace buildings to the ground. His two accomplices escaped, though both were gravely injured. The Palace recaptured James alive."

Kyra let out a sigh of relief, though she wasn't sure if the relief was because James had been recaptured or because he was still alive. "So they have him again." But there was more to the story. Otherwise, Flick wouldn't have looked so disturbed.

"They did nab him. The magistrate was furious, as was the Council, as you might expect. They've decided to stop trying to get information out of him and to make an example of him instead." Flick took a breath. "They've sentenced James to torture and a public execution in two days."

A chill spread over Kyra's skin at Flick's words. For a long moment, she didn't say anything.

"In the city square, as usual?" she finally asked.

"That's the news."

Kyra was familiar with the type of spectacle planned for James. The Palace reserved it for its most notorious criminals, to make an example of the very worst and warn others away. Kyra had gone once out of curiosity, and she'd had nightmares for a solid week afterward. The criminal hadn't been recognizable as a man by the time they'd finished with him, and he'd screamed until he was no longer physically able to continue. She swallowed against the bile suddenly rising in her stomach.

"You're certain of this?" she asked.

"It's all anyone was talking about."

It shouldn't have surprised her. After the Demon Rider raids and the latest escape attempt, it only made sense that the Palace would choose a public and painful way for James to die. But that didn't stop her gut from twisting at the prospect.

"Kyra?" Flick put his hand on her shoulder, forcing her to look at him.

She shook herself. "Sorry."

"What are you thinking?"

If only she knew. Her thoughts about James had always been an inscrutable mass. "I've every reason to hate him," she said slowly. "But his ends were not completely unjust." James had done some inexcusable things. She wouldn't romanticize him as she had before, but they'd come to some sort of understanding in that dungeon, and it didn't feel like the naïve infatuation she used to hold.

"I need to get back into the city," she said.

Flick sat up. "Kyra, you can't let one comment from Leyus push you into risking your life. He might be your father by blood, but he's never done anything for you."

"I in't doing this because of Leyus. Tristam and Malikel are in trouble with the Palace on my account. I need to speak with Tristam, to see if there's any way I can help, and I'd like to—" She'd been about to say that she wanted to talk to James one more time. "I'd like to see if I can learn anything more about the Guild before James dies."

Flick shook his head, massaging the knuckles of one of his hands. "I won't try to stop you. Never does any good."

Was she really that hardheaded? "I'll be careful. I promise."

He smiled at that, and tugged on a strand of her hair. "The problem is, you have a funny idea of what it means to be careful."

## TWENTY-ONE

Getting back into the city wasn't hard, but moving around without being recognized was tricky. Kyra waited until it was dark to scale the city walls. Once inside, she kept her cloak low over her face. She weaved her way through the evening crowds, taking care not to attract anyone's attention. Parchments with her likeness were posted in the larger squares, and Kyra had a nervous moment when a maidservant squinted at her, trying to see beneath her cloak. Kyra affected her most unconcerned expression and walked on. No one chased after her, and she soon found herself staring at the Palace wall.

Perhaps it was her fate to always be sneaking in. She'd had a brief period of legitimacy, when she'd walked in through the gates as if she belonged. But she'd never felt comfortable out in the open, not like she did now. Even her fear of discovery was a thrill of excitement in her veins as she pulled herself over the ramparts and dropped to the ground.

It was still early enough in the evening for people to be about their after-dinner business—guards making their rounds, noblemen and their families out for strolls—so she climbed the closest building to escape the torchlight below. The icy wind whipped around her, buffeting her ears. She could feel her fingers getting numb, so she broke into a run to keep warm.

She was making decent progress along the ledges until her foot slipped out from under her. Kyra gasped and splayed her limbs out wide. She landed lengthwise along the edge, one leg hanging over empty space as she scrambled to grip the stone. Soft conversation and chatter floated up to her from below, and her heart pounded in her ears as she slowly hauled herself back to her feet. She'd thought that the sun had melted all the ice from the buildings, but she'd obviously been wrong.

Kyra proceeded more slowly from there, testing the surfaces before she stepped and sticking to walls that faced the sun during the day. The difference between smooth granite and slick ice was subtle but important. Finally, she stood atop the wall of the inner compound. The prison building was a barely visible shadow in the night sky. As she made her way closer, she passed the burned-out shell of what had once been noblemen's living quarters—Rand's and Bacchus's handiwork. The sight brought uncomfortable memories of The Drunken Dog, and she hurried past. Finally, she looked down on the prison from a nearby ledge and took in the entire scene.

The building was on lockdown. Red Shields stood guard all around the building's perimeter, with six more blocking the doors. Extra torches had been lit along the paths and hung on the walls so that only the very top of the building was dark.

*Make no mistake, Kyra. Someday I'll call in a favor from you, and I'll hold you to it.*

Kyra thought of the Demon Rider raids that James had

instigated, the fire, the injured along the street, the countless left without homes. Those people deserved justice, didn't they?

She counted the guards again and imagined ways of getting past them. Just a game, a thief's mind exercise, as she'd done before with hundreds of other buildings. There were too many Red Shields up front. A diversion might take a few away, but they were probably alert for one. Maybe with some luck she could get into the prison, but getting out with a gravely wounded James would be near impossible.

Another column of guards walked in through the gate. Kyra started to count them too but stopped. She knew in her bones that she wouldn't be going into the prison tonight. Her debt to James did not extend that far. When she finally admitted this to herself, Kyra wasn't sure whether the tugging at her chest was pity, guilt, or grief for the people James had taken from her.

She stood there a while longer, until the chill made her spring into motion. There was one more place she wanted to go. Her heartbeat quickened in anticipation as she approached the building that housed Tristam's quarters. Was he even there, or was he still being held somewhere else? His room was dark through the windows, but he might have simply been out for the evening. Kyra found a spot where an outcropping offered some shelter from the wind. She'd been up there for about half an hour when she heard his voice down below.

It was Tristam, dressed in one of his finer embroidered tunics and a fur cloak. And with him, on his arm, was a woman. Kyra couldn't see her very well from that height, but she could tell that the woman was young and that the luxurious furs lining her cloak were fit for a nobleman's daughter. The two of them stood for a while on the path outside the building until a courtier arrived. Tristam bowed then and kissed the girl's hand before she left with the courtier at her side.

The moment his lips touched her hand, Kyra's chest turned to ice. She'd assumed, with all the upheaval in the Palace, that something like the marriage negotiations would have been suspended. How naïve she'd been.

Tristam watched the girl leave and went inside the building. A short while later, a soft glow came from the window as he lit a lamp. Kyra pressed herself flat against the wall. She'd planned to knock on his window, but she couldn't let Tristam know what she'd seen. She lingered outside until her skin was numb from the wind and finally admitted to herself that she was being ridiculous. She'd come all the way here from the forest. She wasn't going to leave without speaking to Tristam.

It took a couple raps on the shutters for Tristam to notice, but then he pulled them open and peered out the window. His eyes focused quickly on Kyra—he'd gotten much better at spotting her on ledges, though he still did a double take before he moved to make room for her to jump in.

There was such relief in his eyes when he looked at her, and it felt so good to see him alive and well, that for a moment Kyra forgot the noblewoman she'd seen. As soon as her feet touched the floor, he pulled her into a hug, and she gladly returned it, squeezing him as tightly as her frozen limbs would allow. He was blissfully warm, and the fine silk of his tunic was soft against her face. He smelled like warm bread and spices. After a moment, he held her out again at arm's length.

"I've missed you," he said softly, his eyes scanning her. "And you're freezing." Tristam motioned for her to sit down at the table and moved to check the latch on his door. He lingered there for a moment, alert for noises in the hallway.

"I don't hear anyone," said Kyra.

He pulled a blanket from his bed and draped it over her shoulder. It wasn't nearly as warm as his arms had been, but Kyra pulled it tight around her. He scrutinized her, and she did the same to him, studying his face, his posture. He seemed healthy. There was a tired slump to his shoulders, but he was alive and not imprisoned.

"Where have you been?" he asked. "Your landlady had no idea, and neither did Flick's roommates."

"I'm still alive," she said. She filled him in on her flight from the city and where she'd been hiding. "And things at the Palace. How are they? Have you been cleared of suspicion?"

A crease formed between his eyebrows. "I have, but not Malikel. They're still questioning him, and Willem means to drag this out as long as he can."

He didn't direct any accusations at Kyra, which somehow made it worse. "Is there any way I can help?"

He shook his head heavily. "Not unless you can control the minds of the Council." But then he raised his head. "Does the name 'Orvin' mean anything to you?"

Kyra blinked. "Willem's manservant?"

"He came to me with a message for you soon after you disappeared."

Orvin had approached Tristam? She wondered what had persuaded Orvin to trust him. "He was an informant for the Guild. He gave me information a while back, and I asked him to get word to me if he had any more. I was trying to find some way to discredit Willem but didn't get anything before I had to...leave."

There was just the slightest flicker of confusion across Tristam's face. He was wondering why she hadn't told him until now. "Orvin must have decided I was the best way to reach you. I was worried it was a trap, but I finally spoke to him. He says Willem is expecting a messenger eight days from today."

Kyra leaned forward. "One of the private messengers?"

Tristam nodded. "It would be too dangerous to confront him inside the Palace, but Orvin says the messenger stays at an inn when he visits Forge and that he comes into the Palace compound and leaves through the private gate near Willem's residence. I was considering tailing him myself, but I'm not as good at it as you are."

Kyra was finally warming up, and she let the blanket fall from her shoulders. "I'll do it," she said. "I'll have to think about how best to track him. It's a pity I didn't learn more about James's crew of spies during my time with the Guild."

"You heard about James, then?" said Tristam.

"Aye, Flick told me. Is it...certain?"

"The executioner's wagon is set to leave the compound gates at the eighth hour tomorrow."

*The executioner's wagon...* There was still something she might be able to do for James, though she wasn't sure if she had the stomach to see it through. "Is it taking the normal route from the Palace to the city center?"

"As far as I know." Tristam eyed her suspiciously. "Why do you ask?"

"Just curious." She stood. "I should go. I'm…glad that you're all right, Tristam. Flick and the girls are taking shelter with a woman named Mercie just south of the city. If you need to find me, they'll know where I am."

He wrapped her hands in his own. "Take care, Kyra." This time, the thoughts of his betrothed *did* come into her mind, but Kyra pushed them away. There were bigger things at stake.

"Thanks for letting me warm up." She studied his face again as she handed him the blanket, fixing his features to memory.

"I don't think I've ever seen you shiver so much," he said, smoothing the blanket back over his bed. "And you must have scaled walls on colder nights than this."

"It was windy," Kyra said.

"True. Well, maybe you can run extra quickly to stay…" His voice trailed off. The look he turned on Kyra was a little too keen. "You've not been running, have you? Did you have to stay out in the cold somewhere?"

"I…" Kyra trailed off, distracted by the memory of Tristam and Cecile. No sooner after she faltered did she realize that she should have kept talking. Tristam's brow furrowed, and she could see him trying to figure out why Kyra was slow to answer what she realized now had been an innocent question.

Then his eyes widened in a mixture of comprehension and dread. "You saw her, didn't you?"

It wasn't the first time that Kyra wished Tristam weren't quite so observant. Her silence spoke more clearly than any affirmative, and Tristam let out a soft groan. "I'm sorry you had to see that."

"I wasn't spying. You weren't here when I came to find you, and then I saw you return with her." She didn't want to argue with Tristam over this, not when she didn't know when she'd see him again. "She seems nice," Kyra finished lamely, belatedly wondering if it came across as sarcastic.

There was a grim humor in Tristam's eyes as he took in her words. He sat down heavily on his bed. "I have very little to complain about," he said. "She's pleasant and close to me in age."

Kyra didn't want to hear this, but he was staring past her without seeing her.

"Cecile is lovely and talented, and clearly cares about her family." Tristam shook his gaze from whatever he'd been looking at and focused his eyes back on Kyra. "I feel nothing for her," he said simply. "Nor does she feel anything for me. We're both well trained in the courtly arts. We can exchange pleasantries for an hour, and we can smile at each other over dinner. I suppose marriages have been built on less."

Though it pained her to hear about this girl, Kyra also realized now how self-centered she'd been. She'd painted herself as the victim in this scenario, the city girl who would be tossed aside by a nobleman. But she hadn't considered how hard it would be for Tristam. He wasn't some fatpurse who took and discarded women at his whim. He was bound by his family and his duties in a way that Kyra never would be.

She crumpled the hem of her tunic. It was time to grow up. "I said some things I shouldn't have, when we last spoke of your marriage." *Right before I turned into a felbeast, eviscerated a man, and had to flee the city,* she thought ruefully. How had so much happened in so little time? "It was unfair of me to be so upset with you. I understand that you have duties to your family."

He met her eyes with gratitude. "I'm sorry I didn't tell you earlier. I shouldn't have hidden it from you."

Kyra looked to the window. She needed to go. There were preparations to make if she was going to attempt her new plan. But her conversation with Tristam didn't seem quite complete. She swallowed. "Do what you think is best, Tristam. Whatever you decide, I'll still be your friend and comrade-in—"

She didn't get to finish the last few words, because he closed the distance between them, threaded his arms behind her back, and kissed her.

Kyra drew half a breath in surprise before his lips met hers and her mind went blank. They had kissed once before. That had been a stolen moment, shy and uncertain. This time, it was also a stolen moment, but it was far different. There was an urgency in the way he pulled her close, an insistence in the way his lips sought hers, as if they might never do this again. Kyra understood it, because she felt the same. She returned his kiss with equal fervor, her world shrinking down to just the two of them, his hands in her hair and hers tightly clutching his waist. His tongue parted her lips, and she gasped as a shiver danced down her spine and her knees went weak. She could lose herself like this, forget about betrothals and marriage negotiations, forget about what she was going to do right after she climbed out the window.

But, of course, she couldn't. Even as she reached up to cup his face, even as she wished she could pull him even closer, she knew this. They weren't some lovers from a talesinger's ballad, about to run off into each other's arms. The next morning, Tristam would continue his negotiations with the family from Parna, and Kyra would go back into hiding. That is, if Kyra survived the night.

Perhaps Tristam sensed the direction of her thoughts, because he pulled back. He looked as if he wasn't quite sure what had happened. And neither was she, for that matter. Kyra's heart still pounded in her chest, and she was sure her face was just as flushed as his. She couldn't look away from his eyes. Tristam was watching her as if convinced she was about to disappear.

And Kyra supposed she was. She gathered her resolve before it could weaken any further and pushed him away.

"I can't," she said quietly. "And neither can you."

He accepted her words without argument, closing his eyes in resignation. "I'm sorry."

She wasn't sure what he was apologizing for. The marriage negotiations? The kiss? She wasn't sure if it mattered, and she wasn't sure she wanted to know. "I really should go," said Kyra.

He watched her silently as she pushed open the shutters and climbed back out. When Kyra peered back in from the ledge, he'd sunk down into a chair, his forehead resting on his hand. His eyes were open, but his gaze was focused on something Kyra couldn't see.

## TWENTY-TWO

As always, the darkness cleared her mind, and the task before Kyra forced her to focus. In that way, she was grateful for the danger. The need to maintain her balance on the ledges and make plans for her next step was the only thing that could keep Tristam from her thoughts.

The first things she needed were supplies. Here, her knowledge of the Palace, her *thief's* knowledge, proved useful. She broke into a minor storehouse and pilfered some twine, some leftover biscuits, Minadan hot pepper powder, and a few strips of cloth. She wrapped the pepper powder into four loosely tied cloth packets and stowed them in her belt pouch. Then she made her way toward one shack she'd never entered before, one that reeked with the smell of old blood. The guard here was uncharacteristically light for the inner compound. There was no one at the door, and only the occasional patrol. Kyra supposed it made sense. What sane intruder would voluntarily make for the torture master's storage house? The lock gave way without much problem, and Kyra felt her resolve weaken as the door swung open. There were things here that she didn't want to look at or think about, wicked-looking knives and racks, other implements she didn't even recognize that were still crusted with blood. It would not be good to be caught here.

Kyra waited for her eyes to acclimate to what sparse moonlight filtered in through cracks around the door. There was only one wagon, and she recognized it immediately from previous execution marches. It was a platform on wheels with a single pole and crossbeam on top for the prisoner to be lashed to. She had never followed the execution parade, but she knew its path. The wagon would come out of the Palace and wind through the streets, making its way to the merchant's ring before circling back to the city center. People would be gathered on either side, jeering and throwing refuse. It was always very crowded.

Kyra crawled between the wheels and felt around with her hands, hoping for some shelf underneath she could cling to, but she found nothing. She supposed it was too much to wish that the wagon would come ready with a hiding place. She crawled back out and wondered if she was taking too much of a risk. But then she imagined James stretched on a rack in the city square, skin flayed open, and bile rose in her throat. She would try this.

It was too dark to see. Kyra brought out her flint, some dried moss, and a stick, listening carefully for footsteps outside. There was always a chance someone would see light leaking from between the slats of the shed, but she couldn't do this blind. She struck her flint until a spark caught in the moss she'd laid out on the floor, then coaxed the flame to life. In its light, she could barely make out the contours of the wagon. She scanned its surface, looking for slots between planks where she could thread some twine. When she found what she was looking for, she blew out the flame. The rest she would do by touch.

Kyra reached into her belt pouch for four pieces of twine and threaded each one around a plank, tying them into loops. They'd be visible from the side of the wagon, but the wood was rough and uneven in color, and she hoped that everyone would be paying more attention to the prisoner than to the execution cart. She crawled underneath and pulled the loops through, then threaded cloth through them so that two long strips ran along the length of the wagon. She tested whether the strips could hold her, hooking her feet over them and spreading the weight of her chest and torso over the length of her arms. It wasn't comfortable, but she'd be able to hold on long enough. With those preparations in place, Kyra let go again and settled in for a wait. She didn't dare sleep, but she curled up under the wagon and tried to make herself as comfortable as possible on the hard ground.

Gradually, light started to filter in from outside. The padlock securing the outside door clanked, and Kyra hurriedly pulled herself up so she was flat against the bottom of the wagon. She saw a pair of boots walk in. Metal clanged as the boot's owners walked around, rearranging equipment. A few times, he threw something on the wagon, and Kyra felt the thud vibrate throughout the frame. Finally, he pulled the wagon outside. If he noticed the extra weight on the wagon, he gave no indication. He hitched a horse to the front. Then a group of soldiers marched toward the wagon—four sets of booted feet surrounding a pair of bare feet in tattered trousers.

The wagon rocked to and fro as soldiers lashed James to the wagon. The planks above Kyra warped with the extra weight, and she eyed the knots in the cloth that supported her, hoping they wouldn't unravel. James made no noise, and Kyra's stomach tightened as a drop of blood landed on the ground.

It was an agonizingly long wait before the wagon finally started rolling. As they came closer to the Palace gates, Kyra heard the roar of the crowd, the anticipating energy. Then they were past it and surrounded by jeering onlookers.

The cobblestones rolled beneath her, about two hand-widths below her nose. Kyra had to be careful not to stare too long at them, lest they make her dizzy. It would be easy enough to get sick here, with her stomach tight as it was. Though she tried to spread her weight along as much of her body as possible, she felt a light numbness through her arms. Kyra flexed her fingers and shifted her weight, doing her best to loosen up. She was waiting for a certain street just outside the merchants' district, where the road became narrower and the rooftops leaned in close. That was when she would make her move.

It was hard to navigate when she could see only gutters and the occasional building foundation, but she managed to keep track of where she was. The wheels in front of her tossed up stones as they turned, and though she managed to dodge most of them, a few left stinging imprints on her skin. The mud was harder to evade, and Kyra soon gave up on avoiding splatters. Slowly, the wagon neared the bottleneck. Three turns away, then two turns, then one.

Ahead of her, the street narrowed and the Red Shields on either side moved to the wagon's front and back, though there was still enough room along the sides for someone small to squeeze through. Kyra took one last breath. Then she dropped to the ground, scrambled between the still-moving wagon wheels, and pulled herself over the edge.

The scene hit her all at once. The wagon was in a narrow alleyway. Red Shields stood ahead of and behind it, facing a crowd of men, women, and children along the road. The bystanders pressed in on the soldiers, though their screams quieted as Kyra stood up to her full height. She got her first glimpse of James as she drew her dagger. He was, as she'd expected, lashed to the crossbeams on top of the cart. He was thinner than she remembered. There were fresh bruises on his face, and a patch of blood seeped through his tattered trousers above his knee. But his gaze was still quick. In a split second, he took in Kyra's dagger, the Red Shields around them, the hanging rooftops, and the hungry crowd around them. Comprehension lit his eyes.

*Why should they dictate how we live and how we die?*

"Would you choose the way you die?" Kyra's question came out breathless. With the roar of the crowd around her, there was no way he could have made out her words. But she could see that he understood nonetheless.

"Do what you came to do," he said. His gaze was as intense as she'd ever seen it. Was he angry at her? Grateful? Kyra didn't have time to wonder. Red Shields were pointing at her and shouting, and she had to make her move. She closed the distance between them. He caught her eyes as she raised her knife to his throat, and such was the strength he projected that Kyra could not look away. The edge of her blade nicked his skin, and still their gazes remained locked. One stroke, then it would be over, quick and clean. But Kyra couldn't move.

The wagon rocked. Kyra cursed her hesitation and whipped around as a Red Shield pulled himself onto the back edge of the cart. She grabbed a pepper pouch and threw it at him. Her left-handed throw went wide, but the second try caught the soldier square in the face, and he fell backward onto his comrades. Kyra pivoted and threw her remaining pouches at the guards on the other side.

Then, as red pepper dust still hung in the air, Kyra turned, gritted her teeth, and buried her blade in James's stomach.

He shuddered once, the muscles of his throat tightening and his jaw clenching against the pain. As warm blood washed over Kyra's hands, a memory came to her. She was on the floor of James's study, convulsing around his blade as she bled out onto his floor. *You could have gone far,* he'd whispered. The scar on her own abdomen throbbed in recognition.

She heard James's voice again, and it took her a moment to realize that this wasn't from her memory. He was speaking, though Kyra couldn't make out the words. Her body was tangled up with his. She still held her dagger, buried in his stomach, and she'd grasped the back of his neck for leverage. Kyra could feel a layer of sweat on his skin, his pulse growing erratic under her fingers. As he struggled to draw breath, she tilted her head to let him speak into her ear.

"Choose your fight," he said.

Then he slumped into his bindings, and the life left his eyes.

## TWENTY-THREE

There was no time to pause, to wallow in what she had done. No time to clean her dagger, wipe James's blood off her hands, or search his face for any remaining message. The crowd was screaming. The dust had cleared. Two Red Shields, one on either side, jumped onto the wagon. Kyra thrust her knife into her boot and leaped for an overhang, pulling herself up and away as the soldiers reached to grab her.

She sprinted down the row of rooftops, jumping between uneven levels and rolling when she took a long drop. But even as she pulled farther away from the wagon, Kyra realized she'd miscalculated. She'd traveled these rooftops before and knew a path that would take her to the city wall, but she'd underestimated the crowds. They were everywhere, and already, she could hear people shouting to stop the lass on the rooftops. She skidded to a stop at the last house and looked down into the faces of wide-eyed watchers below, packed so tightly she couldn't even see the ground. Kyra turned around to see Red Shields climbing up awkwardly after her. Then the first arrow struck by her feet.

Kyra scrambled away from the edge and crouched as another arrow soared over her head. The way forward was closed to her. Behind her, three Red Shields gained their footing and raced toward her. Kyra hesitated a brief moment, then ran straight at them. The houses along this street had courtyards, and Kyra dropped into one, pressing herself between a row of hedges and the wall. She wasn't very well sheltered here. The hedge was only slightly taller than she was, about three hand-widths from the wall. An overhang from the roof offered some coverage from above, but there was plenty of open space between the roof and the top of the hedge through which someone could see her.

Kyra struggled to calm her breathing as the footsteps above came closer. Her blood ran hot with the battle rage she was coming to expect every time she killed. Her fur called to get out, and Kyra knew instinctively that to change form right now would take no effort at all. She thought for a moment about succumbing to the change, of exploding out of the hedges and onto the soldiers who chased her. But there were so many bystanders around, and she didn't know what she would do to them.

The shouts were all around her now, accompanied by thuds as men dropped onto hard dirt. Kyra peered through a gap in the leaves and counted eight Red Shields, though they moved in and out of view so quickly that she couldn't be sure. It would only be a matter of time before they found her.

She drew her dagger once more. But then, was she really expecting to fight eight swordsmen with a knife? No, there was only one way she could take on all of them. Kyra could feel the heat within her, eager to come out. Could she simply change form and run for the walls? She didn't hate these men like she'd hated Santon. Maybe she could control it this time.

A shadow fell across her. A soldier hung his head and shoulders off the rooftop, looking down at her hiding place. He opened his mouth to call the others.

Before he could speak, Kyra climbed, using the wall and the hedge for footholds, and gripped his tunic. He made an ill-fated grab for the roof but missed, and they both fell, stripping leaves and branches from the hedges. Kyra landed in a crouch. The soldier landed face-first and groaned.

Before he could move again, Kyra jumped on his back and snaked her arm around his neck. A wave of battle fury hit her, the thrill of it as strong as the smell of his fear. Kyra had an overwhelming urge to tighten her grip further, to hold the choke and not let go.

"There's something moving back there," said a voice on the other side of the hedge.

Kyra jumped back from the fallen soldier, trembling at how close she'd come to wringing his neck. As the man fell forward, coughing, she drew his sword and threw it away from both of them.

"Go," she hissed. "Tell your comrades to flee. This in't worth dying over."

She was ready with her dagger as he regained his feet, but he took one last look at her and fled around the hedge. Yells sounded from the other side. Commands. They were planning the best way to surround her. Kyra heard the scrape of swords being drawn, and she cursed the discipline of Palace troops. Soldiers appeared at the ends of the hedge.

"Stay back," she yelled again, but they only raised their swords.

Kyra tossed out one last desperate wish for control before she pulled off her shoes and threw her cloak to the ground.

◌ ◌ ◌

When the shouts and screams first started, Tristam held rank with his fellow Red Shields. They stood at attention along the side of the road, scanning for any signs of resistance and bracing themselves for the rush of people that would surely come when the execution cart passed their stations. He didn't pay much attention to the ruckus at first. It was an execution, after all—a fair amount of rowdiness was to be expected. And frankly, he didn't have much energy left in him for alarm. He hadn't exactly slept well the night before.

Tristam had stayed awake long after Kyra left, unable to forget how she'd felt in his arms and how desperately she'd kissed him back. It had been such a relief to act on his feelings for once, to stop being the responsible son if only for a moment. But once the dust had cleared, things remained the same.

*I can't. And neither can you.* He saw Kyra saying that, her eyes still bright, but grounded now with regret.

Kyra was right, of course. Tristam was to have dinner again with Cecile in another week, and he had no idea how he would look her in the eye, let alone discuss their marriage. Tristam had been brought up with the expectation of serving his family through this type of alliance, and he'd long made his peace with it. But he'd never realized just how hard it would be. He shouldn't have kissed Kyra last night. It only made things worse. But somehow, he couldn't quite bring himself to regret it.

Tristam might have remained lost in his thoughts, but gradually the commotion around him increased until he could no longer ignore it. Tristam pushed his worries aside and peered up the street. The execution cart wasn't here yet, though it should be close if everything was running on schedule. He exchanged a glance with the soldier next to him, who was also starting to look around.

"Think they need reinforcements?" asked the Red Shield.

"I've not heard a call for them," said Tristam.

Then he started to make out words. "Girl...rooftop... monster..."

"Kyra," he whispered. And he knew something was horribly wrong.

"What did you say?"

Tristam stepped out of formation and ran up the road.

Getting to the cart was easy. The road had been cleared, and his fellow soldiers were holding the crowd at bay. Quite a few Red Shields turned in confusion as he ran by. Someone shouted his name, asking him what he thought he was doing, but he just ran faster. The orderly ranks of soldiers broke down as the wagon came into view, and the shouts of the crowd grew deafening. Tristam caught a glimpse of James, hanging limply from the crossbeams. Dead.

Tristam stopped in his tracks, staring in disbelief. Shouts of "girl" and "monster" still rose up at random around him. "Girl crawled out from under the wagon," said an old man. "Gutted him like a fish."

Had Kyra done this? Had she planned to? And *why?* Tristam grabbed a man in the crowd. "Where did the assassin go?"

The man pointed—at the rooftops, naturally. Tristam gritted his teeth and pushed his way into the throng. It was slow going. Even with his official livery and his height, the mob could only part so quickly. He took a rougher approach as he grew more impatient, throwing elbows and ignoring angry comments.

Red Shields ran along the rooftops and dropped out of sight farther on. They had the right idea—the crowd wasn't going to get any thinner. Tristam gave up on the street and pushed his way to a nearby wall. He jumped for an overhang and pulled himself up. Most of the Red Shields he'd seen were gone by now, but he had a vague idea of where they'd disappeared to. Tristam ran, his steps landing too heavily for comfort on the well-crafted roof tiles. He'd heard enough from the crowd to know that they'd recognized Kyra for who she was and what she was. There was no way this could end well.

Tristam was halfway there when he heard the roar, and the blood drained from his face. No. She wouldn't.

He redoubled his speed. His way was once again directed by screams and shouts, and it was easy to find the courtyard where chaos was breaking loose. He skidded to a stop dangerously close to the roof edge and took in the scene below.

She was there. Tristam had seen Kyra twice in this form now—dark brown fur, slender muscular body—and she was backed into a corner by four Red Shields. Tristam's first reaction was relief to see that they wielded swords rather than spears.

But then Kyra growled, a deep-throated snarl that sent shivers down his spine, and he wondered if he was worried for the wrong party.

He lowered himself off the roof and crept closer. *Jump over them, Kyra. Knock them aside and make for the forest.*

Just then, two of the Red Shields attacked. One of them managed to cut Kyra's flank, and she roared in fury. She leaped into their midst, scattering them like pebbles. There was murder in her eyes.

"No!" Tristam shouted. He ran in front of Kyra, holding up his hands. "Kyra, it's me. Don't do this."

She fixed his eyes on him, and what he saw froze him to the core. Last time, after she'd killed Santon, Tristam had still been able to see some humanity in her. He'd spoken to that, and he'd reached her. But this time, he saw none of it. No sign at all that Kyra recognized him. No hint, as she advanced on him, teeth bared, that she even knew who he was.

Tristam drew his sword. Bad idea. At the first flash of steel, Kyra launched herself at him. He dove out of the way and turned to find her engaging now with the other Red Shields. Things were spiraling out of control.

Tristam tossed his sword to the side. It would only make things worse. And then, without stopping to think lest he realize his foolishness, he ran and threw herself onto her back.

Kyra's reaction was immediate. She twisted and snarled as Tristam looped his arms around her neck and hung on for dear life. "Don't do this, Kyra. It's me."

Kyra gave no sign of understanding. She rose up on her hind legs, doing her best to toss him off. Tristam continued talking to her, shouting words he couldn't even make sense of himself. But finally, his grip failed, and she tossed him onto the ground. The impact knocked the breath out of him. He groaned, willing the spots to clear out of his vision. The courtyard had gone quiet. Kyra was staring at him, still growling, tail swishing.

"Leave the city, Kyra," he said. He breathed in dust from his fall and coughed. "Get out of here." Was she that completely gone? Would she kill him right here and now?

A door opened into the courtyard, and new soldiers rushed in, some with spears this time. Kyra whipped around to face them, and Tristam braced himself for what was to come. But then she turned abruptly and ran up a tree. It bowed under her weight, and just as Tristam thought something would snap, Kyra launched herself onto the rooftop and ran for the city walls.

## TWENTY-FOUR

Kyra ran with a speed born of madness. As she leaped off the rooftop and onto the street, people screamed and scattered in her wake. She was tempted to chase them, but Tristam's voice lodged in her mind and she kept running. She cleared the city wall by climbing another tree, then tumbled down the other side. She landed on her feet.

Houses changed to farmland, then gave way to the shelter of the forest. She dodged branches and tree trunks, zigzagging her way through. A pent-up frustration drove her on, a feeling that if she stopped or slowed, she would explode. Kyra spied a raccoon and gave chase, killing it with a snap of her jaws and tearing into its flesh. Only then did her blood cool. Only then did her wits return. She couldn't stay in this shape, but she would freeze if she changed back now.

She limped her way to her cave. The winter air swirled around her as she finally shrank back into her skin. Her limbs ached, and she was covered with cuts and bruises, including one long gash across her ribs. Nothing life-threatening, but they made every movement painful. Kyra stumbled inside, shivering violently, and dressed herself as quickly as she could. This was her last spare tunic.

She crumpled against the sandy cave wall as the memories came back to her. The fight against the guards—had she killed any of them? Then there was Tristam. *Tristam.* How badly had she hurt him?

Kyra's hands were still crusted with James's blood. Somehow, through all the transformations, fighting, and fleeing, it had stayed on. Kyra stared at her fingers until her eyes blurred. What had James been to her? At different times, he'd been a Guildleader, an infatuation, an enemy, and a co-conspirator. And now he was dead at her hands. He'd wanted her to be an assassin. Today he'd been her mark.

Kyra saw again the pain in his face as he'd died. Why had she stabbed him in the stomach? She'd meant to cut his throat, but then the Red Shields had come after her, and she'd simply acted. Kyra had thought to kill him as an act of mercy, but had there been a part of her that sought revenge? Maybe she hadn't been ready to let James forget the pain he'd caused her.

Snow crunched nearby, and Kyra held her breath. Outside, the forest had fallen unnaturally silent. She grabbed her dagger and ran to the cave mouth. Someone stepped out of the trees.

"Tristam?" Kyra asked. Her voice shook.

He stepped fully into view. "You left a trail. I tried to obscure it as best I could." He held out a cloak and a pair of boots—hers. "I don't think anyone saw me grab these."

"Thank you." She came out of the cave and took her things, tucking them under one arm. Tristam's eyes flickered over her, taking in her ragged appearance. He didn't look too good himself. There was dirt on his tunic, and the skin on one side of his face looked raw. But the worst was the caution in his eyes, the way he stood as if he expected her to change shape at any moment.

"I'm so sorry." Kyra's voice broke.

He didn't respond right away, and Kyra wondered if this had finally turned him away from her forever.

"Are you...back to yourself?" he finally asked.

She nodded, closing her eyes. "The Red Shields. How many...?"

"Four had minor injuries to be treated. One lost a great deal of blood but should survive."

Her knees buckled with relief, and she touched a tree for support. "Thank you for stopping me." When she'd faced the soldiers, they'd seemed nothing more than nameless enemies, helpless targets. But they'd had families and children.

"You're shaking," Tristam said. He took her hand and led her back to the cave. She was grateful for his touch and that he didn't refuse to be close to her. But still, he was so careful in the way he moved, so on his guard.

"I thought I could control it," she said. But was that even true? She'd been scared, hemmed in by soldiers, and taking her other form had seemed her only way out. Her life or theirs. She'd made her choice, though there had been eight of them and one of her. "I don't think I should change shape again," she said.

He didn't argue. They sat just inside the cave entrance. The afternoon sunlight came in at an angle and illuminated the dust in front of them.

"How many people have you killed, as a soldier?" she asked.

"Two," he said quietly. "The first time, we happened upon brigands attacking a trade caravan. The second was near my manor. It was the same thing, except they were looting a farm."

"How did it . . . make you feel afterward?"

He took his time answering, as if he knew how much hung in the balance. "It was hard, looking into the eyes of someone who was dying and knowing it was my doing."

Did he feel a rush of power when he killed? An overwhelming desire to draw more blood? She couldn't ask, but she suspected she knew the answer. "James held my eyes when I killed him," she said. "He wouldn't let me look away." Of course James would know what those last moments were like. Of course he'd insist on that last connection.

"Why did you do it?" asked Tristam. "That much planning, that much risk, just to spare him the last few hours?"

"I couldn't let him die like that." It didn't make sense. Even Kyra didn't quite understand the common thread of purpose that bound James and her together. They'd hurt each other so many times, yet some part of her had felt she owed him this. "He said something to me before he died. He told me to choose my fight."

"Your fight?" Tristam echoed. "And what is that?"

She rubbed at her fingers to get the blood off. "I don't know."

"I don't believe you."

He was right. Kyra wasn't as naïve as she used to be. She knew more about the city now and its workings. James had wanted to bring down the entire Council. She wasn't sure what he'd had in mind after that. Anarchy? Establishing himself in power? He hadn't seen fit to share his plans with her, and Kyra suspected she wouldn't have agreed with them. But neither was she happy with the way things were.

"Willem's got to go. It's not enough simply to stop the Demon Rider offensive. I want him out of power."

Tristam was silent for a long moment before he finally spoke again. "I'll help you in any way I can."

He'd spoken so calmly that it took a while for Kyra to recognize the implications. But when they finally sank in, she looked to him in alarm. "Tristam, this is high treason. You've been working so hard to get back to good standing in the Palace, and you've got your marriage negotiations to think about." He'd given up so much for her already.

Tristam stared at the dust swirling in front of them. "You know, before I met you, I never gave much thought to my station in life. I knew I was fortunate, but I didn't really know what it meant. But I have to think now that my good fortune comes with some measure of responsibility, whether it be taking up arms to protect the lowborn or trying to make changes where we can." He paused then. "I suppose we all have to make our choices. This is mine."

It was the type of decision that should have been announced with trumpets and rousing speeches, but instead it was just the two of them hiding in the mouth of a cave, bruised, dirty, and exhausted.

"I won't stop you," said Kyra. "But if you have doubts at any point, you need to tell me."

"What next, then?"

She looked up at him, and their eyes met briefly. It seemed

she was always looking at the space between the two of them. Measuring it, wishing she could bridge it. "James told me once that Willem must be disgraced before he's brought down. I think he's right. We need to discredit him."

"Orvin's mystery messenger, then?" said Tristam.

Kyra nodded. "We'll need to think how best to do it. Flick might be able to help. He's good at flipping pockets." She started going through the possibilities in her head, but her mind wouldn't cooperate. Too much had happened in too short of a time. She wasn't ready to get back on the warpath just yet. "We'll make plans, but can you give me a moment? I can't think straight."

He looked her over again, and there was a softness in his gaze when he nodded. She leaned her head against the cave wall and closed her eyes. She'd only meant to rest a little, but a while later, she was groggily aware of him laying her down on the cave floor and tucking his cloak around her. She reached out and took his hand. His grip felt so comfortable, so solid. And yet, there was caution in his manner that hadn't been there the night before.

"Tristam," she said. "It's not just Cecile that stands between us, is it? Even if I were higher-born, it wouldn't matter. You're scared of what I am."

He didn't answer right away, and his hesitation spoke more than any words he might have said. For a moment she could see it in his eyes, his lingering fear and mistrust of the Demon Riders, something he'd done an admirable job of hiding from her but was nonetheless still there. Kyra looked down, trying to ignore the tightness that had arisen in her chest. "I'm not completely blameless in Santon's death. I hoped he would attack me, and I pretended to be vulnerable so they'd give me the excuse I needed. Part of me liked tearing Santon apart. I'm not proud of it, but I won't hide it from you. I owe you that much."

Tristam looked down at her hand. When he finally spoke, his voice was heavy. "I don't envy you, Kyra. I might have done the same or worse had I been in your shoes."

He was offering her empathy, understanding, friendship. And though a selfish part of her wished for more, Kyra supposed that they didn't have that luxury. Tristam brushed her hair away from her face with the back of his fingers. The featherlight touch left a pleasant tingling on her scalp, and she let her eyes close. "Should you be getting back to the city?" she asked him.

"They won't notice my absence for a few more hours. Sleep for now. I'll be here."

## TWENTY-FIVE

Flick was getting better at spotting Demon Riders in the trees. Or at least he thought he was. He caught hints of movement in the corners of his eyes when he walked near the forest, though when he turned and looked, he never saw anything for certain.

He was out behind Mercie's house this afternoon. There had been a lot of activity on the roads earlier, and Flick suspected something had happened in the city. Mercie had gone in to hear the news, and Flick watched the road, eager to know what had occurred.

But there was that thing that kept moving in his periphery. He supposed he should have been more nervous, but he suspected he knew what it was. Or rather, who it was. Finally, his curiosity got the better of him. "Is anyone there?" he called.

Adele stepped out. Flick grinned. "I'm glad to see you."

She smiled serenely in return, her amber eyes sparkling against her pale skin. That was a first. He couldn't remember her giving him a full smile before.

"Are you well?" she asked.

"I am. Thank you."

They stood looking at each other for a few moments. Finally, Flick gestured to the forest. "I was just taking a walk. Would you like to join me?"

"To see Kyra?"

"No, just watching the road. But there's no reason I must do it alone."

Her eyes brightened at this, and she fell in step beside him. They strolled just inside the line of the forest so Flick could catch glimpses of the road. It was his fourth time meeting Adele now, yet he still felt off balance around her. He'd had his share of sweethearts in the past. Flick never had trouble talking to girls or making them laugh. But then, none of girls he flirted with back in the city had been capable of turning into giant beasts. Not that he thought he was flirting with Adele. Who knew what these people's customs were? It was enough of a triumph that he hadn't yet been mauled to death. But something about this lass fascinated him. Her quick eye and curiosity, her uninhibited openness in expressing her opinion, her never-ending stream of questions for him.

Speaking of which, she was about to ask him another one. He could tell. Flick interrupted her. "You're always asking me about me and my people," he said. "I think it's my turn, don't you?"

A few meetings ago, this sort of question might have made her jump back in alarm. But this time, she simply tilted her head, then nodded. "What would you like to know?"

"Well..." Flick paused. He hardly knew where to start. "What do you do most days?"

"Nights," she corrected. "I hunt at night, and I wander the forest. Sometimes I gather with the others."

"What do you do with them?"

"Talk, tell stories, sing." She reached out and touched a tree branch with her finger as they walked past.

Sing? The idea of Adele as a songbird piqued his interest. "Will you sing something for me?"

He thought he'd have to coax her further, but she launched right into a quick song. Her voice was high and steady. The melody itself was unusual. It went up and down in finer increments than the songs he was used to hearing. It almost reminded Flick of Minadan pipe tunes, the ones said to lull a sleeper into strange and curious dreams, but Adele's tune was livelier and happier.

"You sing beautifully," he said when she finished. "Can you teach me this song?"

She sang a phrase for him to repeat, then covered a smile at his attempt.

"No good?"

"Your pronunciation is not the best," she said gently.

He tried several more times until she deemed his performance satisfactory enough to move on. They continued like this, phrase by phrase, laughing at his mistakes and sending wayward phrases into the trees. He'd almost made it through what he thought was the first stanza when Adele stopped him with a touch to the elbow. She was looking into the forest again.

"Some of your kin?" he asked, suddenly tense. Adele, he was always happy to see. But the others . . .

She stared in that direction, then shook her head. "It's Kyra. And someone else."

Kyra came into view a few moments later. Her face was smudged with dirt, and she moved like it hurt to do so. And was that blood seeping through her tunic?

"Kyra, what happened?" Then he saw Tristam a few steps behind her, looking equally beat-up and still wearing his Red Shield livery.

Kyra looked between Flick and Adele, confused for a moment, and then seemed to put the matter out of her mind. "Have you had news from the city?" she asked.

"Not today. But Mercie went in to find out what the excitement was."

Kyra lowered her eyes. Flick could tell from the way her brows knitted together that the news was big, that it had to do with her, and that he wasn't going to be pleased.

"Out with it," he said.

She spread her hands apologetically. "Things have happened," she said. "And we need your help."


Flick knew that the Palace compound had two main gates, one in the north, and one on the south wall. These were the only ones opened on a regular basis. What he hadn't noticed until tonight was the presence of smaller gates. According to Kyra, these were usually double-locked and guarded, although select noblemen living within those walls had keys. A few hours past midnight, a man had entered through one such gate, and now Flick waited in a nearby alleyway for him to leave.

He heard a faint metallic creak, followed by quick footsteps that echoed down the empty street. Flick ducked deeper into the alley as the man walked past. A few moments later, a shadow passed overhead—Kyra was trailing him on the rooftops. Flick pulled his cloak tighter and settled down to wait.

Kyra dropped off the roof a short while later, landing softly in front of him. Though Flick could not see her face clearly in the darkness, he could hear her panting from exertion. Kyra was dressed for work in a dark tunic and trousers, with her hair tied back in her characteristic ponytail. He'd seen her like this hundreds of times, and after all the craziness of the past few weeks, it was nice to see her back to form.

Flick had been . . . less than pleased to learn what had happened at James's execution. But somehow, after berating Kyra for her harebrained, risky scheme, he'd immediately agreed to help her with another one. Kyra had argued that this new mission was important, and this time, Flick agreed. If there was any way to stop Willem's Demon Rider offensive, they had to try. Flick's conversations with Adele had convinced him that peace with the Makvani was possible, but only if Forge didn't embark on such a disastrous attack.

Kyra dusted off her hands. "The messenger's staying at an inn called The Drowned Cat," she said. "Not the most auspicious name for an inn, is it?"

"Mayhap it refers to the contents of their stew," said Flick.

Kyra stifled a giggle as they made their way to the inn. The windows were dark, and the road was completely silent. They slipped into an alleyway across the street, where Tristam was already waiting.

"I'm guessing he'll leave tomorrow morning to blend in with the other travelers," Tristam said.

Flick handed Kyra a large bag. "If he breaks his fast in the inn's dining room, I'll flip his purse then. And you, my delightful assistant, will need these."

Kyra reached into the bag and fished out a long black wig, a trader's tunic, and a pair of shoes, examining each in turn. Flick grinned when he saw Tristam eyeing the props with curiosity. The wallhugger would be getting quite the education in undercity tactics today.

Kyra rounded the corner with the props. When she came back, she looked taller, thanks to the shoes' well-concealed heels, and she boasted a head of luxurious ebony curls instead of her usual brown ponytail. In the darkness, Flick could barely make out the intricately patterned leather knots decorating her tunic in the style of the southern traders. Trader women were some of the few who might actually eat or stay at an inn. It wasn't the best disguise, but it was the best Mercie had. Flick didn't bother with a costume himself, thinking instead to blend in among the countless tavern-going men. Though he'd grown out his beard since he fled the city. It always made him look quite a bit older.

They took turns watching the inn until light started to shine on the horizon and the city started to stir. When the innkeeper came out to sweep the doorstep, Kyra looked to Flick. "Better if you're already in the dining room when he comes in. Remember what he looks like?"

"Black hair down to his shoulder, a few years older than

me. Small eyes. Mustache." Flick wiped the dust off his cloak. "You're paying for my drink, right?"

Kyra rolled her eyes and handed Flick a few coppers.

"The messenger came in late last night, and he might not be up for a while," said Tristam. "Do you think it'll be suspicious for Flick to be in there so long?"

Flick and Kyra exchanged a glance, and Kyra's lips twitched. "Flick always thinks up something to do." She turned to Flick. "Just, uh, try not to attract too much attention, all right?" The last time Flick had done a day-long stint at an inn, he'd invented a drinking game where each drinker had to be at a higher physical location than the last. The fallout had involved a crowd of people on the roof, multiple bruises, one broken limb (not Flick's), and a warning never to step foot in The Bow-Legged Canary again.

Flick grinned. "Who, me?" And he sauntered off.

After a night out in the cold, the warm air of the inn's dining room felt lovely, and the smell of freshly baked bread wafting out from the kitchen made Flick's stomach growl. The room was about half full as the earlier-rising patrons broke their fast, and Flick settled near a window. The serving girl was a friendly lass with dimpled cheeks who laughed at his jokes. She brought him a plate of sausages, and he tucked into the meal.

He'd just about finished his sausages when he saw his mark. The messenger entered alone and sat down with the bristly body language of someone who didn't want company. Flick washed down his last bite of breakfast with ale, then put a little unsteadiness in his stride and strolled to the messenger's table.

"Fine morning, in't it?" said Flick, sinking onto a stool next to him. The messenger didn't so much as glance at him. Flick had been about to recite some platitudes about delicious food and beautiful serving girls but changed his mind when he saw the man's scowl. "Of course, can't quite enjoy it in this type of establishment. Second-rate food and lazy serving lasses." Flick sent a mental apology to the nice serving girl, grateful she was out of earshot.

Flick studied the man with a careful eye. The messenger was grumpy and standoffish. His clothes were unremarkable in style and color, but his tunic was of surprisingly thick and soft wool, and he wore a finely crafted ring. Flick also noticed that the man's hair and mustache were meticulously trimmed. Most importantly, he carried a small leather bag across his shoulder. That was likely where his message would be.

"That's a fine ring you've got there," Flick said. "Impressive detailing. Must have been made by a master."

The man straightened just the tiniest bit.

"What's the design? Looks like one of the newer fashions out of Parna."

It was just an educated guess, since everything seemed to come from Parna these days. But the messenger regarded him with new consideration. "That's right."

Flick smiled and extended a hand. "I'm Taylon of Forge."

"Robert," said the messenger. No city, no house. Still being careful.

The door opened, and Flick saw Kyra come in and sit at a back table. He averted his eyes and launched into an elaborate story about getting cheated by a trader over a fake silver brooch. Robert's lips curled slightly as the story progressed—the messenger didn't have a high opinion of Flick's eye for goods—but Flick knew he had him. Robert was listening intently, and he'd forgotten all about his earlier attempts to stay aloof.

Flick patted Robert on the shoulder. "I'll wager someone like you wouldn't be fooled by such a simple trick." The pat was a little rougher than it needed to be, and Robert scowled at Flick's drunken clumsiness. As the messenger pulled away, Flick undid the clasp on Robert's bag, looking out the window as he did so. "You've far to travel today?"

Robert followed Flick's gaze. They always did, if he led confidently. "Not too far," the messenger said, oblivious to the fact that Flick had just lifted a piece of parchment from his purse.

Flick tucked the parchment up his sleeve and continued to chatter on. Someone brushed past him—Kyra's scratchy wig tickled the back of his neck. Her fingers skimmed his palm, and he let the parchment drop into her hand.

He spoke to the man a while longer and then pushed back from the table. "Pity that ale never stays with us very long," he said with an embarrassed grin. He made a show of asking for the privy before he went out the door.

Flick found Kyra and Tristam crouched in the alley behind a stack of crates. Kyra had already opened the parchment, and Flick noticed with pride that she'd managed to keep half the seal intact, though the other half had broken into pieces.

"Find anything?" he asked, bending down to join them.

Tristam handed him the opened note. The message inside was written in neat, elegant script.

*All our soldiers are in position and ready for the forest offensive, though the Council is volatile and our plans are far from secure. I need more funds to gain the cooperation of Palace scribes, as well as key members of the defense forces. The more of our own that we have within the Palace, the safer our position will be.*

"That's Willem's handwriting," said Tristam.

Flick read it over one more time, then returned it to Tristam. "Certainly seems underhanded, but what's it mean? Care to enlighten us on the ways of the court?"

Tristam rubbed his temples. "Willem's trying to ensure the success of the Demon Rider offensive—that's clear enough. And looks like he's using bribes to do it. The Council members look to the scribes and army leaders for advice. If Willem controls what they hear, he controls what they think."

Seemed a roundabout way of pulling strings, but Flick supposed everything in the Palace was roundabout. "Who do you think is providing this coin?"

"Hard to tell. My best guess would be some of the minor families outside the city. They'd have the most to gain from an offensive against the Demon Riders."

They were silent for a moment, then Kyra spoke. "If the Council's decision to attack the Demon Riders was influenced by bribery, would that be enough reason to stop the offensive?"

"It might be enough to delay while they investigate further," said Tristam, "and it might be the first step we need to discredit Willem himself. But I'm not sure we have enough proof. This is only one letter, and it's not even signed. Willem's handwriting could easily be faked. And we don't even know who his co-conspirators are."

Flick drummed his fingers against his thigh. "What if you

had the testimony of the messenger? He'll find his purse empty soon enough and come looking for me. Might there be some way to, ah . . . persuade him to cooperate?" He almost felt guilty for suggesting it. Though really, Robert was a rather unpleasant fellow. . . .

Tristam squinted in the direction of the street. "Depends on how his loyalty measures up to his self-preservation. But we'd need someplace to keep him. We can't exactly interrogate him here."

"I could guard him at my cave," said Kyra.

"It'd be better if you had help," said Flick. An idea came to him, and he made a quick decision. Why should Kyra be the only one to come up with harebrained schemes? "I might have friends who could keep an eye on him."

"Are these friends trustworthy?" asked Tristam.

"They've no love for Willem. I'll introduce you and you can decide for yourself."

Tristam looked to Kyra. "What do you think?"

She stared at the parchment. "We've only seven days until the offensive starts. Think we can get the messenger to crack that quickly?"

"Can you think of a better way?" said Tristam.

A vendor on the street outside hawked his hotcakes as the three of them thought this over. Kyra gave a decisive nod. "Let's do it."

They sketched out a quick plan, then Flick returned to the inn, bypassing the dining room this time for the living quarters in back. He climbed the stairs in a rush, as if he were making a hasty exit. No one stopped him, so he ran through the hallways several more times, wondering how long he could keep this up. Finally, Robert stepped around the corner. The man grabbed Flick's collar and forced him against the wall.

Flick raised his hands. "Whoa there, friend." One of the doors in the corridor opened, and a bewildered lodger peered out, only to duck back into his room when Robert glared at him.

The messenger bent his face close to Flick's. "Where is it?"

"Where's what?"

Flick felt the sharp point of a dagger against his side. "The parchment," said Robert.

"I've no idea what you're talking about." Flick bit back a curse as cloth ripped and the dagger skimmed his skin. He was pretty sure Robert had drawn blood. "Search me if you want," he said through gritted teeth. "I've nothing on me." *You owe me, Kyra.*

Flick stayed absolutely still as Robert patted him down. Robert searched him twice, then narrowed his eyes. "It was in my purse when I stepped into the dining room, and gone after you left. No one else came near me except for you." Robert raised the dagger to Flick's throat.

"All right, all right, I took it." Flick didn't have to work hard to sound convincingly panicked. "It's outside. I can give it back. Just—keep that dagger to yourself."

The messenger spun Flick roughly around so they were facing the same direction. A moment later, the knife reappeared at his back. "Slowly," said Robert. "If I suspect anything, your life is forfeit."

They walked in lockstep down the stairs. The lodgers they passed didn't even notice anything was amiss. Once out the door, Flick headed for the alley, and Robert tightened his grip. "Don't try anything."

"Do you want the parchment or not?" said Flick under his breath.

Flick felt a layer of sweat forming over his skin as they stepped into the alley. There was no sign of Tristam or Kyra as they walked past the stack of crates, and he dearly hoped that nothing had gone awry. Flick's gaze settled on a pile of rocks next to the wall. "There, under the rocks."

Robert nudged him closer. "Move them aside slowly."

Carefully, Flick got to his knees and began slowly shifting the rocks in the pile. *Any time now, Tristam...*

Robert grunted behind him, and Flick felt the man's grip go slack. He turned around to see Tristam carefully lowering the messenger's body to the ground. Kyra dropped off the roof, eyed Robert, unconscious on the ground, and breathed a sigh of relief.

"He's alive," said Tristam. "He'll have a headache when he wakes though."

"Cutting it a bit close?" said Flick, shaking out his arms and shoulders. He hadn't realized how tense he'd been.

"Sorry," said Tristam. "With that knife drawn on you, I wanted to make sure he didn't see me coming."

Flick plucked Robert's dagger off the ground and wiped the dust off the blade. "I'm keeping this," he said. "For my troubles."

## TWENTY-SIX

They bound Robert tightly and gagged him while Tristam hurried back to the Palace for a wagon. When the messenger awoke, Kyra showed him her dagger.

"You'll be quiet," she said, conjuring her best imitation of James in his more dangerous moments. "And you won't cause any trouble." The messenger's glare could have sparked kindling, but he made no noise.

A short while later, Tristam pulled up with a wagon full of the fake demon cat heads. "I told them I was going to set up some exercises outside the city," he said. "I suppose I'll have to do that now."

By pulling the wagon right to the alley, they loaded Robert without attracting too many wayward glances. Flick lay down behind him, holding tight to the ropes that bound Robert's wrists. Kyra took her place in front of the messenger, and Tristam covered all three of them with demon cat heads. The hemp sacks smelled like mold, and Kyra could feel Robert's eyes on her in the cramped semidarkness. The messenger exuded fury, and Kyra wondered how they would possibly get him to cooperate before the start of the Demon Rider offensive in seven days.

After a bumpy and stuffy ride out of the city, Tristam pulled the wagon off the road. Flick left to find his friends, and Kyra and Tristam marched Robert to Kyra's cave. Their captive walked stoically in front of them, with Tristam's knife at his back. He was obediently quiet, but his eyes were a bit too keen, and it was with great relief that Kyra saw her cave appear ahead of them.

Kyra scouted it first, then waved Tristam in when she found it empty. Not much light came in from the mouth, and it took a moment for their eyes to adjust to the darkness. It also smelled slightly of cat, and Kyra wondered if Tristam noticed.

Tristam ungagged Robert. "You may sit if you'd like," said Tristam, motioning to the cave wall. The messenger glared at them but carefully lowered himself onto the ground. He pulled his legs away from Kyra when she tried to retie them, but relented after a moment.

"You're from the Forge Council?" said Robert. "I didn't peg that fellow for a Palace man."

"We'll be asking the questions," Tristam said calmly. "Who sent the message to Willem?"

Robert's laugh had a sarcastic edge. "And you expect me to simply lay it all out for you?"

"No, not immediately. But you will. You looked competent with that dagger, but you're a messenger and not a soldier. You aren't sworn to die for your master, and I don't think you mean to. It might take some time for this to sink in, but you'll come around."

Kyra had been on the receiving end of Tristam's interrogations not long ago, and it was strange to be on the other side. Tristam didn't yell or raise his voice, but there was a quiet intensity to the way he spoke that commanded attention. He was also incredibly calm. All their plans hinged on this messenger, but Tristam acted as if he had the upper hand.

"I don't believe you'll kill me," said Robert.

"I won't have to," said Tristam. "The Council will gladly execute you for me. But if you give us useful information, we might be able to speak on your behalf. I can't promise you any specific terms to your sentence, but I can promise you far better than what you'll receive if I turn you in without an admission of guilt. Just tell me which house employs you and whom the message was for."

Kyra heard footsteps outside a few moments before Tristam did. They exchanged a glance, and she slipped out. Flick waited a short distance from the cave mouth, shifting his weight from foot to foot. She could have sworn he looked guilty.

"My friends can help," he said. "And they're right behind me."

"I see." Kyra took a few steps closer, wondering at Flick's manner. "That's good news, in't it?" She stopped as Adele, Pashla, and Mela and a man she didn't recognize came into view. "Flick, that's—"

At that moment, Tristam stepped out of the cave. He took one look at the newcomers and reached for his sword.

"There's no need, Tristam," said Flick. "These are the friends I mentioned."

Tristam had gone rigid. He drew breath sharply to speak, then looked back at the cave mouth. His voice was low when he spoke again, but no less angry. "You didn't mention that your friends were Demon Riders."

"I know," said Flick. He spoke carefully, though there was no hint of apology in his manner. "They're good to help, but you don't have to accept it."

Kyra looked from Flick to Tristam and back again, trying to ignore a feeling of betrayal that was trickling into her consciousness. She wasn't sure what bothered her more, that Flick had obviously hidden this plan from her, or that he'd been the one to think of it when Kyra shared their blood.

Pashla nodded to Kyra in greeting, then looked at Tristam. "I didn't know the knight would be here," she said to Adele.

"I have a name," said Tristam, his voice taut.

"Tristam of Brancel," Pashla said lightly. While her tone didn't exactly convey disrespect, neither did she assign much importance to the utterance. The tension in the circle was palpable, and Kyra couldn't quell the feeling that things were about to unravel. She didn't know what Flick's game was, and the thought of her old friend doing anything behind her back bothered her more than she cared to admit.

It was Adele who spoke first. "Flick tells me that we need this prisoner if we want to stop Forge from sending soldiers into the forest. We will guard him for you. You have our word that he will not escape," she said.

"Your word?" said Tristam. "And what's that worth?" Kyra had to look away at the raw animosity in his voice. If she'd had any doubt as to how he felt about her kin . . .

"We're skilled at watching prisoners, and we're skilled fighters," said Pashla. "This, you should know, since you've been one of our captives, and you've seen how easily we can kill your kind."

Kyra looked to Pashla in disbelief. Was she deliberately goading Tristam, or did she simply not realize what effect her words would have?

Tristam took a step toward Pashla, drawing his sword. "I stood by while you murdered two of my comrades. I will not stand by while you mock their deaths."

"No!" Kyra reached for him as Pashla took a step back. The Demon Riders to either side of her untied their belts.

"Stop now!" Flick could be deafening when he wanted to be, and his shout reverberated through the trees. Everybody froze, and he planted himself between Tristam and Pashla. "We've got the same goals here and enough at stake so that we can't afford to fall apart amongst ourselves."

Tristam's sword hovered a finger's width from Flick's throat. Adele's features blurred and re-formed as she looked between the two of them.

Kyra finally found her voice. "Tristam," she said softly, almost apologetically. "I think Flick's right. The Makvani could do a better job of guarding him than I could by myself."

Tristam's face was still tight with anger. "Can I have a word, Flick?" he said.

"Aye," said Flick, resigned.

Tristam lowered his blade, and the two walked into the trees with the wariness of men about to start a duel. Kyra wondered if she should step in. Both Tristam and Flick knew how high the stakes were. They wouldn't come to blows over this, would they?

"Your friend holds long grudges," came Pashla's low voice at her ear.

Kyra could feel a headache starting to form right in the middle of her forehead, and she found she didn't have the patience for caution or tact. "You killed two of his friends, Pashla. That's more than a grudge to get over."

"They were killed in battle," said Pashla calmly, as if that settled the matter.

Flick and Tristam were arguing and gesticulating, though Kyra couldn't make out the words. At one point, Flick gestured in their direction, and she got the clear impression that he pointed to her rather than the Demon Riders near her. A short while later, her friends returned. Tristam's eyes still flashed, and Flick had the look of someone who'd just weathered a hard storm.

"Everything all right?" Kyra asked. She'd have her own words with Flick later, but right now she just wanted to keep everything from falling apart.

"We accept your help," said Tristam to the Demon Riders.

"We are, in fact, grateful for it," added Flick. Tristam's expression remained stony. "And I have clothes for the guards to change into. Seems it would be prudent not to let"—he jerked his head toward the cave—"know about, uh"—he gestured toward the Makvani.

Things progressed quickly after that. Kyra set up a guard schedule with the Demon Riders while Tristam questioned Robert further. The messenger didn't give him any useful information, but Tristam didn't seem surprised.

"He needs some time to think. They always do," Tristam said to Kyra as he prepared to leave. He'd calmed down since the confrontation earlier, and Kyra had seen him thank Adele for the Makvani's help.

"I certainly needed some time," said Kyra, thinking back to her interrogation and imprisonment at the Palace.

Tristam's eyes went cautiously over her face, and only after searching her features did he relax and meet her eyes. "You know, I still feel guilty about how I treated you," he said.

She smiled wryly up at him. "Why ever for? We've been through enough together. No reason to dwell on past misunderstandings."

They looked at one another, sharing for a moment the memory of when they'd faced off over the interrogation table. And though they had hated each other at the time, thinking back on it now brought Kyra comfort. It was a reason for hope, she supposed, that two people at odds could come so far.

Finally, Tristam looked down. "I should go," he said. "I'll be back when I can. Keep him well fed and sheltered. We need him to believe us when we say we can protect him."

Kyra let out a long, slow breath as she watched Tristam walk away. When he finally disappeared, she covered her eyes with the heel of her hands and arched her back, trying to loosen up her muscles. Footsteps crunched in the snow, and she opened her eyes to see Flick walking toward her, for all the world looking like a dog who'd been caught ransacking the family kitchen.

"So," he said. "Are you ready to yell at me now?"

That was all the encouragement Kyra needed.

"What were you thinking?" She rounded on him, venting all the tension and betrayal she'd been feeling. "They could have slaughtered each other in front of that cave."

Flick bore her words, making no attempt to interrupt her.

"Why'd you do it?" she asked, throwing up her arms. "Why didn't you tell me?" She looked back toward the Demon Riders by the cave. "And have you become bosom friends with Pashla, too?" She finally admitted it. She was jealous of her friend, who picked up allies wherever he went, while it seemed she herself only found more enemies.

She ran out of words and settled for glaring at Flick, who stirred when he realized she was done.

"I'm sorry I didn't tell you," he said, subdued. "I knew Tristam wouldn't agree if I asked him beforehand, and if I'd told you, you'd have been forced to decide whether you wanted to hide it from him. This way, the blame fell squarely on me." He took a breath. "I don't know Pashla well at all. Adele was the one I asked for help, and she found the others."

"And you just decided this was the right thing to do?" Kyra said.

"Can you think of anyone else who could have helped us?"

She couldn't, really, but she wasn't ready to let him off the hook. "Just because things didn't explode today doesn't mean they won't tomorrow."

"I know. But it's worth it." Flick spoke with surprising conviction, and Kyra wondered at it. He sank down onto a fallen log. After a moment, Kyra grudgingly followed his lead.

"Why?" she asked.

Flick stared down at his hands, massaging the knuckles of

his right hand with his left. "Call me foolish, I suppose, but I think it might do some good to work together with these people. I've had a few run-ins with the Makvani now. Truth is, they do look on us humans as something below their regard. But I'm realizing that it's different when they see you face-to-face. That's why I don't think those folk by the cave will hurt me, even if their clanmate was wounded by a soldier this morning. I'm no longer a nameless human to them. And I wonder, if more of them actually spent time with us, maybe something could come out of it."

"You think we could avoid a war?"

Flick sighed and absentmindedly broke a twig off the fallen tree. "I don't think Adele's eager for a fight, and some of the others aren't either. I mean, I'm not naïve. I know this will only make a small difference. But it's better than nothing, in't it?"

His face had such an optimistic cast that Kyra found it hard to hold her grudge. "I hope you're right," she said. "And I hope Tristam can get over what happened today and trust us again."

"Tristam, in particular, needs to get over his fears."

There was a layer of meaning in Flick's tone that caught Kyra's attention. "Why? What do you mean?"

"Oh." For the first time, Flick stumbled on his words. "I just mean . . ."

And Kyra remembered how Flick had pointed at her when he argued with Tristam. The pieces fell together, and she looked incredulously at Flick. "You're not trying to put me and Tristam together, are you? You've been against it from the beginning."

"I was wrong," Flick said. "I admit it. Tristam's a decent fellow. He's not my da, and you are not my ma. I probably should have realized that sooner, and I worry that something I said might have swayed you against him."

Kyra put a hand to her temple. Of all the times for Flick to come around... "You *were* wrong about him," she said. "But it doesn't matter. He's still a nobleman, and he has duties to his family."

"That might be true," said Flick. "But he in't married yet, and who knows what might happen? Things are changing, Kyra. I don't think we can take anything for granted anymore."

Kyra wondered if the fight with the messenger had muddled Flick's brain. But then she followed Flick's gaze to where Adele stood arm in arm with Mela, and she finally understood.

She jabbed her elbow into his rib cage. "Someone's changed your mind, Flick. And it wasn't Tristam."

He saw where she was looking and gave a sheepish smile. "I suppose one's view on forbidden romance changes when it no longer concerns other people."

Even though Kyra had suspected something, it still surprised her to hear Flick confirm it so readily. It hadn't been that long since they'd met, had it? "Is it... mutual between the two of you?" she asked.

He shrugged, eyes still on her. "I'm only now learning their ways. I don't even think they all 'take mates,' as they call it. She'd need the permission of the clan leader. But she enjoys my company, and I've grown rather fond of hers. She's been bringing her friends to meet me. It's been... quite an adventure."

"What will you do?" Kyra asked.

He shrugged. "Who knows what will happen tomorrow or next week, with things the way they are. But we'll live things out day by day. It's all we can do, really." He had a gentleness to his voice that tugged at Kyra's heart.

As if sensing Kyra and Flick talking about her, Adele turned and gave a slight smile. Flick waved.

"In that case, I wish you two the best," said Kyra, giving Flick's shoulders a quick squeeze. Kyra stood and dusted off her clothes, then turned a mischievous eye back toward him. "I do have one question though."

"What?"

"Are you sure you're not smitten with Adele simply because you saw her without her clothes? She does have a lovely figure."

"All right. That's it." Flick rolled up his sleeves and lunged for Kyra, ignoring her squeals as he caught her in a bear hug from behind. "I think you need some lessons in respecting your elders." And he methodically began to turn her upside down. Kyra yelled something about things dropping out of her pockets, but she was laughing too hard for any coherent words to come out. She scrabbled at Flick's legs behind her head, wondering at how the trees looked so much taller from this angle, when she saw the Demon Riders making their way toward the commotion.

"Everything's fine," said Flick. "This is how we show love in our family."

And Kyra didn't have the breath to contradict him.

## TWENTY-SEVEN

Tristam tried not to worry as Robert held out, but the calendar was not on his side. As the date of the offensive ticked closer, units started taking position outside the city, and news of clashes with the Demon Riders came in daily. On his third trip to the cave, Tristam noticed that some of the Demon Riders had dyed the skin of their fingers red. When he asked Kyra about it, she coughed uncomfortably and told him that it was their tradition to do so before battle.

"That bad?" said Tristam.

"They're expecting a war," said Kyra.

The one good result of the approaching Demon Rider offensive was that Malikel resumed his duties with the Council. The magistrate's reasons for reinstating him had more to do with the city's need for wartime leadership than with his own investigations, but any change that got Malikel back on the Council was a good one in Tristam's book. On the first day of Malikel's return, Tristam hung near the Council Room, hoping to speak with the Defense Minister, but Malikel's movements were still closely monitored, and he couldn't get a word with him alone.

Three days before the Demon Rider offensive, Robert finally folded. "I serve the Whitt house," he said. "I've been carrying messages between Lord Whitt and Head Councilman Willem." His well-tailored clothes had become wrinkled and dirty after his days in the cave, and his hair and beard were unkempt.

It took some effort on Tristam's part not to let his relief show. "And what do they discuss?"

"They tell me very little," said Robert. "I simply carry the letters."

He might have been lying. He might have been telling the truth. But Tristam was running out of time. The Whitt household was one of the smaller houses of Forge, halfway to Edlan. They certainly would have had plenty of reason to encourage a Demon Rider sweep. "Will you testify to the Council that you ran messages between Willem and Lord Whitt?"

Robert didn't answer right away, and Tristam allowed the silence between them to stretch. It was like a game of cards, interrogating a hostile prisoner, always trying to hide one's own hand while guessing the opponent's.

"I'll testify," Robert said. "But I want a guard around me at all times. I fear for my life."

"I can arrange that," he said. "We'll take you to the city tomorrow."

He kept his walk at a dignified pace until Robert could no longer see him, then he rushed out to find Kyra. The cave was surrounded by Demon Riders. Each time Tristam returned, it seemed more Makvani loitered in its vicinity—four the first time, then five, then seven. Only one or two at any given time were actually serving a shift. The rest had no obvious reason for being there.

He finally spotted Kyra farther out, walking aimlessly through and around the trees. She looked a little worse for wear these days—her clothes were dusty, and her ponytail had several escaped strands, though she still walked with that graceful, easy stride. She came toward him when he caught her eye, and something must have showed in his expression, because a cautious optimism crossed her face.

"Do you believe him?" asked Kyra after he told her.

"We can't afford not to," he said. "If we want to stop the offensive, we must do something now."

"And you're set on taking it before the Council? It could be bad for you, if they don't believe you." There was real worry in her eyes. The strands of hair that had escaped her ponytail blew across her face. Tristam was tempted to brush them away but thought better of it. He was to have dinner again with Cecile tonight. "It's less dangerous for me than it would be for you."

Kyra pursed her lips but couldn't argue with his reasoning. "Very well, then," she said. She squeezed his hand. "Rest well."

The voices of the Makvani drifted after Tristam as he walked away. As much as he hated to admit it, Flick had been right about asking the Demon Riders to help. The guards had been very helpful. There was no way Kyra could have watched and sheltered Robert nearly as well on her own. He thought back again to his argument with Flick. They had primarily exchanged words over the Makvani, but it was what he'd said about Kyra that stuck in Tristam's mind.

*You think you can keep her separate in your mind from the others. You think she's different,* Flick had said. Or, more accurately, yelled. *But don't you realize Kyra doesn't see it that way? It's killing her to see you hate her kin like this. You'll never truly care for her if you despise her blood.*

Tristam could have argued with Flick. There were many things that made Kyra different from the others. But even if he'd brought those up, he couldn't argue with the look in Kyra's eyes whenever he made his true feelings about the Makvani known. He'd seen it many times, but he'd looked away.

Distracted by his thoughts, Tristam was slow to react when a yellow blur shot out from between the trees and knocked him to the ground. Before Tristam could grab his sword, whatever attacked him had disappeared back into the trees. He climbed to his feet, holding his sword in one hand and his dagger in the other. Had that been a demon cat? No, too small. Whatever had hit him had run into his legs.

He heard some scuffling around him, then saw a gray blur in the trees, circling him. Tristam dropped into a defensive crouch. Footsteps sounded behind him. He turned and almost dropped his sword in shock.

Lettie stood ten paces away from him, as surprised to see him as he was to see her. The girl was bundled up in a wool tunic, trousers, and a cloak. Her cheeks shone red from the cold, and she was taking in big gulps of air, as if she'd been running very hard.

"Lettie!" Tristam said. "What are you doing here?"

The girl gave him a shy smile. "Ho, Tristam."

"Does Kyra know you're out here?" he asked.

"Aye," Lettie said, wiping her nose with the back of her hand. "I'm playing with my friends."

He was about to ask her to explain further when two young demon cats, the yellow blur and the gray blur, crept out and did their best to hide behind Lettie—not incredibly effective given their size. The yellow one peeked out occasionally to stare at Tristam but retreated whenever Tristam looked back.

"And these are your... friends?" Tristam asked.

Lettie blinked up at him. "Flick was worried too, but he still lets us play. All the Demon Riders watch us." She pointed to the yellow one. "This is Libena, and her brother is Ziben." Lettie turned to address Libena. "Tristam's nice. You can let him pet you."

He really would have preferred not to, but Lettie was beaming up at him and he couldn't bring himself to refuse. It did help that these cubs had features clearly marking them as babies—large head and eyes, and soft, downy fur. The gray one crept closer, step by step, and finally rubbed his flank against Tristam's knees. Ziben was about three times the size of a house cat, and Tristam reached out carefully to stroke his back. The kitten yawned, revealing tiny, sharp fangs.

"I told you Tristam was nice," said Lettie smugly.

Following her brother's bravery, Libena circled closer. She was considerably larger, standing as high as Tristam when he was on one knee. When she leaned against Tristam's back, it took some effort on his part not to be knocked over. Both cats sniffed at him, sticking their noses in his face. Ziben's chest was rumbling. Was that a *purr*?

Eventually, the two kittens lost interest. Libena moved away first, and Ziben soon followed suit. Libena stepped toward the trees and looked expectantly at Lettie.

"Good-bye, Tristam!" said Lettie, and ran off after them.

He watched them disappear, feeling as if he had come out of some bizarre dream. His cloak was covered with strands of gray and yellow fur.

"It is interesting, isn't it?" said a new voice behind him. "How easy it is for the younger ones to fall into new patterns."

A prickle passed over the skin of Tristam's arms and neck, and he turned around to face Pashla. He didn't reach for his weapon—that would have violated the unspoken truce between them. But it was hard to be civil to the woman who had stood by calmly while her companion killed Jack, and who had wounded Martin and delivered him to his death.

"I won't lie," he said. "I worry about Lettie's safety."

"As do Kyra and Flick, but the girl is stronger than she looks," said Pashla. "Lettie and the kittens have become fast friends. There are some among our own number who object to this, but others urge them to let Libena and Ziben pick their own companions." Pashla paused. "Kyra and Flick hope for peace between our peoples. Do you share that hope?"

It would have been safest to lie to her, but to do so seemed a betrayal of Jack's and Martin's memory. "I hope for peace," said Tristam. "But I cannot see how it could come to pass, if your people view us as mere animals to be slaughtered."

"And your people, how do they view us?" asked Pashla. "Are we worthy of friendship and understanding, or are we simply monsters to be destroyed? Virtue does not solely reside with your people, nor does brutality reside solely with mine. We live and die by our honor, courage, and loyalty. Can you say the same for Forge?"

"I won't deny your courage," said Tristam. "But your people take pleasure in bloodshed. I've seen what you do in battle when your rage overtakes you."

"And what about Kyra?" asked Pashla. "Do you shun her because she succumbs on occasion to her instincts?"

Pashla's question silenced him. To have yet another person bring up Kyra like this . . . Tristam swallowed and couldn't think how to respond.

Pashla took a step closer to him, and then another, until the two of them stood almost toe to toe. She was tall for a woman, and their eyes were almost level when she spoke again. "If you can trust Kyra, then you can learn to trust us. If you cannot trust us, then perhaps you do not really trust her."

Tristam met her gaze and finally found his voice. "Fair point," he said. And he stepped away.

Pashla stayed where she was, and her gaze seemed to go right through his skin. "I do understand what it's like to lose a friend in battle," she said quietly. "I do have sympathy for your loss."

Was she trying to make amends? Even now, Pashla's words brought back the sheer horror of those fateful encounters. Jack had died silently, but Martin's screams would forever be etched in Tristam's memory.

"Thank you." He couldn't give her more than that. Not yet.

Pashla inclined her head at his words. "Our ways are different," she said. "But perhaps we can learn from the kittens."

And then she too disappeared into the forest.

"I understand it's been a trying week for all of us," said Cecile of Routhian. "But I do require a minimal amount of effort from you, Tristam, if we are to carry on a conversation."

The impatience in Cecile's voice was mild, but it jarred Tristam to attention nonetheless. It was the first time he'd seen anything but perfect poise from her. The two of them sat in a private dining room on the Palace grounds. A servant had just brought them each a small bowl of lemon curd to finish up the meal.

"I'm sorry," he said, rubbing his forehead. He'd struggled all evening to be present with her, but there were simply too many thoughts going through his mind: his conversation with Pashla, Robert's confession, tomorrow's Council meeting... "I've been inexcusably rude. Forgive me."

Cecile was quite pretty, with flax-colored hair and large green eyes that shone with intelligence. She usually held herself and spoke in a way that projected serenity, though now there was strain around her eyes and a tightening at the corners of her mouth. She placed her spoon back onto the table and looked him in the eye.

"Kyra of Forge is alive, isn't she?" she said. "And you've been in contact with her."

It was only by a small miracle that Tristam didn't drop his own spoon.

Cecile smiled sadly at his surprise. "When you're alone in a foreign court, you pay attention to the gossip, especially when they concern your prospective husband. I've known from the very beginning that your heart wasn't in these negotiations."

Tristam lowered his spoon into his bowl. He felt like the lowest kind of human being, and he couldn't find it in himself to keep up the pretense. He looked Cecile in the eye. "I have a great deal of respect for you, my lady, so I won't attempt to deny anything you've said. And I have no excuses for myself. Though you should know that Kyra and I do not intend to . . . pursue our relationship, if you and I were to marry."

Cecile took a delicate bite of lemon curd, eyeing him thoughtfully. "I believe you," she said finally. "And that says something about my regard for you, as I would not believe those words from many other men."

It surprised Tristam how calmly she was taking this. Sure, he'd known that she wasn't in love with him, but it still must hurt one's pride, if nothing else, to learn that one's betrothed already had feelings for someone else. "If you . . . find that you no longer wish to continue the negotiations, I can send word to—"

Cecile stopped him with a hand on his wrist, touching him in a way that was authoritative rather than flirtatious. "Do your feelings for Kyra change your family's need for help against the Demon Riders?"

Tristam grimaced. "No. I suppose not."

She withdrew her hand. "Nor does it change my family's ambitions. I was raised in the court just as you were, and I know my duties. I believe you to be good and honorable. There's no reason to believe another match for me would turn out better." She met his eyes with a wry smile. "We're both affected by things out of our control. But we make the best of it, don't we?"

Her candor was refreshing, even if her words contained unpleasant truths. "You're a better woman than I deserve, Cecile."

She inclined her head, smiled, and did not contradict him. The door opened, and a servant announced the arrival of the courtier who would escort Cecile back to her quarters.

Tristam left dinner with Cecile's words circling in his head. He found he respected her more after that frank exchange, though the open-eyed pragmatism of her words seemed sad. But she was right. The circumstances surrounding their marriage alliance remained unchanged.

Tristam was marginally successful in focusing his thoughts as he made his way to the Red Shield barracks, where a few quick inquiries led him to Fitz. The young man blinked when Tristam asked for a private word with him but agreed readily enough.

"I have a favor to ask," said Tristam when they were out of earshot of the barracks. "It would help Malikel and Forge, but it's of questionable legality."

Fitz's eyes widened. "Looking to get yourself demoted again, milord?"

Tristam thought back to his earlier conversations with Fitz and hoped that his impression of the Red Shield's character and loyalties was accurate. "I have a prisoner who has information about Willem's misdeeds. I need someone to guard him while I speak to the Council. If things go wrong, I'll do my best to ensure any blame falls on me, but I can't promise I'll succeed."

Fitz leaned back on his heels and considered Tristam's words. "If it'll help Sir Malikel, I'll do my part." Then he grinned. "What's a soldier's life without risk, right?"

Tristam took Robert back to Forge early the next morning and left him in Fitz's care. Then he attended the Council meeting, carrying the message that he, Kyra, and Flick had confiscated from Robert. At the end of every Council meeting, the Head Councilman traditionally announced an opportunity for any citizen to raise an issue before the Council. It was an old law, and admirable in its designation of the Council as a government that listened to all. In practice though, because only a very special portion of the population was even allowed in the Palace compound, much less the Council Room, the definition of "any citizen" was much narrower than the wording suggested.

Nobody paid Tristam much mind as he slipped into the Council Room. Malikel had taken the stage to discuss preparations for the forest sweep. When the discussion ended, Willem gave the customary closing. "If any citizen of Forge would like to make a petition before the Council, he may take the stage now."

It was now or never.

"I have a petition," he said loudly, getting to his feet. He was painfully aware of the Council members swiveling their heads to look at him. Tristam walked up the aisle with as much dignity as he could muster. Willem looked at him with thinly veiled annoyance. "A petition, Tristam of Brancel?"

"Some information has come into my possession, and I would like to present it to the Council."

"It is your right," said Willem drily. "Go ahead."

"I received word of a messenger carrying a private missive into the Palace compound. I, along with some companions, intercepted this message and found that a leader of Forge was conspiring to unlawfully influence the decisions of the Council." In the corner of his eye, he saw Malikel sit up straighter. He dearly hoped that his commander would approve of what he was about to do.

"That's a very vague report," said Willem. "Who was your informant?"

"My informant wishes to remain anonymous, Your Grace, but the note itself requests gold to sway scribes, soldiers, and other people within Forge. It suggests that the Council's vote to attack the Demon Riders was corrupted by bribery." Tristam produced the parchment out of his pocket. "Here is the original note, if the Council would like to inspect it."

Willem held out a hand. "Give it here."

"I'm afraid I can't do that, Your Grace." Willem shifted in surprise, and Tristam felt his heart pound against his rib cage. Even after all this, he wasn't used to direct insubordination, and his body was letting him know it.

"You refuse?" asked Willem.

"I refuse because the messenger entered the Palace compound from your private gate, and the note is written in your handwriting."

The Council Room erupted in shouts. Willem pounded his gavel to regain the floor. "Let me see if I understand you,

Tristam. You are accusing me of treason against Forge, the city in which I already hold the highest office."

Tristam raised his voice. "With all due respect, Your Grace, you are indeed Head Councilman, but the Demon Rider offensive was a close vote, and there was plenty of motivation on either side to sway it."

Lord Perce of Roll, a Council member who had voted against Willem, raised his hand. "These are serious allegations you bring against the Head Councilman. Do you have any evidence?"

"I will gladly hand over this note to a neutral third party."

"May I see it?"

Tristam handed the message to Perce, who looked it over. "The note reads as Tristam says, but it contains no signature, and the seal is not one I recognize." He looked back at Tristam. "Do you have any stronger evidence?"

Tristam nodded to a manservant waiting near the door and hoped that Fitz was still outside. "I have the testimony of the messenger."

This time, he did see a flicker of worry across Willem's face. A moment later, Fitz stepped into the room with Robert in tow. The messenger faltered when he saw Willem, and Fitz had to drag him the remainder of the way. *Don't lose your nerve,* thought Tristam.

"This is the messenger whom I followed from the Palace walls to an inn not far away. He has confessed to taking messages between Head Councilman Willem and Whitt Manor."

Tristam could see observers in the Council Room looking around, probably trying to see if Lord Whitt had any representatives in attendance. Tristam doubted he did. Whitt didn't have a strong presence within the city.

Perce addressed the messenger. "What is your name?"

"Robert, sir. Of Forge." The messenger couldn't seem to take his eyes from Willem, who was studying him with an intense, cold gaze.

"And do you confirm what Tristam of Brancel has said? Did you, in fact, receive this message from the Head Councilman to deliver to Lord Whitt?"

The messenger was still staring at Willem. His jaw worked, but he didn't speak. Tristam focused everything he had on Robert, willing him to follow through.

"Please answer the question," Perce repeated.

The messenger licked his lips. "No," he said. "The parchment that Tristam claims to have found on me was a plant that he created himself. He tried to pay me to testify against Willem."

Tristam struggled to maintain his composure as the room once again dissolved into murmurs. Of course that was what Robert would say. What did Tristam have to threaten him with that didn't pale against the Head Councilman's influence?

Willem sat back in his seat. "I believe we've taken care of that," he said. "I will be requesting a full investigation into Tristam for bringing false charges against me."

Malikel cleared his throat. "May I suggest that the messenger might not be trusted to give a truthful testimony in front of the accused?"

"How much longer must we put up with this nonsense?" said Willem. "We have preparations to make. Tristam of Brancel has already wasted enough of our time in a clear effort to delay our attack on the barbarians. I move to dismiss discussion of this subject to a later time."

It was a close vote, but it came out in Willem's favor. Willem looked pointedly at Tristam. "You are dismissed, soldier."

There was finality to that command, and there was nothing Tristam could do except bow and walk away. Robert, still in Fitz's grip, avoided Tristam's gaze as he passed. Tristam tried his best to hold his head high on his way to the door, fighting the despair that was starting to take root in his stomach. They had staked so much on this. What could they do now?

Tristam was so caught up in his own frustrations that he didn't notice that someone was trying to talk to him. When he finally realized someone had spoken his name, he turned to see a young servant girl looking urgently up at him. He returned her gaze, surprised to be approached so by one of the staff. She looked familiar.

"Lord Tristam," she said, her voice low. "Can anyone speak in front of the Council?"

"Anyone?" he echoed dumbly before he finally made sense of her question. "Anyone, yes. But only before Willem closes the meeting."

She nodded then, and her face took on a mask of determination. Tristam watched in bemusement as she made straight for the herald. The two exchanged a few words, and she seemed to be arguing with him, though Tristam couldn't make out what was said.

Finally, the herald drew breath for an announcement. "Darylene of Forge would like to make a statement before the

Council." His voice lacked his usual confidence, and he glanced uncertainly at the serving girl behind him.

"What is the meaning of this? We've had enough oddities today," said Willem. Tristam was surprised to hear alarm in Willem's voice, given the cool disdain with which the Head Councilman had responded to Tristam's accusations. Then Tristam recognized the girl. Darylene of Forge was Willem's mistress.

"We haven't closed the Council meeting yet," said Malikel. "The lady has a right to speak."

Darylene didn't look at all at ease in front of the Council. She glanced from Councilman to Councilman, though she seemed to studiously avoid Willem's gaze. "I'm sorry, milords," she said. She sounded younger than she looked. Tristam had thought her older because of her association with Willem, but he now realized she was probably close to his own age, if not younger. "I've been listening to the young lord's testimony, and I can tell you that he's both right and wrong.

"I am...privy to some of the Head Councilman's private dealings," she continued. Some knowing glances passed between the Councilmen, and a few snickers sounded from the observing benches. It took no small amount of courage, Tristam thought, to brave such scrutiny.

Darylene waited for the room to quiet. "The messenger Robert of Forge is, in truth, Robert of Edlan. He lied about working for Whitt Manor. He has actually been carrying messages directly between Sir Willem and Duke Symon of Edlan. They have been working together to overthrow Forge's Council."

Pandemonium. Willem shouted something about the girl having lost her mind, and Malikel called for order as Tristam struggled to understand what he'd heard. Had he misread the message from Willem?

"The girl tells lies," said Willem. "She must be in the employ of my enemies."

"Lies or not, they must be investigated," said Malikel. "Darylene, do you have any evidence?"

Darylene looked to Willem, who was staring at her with barely controlled rage. "There's a compartment in the floor of his sitting room, next to the fireplace. You can access it if you pry up the floorboards. You will find other messages there from those he's been contacting in Edlan."

"This is preposterous," said Willem. "A clear attempt to distract from the coming offensive. I move to dismiss this Council meeting."

"Not yet, Willem," said a Councilman in the second row. "The girl gave us information that can be easily confirmed. It is only reasonable to do so." Tristam began to feel some hope. At least the Council members were taking these accusations seriously now.

"I agree." Malikel raised his voice. "Seal the doors. Don't let anyone come in or out of this room until we've verified Darylene's claims. I'm sure you'll agree, Willem, that the best way to dismiss these claims beyond doubt is to verify them now."

Willem gave Malikel a long, measured look, and then nodded. "Very well, if you are to accuse me, then let us go investigate these charges. Do you claim this investigation under your purview, Malikel?"

"I will verify the allegations as Defense Minister. I believe protocol also requires the presence of the accusers, Darylene and Tristam."

"Will you take guards too, lest I turn violent upon discovery of my misdeeds?" A layer of scorn laced Willem's voice.

"The usual escort of Red Shields should be enough," said Malikel mildly.

Willem nodded to the Red Shields lining the side of the room, and four stepped forward. The Head Councilman turned his eye to Tristam and then to Darylene, who stood braced against Willem's fury as if it might knock her over. "Let's get this farce over with."

Willem led the way across the Palace grounds to his private living quarters. It was a small, detached building in the inner compound, unremarkable on the outside, though the inside was luxuriously decorated with tapestries, carvings, and marble statues. Nobody spoke. The Head Councilman exuded an aura of fury and kept a few steps in front of everyone else. Malikel trailed behind him, calm but focused, and Darylene followed after. Tristam wished he could talk to her, find out more about what she was thinking, but she studiously avoided his gaze.

"Are we headed to my bedchamber?" asked Willem.

"Is that correct, Darylene?" said Malikel.

She gave a barely discernible nod.

Willem led them up a flight of stairs, where a manservant opened a pair of tall oak doors. The suite within was large and opulent. A four-poster bed took up the center of the room. The walls, the rug, and the linens on the bed were all decorated in maroon with gold accents.

"By the fireplace," said Malikel.

One of the Red Shields bowed and knelt near the fireplace, running his hands along the floorboards. "I don't feel anything," he said.

"To your left," said Darylene. "Feel for a raised portion along the floor."

"By all means, search your best, soldier," said Willem. "There's nothing to be afraid of."

The Red Shield paused in his search, fingers curving against an edge Tristam couldn't see. The soldier jiggled something, and then there was the clear sound of a wood panel sliding away. Tristam's breath caught. He'd believed the girl, but somehow he still hadn't expected the Red Shield to find anything.

"What is that?" said Malikel, walking toward him. The Red Shield was frowning at a box in his hands. "It's a compartment, just as the lass said."

"Let me see," said Malikel, reaching for the box.

"Now," said Willem.

The Red Shield handed Malikel the box. And then, as the Defense Minister's hands were occupied, the Red Shield drew his dagger and thrust it toward Malikel's stomach.

## TWENTY-EIGHT

Darylene screamed. Tristam shouted Malikel's name and took a step forward, so intent on his commander that he almost didn't see the man coming at him from the side. Tristam ducked out of the way just in time to avoid being gutted. He pivoted to face his attacker. It was another of the Red Shields who had accompanied them. Had Willem managed to turn them all? Tristam drew his dagger, extremely grateful that he'd kept it on him this morning. When his attacker came at him again, he stepped around the Red Shield's knife hand and grabbed his wrist, pulling the man past him and sinking his own blade deep between his opponent's ribs. He pulled his dagger free and threw the man to the ground.

Tristam cast about, breathing heavily, trying to get his bearings. The man who'd attacked him lay on the ground in front of him. Darylene stood pressed against the wall. There were blood spatters on her face and gown, but she looked otherwise uninjured. Malikel crouched with his hand pressed to his side. The mysterious box sat on the ground not far from him, and next to the box lay the body of the soldier who had attacked the Defense Minister. The room was otherwise empty. Willem and the remaining two Red Shields were nowhere to be seen.

"Malikel!" Tristam ran to his commander's side.

The older man groaned. "It's not as deep as it could have been," he said. "Must have glanced off one of my ribs. Help me bind it."

Darylene came forward with a strip of fabric she'd torn from the bed linens. Tristam thanked her and set about wrapping Malikel's chest.

"Quickly, Tristam," said Malikel. "Did anyone see what happened to Willem?"

"He ran, with the two Red Shields after him," said Darylene.

Malikel exhaled sharply through his nose as Tristam pulled the makeshift bandages tight. "All four of the guards were loyal to Willem?"

"I don't think so," said Darylene. "Three of them were, and the fourth chased Willem when he fled."

Tristam secured the bandages, and Malikel gripped his arm. "A hand, please." Tristam had doubts about whether his commander should be standing and moving, but he obeyed. The Defense Minister regained his feet and nodded toward the door. "We need to get word to the Council."

Darylene took the hard-earned box of evidence, and Tristam ducked under Malikel's arm. They slowly made their way out, Tristam sneaking surreptitious glances at his commander to see how he fared. Malikel moved as if it pained him, but at least he was supporting much of his own weight.

Tristam drew his dagger as they stepped into the corridor. It was eerily silent in Willem's house. As they made their way down the staircase, Tristam caught sight of a few servants running away. As he neared the front door, Tristam heard noises from outside—shouts, yells, and the clash of weapons. Malikel frowned.

Tristam stopped. "With your permission, sir, I'll go scout."

Tristam wished he had his sword. The dagger wasn't going to do much good against enemy soldiers. Willem's doorman was long gone, so Tristam reached for the doorknob and hoped for the best.

He opened the door to a battle in full swing. Soldiers clashed swords while Palace staff did their best to flee the fighting. Tristam looked around in confusion as battle cries and screams assaulted his ears. Were they invaded? Had the enemy breached their walls so easily? But then he realized what had really happened. The three Red Shields who'd attacked Malikel were obviously not the only traitors in the compound.

There was a cluster of four soldiers fighting just a short distance away. At first, Tristam had trouble distinguishing sides because they all wore Forge livery. Then he saw that two of the soldiers had blue armbands. Edlan blue.

*I need more funds to gain the cooperation of Palace scribes, as well as key members of the defense forces,* Willem's note had said. Tristam had thought it a roundabout way of swaying Council votes, but Willem had actually been using the bribes to hide Edlan troops within Forge. There had been such confusion in the Palace lately, with the extra conscripts from the city. A few well-placed bribes to scribes and Red Shield commanders, a few altered documents… *The more of our own that we have within the Palace, the safer our position will be.*

A body sporting a blue armband lay beside one of the pathways. Tristam swallowed against his disgust and took the man's sword. Its balance was different from his own, but it would have to do.

The men outside Willem's house were still fighting. One of the true Red Shields had fallen, and his comrade was backed against a shrub, trying to fend off two enemies. Tristam cut one of the traitors down from behind. The remaining Edlan soldier turned to gape, and the cornered Red Shield ran him through. For a moment, Tristam and the Red Shield stared at each other, catching their breath.

"Thank you," said the soldier.

"That was an impressive fight. I'm Tristam of Brancel," said Tristam.

"Claren of Forge."

They looked to the neighboring courtyard. There, five Red Shields closed in on three Edlan fighters. A line of soldiers rounded the corner, and Tristam raised his sword, only to cautiously lower it again when he saw no sign of Edlan blue. Forge soldiers still outnumbered the Edlanese, at least in this part of the Palace.

"How widespread is the fighting?" asked Tristam.

"All over the Palace grounds. There must have been some kind of signal."

"The Defense Minister is wounded," Tristam said. "Can you help?"

They rushed back to Willem's house. Tristam had just thrown the door open when he heard new shouts.

"Forge men, to the city wall! Edlan's army is at the gates!"

Kyra waited out the morning as close to the city as she dared. She climbed a tree overlooking the main road and ducked behind the trunk whenever a traveler passed by. She tried not to dwell on her worries, but it became harder as the sun climbed steadily overhead. What had become of Tristam? Would the Council believe him? She had ample time to think up worst-case scenarios, but she didn't dare go into the Palace, at least not until dark. The last thing they needed was for her to create more trouble by getting impatient.

She heard footsteps approaching, not from the main road, but from the forest below her. Kyra froze stock-still. There wasn't nearly as much cover for her in the winter. She hoped whoever was coming would not think to look up.

It turned out to be another one of Willem's forest patrols. Kyra stayed silent as the men passed below her, and they were none the wiser. She watched them gather on a plot of farm-land just outside the forest boundary. There they stood, wait-ing. Some tended to their weapons, while others simply milled about. After a while, Kyra turned her attention away from them and resumed watching the main road.

It wasn't until a second group came and joined the first that Kyra began to wonder. And then a third, fourth, and fifth group came as well. Soon there were a hundred men standing on that field. Kyra watched as a man came walking from the opposite direction—the owner of the farm, Kyra guessed, and she was suddenly scared for him. The gathered soldiers had also noticed the farmer, and one of them went out to meet him. Words were exchanged. Kyra couldn't hear them, but they were obviously not friendly. The soldier drew his weapon and Kyra stifled a gasp, but he didn't strike. The farmer retreated.

As the one soldier rejoined the rest of the group, Kyra gave up completely on watching the main road and focused on these men. They were taking tunics out of sacks now and putting them on. The tunics were colored deep blue. Edlan blue.

This time Kyra did gasp, and it was only the men's lack of attention that kept her from discovery. Puzzle pieces fell in place in her mind. She remembered the group of soldiers who had stumbled upon her family with Pashla and Adele in the forest. They'd looked like seasoned soldiers instead of peasants. One had told Kyra that "His Grace" didn't want people in the forest. It was a funny way to put things, since Forge citizens almost always referred to the Council as a whole. The man had been an Edlan soldier hiding under the guise of Willem's Demon Rider offensive. Did Willem know about this? If Willem had betrayed the city, what had happened to Tristam and Malikel?

The gathered soldiers were dressed now, and they began to march toward Forge. Kyra waited until they had gone some distance, then came down from her hiding place and trailed them. When she came out of the trees, her heart almost stopped. From her vantage point, she had only seen one group of soldiers. But now that she was in open farmland, she could see multiple companies taking up formation and converging on the main road. The muted thuds of their boots carried over the fields.

Kyra shielded her eyes and squinted toward the city. The gates still looked to be open. Did the Palace have any idea what was happening?

No, they likely did not.

In front of her, the soldiers marched at a quick pace, and people took notice. Those on the road and fields ran, some retreating into their houses and others running for the city gates. One older man shouted defiantly at the troops. Two Edlan soldiers cut him down.

Finally, the call of bugles drifted from the city, and the gate began to close. Soldiers, just dots from this distance, ran along the parapets. Kyra breathed a sigh of relief. Someone had sounded the alarm.

But the Edlan troops continued to march.

⊠ ⊠ ⊠

Disgraceful. That was how Malikel had described Forge's response to the attack. Yes, they had been betrayed. Yes, they'd had little warning of Edlan's approaching troops. But still, the Palace's forces had been far too slow to react. Messages between wall sentries and the Palace had gone astray. Commands had been dithered over and questioned. Tristam himself had been shocked at how greatly the forces' discipline had fallen short of what it should have been. Part of it was due to Malikel's removal from command. Part of it had been the confusion sowed by Willem's schemes. But whatever the reason, the city was in dire straits.

The watch had barely managed to close the city gates in time, and archers were still running to their stations. Tristam stood on the parapets next to Malikel, surveying the scene outside the city. The main road led out from the gates. On a

313

normal day, Tristam would have been able to follow it with his eyes as it passed houses, then farmland, until it disappeared into the forest. Today though, the road was blocked by Edlan soldiers. Rows of them, lined up in formation on the road and spilling into the farmland on either side. Scouts had confirmed that Edlan had blocked the roads to the south as well. Groups of people fled their homes with hastily wrapped bundles on their backs, some running for the protection of Forge's walls, and others for the forest.

"Edlan could have taken the city," said Malikel. "If they'd wanted to, they could have marched right in." There had been some confusion about who would act as Head Councilman after Willem's defection. The laws indicated Malikel, but none of the laws took into account what to do if the second in line was currently under investigation. In the end, Malikel had been given temporary authority until the Edlanese were defeated.

"Why do you think they didn't?" asked Tristam.

"Willem is a man of Forge at heart. He doesn't want to see it looted or damaged."

"Do you think he made it out of the city?"

"I think so. I believe you forced his hand, Tristam. He most likely didn't mean to trigger any attack until after the forest offensive began. He could have picked off or captured our own soldiers in the forest with his own, and we would have blamed the Demon Riders. Once we were sufficiently weakened, he would have sprung his trap. Our position now isn't good, but at least we have our forces intact within the city."

"What do you think Willem wants?" Tristam asked.

"He'll tell us himself, soon enough."

An hour later, several riders rode toward the city, escorted by a contingent of Edlan soldiers. They came to a halt just outside of arrow range and raised a flag of parley.

"Come with me, Tristam," said Malikel.

Malikel assembled a contingent of ten guards, and Tristam took up ranks with them. The gate was pulled open, and they rode out. Tristam did his best to ride proud. Not the easiest thing to do when an entire army was spread out in front of him, but he had to trust his comrades on the wall behind him to watch for signs of betrayal. At least the skies were clear today, and they had an unimpeded view.

As they came closer to the other party, Tristam finally made out their faces. Lord Alvred, the Defense Minister of Edlan, led the party on a giant black war stallion. And next to him was Willem.

*Traitor.* Tristam looked over at Malikel, trying to see his commander's reaction, but the fur lining of Malikel's cloak blocked his view.

"Alvred," Malikel said pleasantly. "I didn't expect to see you again so soon. Was our hospitality not up to your standards?"

Alvred's mustache twitched humorlessly. "We both serve our cities, Malikel. You know that as well as I."

"If we're dispensing with pleasantries, I'll address my former Head Councilman directly," said Malikel. "What do you want, Willem?" Malikel spoke loud enough to be heard by all nearby, and Tristam wondered whether it hurt his wounded ribs.

Willem, to his credit, didn't look as smug as Tristam had expected him to, though he regarded Malikel with the confidence that came with knowing he had the upper hand. "You know you can't win this, Malikel. We have more troops, and we have the strategic advantage now that we're in position. You have no allies who will come to your help. We can either drag this out and let the people suffer, or we can solve things quickly."

"What are your terms?" asked Malikel.

"You and the rest of the Council will sign a measure ceding power to me as Duke of Forge. I have no wish to harm any of you, though you will be required to live out your lives outside of the three cities."

"Head Councilman wasn't enough, Willem?" An edge finally found its way into Malikel's voice. "You want to wield absolute power?"

"Our Council is fundamentally flawed. We spend most of our time in deadlock or undoing one another's efforts. That's no way to rule a city."

"And, of course, you'll be the one to lead Forge to a glorious future." Malikel looked to Alvred and the Edlan officials behind him. "What are you giving Edlan for their help? Better trade?"

"Among other things."

"And you're confident they won't stab you in the back once their soldiers have breached our walls?"

Willem drew himself to his full height atop his horse. "Do you think me so incompetent? I have safeguards in place."

Tristam wondered what those safeguards might be. Willem must have cultivated favor with Edlan houses as well, enough so that they would support him against any possible double cross from Symon.

"Let's not drag this conversation on," said Willem. "Will you take my terms or not?"

"Of course not," said Malikel.

"Perhaps, then, you will change your mind in a few weeks."

There was an emergency Council meeting that evening. As Red Shields carted off bodies from the battle within the Palace walls, and others scoured the ranks for any remaining Edlan imposters, the nineteen remaining Council members faced off and yelled at each other. Councilman Caldre argued vociferously for a head-on charge against the Edlanese army, while Malikel dismissed this as suicidal. Another Councilman suggested sending for help from Parna, but even Tristam knew that Parna would happily remain neutral while Edlan and Forge weakened themselves. And they'd make plenty of money selling supplies to both parties.

The problem was, there were no good solutions. The Council knew this, but as men used to power, they couldn't come to terms with that fact. So they continued on with their posturing. They wouldn't come to an agreement tonight, and by now, Tristam wished they would simply agree to go to sleep. He supposed he could ask to be excused. He'd given his testimony to the Council hours ago, and they hadn't asked for him since. But tired and disheartened as he was, he couldn't bring himself to leave.

The first time he heard someone knock on the window next to him, he thought he'd just imagined it. But he heard it again, in the silence between Councilman Caldre bringing up another impossible strategy and Councilman Perce ruling it out. A definite tapping—he wasn't deluding himself. He casually stood and made his way over to the window.

"Kyra?" he whispered, still not quite believing it.

There was a soft tap on the shutters in reply.

Tristam's rush of elation was quickly tempered by incredulity over what Kyra had done. She'd been in the forest, hadn't she? Had she snuck past enemy lines and somehow into the city itself? True, she did have the cover of night, and Palace forces had better things to do now than look for her, but it was still reckless. And what was she doing here, anyway?

"Back corridor," he said. "I'll meet you there."

He slipped out of the room and circled around to the servants' corridor. As he'd hoped, it was empty at this hour. There was a small window, and he pushed the shutters open. After a moment, he saw a familiar outline in the darkness and stepped back to let her in.

Kyra jumped in silently, her body taut and her eyes actively searching the corridor for threats. Her hands, when he took them, were ice-cold, and he wrapped them in his own. "I can't believe you snuck in like this."

"I'm just glad you're safe. What happened?"

Tristam recounted the Council meeting and Willem's betrayal. Had it all occurred in one day? Anger built in Kyra's eyes as he spoke. She pulled away from him and started pacing the corridor.

"I didn't think Willem would go this far," said Kyra. "I thought he at least cared for the city."

"Well, the army hasn't attacked yet."

She turned to him, her gaze fierce. "I watched Edlan soldiers kill an old man today. His blood is on Willem's hands, as is the blood of the soldiers who died in the Palace today. Is there any way for us to break the siege?"

"There's posturing and debate in the Council, but no," said Tristam. "We have nothing except for the prospect of a long and drawn-out engagement."

Kyra seemed to waver over some decision before her eyes regained their focus. "I need to talk to Malikel, if he'll speak with me."

"You have news?"

"A proposal. A far-fetched one," she admitted, with an apologetic shrug. "But at this point, I don't see how it could hurt."

When Tristam returned to the Council Room, he found Malikel listening intently to the debate, leaning over his table and looking from speaker to speaker with a gaze that could have bored holes in the wall. It was easy to forget that the man had been stabbed that morning. Malikel shook out of his focus as Tristam came to his side.

"Are you able to leave the Council meeting?" Tristam asked softly. "There's someone who wants to talk to you."

"Is it important?" said Malikel.

"It's Kyra."

The briefest flicker of surprise crossed Malikel's face, and then he nodded and followed Tristam out of the room. The Council debate continued without a pause.

Kyra was visibly nervous when Tristam and Malikel came back. She stood close to the window, and her posture was such that she looked ready to spring back out at the slightest provocation. Malikel seemed to sense this and stopped a good distance away.

"Kyra," he said simply.

"I'm sorry I hid what I was," said Kyra. "I didn't mean for you to pay the price for my secret."

"There's no use dwelling on what has happened already," said Malikel. "Best we can do is move forward."

Malikel's response was so mild that Tristam couldn't help but interrupt. "You knew what Kyra was, didn't you? Why didn't you confront us outright?"

"I took a gamble. True service can't be forced." He fixed his eyes on Kyra. "Tell me if my gamble paid off."

Relief washed over Kyra's countenance, followed by resolve. "I've an idea for breaking the siege. It's a last-ditch effort, but if what Tristam tells me is right, you don't have many choices. I'm now in contact with the Demon Riders. I can carry a petition to them if you'd like."

"Why do you think an appeal to the Demon Riders would work when they wouldn't even talk to us before?" said Malikel.

"Because they've been taking losses. I think they're starting to see that they can't carry on a war against the humans here, even with their increased numbers." Kyra looked in the direction of the Council Room as muted shouts echoed down the corridor. "I also . . . have reason to believe that Leyus may be more kindly disposed toward humans than I first thought."

"How do you know this?" asked Malikel.

Something flickered in Kyra's eyes. "I know you don't like

secrets, and I'll do my best to be honest with you. But let me keep this one."

Malikel leveled a long gaze at Kyra. "Say we attempt this—what's your plan? The Demon Riders will want something in return," said Malikel.

"Peace might appeal to them, now that some of their number have been injured. They want adequate hunting and a place to live." Kyra looked to Tristam as she said this, obviously bracing for an objection from him. When he said nothing, her surprise was more damning than anything Flick or Pashla could have said.

Malikel's brow furrowed in concentration. "We could offer the Demon Riders protected hunting in a portion of our forest, and terms of trade for what they cannot get."

"Can I get the Council's word on this?" asked Kyra. "Will you pass a resolution to negotiate peace with the Demon Riders if they help defeat Edlan?"

"I will need to bring it before them," said Malikel. "This is a decision that must be made by all of us."

## TWENTY-NINE

Edlan didn't have enough forces to completely surround Forge. They'd set up their encampment across the main road, and intermittent patrols formed a porous perimeter around the rest of the city. Kyra could have avoided the camp entirely and dealt simply with the patrols, but she wanted to get a better look at what Forge was up against.

She skirted the outer edge of the Edlan camp as she left the city. The soldiers had dug trenches at the borders of their camp and were in the process of fortifying them with sharpened stakes. Kyra saw a few catapults, but not enough to suggest an imminent attack on the walls. Talk and laughter filtered out to Kyra as she passed. There were many soldiers and many campfires, but even from her limited vantage point in the darkness, she could see that activity centered on one central campfire and a large tent set up next to it. Kyra recognized Alvred, the Defense Minister, and Willem holding court there. Pages and squires attended them, and messengers came back and forth from other parts of the camp. She watched for a while and then headed for the safety of the trees.

Kyra ran deeper into the woods until she was absolutely sure that the soldiers were behind her. Then she stopped and cast about in the darkness. What was her plan? She had to find Leyus, somehow persuade him to help, and then lead an attack on the Edlan forces. It had seemed less ludicrous when she'd proposed it to Malikel.

She wandered awhile, calling out a few times, but there was no response. If any Demon Riders watched her, they weren't interested in helping her. Well, there was one other way to find the clan.

Kyra looked around one last time, peeled off her clothes, and tied them as best she could into a bundle. Her fur came easily, but she shuffled from foot to foot after her shape settled, unsure of what exactly to do. She'd made plenty of sounds in her fur before, but never on purpose. She experimented with something that sounded like a mix between a growl and a bark, and then threw her head back.

The roar reverberated through the forest, and Kyra couldn't quite believe that such a sound had come from her throat. She waited, and for a long time there was nothing. But then, in the distance, there came a faint response. It was far away, but Kyra knew immediately which way to go. She carefully picked up her clothes in her teeth and loped off.

Her sense of direction never wavered. Soon enough, she smelled other demon cats nearby and saw movement in the trees ahead of her. Kyra stopped and changed back into her somewhat slobbery clothes. She had just fastened her cloak when she noticed two Demon Riders watching her.

"Is Leyus here?" she asked.

One of the two, a man around Leyus's age, gestured toward the trees to Kyra's left, though his expression conveyed that he was simply answering her question and not extending an invitation. Kyra heard him fall in step behind her.

There was a surprising number of Demon Riders milling about. Kyra counted about twenty-two in their skin and about half that number in their fur. Kyra thought she spotted Adele at the edge of the group, and near the middle of the pack, a tawny-yellow cat looked up sharply at Kyra's arrival. Pashla.

Leyus—*her father*—sat beneath a tree, one arm propped up on his knee. Next to him sat Havel and Zora. There was something about the body language among the three of them as they talked. Kyra could tell that these were old friends, and she found their easy familiarity with one another almost as intimidating as the power they wielded.

Leyus's expression as he watched her come closer was one of controlled impatience. To Kyra's surprise, it wasn't Leyus who spoke first, but Havel, and he spoke the language of the three cities.

"She cannot stay away," he said, his eyes bright with interest. "Blood calls to blood."

"It is of no consequence," said Leyus. "The girl has chosen her loyalties."

Loyalties. Of course. Kyra had a task to do. "I'm here on behalf of the Palace," she said. "They want to offer an alliance."

Leyus exchanged a glance with Havel, as if Kyra had confirmed his words. Kyra looked at Leyus, then Havel and Zora. "I was born of two different groups, raised by a third, and recruited by a fourth. I belong to no one, but I serve those whom I see fit. Right now, I serve the Council. I know you don't think highly of the humans, but you must hear this message if you want your clans to survive."

Zora turned a languid gaze to Leyus. "Are you in the habit of negotiating with humans?"

"Only those who prove useful," said Leyus.

"They are untrustworthy. Remember what happened with Maikana," said Zora.

Kyra momentarily forgot about her mission. "You knew my mother?" she asked, fully aware that her voice came out a breathless whisper.

The three Makvani exchanged looks, and their silence was more telling than anything they could have said.

"What happened?" said Kyra. She was overstepping bounds, she knew it. But she didn't care.

The woman picked up a stick and drove it into the snow, giving Kyra a pointed glance as she did so. "Your mother forced us out of our homeland."

At this, Leyus made a noise in his throat. "Mind your words, Zora. We would have done the same, had we been in her position." Once again Kyra sensed an undercurrent of emotion. Leyus wasn't as hardened toward humans as he pretended to be. He'd loved a human woman once—her *mother*. Kyra had an opening here, if she didn't ruin her opportunity.

"Is it really so unthinkable to make an alliance with the humans? The man whose message I bear, his name is Malikel. He's an honorable man who won't break his word. Wouldn't it be better to help each other rather than destroy each other?"

Leyus looked at her for a long moment. "What does he propose?"

Kyra plunged into an explanation of what had happened around Forge. Not much of it seemed to surprise Leyus. He knew that the troops out here were from the northern city of Edlan and that they were planning an attack on Forge.

"The Edlan forces are settling in for a drawn-out siege. This buys you time against Willem's forest offensive, but it'll only be a matter of days or weeks before these Edlan troops start causing you trouble. They'll be in the same forest, hunting the same game. Truth is, no matter how this fight turns out, the victors will still outnumber you by far. And eventually, they will defeat you too."

She wondered if she was in danger of insulting him again, but Leyus simply regarded her. "And what does Malikel propose instead?"

"He would have your help breaking the siege. Your people are quick and familiar with the forest. If you create enough trouble for the troops, Edlan will retreat. In return, Forge will cede to you a portion of the forest where you can live and hunt undisturbed. He'll also provide help in the form of workmen and supplies to help you make a real home."

Leyus was silent as he weighed her words. "No," he said firmly. "We will not risk our lives for the promises of a human official we do not know."

"But—"

"I've made my decision. I want nothing more from you." When Kyra opened her mouth to protest again, he cut her off. "I think it's time for you to leave."

There was no hint of compromise in his voice, and Kyra's objections died in her throat. Havel and Zora watched her with equally unyielding gazes. As Kyra turned away, she racked her mind for an alternative, some other way to convince Leyus, but she came up with nothing. That was when she noticed Adele coming toward them.

The young clanswoman walked right past Kyra and bowed deeply in the Makvani fashion, running three fingers down the front of her throat. "Forgive me, clan leader," she said. "I couldn't help but overhear the halfblood's request. I would like to help her, if I may."

Leyus sat up straighter. "That is an unusual request, Adele. How do you plan to help her?"

"I would fight for her, against the Edlan troops."

"By yourself? Why lend them your strength?"

Adele lowered her gaze, and Kyra imagined a slight flush on the young woman's cheeks. "I would like to see peace between our people and the humans on this side of the mountain."

"And you want this enough to risk your life for them?"

Adele raised her eyes to Leyus, and her voice was clear when she responded. "I want this enough that I am willing to take this to Challenge if you forbid me to go."

There were gasps and murmurs, and Kyra realized that many of the Makvani had gathered around to listen. The Challenge was a right of anyone of Makvani blood, an opportunity to fight to the death on behalf of a petition. If Adele claimed a Challenge here, it would be against Leyus or someone of his choosing. Kyra had seen Leyus fight. He was almost twice Adele's size, and far stronger. As unfamiliar as she was with Makvani customs, Kyra knew that Adele had just said she would rather die than lose her chance for peace with the humans. Why was she doing this? Was this all for Flick?

"Adele." Pashla's voice rang out from the back. The older woman came to her side, acknowledging Kyra with a nod before she too addressed Leyus. "I also beg permission to help Kyra in her quest. And I too am willing to Challenge for it."

Leyus had risen to his feet by now, his arms crossed over his chest. His brow was furrowed, but he didn't look angry. "The two of you, then. Is there anyone else who wishes permission to go with the halfblood?"

*Halfblood*, Kyra thought. He still spoke of her as if she were a stranger to him.

"I would," said a new voice. Kyra recognized Mela, Adele's friend. A few others also stepped out, mostly younger clansfolk, several of whom looked familiar.

Leyus looked over each one of them. "You understand that this is no paltry raid. This army comes in great numbers, and they are well armed." There were a few nods. By now, almost all the Demon Riders had gathered around to watch. When Leyus spoke again, his words were to the volunteers, but his voice was loud enough for all gathered to hear. "You have my permission. Fight as you will. And if you succeed in breaking the siege, I will consider negotiating peace with Forge."

All in all, there were twelve of them: Kyra, Pashla, Adele, Mela, three other women, and five men. They were all young. Several were friends of Adele's or had spoken with Flick. Most were from Leyus's clan—three were from the other. When Kyra asked one of them why he was helping, he replied, "We've been sleeping in trees and eating raw meat for over a year now to stay hidden from the human troops. If there's a better way, I would like to find it."

She was grateful for their help, but still, there were only twelve of them against over a thousand troops. What good could they possibly do?

"I'd imagined surprising these soldiers with two hundred demon cats at my back, but we can't do that now," Kyra told Flick. He'd found her in the forest soon after Kyra left Leyus with her recruits. Mercie, Lettie, and Idalee had taken shelter with friends farther from the city, but he chose to stay with Kyra and her band of Makvani fighters. Whenever Flick wasn't talking with Kyra, he was at Adele's side. Kyra wondered if he knew that Adele had been willing to fight a Challenge to win her right to be here. It seemed too personal a thing for Kyra to disclose.

"If you can't attack them directly, mayhap you could weaken their position some other way," said Flick. "Their supplies, perhaps?"

"That might work," said Kyra. "But I know nothing about the Edlan supply caravans."

"What about that trader Craigson? He's from Edlan, in't he?"

Kyra considered his words. Craigson did live close to Edlan, and he bore no particular loyalty to its Duke. "I'll go speak with him."

Though the trader camp lay outside the line of Edlan soldiers, Kyra wasn't surprised to find them readying their wagons to leave. A potential battlefield wasn't exactly the best place to winter. Craigson was bundling up cooking supplies when Kyra arrived, and he beckoned her closer.

"I'm glad you found us," he said. "I was regretting having to leave without a final word with you."

"I'm afraid I'm not here to talk about my past," said Kyra. "Things have become more complicated since then."

"Aye, it has. What might I do for you, then?"

Craigson listened with sharp-eyed intelligence as Kyra told him what had happened. "We'd like to avert a war," she said. "Do you think we could stall the army by stopping their caravans?"

"I reckon you could," he said. "The Edlan army gets its supplies from wagon trains that come down from the north. The trains are heavily armed, of course, but man for man they'd be easier to go up against than actual soldiers. What you really want to do is destroy the wagons along with the supplies in them. That would make it harder for them to recover." Craigson paused to roll a bundle tight. "They're friendly folk, the supply caravanners. I hate to think of them coming to harm, but I suppose they knew that risk when they took the job."

"How big are the wagon trains?" asked Kyra.

"Ten to fifteen wagons, with two to four men manning each wagon."

Kyra did some figuring in her head. One demon cat could probably handle one wagon, especially if they attacked at night. The image of demon cats leaping out of the darkness onto unsuspecting caravanners left an uneasy feeling in her stomach.

Craigson's gaze lingered on her face, though Kyra got the impression that he was actually seeing something in his mind's eye. "You know, your mother once led a small force against a much stronger one."

"Did she win?" asked Kyra.

"She drove the Makvani here, didn't she? Maikana was a strong leader."

Kyra picked up a piece of charcoal from the fire pit and rolled it between her fingers. She knew he meant well, but Craigson's words only made her feel smaller. "To be honest, Craigson, I've got enough people telling me how wonderful my ma was. Please tell me she made mistakes too."

To her surprise, Craigson laughed. "Mistakes? Maidy, your ma's first year as her village Guide was one mistake after another. If she hadn't made mistakes, you wouldn't be here." He paused and lowered his voice. "Though she loved you dearly. It near broke her heart when she had to give you to me, and that was with the understanding that you'd be back when the drought ended."

Kyra latched onto Craigson's final words. "She did love me, then? She didn't hate me, for what I was?"

Craigson's eyes were soft with compassion. "She worried about what you'd become, but it didn't stop her from loving you and hoping for the best. Maikana didn't always know what to do, and she made many, many mistakes. But she loved her village, even when the villagers didn't love her, and when she fell down, she always got up again."

Craigson's words reminded Kyra of the conversation she'd had with Malikel, when the Defense Minister had told her he stayed in Forge because he had work to do, despite the mistrust he faced from some. Kyra wondered about herself. Did she love

Forge that much? There were certainly parts that she loved—the gutter rats, the southwest quadrant, the streets and rooftops that were as familiar to her as Flick's laugh or Lettie's smile. Was that enough to make it worth fighting for?

"Thank you Craigson. For everything," she said.

Craigson took her hand in his own. His skin was callused and dry, but his grip was warm. "I'll likely return to Edlan for the rest of the winter. When this all calms down, come find me, and we'll talk more."

Twelve was too large a number to convene for long, and the Makvani grew restless to disperse. It was decided that they would set scouts farther up the road to watch for the caravans. When one came close, the scout would reconvene them.

Flick pointed out that it wouldn't be enough just to stop the caravans, since stores from nearby farms could feed the army for a few weeks at least. He volunteered to carry a message to those still around and rally them to hide their food stores.

"It's the least I could do," he said, rubbing his bearded chin with his fingers. Between the facial hair and the lengthening curls atop his head, he was starting to look rather wild. "To be honest, I feel rather useless. I'd much rather be taking down wagon trains with the rest of you, if only I had the claws to do it."

"Don't feel guilty," said Kyra, thinking of all the Makvani who had come to her aid because of Flick. "You've already done much more than you realize."

When the signal came the next evening, Kyra was still

half-asleep in her cave. If she'd been in her skin, she might have missed it completely, but she'd slept in her fur, and instinct pulled her awake. Once again Kyra knew exactly where the roar had come from. It was a new thrill, bounding through the trees toward the others and seeing the branches rush by. When she sensed motion in her periphery and her nose picked up the smell of other demon cats, the fur along her spine prickled in recognition. She had never been in her cat form around so many others before, and the unexpected feeling of kinship surprised her.

They gathered in a small clearing. When they had all changed into their skin and dressed, the scout spoke. "There is a caravan on its way. I think they will camp here tonight and meet the army tomorrow."

"They'll be most vulnerable when they sleep," said Kyra. "Pashla and I will go closer and get a better look at how they're positioned. We can attack when the moon sets."

A few of the gathered Makvani bowed to her, running one finger down the front of their necks. Then all except Pashla scattered into the trees.

Kyra stared after them, wondering at this honor they paid her, before she returned her thoughts to the matter at hand. She spoke to Pashla. "I prefer to scout in my skin, if you don't mind."

"You lead the way," said Pashla.

The scout had pointed them toward the road slightly north of them, so Kyra set off in that direction with Pashla walking silently alongside her. It didn't take long for them to hear voices and see campfires in the distance. They slowed and Kyra pointed to a tree. When Pashla nodded, Kyra led the way up.

She wasn't surprised to see that Pashla climbed well in her skin. In a few moments, they were both high enough to get a good view of the wagon train.

Like the scout had said, there were ten wagons, circled now for the night. Armed guards ringed the outside, while those inside tended to animals and prepared food.

"Where will they sleep?" asked Pashla.

"Under the wagons, I'd think," said Kyra. "The wagons themselves are likely too full to fit any people."

Pashla watched the wagons with the sharp gaze of a predator. "We'll fall on the guards from the trees above. They won't be expecting it, and they won't be able to see us coming. But it's still a large number of enemies for the twelve of us. We'll all have to be in our fur, if we want our best chance of surviving to fight again. You too, Kyra."

"I know," she said. The idea didn't sit well with her, but if she was to lead the raid, she would have to fight as the others did.

She and Pashla returned to her crew and made plans to meet again after the moon set. When the rest of the group left, Pashla stayed behind.

"You're not leaving?" asked Kyra.

"I think it's best if you're not alone," said Pashla.

She was grateful for Pashla's company, though the two of them didn't say much. Pashla seemed lost in her own thoughts while Kyra sat against a tree and scribbled diagrams on the ground with a stick. She couldn't stay still and got up frequently to pace.

"Something worries you," said Pashla.

Kyra took a moment to choose her words. "People will die in these raids," she said. "Both ours and theirs."

"Is it really so bad a thing to die in battle?" said Pashla. "There's a saying amongst our people: 'It is better to die honorably and render yourself immortal than live to old age and fade to dust.'"

"It in't quite the same," said Kyra. "You joined the fight because you think it's worth fighting. But most of the soldiers in this war fight under orders. Some might truly care for the cause, but others serve because it's the best way to feed their families, and still others were conscripted. So many lives stand to be lost, and it's all for the ambitions of a few." And there was more. It was becoming clear to Kyra that there would be no turning back from this. If she changed shape and fell on the caravan with the others, there would be no Tristam this time to keep her in line. She would take pleasure in the slaughter. She would lose herself in the act of war, and the men in the caravan would die gruesome, painful deaths.

Pashla laid a hand on her arm. "We have all agreed to follow you. If you've changed your mind about attacking the Edlan troops, then we don't have to continue on with our plans."

It was tempting, but Kyra shook her head. "No, we continue with the plan. I don't see any better way. I do love Forge, and if we hand it over to Willem, more people will be hurt in the long run. More people will go hungry, or lack for medicine..."

Kyra stopped short when she realized that the words coming out of her mouth were not her own. *Did the fire take more than what the Palace would have taken eventually? Lives lost when folk can't buy medicine and food. Homes lost because the fatpurses forever grab for more.* James had been talking about his Demon Rider raid, the one that killed Bella. Kyra had confronted him in a rage, unable to understand how he could have done something that took so many lives. *Oh, James, if you could see me now.* Here she was a few months later, in the forest among her fellow Makvani, orchestrating an attack of her own and justifying it with his words.

Something crunched in the snow around her. Perhaps Kyra was becoming attuned to her kin, because she immediately knew that another Demon Rider had come. Still, it was Pashla who recognized the newcomer first.

"Leyus," she said, and bowed as he came out.

There was something about the clan leader. Wherever he went, he gave the impression that the territory belonged to him and everybody was there at his will. Kyra wondered what kind of greeting she would have given him if she had been raised as his daughter. Was there a different bow?

"I will have a word with Kyra," Leyus said.

"Of course," Pashla said, and retreated.

In the past, being left alone with Leyus would have frightened Kyra, but knowing the truth made her bold. Kyra found that she no longer feared Leyus. Nor did she worry about losing his good opinion. He'd already made it clear that she didn't have it.

Leyus took his time before speaking, gazing down at her like a potter searching a vessel for flaws. "You're planning to raid the army caravan tonight," Leyus said.

"Aye," she said. It was hard not to fidget under his scrutiny.

What was Leyus doing here? "It seemed the best way to hurt the Edlan troops."

He walked a slow arc in the snow in front of her, gazing into the forest beyond. "Had you been raised in a clan, as my heir, I would have trained you to lead your people into battle."

*Your people.* What would it have been like to grow up as the daughter of a Makvani clan leader? She imagined herself hunting beside Pashla, learning to fight in preparation for her first Challenge. Would she have been friends with Adele? Would she look upon humans as lower beings and despise that part of herself?

"But I wasn't raised your heir, was I?" She'd grown up in the gutter, about as far from leading a desert village or a Makvani clan as she could get. "And I only have eleven fighters to lead into battle."

"Do you pity yourself, that I did not give you more help? A true leader would not rely on the charity of others."

And here it was again, another reminder that she didn't measure up. "And I suppose you'd rather have me kill all the Edlan soldiers with my bare hands," Kyra said bitterly. "Or was I supposed to have inspired more of your people to follow me?"

"I'd rather have you know yourself and your own strengths, and to act with purpose. That is the first lesson I would have taught you, had I raised you." There was no sentimentality in Leyus's voice, just his direct and unflinching words. Anger stirred in Kyra's chest. Would it kill him to express even some scrap of regard for her? Some minuscule hint of happiness to have discovered the daughter he'd lost?

"I'm sorry I wasn't there to learn your lessons," she said. She kept her voice low and cold so it wouldn't quaver. "But I will do my best with the things I've learned in the life I've had. I must ask you to leave now, as we have many preparations to make."

"To have command of eleven of your kin is no small thing. Use your power wisely."

He left her then, and as soon as he was out of sight, Kyra took her frustrations out on a nearby tree, kicking and pummeling it with her fists. What she really wanted to do was scream, but she retained at least the presence of mind to remain quiet. Her shoes were soft leather and the tree was sturdy, so all she managed to do was bruise her toes and send shooting pains up her elbow. At some point during her tantrum, Pashla came to stand next to her and quietly watched until Kyra was still again.

"If this is what it's like to have a father," said Kyra under her breath, "I'd rather go back to being an orphan."

"He does wish you to succeed, Kyra," Pashla said. "He would not have come to speak to you if he did not care."

Pashla's voice was as calm and smooth as a healer's balm, yet Kyra resisted her words. "If he wanted me to succeed, he could have given me more help. Instead, he lists my failures and gives me useless advice."

"To know your strengths and act with purpose is not useless advice," Pashla said. So she'd been eavesdropping.

"I know my strengths, and they're nothing like what I need to see this through. I'm a thief. I climb rooftops, I slip into windows, and I steal things." Her voice got louder as she spoke. "I've no idea how to lead fighters into battle, and with this coming raid, I feel like I'm running headlong toward the edge of a precipice."

"Then perhaps our plan is the wrong one," Pashla said.

Pashla's words surprised her. Kyra supposed she'd expected the clanswoman to be in favor of a raid and nothing else.

"You think so?" Kyra asked. "But what else is there?"

"I don't know. You are not like us."

Well, that was one thing the two of them could agree upon. Kyra sank down into the snow and leaned back against a tree, paying no heed to the cold seeping into her trousers or the rough bark pulling at her hair. She stayed like that for a long while, eyes closed, simply trying to hold on to what sanity she had left. Then she sat bolt upright.

"What is it?" asked Pashla.

"I have an idea," said Kyra. It had come to her suddenly, but as soon as it came to mind, she knew it was the right one. It would be dangerous, but it was something she could attempt with a clear conscience. Perhaps Flick was right. Whatever she was, whatever hidden pasts she discovered, in the end she would always be the thief girl that he met on the streets so long ago.

Kyra turned to Pashla. "Cancel the raid. I've a new plan." Leyus would probably tell her that her decision was driven by fear of what she was, but it wasn't fear that motivated her this time. It was confidence—in what she was, and more importantly, in knowing what she wanted to be. "I'm going into the enemy camp," she said. "And I'm doing it in my skin."

## THIRTY

Flick didn't like the idea, of course. He never liked anything that placed Kyra in danger, and this would be far riskier than a caravan raid.

"You know, you don't always have to pick the most foolhardy way forward," he told her.

"But if it works, it could end it all before it begins," said Kyra.

The plan was simple. The easiest way to control an army was to control its leaders, and the leaders currently resided in a large tent at the center of Edlan's encampment. If someone were to, say, steal the leaders and turn them over to Forge, then Edlan's army would have newfound motivation to retreat.

Of course, an army encampment was perhaps the very definition of "well guarded." Kyra was fairly confident she could get in. She wasn't nearly as confident that she could get back out, but she had to try. They had so much to gain if she succeeded.

She risked a trip back into the city and relayed her plan to Tristam and Malikel. "If all goes well, I'll deliver Willem to your gates tomorrow night. My Demon Riders will be waiting outside the camp to guard my initial retreat, and I'll need troops from Forge stationed by the city to guard the final stretch. If things do not go to plan..." She paused here and avoided Tristam's eyes. "All the Demon Riders with me are dedicated to this task. They can carry out raids on the Edlan supply caravans even if I can't help them."

"I will have a unit by the gates ready to come to your defense," said Malikel.

"Thank you." She finally looked at Tristam then. She could see the effort it took for him not to object to her plan, and his struggle tugged at her chest. Kyra swallowed and met his gaze. "This is war. We do what we must."

She left before her resolve could weaken further.

Kyra tried her best to get plenty of rest the next day, though her nerves didn't allow her to sleep for very long. When she could no longer stay still, she paced the ground in front of her cave. She'd just about churned the snow into mud when Adele and Pashla appeared.

"We will go with you tonight," said Pashla.

Kyra's initial reaction was to refuse. "I can't in good conscience make you run a mission in your skin."

"We have stake in this as well," said Adele.

"You can't subdue both Alvred and Willem by yourself," said Pashla. "And your plan does work better with us in our skin."

Once she gave up trying to dissuade them, Kyra had to admit that they were right.

They set out late that night, after the moon had set. Kyra had Pashla and Adele darken their clothes with mud to blend in. Then they walked silently to the forest edge, where they could see the campfires of the Edlan army. Kyra looked back to check that the other two were still with her, then set off on a slow jog toward the camp. The women fell easily behind her—Kyra's own stealth, after all, was a legacy of their blood. But though the clanswomen were quiet, they still looked to her as they neared the edge of the encampment. As Kyra watched the guards go by, waiting for an opening, she sensed that her companions couldn't read the intention in a sentry's footsteps or predict where he would look next. The clanswomen didn't have Kyra's lifelong experience breaking into guarded places, but they watched her carefully, and Kyra led the way into the camp, trailed by two impossibly graceful shadows.

The ground of the camp was muddy and wet; all the snow had long been trampled away. The muck was slick in some places, while others times it sucked at their shoes. The three of them passed campfires at regular intervals, all burning low. Kyra steered clear of the occasional groggy soldier who got up to feed the flames.

The center of command was a large tent near the physical center of the camp. Kyra could see its shadow looming in the dim moonlight. Little by little, from one patch of darkness to the next, they made their way closer. There was a sentry at the tent flap standing next to one of the few torches around. Kyra motioned to Pashla. They approached him from opposite sides, skirting along the edges of the tent until they stood just outside the light cast by the torch. Kyra could barely see Pashla's form as the clanswoman bent down, picked a rock off the ground, and let it drop. The sentry turned toward the sound, alert but not alarmed. Kyra ran while his back was turned and brought the hilt of her dagger down on the back of his head. He grunted, and Kyra snaked her arms under his armpits as he crumpled to the ground. Adele rushed in to help drag the body out of the torchlight. The sentry had a partner, who circled around from the other side of the tent. When he saw Kyra and Adele, he drew breath to shout but pitched forward before any sound left his mouth. Pashla bear-hugged him from behind and eased him to the ground.

"Ho, what's happening there?" came a shout from across the camp.

Sweat broke out over Kyra's skin. "We have to get them now," she said.

She drew her dagger and rushed into the tent. It was dark inside, and Kyra barely caught the glint of metal as a man charged at her with a blade. Kyra shouted a warning as she sidestepped his swipe. He moved with the clumsiness of someone who'd just woken. When he stumbled, Kyra saw her opening and slashed at his knife arm. He dropped the blade and clutched his arm, swearing.

Kyra pressed her knife to his throat, and for the first time, got a good look at her opponent's face. He'd trimmed his mustache since she last saw him, but there was no mistaking Edlan's Minister of Defense. Lord Alvred's eyes widened in recognition as he took in her features. Around her, the scuffling died down. As Kyra's eyes adjusted to the darkness, she saw that Pashla had Willem facedown on his bedroll, her knee on his spine and her dagger pointed at the base of his skull. Adele stood alert by the tent flap.

"Adele, rope," said Kyra. Her heart pounded so loudly it was a wonder the entire camp couldn't hear it.

Pashla shifted her weight so Adele could bind Willem's wrists. The Head Councilman glared at Kyra as Adele pulled the knots tight. His gray-streaked hair was messy and tangled from the scuffle.

"Do you really expect to get out of here alive?" asked Willem.

"Your fate will be tied to ours," Kyra said. When Adele finished binding Willem's arms, she stepped toward Kyra and Alvred, rope in hand.

"Kyra, take care!" said Pashla as someone threw open the tent flap. Kyra tightened her grip on Alvred as she turned. Three Edlan soldiers stood at the entrance with swords drawn. Several more stood behind them.

"Drop your weapons or your commanders die," she said, her voice sharp in her ears.

"Do as she says," said Alvred in his low, booming shout, and the others obeyed.

Well, it was too late for rope now. "Clear a path," said Kyra. Slowly, the soldiers parted. Kyra turned Alvred around so he faced away from her and nudged him to start moving. She stepped out first, followed by Pashla and Willem, with Adele bringing up the rear. It was awkward progress. He was much larger than she was, and Kyra had to reach up to get her dagger to his throat. Her arm quickly began to get sore, and sweat from his skin soaked into her clothes.

Kyra scanned the soldiers around her as they walked. This couldn't last forever. There were too many soldiers, and too few hostages. Her spine prickled—she expected an arrow in her back any moment. When Alvred lagged, she pressed the blade closer to his throat, nudging him forward. Slowly, ever so slowly, they made their way to the edge of the camp. Her arms burned. She could see the forest now when she peered around Alvred's bulk. Almost there. They just needed the shelter of the trees.

Something whistled through the air, followed by a woman's cry. Kyra turned just in time to see Adele fall to her knees, an arrow shaft sticking out her back.

"Adele!" she shouted. At that moment, Alvred broke free and struck her hard in the stomach. Kyra fell to the ground, retching. Alvred grabbed for her dagger, but she snatched it away just in time.

"Lord Alvred!"

A soldier handed Alvred a mace, an evil-looking club with a steel-coated head. Kyra dove to the side as he raised it high and brought it down. He missed the first time and the second, but his third blow came down squarely on her right hip.

Kyra screamed, and for a moment she couldn't see anything for the pain. When her vision cleared, Alvred was closing in for another blow. She tried to scoot away, and realized with horror that she couldn't move her leg at all.

A roar split the air and a demon cat charged into the fray, coming to a stop protectively above Adele. Two more came after and stood tail-to-tail with the first, fangs bared and snarling dangerously. For a moment, everyone stared. Then the demon cats disappeared behind a wave of soldiers. Alvred raised his mace once more, and Kyra hopelessly threw her arms in front of her face.

"Stand back!" Suddenly, Pashla was next to her, still with Willem firmly in her grasp. How had she managed to hold on to her hostage in all that chaos? Alvred hesitated, and in that moment someone's arms threaded under Kyra's and pulled her to her feet. She cried out again as the movement jarred her leg. Then she realized it was Flick holding her.

"Easy, Kyra." His voice was a safe harbor she could cling to. "Let's get you to safety."

"To the trees," said Pashla, dragging Willem in that direction. Flick threw Kyra over his shoulder and hurried after the clanswoman. Kyra buried her face in his chest to keep from screaming. Every step he took was agony. Two swordsmen gave chase, but a demon cat jumped in front of them, cutting off pursuit.

The sounds of battle followed them into the forest. "Our people won't last long," Kyra said. And Adele. Was she alive?

Pashla forced Willem to his knees in front of her. "We must get him to Forge."

She was right. If the Edlanese recovered Willem, all their efforts would have been in vain. "Pashla," she said. "I can't walk, much less run. You must bring him to the gates."

Pashla's eyes flickered quickly over Kyra, and then she undid her tunic as Flick lowered Kyra to the ground. When Pashla regained her form, Flick hoisted Willem onto her back and secured him with rope. The Head Councilman's attempts to resist met with two solid clouts to the head. Willem swore at Flick but stopped fighting.

Finally, Flick pulled the rope tight. When Pashla bent her

head around to check Flick's progress, he patted her on her flank. "Go," he said. "Run quickly."

Pashla took off with a bound, zigzagging through the trees. Kyra watched her disappear, then turned back toward the battle, trying to see between the trees to the chaos beyond. Demon cat growls split the air. Swords clanged as fur and steel flashed in and out of view.

Kyra drew the deepest breath she could. "Retreat!" she yelled. "Makvani retreat!"

The battle continued on, and she wondered if anyone had heard her. Then a demon cat ran for the trees and knelt in front of Kyra.

"Hang on," said Flick as he lifted her onto its back and climbed on behind her. Another demon cat came on its tail, and Kyra was light-headed with relief to see a very pale Adele clinging to its back. Other demon cats followed, turning around several times to fend off pursuers. The demon cat Kyra was riding looked around at the gathered Makvani and let out a roar. And then, as one, the beasts ran into the forest.

🁢 🁢 🁢

Tristam stood at attention outside the city gate, facing the empty road. He might as well have been sitting in a root cellar for all he could discern in the darkness. Tristam knew from Malikel's strategy charts that fifty Red Shields stood to his left, armed with spears. To his right came the occasional whinny and snort from the horses of twenty cavalrymen. Sir Rollan stood in command at the front, while Malikel oversaw everything from the wall.

"Disturbance in the enemy camp," came a lookout's voice from above.

Perhaps it was good that his position required absolute still-ness, because otherwise Tristam would have worn down the road with his nervous energy. Of all the schemes Kyra had come up with so far, this had to be the most brazen, and he couldn't quiet the fear that her luck would finally run out. What was this "disturbance" in the enemy camp? Panic at finding their leader gone, or celebration at capturing an intruder?

"Light the torches," Rollan commanded. "Put them in place."

A ripple of readiness went through the troops. All around him, there was the sound of flint striking. A warm glow illumi-nated the troops as sparks caught on pitch-coated wood. Each cavalry man took two torches and rode down the road to place them in stands before returning to formation. They all waited, growing more and more tense as the shadows formed and dis-sipated on the newly lit road.

"A rider, sir," came the lookout's voice, sharp now. "No, a demon cat. With a single rider. A man."

"Tristam," said Rollan. "Is it Kyra?"

Tristam squinted down the road. He could make out the rider now, and his steed was definitely a demon cat. As the beast passed the torches though, he saw that the fur was tawny yellow.

"It's not Kyra, sir," he said. "Wrong color." Was it Pashla? "I think it may be one of her allies."

"Spearmen, take formation, but don't attack." Rollan

delivered his orders with confident ease, and his composure seemed to rub off on the troops around him. "Tristam, speak immediately if you see anything untoward."

"Yes, sir," he said. Where was Kyra? A knot formed in his stomach. *Concentrate on your task.*

"It's Willem tied to the beast's back," called the lookout.

The felbeast slowed as it neared them and approached carefully with its head lowered and ears flat. Willem was indeed tied to its back. He must have been captured while he was asleep because he wore only a plain wool tunic and trousers. And though Willem's face was turned partially away, Tristam could clearly see the rage etched in his features. Tristam almost felt sorry for him. What a fall it must be for a Head Councilman to be delivered to his city gates like a sack of flour.

Red Shields formed a half circle around the demon cat and raised their spears as it came closer. The beast stopped and eyed the weapons warily. Tristam was almost certain now that it was Pashla.

"Sir Rollan," said Tristam. "May I cut the hostage from the beast's back?"

"You may."

Pashla knelt as Tristam approached. Willem glared but didn't say anything as Tristam surveyed the ropes and cut the ones that tied him to Pashla. Willem slid to the ground, and several Red Shields lifted him to his feet.

"The cat's changing shape," a man said.

Apparently, Red Shield discipline couldn't match the sight of a demon cat transforming before their eyes, because shouts and exclamations rose up all around. As Pashla shrank down,

Tristam unclasped his cloak and threw it over her shoulders. She gathered the cloak around her and looked calmly at the troops before settling her eyes on Tristam.

"Thank you," she said.

It was on his tongue to ask about Kyra, but the gate opened just then, and Malikel walked out. He was flanked by soldiers, and he looked, every inch of him, like a leader of men. He faced Willem, who stood with his hands bound in front of him. A Red Shield held each arm.

"That was cleverly done, Malikel," said Willem, his voice crisp. "And what happens now?"

"That is something we'll have to discuss." Malikel turned to Pashla. "We are grateful," he said with dignity, "though we'd expected Kyra to come."

"She was injured in the fighting," said Pashla.

"How badly was she wounded?" asked Tristam. His need to know outweighed his adherence to protocol.

"She is alive," said Pashla. "And she is unlikely to die from the wounds she'd received when I left. Beyond that, I do not know."

It was a small relief, but not exactly happy news.

"You are welcome to take shelter within our walls tonight," said Malikel.

Pashla shook her head. "If you have no further need for me, I will return to my clan."

"Very well, then. We are indebted to your people." Malikel addressed the men holding Willem. "Take the prisoner back to the Palace."

As Malikel and Willem disappeared into the city, Pashla stepped back from the soldiers around her. She handed Tristam's cloak to him, her shape blurring. The spearmen around her squared their stances as she fell on all fours, but Pashla simply turned and raced away.

There was a collective release of tension amongst the troops as Pashla left.

"Return to formation," commanded Rollan. "Head back through the gate."

Tristam turned with the rest of his comrades toward the city. He realized now that he should have asked Pashla to take him to Kyra, but it was too late. As the first soldiers started to march, the lookout called down again.

"Sir Rollan," he said. "I see troops riding toward the city. Edlan riders, carrying torches."

Tristam turned, as did the men around him. Dots of torchlight bobbed in the distance, illuminating men on horseback. They were riding down the road to the city, though now they stopped and fanned into a half circle, as if they were surrounding something. A demon cat. Pashla.

"All troops retreat into the city." Rollan's voice rang over the troops. "Close the gates."

Tristam looked to Rollan in disbelief. Were they simply going to leave Pashla to her fate? The soldiers around him started marching again, but Tristam didn't move. When the soldier behind Tristam stepped around him, Tristam broke out of the stream, elbowing his way to Rollan's horse.

"Rollan," he said. "There must be at least ten horsemen out there. Pashla can't face them all."

"We're tasked with securing the city." Rollan barely gave Tristam a sideways glance as he observed the retreat.

Tristam looked back out toward the Edlan soldiers. One horseman lowered a spear and charged Pashla. She jumped aside just in time, then twisted around to rake her claws across the horse's flank. The torchlight played off her fur as the other horsemen formed a loose circle around her, cutting off any escape.

"She just saved our city," said Tristam. "And we leave her now to the enemy?"

A spasm of irritation crossed Rollan's face. "You forget your place, soldier."

Tristam suppressed the urge to pull Rollan off his horse. Not three months ago, he'd have been commanding troops alongside him. But it was clear that Rollan would not have his authority challenged. In the distance, Pashla roared, and the Edlan horses danced apart. Was she limping?

That was when Tristam noticed that the knight next to Rollan was not on his horse. Tristam wasn't sure why the man had dismounted, but an idea came to him. *Well, I suppose there are more important things than regaining my knighthood.*

Tristam pushed his way toward the steed before he could change his mind. The horse's rider stood nearby, still holding his lance. Tristam grabbed the weapon and knocked the man aside. Before anyone realized what was happening, Tristam had pulled himself into the horse's saddle and urged the creature forward with a kick. Over the pounding of his horse's hooves, he heard Rollan yelling after him. He looked over his shoulder to see several Forge cavalrymen giving chase. Were they coming to help him or knock him off his horse? He wasn't about to wait and find out.

The Edlan troops had seen the Forge soldiers coming by now, and five of them turned their horses to face them. Tristam could see Pashla beyond them, definitely limping as she charged her enemies. She roared once, and the sound quickened his blood.

Tristam leveled his spear, shouted a war cry, and braced for impact.

The felbeast Kyra rode had a smoother stride than a horse, but every leap it took still sent agony shooting through her limbs. She gritted her teeth and tried to convince herself it didn't hurt. As they ran farther away from the troops, she started to feel light-headed, as if she had lost a lot of blood. But she wasn't bleeding, was she? Not on the outside at least. Her awareness started to leave her. She began listing to the side, but Flick tightened his arms around her and kept her from falling. She was aware of other demon cats around her, also fleeing, but as time passed, she no longer had the energy to think about them or anything else.

She wasn't sure how long they rode. By the time they slowed, she was drifting in and out of consciousness. She felt a breeze at her back and realized that Flick was no longer behind her. Strong arms lifted her off her steed. Flick? No. It was Leyus who looked down at her, his expression grave. And then she drifted again.

The next thing she knew, she lay on a fur spread over the ground. New hands and voices tended to her. Someone was cutting the clothes from her body. A man spoke. Not Leyus this time, but she couldn't place the voice. "Kyra, change into your fur."

She tried to ignore him at first. Change now? She could hardly lift her head. She closed her eyes and tried to sleep, but someone shook her. She realized she was shivering without her clothes.

"Change into your fur, Kyra," said the voice again, more commanding this time. "Then you can rest."

Kyra obeyed just so that he would leave her alone. The spark of her other form was hard to find by now, and everything around her seemed dim. But finally she grabbed on and coaxed it stronger. Welcome warmth spread through her body. And then it was too much for her, and she slept.

Kyra awoke disoriented. She was in her fur, but not in her cave. There was no strength in her limbs. Pain still radiated from her hip, although it was not nearly as bad as it had been before. Kyra shook the fog out of her mind and climbed slowly to her feet.

She was in the forest, and the angle of the light suggested it was afternoon. Some demon cats lay a stone's throw away, tended by their kin. A few other Makvani stood nearby in human form. Their voices carried easily over the snow, but Kyra couldn't understand the words.

It was too painful to put weight on her back leg, so she hobbled awkwardly forward on three. She'd only made it a few paces when someone approached her. It took her a moment to recognize Havel, the leader of the new clan. He greeted her with a friendly tone and held out a tunic. Kyra understood that he wanted her to change into her skin.

She obeyed. Her weight shifted as she changed, and the resulting pressure on her injured leg would have made her lose her balance if Havel hadn't steadied her shoulder. When Kyra stabilized, he handed her the tunic, and she pulled her arms through, too disoriented to be concerned about modesty.

"How do you feel?" Havel asked.

There was warmth in his voice, and Kyra recognized it as the one who had commanded her to change shape the night before. "Was it you who cared for me last night?"

Havel inclined his head. "I served as a healer for your father long ago. He still asks me for help, in cases that are important to him." He met Kyra's eyes as he said the last part, and the meaning was not lost on her. Nor had she forgotten the worry in Leyus's brow as he'd lifted her off the demon cat last night.

"Is Leyus still here?" asked Kyra.

"No, not at the moment."

Perhaps that was just as well. She'd wished for some sign that her father cared for her, but the thought of facing him and having this new knowledge shaken was too frightening.

Now that she was in her skin, worries came crowding back. Where was she? What was the outcome of the battle last night? And—a new urgency hit her—who had been hurt?

"Flick and Adele, are they safe?"

"Flick is unharmed," said Havel. Maybe it was something about Makvani healers, but Kyra felt at ease with Havel. The edge of aggression carried by most of his kin seemed softened in him. "Adele lost a good deal of blood, but she will live. Flick has been either at her side or yours all day."

Kyra closed her eyes, relieved. "And Pashla? Did she convey Willem to Forge?"

Here, Havel's countenance darkened. "We have no news of Pashla. Our scouts have been watching the Edlan troops, and they say the Defense Minster Malikel met with the Edlan leader this morning. Edlan troops are packing up their camp, so we can only guess that Pashla succeeded. But we do not know where she is."

Kyra thought back to the determination in Pashla's face when she'd changed shape to convey Willem to the city. She would have done her utmost to get him there. A chill went through Kyra, and she looked into the trees, wishing she could somehow see through them to the city.

"How is your leg?" Havel asked.

Kyra realized she'd been silent for a long time. "It doesn't hurt nearly as much as it did last night," she said. "But I can't put weight on it."

"Lord Alvred is a strong man. The blow crushed the bones of your hip and caused you to bleed in your abdomen. We had you change shape so the bone fragments would go back to their proper place, but it does not always work, especially in someone who does not share all our blood. We'll have someone cut you a staff to use while you recover. In the early days, you might find it easier to move around in your fur."

Someone shouted in the distance just then. It didn't sound like an alarm, more like a sentry's report. Havel looked toward the sound. "We may have more news now."

There was someone coming through the trees—someone tall, who walked like a soldier. He carried a long, rolled blanket across his arms, and a horse trailed behind him. Kyra squinted. Was that...

"Tristam!" Kyra shouted. Only at the last minute did she remember that she couldn't run to him. His eyes fixed on her, and his entire body sagged with relief.

It was awkward, standing and waiting for him to get to her. She found herself leaning forward, impatient to talk to him. Tristam couldn't walk very quickly because of what he carried, and as he came closer, Kyra felt a rising dread. Tristam's steps were heavy, and his eyes did not signal good news. Kyra turned to Havel, only to realize that the man had slipped away.

Tristam came to a stop in front of Kyra and laid his burden on the ground in front of her. For a long moment, they stared at each other. She longed to throw her arms around him, but it was too strange, with all the Makvani around.

"I heard you were injured," he said.

"Alvred's got a deadly mace arm," she said. "But Flick got me out alive." She gestured weakly toward herself. "I...can't walk very well at the moment."

"I'm glad you're alive," said Tristam. He started to reach for her but curled his hand into a fist and lowered it to his side as he stared down at the ground in front of him. When he spoke again, the words came out deliberately, as if he had to push them out before his resolve failed. "We had a unit waiting outside the gate for your arrival." he said, his voice low and even. His eyes were clouded with anguish. "Pashla made it to us with Willem on her back. But when she tried to return to the forest, she ran across a group of Edlan horsemen."

He stopped then, and Kyra felt something cold grip her

chest. She looked down at the rolled blanket on the ground. She'd known what it was. But still she'd hoped...

"I'm sorry, Kyra," Tristam said. "I tried to help her, and several of our knights as well. But we were too late." He kneeled then and pulled up one edge of the blanket to reveal Pashla's face.

Pashla's eyes were closed, her skin pale and bloodless, and Kyra found she couldn't breathe. She started to kneel down beside Pashla but stopped when pain shot through her hip. Tristam reached out to steady her, and slowly, she eased herself onto the snow.

The battle at the enemy camp played over and over in Kyra's mind. The arrow in Adele's back. Lord Alvred's mace coming down on Kyra's hip. The chaos that had led to Pashla taking her place.

"It should have been me," Kyra said. There was a lump in her throat that didn't move when she swallowed.

"The tides of battle cannot be predicted by any of us," said Tristam. "Don't blame yourself for the hand of fate."

He spoke the words as if he knew the grief they addressed. And Kyra supposed he did. His fellow knights had probably told him the same thing when Jack and Martin had died.

Kyra reached out to adjust the blanket around Pashla. Her fingers brushed against Pashla's cheek. The flesh was cold, as icy as the snow around them, and Kyra snatched her hand back with a gasp. The difference between that frozen shell and Pashla's warm, gentle touch was so stark that it felt like a cruel joke.

And that was when it sank in. This body was all that was left of the woman who had saved Kyra's life and nursed her back from near death. The woman who had fought for her, taught her the secrets of her Makvani blood, and forgiven Kyra when she returned to the humans. Kyra felt a burning beneath her eyelids. She fought it for a while, but when Tristam came and placed an arm around her shoulders, Kyra buried her face in his chest and let the tears come. He held her wordlessly through the sobs, occasionally rubbing her back, until finally she wiped her eyes and pulled away.

"Pashla and I," said Tristam, "we had our differences. But it was not my wish to see her fall."

"Did you speak to her before she died?" Kyra asked.

Tristam's nod was so slight that she almost didn't see it. "She asked me to take her body back to the clan."

Kyra stared down at Pashla's face, stern and beautiful, mysterious even in death. *What are you thinking, Pashla?* "She thought it an honor to die in battle for a cause she believed in. I hope she found this fight worthwhile."

"I think she did," said Tristam. "I know she did."

Kyra closed her eyes and breathed a silent thank-you and good-bye. Then she once again covered Pashla with the blanket and let her sleep.

The clan burned Pashla's body, with each member contributing a branch for the fire. In addition to Pashla, they mourned the deaths of two others who had been in Kyra's band of twelve. Those two had perished in the enemy camp, and there was no way to recover their remains.

Over the next few days, Tristam came often with news from Forge. The morning after Willem's capture, messengers had been dispatched to the Edlan troops with orders from the captive Willem to call off the siege. While some of Edlan's commanders might have been tempted to continue their attack even without their original ally, Willem had enough relatives in Edlan, including the Duke himself, who did not wish to see him harmed. The Edlan troops began their long march back a few days later. Malikel dispatched scouts to make sure they had gone, and after a few days, it was declared that the Edlan invaders had returned to their own city. Willem himself would be tried in front of the Council for treason.

"The Council voted to keep Malikel in his position as Head Councilman," said Tristam. "In part, he has Willem to thank for it. When your most vocal enemy turns out to be a traitor to the city, it tends to boost your credibility." Tristam paused. "Malikel requests that you return to Forge to speak with him, and he promises you safe passage into the Palace, should you take his request."

The promise of safe passage was important because Kyra was in no condition for any daring escapes at the moment. Her leg had healed to the point where she could walk with a crutch. It was a relief to be able to get around at all, but rooftop running was going to be out of her repertoire for a while.

Havel told her he wasn't sure what trajectory her recovery would take. "Your bones were crushed severely, and you're of mixed blood," he said. "The pain will lessen with time, but I don't know how far the healing will go. It may never return to the way it was before. You have to be prepared for that."

It was the uncertainty that scared her. Not knowing how the future would look, whether she'd be able to climb or run.

But Kyra also remembered that she was alive, when Pashla and two others had died for a plan that she'd proposed. It wasn't an easy thing to forget. Every conversation with Havel reminded her of Pashla, and how the clanswoman had also nursed Kyra back to health not long ago.

Two weeks after the big battle, Kyra accepted Malikel's invitation, and Tristam brought a cart to convey her to the Palace. It felt strange to be sitting up straight in the back of a wagon, rather than being smuggled under a blanket, as she had done so many times before. Tristam wore plain clothes as he drove, and though she got some curious looks, nobody made a noticeable commotion about recognizing her.

Once they reached the Palace though, things were different. The gate guards looked on her with thinly disguised fear, and Red Shields within sight kept their hands close to their weapons. Tristam stopped the cart near Malikel's building and offered her an arm. Kyra did her best to walk with her chin up the rest of the way.

Malikel looked older than Kyra remembered, or perhaps it was just the circles under his eyes. Kyra thought she saw more gray in his beard as well, but that was impossible in just a few days, wasn't it? The new Head Councilman thanked Tristam and dismissed him, then motioned for Kyra to sit down across from him at his desk.

"The city thanks you for your role in breaking the Edlan siege," he said, folding his hands in front of him. "Without your help, many more would have suffered."

"I heard about the Council vote," said Kyra. "I'm glad you've taken over Willem's position."

"Thank you. Though I'm guessing you've gathered by now that I've not summoned you here to exchange pleasantries."

"No, I suppose not," said Kyra. Had it been any other man who'd invited her back, she might have suspected a trap. But she believed Malikel honorable.

"I won't mince words, Kyra. You've always been a challenge as far as our laws are concerned. You've committed considerable transgressions, yet at the same time, you've performed great services for the city. You're responsible for the death of Santon of Agan and the assassin James. You also wounded many men, including Dalton of Agan and several Red Shields at James's execution. The Council could not simply pardon those crimes, even with your services to the city. Perhaps if you had an otherwise blameless record, but you've already been pardoned for one murder, and now that the truth of your bloodlines is known... I'm afraid it's impossible."

Kyra bowed her head at the mention of the murder she'd already been pardoned for, the manservant she'd accidentally killed when she worked for James. Of all she'd ever done, it was the one thing Kyra wished most she could undo, and she suspected it would haunt her for the rest of her life. "Does your promise of safe passage still stand, then?"

Malikel looked her over with an appraising eye. "I assure you, I have no desire to drag you into our dungeons. Nor would I want to take the losses in soldiers and guards should I attempt to do so. My promise of safe passage is sincere."

She waited. There was more. She knew there was more.

Malikel met her eye. "It brings me no joy to do this, but the Council has voted to exile you from Forge. You'll be conveyed out of this city, but after this, you will only be allowed within the city's walls under strict guard."

It took a moment for Malikel's words to sink in. And then she stared at him in disbelief. "You're exiling me from Forge? If it wasn't for me, you wouldn't have a city to exile me from."

"I know Kyra, and I'm sorry—"

She interrupted him angrily. "You're sorry, but you're bound by the decisions of the Council. Just as you were when the magistrate pardoned Santon for beating my sister to near death. This in't about the law, is it? It's about how the Council won't trust a halfblood Makvani in their city." *Not just any halfblood Makvani*, said a traitorous voice in her head. *A halfblood who's killed three men and thrown the city into chaos more than once.* She still thought the Council's decision was motivated by fear, but she couldn't deny that the case against her was substantial.

She collapsed back into her chair. "So nothing's changed," she said. "I'm still a criminal. The Council makes its decisions, and the city continues as before. Somehow I'd thought, with Willem gone and you in his place..."

Malikel pushed a piece of parchment across the table. Kyra had half a mind to throw it back at him, but she grudgingly looked it over. It was a Palace document, from one of the city magistrates. Something about a trial to be planned. And the accused was named...

"Douglass and Dalton of Agan will be tried for assaulting Idalee," said Malikel. "The magistrate conducted a further investigation into the case and determined that the initial ruling was unduly influenced by political factors. In addition, other victims have come forth with complaints against the brothers, and the magistrate is investigating them all.

"The Agan brothers will not be the only ones investigated. Others who enjoyed immunity under Willem are being held accountable as well. It will be a busy season for the magistrates." Malikel waited for Kyra to finish looking over the parchment. "Things are changing, Kyra. Though they progress slowly, in fits and starts. You're not the first to find this frustrating. My predecessor in this position found it so as well, and in fact engineered a plan to change our system of government." Malikel's lips twitched in the slightest of smiles. "I heard that the plan did not go well for him."

Though Kyra couldn't bring herself to smile back, she couldn't deny the irony. "It's funny," she said. "Remember the conversation we had, about serving the city even though not everyone within it would care to have us? What I did to break the siege, I did because I'd finally decided I agreed with you."

"And you can still serve the city, if you wish," said Malikel. "Which brings me to the last thing I wanted to discuss with you. I'm ready to follow through on the promises we made to the Makvani and discuss peace."

That, at least, was good news. "I can convey your message to Leyus."

"Thank you," said Malikel. "Given the times that lie ahead, I see the need for a go-between for our two peoples. An emissary, of sorts, and preferably someone who is familiar with both societies." He glanced significantly at Kyra.

She bristled. "And you would like me to do this? Why should I?"

"There's no reason why you should. I won't try to convince you that you owe it to the city or create some other sense of false responsibility. You owe Forge nothing, but you can do some good if you want to. The choice is yours."

Kyra gazed across the desk at him. It was tempting to throw a refusal in his face, but the less hotheaded part of her urged her to pause. The thought of peace between Forge and the Makvani—cooperation, even—was a good one.

"I'll think on it," said Kyra.

"That's all we can ask," said Malikel.

When Tristam came to convey her back out of the city, she could tell he was curious about what had transpired.

"Malikel didn't tell you why he called me in?" said Kyra.

"No," said Tristam. "He didn't share anything."

She supposed it was no big secret. Tristam would find out about her exile soon enough. "Let's leave the Palace first, and then I'll tell you."

He helped Kyra into the wagon. As he walked to the front, Kyra called to him. "Tristam."

He turned.

"Do you mind if we take a different route out of the city this time?"

"I suppose," he said, looking slightly perplexed. "How would you like to go?"

She let out a slow breath as the full implications of the Council's sentence finally hit her. "Bring the wagon by the southwest quadrant. I'd like to see The Drunken Dog."

Kyra accepted Malikel's offer to act as emissary between the Makvani and Forge. Sometimes the Head Councilman met with her outside the city. Other times, a contingent of Red Shields escorted her from the gate to the Palace. Her first job was to arrange a meeting to begin peace negotiations, and after a few proposals and counterproposals, the leaders agreed to meet on a patch of farmland bordering the forest.

Each group brought a contingent of five. Leyus, Havel, Zora, Adele, and Mela formed the Makvani contingent, while Malikel brought Tristam and three members of the Council. Kyra was there as well, the only person present who was not affiliated with either party. She arrived first and watched nervously as the two groups came to the meeting place, then held her breath as Malikel and Leyus shook hands. The Forge contingent set up a tent for shelter, and the Makvani provided deer hides to sit on. Kyra noticed Adele glancing over her shoulder toward the forest before stepping into the tent. When Kyra followed her gaze, she saw Flick watching from the trees. He winked at Kyra when he saw her looking, and the sight somehow made her more optimistic about the way things would go.

It was a long day, and there were several tense moments, but by the end of it, the two groups had the beginnings of a peace agreement. Malikel and Leyus shook hands one more time before they parted.

"I feel hopeful about this direction," said Malikel. "If any concerns should arise before the next time we meet, have Kyra convey a message to the city. I trust she has been satisfactory thus far as an emissary?"

Leyus looked at Kyra and gave the slightest of nods. "Yes," he said. "She has done well." Their eyes met, and just for a moment, something passed between them, a hint of understanding between father and daughter. It wasn't the stuff of talesinger ballads, but it gave Kyra hope. Perhaps someday she'd come to know him better, learn about his past and the mysterious woman he'd left on the other side of the Aerins. Someday.

Kyra initially took up residence again in her cave, but she eventually found a small cottage near the forest, far enough removed from other houses that they didn't have to worry about fearful neighbors. Lettie and Idalee moved back in with her from Mercie's house. Lettie took to the spot immediately, as it gave her a chance to stay near her new playmates. As spring came, Idalee started a small garden. Though the girl enjoyed tending it, Kyra guessed that Idalee might move back to Forge when she was older. She missed the bustle of the city, as did Kyra.

As was the case with their previous quarters, Flick was still a semipermanent fixture at the cottage. These days, however,

Kyra wasn't sure if he came by their house because she, Lettie, and Idalee were there or because it was convenient to the forest, and to Adele. The Makvani themselves didn't build permanent houses, though they crafted large, sturdy tents that they set up where they wished.

One morning, when Idalee and Lettie had gone to buy seeds for the garden, someone knocked on Kyra's door. Kyra thought it was one of the Makvani, and it was a few seconds before she recognized the human woman who greeted her. Darylene of Forge looked very different than she had when Kyra had seen her last. Her thick chestnut hair was bound back, and she wore an unassuming dress of undyed linen. But though she dressed to blend in, Willem's former mistress was still stunningly beautiful.

"I'm sorry to visit unexpectedly," Darylene said. "May I come in?"

It took Kyra a moment to get over her surprise, but she waved Darylene in and motioned for her to sit down. Kyra offered her a cup of tea, and Darylene accepted.

An awkward silence stretched between them then, and Kyra was grateful that she could busy herself with the stove. She knew by now that she'd been unfair in her initial animosity toward Darylene, and she was also well aware of the girl's role in Willem's overthrow. But still, old impressions were hard to get over, and Kyra didn't know what to say to Darylene, much less why she was here.

"I trust you are well?" Kyra asked when the tea was finally poured.

Darylene nodded. She still moved and held herself like

an elegant lady. Kyra could see why she might have caught Willem's eye. "Things progress well. I no longer work in the Palace. There's too much talk. Half the nobles deem me a traitor, while others treat me like a former trophy of Willem's to be won and flaunted," said Darylene. "As for my fellow servants, they've never had much use for me, and turning Willem in wasn't enough to earn their good opinion. It all grew to be too much."

Kyra could imagine.

Darylene brushed a stray curl from her face, then continued. "It probably won't surprise you that Willem provided for my material needs while I was his companion. And it was a big reason why I hesitated to say anything about Willem's crimes. It was selfish of me, I know, but I had a brother and sister who depend on me, and what I made as a servant in the Palace was not enough." She gave a sad smile. "Why worry about the fate of the city when my own family was fed?"

"You have siblings?" asked Kyra.

"Yes." Darylene's eyes softened when she spoke of them. "Ava is ten and Derek is eight. We're very close, since my ma and pa passed."

Kyra thought of Idalee and Lettie. "They're lucky to have you." And she found that she meant it.

Darylene smiled then and looked down at her tea. "It's . . . hard for us to stay in the city after all that has happened. I think I need to take my family and leave, at least for a while. James said you could help me with supplies, coin, and arrangements."

At first, Kyra thought she'd misheard what Darylene had said. "James?" Kyra asked. "The Head of the Assassins Guild?"

Darylene nodded. "When he escaped from prison, he came to speak with me. He'd somehow found out that I had proof of Willem's misdeeds. He said . . . that if I ever decided to turn Willem in, I could ask you for help getting back on my feet."

Kyra stared at Darylene, unable to respond.

*Someday I'll call in a favor from you, and I'll hold you to it.*

So he'd decided that Kyra was the best person to help Darylene. Kyra supposed he was right. Compared to Bacchus or even Rand, she was the one most likely to see Darylene safely off to a new life.

"I'll need some time to make arrangements and call in some favors," said Kyra. "But I'll see it done. Come back in three days, and we can talk further."

Darylene took Kyra's hands and squeezed them. "Thank you," she said.

Kyra looked down, wondering if Darylene had any idea how deeply Kyra's distaste for her had run before. "Thank you for what you did," said Kyra. "Who knows where the city would be now if you hadn't come forward."

"I should have done so earlier, but I didn't have the courage." Darylene paused. "I know you must hate him, but Willem was kind to me. I'm not sure I can say I loved him, but I respected him. He was a proud man, with a vision for Forge to be a beacon to the surrounding cities. Willem had the kind of ambition and foresight that few men ever dreamed of, much less acted on." Darylene's gaze went distant for a moment. "But James was persuasive when we spoke. Eventually, I realized I couldn't stay silent."

"He was a very persuasive man," said Kyra.

"Did you . . . know James well?" Darylene asked. "I got the impression that he was a hard man to know."

"I don't think he revealed much of himself to anyone," said Kyra. She once again heard James's whispered words. *Choose your fight.* And Kyra felt something in her chest. Not quite grief, but not far from it either. "James kept his secrets close, and we didn't always agree. But I learned much from him."

Kyra's injuries continued to heal. As the weather grew warmer, she became able to move around without a cane. She almost had a normal stride now, though larger steps pained her, as did the few hours before a coming storm. She experimented a bit with running, but her hip had a troublesome tendency to lock up unexpectedly, forcing her to react quickly to keep from tumbling to the ground.

At Flick's and Idalee's insistence, she didn't try to climb, though as the months passed, she grew restless. Finally, one warm morning when Lettie had gone into the forest and Idalee had gone to the market, Kyra paused while sweeping the doorstep and found herself gazing longingly at the overhanging eave of her roof. She looked around one more time, assuring herself that there was no one nearby, and then jumped for it. She missed by quite a distance—it would have been a stretch even in her uninjured days. But there was always the windowsill, which she climbed by leading with her left leg. From there, it was a precarious moment as she jumped again for the overhang, but this time her fingers caught, and she pulled herself over.

She straightened to her full height and couldn't help but grin. A light breeze blew through her hair, and she turned her face to enjoy the sun.

She walked a leisurely circle around the edge of the roof. Flick would have scolded her, but she knew she could catch herself if she stumbled. After one loop, she climbed to the top and walked along the ridgeline, pausing a few times to readjust her balance when her hip locked. But she didn't fall, and she felt lighter than she had in a long time. Finally, she decided it was enough climbing for the day. Kyra settled down next to the chimney and watched the road. It was a crisp morning, and only the occasional farmer or horseman passed by. She'd been up there almost an hour when she recognized the next person coming down the bend.

It took her a while to be sure it was Tristam. He'd been gone the past couple of months. As soon as Edlan retreated and peace with the Makvani became likely, Lord Brancel had called Tristam home to help rebuild the damage from the Demon Rider attacks. In addition to helping his family, there was another reason for him to leave court for a while. The Council had stripped Tristam of his knighthood for two more years as punishment for disobeying Rollan's orders, and his absence gave the resultant gossip some time to settle down.

As Tristam came closer, his eyes locked on her roof, and he smiled and waved. Kyra waved back.

He came to a stop at the corner of the house. "How's the breeze up there?" he asked.

"Quite nice," said Kyra. She made her way to the edge and lowered herself down, making sure to land on her good leg. He caught her in a big embrace as soon as she touched the ground, and she squeezed him tightly back.

"Are you returned for good now?" she asked.

"Yes," he said. "I've done about all I can back at Brancel."

Kyra pulled back and looked him over. "Home life has agreed with you. You're looking rather handsome." It was true. The shadows that had weighed him down over the past months had lifted, and his eyes were bright. And though he'd lost some weight over the stressful winter, the time at Brancel had filled out his chest and shoulders again.

Tristam's mouth quirked, and his gaze drifted over Kyra's face in a way that made her stomach tingle. "You're looking very well yourself."

Kyra invited him in and offered him tea and a piece of the cake Idalee had baked that morning. The girl's cooking was rivaling Bella's these days.

"Things are much better at the manor," he told Kyra as they sat down at her table. "There's still the occasional raid from the rebellious Demon Rider, but the number has dropped enough so that our family can handle the defense."

"That's good to hear," said Kyra. "And your family, they are well and safe?"

"They are all well," he said. "Henril will be returning to his post in the border patrols. Lorne will stay with Father a while longer." He hesitated for a moment. "I . . . sent a message to Lord Salis in Parna with my regrets. Lady Cecile is a beautiful, intelligent, and amiable woman, but I do not think we would make a good match."

Kyra had been drinking her tea, and she was grateful she

had an excuse not to look at Tristam. She took a long sip while she composed herself behind the mug. "Will they take offense?" she asked.

"The family was not pleased, since we'd spent so much time on the negotiations, though my most recent demotion did make me a less favorable match." He gave a wry smile. "Apparently, even Parnan families care about court reputation if it gets bad enough. As for Cecile..." And here he paused. "I didn't know her well, but I think she might be happy for me. I can only wish her the best."

Kyra wrapped her mug in her hands. It threatened to scald her skin, but she was too distracted to mind. "So that gives you some respite, then, before your da and your ma start thinking about another match for you."

This time it was his turn to look down. He'd eaten his whole piece of cake, and he stirred the crumbs with his fork. "I've been speaking to them about other matches. They've always been reasonable on the subject of marriage, and now that our manor is no longer under direct attack, they were happy to hear my thoughts. We've talked about the new peace agreement with the Demon Riders. We're hopeful that even if things don't go completely smoothly from here on out, there might at least be some basis for coexisting." He paused, and when he spoke again, it was with the expression of a man scaling a cliff without a safety rope. "I... mentioned to them that it might be good, though perhaps unconventional, to think about a match with one of their number."

Kyra let go of her mug and wiped her damp hands on her trousers. Her heart beat strange rhythms against her rib cage.

"Well, don't set your sights on Adele," she said. Her voice didn't sound like her own. "Flick is a decent brawler, even if he doesn't have a knight's training."

Tristam smiled at that, though his eyes were still uncertain. "No, I don't have my sights set on Adele."

It would have been easier to continue teasing him, but as Kyra met his eyes, she found it hard even to breathe, much less say anything clever. "I see..."

She swallowed, but it didn't make her mouth any less dry. A long moment of silence stretched between them. Bits of birdsong drifted in through the windows, and still neither of them spoke.

Tristam cleared his throat. "I'm not asking you to marry me right away, of course. I mean, I've been gone a while, and with everything that has happened...I just thought...well..." He laughed at himself then, and put his fork down to take a deep breath and pull himself together. When he spoke again, his voice was calm but strong. "I love you, Kyra. You know that, don't you? And I'd fight for a future for us, if you'll have me."

What a difference a few words made. The cottage itself seemed to hold its breath, waiting for her reply. "And what about what I am?" she asked quietly. "Would you tie yourself to someone like me?"

Tristam rubbed his jaw. The bruise was gone, but Kyra would always remember striking him there. "I've seen you struggle with your bloodlines, and I will always have tremendous respect for what you can do." He stopped and looked her in the eye. "I also trust you with my life. I hope you can do the same with me."

He spoke the words with conviction, and Kyra found that she believed him. How things had changed since their first encounter, when he'd tackled her in the Palace courtyard. She'd been a common thief, and he had been dead set on destroying her. Kyra reached over and covered his hands with her own. "I do trust you."

They smiled at each other then and stood up at the same time. The table was still between them. Tristam started to walk around to her side, but she stopped him with a touch on the arm. The table's height had caught her eye. Kyra kicked off her shoes and hoisted herself up. She had to put more weight on her arms to accommodate her hip, but she jumped up quickly without knocking any dishes to the ground. From there, it was just a short hop to land in front of Tristam. He ringed her waist with his arms, his touch setting off a pleasant shiver that swept to the tips of her toes. Tristam looked down at her, amused.

She shrugged. "I'm still getting a feel for what I can do."

"And was that a difficult climb, master thief?"

She wrapped her arms around him and pulled him close. He was wonderfully warm. "Horribly difficult, but worth it."

Tristam bent his face down toward hers then, and she closed her eyes. Her skin prickled at his nearness, and she let out a contented sigh. Then, after what seemed like forever, his lips brushed hers, and they put off the rest of their talking until later.

## ACKNOWLEDGMENTS

Whisper the word "sequel" into a debut author's ear and she'll likely jump five feet into the air and flee wild-eyed into a corner. Writing *Daughter of Dusk* was a very different experience from *Midnight Thief*, as I made the transition from writing for my own enjoyment to delivering a book under contract while my newfound (and wonderful) readers waited in the wings. Thankfully, I had a fantastic team of people steering me safely into port.

My editor, Rotem Moscovich, shepherded this manuscript from early outlines to final draft, providing insightful guidance the entire way. Julie Moody, Jamie Baker, and the rest of the team at Hyperion were instrumental to the process as well.

My agent, Jim McCarthy, kept me sane and assured me, time after time, that each draft was not as horrible as I believed.

My longtime critique group, Courtyard Critiques, offered encouragement and suggestions on my first draft as it came out, three thousand words at a time: Amitha Knight, Rachal Aronson, Jennifer Barnes, and Emily Terry.

First-round beta readers kindly slogged through the original (boring) beginning and offered key insights for restructuring every plot arc: Lauren James (*Love is not a triangle*), Andrea Lim (jukeboxmuse.com), Anya (*On Starships and Dragonwings*), Stephenie Sheung (*The BiblioSanctum*), Tabitha Jensen (notyetread.com), Summer McDaniel (*Blue Sky Shelf*), Alyssa Susanna (*The Eater of Books!*), and Maja (*The Nocturnal Library*).

Second-round beta readers pushed me to polish every scene and campaigned (successfully) for more sparks between Kyra and Tristam: Faye M. (*The Social Potato*), Jenna DeTrapani, April Choi, Amy Hung, Lianne Crawford, Emily Lo Gibson, Bekah (*Awesome Book Nuts*), Kelsey Olesen, and Lisa Choi, MD.

Thanks to several authors' loops for wisdom and laughs: The Fourteenery, One Four Kidlit, and YA Binders.

And of course, love and gratitude to my husband for being a (captive) sounding board on everything from plot ideas to copy edits (and, to his credit, he was only slightly insufferable when his grammar or vocabulary proved better than mine), and my parents, in-laws, extended family, and friends for their constant excitement and support on this journey. You make a girl feel loved.

## ABOUT THE AUTHOR

JOHN TIPPLE is Professor of History at California State College at Los Angeles. He previously taught at Stanford where he received his Ph.D. degree. He is the author of THE NEW ORDER: ALEXANDER HAMILTON AND THOMAS JEFFERSON and THE PROBLEMS OF PROGRESS: ANDREW CARNEGIE AND HENRY GEORGE.

Professor Tipple is writing a four-volume work, THE PRAGMATIC NATION: A HISTORY OF AMERICAN SOCIAL THOUGHT SINCE 1865, of which CRISIS OF THE AMERICAN DREAM is the first published volume.

c

JOHN ord TIPPLE

# Crisis of the American Dream

## A History of American Social Thought
## 1920 – 1940

PEGASUS/NEW YORK

HN
64
.T56

# Foreword

Within the compass of four volumes, *The Pragmatic Nation: A History of American Social Thought Since 1865,* I have attempted to give an account of the important ideas which have influenced the political, economic, and social development of modern America. In choosing the readings in these volumes I have not been greatly concerned with literary values but have tried to treat of ideas in their meaningful social context, making my selections solely on the basis of their intrinsic worth as clear and valid expressions of the dominant ideas of the time. The main divisions of the study reflect major changes in the outlook and material framework of American society. Volume I, *The Great Money Machine,* begins after the Civil War and follows the evolution of the United States from a simple agricultural and commercial society to an industrial economy created by and ideologically dependent upon the findings of nineteenth-century science. Volume II, *The Capitalist Revolution,* is concerned with the overthrow of the established system and practices of individualistic capitalism by the organized power of corporate capitalism and with the pragmatic revolt against traditionalism that followed in its wake. The present volume, *Crisis of the American Dream,* third in historical sequence, carries the account through the boom days of the twenties and the depression-ridden thirties, marking the collapse of the business order and the faltering emergence of the welfare state. Volume IV, *The Paradox of Power*, considers the contemporary conflict between the individual and the organization and the search for assurance in a technological society.

The task of measuring the historical significance of ideas is an extremely difficult one. Perhaps the most vexing question for the historian to answer is: What portion of the public was moved by and won for a particular idea? Yet ideas have consequences, and this pragmatic consideration has been my chief criterion. As Justice Holmes observed, "Every idea is an incitement. It offers itself for belief and if believed it is acted upon." Important ideas are consequential ideas, whether they come from politicians or professors, businessmen or philosophers. The active American mind has never been confined to the genteel tradition of academies but has taken ideas wherever it found them, from the market place as well as the lecture hall. The historian, being a product of his time, faces the additional danger of reading into history the ideas and opinions of a later day. In this sense, there is considerable truth in Voltaire's witticism: "History is only a pack of tricks we play on the dead." The best defense against playing such tricks on the dead is to let the living speak for themselves, as I have tried to do by introducing contemporary writing within the historical context of the time.

Essentially history is concerned with the dialectical struggle between persistence and change, between the old and the new. For every accepted idea there are always a host of challengers or rival "truths" competing for acceptance at any given time in history. Therefore, to bring into this study a genuine sense of historical dynamism, I have endeavored to follow the example of history itself by presenting with every dominant idea a counter-idea which, if not its direct antithesis, offers another point of view. To capture the authentic flavor of the times, the major issues are documented by excerpts from contemporary writings which follow each section and which are indicated by an asterisk at the appropriate point in the text. By giving the losing as well as the winning side and by allowing the proponents to speak for themselves, I have sought to avoid the dishonest practice of presenting the regnant American ideology as a homogeneous body of unchallengeable "truths" resting upon the nearly unanimous consent of history.

I am, of course, heavily indebted to the critical historians and the many students of American society who have enabled me to build upon their careful research. Especially am I indebted to my wife, Edith, for practical and spiritual aid and to John Jensen of Pegasus for invaluable editorial advice.

J.T.

*Santa Barbara, June 4, 1967*

# Table of Contents

ix

CHAPTER FOUR: The Materialistic Faith, 221

CHAPTER FIVE: Liberalism and Democracy, 275

# Introduction

Since colonial days, Americans had boasted that man would find, and in this country had largely found, the good life that was denied to the antiquated and corrupt nations of the old world. Although poverty had proved to be the all-pervasive fact of history, its reality never had been truly accepted by good Americans who, as the fortunate possessors of a new land with unlimited natural wealth, held to the stubborn belief that the right of all Americans to share, and to share increasingly, in the gains of industry and progress was sanctioned by higher law.

This vision of America as a materialistic heaven on earth where man could realize his highest aspirations amid abundance had become, by the 1920's, an indispensable part of the American dream. A kind of "virtuous materialism," the American dream envisaged the establishment of a new order of universal prosperity which would not corrupt but would energize the soul, freeing man for higher and finer things. That was why, as Tocqueville remarked, every new method that led by a shorter road to wealth, every machine that spared labor, every invention that diminished the cost of production, every discovery that facilitated pleasures or added to comforts, seemed to Americans to be the grandest effort of the human intellect. That was why, also, wide-awake Americans in the twenties with their automobiles, radios, vacuum cleaners, telephones,

13

bathtubs, subways, steam shovels, tractors, and automatic lathes believed universal prosperity was an accomplished fact. For ten thousand years mankind had been struggling toward this materialistic Eden, and only in the United States did the goal appear in sight.

The American outlook was dominated by the youthful dream that anybody could become a millionaire. Widespread stories of fabulous fortunes made overnight in stocks or real estate so excited the normal desire to get rich quick that most Americans, along with President Hoover, were convinced the end of the rainbow was just around the corner. At the height of prosperity, the *Ladies Home Journal* ran an article by John J. Raskob, a General Motors executive, entitled "Everybody Ought to Be Rich," and nearly everyone tried. Money-mad Americans feverishly chased the elusive dollar from Wall Street to the Florida swamplands, trying everything from advertising to bootlegging, selling anything from "The Skin You Love to Touch" to a happy life in Christ, always hoping in the end to "put it over" by promising much and giving little.

Then, with terrible suddenness, the Wall Street crash of 1929 and the ensuing depression turned the dream of universal prosperity into a horrible nightmare. Americans woke from their patriotic slumbers to find themselves in a stricken land of empty factories and idle machines where fear vanquished hope, and hunger and poverty stalked the streets. The national quest no longer was the high-flown pursuit of millions but the down-to-earth demand for a job and enough to eat. The temper of the disillusioned thirties was no less materialistic, perhaps more so, but it was more realistic. Where the American of the 1920's innocently pursued a private materialistic heaven, trusting his extravagant hopes to the unfailing beneficence of providence, his more worldly counterpart ten years later faced the cold-hearted reality of depression and tried by rational means to achieve collective security here and now.

Essentially the conflict of these years was over the nature of the good society. In the twenties the contest was between the victorious supporters of "normalcy" and social reformers fighting for equal rights. In the thirties, with positions now reversed, the debate was between the triumphant political activists of the New Deal and disinherited individualists united in bitter resistance to the general welfare state. These conflicting points of view ran like contrapuntal themes through both decades and were a distinctly American version of the eternal struggle between those who accept and support the status quo and those who are critical of the existing order and advocate change.

Yet, though the specific problems were new, the issues were, for the most part, old. The battle cries had been sounded half a century before, and the battle lines drawn during the Progressive era. The individualistic rhetoric of the defenders of the economic system and the critics of the New Deal was drawn from the doctrines of nineteenth-century liberalism. Though almost totally irrelevant to the modern technological economy, the habits of mind and action of the earlier period still persisted and operated to retard social change in the interests of a narrowly construed economic liberty. Not that those who accepted the existing state of things in the twenties were completely opposed to progress, rather they envisaged progress as continuous technological change taking place in an immutable social order. Similarly, the fighting faith of their opponents—the parlor liberals of the twenties and the militant New-Dealers of the thirties—could be traced to late nineteenth- and early twentieth-century critics of laissez-faire who believed human advancement demanded social change to meet the unforeseen exigencies of technical progress. Their belief that liberal democratic values could be achieved in a complex industrial society only by practical state action had been advanced earlier by Henry George, Lester Ward, Simon Patten, Herbert Croly, and Walter Weyl.

Although the New Deal was collectivist rather than individualistic in temper and national instead of local in terms of action, its programs and theories had been largely worked out in the past. The acceptance and regulation of big business called for by Theodore Roosevelt's New Nationalism reappeared in the National Industrial Recovery Act, while the antitrust point of view of Woodrow Wilson's New Freedom emerged once again in the Public Utilities Holding Company Act and the Temporary National Economic Committee. But, though borrowing from the two major strains of Progressivism, the interventionist program of the New Deal owed much more to Hamiltonian mercantilism and to its modern manifestation during World War I. The wartime experience of economic mobilization provided not only the example for many of the emergency agencies but also the democratic rationale for fighting the depression. Hoover's Reconstruction Finance Corporation, for example, was frankly modeled after the War Finance Corporation, just as Roosevelt's National Recovery Administration rested squarely on the example of the War Industries Board. Both Presidents, moreover, employed the metaphor of war to mobilize public opinion for government intervention in the economy. In short, the New Deal like its more modest predecessor was in its methods and aims a traditional answer to a radical dilemma.

As long as Americans had believed they were able to fulfill their ideal of the good life merely by keeping intact their political institutions and by the selfish pursuit of private ends, their allegiance to the achievement of a better American future had been, as Herbert Croly once suggested, more a matter of words than deeds. But Americans of the twenties who had looked upon democracy merely as the end product of mass production and had confidently expected ethical rejuvenation as a by-product of prosperity found themselves in the thirties confronted by an overproduction of things and a shortage of values. With a deep sense of national failure, they discovered they must, as a nation, redefine their faith and give it democratic shape and intelligent direction. The American dream was no longer to be propagated merely by words—it was to be fulfilled not by more economic freedom but by a measure of social discipline, not by greater trust in immutable laws but by more confidence in the ability of Americans to control what they had created.

# The Businessman
# and the Politician

I

America in the 1920's belonged to the businessman. Literally and spiritually, the businessman owned the country. "There is no doubt," rejoiced *Nation's Business*, the organ of the United States Chamber of Commerce, "that the American business man is the foremost hero of the American people today." Amid booming prosperity, the head of the Chamber's civic development department proudly proclaimed the American businessman to be "the most influential person in the nation . . . perhaps the most influential figure in the world." From across the ocean the London *Times* and other European journals confirmed the claim, applauding American industry for raising up "a race of supermen."[1]

If the businessman had "made good," the politician was in disgrace. After all of President Wilson's lofty moralizing, the results had been profoundly disappointing to the American people. The "peace," even more than the war, had been a disillusionment. Even those who had believed in the war were appalled by a peace which promised merely a lull of temporary exhaustion and of preparation for more destructive and futile wars to come. The League of Nations, at best, seemed to offer only mocking hopes of avoiding new wars, and after endless wrangling between the President and Congress, it had become a pumped-up issue the people were tired of hearing about. As a consequence, those Americans who had entrusted their dreams of a better world to soldiers and politicians felt hopelessly betrayed and deluded. Their disenchantment with the politician was cruelly manifested by "poor Woodrow's astounding unpopularity," a dramatic reversal of public opinion which startled even the cynical Henry L. Mencken, the popular wit of the day. The President, Mencken observed, had come from Paris in 1919 "ranking with the master-minds of the ages" and then, less than a year later, was regarded by everyone save a few fanatics as "a devious and foolish fellow, whom the nation will be well rid of on March 4."[2]

The default of political leadership was declared by *American Industries,* speaking for the National Association of Manufacturers, to be "the one conspicuous failure of American life." As *Nation's Business* reminded its readers, it was because of the inability of the politician to meet the needs of society that the businessman now occupied "a position of leadership which the business man had never held before." The coming age was his, but the businessman was warned that "he was on trial" and, like his political predecessor in leadership, must expect to answer for his stewardship.[3]

While politics had seemingly degenerated, American business had made conspicuous progress. For about two years before the United States declared war against Germany, American industry had begun to prosper by the sale of goods to the European belligerents. Profits were enormous, for the hard-pressed Allies were ready to pay virtually whatever the producers asked. As sole purchasing agent for Great Britain and France, J. P. Morgan & Company ladled out billions of dollars in war orders to great American manufacturing corporations. Within three months, for instance, Bethlehem Steel received two huge orders, one for $83 million and another for $63 million, and the profits of United States Steel jumped from $76 million in 1912–1914 to $478 million in 1917.[4] Because of such tremendous profits, American capitalism, which had always been Europe's debtor, emerged from the war as the world's greatest creditor.

The twenties likewise proved to be very good years for business. After a short postwar depression, production, profits, and consumption rose spectacularly. Although there was a virtually permanent depression in agriculture and considerable unemployment in some distressed mining and manufacturing areas, dividends and real wages were high and rising. True, the richer were getting richer much faster than the poor were getting less poor, but the *average* level of living in the United States was undoubtedly the highest in the world. The federal budget showed a surplus year after year, and the federal debt was steadily reduced. As stock prices rocketed skyward in 1929, it appeared to the casual observer that America was on the way to becoming the richest nation in history, and credit for this booming prosperity went to the businessman.

Powerful and unashamed, the American businessman acknowledged the tribute and, basking in popular adulation, forgot that not many years before he had been held up to public scorn as a capitalist villain and robber baron. Good times brought forgiveness. Business was entering a new era, said the Chicago *Daily News*: "the period of prosecution and restriction is over."[5] Business was taking charge of the country, business was running the world, but, as a writer in *Harper's* observed, business had changed; it was not the same as thirty, twenty, or even ten years ago. "The world is becoming spiritualized. Business shows it." As faith in business as a way of life spread throughout the country, the belief flourished that the businessman "can do what governments cannot." Business was exalted as the chief instrument of society, and government was relegated to an inferior role. "Who are the managers of the United States in these days?" asked *Life* magazine. "Who take care of undertakings that they think are necessary and put them through? Who but the managers of the industrial enterprises of the country?" On the basis of actual performance— its contribution to the well-being of society—business was adjudged the most important institution of America.[6]

Among Americans the feeling grew that the central institutions of society were economic rather than political. Unlike government, it was argued, economic institutions wielded power primarily over things rather than people; therefore, economic power was less oppressive and more democratic than political power ever could be. True democracy, the readers of *Nation's Business* were told, was thus economic rather than political: "The 'voters' are the people who spend money for goods. Their dollars are their votes. By the aid of prices the people 'elect' the producers who will serve them; they also 'elect' the kinds of goods to be made and the amount of employment for the wage earners. By the aid of prices the people decide what industries shall have capital; they determine who will make profits and who shall go 'broke.'" Since suffrage was universal under economic democracy—insofar as the individual's dollars were his votes—the power of business was not to be feared because in actuality "the people organize and direct the whole business and industrial system." From this argument it followed logically that government was not even a "necessary evil" but an unnecessary extravagance. So appealing was this point of view to the editors of *American Industries* that they quoted the praiseful article from *Life* with added emphasis, answering affirmatively the question: "*Are we approaching a millennium in which visible government will not be necessary and in which the job of running the world will slip away from obstructive politicians and be taken over by men trained in the shop?*" Thus, it would

appear, American businessmen shared with Karl Marx the
hopeful expectation that government would eventually
wither away.[7]

If, as the businessman insisted, the main institutions of
society were economic rather than political, then there was
little or no room for either the politician or the political
party. "The professional agitator or politician can hardly
be expected to know where business is striving to get as
well as business itself." Not only did the direction of business affairs require an expertise that no politician could
be expected to have, but there was also a marked disparity
in the comparative capacities of the businessman and the
politician. Put bluntly, businessmen had "better ability and
philosophy" and were "more useful than writers, soap box
orators, politicians and statesmen." Since the beginning of
the industrial period, about 1870—it was explained in *American Industries*—"the men of real ability in the United States
have devoted their time, their energy, and their money to
the pursuit of wealth." Business experience itself, as James
Prothro has pointed out, was thought also to exert an ele-
vating influence which enhanced this original superiority:
first, by bringing out "the best side of a man"; second, by
implanting a tolerance toward "the weaknesses of their
fellow men"; third, by developing a realistic outlook free
from sentimentality.[8]

## II

By comparison, politicians as a class were deemed an
unsavory lot. As most businessmen saw it, politics was the
sort of occupation that appealed to "men who would rather
agitate than work" and so attracted "a distinctly cheap
and parasitic class." Consequently, though success was the
only criterion of ability in business, the opposite was true
in politics. Unlike business, the political experience was
regarded as essentially degrading. Instead of bringing out
the best side of a man, it brought out the worst, for suc-

cess in politics meant demagoguery, the unprincipled courting of popular favor; instead of cultivating a tolerance of
the weaknesses of men, politics preyed upon them; instead
of inculcating a realistic outlook, it encouraged a maudlin
sentimentality which distorted "the simple facts of life"
and subverted whatever habits of thrift, common sense,
and economy the people naturally had.[9] Apparently the
businessman's low estimate of the politician was shared
by most Americans in the 1920's. When a reporter asked
students, "How many of you are going into politics?" the
question brought instantly the most derisive of laughs.
Though there might be excuses for the bootlegger and gang-
ster, the politician seemed to be the only man in America
for whom no legitimate defense could be made.[10]

If the politician was scorned, the political party was
dreaded. To businessmen, the political party, being nothing
more than a gang of self-seeking incompetents, displayed
all the vices of the individual politician writ large, plus
an infinitely greater capacity to inflict damage. As for the
business and financial world, said the *Wall Street Journal*,
"The less it has to do with politics, the better it is pleased."
With the common run of politicians, the president of the
National Association of Manufacturers told fellow industrialists, "it has ceased to be a question of what is good for
the country, what is American, or what is constitutional.
It is rather what is best for the party and for his own political self-perpetuation."[11] If government dominated by
political groups was incapable of "broad, sound national
policies," no group was more obviously dedicated to the
public interest than American business. Said the president
of the Chamber of Commerce, "The individual welfare of
all the people is wrapped up today as never before in a
proper understanding· and proper relationship between
government and business."[12]

To business leaders, the "proper relationship" between
business and government meant simply that the direction
of America should be in the hands of its most successful

institution. Organized business should replace the political party as the force directing the machinery of government. For the maximum benefit of all of the people, government need only respond to business views expressed "without color or self-interest," and the proper relationship would be automatically established. As announced at the National Association of Manufacturers' convention of 1920, "The crying need of the hour" was "a business government for a business people."[13]

And then, almost magically, out of the darkness and chaos of politics came Warren G. Harding with the right answer. "This is essentially a business country," said the Republican presidential candidate. "That is why we need business sense in charge of American administration." Instead of concerning himself with the "impossible democracy" of Wilson, President Harding declared the aim of his administration was to "get back to the methods of business." Harding's willingness to accept business ideas as his own was matched and even exceeded by his successor in the White House, Calvin Coolidge. Where the more loquacious Harding had said, "The business of America is the business of everybody in America," Coolidge with typical Yankee bluntness went straight to the point, saying, "The business of America is business."[14] The perfect coincidence of Coolidge's views with those of business led the *Wall Street Journal* to comment: "Never before, here or anywhere else, has a government been so completely fused with business."[15]

Although Coolidge was rightly regarded as "the businessman's president," he was still a politician by trade, and not until the election of Herbert Hoover in 1928 did the old dream of "a businessman in the White House" approach complete realization. As *Nation's Business* noted with enthusiasm, "Mr. Hoover, the engineer in politics, is a business man—plus." Like Harding and Coolidge, Hoover showed during the campaign that he had a "proper understanding" of the "proper relationship" between government and business by lauding "the wise policies" of his Republican predecessors which had "introduced a new basis in government." His election, both the *Nation* and the *New Republic* grudgingly conceded, marked the conversion of the vast majority of Americans to the political creed of the businessman. "The historical role of Mr. Hoover is apparently to try the experiment of seeing what business can do when given the steering wheel. Mr. Hoover insists that there should be a steering wheel, but he will also let business do the driving." With Hoover politics was an adjunct of business, and he was thoroughly convinced there were virtually no limits to the progress that could be obtained through the understanding cooperation of government in business.[16]

"We in America today," Herbert Hoover said confidently on the eve of his election in 1928, "are nearer to the final triumph over poverty than ever before in the history of any land. The poorhouse is vanishing from among us. We have not yet reached the goal, but, given a chance to go forward with the policies of the last eight years, we shall soon with the help of God be in sight of the day when poverty will be banished from this nation."[17]

# III

President Hoover had been in the White House only seven months when the business and financial world was shaken by the greatest stock-market crash in history. In a few devastating weeks thirty billion dollars disappeared in thin air, and with it vanished the American dream of unending prosperity. Not only did millions of investors lose their lifetime savings overnight, but thousands of banks and corporations, which only weeks before had seemed as sound as bedrock, were forced into bankruptcy and crashed like a great avalanche down the Main Street of every city and town in America sweeping smaller businesses before them. Debts mounted, purchases dropped, factories shut down, workers lost their jobs, wages and prices were slashed. Farmers, already hard hit, were unable to meet their debts and faced mortgage foreclosures. As the depression deepened, national income fell to almost half the level of 1929, unemployment climbed steadily upward, and across the nation tattered breadlines became a permanent feature in city streets.

For the average American the widespread loss of employment was beyond doubt the most conspicuous disaster of the Great Depression. As ex-President Coolidge sagely remarked at the time, "When more and more people are thrown out of work, unemployment results." [18] Immediately after the stock-market crash in the fall of 1929 unemployment was said to have jumped in two weeks from 700,000 to 3,100,000. By 1933, when Hoover left the presidency, the mounting flood of joblessness had reached fifteen million, and one out of every three wage or salary earners in the United States was totally without work. Of course, this proportion was not evenly distributed throughout the country. Some areas were much harder hit than others. For example, in 1932 it was reported that in a small town in southern Illinois only two persons of the population of 1350 had jobs. Nor did unemployment figures account for those working only part time or those who were self-employed but without any income.

Statistics, however, are bloodless and unable to convey the incalculable human cost of unemployment. Enforced idleness not only destroyed purchasing power, but broke the spirits of once industrious and resourceful Americans, undermined their health, and robbed them of self-respect. Once meager savings were depleted, debts piled up, rents or mortgages went unpaid, and families were turned into the streets. The situation of millions of jobless Americans was summed up by the report of the California Unemployment Commission:

Many households have been dissolved; little children parceled out to friends, relatives, or charitable homes; husbands and wives, parents and children separated, temporarily or permanently. Homes in which life savings were invested and hopes bound up have been lost never to be recovered. Men, young and old, have taken to the road. They sleep each night in a new flophouse. Day after day the country over, they stand in the breadlines for food which carries with it the suggestion "move on, we don't want you." In spite of the unpalatable stew and the comfortless flophouses, the army of homeless grows alarmingly. Existing accommodations fail to shelter the homeless; jails must be opened to lodge honest job-hunters. Destitution reaches the women and children. New itinerant types develop: "women vagrants" and "juvenile transients." There are no satisfactory methods of dealing with these thousands adrift. Precarious ways of existing, questionable methods of "getting by" rapidly develop. The law must step in and brand as criminals those who have neither desire nor inclination to violate accepted standards of society.[19]

Even for those who had not joined the "migration of despair" and were listed as "employed" there was little security or hope for the future. To a fortunate few one manufacturing company in Detroit paid men ten cents and women four cents an hour; while others not so lucky stood on street corners shining shoes or peddling apples in the shivering cold.

For these millions of bewildered and disillusioned Americans there was little hope of relief. After several months of depression neither private charity nor local government could begin to cope with the widespread poverty and hunger. Washington offered no help, for President Hoover firmly believed that relief was the responsibility of state and local government only. Federal relief, he told distressed Americans, would destroy "character" and strike at "the roots of self-government." Not until the summer of 1932, after three bitter winters of depression, did Hoover consent to any federal relief action. In the meantime, bleak settlements known ironically as "Hoovervilles" sprang up all across the country in vacant lots and on the outskirts of cities. "Anyone who wants actually to see civilization creaking," the *New Yorker* reported in the spring of 1932, "will do well to visit the corner of West and Spring Streets. . . . There is a whole village of shacks and huts there, made of packing boxes, barrel staves, pieces of corrugated iron, and whatever else the junkman doesn't want, and the people who live there do so because the New York Central hasn't gotten around to driving them off." [20]

Without adequate clothing, shelter, or food, human suffering reached tragic proportions. In the rural communities of West Virginia, where distress was intense, Quakers providing relief weighed undernourished children and fed only those who were more than ten percent underweight; in New York City in 1931 there were ninety-five deaths from starvation. While one family lived for weeks on flour and water paste, others hunted the garbage cans of their more affluent neighbors. "One vivid, gruesome moment of those dark days we shall never forget," wrote a shocked reporter, describing conditions in Chicago in the late spring of 1932. "We saw a crowd of some fifty men fighting over a barrel of garbage which had been set outside the back door of a restaurant. American citizens fighting for scraps of food like animals!" In other parts of the country there were "hunger riots" in which several hundred unemployed men and women raided grocery stores, smashing plate glass windows and helping themselves to meat and canned goods.[21]

Despair reached a peak in the summer of 1932 when some twenty thousand homeless, penniless veterans descended on Washington, D.C. Gathering spontaneously from all over the nation, jobless ex-soldiers hitch-hiked, "road the rods," or came in old jalopies to lobby for passage of a veterans' bonus bill. At first Washington tolerated the Bonus Army, allowing them to set up a makeshift community or "Hooverville" within sight of the White House; but after the bill failed in the Senate and many veterans stayed

The crisis of one American's dream—no money, no work, no hope. For millions like him the great depression was a personal tragedy. With no way out, job gone or business bankrupt, the once industrious and resourceful citizen who had always earned his own way lost faith in himself and society.

---

on—having no place to go—President Hoover called out the U.S. Army to disperse them. Under command of General Douglas MacArthur and his aide, Major Dwight D. Eisenhower, the troops attacked with tanks and tear gas, driving thousands of unarmed veterans and their wives and children before them and setting fire to the ramshackle huts. There was virtually no resistance, but two veterans were shot to death, two policemen received fractured skulls, a bystander was shot in the shoulder, a veteran's ear was severed by a cavalry saber and another veteran was bayoneted in the hip, a dozen persons were injured by bricks and clubs, and more than a thousand gassed. On the next day reporters were told that "the President was pleased," but public reaction was shock and dismay.[22]

IV

Something was gravely wrong in America. There was poverty amid plenty, hunger in the midst of abundance, and hopelessness in a land of boundless opportunity. Homeless people slept in doorways or on park benches while houses and warm apartments sat empty. In the cities people starved in the shadow of bulging warehouses; in the country farmers burned great piles of wheat and slaughtered surplus cows, hogs, sheep, leaving the carcasses for the buzzards. Broken, spiritless men, jobless for two or three years, huddled in dreary lines before soup kitchens and stared mutely at the ghostly factories whose dusty, unmanned machines were capable of producing shoes, clothes, all the countless things they needed so desperately. "Society," Alfred Kazin remarked, "was no longer a comfortable abstraction, but a series of afflictions." America in depression presented such a melancholy spectacle to the world that, in 1931, natives of the Cameroons in West Africa sent over $3.77 for the relief of "the starving." Yet, by all counts, the United States was still the richest nation in the world— possessing abundant resources, unexcelled "know-how," a plentitude of skilled labor, and an unlimited capacity to produce.[23]

The devastating contrast between Hoover's promise in 1928 of two chickens in every pot and two cars in every garage and the hard actualities of unemployment, breadlines, and bankruptcies in 1932 forced Americans to take a new look at their economic system. Now for the first time they clearly saw serious flaws in the economy which hitherto had been overlooked or concealed by the brilliant razzle-dazzle of the stock market. The crash had not only exposed a heavily overloaded corporate structure capitalized on future prosperity a generation in advance, but also disclosed the fact that American business in the twenties had sheltered an exceptional number of promoters, grafters, swindlers, impostors, and frauds—an ethical phenomenon characterized by John Kenneth Galbraith as "a kind of flood tide of corporate larceny." Testimony before the U.S. Senate Committee on Banking and Currency brought to light "a shocking corruption in our banking system, a widespread repudiation of old-fashioned standards of honesty and fair-dealing in the creation and sale of securities, and a merciless exploitation of the vicious possibilities of intricate corporate chicanery." Samuel Insull, who had been celebrated as a "financial miracle-maker" and nationally respected as suzerain of a vast and labyrinthine utilities empire, had taken flight to escape criminal trial and left behind bewildered investors holding billions in worthless securities; and not long afterward, the president of the New York Stock Exchange, Richard Whitney, was convicted and sent to Sing Sing Prison for appropriating his clients' funds.[24]

Businessmen generally, however, refused to accept responsibility for the depression. While they had eagerly and proudly taken credit for prosperity, they blamed the depression upon impersonal forces beyond their control. In fact, business leaders tended to disclaim that there were any economic problems at all. In the face of widespread suffering, Andrew Mellon, one of the "biggest" of big businessmen, said, "I do not believe . . . there is anything fundamentally wrong with the social system." With the nation plunging into the worst depression in its history, the president of the National Association of Manufacturers assured hungry and jobless Americans that he saw nothing "to weaken the confidence of understanding minds in the essential parts of our American economic system." So-called "economic" problems, it was suggested, were "fundamentally moral problems," and could be more easily solved if approached with that understanding. Rather than engaging in misguided schemes of unemployment relief, the government was urged to address itself to the problem of crime. Obviously, as James Prothro remarked, the business community—

in alarm for its prestige and profits—had to a considerable extent lost contact with reality.[25]

Under these damaging circumstances, the stock of the American businessman fell to an all-time low. If in 1929 he had been at the pinnacle of popularity, by 1932 he was almost completely discredited. Distrusted, his prestige gone, the businessman sought a comfortless anonymity. "It is almost literally true," said *Christian Century*, "that, in the realm of industry and finance, there are no more big names." The general public no longer believed business leadership had any necessary relation to the general welfare. Where once the leader in corporate finance and industry had been superstitiously regarded as a kind of superman endowed with super-intelligence and preternatural shrewdness, now the businessman was described as "abysmally ignorant" and charged with seldom having troubled himself to understand the economic system under which he operated. How far down the road of disillusionment the American people had traveled since October, 1929, was unexpectedly revealed by the investment analyst and respected business authority, John Moody, who announced in 1932: "Today the superman superstition is a wreck; things have gone so far that even the supermen themselves have lost faith in their own wisdom and judgment; blunder after blunder has been their portion since 1927, and most of them have recently been throwing up their arms in despair. They are now admitting that they are just ordinary 'damned fools,' after all. And they are largely right, perhaps for the first time in their lives."[26]

Plainly the businessman's complacency had been shattered, and the "big men" of Wall Street and industry seemed as bewildered as anyone else. Most business leaders, Dun & Bradstreet found, were without plans and slow in discussing termination of the depression. Richard Whitney, head of the New York Stock Exchange, proposed leaving it to the law of supply and demand to right things, while the industrialist Harvey S. Firestone said that the application of the Golden Rule would bring revival. Walter P. Chrysler, auto magnate, urged American consumers—at least half of whom were broke, on relief, and unemployed—to "buy now," and Henry Ford offered tenuous consolation by declaring the slump to be "more wholesome" than false prosperity. Andrew Mellon, multimillionaire head of the Treasury under Coolidge and a business leader celebrated for his financial acumen, candidly admitted: "None of us has any means of knowing when and how we shall emerge from the valley of the depression." And Charles M. Schwab of Bethlehem Steel, who had been one of the clarion voices of prosperity, frankly confessed: "I'm afraid, every man is afraid."[27]

With business leadership bankrupt, the country turned again to the politician and government for a way out. The people seemed to have lost interest in business goals, but were showing a new interest in national economic planning. As some conservatives noted with alarm, there appeared to be a growing tendency to exalt the power of political action over economic conditions. Instead of an economic policy of no "dictation or interference by the Government with business" which Hoover had proudly announced to the Chamber of Commerce after the 1929 crash, the public and, astoundingly enough, the Chamber itself now favored cooperation under government control. Although the professional politician was still depreciated, the incoming Roosevelt administration brought a new group to Washington in 1933. The new politician, as W. M. Kiplinger of the well-known letter bureau noted, was a different breed. There was no average type; there were professors, lawyers, economists, an endless stream of "bright young men." Most had become politicians only recently, and the majority were amateurs at the business of governing. They were a new set of officials with a new set of ideas. Although the "brain trust," as the group of young intellectuals around the President were known, was composed of men with all sorts of theories, the guiding idea of this new political leadership, as one of them admitted, was "to make political power ascendant over business or economic power—perhaps temporarily, perhaps permanently." They were united in the belief that government must intervene directly and do something to relieve national distress. Since the business hierarchy was obviously not up to the task, government must take over.[28]

CHAPTER ONE

# Back to Normalcy

## I

After the Armistice of November, 1918, the earnest desire of millions of Americans was to pick up life where they had left off, to resume the old familiar pattern of living with as little interruption as possible. But, to their frustration, they found the way to the past blocked. War unsettles all things, and though the United States had escaped physical devastation, two years of contrived hate, calculated destruction, and mass murder had left the country in a state of emotional shell shock. The forces of war, world events, and new developments at home had all conspired to change America.

War, "the devil's answer to human progress," wrote William Allen White, had left America disorganized and demoralized. After the Armistice, war contracts had been abruptly canceled, production dropped precipitately, and thousands of workers in war industries were suddenly jobless. Reconversion of the country's vast industrial system to peacetime uses was left to chance, and the resulting economic instability and hardship was further complicated by the ill-timed dumping of some 4,000,000 ex-soldiers into the already burdened labor market. Abandoned by an ungrateful nation and turned out of the army to shift for themselves, embittered jobless veterans swelled the ranks of discontented Americans who stood helplessly by while wartime prosperity vanished in a cloud of upward spiraling prices. By late 1919 the purchasing power of the prewar dollar had shrunk from 100 to 45. Food costs had jumped 84 percent, clothing 114.5 percent, and furniture 125 percent. For the average American family the cost of living was 99 percent higher than it had been before the beginning of the war in 1914. Hardest hit were salaried people who were worse off than at any time since the Civil War. While the white-collar class struggled gamely, if vainly, against the rising cost of living, organized labor, which had made great gains during the war, fought to hold its position, demanding higher wages and going out on strike to get them. In 1919 alone there were 3600 strikes involving more than 4,000,000 workers. There seems little doubt that rampant inflation was behind much of the industrial unrest, and had the government made any attempt or shown any inclination to deal realistically with the economic instability caused by reconversion, demobilization, and inflation, widespread discontent might have been avoided. As it was, however, the Wilson administration—obsessed with the troubles of Europe—ignored social and economic difficulties at home. The result was that the social pressures building up finally erupted in an explosive series of bombings, riots, and lynchings which, along with strikes, convinced many frightened Americans that revolution was here. Bewildered and frustrated, the American people looked angrily for the devil and, not finding him, invented one—the Bolshevik.[1]

So began the great witch-hunt of 1919–1920. In part an escape from personal tensions, the Red Scare was chiefly a crowd manifestation, a carry-over of war-bred fears and passions into the problems of peace. As Wilson had predicted, war would brutalize America. "Once lead this people into war," he told the editor of the New York *World*, "and they'll forget there ever was such a thing as tolerance." Certainly, under leadership of the President, the government by rigid suppression of dissident opinion and by organized propaganda had done everything it could to inculcate hate, prejudice, and 100% Americanism on a massive scale. In the patriotic vocabulary of hatred the villain had been the German Kaiser; in the hysterical liturgy of 1919 it was the Russian Bolshevik. "Reds" replaced "Huns" as the target of patriotic bigotry, and almost overnight "Bolshevik" became the epithet for all that was evil and wrong in America. Liberals and radicals, progressives and revolutionaries, reformers and crackpots—all those who did not particularly agree with the way things were going—were tagged "Bolsheviki" and subjected to persecution. Instead of making scapegoats of pacifists, slackers, and draft-dodgers, self-styled super-patriots and former spy-chasers turned on persons and groups whose opinions they hated and feared, demanding with vehement intolerance their absolute loyalty to the status quo.[2]

Although the menace of Bolshevism was greatly exaggerated, popular fears were not entirely groundless. Behind the smoldering threat of revolution there were real live Bolsheviks who, in the first vainglorious hours of success, had boasted that the Russian Revolution of 1917 was but the first step in the world-wide overthrow of capitalism. Under the slogan "Workers of the World unite, you have nothing to lose but your chains," the Bolsheviks launched a propaganda offensive calculated to strike terror into the hearts of uneasy capitalists everywhere. By words, and not by deeds—for the Russian revolutionaries had not yet gained complete control at home—the Third International challenged world capitalism and urged the proletariat to seize power, arm the workers, and abolish private property. Concerned over the aggressive program of Bolshevism, alarmed capitalists prevailed upon President Wilson to send small forces of American troops to both northern Russia and Siberia in 1918, and though this "limited intervention" was largely a sop to conservative fears and was short-lived, it served nonetheless to dramatize the issue in the United States, and to heighten tensions between American radicals and conservatives. Sensational horror stories in the conservative press claiming the Bolsheviki had an electric guillotine that lopped off five hundred heads an hour and portraying Bolshevik rule as a "compound of slaughter, confiscation, anarchy, and universal disorder" were countered in left-wing journals by fulsome praise for the Bolshevik revolution and charges that capitalistic imperialism was seeking to destroy the only true "people's government" that existed.[3]

Fear of subversion led to a mounting clamor for government action. Under normal conditions, the existence in the United States of a radical minority of some 70,000 hard-core Communists probably would not have caused much alarm, but a succession of unusual and spectacular events beginning with the Seattle general strike of 1919 and followed by a rash of bombing incidents and May Day riots in various cities across the nation brought Attorney General A. Mitchell Palmer into the crusade against the Reds in the fall of 1919. Under his direction and using the specially created Federal Bureau of Investigation as an anti-radical task force, the federal government launched a nationwide purge of radicals which was conducted in such an aggressive, lawless fashion that it was labeled "Palmer's Reign of Terror." Early in January, 1920, the Department of Justice rounded up more than four thousand suspected radicals, holding them incommunicado and treating many with extreme brutality. Attorney General Palmer justified his actions on the basis of imminent revolution, maintaining that only by such militant tactics could the advance of "red radicalism" be halted in the United States.*

In such an atmosphere of intolerance, "Americanism" was perversely applied to anything representing the status quo, while patriotism became an excuse for any illiberal action by economic and political conservatives. Vigilante groups of super-patriots from the newly formed American Legion or the recently resurrected Ku Klux Klan often

---

*A. Mitchell Palmer, *The Case Against the "Reds."* See page 55.

took matters into their own hands, beating, torturing, and, in a few instances, lynching persons suspected of being less than 100% Americans. As the hysteria grew, school teachers, college professors, clergymen, public officials, and other prominent citizens were bullied, smeared, and subjected to outrageous restrictions. Yale, Radcliffe, and Vassar were condemned as hotbeds of Bolshevism, and the American Civil Liberties Union was disparaged as a "Bolshevik front." Middle-class intellectuals who read Karl Marx or liberal reformers who objected to vigilante injustices were branded "Parlor Reds" and proclaimed to be more dangerous than the "nut" who throws a bomb. Despite warnings from the newspapers that the government might be carrying this "anti-red business" too far, Attorney General Palmer exploited the issue of radicalism for all it was worth, partly out of genuine fear of Communist subversion but also to advance his political ambitions. Palmer finally overreached himself, however, by direly predicting an impending "Red" revolution on May 1, 1920. There were sensational headlines and feverish precautions, but not a single disturbance took place in the entire nation. After the May Day fiasco, which was denounced in newspapers as a "mare's nest hatched in the Attorney General's brain," there was growing criticism of the government's anti-red activities. Twelve of the nation's most prominent lawyers issued a report condemning the "utterly illegal acts" of the Department of Justice and charging that it had violated the Constitution by inflicting cruel and unusual punishments, making arrests without warrant, engaging in unreasonable searches and seizures, compelling persons to be witnesses against themselves, and misusing the office of Attorney General by issuing anti-radical propaganda patently designed to affect public opinion in advance of court decisions.[4] Among these outspoken critics was Professor Zechariah Chafee, Jr., of Harvard, who also published independently a vigorous defense of free speech in which he argued that there

## Soak It Hard

McCall in *The Portland Telegram*, Portland, Oregon

In the national hysteria following the war America became obsessed by the specter of "Bolshevism." Haunted by fear of revolution, vigilante bands of super-patriots from the newly formed American Legion beat, bullied, and in some cases lynched persons suspected of being less than 100% Americans.

was both an individual interest and a social interest in the attainment of truth.°

# II

Though the Red Scare collapsed, the crusade for 100% Americanism continued through most of the decade. The herd demand for conformity, the marked dislike of any variation in thought or action, and the "joyful willingness to use force to eradicate such differences" were all, as George Mowry observed, part of the end product of mass mental conscription during the war.[5] In such an intellectual environment persecution was bound to flourish. Wartime intolerance was kept alive by organized hate-groups, the most vicious and insidious of which was the Ku Klux Klan. Dedicated to the ideal of "pure American-ism," the Klan fed upon the pet hatreds and fears of white Anglo-Saxon Protestants—against Catholics, "nig-gers," Jews, and foreigners. Reactivated in Georgia in 1915, the Klan limped along until 1919–1920, when, nourished by the hysteria and violence of those postwar years, it grew to gigantic proportions. By 1924 its membership reached the staggering total of four and a half million, and its political influence was a force to be reckoned with in the South, the Midwest, and on the Pacific Coast. Not only did the Klan's gospel of hate and bigotry succeed by inflaming white against black and yellow, gentile against Jew, Protestant against Catholic, but its preposterous mum-mery—the secret ritual, the flaming cross, the white robe and hood, the Grand Goblins, King Kleagles, and Imperial Wizards—had great sales appeal for simple-minded adults who for ten dollars could find adventure and excitement by becoming a Knight of the Invisible Empire. Retailing

°Zechariah Chafee, Jr., *The Case for Free Speech*. See page 62.

hate, it turned out, was a profitable business, reportedly netting more than twenty million dollars to the original promoters.

The Klan, as the Imperial Wizard Hiram Wesley Evans made embarrassingly clear, was pledged to preserve the white race and Anglo-Saxon culture from mongrelization and contamination, and was prepared, if necessary, to take direct action.° In Alabama, for instance, the Klan's fight for "Americanism" led to: "A lad whipped with branches until his back was ribboned flesh; a Negress beaten and left helpless to contract pneumonia from exposure and die; a white girl, divorcée, beaten into unconsciousness in her own home; a naturalized foreigner flogged until his back was a pulp because he married an American woman; a Negro lashed until he sold his land to a white man for a fraction of its value." From all over the country came similar reports of Klan beatings and atrocities, while the forces of law and order, in most instances, scrupulously observed a strict neutrality.[6]

As always, the chief victim of intolerance was the Negro. Although Henry Ford—the American Janus whose rural bigotry was financed by the proceeds of mass-production—purveyed fantastic lies about the intrigues of "international Jewry" in his Dearborn *Independent,* going so far in anti-Semitism as to declare Einstein a "colossal humbug," the Jew in the United States was never subjected to the widespread persecution that dogged the Negro. During the war Negroes had been accepted in the military services, and there had been a great northward migration of Negroes in search of high wages in the war industries. As more and more Negroes invaded the factories and slums of northern cities, racial tensions built up. White workers, jealous of their status, resented the competition of black laborers and excluded them from unions. After the Armistice Negroes were pushed out of the more desirable jobs they had held during the manpower shortage of the war years, but

°Hiram Wesley Evans, *The Klan's Fight for Americanism.* See page 68.

the taste of temporary prosperity and partial acceptance
as workers and soldiers which had given the Negroes new
hope had also inspired a new disposition to fight against
racial discrimination. The result was an explosion of interracial strife, the worst the nation had ever seen. During
the first year following the war, more than seventy Negroes
were lynched in the South, some of them veterans still
in uniform; and in the "Red Summer" of 1919 race riots
broke out in twenty-five American cities. In Washington,
D.C., and Chicago, mobs took over the cities for days—
whites and Negroes beating, stabbing, shooting one another
in the streets. For nearly a week, Chicago was in a virtual
state of civil war, and when order was finally restored,
it was found that fifteen whites and twenty-three Negroes
had been killed, five hundred thirty-seven people injured,
and a thousand left homeless and destitute.

Tragically futile, roughly suppressed, these postwar protests by an urban Negro minority marked a new disposition to revolt against the philosophy of accommodation
that had dominated Negro thought since the beginning of
the twentieth century. To black slum-dwellers confronted
with the hopeless prospect of a lifetime of poor housing,
mass unemployment, and racial persecution, the only way
out seemed to be offered by Marcus Garvey, an ambitious
West Indian Negro who came to the United States in 1916.
Appealing to the growing despair among black Americans,
Garvey renounced all hope of any assistance or understanding from the whites: "For over three hundred years
the white man had been our oppressor, and he naturally
is not going to liberate us to the higher freedom—the truer
liberty—the truer Democracy. We have to liberate ourselves."

Not only did Garvey repudiate Booker T. Washington's
policy of conciliation and gradualism, he denounced
practically the entire Negro leadership, rejecting the militant elitism of W. E. B. DuBois along with the more moderate black-and-white alliance of the N.A.A.C.P. Both were
spurious because, said Garvey, the Negro could never ex-

The Indispensable Weekly
The Voice of the Awakened Negro—The Peerless Paper

THE

Guaranteed Circulation 50,000
Reaching the Mass of Negroes Throughout the World

# Negro World

ONE GOD, ONE AIM, ONE DESTINY

A Newspaper Devoted Solely to the Interests of the Negro Race

VOL. VIII. No. 24      NEW YORK, SATURDAY, JULY 31, 1920      PRICE, THREE CENTS IN GREATER NEW YORK; FIVE CENTS ELSEWHERE IN THE U. S. A.; TEN CENTS IN FOREIGN COUNTRIES.

## GREAT WORLD CONVENTION OF NEGROES

### Members of the Race From All Parts of the World to Assemble at Liberty Hall, New York, Sunday, August 1, at 10 A. M.—Biggest and Most Representative Assemblage in History of the Race

## CONSTITUTION OF NEGRO LIBERTY IS TO BE WRITTEN

The Negro World, July 31, 1920. from World's Work, XLI, December 1920, p. 161

pect to gain social equality in this country by political agitation of any kind. Garvey taught that Negroes, instead of trying to be "white folks' niggers," should take pride in purity of race, exalting black over white and even deprecating the light-brown skins of people like DuBois, who was of mixed ancestry. The prejudice of the white race against the black race, he insisted, was due not so much to color as to condition—"because as a race, to them, we have accomplished nothing; we have built no nation, no government; because we are dependent on them for our economic and political existence." The only thing left for the Negroes to do, therefore, was to organize the world over and to build up a mighty nation of their own in Africa. Until the black man reached that point of independence, Garvey declared, he would count for nothing.° As World War I had freed many subject peoples, so he prophesied the next war would bring a changed world politically in which "Africa for the Africans" was no longer a dream but a progressive reality. Despite strong opposi-

°Marcus Garvey, The Negro's Struggle for Survival. See page 75.

"Black ideals, black industry, black United States (of Africa), and black religion," Marcus Garvey told his followers, was the only solution to the Negro problem. So marchers in the great parade which opened the annual fifth convention of the Provisional Republic of Africa carried this painting of the Ethiopian Christ.

---

tion from middle-class Negroes and intellectuals, Garvey was able to attract a larger following than any Negro leader in America. Membership in his Universal Negro Improvement Association reputedly ran as high as several million. With amazing drive Garvey organized cooperative enterprises—grocery stores, laundries, restaurants, hotels, a steamship line—and printed his own newspaper, which had wide circulation among Negroes. Although after a few years his grandiose schemes collapsed due to poor judgment and possible fraudulent practices, Garvey's success, as Gunnar Myrdal pointed out, not only proved it was possible to activate the Negro masses but testified to the great unrest in the American Negro community which, DeBois predicted, would some day "burst in fire and blood."[7]

# III

Behind the floggings, church burnings, and lynchings were the fears of poorer and less educated white folk who were attempting desperately to stem the tide of change that threatened the mores and beliefs of small-town America. The Ku Klux Klan, prohibition, funda-mentalism, and xenophobia were, as Walter Lippmann perceived, "an extreme but authentic expression of the politics, the social outlook, and the religion of the older American village civilization making its last stand against what looks to it like an alien invasion." This alien invasion was in fact the new urban civilization with its radical ideas, cosmopolitan ways, and its irresistible economic and technical power. Beer and Bolshevism, Darwinism and the Bible, the Pope and Nordic supremacy were all part of a mythology which expressed symbolically the impact of a vast and dreaded social change.[8]

Just as the Klan's intimidation of the Negro in the South was an attempt to use terror to preserve an archaic social system, so the campaign in certain rural localities to pre-vent the teaching of Darwinism was an effort to resist urban forces of change, to erect legal barriers against a scientific rationalism that threatened to undermine the spiritual foundations of the village civilization. Since most of the nation thought the question of evolution had been settled some fifty years before, the country was startled, and completely fascinated, by the breaking out in 1925 of the old controversy between science and Christian funda-mentalism. In the little mountain town of Dayton, John T. Scopes, a high school biology teacher, was brought to trial for violating a Tennessee statute which forbade the teach-ing in public schools of any theory that denied "the con-ception of the divine creation of man as put in the Bible" and held in its stead that man was "descended from a lower order of animal."

Immediately dubbed the "Monkey Trial" by an opportunistic press, the case attracted international attention. To Scopes' defense came Clarence Darrow, nationally renowned defense lawyer and an admitted agnostic, while William Jennings Bryan, the folk-hero of rural America since 1896 and more recently named the "Fundamentalist Pope" by H. L. Mencken, was retained to assist the prosecution. In a bitter cross-examination, Bryan, who had denounced evolution as "a bloody, brutal doctrine" and vowed a "duel to the death," attacked the defense for trying "to

---

In the bizarre "Monkey Trial" at Dayton, Tennessee, in 1925, Clarence Darrow (in galluses), representing the A.C.L.U., defended John T. Scopes (seated behind Darrow in shirtsleeves, with folded arms) against the charge of teaching evolution. More than a skirmish between religious Fundamentalists and Modernists, it was the last stand of the older rural civilization against the radical ideas and alien ways of the new urban civilization.

cast ridicule on everybody who believes in the Bible."* In
retaliation, Darrow, after lashing out against "this foolish,
mischievous, and wicked act," proclaimed that his only
purpose was to prevent "bigots and ignoramuses from controlling the education of the United States."†

Yet the trial was not simply a contest between the
forces of religious bigotry and intellectual freedom, though
this was an important issue. In this bizarre war between
country and city, the quixotic provincialism of Bryan was
pitted against the urbane sarcasm of Darrow, a truly mun-
dane belief in religion against an almost superstitious faith
in science. Although the anti-evolutionists won the Scopes
case, they were defeated in the long run, for the world-
wide derision aroused by the trial destroyed evolution as a
valid intellectual issue. Science had become the chief power
in modern civilization, and, said the *New Republic*,
"Theoretically it is possible for a man or a state to prefer
the civilization of bygone days to his own. But practically,
no one does and no one can. . . ." Bryan, having become
a pathetic figure of fun, died soon afterward. But his last
battle was more than a mere exercise in fanaticism. He
had at any rate, remarked Lippmann, fought "for the
memory of a civilization which in its own heyday, and by
its own criteria, was as valid as any other."[9]

The crusade to preserve America as it was found political expression in the presidential election of 1920. The
people—after eight years of Wilson and fighting for principles, first at home and then abroad—were "tired of issues,
sick at heart of ideals, and weary of being noble." We
Americans, said Alvin Johnson, "thought we were settling
the world, but straightway it became more unsettled than
ever. We thought we were winning undying gratitude
from mankind, but returned travelers keep telling us that
America is unpopular everywhere. . . . We thought we
were attaining a new national unity, but sectionalism and

*William Jennings Bryan, *Faith of Our Fathers*. See page 80.
†Clarence Darrow, *In Defense of Reason*. See page 88.

class feeling are more rampant than ever before. We have our inflated cost of living, our crushing taxation, our discount on government bonds to remind us of our participation in great events. But we'd like to forget it all." Things had gone amiss; and the American people, afraid of the future and plagued by unfamiliar problems, sought to escape their troubles by turning back the hands of time.[10]

# IV

Rightly sensing the underlying temper of the country, the Republicans nominated Senator Warren G. Harding for the Presidency. An almost perfect specimen of the average 100% American, Harding personified himself as "Main Street come to Washington." Main Street was for him "the epitome of success, soundness, enterprise, orthodoxy, every worthy quality which he had in mind when he rolled out his unctuous encomiums of Americanism." Harding, wrote Lippmann, was distinguished by the fact that nothing distinguished him. "Put him into the White House," declared Mencken, "and you will put every president of every Chamber of Commerce into the White House, and every chairman of every Y.M.C.A. boob-squeezing drive, and every sales manager of every shoe factory, and every reader of the *Saturday Evening Post* and every abhorrer of the Bolsheviki." As befitted a modest, home-loving, small-town American, Harding conducted an informal campaign from his front porch where he smiled at visitors and shook hands with a firm grip.[11]

In politics and economics Harding stood just about where McKinley did in 1900. "Harding stands for a kind of candid and unpretentious reaction that everyone can respect, and that a great many people desire," said the *New Republic*. He was, the *Nation* grumbled, "McKinley come to life again," and the Washington *Post* concurred, finding the comparison "excellent." "Harding is of the McKinley type—safe, sound, courageous, and always ready to listen

Disillusioned by the failure of Wilson's crusade to make the world safe for democracy and fearing foreign control by the League of Nations, Americans in the presidential election of 1920 voted for a return to "normalcy" and isolationism.

to counsel." Acting as if nothing had occurred in the past two decades, Republican leaders had turned to Ohio for another negative statesman to be the safe and sound apostle of business as usual. In economics, Harding was regarded as having "reached the benevolent capitalist stage"; in politics, the candidate proclaimed his sincere devotion to an "idealism of a simple and old-fashioned kind" which sought "a new freedom from too much government in business and not enough business in government."* Turning his back upon the "folly, waste, grotesque experimentation" of the Wilson administration, Senator Harding plumped resolutely for the *status quo pro ante:* "America's present need is not heroics, but healing; not nostrums but normalcy; not revolution, but restoration; not agitation, but adjustment; not surgery, but serenity; not the dramatic, but the dispassionate; not experiment, but equipoise; not submergence in internationality, but sustainment in triumphant nationality." No one need fear the ultimate outcome, promised Harding, because "immutable laws have challenged the madness of all experiment."[12]

The only significant alternative in 1920 to Harding's banal appeal for "normalcy" came from Eugene V. Debs. Regarded as the "leading presidential impossibility," Debs was in the Atlanta federal prison when he was selected to run for the fifth time as the Socialist candidate for President. Along with a handful of prominent Americans—William Jennings Bryan, Jane Addams, Senators La Follette and Norris—Debs had opposed the preparedness drive and battled for true neutrality. When the United States joined the Allies, Debs refused to go along, and after a speech at Canton, Ohio, in 1918 in which he contended it was not a war for national defense but a war for capitalist profits, he was arrested, convicted, and sentenced to ten years imprisonment for treason. Ironically, barely a year later, President Wilson publicly expressed the same point of view: "Is there any man here or woman—let me say is there any child—who does not know that the seed of war in the modern world is industrial and commercial rivalry? . . . This

---

*Warren G. Harding, *Back to Normalcy*. See page 94.

was a commercial war." Yet, despite recommendation from Attorney General Palmer, Wilson adamantly refused to pardon Debs.[13]

Popularly regarded as a senseless martyr to his convictions rather than a criminal, Debs was described by the *New York Times* as a "man of great kindliness and of excellent private character, qualities which have caused a degree of love for him almost amounting to worship among his followers." But for all his good qualities, Debs was still an untamed revolutionist. From his jail cell he stubbornly declared for Lenin's Third International, telling a reporter from the New York *World*, "I am heart and soul with the Russian revolution." As a "catastrophic revolutionary," Debs was committed to the dictatorship of the proletariat but believed it possible that by peaceful revolution—ballots not bullets—American workers could take over the industrial system and run it for use and not for profit. There seems little doubt that the choice of Debs as a presidential candidate was a personal tribute rather than an acceptance of his ideas of social revolution, for American Socialists were basically conservative, and the convention which chose Debs and drew up the platform was dominated by the moderate wing of the party. Though more radical than his supporters, Debs endorsed the platform which, Socialist dogma aside, offered a provocative program for social democracy, proposing among other things full civil, political, and educational rights for Negroes.°

But, infected with anti-radical hysteria, the American people were in no mood for change. Psychopathic fears of radicalism reached such a fever-pitch in 1920 that during a trial of some Communists at Boston the government expert unwittingly branded a section read from President Woodrow Wilson's *The New Freedom* as good Communist doctrine and pronounced it just cause for the deportation of the author. In New York five duly elected Socialist

---

°Eugene V. Debs, *A Last Call for Revolution*. See page 98.

representatives were unlawfully denied seats in the state
assembly, and shortly afterward the Socialist party was
declared illegal and its candidates barred from the state
ballot. Perhaps the most graphic indication of the prevailing state of mind was the controversial trial of two Italian-
born anarchists, Sacco and Vanzetti, who though allegedly
sentenced to death for robbery and murder were seemingly
convicted by a Massachusetts jury for the dual crime of
being pacifists and radicals. With nonconformity a political
and social crime, Debs had no expectation of being elected.
Election results confirmed the observation of Paris *Le
Matin* that Socialism in the United States was "exotic and
alien," for Debs polled less than a million votes as compared
to the twenty-five million votes cast for his more conventional Republican and Democratic opponents.[14]

With President Harding in the White House the people
could once more relax, secure in the belief they were back
on the American way. Although less than one-half of the
electorate bothered to vote, they decisively chose restoration over revolution. In every previous election since 1896,
at least one of the major parties had offered a candidate
who believed that the public welfare demanded more or
less drastic changes in national organization and policy.
In 1920, however, neither the Republicans nor the Democrats made an honest bid for progressive support, a fact
which, for Herbert Croly, was a sign of political bankruptcy and meant the eclipse of liberalism and progressivism
as an effective force in American politics. Harding's frank
resurrection of McKinley Republicanism was, under these
conditions, an honest avowal of political neutrality. "We
must strive for normalcy to reach stability" was meaningless rhetoric, and his clarion cry to "Stabilize America
first, prosper American first, think of America first, exalt
America first!" was comfortingly non-controversial. A vote
for Harding was an empty hurrah for McKinley—a post-
ponement of issues, not an evasion.[15]

As a formula for the good society, normalcy equated

national happiness with business prosperity and, in its more
obvious sense, was a condition which could be expressed
in concrete facts and figures; but, in a subtle and perhaps
more important sense, it was a psychological condition,
a national state of mind. As a member of the cabinet suggested, the "curing and restorative qualities of President
Harding's personality" had affected the spiritual temper of
the country. Certainly it seemed that the nation, like the
President, proposed to cure excitement with serenity, to
meet injustice with platitudes, to overcome greed with innocence, and in childlike faith to conquer change with
nostalgia.[16]

# Readings:

# Back to Normalcy

## A. Mitchell Palmer (1872–1936)

*Ambitious, dogmatic, and combative, he was known as the "Fighting Quaker." From 1919 to 1921, as Attorney-General in Wilson's cabinet, he achieved great notoriety fighting labor unions and chasing suspected radicals. Bitterly denounced in liberal circles for his unconstitutional actions at the time of the Red Scare and charged with mishandling some $600 millions in alien property, he spent his last months in office facing congressional investigating committees. Cleared of all charges of dishonesty and malfeasance, he retired in 1921 from public life but not from politics. In 1932 he supported Franklin D. Roosevelt and was credited with writing most of the campaign platform.*

## THE CASE AGAINST THE "REDS"

In this brief review of the work which the Department of Justice has undertaken, to tear out the radical seeds that

From *Forum*, LXIII (Feb., 1920), 173–5, 181–5.

have entangled American ideas in their poisonous theories, I desire not merely to explain what the real menace of communism is, but also to tell how we have been compelled to clean up the country almost unaided by any virile legislation. Though I have not been embarrassed by political opposition, I have been materially delayed because the present sweeping processes of arrests and deportation of seditious aliens should have been vigorously pushed by Congress last spring. The failure of this is a matter of record in the Congressional files.

The anxiety of that period in our responsibility when Congress, ignoring the seriousness of these vast organizations that were plotting to overthrow the Government, failed to act, has passed. The time came when it was obviously hopeless to expect the hearty co-operation of Congress, in the only way to stamp out these seditious societies in their open defiance of law by various forms of propaganda.

Like a prairie-fire, the blaze of revolution was sweeping over every American institution of law and order a year ago. It was eating its way into the homes of the American workman, its sharp tongues of revolutionary heat were licking the altars of the churches, leaping into the belfry of the school bell, crawling into the sacred corners of American homes, seeking to replace marriage vows with libertine laws, burning up the foundations of society.

Robbery, not war, is the ideal of communism. This has been demonstrated in Russia, Germany, and in America. As a foe, the anarchist is fearless of his own life, for his creed is a fanaticism that admits no respect of any other creed. Obviously it is the creed of any criminal mind, which reasons always from motives impossible to clean thought. Crime is the degenerate factor in society.

Upon these two basic certainties, first that the "Reds" were criminal aliens, and secondly that the American Government must prevent crime, it was decided that there could be no nice distinctions drawn between the theoretical ideals of the radicals and their actual violations of our national laws. An assassin may have brilliant intellectuality, he may be able to excuse his murder or robbery with fine oratory, but any theory which excuses crime is not wanted in America. This is no place for the criminal to flourish, nor will he do so, so long as the rights of common citizenship can be exerted to prevent him.

### Our Government in Jeopardy

It has always been plain to me that when American citizens unite upon any national issue, they are generally right, but it is sometimes difficult to make the issue clear to them. If the Department of Justice could succeed in attracting the attention of our optimistic citizens to the issue of internal revolution in this country, we felt sure there would be no revolution. The Government was in jeopardy. My private information of what was being done by the organization known as the Communist Party of America, with headquarters in Chicago, of what was being done by the Communist Internationale under their manifesto planned at Moscow last March by Trotzky, Lenine and others, addressed "To the Proletariats of All Countries," of what strides the Communist Labor Party was making, removed all doubt. In this conclusion we did not ignore the definite standards of personal liberty, of free speech, which is the very temperament and heart of the people. The evidence was examined with the utmost care, with a personal leaning toward freedom of thought and word on all questions.

The whole mass of evidence, accumulated from all parts of the country, was scrupulously scanned, not merely for the written or spoken differences of viewpoint as to the Government of the United States, but, in spite of these things, to see if the hostile declarations might not be sincere in their announced motive to improve our social order. There was no hope of such a thing.

By stealing, murder and lies, Bolshevism has looted Russia not only of its material strength, but of its moral force. A small clique of outcasts from the East Side of New York has attempted this, with what success we all know. Because a disreputable alien—Leon Bronstein, the man who now calls himself Trotzky—can inaugurate a reign of terror from his throne room in the Kremlin; because this lowest of all types known to New York can sleep in the Czar's bed, while hundreds of thousands in Russia are without food or shelter, should Americans be swayed by such doctrines?

Such a question, it would seem, should receive but one answer from America. . . .

### Will Deportations Check Bolshevism?

Behind, and underneath, my own determination to drive from our midst the agents of Bolshevism with increasing vigor and with greater speed, until there are no more of them left among us, so long as I have the responsible duty of that task, I have discovered the hysterical methods of these revolutionary humans with increasing amazement and suspicion. In the confused information that sometimes reaches the people, they are compelled to ask questions which involve the reasons for my acts against the "Reds." I have been asked, for instance, to what extent deportation will check radicalism in this country. Why not ask what will become of the United States Government if these alien radicals are permitted to carry out the principles of the Communist Party as embodied in its so-called laws, aims and regulations?

There wouldn't be any such thing left. In place of the United States Government we should have the horror and terrorism of bolsheviki tyranny such as is destroying Russia now. Every scrap of radical literature demands the overthrow of our existing government. All of it demands obedience to the instincts of criminal minds, that is, to the lower appetites, material and moral. The whole purpose of communism appears to be a mass formation of the criminals of the world to overthrow the decencies of private life, to usurp property that they have not earned, to disrupt the present order of life regardless of health, sex or religious rights. By a literature that promises the wildest dreams of such low aspirations, that can occur to only the criminal minds, communism distorts our social law.

The chief appeal communism makes is to "The Worker." If they can lure the wage-earner to join their own gang of thieves, if they can show him that he will be rich if he steals, so far they have succeeded in betraying him to their own criminal course.

Read this manifesto issued in Chicago:

THE COMMUNIST PARTY MANIFESTO

The world is on the verge of a new era. Europe is in revolt. The masses of Asia are stirring uneasily. Capitalism is in collapse. The workers of the world are seeing a new light and securing new courage. Out of the night of war is coming a new day.

The spectre of communism haunts the world of capitalism. Communism, the hope of the workers to end misery and oppression.

The workers of Russia smashed the front of international Capitalism and Imperialism. They broke the chains of the terrible war; and in the midst of agony, starvation and the attacks of the Capitalists of the world, they are creating a new social order.

The class war rages fiercely in all nations. Everywhere the workers are in a desperate struggle against their capitalist masters. The call to action has come. The workers must answer the call!

The Communist Party of America is the party of the working class. The Communist Party proposes to end Capitalism and organize a workers' industrial republic. The workers must control industry and dispose of the product of industry. The Communist Party is a party realizing the limitation of all existing workers' organizations and proposes to develop the revolutionary movement necessary to free the workers from the oppression of Capitalism. The Communist Party insists that the problems of the American worker are identical with the problems of the workers of the world.

These are the revolutionary tenets of Trotzky and the

Communist Internationale. Their manifesto further embraces the various organizations in this country of men and women obsessed with discontent, having disorganized relations to American society. These include the I.W.W.'s, the most radical socialists, the misguided anarchists, the agitators who oppose the limitations of unionism, the moral perverts and the hysterical neurasthenic women who abound in communism. The phraseology of their manifesto is practically the same wording as was used by the Bolsheviks for their International Communist Congress.

Naturally the Communist Party has bored its revolutionary points into the Socialist Party. They managed to split the Socialists, for the so-called Left Wing of the Socialist Party is now the Communist Party, which specifically states that it does not intend to capture the bourgeoisie parliamentary state, but to conquer and destroy, and that the final objective, mass action, is the medium intended to be used in the conquest and destruction of the bourgeoisie state to annihilate the parliamentary state, and introduce a revolutionary dictatorship of the Proletariat. . . .

There is no legislation at present which can reach an American citizen who is discontented with our system of American Government, nor is it necessary. The dangerous fact to us is that the Communist Party of America is actually affiliated and adheres to the teaching program and tactics of the 3d Internationale. Consider what this means.

The first congress of the Communist Nationale held March 6, 1919, in Moscow, subscribed to by Trotzky and Lenine, adopted the following:

This makes necessary the disarming of the bourgeoisie at the proper time, the arming of the laborer, and the formation of a communist army as the protectors of the rules of the proletariat and the inviolability of the social structure.

When we realize that each member of the Communist Party of America pledges himself to the principles above set forth, deportation of men and women bound to such a theory is a very mild reformatory sentence.

### Have the "Reds" Betrayed Labor?

If I were asked whether the American Federation of Labor had been betrayed by the "Reds," I should refer the inquiry to the manifesto and constitution of the Communist Party of America, in which, under the heading, "Revolutionary Construction," the following paragraph appears:

But the American Federation of Labor, as a whole, is hopelessly reactionary. At its recent convention the A. F. of L. approved the Versailles Peace Treaty and the League of Nations, and refused to declare its solidarity with Soviet Russia. It did not even protest the blockade of Russia and Hungary! This convention, moreover, did all in its power to break radical unions. The A. F. of L. is united with the Government, securing a privileged status in the governing system of State Capitalism. A Labor Party is being organized—much more conservative than the British Labor Party.

It has been inferred by the "Reds" that the United States Government, by arresting and deporting them, is returning to the autocracy of Czardom, adopting the system that created the severity of Siberian banishment. My reply to such charges is, that in our determination to maintain our government we are treating our alien enemies with extreme consideration. To deny them the privilege of remaining in a country which they have openly deplored as an unenlightened community, unfit for those who prefer the privileges of Bolshevism, should be no hardship. It strikes me as an odd form of reasoning that these Russian Bolsheviks who extol the Bolshevik rule, should be so unwilling to return to Russia. The nationality of most of the alien "Reds" is Russian and German. There is almost no other nationality represented among them. . . .

It is my belief that while they have stirred discontent in

our midst, while they have caused irritating strikes, and while they have infected our social ideas with the disease of their own minds and their unclean morals, we can get rid of them! and not until we have done so shall we have removed the menace of Bolshevism for good.

# Zechariah Chafee, Jr. (1885–1957)

*Appointed to the law faculty of Harvard University in 1916, he wrote his well-known defense of free speech largely by accident. As a young assistant professor hard up for money, he warmly welcomed an offer by the* New Republic *in 1918 to write an article on the Espionage Act cases. Later, because of the interest it aroused, it was expanded into a book. His argument was not chiefly a legal one, nor did he place his confidence in the courts alone. In his opinion, the protection of freedom of speech rested primarily with people of sound minds rather than with sound laws.*

## THE CASE FOR FREE SPEECH

And though all the winds of doctrine were let loose to play upon the earth, so Truth be in the field, we do injuriously by licensing and prohibiting to misdoubt her strength. Let her and Falsehood grapple; who ever knew Truth put to the worse, in a free and open encounter?—Milton, *Areopagitica.*

Never in the history of our country, since the Alien and Sedition Laws of 1798, has the meaning of free speech been

Reprinted by permission of the publishers from Zechariah Chafee, Jr., *Free Speech in the United States* (Cambridge, Mass.: Harvard University Press), pp. 3, 30–5. Copyright, 1941, by the President and Fellows of Harvard College. First published in 1920.

the subject of such sharp controversy as to-day. Over nineteen hundred prosecutions and other judicial proceedings during the war, involving speeches, newspaper articles, pamphlets, and books, have been followed since the armistice by a widespread legislative consideration of bills punishing the advocacy of extreme radicalism. It is becoming increasingly important to determine the true limits of freedom of expression, so that speakers and writers may know how much they can properly say, and governments may be sure how much they can lawfully and wisely suppress. . . .

It is now clear that the First Amendment fixes limits upon the power of Congress to restrict speech either by a censorship or by a criminal statute, and if the Espionage Act exceeds those limits it is unconstitutional. It is sometimes argued that the Constitution gives Congress the power to declare war, raise armies, and support a navy, that one provision of the Constitution cannot be used to break down another provision, and consequently freedom of speech cannot be invoked to break down the war power. I would reply that the First Amendment is just as much a part of the Constitution as the war clauses, and that it is equally accurate to say that the war clauses cannot be invoked to break down freedom of speech. The truth is that all provisions of the Constitution must be construed together so as to limit each other. In a war as in peace, this process of mutual adjustment must include the Bill of Rights. There are those who believe that the Bill of Rights can be set aside in war time at the uncontrolled will of the government. The first ten amendments were drafted by men who had just been through a war. The Third and Fifth Amendments expressly apply in war. A majority of the Supreme Court declared the war power of Congress to be restricted by the Bill of Rights in *Ex Parte* Milligan, which cannot be lightly brushed aside, whether or not the majority went too far in thinking that the Fifth Amendment would have prevented Congress from exercising the war power under the particular circumstances of that case. If the First Amendment is to mean anything, it must restrict powers which are expressly granted by the Constitution to Congress, since Congress has no other powers.* It must apply to those activities of government which are most liable to interfere with free discussion, namely, the postal service and the conduct of war.

The true meaning of freedom of speech seems to be this. One of the most important purposes of society and government is the discovery and spread of truth on subjects of general concern. This is possible only through absolutely unlimited discussion, for, as Bagehot points out, once force is thrown into the argument, it becomes a matter of chance whether it is thrown on the false side or the true, and truth loses all its natural advantage in the contest. Nevertheless, there are other purposes of government, such as order, the training of the young, protection against external aggression. Unlimited discussion sometimes interferes with these purposes, which must then be balanced against freedom of speech, but freedom of speech ought to weigh very heavily in the scale. The First Amendment gives binding force to this principle of political wisdom.

Or to put the matter another way, it is useless to define free speech by talk about rights. The agitator asserts his constitutional right to speak, the government asserts its constitutional right to wage war. The result is a deadlock. Each side takes the position of the man who was arrested for swinging his arms and hitting another in the nose, and asked the judge if he did not have a right to swing his arms in a

---

*United States Constitution, Art. I, § 1: "All legislative powers herein granted shall be vested in a Congress." Amendment X: "The powers not delegated to the United States by the Constitution, nor prohibited by it to the States, are reserved to the States respectively or to the people."

"This government is acknowledged by all to be one of enumerated powers. The principle that it can exercise only the powers granted to it, would seem too apparent."—Marshall, C.J., in McCulloch v. Maryland, 4 Wheat. (U.S.) 316, 405 (1819). See also Taney, C.J., in Ex parte Merryman, Taney, 236, 260 (1861), and Brewer, Jr., in Kansas v. Colorado, 206 U.S. 46, 81 (1907).

free country. "Your right to swing your arms ends just where the other man's nose begins." To find the boundary line of any right, we must get behind rules of law to human facts. In our problem, we must regard the desires and needs of the individual human being who wants to speak and those of the great group of human beings among whom he speaks. That is, in technical language, there are individual interests and social interests, which must be balanced against each other, if they conflict, in order to determine which interest shall be sacrificed under the circumstances and which shall be protected and become the foundation of a legal right. It must never be forgotten that the balancing cannot be properly done unless all the interests involved are adequately ascertained, and the great evil of all this talk about rights is that each side is so busy denying the other's claim to rights that it entirely overlooks the human desires and needs behind that claim.

The rights and powers of the Constitution, aside from the portions which create the machinery of the federal system, are largely means of protecting important individual and social interests, and because of this necessity of balancing such interests the clauses cannot be construed with absolute literalness. The Fourteenth Amendment and the obligation of contracts clause, maintaining important individual interests, are modified by the police power of the states, which protects health and other social interests. The Thirteenth Amendment is subject to many implied exceptions, so that temporary involuntary servitude is permitted to secure social interests in the construction of roads, the prevention of vagrancy, the training of the militia or national army. It is common to rest these implied exceptions to the Bill of Rights upon the ground that they existed in 1791 and long before, but a less arbitrary explanation is desirable. Not everything old is good. Thus the antiquity of peonage does not constitute it an exception to the Thirteenth Amendment; it is not now demanded by any strong social interest. . . . The Bill of Rights does not crystallize

antiquity. It seems better to say that long usage does not
create an exception to the absolute language of the Constitution, but demonstrates the importance of the social interest
behind the exception.

The First Amendment protects two kinds of interests in
free speech. There is an individual interest, the need of
many men to express their opinions on matters vital to them
if life is to be worth living, and a social interest in the attainment of truth, so that the country may not only adopt
the wisest course of action but carry it out in the wisest way.
This social interest is especially important in war time.
Even after war has been declared there is bound to be a
confused mixture of good and bad arguments in its support,
and a wide difference of opinion as to its objects. Truth can
be sifted out from falsehood only if the government is vigorously and constantly cross-examined, so that the fundamental issues of the struggle may be clearly defined, and the
war may not be diverted to improper ends, or conducted
with an undue sacrifice of life and liberty, or prolonged
after its just purposes are accomplished. Legal proceedings
prove that an opponent makes the best cross-examiner. Consequently it is a disastrous mistake to limit criticism to those
who favor the war. Men bitterly hostile to it may point out
evils in its management like the secret treaties, which its
supporters have been too busy to unearth. If a free canvass-
ing of the aims of the war by its opponents is crushed by
the menace of long imprisonment, such evils, even though
made public in one or two newspapers, may not come to
the attention of those who had power to counteract them
until too late.

The history of the last five years shows how the objects
of a war may change completely during its progress, and
it is well that those objects should be steadily reformulated
under the influence of open discussion not only by those who
demand a military victory, but by pacifists who take a different view of the national welfare. Further argument for
the existence of this social interest becomes unnecessary if

we recall the national value of the opposition in former wars.

The great trouble with most judicial construction of the Espionage Act is that this social interest has been ignored and free speech has been regarded as merely an individual interest, which must readily give way like other personal desires the moment it interferes with the social interest in national safety. . . . The failure of the courts in the past to formulate any principle for drawing a boundary line around the right of free speech has not only thrown the judges into the difficult questions of the Espionage Act without any well-considered standard of criminality, but has allowed some of them to impose standards of their own and fix the line at a point which makes all opposition to this or any future war impossible. For example:

No man should be permitted, by deliberate act, or even unthinkingly, to do that which will in any way detract from the efforts which the United States is putting forth or serve to postpone for a single moment the early coming of the day when the success of our arms shall be a fact.°

The true boundary line of the First Amendment can be fixed only when Congress and the courts realize that the principle on which speech is classified as lawful or unlawful involves the balancing against each other of two very important social interests, in public safety and in the search for truth. Every reasonable attempt should be made to maintain both interests unimpaired, and the great interest in free speech should be sacrificed only when the interest in public safety is really imperiled, and not, as most men believe, when it is barely conceivable that it may be slightly affected. In war time, therefore, speech should be unrestricted by the censorship or by punishment, unless it is clearly liable to cause direct and dangerous interference with the conduct of the war.

°United States *v.* "The Spirit of '76," 252 Fed. 946. Another good example is United States *v.* Schoberg, Bull. Dept. Just., No. 149.

# Hiram Wesley Evans (1879–    )

*A Texan born, a dentist by profession, and a thirty-second degree Mason, he supposedly represented the reform leadership in the Klan. Taking over in the early twenties after a congressional investigation had revealed wholesale corruption and graft, he cleaned up finances and tried to create a new image of the Klan as a law-abiding, peace-loving organization. Although as Imperial Wizard he officially disavowed violence, his directives apparently were not always heeded by local Klansmen. Deeply suspicious of liberals and intellectuals, he identified with the common people, appealing to their ignorance and prejudices, and at times displayed a remarkable intellecutal naiveté. For instance, when asked why the Klansmen did not parade with their hoods raised, he replied, "The morale of the Klan would kill itself."*

# THE KLAN'S FIGHT FOR AMERICANISM

The Ku Klux Klan is an organization which gives expression, direction and purpose to the most vital instincts, hopes and resentments of the old stock Americans, provides them with leadership, and is enlisting and preparing them for militant, constructive action toward fulfilling their racial and national destiny. . . . The Klan literally is once more the embattled American farmer and artisan, coordinated into a disciplined and growing army, and launched upon a definite crusade for Americanism! . . .

From *North American Review*, CCXXIII (Mar., 1926), 49–56, 60–1.

We are a movement of the plain people, very weak in the matter of culture, intellectual support, and trained leadership. We are demanding, and we expect to win, a return of power into the hands of the everyday, not highly cultured, not overly intellectualized, but entirely unspoiled and not de-Americanized, average citizen of the old stock. Our members and leaders are all of this class—the opposition of the intellectuals and liberals who held the leadership, betrayed Americanism, and from whom we expect to wrest control, is almost automatic.

This is undoubtedly a weakness. It lays us open to the charge of being "hicks" and "rubes" and "drivers of second hand Fords." We admit it. Far worse, it makes it hard for us to state our case and advocate our crusade in the most effective way, for most of us lack skill in language. Worst of all, the need of trained leaders constantly hampers our progress and leads to serious blunders and internal troubles. If the Klan ever should fail it would be from this cause. All this we on the inside know far better than our critics, and regret more. Our leadership is improving, but for many years the Klan will be seeking better leaders, and the leaders praying for greater wisdom. . . .

But we have no fear of the outcome. Since we indulge ourselves in convictions, we are not frightened by our weaknesses. We hold the conviction that right will win if backed with vigor and consecration. We are increasing our consecration and learning to make better use of our vigor. We are sure of the fundamental rightness of our cause, as it concerns both ourselves and the progress of the world. We believe that there can be no question of the right of the children of the men who made America to own and control America. We believe that when we allowed others to share our heritage, it was by our own generosity and by no right of theirs. We believe that therefore we have every right to protect ourselves when we find that they are betraying our trust and endangering us. We believe, in short, that we have the right to make America *American* and for Americans. . . .

Our critics have accused us of being merely a "protest movement," of being frightened; they say we fear alien competition, are in a panic because we cannot hold our own against the foreigners. That is partly true. We are a protest movement—protesting against being robbed. We are afraid of competition with peoples who would destroy our standard of living. We are suffering in many ways, we have been betrayed by our trusted leaders, we are half beaten already. But we are not frightened nor in a panic. We have merely awakened to the fact that we must fight for our own. We are going to fight—and win!

The Klan does not believe that the fact that it is emotional and instinctive, rather than coldly intellectual, is a weakness. All action comes from emotion, rather than from ratiocination. Our emotions and the instincts on which they are based have been bred into us for thousands of years; far longer than reason has had a place in the human brain. They are the many-times distilled product of experience; they still operate much more surely and promptly than reason can. For centuries those who obeyed them have lived and carried on the race; those in whom they were weak, or who failed to obey, have died. They are the foundations of our American civilization, even more than our great historic documents; they can be trusted where the fine-haired reasoning of the denatured intellectuals cannot.

Thus the Klan goes back to the American racial instincts, and to the common sense which is their first product, as the basis of its beliefs and methods. The fundamentals of our thought are convictions, not mere opinions. We are pleased that modern research is finding scientific backing for these convictions. We do not need them ourselves; we know that we are right in the same sense that a good Christian knows that he has been saved and that Christ lives—a thing which the intellectual can never understand. These convictions are no more to be argued about than is our love for our children; we are merely willing to state them for the enlightenment and conversion of others.

There are three of these great racial instincts, vital elements in both the historic and the present attempts to build an America which shall fulfill the aspirations and justify the heroism of the men who made the nation. These are the instincts of loyalty to the white race, to the traditions of America, and to the spirit of Protestantism, which has been an essential part of Americanism ever since the days of Roanoke and Plymouth Rock. They are condensed into the Klan slogan: "Native, white, Protestant supremacy."

First in the Klansman's mind is patriotism—America for Americans. He believes religiously that a betrayal of Americanism or the American race is treason to the most sacred of trusts, a trust from his fathers and a trust from God. He believes, too, that Americanism can only be achieved if the pioneer stock is kept pure. There is more than race pride in this. Mongrelization has been proven bad. It is only between closely related stocks of the same race that interbreeding has improved men; the kind of interbreeding that went on in the early days of America between English, Dutch, German, Huguenot, Irish and Scotch.

Racial integrity is a very definite thing to the Klansman. It means even more than good citizenship, for a man may be in all ways a good citizen and yet a poor American, unless he has racial understanding of Americanism, and instinctive loyalty to it. It is in no way a reflection on any man to say that he is un-American; it is merely a statement that he is not one of us. It is often not even wise to try to make an American of the best of aliens. What he is may be spoiled without his becoming American. The races and stocks of men are as distinct as breeds of animals, and every boy knows that if one tries to train a bulldog to herd sheep, he has in the end neither a good bulldog nor a good collie.

Americanism, to the Klansman, is a thing of the spirit,

a purpose and a point of view, that can only come through instinctive racial understanding. It has, to be sure, certain defined principles, but he does not believe that many aliens understand those principles, even when they use our words in talking about them. Democracy is one, fairdealing, impartial justice, equal opportunity, religious liberty, independence, self-reliance, courage, endurance, acceptance of individual responsibility as well as individual rewards for effort, willingness to sacrifice for the good of his family, his nation and his race before anything else but God, dependence on enlightened conscience for guidance, the right to unhampered development—these are fundamental. But within the bounds they fix there must be the utmost freedom, tolerance, liberalism. In short, the Klansman believes in the greatest possible diversity and individualism within the limits of the American spirit. But he believes also that few aliens can understand that spirit, that fewer try to, and that there must be resistance, intolerance even, toward anything that threatens it, or the fundamental national unity based upon it.

The second word in the Klansman's trilogy is "white." The white race must be supreme, not only in America but in the world. This is equally undebatable, except on the ground that the races might live together, each with full regard for the rights and interests of others, and that those rights and interests would never conflict. Such an idea, of course, is absurd; the colored races today, such as Japan, are clamoring not for equality but for their supremacy. The whole history of the world, on its broader lines, has been one of race conflicts, wars, subjugation or extinction. This is not pretty, and certainly disagrees with the maudlin theories of cosmopolitanism, but it is truth. The world has been so made that each race must fight for its life, must conquer, accept slavery or die. The Klansman believes that the whites will not become slaves, and he does not intend to die before his time.

Moreover, the future of progress and civilization depends on the continued supremacy of the white race. The forward movement of the world for centuries has come entirely from it. Other races each had its chance and either failed or stuck fast, while white civilization shows no sign of having reached its limit. Until the whites falter, or some colored civilization has a miracle of awakening, there is not a single colored stock that can claim even equality with the white; much less supremacy.

The third of the Klan principles is that Protestantism must be supreme; that Rome shall not rule America. The Klansman believes this not merely because he is a Protestant, nor even because the Colonies that are now our nation were settled for the purpose of wresting America from the control of Rome and establishing a land of free conscience. He believes it also because Protestantism is an essential part of Americanism; without it America could never have been created and without it she cannot go forward. Roman rule would kill it. . . .

Let it be clear what is meant by "supremacy." It is nothing more than power of control, under just laws. It is not imperialism, far less is it autocracy or even aristocracy of a race or stock of men. What it does mean is that we insist on our inherited right to insure our own safety, individually and as a race, to secure the future of our children, to maintain and develop our racial heritage in our own, white, Protestant, American way, without interference. . . .

In the National Government our interest is along the same lines, with special emphasis on anti-alien and pro-American legislation. Also, far more than in local affairs, we take pains to support men who understand and are loyal to the best American traditions. Apart from that the Klan takes no interest in any government matters except those having a direct bearing on decency and honesty. . . .

The Negro, the Klan considers a special duty and problem of the white American. He is among us through no wish of his; we owe it to him and to ourselves to give him full protection and opportunity. But his limitations are evident; we will not permit him to gain sufficient power to control our civilization. Neither will we delude him with promises of social equality which we know can never be realized. The Klan looks forward to the day when the Negro problem will have been solved on some much saner basis than miscegenation, and when every State will enforce laws making any sex relations between a white and a colored person a crime. . . .

The most menacing and most difficult problem facing America today is this of the permanently unassimilable alien. The only solution so far offered is that of Dr. Eliot, president emeritus of Harvard. After admitting that the melting pot has failed—thus supporting the primary position of the Klan!—he adds that there is no hope of creating here a single, homogeneous race-stock of the kind necessary for national unity. He then suggests that, instead, there shall be a congeries of diverse peoples, living together in sweet harmony, and all working for the good of all and of the nation! This solution is on a par with the optimism which foisted the melting pot on us. Diverse races never have lived together in such harmony; race antipathies are too deep and strong. If such a state were possible, the nation would be too disunited for progress. One race always ruled, one always must, and there will be struggle and reprisals till the mastery is established—and bitterness afterwards. And, speaking for us Americans, we have come to realize that if all this could possibly be done, still within a few years we should be supplanted by the "mere force of breeding" of the low standard peoples. We intend to see that the American stock remains supreme.

# Marcus M. Garvey (1887–1940)

*A Jamaican Negro, he became convinced that he had a mission as leader of the black race when he read* Up from Slavery, *the autobiography of Booker T. Washington. In 1916 he moved to New York where in a few years he had gathered a mass following of several million Negroes. The climax of his astonishing American career occurred in 1920 when he presided over a mammoth international convention in New York, representing Negroes from all parts of the world. His triumph, however, was short-lived. Though personally honest and sincere, he was inexperienced in business matters and unwise in the choice of some of his subordinates. As a result, in 1923 he was tried and sentenced for mail fraud. Although his sentence was commuted by President Coolidge, he was deported in 1927 and never regained his popular following.*

# THE NEGRO'S STRUGGLE FOR SURVIVAL

Surely the soul of liberal, philanthropic, liberty-loving, white America is not dead.

It is true that the glamor of materialism has, to a great degree, destroyed the innocence and purity of the national conscience, but still, beyond our politics, beyond our soulless industrialism, there is a deep feeling of human sympathy that touches the soul of white America, upon which the un-

From *The Philosophy and Opinions of Marcus Garvey* (New York: The Universal Publishing House, 1923), pp. 1–6.

fortunate and sorrowful can always depend for sympathy, help and action.

It is to that feeling that I appeal for four hundred million Negroes of the world, and fifteen millions of America in particular.

There is no real white man in America, who does not desire a solution of the Negro problem. Each thoughtful citizen has probably his own idea of how the vexed question of races should be settled. To some the Negro could be gotten rid of by wholesale butchery, by lynching, by economic starvation, by a return to slavery, and legalized oppression, while others would have the problem solved by seeing the race all herded together and kept somewhere among themselves; but a few—those in whom they have an interest—should be allowed to live around as the wards of a mistaken philanthropy; yet, none so generous as to desire to see the Negro elevated to a standard of real progress and prosperity, welded into a homogeneous whole, creating of themselves a mighty nation, with proper systems of government, civilization and culture, to mark them admissible to the fraternities of nations and races without any disadvantage. . . .

Negroes are human beings—the peculiar and strange opinions of writers, ethnologists, philosophers, scientists and anthropologists notwithstanding. They have feelings, souls, passions, ambitions, desires, just as other men, hence they must be considered.

Has white America really considered the Negro in the light of permanent human progress? The answer is NO.

Men and women of the white race, do you know what is going to happen if you do not think and act now? One of two things. You are either going to deceive and keep the Negro in your midst until you have perfectly completed your wonderful American civilization with its progress of art, science, industry and politics, and then, jealous of your own success and achievements in those directions, and with the greater jealousy of seeing your race pure and unmixed, cast him off to die in the whirlpool of economic starvation, thus

getting rid of another race that was not intelligent enough
to live, or, you simply mean by the largeness of your hearts
to assimilate fifteen million Negroes into the social fraternity
of an American race, that will neither be white nor black!
Don't be alarmed! We must prevent both consequences. No
real race loving white man wants to destroy the purity of his
race, and no real Negro conscious of himself, wants to die,
hence there is room for an understanding, and an adjustment.
And that is just what we seek.

Let white and black stop deceiving themselves. Let the
white race stop thinking that all black men are dogs and
not to be considered as human beings. Let foolish Negro
agitators and so-called reformers, encouraged by deceptive
or unthinking white associates, stop preaching and advocating
the doctrine of "social equality," meaning thereby the social
intermingling of both races, intermarriages, and general
social co-relationship. The two extremes will get us nowhere,
other than breeding hate, and encouraging discord, which
will eventually end disastrously to the weaker race.

Some Negroes, in the quest of position and honor, have
been admitted to the full enjoyment of their constitutional
rights. Thus we have some of our men filling high and responsible government positions, others, on their own account,
have established themselves in the professions, commerce
and industry. This, the casual onlooker, and even the men
themselves, will say carries a guarantee and hope of social
equality, and permanent racial progress. But this is the mistake. There is no progress of the Negro in America that is
permanent, so long as we have with us the monster evil—
prejudice.

Prejudice we shall always have between black and white,
so long as the latter believes that the former is intruding
upon their rights. So long as white laborers believe that
black laborers are taking and holding their jobs, so long as
white artisans believe that black artisans are performing the
work that they should do; so long as white men and women
believe that black men and women are filling the positions

that they covet; so long as white political leaders and statesmen believe that black politicians and statesmen are seeking
the same positions in the nation's government; so long as
white men believe that black men want to associate with,
and marry white women, then we will ever have prejudice,
and not only prejudice, but riots, lynchings, burnings, and
God to tell what next will follow! . . .

In another one hundred years white America will have
doubled its population; in another two hundred years it will
have trebled itself. The keen student must realize that the
centuries ahead will bring us an over-crowded country; opportunities, as the population grows larger, will be fewer;
the competition for bread between the people of their own
class will become keener, and so much more so will there be
no room for two competitive races, the one strong, and the
other weak. To imagine Negroes as district attorneys, judges,
senators, congressmen, assemblymen, aldermen, government
clerks and officials, artisans and laborers at work, while
millions of white men starve, is to have before you the bloody
picture of wholesale mob violence that I fear, and against
which I am working.

No preaching, no praying, no presidential edict will control the passion of hungry unreasoning men of prejudice
when the hour comes. It will not come, I pray, in our
generation, but it is of the future that I think and for which
I work.

A generation of ambitious Negro men and women, out from
the best colleges, universities and institutions, capable of
filling the highest and best positions in the nation, in industry,
commerce, society and politics! Can you keep them back?
If you do so they will agitate and throw your constitution in
your faces. Can you stand before civilization and deny the
truth of your constitution? What are you going to do then?
You who are just will open the door of opportunity and say
to all and sundry, "Enter in." But, ladies and gentlemen,
what about the mob, that starving crowd of your own race?
Will they stand by, suffer and starve, and allow an opposite,

competitive race to prosper in the midst of their distress? If you can conjure these things up in your mind, then you have the vision of the race problem of the future in America.

There is but one solution, and that is to provide an outlet for Negro energy, ambition, and passion, away from the attractions of white opportunity and surround the race with opportunities of its own. If this is not done, and if the foundation for same is not laid now, then the consequence will be sorrowful for the weaker race, and disgraceful to our ideals of justice, and shocking to our civilization.

The Negro must have a country and a nation of his own. If you laugh at the idea, then you are selfish and wicked, for you and your children do not intend that the Negro shall discommode you in yours. If you do not want him to have a country and a nation of his own; if you do not intend to give him equal opportunities in yours, then it is plain to see that you mean that he must die, even as the Indian, to make room for your generations.

Why should the Negro die? Has he not served America and the world? Has he not borne the burden of civilization in this Western world for three hundred years? Has he not contributed of his best to America? Surely all this stands to his credit. But there will not be enough room and the one answer is "find a place." We have found a place; it is Africa, and as black men for three centuries have helped white men build America, surely generous and grateful white men will help black men build Africa.

And why shouldn't Africa and America travel down the ages as protectors of human rights and guardians of democracy? Why shouldn't black men help white men secure and establish universal peace? We can only have peace when we are just to all mankind; and for that peace, and for the reign of universal love, I now appeal to the soul of white America. Let the Negroes have a government of their own. Don't encourage them to believe that they will become social equals and leaders of the whites in America, without first on their own account proving to the world that they are capable of evolving a civilization of their own. The white race can best help the Negro by telling him the truth and not by flattering him into believing that he is as good as any white man without first proving the racial, national, constructive metal of which he is made.

Stop flattering the Negro about social equality, and tell him to go to work and build for himself. Help him in the direction of doing for himself, and let him know that self-progress brings its own reward.

# William Jennings Bryan (1860-1925)

*At the time of the Scopes trial, the once prodigious "Boy Orator of the Platte" was definitely an old man, and his great days were behind him. Having early demonstrated his superior powers as an orator on Chautauqua platforms, he won the Democratic Presidential nomination in 1896 with his famous "Cross of Gold" speech. From 1896 until 1912 he was the virtually undisputed leader of the Democratic party, running three times as its unsuccessful Presidential candidate. His last public office before slipping into near oblivion was Secretary of State in Wilson's cabinet, from which he resigned because of differences over his stand for strict neutrality. Perhaps, as Mencken said, Bryan lived too long. "He came into life a hero, a Galahad, in bright and shining armor. He was passing out a poor mountebank."*

From a proposed address in defense of Tennessee's law against the teaching of evolution in the public schools which was never given because arguments to the jury by counsel on both sides were dispensed with by agreement. Reprinted in *World's Most Famous Court Trial* (Cincinnati: National Book Co., 1925), pp. 321-5, 337-8.

# FAITH OF OUR FATHERS

Demosthenes, the greatest of ancient orators, in his "Oration on the Crown," the most famous of his speeches, began by supplicating the favor of all gods and goddesses of Greece. If, in a case which involved only his own fame and fate, he felt justified in petitioning the heathen gods of his country, surely we, who deal with the momentous issues involved in this case, may well pray to the Ruler of the universe for wisdom to guide us in the performance of our several parts in this historic trial.

Let me, in the first place, congratulate our cause that circumstances have committed the trial to a community like this and entrusted the decision to a jury made up largely of the yeomanry of the state. The book in issue in this trial contains on its first page two pictures contrasting the disturbing noises of a great city with the calm serenity of the country. It is a tribute that rural life has fully earned.

I appreciate the sturdy honesty and independence of those who come into daily contact with the earth, who, living near to nature, worship nature's God, and who, dealing with the myriad mysteries of earth and air, seek to learn from revelation about the Bible's wonder-working God. I admire the stern virtues, the vigilance and the patriotism of the class from which the jury is drawn, and am reminded of the lines of Scotland's immortal bard, which, when changed but slightly, describe your country's confidence in you:

> "O Scotia, my dear, my native soil!
>   For whom my warmest wish to Heaven is sent,
> Long may thy hardy sons of rustic toil
>   Be blest with health, and peace, and sweet content!
> "And, oh, may Heav'n their simple lives prevent
>   From luxury's contagion, weak and vile!
> Then, howe'er crowns and coronets be rent,

A virtuous populace may rise the while,
And stand, a wall of fire, around their much-loved isle."

Let us now separate the issues from the misrepresentations, intentional or unintentional, that have obscured both the letter and the purpose of the law. This is not an interference with freedom of conscience. A teacher can think as he pleases and worship God as he likes, or refuse to worship God at all. He can believe in the Bible or discard it; he can accept Christ or reject Him. This law places no obligations or restraints upon him. And so with freedom of speech; he can, so long as he acts as an individual, say anything he likes on any subject. This law does not violate any right guaranteed by any constitution to any individual. It deals with the defendant, not as an individual, but as an employee, an official or public servant, paid by the state, and therefore under instructions from the state.

### Right of the State to Control Public Schools

The right of the state to control the public schools is affirmed in the recent decision in the Oregon case, which declares that the state can direct what shall be taught and also forbid the teaching of anything "manifestly inimical to the public welfare." The above decision goes even farther and declares that the parent not only has the right to guard the religious welfare of the child, but is in duty bound to guard it. That decision fits this case exactly. The state had a right to pass this law, and the law represents the determination of the parents to guard the religious welfare of their children.

It need hardly be added that this law did not have its origin in bigotry. It is not trying to force any form of religion on anybody. The majority is not trying to establish a religion or to teach it—it is trying to protect itself from the effort of an insolent minority to force irreligion upon the children under the guise of teaching science. . . .

Religion is not hostile to learning, Christianity has been the greatest patron learning has ever had. But Christians know that "the fear of the Lord is the beginning of wisdom" now just as it has been in the past, and they therefore oppose the teaching of guesses that encourage godlessness among the students.

Neither does Tennessee undervalue the service rendered by science. The Christian men and women of Tennessee know how deeply mankind is indebted to science for benefits conferred by the discovery of the laws of nature and by the designing of machinery for the utilization of these laws. Give science a fact and it is not only invincible, but it is of incalculable service to man. If one is entitled to draw from society in proportion to the service that he renders to society, who is able to estimate the reward earned by those who have given to us the use of steam, the use of electricity, and enabled us to utilize the weight of water that flows down the mountainside? Who will estimate the value of the service rendered by those who invented the phonograph, the telephone and the radio? Or, to come more closely to our home life, how shall we recompense those who gave us the sewing machine, the harvester, the threshing machine, the tractor, the automobile and the method now employed in making artificial ice? The department of medicine also opens an unlimited field for invaluable service. Typhoid and yellow fever are not feared as they once were. Diphtheria and pneumonia have been robbed of some of their terrors, and a high place on the scroll of fame still awaits the discoverer of remedies for arthritis, cancer, tuberculosis and other dread diseases to which mankind is heir.

Christianity welcomes truth from whatever source it comes, and is not afraid that any real truth from any source can interfere with the divine truth that comes by inspiration from God Himself. It is not scientific truth to which Christians object, for true science is classified knowledge, and nothing therefore can be scientific unless it is true.

### Evolution Not Truth; Merely an Hypothesis

Evolution is not truth; it is merely an hypothesis—it is millions of guesses strung together. It had not been proven in the days of Darwin; he expressed astonishment that with two or three million species it had been impossible to trace any species to any other species. It had not been proven in the days of Huxley, and it has not been proven up to today. It is less than four years ago that Prof. Bateson came all the way from London to Canada to tell the American scientists that every effort to trace one species to another had failed—every one. He said he still had faith in evolution, but had doubts about the origin of species. But of what value is evolution if it cannot explain the origin of species? While many scientists accept evolution as if it were a fact, they all admit, when questioned, that no explanation has been found as to how one species developed into another. . . .

But while the wisest scientists cannot prove a pushing power, such as evolution is supposed to be, there is a lifting power that any child can understand. The plant lifts the mineral up into a higher world, and the animal lifts the plant up into a world still higher. So, it has been reasoned by analogy, man rises, not by a power within him, but only when drawn upward by a higher power. There is a spiritual gravitation that draws all souls toward heaven, just as surely as there is a physical force that draws all matter on the surface of the earth towards the earth's center. Christ is our drawing power; He said, "I, if I be lifted up from the earth, will draw all men unto Me," and His promise is being fulfilled daily all over the world.

It must be remembered that the law under consideration in this case does not prohibit the teaching of evolution up to the line that separates man from the lower forms of animal life. The law might well have gone farther than it does and prohibit the teaching of evolution in lower forms of life; the law is a very conservative statement of the people's opposition to an anti-Biblical hypothesis. The defendant was not content to teach what the law permitted; he, for reasons of his own, persisted in teaching that which was forbidden for reasons entirely satisfactory to the law-makers. . . .

Does it not seem a little unfair not to distinguish between man and lower forms of life? What shall we say of the  intelligence, not to say religion, of those who are so particular to distinguish between fishes and reptiles and birds, but put a man with an immortal soul in the same circle with the wolf, the hyena and the skunk? What must be the impression made upon children by such a degradation of man? . . .

But it is not a laughing matter when one considers that evolution not only offers no suggestions as to a Creator but tends to put the creative act so far away as to cast doubt upon creation itself. And while it is shaking faith in God as a beginning, it is also creating doubt as to a heaven at the end of life. Evolutionists do not feel that it is incumbent upon them to show how life began or at what point in their long-drawn-out scheme of changing species man became endowed with hope and promise of immortal life. God may be a matter of indifference to the evolutionists and a life beyond may have no charm for them, but the mass of mankind will continue to worship their Creator and continue to find comfort in the promise of their Savior that He has gone to prepare a place for them. Christ has made of death a narrow, star-lit strip between the companionship of yesterday ánd the reunion of tomorrow; evolution strikes out the stars and deepens the gloom that enshrouds the tomb.

If the results of evolution were unimportant, one might require less proof in support of the hypothesis, but before accepting a new philosophy of life, built upon a materialistic foundation, we have reason to demand something more than guesses; "we may well suppose" is not a sufficient substitute for "Thus saith the Lord." . . .

In 1900—twenty-five years ago—while an international peace congress was in session in Paris, the following editorial appeared in *L'Univers:*

"The spirit of peace has fled the earth because evolution has taken possession of it. The plea for peace in past years has been inspired by faith in the divine nature and the divine origin of man; men were then looked upon as children of one Father, and war, therefore, was fratricide. But now that men are looked upon as children of apes, what matters it whether they are slaughtered or not? . . ."

Let us, then, hear the conclusion of the whole matter. Science is a magnificent material force, but it is not a teacher of morals. It can perfect machinery, but it adds no moral restraints to protect society from the misuse of the machine. It can also build gigantic intellectual ships, but it constructs no moral rudders for the control of storm-tossed human vessels. It not only fails to supply the spiritual element needed but some of its unproven hypotheses rob the ship of its compass and thus endangers its cargo.

In war, science has proven itself an evil genius; it has made war more terrible than it ever was before. Man used to be content to slaughter his fellowmen on a single plane —the earth's surface. Science has taught him to go down into the water and shoot up from below and to go up into the clouds and shoot down from above, thus making the battlefield three times as bloody as it was before; but science does not teach brotherly love. Science has made war so hellish that civilization was about to commit suicide; and not we are told that newly discovered instruments of destruction will make the cruelties of the late war seem trivial in comparison with the cruelties of wars that may come in the future. If civilization is to be saved from the wreckage threatened by intelligence not consecrated by love, it must be saved by the moral code of the meek and lowly Nazarene. His teachings, and His teachings alone, can solve the problems that vex the heart and perplex the world.

The world needs a Savior more than it ever did before, and there is only one Name under heaven given among men whereby we must be saved. It is this Name that evolution degrades, for, carried to its logical conclusion, it robs Christ of the glory of a virgin birth, of the majesty of His deity and mission and of the triumph of His resurrection. It also disputes the doctrine of the atonement.

It is for the jury to determine whether this attack upon the Christian religion shall be permitted in the public schools of Tennessee by teachers employed by the state and paid out of the public treasury. This case is no longer local, the defendant ceases to play an important part. The case has assumed the proportions of a battle-royal between unbelief that attempts to speak through so-called science and the defenders of the Christian faith, speaking through the legislators of Tennessee. It is again a choice between God and Baal; it is also a renewal of the issue in Pilate's court. . . .

Again force and love meet face to face, and the question, "What shall I do with Jesus?" must be answered. A bloody, brutal doctrine—Evolution—demands, as the rabble did nineteen hundred years ago, that He be crucified. That cannot be the answer of this jury representing a Christian state and sworn to uphold the laws of Tennessee. Your answer will be heard throughout the world; it is eagerly awaited by a praying multitude. If the law is nullified, there will be rejoicing wherever God is repudiated, the Savior scoffed at and the Bible ridiculed. Every unbeliever of every kind and degree will be happy. If, on the other hand, the law is upheld and the religion of the school children protected, millions of Christians will call you blessed and, with hearts full of gratitude to God, will sing again that grand old song of triumph:

> "Faith of our fathers, living still,
> In spite of dungeon, fire and sword;
> O how our hearts beat high with joy

Whene'er we hear that glorious word—
Faith of our fathers—holy faith;
We will be true to thee till death!"

# Clarence Darrow (1857-1938)

*A famous criminal lawyer, he was started on his
career in the 1890's by the liberal governor of
Illinois, John Peter Altgeld. Noted for his defense
of unpopular causes, he defended, at one time
or another, the eight anarchists in the Haymar-
ket case, Eugene Debs and the American Railway Union, Big Bill Haywood of the Western
Federation of Miners, the McNamara brothers
who bombed the anti-union Los Angeles Times,
and the "thrill-murderers" Loeb and Leopold
before he confronted the aging Bryan in 1925.
A defense lawyer by conviction, his trial arguments were based on his philosophic view that
men acted in response to social and physiological forces which they could not control and
usually did not recognize.*

# IN DEFENSE OF REASON

I remember, long ago, Mr. Bancroft wrote this sentence,
which is true: "That it is all right to preserve freedom in
constitutions, but when the spirit of freedom has fled from
the hearts of the people, then its matter is easily sacrificed under law." And so it is, unless there is left enough
of the spirit of freedom in the state of Tennessee, and in
the United States, there is not a single line of any constitution that can withstand bigotry and ignorance when it

---

From the second day's proceedings as recorded in the *World's Most Famous
Trial* (Cincinnati: National Book Co., 1925), pp. 75, 77-8, 82-4, 87.

seeks to destroy the rights of the individual; and bigotry and ignorance are ever active. Here, we find today as brazen and as bold an attempt to destroy learning as was ever made in the middle ages, and the only difference is we have not provided that they shall be burned at the stake, but there is time for that, Your Honor, we have to approach these things gradually. . . .

What is the Bible? . . . It is a book primarily of religion and morals. It is not a book of science. Never was and was never meant to be. Under it there is nothing prescribed that would tell you how to build a railroad or a steamboat or to make anything that would advance civilization. It is not a textbook or a text on chemistry. It is not big enough to be. It is not a book on geology; they knew nothing about geology. It is not a book on biology; they knew nothing about it. It is not a work on evolution; that is a mystery. It is not a work on astronomy. The man who looked out at the universe and studied the heavens had no thought but that the earth was the center of the universe. But we know better than that. We know that the sun is the center of the solar system. And that there are an infinity of other systems around about us. They thought the sun went around the earth and gave us light and gave us night. We know better. We know the earth turns on its axis to produce days and nights. They thought the earth was 4,004 years before the Christian Era. We know better. I doubt if there is a person in Tennessee who does not know better. They told it the best they knew. And while suns may change all you may learn of chemistry, geometry and mathematics, there are no doubt certain primitive, elemental instincts in the organs of man that remain the same, he finds out what he can and yearns to know more and supplements his knowledge with hope and faith.

That is the province of religion and I haven't the slightest fault to find with it. . . .

The state by constitution is committed to the doctrine of education, committed to schools. It is committed to teaching and I assume when it is committed to teaching it is committed to teaching the truth—ought to be anyhow—plenty of people to do the other. It is committed to teaching literature and science. My friend has suggested that literature and science might conflict. I cannot quite see how, but that is another question. But that indicates the policy of the state of Tennessee and wherever it is used in construing the unconstitutionality of this act it can only be used as an indication of what the state meant and you could not pronounce a statute void on it, but we insist that this statute is absolutely void because it contravenes Section 3, which is headed "the right of worship free." . . . If this section of the constitution which guarantees religious liberty in Tennessee cannot be sustained in the spirit it cannot be sustained in the letter. What does it mean? What does it mean? I know two intelligent people can agree only for a little distance, like a company walking along in a road. They may go together a few blocks and then one branches off. The remainder go together a few more blocks and another branches off and still further some one else branches off and the human minds are just that way, provided they are free, of course; the fundamentalists may be put in a trap so they cannot think differently if at all, probably not at all, but leave two free minds and they may go together a certain distance, but not all the way together. There are no two human machines alike and no two human beings have the same experiences and their ideas of life and philosophy grow out of their construction of the experiences that we meet on our journey through life. It is impossible, if you leave freedom in the world, to mold the opinions of one man upon the opinions of another—only tyranny can do it—and your constitutional provision, providing a freedom of religion, was meant to meet that emergency. I will go further—there is nothing else—since man—I don't know whether I dare say evolved—still, this isn't a school—since man was created out of the dust of the earth—out of hand—there is nothing else,

Your Honor, that has caused the difference of opinion, of bitterness, of hatred, of war, of cruelty, that religion has caused. With that, of course, it has given consolation to millions.

But it is one of those particular things that should be left solely between the individual and his Maker, or his God, or whatever takes expression with him, and it is no one else's concern.

How many creeds and cults are there this whole world over? No man could enumerate them. At least as I have said, 500 different Christian creeds, all made up of differences, Your Honor, every one of them, and these subdivided into small differences, until they reach every member of every congregation. Because to think is to differ, and then there are any number of creeds older and any number of creeds younger, than the Christian creed, any number of them, the world has had them forever. They have come and they have gone, they have abided their time and have passed away, some of them are here still, some may be here forever, but there has been a multitude, due to the multitude and manifold differences in human beings, and it was meant by the constitutional convention of Tennessee to leave these questions of religion between man and whatever he worshiped, to leave him free. Has the Mohammedan any right to stay here and cherish his creed? Has the Buddhist a right to live here and cherish his creed? Can the Chinaman who comes here to wash our clothes, can he bring his joss and worship it? Is there any man that holds a religious creed, no matter where he came from, or how old it is or how false it is, is there any man that can be prohibited by any act of the legislature of Tennessee? Impossible? The constitution of Tennessee, as I understand, was copied from the one that Jefferson wrote, so clear, simple, direct, to encourage the freedom of religious opinion, said in substance, that no act shall ever be passed to interfere with complete religious liberty. Now is this it or is not this it? What do you say? What does it do? . . . Can a legislative body say, "You cannot read a book or take a lesson, or make a talk on science until you first find out whether you are saying against Genesis." It can unless that constitutional provision protects me. It can. Can it say to the astronomer, you cannot turn your telescope upon the infinite planets and suns and stars that fill space, lest you find that the earth is not the center of the universe and there is not any firmament between us and the heaven. Can it? It could—except for the work of Thomas Jefferson, which has been woven into every state constitution of the Union, and has stayed there like the flaming sword to protect the rights of man against ignorance and bigotry, and when it is permitted to overwhelm them, then we are taken in a sea of blood and ruin that all the miseries and tortures and carrion of the middle ages would be as nothing. They would need to call back these men once more. But are the provisions of the constitutions that they left, are they enough to protect you and me, and everyone else in a land which we thought was free? Now, let us see what it says: "All men have a natural and indefeasible right to worship Almighty God according to the dictates of their own conscience."

That takes care, even of the despised modernist, who dares to be intelligent. "That no man can of right be compelled to attend, erect or support any place of worship, or to maintain any minister against his consent; that no human authority can in any case whatever control or interfere with the rights of conscience in any case whatever"—that does not mean whatever, that means, "barring fundamentalist propaganda." It does not mean whatever at all times, sometimes maybe—and that "no preference shall be given by law to any religious establishment or mode of worship." . . .

And along comes somebody who says we have got to believe it as I believe it. It is a crime to know more than I know. And they publish a law to inhibit learning. Now, what is in the way of it? First, what does the law say? This law says that it shall be a criminal offense to teach in the public schools any account of the origin of man that is in conflict with the divine account in the Bible. It makes the Bible the yard stick to measure every man's intellect, to measure every man's intelligence and to measure every man's learning. Are your mathematics good? Turn to I Elijah ii, is your philosophy good? See II Samuel iii, is your astronomy good? See Genesis, Chapter 2, Verse 7, is your chemistry good? See—well, chemistry, see Deuteronomy iii-6, or anything that tells about brimstone. Every bit of knowledge that the mind has, must be submitted to a religious test. Now, let us see, it is a travesty upon language, it is a travesty upon justice, it is a travesty upon the constitution to say that any citizen of Tennessee can be deprived of his rights by a legislative body in the face of the constitution. . . .

If today you can take a thing like evolution and make it a crime to teach it in the public school, tomorrow you can make it a crime to teach it in the private schools, and the next year you can make it a crime to teach it to the hustings or in the church. At the next session you may ban books and the newspapers. Soon you may set Catholic against Protestant and Protestant against Protestant, and try to foist your own religion upon the minds of men. If you can do one you can do the other. Ignorance and fanaticism is ever busy and needs feeding. Always it is feeding and gloating for more. Today it is the public school teachers, tomorrow the private. The next day the preachers and the lecturers, the magazines, the books, the newspapers. After while, Your Honor, it is the setting of man against man and creed against creed until with flying banners and beating drums we are marching backward to the glorious ages of the sixteenth century when bigots lighted fagots to burn the men who dared to bring any intelligence and enlightment and culture to the human mind.

# Warren G. Harding (1865-1923)

*Twenty-ninth President of the United States, he
was a genial, handsome, densely ignorant man
whose life seemed to be directed by expediency
rather than conviction. As William Allen
White observed, "At best he was a dub who had
made his reputation running with the [Republi-
can] political machine in Ohio, making Memorial Day addresses for the Elks, addressing
service clubs—the Rotarians, Kiwanians, or
the Lions—uttering resounding platitudes, and
saying nothing because he knew nothing."
The major achievement of his administration,
the Washington Naval Conference for naval
limitation, was largely forgotten in the
scandalous exposures after his death of corruption in the major departments of government,
which stamped his administration as both corrupt and incompetent.*

## BACK TO NORMALCY

My Countrymen: When one surveys the world about him
after the great storm, noting the marks of destruction
and yet rejoicing in the ruggedness of the things which
withstood it, if he is an American he breathes the clarified
atmosphere with a strange mingling of regret and new
hope. We have seen a world passion spend its fury, but
we contemplate our Republic unshaken, and hold our civilization secure. Liberty—liberty within the law—and civilization are inseparable, and though both were threatened we
find them now secure; and there comes to Americans the

From Inaugural Address of President Warren G. Harding, *Congressional Record*, 67th Cong., Spec. sess., Mar. 4, 1921, LXI, pt. 1, 4–6.

profound assurance that our representative government is the highest expression and surest guaranty of both. . . .

The recorded progress of our Republic, materially and spiritually, in itself proves the wisdom of the inherited policy of noninvolvement in Old World affairs. Confident of our ability to work out our own destiny, and jealously guarding our right to do so, we seek no part in directing the destinies of the Old World. We do not mean to be entangled. We will accept no responsibility except as our own conscience and judgment, in each instance, may determine.

Our eyes never will be blind to a developing menace, our ears never deaf to the call of civilization. We recognize the new order in the world, with the closer contacts which progress has wrought. We sense the call of the human heart for fellowship, fraternity, and cooperation. We crave friendship and harbor no hate. But America, our America, the America builded on the foundation laid by the inspired fathers, can be a party to no permanent military alliance. It can enter into no political commitments, nor assume any economic obligations which will subject our decisions to any other than our own authority. . . .

Since freedom impelled, and independence inspired, and nationality exalted, a world supergovernment is contrary to everything we cherish and can have no sanction by our Republic. This is not selfishness; it is sanctity. It is not aloofness; it is security. It is not suspicion of others; it is patriotic adherence to the things which made us what we are. . . .

Our supreme task is the resumption of our onward, normal way. Reconstruction, readjustment, restoration—all these must follow. I would like to hasten them. . . .

We contemplate the immediate task of putting our public household in order. We need a rigid and yet sane economy, combined with fiscal justice, and it must be attended by individual prudence and thrift, which are so essential to this trying hour and reassuring for the future.

The business world reflects the disturbance of war's reaction. Herein flows the lifeblood of material existence. The economic mechanism is intricate and its parts interdependent, and has suffered the shocks and jars incident to abnormal demands, credit inflations, and price upheavals. The normal balances have been impaired, the channels of distribution have been clogged, the relations of labor and management have been strained. We must seek the readjustment with care and courage. Our people must give and take. Prices must reflect the receding fever of war activities. Perhaps we never shall know the old levels of wage again, because war invariably readjusts compensations, and the necessaries of life will show their inseparable relationship, but we must strive for normalcy to reach stability. All the penalties will not be light nor evenly distributed. There is no way of making them so. There is no instant step from disorder to order. We must face a condition of grim reality, charge off our losses, and start afresh. It is the oldest lesson of civilization. I would like Government to do all it can to mitigate; then, in understanding, in mutuality of interest, in concern for the common good, our tasks will be solved. No altered system will work a miracle. Any wild experiment will only add to the confusion. Our best assurance lies in efficient administration of our proven system.

The forward course of the business cycle is unmistakable. Peoples are turning from destruction to production. Industry has sensed the changed order and our own people are turning to resume their normal, onward way. The call is for productive America to go on. I know that Congress and the administration will favor every wise Government policy to aid the resumption and encourage continued progress.

I speak for administrative efficiency, for lightened tax burdens, for sound commercial practices, for adequate credit facilities, for sympathetic concern for all agricultural problems, for the omission of unnecessary interference of Government with business, for an end to Government's experiment in business, and for more efficient business in government administration. With all of this must attend a mindfulness of the human side of all activities, so that social, industrial, and economic justice will be squared with the purposes of a righteous people. . . .

If revolution insists upon overturning established order, let other peoples make the tragic experiment. There is no place for it in America. When world war threatened civilization we pledged our resources and our lives to its preservation, and when revolution threatens we unfurl the flag of law and order and renew our consecration. Ours is a constitutional freedom where the popular will is the law supreme and minorities are sacredly protected. Our revisions, reformations, and evolutions reflect a deliberate judgment and an orderly progress, and we mean to cure our ills, but never destroy or permit destruction by force. . . .

We would not have an America living within and for herself alone, but we would have her self-reliant, independent, and ever nobler, stronger, and richer. Believing in our higher standards, reared through constitutional liberty and maintained opportunity, we invite the world to the same heights. But pride in things wrought is no reflex of a completed task. Common welfare is the goal of our national endeavor. Wealth is not inimical to welfare; it ought to be its friendliest agency. There never can be equality of rewards or possessions so long as the human plan contains varied talents and differing degrees of industry and thrift, but ours ought to be a country free from great blotches of distressed poverty. We ought to find a way to guard against the perils and penalties of unemployment. We want an America of homes, illumined with hope and happiness, where mothers, freed from the necessity for long hours of toil beyond their own doors, may preside as befits the hearthstone of American citizenship. We want the cradle of American childhood rocked under conditions so wholesome and so hopeful that no blight may touch it in its development, and we want to provide that no selfish interest, no material necessity, no lack of opportunity, shall prevent the gaining of that education so essential to best citizenship.

There is no short cut to the making of these ideals into glad realities. The world has witnessed, again and again, the futility and the mischief of ill-considered remedies for social and economic disorders. But we are mindful today, as never before, of the friction of modern industrialism, and we must learn its causes and reduce its evil consequences by sober and tested methods. Where genius has made for great possibilities, justice and happiness must be reflected in a greater common welfare.

# Eugene V. Debs (1855-1926)

*A perennial rebel and martyr, he began his career as a locomotive fireman and, in 1893, was made president of the American Railway Union. After the union was broken in the Pullman Strike of 1894, he was convicted and imprisoned on a juridical sophism. When released, he helped organize the Socialist party and was five times its candidate for President. As Ray Ginger has pointed out, he never doubted his moral responsibility for the welfare of his brothers and was convinced the common people were being crucified by an outmoded economic system. Though an advocate of class-conscious industrial unionism and a founder of the International Workers of the World, he broke with the revolutionary union when it resorted to force and violence. A sincere, perhaps naïve reformer, he always spoke his mind, regardless of consequences. Because in 1918 he had frankly told Americans: "Quit going to war. Stop murdering one another for the profit and glory of the*

*ruling classes. Cultivate the arts of peace.*
*Humanize humanity. Civilize civilization," he*
*was sent to jail for obstructing the conscription*
*act.*

# A LAST CALL
# FOR REVOLUTION

In the national campaign of 1920 the Socialist Party calls upon all American workers of hand and brain, and upon all citizens who believe in political liberty and social justice, to free the country from the oppressive misrule of the old political parties, and to take the government into their own hands under the banner and upon the program of the Socialist Party.

The outgoing administration, like Democratic and Republican administrations of the past, leaves behind it a disgraceful record of solemn pledges unscrupulously broken and public confidence ruthlessly betrayed.

It obtained the suffrage of the people on a platform of peace, liberalism and social betterment, but drew the country into a devastating war, and inaugurated a régime of despotism, reaction and oppression unsurpassed in the annals of the republic.

It promised to the American people a treaty which would assure to the world a reign of international right and true democracy. It gave its sanction and support to an infamous pact formulated behind closed doors by predatory elder statesmen of European and Asiatic imperialism. Under this pact territories have been annexed against the will of their populations and cut off from their sources of sustenance; nations seeking their freedom in the exercise of much heralded right of self-determination have been

---

From the Socialist Party Platform of 1920 in Kirk H. Porter and Donald B. Johnson, eds. *National Party Platforms* (Urbana: University of Illinois Press, 1961), pp. 238–41. Reprinted by permission of the publisher.

brutally fought with armed force, intrigue and starvation blockades.

To the millions of young men, who staked their lives on the field of battle, to the people of the country who gave unstintingly of their toil and property to support the war, the Democratic administration held out the sublime ideal of a union of the peoples of the world organized to maintain perpetual peace among nations on the basis of justice and freedom. It helped create a reactionary alliance of imperialistic governments, banded together to bully weak nations, crush working-class governments and perpetuate strife and warfare.

While thus furthering the ends of reaction, violence and oppression abroad, our administration suppressed the cherished and fundamental rights and civil liberties at home.

Upon the pretext of war-time necessity, the Chief Executive of the republic and the appointed heads of his administration were clothed with dictatorial powers (which were often exercised arbitrarily), and Congress enacted laws in open and direct violation of the constitutional safeguards of freedom of expression.

Hundreds of citizens who raised their voices for the maintenance of political and industrial rights during the war were indicted under the Espionage Law, tried in an atmosphere of prejudice and hysteria and are now serving inhumanly long jail sentences for daring to uphold the traditions of liberty which once were sacred in this country.

Agents of the Federal government unlawfully raided homes and meeting places and prevented or broke up peaceable gatherings of citizens.

The postmaster-general established a censorship of the press more autocratic than that ever tolerated in a régime of absolutism, and has harassed and destroyed publications on account of their advanced political and economic views, by excluding them from the mails.

And after the war was in fact long over, the administration has not scrupled to continue a policy of repression and terrorism under the shadow and hypocritical guise of war-time measures.

It has practically imposed involuntary servitude and peonage on a large class of American workers by denying them the right to quit work and coercing them into acceptance of inadequate wages and onerous conditions of labor. It has dealt a foul blow to the traditional American right of asylum by deporting hundreds of foreign-born workers by administrative order, on the mere suspicion of harboring radical views, and often for the sinister purpose of breaking labor strikes.

In the short span of three years our self-styled liberal administration has succeeded in undermining the very foundation of political liberty and economic rights which this republic has built up in more than a century of struggle and progress.

Under the cloak of a false and hypocritical patriotism and under the protection of governmental terror the Democratic administration has given the ruling classes unrestrained license to plunder the people by intensive exploitation of labor, by the extortion of enormous profits and by increasing the cost of all necessities of life. Profiteering has become reckless and rampant, billions have been coined by the capitalists out of the suffering and misery of their fellow men. The American financial oligarchy has become a dominant factor in the world, while the condition of the American workers has grown more precarious.

The responsibility does not rest upon the Democratic party alone. The Republican party, through its representatives in Congress and otherwise, has not only openly condoned the political misdeeds of the last three years, but has sought to outdo its Democratic rival in the orgy of political reaction and repression. Its criticism of the Democratic administrative policy is that it is not reactionary and drastic enough.

America is now at the parting of the roads. If the outraging of political liberty and concentration of economic power into the hands of the few is permitted to go on, it can have only one consequence, the reduction of the country to a state of absolute capitalist despotism.

We particularly denounce the militaristic policy of both old parties, of investing countless hundreds of millions of dollars in armaments after the victorious completion of what was to have been the "last war." We call attention to the fatal results of such a program in Europe, carried on prior to 1914, and culminating in the Great War; we declare that such a policy, adding unbearable burdens to the working class and to all the people, can lead only to the complete Prussianization of the nation, and ultimately to war; and we demand immediate and complete abandonment of this fatal program.

The Socialist Party sounds the warning. It calls upon the people to defeat both parties at the polls, and to elect the candidates of the Socialist Party to the end of restoring political democracy and bringing about complete industrial freedom. . . .

To achieve this end the Socialist Party pledges itself to the following program:

### 1.  Social

1.   All business vitally essential for the existence and welfare of the people, such as railroads, express service, steamship lines, telegraphs, mines, oil wells, power plants, elevators, packing houses, cold storage plants and all industries operating on a national scale, should be taken over by the nation.

2.   All publicly owned industries should be administered jointly by the government and representatives of the workers, not for revenue or profit, but with the sole object of securing just compensation and humane conditions of employment to the workers and efficient and reasonable service to the public.

3. All banks should be acquired by the government, and incorporated in a unified public banking system.

4. The business of insurance should be taken over by the government, and should be extended to include insurance against accident, sickness, invalidity, old age and unemployment, without contribution on the part of the worker.

5. Congress should enforce the provisions of the Thirteenth, Fourteenth and Fifteenth Amendments with reference to the Negroes, and effective federal legislation should be enacted to secure to the Negroes full civil, political, industrial and educational rights.

### 2. *Industrial*

1. Congress should enact effective laws to abolish child labor, to fix minimum wages, based on an ascertained cost of a decent standard of life, to protect migratory and unemployed workers from oppression, to abolish detective and strike-breaking agencies and to establish a shorter work-day in keeping with increased industrial productivity.

### 3. *Political*

1. The constitutional freedom of speech, press and assembly should be restored by repealing the Espionage Law and all other repressive legislation, and by prohibiting the executive usurpation of authority.

2. All prosecutions under the Espionage Law should be discontinued, and all persons serving prison sentences for alleged offenses growing out of religious beliefs, political views or industrial activities should be fully pardoned and immediately released.

3. No alien should be deported from the United States on account of his political views or participation in labor struggles, nor in any event without proper trial on specific charges. The arbitrary power to deport aliens by administrative order should be repealed.

4.   The power of the courts to restrain workers in their struggles against employers by the Writ of Injunction or otherwise, and their power to nullify congressional legislation, should be abrogated.

5.   Federal judges should be elected by the people and be subject to recall.

6.   The President and the Vice-President of the United States should be elected by direct popular election, and be subject to recall. All members of the Cabinet should be elected by Congress and be responsible at all times to the vote thereof.

7.   Suffrage should be equal and unrestricted in fact as well as in law for all men and women throughout the nation.

8.   Because of the strict residential qualification of suffrage in this country, millions of citizens are disfranchised in every election; adequate provision should be made for the registration and voting of migratory workers.

9.   The Constitution of the United States should be amended to strengthen the safeguards of civil and political liberty, and to remove all obstacles to industrial and social reform and reconstruction, including the changes enumerated in this program, in keeping with the will and interest of the people. It should be made amendable by a majority of the voters of the nation upon their own initiative, or upon the initiative of Congress.

# CHAPTER TWO

# Dollar Democracy

I

The American people had traveled along the road to normalcy slightly more than two years when, in 1923, President Harding unexpectedly died and was succeeded by Vice President Calvin Coolidge. Considered "a pre-eminently safe man," Coolidge had certified his orthodoxy by his candid veneration of the dollar and proved his patriotism by publishing an anti-radical tract entitled "Are the 'Reds' Stalking Our College Women?" He had been catapulted into the headlines by his resolutely unsympathetic attitude toward the Boston police strike of 1919, when as Governor of Massachusetts he dispatched a telegram to Samuel Gompers, head of the American Federation of Labor, refusing arbitration and maintaining, "There is no right to strike against the public safety by anybody, anywhere, anytime." The country's newspapers applauded, and overnight Coolidge became a national hero. On the strength of this opportune slogan Coolidge was started on his way to the White House.[1]

Unlike the jovial Harding, who had wallowed in "equivocal verbosity," Coolidge was publicly taciturn and sourly Puritanical, but like his predecessor Coolidge displayed an almost mystical devotion to the status quo. Change, he firmly believed, resulted in more harm than good. "Four-fifths of all our troubles in this life would disappear," he once remarked, "if we would only sit down and keep still." With Coolidge, commented Lippmann, inactivity was a political philosophy and a party program. Not merely a soft and easy desire to let things slide, it was "a grim, determined, alert inactivity" which kept the President occupied constantly at the task of neutralizing and thwarting political activity wherever it showed signs of life. This policy of "active inactivity" suited the mood and certain needs of the country admirably. Everybody who was making money wanted to let well enough alone. Prosperous America, it was said, "wanted above everything the status quo," and "was worshiping on padded knee the God of things as they were."[2]

But while a national policy of political inactivity suited the business interests, it did not suit organized labor, which was kept at a disadvantage under the status quo. Partly as a result of the Red Scare, labor had been driven into a hopeless position in the twenties. Not only had the labor movement been badly mauled in 1919–1920, losing more than a million members in two years, but lingering public suspicion of labor radicalism after the bitterly controversial Steel Strike of 1919 was used by employer groups to frustrate unionism. Though Scare-inspired prejudice against aliens had led to restrictive immigration laws in 1924, any potential benefits as far as labor was concerned were wasted in a hostile social climate which stressed individualism and had no use for collective action.

By launching a nationwide propaganda drive identifying organized labor's insistence upon the closed shop as "un-American," employer organizations—notably the National Association of Manufacturers with assistance from the Bankers Association and the United States Chamber of Commerce—were able to severely cripple labor unionism. In a flood of anti-labor literature distributed to the press, churches, banks, schools, colleges, businesses, and to local chambers of commerce, unionism and un-Americanism were made to appear synonymous, while at the same time business was apotheosized as the champion of the open shop or the "American Plan," as it was now popularly labeled, which was skillfully presented as the major bulwark against the "Soviet methods" and the "subversive foreign concept" of unionism.[3]

Though the public was led to believe that anything less than the open shop was "un-American" and "un-patriotic," the real issue was not radicalism, but the much more basic question of union versus no union. Allegedly the open shop was one "with equal opportunity for all and special privileges for none," where non-union and union men received the same treatment, but actually in most cases so-called "open" shops were normally non-union shops. Anti-union employers were not only relieved of the obligation to hire only union members, but, more important from management's point of view, they were in the very advantageous position of being able to bargain on an individual rather than a collective basis. Behind the "patriotic" propaganda of the open shop was the employer's knowledge that without the closed or union shop it was impossible for labor to organize American industry. As open-shop sentiment gained wide support among the public and the press, business leaders pressed their advantage:[4] E. H. Gary, chairman of United States Steel, was reported in the *New York Times* as saying he saw no necessity for labor unions at present; and Charles N. Fay, prominent utilities executive and former vice-president of the N.A.M., told businessmen the time was now ripe for strict government control of labor.*

If America in the twenties was an employer's paradise, a major reason was the hostile attitude of the courts and the law toward labor. From the viewpoint of the law organized labor, unlike organized business, was not accepted as a legitimate institution of American society. Though in

*Charles N. Fay, *No Right to Strike*. See page 122.

theory the law treated both sides equally, in reality the law and the existing economic situation favored the employer: "The law recognized the equal freedom of the employers to destroy labor organizations and to deny the right of employees to join trade unions. An employer could coerce or threaten his employees to keep them from organizing. He could discharge them if they joined a union, and he could refuse to hire anyone who was a member. He could decline to deal with any union of his employees or to recognize the organization or any of its officers or agents as representatives of the employees. He was free to organize a company union of his own and force his employees to join it." Labor's actions, on the other hand, were severely limited. For instance, labor's chief weapon, the strike, was illegal if the court did not approve its purpose—and usually the courts did not approve of strikes for union recognition or for the closed shop. Equally crippling were the restrictions fixed by the courts upon the conduct of strikers: threats, coercion, intimidation (including psychic intimidation) were unlawful but so were boycotts and most picketing. Chief Justice Taft declared even peaceful picketing illegal on grounds that the word "picket" was "sinister" and suggested "a militant purpose."[5]

Beyond doubt, the two most powerful weapons used by the courts were the injunction and the Sherman Act. Usually invoked under the anti-trust provisions of the Sherman Act (which originally had been intended to apply only to the monopolistic practices of big business), the injunction commonly prohibited the employment of force, coercion, and intimidation; prevented or regulated picketing; barred boycotts, trespass, use of the epithet "scab," and payment of strike benefits. Sometimes the court order went so far as to forbid workers to strike or the union to hold meetings. The height of absurdity was reached in Iowa in 1930 when an injunction, in effect, prohibited a striker from telling his wife there was a controversy over wages and put him into contempt of court if he did so. Even though the Clayton

Act passed in 1914 during the first Wilson administration—
and rashly hailed as labor's Magna Carta—had specifically
forbidden application of anti-trust laws to labor organizations and prohibited use of injunctions in labor disputes,
the courts by various legal evasions nevertheless issued
more injunctions and applied the anti-trust laws against
labor in more cases in the 1920's than in any similar period
of American history. In short, under these adverse circumstances, all that American laborers had was a right to try
to organize if they could get away with it; and whether
they could or not depended in last measure upon the
courts.[6]

Without public confidence and unable to gain any sympathy from either government or the courts, the position
of organized labor steadily deteriorated in the twenties.
Magazines and newspapers were full of articles and editorials with such titles as "The Collapse of Organized Labor,"
"Decline of Organized Labor in America," and "The Twilight of the A. F. of L." By 1930 union membership
amounted to barely 10 percent of the labor force, about
half that of 1920, and great segments of American industry were completely unorganized, including such important
industries as steel, automobiles, rubber, textiles, and electri-
cal equipment. With real wages and salaries rising 20.6
percent between 1923 and 1929, there was little incentive
to organize among skilled workers, and under mounting
pressure from business and the press the attitude of organized labor shifted from militancy to respectability. Labor
leadership pursued a gentle policy of "concord rather than
conflict" so successfully that thousands of abandoned American workers would have readily agreed with Mencken that
the A. F. of L. was not a labor organization at all but
"simply a balloon mattress interposed between capital and
labor to protect the former from the latter."[7]

The most graphic portrayal of the plight of unionism in
the twenties was the fate of the United Mine Workers.
In 1920 the union was the largest and most powerful in

America; at the end of the decade, it lay in ruins. The initial cause of its extraordinary decline was a falling market brought about by an overproduction of coal. As coal prices plunged downward, mine operators sought to cut the wages of miners, two-thirds of whom according to the U.S. Coal Commission were already earning less than a living wage. The union under John L. Lewis balked, vowing "No Backward Step!" In insisting on the maintenance of an American wage standard in the coal fields, Lewis argued, the UMW was only acting according to the theory of the free-enterprise system—"that the ultimate prosperity of all is best assured by the utmost endeavor of each to better his own condition."°

Certainly living conditions of the miners were far below the American standard. After visiting 800 mining communities in 1923, of which 713 were company-owned, representatives of the U.S. Coal Commission found housing generally poor: "In the worst of the company-controlled communities the state of disrepair at times runs beyond the power of verbal description or even of photographic illustration, since neither words nor pictures can portray the atmosphere of abandoned dejection or reproduce the smells. Old, unpainted board and batten houses—batten going or gone, and boards fast following, roofs broken, porches staggering, steps sagging, a riot of rubbish, and a medley of odors—such are features of the worst camps." In company-owned dwellings less than three percent had bathtubs or toilets, fewer than fourteen percent running water. But far worse than living in squalor and filth, the miner living in a company town usually forfeited his right to citizenship, lost the rights of free speech and free assemblage, and if he complained of any grievance, he was liable to be summarily dismissed and blacklisted, and his family turned out into the street.[8]

When Lewis refused to agree to a wage reduction, the

°John L. Lewis, *The Miners' Fight for American Standards*. See page 127.

operators set about the systematic destruction of the union. Although John D. Rockefeller, Jr., publicly denounced the labor policy of the operators as "both unwise and unjust," his was a lone voice among mine owners. Like the Railroad Labor Board, most of them were inclined to regard the theory of "the living wage" as "a bit of mellifluous phraseology" and no doubt felt that its application would bring the nation's industry to "communistic ruin." The offensive was taken by the Pittsburgh Coal Company, the largest producer in the country, which had recently passed into the hands of the Mellon banking interests (Treasury Secretary Andrew Mellon and his brother owned 25 percent of the stock). After having had a contract with the miners for thirty-five years, the company closed down in 1924 and then a year later, in violation of its agreement, reopened on a non-union basis. When the UMW struck to enforce the contract, Pittsburgh Coal evicted the miners and their families from company houses and brought in Negro and white strikebreakers, employing armed guards for their protection—many of whom were thoughtfully provided by the Governor of Pennsylvania. War broke out in the coal fields, and how many lives were lost from starvation and violence will never be known. But, as a reporter from the New York *Daily News* discovered, conditions were almost beyond belief:

I have just returned from a visit to "Hell-in-Pennsylvania." I have seen horrible things there; things which I almost hesitate to enumerate and describe. I can scarcely expect my story to be believed. I did not believe it myself when the situation was first outlined to me. Then I went into the coal camps of western and central Pennsylvania and saw for myself.

. . . Many times it seemed impossible to think that we were in modern, civilized America.

We saw thousands of women and children, literally starving to death. We found hundreds of destitute families living in crudely constructed bare-board shacks. They had been evicted from their homes by the coal companies. We unearthed a system of despotic tyranny reminiscent of Czar-ridden Siberia at its worst. We found police brutality and industrial slavery. We discovered the weirdest flock of injunctions that ever emanated from American temples of justice.

We unearthed evidence of terrorism and counterterrorism; of mob beatings and near lynchings; of dishonesty, graft, and heartlessness. . . .

The mine fields are a bubbling cauldron of trouble. If it boils over—and it threatens to do so—blood must flow freely and many lives pay the forfeit.

---

When the United Mine Workers tried to organize West Virginia in 1924, they ran into determined resistance from mine operators. Union miners attempting to march into non-union areas were met by a force of 2,000 men, including state troopers with machine-guns and tanks.

United Press International, Inc.

As Irving Bernstein has noted, the combination of armed power and starvation virtually destroyed the union. By 1928 the UMW bargained for only twenty percent of the nation's bituminous miners, and wages had dropped from $7.50 to as little as $1.50 a day.[9]

# II

The miners were not the only group outside the orbit of the business boom. Nearly eleven million Americans engaged in farming were left behind when the Harding-Coolidge prosperity bandwagon started rolling. Like labor, the farmers as a class had prospered during the war; like labor, they had suffered badly in the postwar depression. But while the skilled laborer made a recovery—real wages rose and employment in manufacturing industries declined only slightly—for most of the decade the farmer knew only distress. Between 1920 and 1932, total farm income dropped 66⅔ percent. Although President Coolidge piously maintained that the government was devoted to the promotion of "business" in the all-inclusive sense of employer and employee, industry and agriculture, facts proved otherwise.* As farm leaders complained, the interests of the farmers were either ignored or evaded by those responsible for the direction of national policies. While endorsing positive aid to business and industry, President Coolidge opposed bills intended to help distressed farmers, taking the position that the farmer should not depend upon governmental price-fixing (as industry did upon the protective tariff) but that simple and direct methods put into operation by the farmer himself were the only real sources of restoration. Such obvious discrimination by government produced a political insurrection.[10]

Charging as had William Jennings Bryan in 1896 that the definition of the businessman had been made too limited,

---

*Calvin Coolidge, *Government and Business*. See page 133.

Senator Robert M. La Follette of Wisconsin emerged in 1924 as the national champion of the forgotten farmer and the downtrodden laborer. In the complacent twenties Senator La Follette was still a fighting liberal, and as presidential candidate of the Progressive party, he demanded in a platform which he himself wrote a drastic redistribution of economic power and opportunity.° His program, the *New Republic* reported, was "a frank demand for a better recognition of the economic interests of two large classes which are considered to have been the victims of economic discrimination from the government as conducted both by the Democratic and Republican parties—the farmers and wage-earners." Like the Populists of an earlier day, La Follette found the existing economy was too largely a one-class economy and the existing state too largely a one-class state, and so he declared "the one paramount issue of the 1924 campaign" was to "break the combined power of the private monopoly system over the political and economic life of the American people."[11]

Though the cry of "monopoly" had an old familiar ring, this was a different brand of Progressivism. Where the Progressivism of twelve years before had been a spontaneous, idealistic program of political action based upon the assumption that the American commonwealth was a complete and essentially classless democracy, the Progressivism of 1924, by contrast, was "a calculated, determined experiment in group resistance to the economic and social classes in control of political authority." Rather than mere political revivalism, it was a kind of economic *macht-politik*, a frank acceptance of power politics. The machinery of the federal government had been used for the benefit of industry, finance, and commerce, and it was only just—the new Progressives argued—that it be used for labor and agriculture. When their argument was hypocritically denounced as "un-American" and "a vicious European prac-

°Robert M. La Follette, *Government and the People*. See page 139.

tice," especially by those who had been in the habit of receiving such legislative favors, La Follette countered by pointing out that similar invasions of economic law were committed daily by other private groups: "We have built up in this country an artificial business structure which throttles the natural law of supply and demand. The price of steel is fixed by private interests. The price of cloth is fixed by private interests. In virtually every line of manufactured commodities a few interests fix the prices. The conservatives, so-called, have nothing to say about that. They support it. But when it is proposed that the government fix prices to save from destruction the great agricultural industry, upon which the country is absolutely dependent, these conservatives throw up their hands in terror."

These Progressive demands of the mid-twenties marked the recasting of the old Wilsonian formulas and the creation of new ones patterned after the Populist program of the nineties. Instead of putting their faith in trust-busting with the hope that this would either preserve or restore a healthy state of competition, the farmers "tossed such thoughts out of the window" and called for restrictive devices patterned after those which had proved so beneficial to big business—tariff, restricted production, price control, cooperative marketing. If big business by its own efforts and those of government could be insured against the hazards of competition, then conceivably agriculture and labor, both perilously exposed to the risks of the market, could also be protected. The farm Progressives, like their Populist forebears, openly identified the state as the primary economic force in American society, clearly perceiving it to be the arbiter of advantage or the instrument of exploitation.[12]

While prospects for third parties in the United States have never been very promising, in 1924 there were at least some grounds for hope. The Harding ideal of normalcy—that government existed primarily to bring prosperity to business—had been notoriously successful. When elected,

Harding had promised to take the government out of business, but what he really meant, said the *Nation,* was that he would "put the government *into* business; that it would become the ally and partner of the get-rich-quick men, the speculators, and the promoters." In its short life of two years and five months, the Harding administration was responsible "for more concentrated robbery and rascality than any other in the whole history of the Federal Government." Early in 1924 Congressional committees brought to light scandals in the departments of Justice, Navy, and the Interior, in the Veterans Bureau, and in the Office of the Alien Property Custodian. The major scandal involved the secret leasing of naval oil reserve lands to private interests led by Harry F. Sinclair and Edward L. Doheny. Senate investigation disclosed that Secretary of the Interior Albert B. Fall had received a $25,000 "loan" from Sinclair and $100,000 from Doheny. Though Fall, the politician, was convicted of bribery, sentenced to one year in prison, and fined $100,000, the two businessmen were acquitted, which would seem to confirm the old Biblical adage that it is "more blessed to give than to receive."[13]

Adopting a policy of silence concerning the scandals, President Coolidge and the Republican party couched their election appeal in terms of prosperity, tax reduction, and freedom of business enterprise. The issue in 1924, Coolidge declared, was "whether America will allow itself to be degraded into a communistic or socialistic state or whether it will remain American." But, from his point of view, Providence had already decreed the outcome. American institutions compelled the loyalty and support of the people because they were founded on righteousness and because they were profitable. "You believe in [America]," the President told his countrymen, because "it is right" and because "it has paid." Under the slogan "Coolidge or Chaos" the Republicans scared millions of timid, ignorant, and uneasy voters into agreeing with them. The business-oriented press branded La Follette "an enemy to the country" be-

GONE DRY

—Sykes in the Philadelphia *Evening Public Ledger.*

Sykes in the Philadelphia *Evening Public Ledger,*
from *Literary Digest,* November 15, 1924, p. 10

In the presidential election of 1924, Senator Robert M. La Follette ran as the champion of the forgotten farmer and down-trodden worker, but despite lurid scandals and opposition from organized labor, the meretricious combination of Coolidge and prosperity proved invincible.

cause of his opposition to American participation in the war, successfully misrepresented his program as "half-baked" Communism, and slurringly insinuated that Soviet Russia was financing his campaign. In spite of the wholesale scandals under the Republican regime and though the A. F. of L. timidly endorsed the Progressives, the meretricious combination of Coolidge and prosperity proved invincible. La Follette lost to the business candidate by more than ten million votes.[14]

## III

No doubt Republican smears cost La Follette many votes, but millions of Americans preferred to play safe with Coolidge because they were politically indifferent. They did not look to the Progressives for relief from poverty and economic servitude because, remarked Lippmann, most of them were finding it by themselves. With prosperity still fairly widely diffused, there was no pressing reason for an alignment of "haves" and "have nots." The system was not yet bankrupt—even though its liabilities already threatened to exceed its assets. It was still a going concern, enormously serviceable and with many valuable unexhausted reserves.[15]

Although the Chamber of Commerce advertised the ideal of "Service" and the National Association of Manufacturers made much of the "spirit of human brotherhood" in industry, the business politics of the twenties placed stubborn limitations on social and economic progress. In Mr. Coolidge's utopia, the rich businessman was not so much an oppressor of the poor as an instrument of divine Providence. As the President explained it, "More and more men are seeking to live in obedience to the law of service under which those of larger possessions confer larger benefits upon their fellow men. The greater their power the greater their service."[16] Under this conception there was to be, on the part of government, the least possible interference with private affairs. Self-reliance and private initiative could be safely stimulated because the social system carried within itself the remedy for its own disorders. These hoary concepts of laissez-faire capitalism were redefined in the twenties by Julius H. Barnes, president of the U.S. Chamber of Commerce, as the "Philosophy of Fair Play."*

As promulgated, the ideal of fair play assumed that all members of society were playing the same game under the same rules with government acting as an impartial umpire; in play, however, the game was usually "fixed." Team play between government and business to bridge the obstacles of trade was allowed, but for non-business classes to seek favors from government was to break the rules of the game. The equivocal nature of the business commitment to "fair play" was clearly revealed in a statement of principles adopted by the Chamber of Commerce in 1921. Although the first article of faith affirmed that "individual initiative, . . . stimulated by active and free competition,

---

*Julius H. Barnes, *The Philosophy of Fair Play.* See page 146.

is the guarantee of sound national progress," the tenth confirmed with equal conviction that a "proper function of government is to render service to business where such service cannot adequately be provided by individual initiative." The way it worked out, the faithful public stood complacently by while their business rulers self-righteously availed themselves of the services of government. Under the prevailing interpretation of the rules of the game, the Harding and Coolidge administrations raised the tariff rates thirty-two times for favored industries, and in line with the Mellon plan of shifting taxes from the rich to the poor, the government repealed the excess-profits tax, cut inheritance taxes, and reduced the maximum income tax on big taxpayers from 65 to 20 percent.[17]

The outcome, after nearly ten years of such "fair play," was an economy in which the share of the income of the top 10 percent had been increasing until it reached nearly 48 percent of the national total by 1929, while that of the lowest 10 percent had been steadily falling. That same upper 10 percent had amassed 86 percent of the total savings as compared to the 2 percent put aside by 80 percent of the nation. In the golden year of prosperity 1929, the Brookings Institution disclosed that only 2.3 percent of American families had annual incomes of over $10,000, 71 percent less than $2500, and 60 percent less than $2000. At 1929 prices, economists estimated that $2000 a year was sufficient to supply only basic necessities—any income below that represented poverty. Hence, in 1929, approximately 60 percent of American families were estimated to be living in or on the edge of poverty.[18]

Although heralded as a New Era in business, the twenties revealed that American business in general was not yet aware of its social responsibilities. There was never a lack of sporadic examples of business benevolence—cafeterias, swimming pools, glee clubs, baseball teams, group-insurance plans, and even profit-sharing schemes for employees—but such programs were never widely realized, being usually confined to a few large corporations. Though, on the one hand, *Fortune* might exalt "the new capitalism" as "a social conception as radical as Stalinism in its ultimate purpose," on the other, the spectacle of U.S. Steel working its employees an average of 54.6 hours a week in 1929 and denying them an equitable share in prosperity (between 1923 and 1929 weekly earnings fell while profits almost doubled) belied serious recognition of the wage-earner as "a purchaser, a partner, and the key to production." While the new emphasis upon human relations in industry reflected, in part, a growing awareness of the relationship between the morale of the work force and its productive efficiency, its central purpose was, as always, the avoidance of trade unionism. Further, the highly publicized paternalism which surrounded such activities tended to obscure rather than to define the interest of the workers in the improvement of their own status. To a good many employers it was merely a shrewd method of flattering employees into believing they had something to do with the determination of industrial conditions without according them any real power. Yet it cannot be denied that where programs of welfare capitalism were seriously undertaken working conditions improved, employment was steadier, and workers developed a closer attachment to the employer. But, as *Fortune* emphasized, it was still paternalism, and paternalism "fails more often than it succeeds," because it refuses to come to grips with the main issue.[19]

The main issue, R. H. Tawney pointed out, was not merely that a large number of workers derived a meager and precarious livelihood from industries which yielded a small minority of persons considerable affluence, but that it involved "a position of privilege among the latter, and subordination among the former." "Kiss Me Clubs," the workers' derogatory term for company unions, and all the other trappings of benevolent autocracy were no substitute for industrial democracy. Wages, hours, the day-to-day problems of the worker, it was argued, involved "political" considerations—"self-determination, the consent of the governed, and a voice for the wage earner."[20]

While industry since the Industrial Revolution had been developing in the direction of autocracy, politics had been developing in the direction of democracy. Industrial democracy, therefore, was regarded as inevitable because political power had been given to the workers. Once given a consciousness of their power and a solidarity of purpose, the workers could get by political means most of these things they were now unable to obtain by industrial means. If business leaders did not adapt themselves, did not follow political democracy with industrial democracy—warned Edward A. Filene, a liberal businessman of Boston—then the workers would use their political power as a means of getting industrial democracy.*

*Edward A. Filene, *Business and Social Progress.* See page 150.

# Readings:

# Dollar Democracy

## Charles Norman Fay (1848–1944)

> *A Phi Beta Kappa from Harvard, he achieved some prominence writing on public affairs from the elitist viewpoint of a former public utilities executive, a vice-president of the National Association of Manufacturers, and as a member of the Chamber of Commerce. His views were strongly anti-labor and anti-government, and his constant theme was that American businessmen should take over the direction of the country because the workers and voters did not have the ability to think for themselves.*

## NO RIGHT TO STRIKE

Our existing labor situation demands a change. There are, according to the census, some 42 million "gainfully employed" workers of both sexes, over 10 years of age, in the United States. About 24 million of them (viz., in agriculture, trade, the professions, civil and domestic service) are and

---

From *Business in Politics, Suggestions for Leaders in American Business* (Cambridge: Cosmos Press, Inc., 1926), pp. 34–5, 37, 39–42, 44–5.

probably will remain practically out of reach of labor organization. Of the 18 million in employments that *can* be "organized," about 3½ million actually are enrolled in some thousands of unions, mainly affiliated with one or other of the American Federation of Labor, the Railway Brotherhoods, the Amalgamated Clothing Workers and the I. W. W. That is, about one in every five of the organizable workers are actually organized—about one in twelve of all workers—and not far from one in twenty-four of the whole population (83 million) over 10 years of age. The locomotive engineers are said to head the list, 96 percent organized. The percentage in other skilled trades is not nearly so great, and averages apparently about 40 percent in most crafts.

Nevertheless, *by the simple device of nation-wide craft organization,* enough of the members of any single skilled craft (such as the Railway Workers or the United Mine Workers) can conspire to quit work simultaneously, seriously to cripple production or transportation, for instance, of coal, food, etc.; and in a very few days or weeks can freeze or starve many millions of helpless and unoffending people throughout the regions "struck."

In most crafts, however, the *majority* of workers are *unorganized;* and, if left free to take the jobs abandoned by the conspirators, and accept the wages refused by them, they sooner or later are very sure to do so—that is, when wages and conditions offered are those current in the neighborhood—and the strike fails.

It is, indeed, so essential to the success of a strike to prevent the free flow of free labor to the jobs vacated, that the whole policy and practice of trades unionism is built upon three main principles: (1) the solidarity of, and the monopoly of work by, union labor; (2) the denial of the right to work of nonunion men; and (3) the physical, social and political *coercion* of workers, employers and public outside of the unions, by absolute prevention of nonunion work.

The union man is taught to believe that the job he quits while on strike *nevertheless remains his job,* which no other worker has any right to take. He is taught to call the nonunion worker by the vile name of "scab"; and to consider it no crime to kill or maim the man who would take *his* place, or to dynamite the plant of the employer who would offer it to any one but himself, and on his own terms, or to terrorize all who would deal with that employer. "The right to *organize,*" and to *strike,* and thus to *coerce,* by stopping work, and preventing its performance by other hands, *"come what may in industry,"* is guaranteed, so runs the Gompers gospel, by the Constitution of the United States to every working man; while any limitation thereof, by the law or the courts, is "wage slavery," industrial serfdom! But that gospel is false! . . .

Now, Mr. Gompers and his lieutenants in the American "labor movement" have strenuously stretched this right, as recognized by the courts—of a group of employees to quit *their particular employer collectively*—into the so-called "right to organize"; that is, the right to *combine any or all of the employees of any or all employers in any or all crafts* into *nation-wide* unions and federations, prepared and financed, far in advance, to strike and hold up *entire* trades or industries, whole cities, whole regions, even the entire country, *for wages or conditions better than those obtainable without coercion in the open labor market.* This they have done, well knowing that the cost incurred must be passed along to and borne by the whole public, *and they openly say so!* . . .

You [the members of the Chambers of Commerce and the great Business Associations throughout the United States] are not only able, but are deeply interested, it seems to me, to stir up a public demand both on Congress and the state legislatures for laws declaring, as Governor Coolidge declared during the Boston police strike, *that there is no right to strike against the public safety.* You might well go still farther, in this land of free government, and teach the voters that *there is no right to strike against the public pocket.* The great American people is surely not so feeble as to let itself forever be "held up" at will by this or that minute but "organized" minority.

There seems to me a clear moral as well as legal distinction to be drawn between what might be called the *retail* and the *wholesale* organization of labor. Let us grant, for the sake of argument (though it is usually untrue), that the poor workingman is at such a practical disadvantage in dealing with his rich employer, that it is natural and fair to let him combine with fellow workmen *in the same shop* to "bargain collectively" for them all; and thus throw their collective need of many jobs into the scale, against his collective need of many workers. Also, let us grant that an isolated combination of workers, against an isolated employer here and there, is a matter of comparative indifference to the public; a local effort, in which most of us have no great concern. Then let us grant that under such conditions the public, the law and the courts are apt to deal kindly with the workman on strike, and to ignore the oldtime law forbidding combination in restraint of trade. The thing might be called "retail" organization of labor and be winked at as fairly legitimate.

But, suppose such an organization to be *expanded, to cover a whole industry*—is not then the single employer, are not all employers, and the public, put at unfair disadvantage? Take the case of the United Mine Workers; which is a vast army of occupation of all the great coal mines of the country, except a few in West Virginia and Kentucky, which thus far refuse to unionize. Suppose (as has often occurred, both in anthracite and bituminous coal) that it is the open purpose of this half-million army *to hold up coal supply* now and again, until its demands are enforced by reason of coal famine, *and at public expense!* . . . *Do you think 110 million Americans will always sit still, while half a million coal miners or railway workers freeze or starve the crowd into paying hold-up wages far above what the open market pays the rest of us?*

It is my own conviction that public opinion is ripe for lawful control of organized labor. The right to "organize" and to "strike" against an individual employer may as heretofore be conceded as a reasonable makeweight in "collective bargaining"—*to those who desire to bargain in that way*, without limiting the freedom of those who prefer to bargain individually. *But the time has come for the law to put an end to organization of whole crafts against the whole public! . . .*

But, gentlemen, *the mass of the people will never, or else but slowly, learn that fact from the politicians*, who naturally cater to the organized labor vote. Nor will they learn it from the press (which echoes talk, but seldom starts it), *until some conspicuous personage or organization first proclaims it.* I submit once more that *you* are the national leaders, conspicuous individually and by your great associations, who best understand the economic and constitutional rights both of the workers you employ and the customers you serve—that is, those of the whole people. It is my conviction that you ought, for the common good as well as your own peace and profit, to take the initiative in this important matter. The time has fully come to *suppress by law all wholesale organization of labor*, for the purpose of fixing wages, or controlling, limiting or preventing work, production or transportation; *that is, organization involving the employees of more than one and the same employer.*

And for consistency it is time, too, to repeal the provisions of the Clayton Act exempting farmer and labor organizations from the penalties of the laws against combination in restraint of trade. . . .

It is the psychological moment—with coal and building and garment workers' strikes impending upon an unoffending people, whose declared intent it is to starve or freeze the public into submission *not only by stopping work* of production and transportation by the strikers themselves, but by *preventing, no matter how,* the willing work of others—it is, I repeat, the perfect moment to rouse that public in its own defense. I urge you, gentlemen of the great associations, to go to the press, to Congress and the legislatures, for the embodiment in law of Calvin Coolidge's celebrated dictum—perhaps omitting the word "safety"— that *there is no right to strike against the public, by anybody, anywhere, anytime.* For, I think, the day of reckoning has fully come, when the American people, having learned not to confuse conspiracy against the community with mutual benefit work, will clearly distinguish between selfishness and liberty, between class and democracy; and will serve notice on organized labor that no fraction of the public is strong enough to plunder the whole. Especially is it your duty and privilege, as broadly educated men, to teach your less informed fellow citizens the needed lesson in morals, economics and politics—that no man or group of men ought to or can get more out of the community by doing less for the community.

# John L. Lewis (1880-       )

*A fearless, aggressive labor leader, he was born into a poor Welsh mining family in Iowa. At fifteen, he went down into the mines, digging coal in Colorado, Wyoming, and Montana, copper in Arizona, and silver in Utah. After helping to drag the mutilated bodies of 236 miners from the hazardous Union Pacific Mine at Hannah, Wyoming, in 1905, he turned his efforts to unionism, becoming president in 1920 of the United Mine Workers, the then largest and most powerful union in America. Following Samuel Gompers' doctrine that tactics, not ideals, made*

*a labor movement, he operated opportunistically,*
*as Irving Bernstein said, "compromising only*
*with reality." Since he believed the world was*
*not amenable to persuasion, he had no faith in*
*arbitration and placed his reliance on power*
*alone. This ruthless faith eventually made him*
*the most powerful labor leader in America.*

# THE MINERS' FIGHT FOR
# AMERICAN STANDARDS

Primarily the United Mine Workers of America insists upon
the maintenance of the wage standards, guaranteed by the
existing contractual relations in the industry, in the interests
of its own membership. It is acting in that respect exactly
as any other individual, organization, or corporation would
do under like circumstances. The theory of our system of
free enterprise is that the ultimate prosperity of all is best
assured by the utmost endeavor of each to better his own
condition. Trade unionism is an integral part of the existing
system of industry first called by its critics capitalism. The
word once used in reproach has in these times been adopted
with pride by the advocates and defenders of the system,
as was the case in regard to great religious sects and political parties, which adopted as badges of honor the names
first hurled at them as epithets.

Distrust and hostility toward the business system wane
as it is becoming better understood how the general prosperity and individual and family welfare of modern peoples
has been increased by the use of capital in production to
multiply the productive power of man's labor, whether of
hand or brain. Trade unionism is a phenomenon of capitalism
quite similar to the corporation. One is essentially a pooling of labor for purposes of common action in production

From *The Miners' Fight for American Standards* (Indianapolis: Bell Publishing
Co., 1925), pp. 40–1, 43–9, 51–2.

and in sales. The other is a pooling of capital for exactly the same purposes. The economic aims of both are identical —gain.

The strange survival of pre-capitalist mentality that makes so many persons subconsciously resent high wages for workingmen, or action by workingmen, to better their condition, while lauding exactly similar efforts by capital to get more profits and avoid losses, is back of these demands that labor act upon other motives than are expected of capital and voluntarily sacrifice its wages to increase the profits of others. It is the feudal mind speaking in a capitalist age.

But in insisting on the maintenance of an American wage standard in the coal fields the United Mine Workers is also doing its part, probably more than its part, to force a reorganization of the basic industry of the country upon scientific and efficient lines. The maintenance of these rates will accelerate the operation of natural economic laws, which will in time eliminate uneconomic mines, obsolete equipment and incompetent management.

Any concession of wage reductions will serve to delay this process of reorganization, by enabling the unfit to hold out a little longer. . . .

Finally in its refusal to countenance any backward step on the wage question the United Mine Workers of America is doing its part to maintain the general prosperity of the United States and all the people in it.

Nothing is more significant of the revolution in economic thinking and methods of study, that has followed the swing of economic thought toward the study of the science from the consumption standpoint, and from the accumulation of accurate statistical measurements of the national income and consumption of goods, than the change in attitude on the wage question.

That the purchasing power of the American masses is the pivot upon which our whole economic system turns, and that a reduction in that purchasing power is instantly registered, not only in the distress of the masses but the shrinkage of profits and the destruction of capital values, has become so evident in the post-war period that it is becoming quite difficult to find advocates of the low wage theories, formerly so popular among financiers and industrial management. . . .

In every discussion of business prospects now, the rate of employment is featured and every gain in employment is noted as an augury of better business, because of the increased purchasing power that it implies.

If a wage cut is noted, the attempt is always made to minimize its effect upon the prospects of business by arguments to show that this particular class of wages is higher than the general level. Seldom is it argued now that a reduction of the general level would be beneficial.

In defense of any cut, it is argued that by a balancing process, not only the labor affected, but all labor, may expect a renewed advance toward higher levels yet.

The professional enemies of organized labor, the open shop organizations, say next to nothing now about lower wages. Only a few years ago it was their great selling argument. Cities which have been long noted for the open shop proclivities of their chambers of commerce, among them Los Angeles, no longer advertise to the world that they have low wage rates. Capital it seems can no longer be lured to low wage communities, because capital is becoming ever more concerned with selling what it produces, and it knows that its sales will be restricted in low wage markets.

Perhaps it is in the advertising field that this revolution in economic thought can be seen best.

Advertising under modern conditions has become almost the life of great new industries, that have sprung up as a result of recent advances of science. Advertising is no longer a mere mode of selling. It has become an instrument for the education of the people into new desires and demands. In seeking customers, the newspapers and advertising agencies themselves have become great advertisers of their market areas. What do they feature most—the pay-rolls and high wages of the industries in their cities and states.

Not only has American economic thought and business practice swung around to the high wage theory, but American domestic and foreign governmental policies are more and more in tune with it.

The working people are admonished almost daily by statesmen and the newspapers of the high wage rates here, as compared to those abroad. We have been shown in tables and diagrams how the higher wage rate of the American worker is accounted for by the greater amount of power per man employed in moving the machinery with which he works, and how the wage rates of the various countries compare to the amount of capital per worker invested.

In all these studies it is assumed as a matter of course, that the worker not only is entitled to share in this greater production, but it is also admitted that if he did not share in such a manner that he could as a consumer help to adequately dispose of the product, the whole system would crash to pieces.

Almost unanimous recognition of these facts, which a generation ago were pooh-poohed by Gradgrind economists and scouted as trade union heresies, has so colored our political activities that Congress passed the recent immigration restriction law by an overwhelming majority. Fifty years ago business interests almost succeeded in defeating labor's demand for the exclusion of Chinese coolie labor and the economists of that day denounced the effort to maintain a high wage standard as economic suicide.

In the matter of wages, the prosperity of the United States today in contrast to the crippled industries of the nations which cling to the low wage fallacies is the crag of fact against which all the theories of a contrary nature have been broken to bits.

High paid American skilled labor can sell its machine-made wares in China and Japan. Our exports of manufactures have been steadily increasing in competition with the cheapest labor in the world.

Our foreign trade experts tell us that the cheap labor countries will never catch us, as long as we keep our lead in the method we have inaugurated—mass production. Mass production can only be maintained by a purchasing power in the home market sufficient to make it possible.

Yet in the face of this almost universal recognition of the vital importance of maintaining American purchasing power in order to keep up our productive pace, it is proposed to inaugurate a cheap labor system in the industry upon which all the others depend—the mining of coal. The absurdity, nay the effrontery of the demand is staggering—when it is examined in the light of what is happening in every other department of industry and in home and foreign trade. . . .

The United Mine Workers would be false not only to itself, but a traitor to the future of America, if it allowed this great industry to fade out of the American picture and, by its maladjustment to the rest of the industrial machine, halt the progress now being made toward a substantial degree of industrial democracy.

For rest assured that if the mining industry be long kept out of pace with the rest of America, out of gear with the big machine, it will slow up the whole works. The industrial system is too closely interdependent to admit of such incongruities being long maintained. . . .

When the United Mine Workers of America declares that it will take no backward step, this great Union speaks in unison with the heart beats of America, and puts into economic language the very essence of the American spirit.

# Calvin Coolidge (1872–1933)

*The thirtieth President of the United States, he
was a dull, taciturn, Puritanical Yankee who
had no noticeable bad habits except an addic-
tion to long afternoon naps in the White House.
After becoming President on Harding's death, he
was elected again in 1924 as the businessman's
choice. Declaring he did not "choose to run" in
1928, he told Congress on Dec. 4 of the same
year, "The country . . . can anticipate the future
with optimism." Then, opportunely, he slipped
out of Washington before the 1929 crash.*

## GOVERNMENT AND BUSINESS

This time and place naturally suggest some consideration
of commerce in its relation to Government and society. We
are finishing a year which can justly be said to surpass all
others in the overwhelming success of general business.
We are met not only in the greatest American metropolis,
but in the greatest center of population and business that
the world has ever known. If any one wishes to gauge the
power which is represented by the genius of the American
spirit, let him contemplate the wonders which have been
wrought in this region in the short space of 200 years. Not
only does it stand unequaled by any other place on earth,
but it is impossible to conceive of any other place where
it could be equaled.

The foundation of this enormous development rests upon
commerce. New York is an imperial city, but it is not a
seat of government. The empire over which it rules is not

Address before the Chamber of Commerce of the State of New York, New York
City, November 10, 1925, from *Foundations of the Republic: Speeches and Addresses of Calvin Coolidge* (New York: Charles Scribner's Sons, 1926), pp. 317–
22. Reprinted by permission of the publishers.

political, but commercial. The great cities of the ancient world were the seats of both government and industrial power. The Middle Ages furnished a few exceptions. The great capitals of former times were not only seats of government but they actually governed. In the modern world government is inclined to be merely a tenant of the city. Political life and industrial life flow on side by side, but practically separated from each other. When we contemplate the enormous power, autocratic and uncontrolled, which would have been created by joining the authority of government with the influence of business, we can better appreciate the wisdom of the fathers in their wise dispensation which made Washington the political center of the country and left New York to develop into its business center. They wrought mightily for freedom.

The great advantages of this arrangement seem to me to be obvious. The only disadvantages which appear lie in the possibility that otherwise business and government might have had a better understanding of each other and been less likely to develop mutual misapprehensions and suspicions. If a contest could be held to determine how much those who are really prominent in our government life know about business, and how much those who are really prominent in our business life know about government, it is my firm conviction that the prize would be awarded to those who are in government life. This is as it ought to be, for those who have the greater authority ought to have the greater knowledge. But it is my even firmer conviction that the general welfare of our country could be very much advanced through a better knowledge by both of those parties of the multifold problems with which each has to deal. . . .

While I have spoken of what I believed would be the advantages of a more sympathetic understanding, I should put an even stronger emphasis on the desirability of the largest possible independence between government and business. Each ought to be sovereign in its own sphere. When government comes unduly under the influence of business, the tendency is to develop an administration which closes the door of opportunity; becomes narrow and selfish in its outlook, and results in an oligarchy. When government enters the field of business with its great resources, it has a tendency to extravagance and inefficiency, but, having the power to crush all competitors, likewise closes the door of opportunity and results in monopoly. . . .

While there has been in the past and will be in the future a considerable effort in this country of different business interests to attempt to run the Government in such a way as to set up a system of privilege, and while there have been and will be those who are constantly seeking to commit the Government to a policy of infringing upon the domain of private business, both of these efforts have been very largely discredited, and with reasonable vigilance on the part of the people to preserve their freedom do not now appear to be dangerous.

When I have been referring to business, I have used the word in its all-inclusive sense to denote alike the employer and employee, the production of agriculture and industry, the distribution of transportation and commerce, and the service of finance and banking. It is the work of the world. In modern life, with all its intricacies, business has come to hold a very dominant position in the thoughts of all enlightened peoples. Rightly understood, this is not a criticism, but a compliment. In its great economic organization it does not represent, as some have hastily concluded, a mere desire to minister to selfishness. . . . It is something far more important than a sordid desire for gain. It could not successively succeed on that basis. It is dominated by a more worthy impulse; it rests on a higher law. True business represents the mutual organized effort of society to minister to the economic requirements of civilization. It is an effort by which men provide for the material needs of each other. While it is not an end in itself, it is the important means for the attainment of a supreme end. It rests squarely on the law of service. It has for its main reliance truth and faith and justice. In its larger sense it is one of the greatest contributing forces to the moral and spiritual advancement of the race.

It is the important and righteous position that business holds in relation to life which gives warrant to the great interest which the National Government constantly exercises for the promotion of its success. This is not exercised as has been the autocratic practice abroad of directly supporting and financing different business projects, except in case of great emergency; but we have rather held to a democratic policy of cherishing the general structure of business while holding its avenues open to the widest competition, in order that its opportunities and its benefits might be given the broadest possible participation. While it is true that the Government ought not to be and is not committed to certain methods of acquisition which, while partaking of the nature of unfair practices, try to masquerade under the guise of business, the Government is and ought to be thoroughly committed to every endeavor of production and distribution which is entitled to be designated as true business. Those who are so engaged, instead of regarding the Government as their opponent and enemy, ought to regard it as their vigilant supporter and friend. . . .

It is my belief that the whole material development of our country has been enormously stimulated by reason of the general insistence on the part of the public authorities that economic effort ought not to partake of privilege, and that business should be unhampered and free. This could never have been done under a system of freight-rate discriminations or monopolistic trade associations. These might have enriched a few for a limited period, but they never would have enriched the country, while on the firmer foundation of justice we have achieved even more ample individual fortunes and a perfectly unprecedented era of general prosperity. This has resulted in no small part from the general acceptance on the part of those who own and control the wealth of the Nation, that it is to be used not to oppress but to serve. It is that policy, sometimes perhaps imperfectly expressed and clumsily administered, that has animated the National Government. In its observance there is unlimited opportunity for progress and prosperity.

It would be difficult, if not impossible, to estimate the contribution which government makes to business. It is notorious that where the government is bad, business is bad. The mere fundamental precepts of the administration of justice, the providing of order and security, are priceless. The prime element in the value of all property is the knowledge that its peaceful enjoyment will be publicly defended. If disorder should break out in your city, if there should be a conviction extending over any length of time that the rights of persons and property could no longer be protected by law, the value of your tall buildings would shrink to about the price of what are now water fronts of old Carthage or what are now corner lots in ancient Babylon. It is really the extension of these fundamental rights that the Government is constantly attempting to apply to modern business. It wants its rightful possessors to rest in security, it wants any wrongs that they may suffer to have a legal remedy, and it is all the time striving through administrative machinery to prevent in advance the infliction of injustice.

These undoubtedly represent policies which are wise and sound and necessary. That they have often been misapplied and many times run into excesses, nobody can deny. Regulation has often become restriction, and inspection has too frequently been little less than obstruction. This was the natural result of those times in the past when there were practices in business which warranted severe disapprobation. It was only natural that when these abuses were reformed by an aroused public opinion a great deal of prejudice which ought to have been discriminating and directed only at certain evil practices came to include almost the whole domain of business, especially where it had been gathered into large units. After the abuses had been discontinued the prejudice remained to produce a large amount of legislation, which, however well meant in its application to trade, undoubtedly hampered but did not improve. It is this misconception and misapplication, disturbing and wasteful in their result, which the National Government is attempting to avoid. Proper regulation and control are disagreeable and expensive. They represent the suffering that the just must endure because of the unjust. They are a part of the price which must be paid to promote the cause of economic justice.

Undoubtedly if public vigilance were relaxed, the generation to come might suffer a relapse. But the present generation of business almost universally throughout its responsible organization and management has shown every disposition to correct its own abuses with as little intervention of the Government as possible. This position is recognized by the public, and due to the appreciation of the needs which the country has for great units of production in time of war, and to the better understanding of the service which they perform in time of peace, . . . a new attitude of the public mind is distinctly discernible toward great aggregations of capital. Their prosperity goes very far to insure the prosperity of all the country. The contending elements have each learned a most profitable lesson.

This development has left the Government free to advance from the problems of reform and repression to those of economy and construction. A very large progress is being made in these directions. [As a result] our country is in a state of unexampled and apparently sound and well distributed prosperity.

# Robert M. La Follette (1856-1925)

*Liberal statesman and a leading Progressive, he fought against entrenched political groups to become governor of Wisconsin in 1901 and was twice reelected. His program, based upon direct appeal to the people, was known as the "Wisconsin idea" and served as a model of progressive government. In 1906 he took a seat in the U.S. Senate to which he was reelected three times. He drafted the program for the National Progressive Republican League, campaigned for the Progressive nomination in 1912, but lost to Theodore Roosevelt, partly as a result of a physical breakdown. He opposed the declaration of war with Germany, but supported most of the war measures. As a liberal leader in postwar years, he proposed the resolution for a Senate inquiry into Teapot Dome and other oil leases made during the Harding administration.*

## GOVERNMENT AND THE PEOPLE

The great issue before the American people today is the control of government and industry by private monopoly.

For a generation the people have struggled patiently, in the face of repeated betrayals by successive administrations, to free themselves from this intolerable power which has been undermining representative government.

Through control of government, monopoly has steadily extended its absolute dominion to every basic industry.

In violation of law, monopoly has crushed competition, stifled private initiative and independent enterprise, and

From the Progressive Party Platform of 1924, Kirk H. Porter and Donald B. Johnson, eds., *National Party Platforms, 1840–1956* (Urbana: University of Illinois Press, 1956), pp. 252–5. Reprinted by permission of the publisher.

without fear of punishment now exacts extortionate profits upon every necessity of life consumed by the public.

The equality of opportunity proclaimed by the Declaration of Independence and asserted and defended by Jefferson and Lincoln as the heritage of every American citizen has been displaced by special privilege for the few, wrested from the government of the many.

That tyrannical power which the American people denied to a king, they will no longer endure from the monopoly system. The people know they cannot yield to any group the control of the economic life of the nation and preserve their political liberties. They know monopoly has its representatives in the halls of Congress, on the Federal bench, and in the executive departments; that these servile agents barter away the nation's natural resources, nullify acts of Congress by judicial veto and administrative favor, invade the people's rights by unlawful arrests and unconstitutional searches and seizures, direct our foreign policy in the interests of predatory wealth, and make wars and conscript the sons of the common people to fight them.

The usurpation in recent years by the federal courts of the power to nullify laws duly enacted by the legislative branch of the government is a plain violation of the Constitution. Abraham Lincoln, in his first inaugural address, said: "The candid citizen must confess that if the policy of the government, upon vital questions affecting the whole people, is to be irrevocably fixed by decisions of the Supreme Court, the people will have ceased to be their own rulers, having to that extent practically resigned their government into the hands of their eminent tribunal." The Constitution specifically vests all legislative power in the Congress, giving that body power and authority to override the veto of the president. The federal courts are given no authority under the Constitution to veto acts of Congress. Since the federal courts have assumed to exercise such veto power, it is essential that the Constitution shall give the Congress the right to override such judicial veto, otherwise the Court will make itself master over the other coordinate branches of the government. The people themselves must approve or disapprove the present exercise of legislative power by the federal courts.

The present condition of American agriculture constitutes an emergency of the gravest character. The Department of Commerce report shows that during 1923 there was a steady and marked increase in dividends paid by the great industrial corporations. The same is true of the steam and electric railways and practically all other large corporations. On the other hand, the Secretary of Agriculture reports that in the fifteen principal wheat growing states more than 108,000 farmers since 1920 have lost their farms through foreclosure or bankruptcy; that more than 122,000 have surrendered their property without legal proceedings, and that nearly 375,000 have retained possession of their property only through the leniency of their creditors, making a total of more than 600,000 or 26 percent of all farmers who have virtually been bankrupted since 1920 in these fifteen states alone.

Almost unlimited prosperity for the great corporations and ruin and bankruptcy for agriculture is the direct and logical result of the policies and legislation which deflated the farmer while extending almost unlimited credit to the great corporations; which protected with exorbitant tariffs the industrial magnates, but depressed the prices of the farmers' products by financial juggling while greatly increasing the cost of what he must buy; which guaranteed excessive freight rates to the railroads and put a premium on wasteful management while saddling an unwarranted burden on to the backs of the American farmer; which permitted gambling in the products of the farm by grain speculators to the great detriment of the farmer and to the great profit of the grain gambler.

Awakened by the dangers which menace their freedom

and prosperity the American people still retain the right and courage to exercise their sovereign control over their government. In order to destroy the economic and political power of monopoly, which has come between the people and their government, we pledge ourselves to the following principles and policies:

## The House Cleaning

We pledge a complete housecleaning in the Department of Justice, the Department of the Interior, and the other executive departments. We demand that the power of the Federal Government be used to crush private monopoly, not to foster it.

## Natural Resources

We pledge recovery of the navy's oil reserves and all other parts of the public domain which have been fraudulently or illegally leased, or otherwise wrongfully transferred, to the control of private interests; vigorous prosecution of all public officials, private citizens and corporations that participated in these transactions; complete revision of the water-power act, the general leasing act, and all other legislation relating to the public domain. We favor public ownership of the nation's water power and the creation and development of a national super-water-power system, including Muscle Shoals, to supply at actual cost light and power for the people and nitrate for the farmers, and strict public control and permanent conservation of all the nation's resources, including coal, iron and other ores, oil and timber lands, in the interest of the people.

## Railroads

. . . We declare for public ownership of railroads with definite safeguards against bureaucratic control, as the only final solution of the transportation problem.

## Tax Reduction

We favor reduction of Federal taxes upon individual incomes and legitimate business, limiting tax exactions strictly to the requirements of the government administered with rigid economy, particularly by curtailment of the eight hundred million dollars now annually expended for the army and navy in preparation for future wars; by the recovery of the hundreds of millions of dollars stolen from the Treasury through fraudulent war contracts and the corrupt leasing of the public resources; and by diligent action to collect the accumulated interest upon the eleven billion dollars owing us by foreign governments.

We denounce the Mellon tax plan as a device to relieve multi-millionaires at the expense of other tax payers, and favor a taxation policy providing for immediate reductions upon moderate incomes, large increases in the inheritance tax rates upon large estates to prevent the indefinite accumulation by inheritance of great fortunes in a few hands; taxes upon excess profits to penalize profiteering, and complete publicity, under proper safeguards, of all Federal tax returns.

## The Courts

We favor submitting to the people, for their considerate judgment, a constitutional amendment providing that Congress may by enacting a statute make it effective over a judicial veto.

We favor such amendment to the constitution as may be necessary to provide for the election of all Federal Judges, without party designation, for fixed terms not exceeding ten years, by direct vote of the people.

## The Farmers

We favor drastic reduction of the exorbitant duties on manufactures provided in the Fordney-McCumber tariff legislation, the prohibiting of gambling by speculators and profiteers in agricultural products; the reconstruction of the Federal Reserve and Federal Farm Loan Systems, so as to eliminate control by usurers, speculators and international financiers, and to make the credit of the nation available upon fair terms to all and without discrimination to business men, farmers and home-builders. We advocate the calling of a special session of Congress to pass legislation for the relief of American agriculture. We favor such further legislation as may be needful or helpful in promoting and protecting cooperative enterprises. We demand that the Interstate Commerce Commission proceed forthwith to reduce by an approximation to pre-war levels the present freight rates on agricultural products, including live stock, and upon the materials required upon American farms for agricultural purposes.

### Labor

We favor abolition of the use of injunctions in labor disputes and declare for complete protection of the right of farmers and industrial workers to organize, bargain collectively through representatives of their own choosing, and conduct without hindrance cooperative enterprises.

We favor prompt ratification of the Child Labor amendment, and subsequent enactment of a Federal law to protect children in industry. . . .

### War Veterans

We favor adjusted compensation for the veterans of the late war, not as charity, but as a matter of right, and we demand that the money necessary to meet this obligation of the government be raised by taxes laid upon wealth in proportion to the ability to pay, and declare our opposition to the sales tax or any other device to shift this obligation onto the backs of the poor in higher prices and in-

creased cost of living. We do not regard the payment at
the end of a long period of a small insurance as provided
by the law recently passed as in any just sense a discharge
of the nation's obligations to the veterans of the late
war. . . .

### Popular Sovereignty

Over and above constitutions and statutes and greater
than all, is the supreme sovereignty of the people, and with
them should rest the final decision of all great questions
of national policy. We favor such amendments to the
Federal Constitution as may be necessary to provide for
the direct nomination and election of the President, to extend the initiative and referendum to the federal government, and to insure a popular referendum for or against
war except in cases of actual invasion.

### Peace on Earth

We denounce the mercenary system of foreign policy
under recent administrations in the interests of financial
imperialists, oil monopolists and international bankers,
which has at times degraded our State Department from
its high service as a strong and kindly intermediary of defenseless governments to a trading outpost for those interests
and concession-seekers engaged in the exploitations of
weaker nations, as contrary to the will of the American
people, destructive of domestic development and provocative of war. We favor an active foreign policy to bring
about a revision of the Versailles treaty in accordance with
the terms of the armistice, and to promote firm treaty
agreements with all nations to outlaw wars, abolish conscription, drastically reduce land, air and naval armaments,
and guarantee public referendum on peace and war.

# Julius H. Barnes (1873-1959)

*A close friend of Herbert Hoover and one of the nation's leading industrialists, he became best known to the public as president of the United States Chamber of Commerce, a post that he held from 1921 to 1924. In his statements and speeches he revealed himself as a staunch supporter of rugged individualism, attributing the advance of American industry to a general adherence to the theory of private ownership rather than government control.*

## THE PHILOSOPHY OF FAIR PLAY

If one should attempt to define the American social and political philosophy in a single phrase it might be described as the PHILOSOPHY OF FAIR PLAY.

In America the various sports of our youth teach the principles of team play and of fair play. On every baseball diamond and football field the qualities of fortitude and courage and fair play, inspired by loyalty to club or town or college, are instilled in our young men.

Americans, therefore, clearly recognize that it is a violation of this fair play when combinations of wealth and power are made to the detriment of the public. And it was to preserve the national policy of fair play that the theory of government regulation was evolved.

This regulation, however, which controls practices and affects earnings, must, in the national interest, be restrained and wise and generous. It must attract the enlistment of capital and the service of superior individual ability in

---

From Julius H. Barnes, *The Genius of American Business* (New York: Doubleday, Page & Co., 1924), pp. 6-13.

order that regulated industry may march in step with non-regulated industry in the development of economies and of service.

It is not fair play for the necessary power of regulating those public services which inevitably possess the character of monopoly—such as railroad, traction services, or other public utilities—to be administered with such a narrow view of selfish interest and in such total disregard of solemn responsibility that the investments which created these public services will be undermined or destroyed. There is every evidence, however, that we have passed the era of unfair and short-sighted, over-rigid regulation, and that we are dealing with regulated public services with a more enlightened vision of fair play.

It is not fair play for the State to overman public-service corporations for political support, provide service below the actual cost of operation, and make up the resultant deficit from the assessment of public moneys raised through taxation.

It is not fair play for special sections of our people, numerically strong, to levy, through unequal and unwise taxation, and in a spirit of envy and resentment, an unfair burden, against those other groups more fortunate than themselves.

The range of employment opportunity is constantly widened with the establishment of new enterprises; and taxation which destroys the human incentive of prospective earnings against the unusual hazards of new ventures, and which stifles the willingness to take the risks of new business ventures, is unwise as well as a violation of fundamental fair play.

It is not fair play for a group of men temporarily in a position of authority in national legislation to vote, for any purpose, gigantic appropriations from the national treasury and then seek to avoid the responsibility of providing the revenues from which those appropriations can be paid. In fact, to leave to their successors the perplexing problem of providing the means of payment, while they short-sightedly seek the present approval of those who benefit by their reckless draft upon the public funds, is a distressing violation of the principles of fair play.

It is not fair play for a government exercising exclusive authority to issue currency denominations in which are recorded the savings of thrift and self-denial—the provision of life insurance protection for survivors—and on the stability of which depends the healthy functioning of trade and commerce, on which in turn rest employment and opportunity, and, therefore, the happiness and content of its peoples deliberately to inflate or deflate the value of that traditional measure of value with its resultant distress and disaster.

It should be America's chief pride, in these recent years of reckless currency inflation in other lands, that its record has been one of intelligent effort to keep stable its currency; and this has been the greatest contribution on the part of the Government to the preservation of fair play. . . .

It is not fair play to-day for organizations of men, associated for lawful activities and rightful ends, to stand unequal before the law. No exceptions should be made for organizations of labour or organizations of growers. The time will come, and soon, when these inequalities will be removed because they violate the fundamental human sense of fair play.

It is not fair play for organizations of men to deny the right to work to men who hold views different from theirs. It is increasingly clear that public opinion condemns organizations that, by force and violence, offend thus the public sense of fair play.

It is not fair play for organizations, with whatever claim of proper purpose, to avoid their own responsibility by shrouding their identity behind the mask and hood. Organizations of that character can maintain their existence only if the community departs entirely from the ideals which preserve fair play.

It is not fair play that either from human laws or from social customs, a system should be evolved which would encase a man in the social stratum in which he has been placed by the accident of birth.

In the Old World this rigid caste system freezes into social strata and strifles individual talent and ambition. It is, in fact, the cause of and the excuse for the injection into government of organizations frankly devoted to the interest of a single section of their people. But where no doors are closed by accident of birth or station against those possessed of superior ability or devoted to superior effort there is no excuse for the formation of political influence on the basis of trade or social position.

Labour parties or farm blocs have no lasting place under the American conditions of fair play. . . .

Organized business does not arrogate to itself a superiority of understanding of the ethics of fair play, nor does it plume itself as expressly the champion of that cause which carries a deep appeal to men of every station. Organized business, however, responsible not only for its own well-being, but because of its position as largely the director of industry, and, therefore, responsible for the opportunities and employment of many times its number, has an especially keen appreciation of the atmosphere in which human activities may prosper.

Organized business has keenly appreciated that the incentive to all effort rests on the confidence that superior service, in any form, will be rewarded, and those rewards secured and protected.

Under conditions of absolute fair play between individuals, society apportions through the processes of trade a sure and fair reward to those individuals who serve it best by new inventions, or superior ability in production, or superior methods of distribution.

In our short national history, under the stimulus of this individualistic fair play, we have led the world in applying science and invention through the service of industry to the enlargement of human comfort and contentment.

# Edward A. Filene (1860–1937)

*As head of a prominent Boston department store, he introduced a series of innovations in merchandising and personnel management which brought him a fortune and proved to him that the efficient performance of a needed social service would bring the best long-run business profit. Always receptive to new ideas, he encouraged profit-sharing, unemployment and medical insurance, and credit-unions for workers. Although he was one of the founders of the United States Chamber of Commerce, he broke openly with the organization in 1936 when he became impatient with what seemed to him to be the unenlightened and self-destructive opinions expressed by its business leadership.*

## BUSINESS AND SOCIAL PROGRESS

I believe that the modern business system, despised and derided by innumerable reformers, will be both the inspiration and the instrument of the social progress of the future. Such a statement cannot go far without encountering vigorous dispute. The air is filled with voices asserting that the modern business system stands squarely across the path that leads to a decent social order. On all hands there are men

From *The Way Out* (Garden City: Doubleday, Page & Co., 1926), pp. 29–32, 34–6, 39–40, 43–7.

who contend that we can assure social progress only by destroying the business system and reorganizing our life upon a communistic or near communistic basis. And multiplied thousands of men and women who are far from being communists indict the modern business system as the tyrant rather than the tool of mankind.

Now, I am under no delusion about the social efficiency of our industrial civilization. Despite the fact that science is daily making life more livable and interesting, daily devising ways and means for shifting burdens from the backs of men to the backs of machines, daily widening the range of men's interests by rapid transportation and communication, and broadening the scope of existence generally, the time of the majority of mankind is still occupied almost entirely in the business of providing food, clothing, and shelter, with little time or training for lifting life to a higher level—even if the means were at hand. This is plainly indefensible, if it is to be accepted as the inevitable result of the business system; . . . yet I am convinced that the social progress of the future will be achieved not by the destruction of the business system but by its further and finer development. The modern business system is at present more or less lawless, but the pressure of necessity during the next ten or twenty years will enforce its reform. Unless I wholly misinterpret the signs of the time, we are now in the morning hours of a period in which business men, in order to survive and succeed, will be compelled to adopt the sort of policies that will give us an increasingly better social order. During the next ten or twenty years we shall come to see from practical experience that there is nothing necessarily contradictory between successful business and social progress. Success in both will demand the same principles and the same practices. Commercial success and social welfare, in the days ahead, will stem from the same root.

The average man and the average student of social con-

ditions too often start with the premise that business by
its very nature is anti-social. Certainly conspicuous business
success has been so regarded. And we are obliged to admit
that much of it in the past has been. But the point I want
to make is that business must henceforth function in a
changed world—a world in which good business policies
will be found to be good social policies.

What I mean concretely is this: Social progress demands
coöperation, the modification or—to borrow a word from
the psychoanalyst—the sublimation of the class struggle, the
access of every man, woman, and child to a decently adequate supply of the necessities of life, and the release of
the individual from the things that prevent his living a
creative and contented life. In the past, successful business has often blocked the way to a realization of these
socially necessary ends. But coming conditions are going
to compel business men to make changes in policy and in
action that will result in just these things. The business
policies that will enable men to make the big business
successes of the next ten or twenty years will produce
these things as by-products. . . .

In times past, business could be successful despite many
anti-social policies and practices, because society was not
in the tight corner it is in today. The business man of the
past was in very much the same position as the pioneer
who could afford to be recklessly wasteful in a virgin land.
Business, until now, has been on what might be called a
pioneering spree. Only lately have economy and the wisest
possible handling of men and material become absolute
essentials to business success.

As H. G. Wells makes a character in one of his later
novels say, "In the days before the war it was different.
A little grabbing or cornering was all to the good. All to
the good. It prevented things being used up too fast. And
the world was running by habit; the inertia was tremendous. You could take all sorts of liberties. But all this is
altered. We're living in a different world."

We are, indeed, living in a different world. In place of abundance we have shortage in most nations. Instead of a simple world with lots of elbow room we have a world complicated and crowded. In place of dominant captains of industry and docile labourers we have captains of industry in insecure seats and a labour mass become articulate and conscious of its political and economic power. In short, we are now living in a world in which the reckless and wasteful methods of the exploiter are a social menace and the creative methods of the scientific, socially minded business man a social necessity. . . .

The wise business man, seeing that we have passed the time when reckless, wasteful, exploitative, and anti-social methods could be made profitable, will, as I have suggested, turn to the scientific development of business. He will do this not merely because a new social conscience constrains him but primarily because sound business intelligence and competition force him to do it. When the character in Mr. Wells's novel said that we were living in a new world, he went on to say, "It's a new public. It's—wild. It'll smash up the show if we go too far." Now, I am not suggesting that the business man will or should base all his policies upon the fear of social revolution. I am saying only that the new economic and social conditions that have come as a result of the increasing industrialism, the increasing complexity, and the increasing interdependence of society, that the particular economic muddle of transition into which the war plunged the world, and especially the newly awakened mind of labour, all mean that the business of the future cannot be commercially successful unless it is socially sound. . . .

But the one thing that makes business predominantly the instrument for social progress—if we only use it wisely— is the fact that business men control the progress of this country. They control the progress of the country not because they are either geniuses or pirates or because they have joined in any dark plot to capture and loot the com-

mon people. They are neither more grasping nor more public spirited than other men. They control the progress of
the country simply because this is an industrial nation and
their hands happen to be on the levers of power.

Whether they are blundering or brilliant, whether they
are actuated by sinister motives or by social vision, they
still control the processes of production, distribution, and
consumption. And these three processes touch our lives at
more points and oftener than all the torch-light processions,
congressional debates, and reform movements that have
taken place since the first politician mounted the stump
and the first reformer challenged the status quo. What
business men think and do about production, distribution,
and consumption is therefore the most important single
factor to be considered in any study of the possible arrest
or advancement of social progress. It is not so much the
attitude of business men toward "public questions" as it
is their attitude toward "business questions" that counts in
the history of social advance. . . .

The successful businesses of the future will be the businesses that improve the processes and reduce the costs of
production, rid distribution of its present indefensible wastes,
bring the price of the necessities of life lower and lower,
shorten the hours of labour and enlarge the margin of
leisure, eliminate periodic depressions and recurrent unemployment, limit the area of the industrial battlefield and
enlarge the floor space of the council chamber, create
better and better working conditions, pay higher real wages,
and increase the comfort and prosperity of both their employees and their customers.

These are the things that the facts prove will be not op-
tional but obligatory upon the business man who wants to
succeed in a big way during the next ten or twenty years.
And these are the things that will give us decent social
progress.

CHAPTER THREE

# Collapse of the
# Old Order

## I

Prosperity in the twenties had come to mean a rate of
advance rather than an actual state of affairs. A progressive concept, the more abundant life in America was regarded as a constantly accelerating process measured in
gross output of goods. Rising statistics, like new skyscrapers,
proclaimed American technology the wonder of the world.
Between 1919 and 1929, horsepower per worker in manufacturing shot up 50 percent and output per man hour 72
percent; and in the short seven years before 1929, production expanded 34 percent, and national income nearly
doubled. Equally impressive was the upward climb of security prices and the fantastic activity in Wall Street. Sales
on the New York Stock Exchange leaped from 236 million
shares in 1923 to 1,125 million in 1928, an amazing phenomenon hailed by an astonished financial expert as "an
economic revolution of the profoundest character." With
"a new age" in the offing, political problems were forgotten, and more and more Americans were inclined to
explain their society in terms of productivity, profits, and
stock-market quotations.[1]

This economic revolution, New Era publicists argued, was bringing an equality of prosperity to the American people which few reformers had ever believed possible. Not only was wealth increasing at a rapid rate, but, they claimed, never before had so much purchasing power been put into the hands of the masses. By 1928, even former critics of the business system were lulled into conceding that the prospects were pleasing. "Big business in America," granted Lincoln Steffens, once a hard-hitting opponent of plutocracy, "is producing what the Socialists held up as their goal: food, shelter, and clothing for all." Practice had moved faster than theory, wrote Walter Lippmann. "The more or less unconscious and unplanned activities of businessmen are for once more novel, more daring, and in general more revolutionary than the theories of the progressives."[2] According to the optimistic views of Harvard economist Thomas Nixon Carver, who equated capitalism with the security of private property, we were in way of establishing a kind of economic democracy in the United States without resorting to the "socialistic" intervention of government in the economy.[*]

Then came the crash of 1929, and the vaunted "economic revolution" turned overnight into an economic debacle. Americans made the sudden shocking discovery that not only had "equal prosperity" been an illusion but the "New Era" had turned out to be the same old story of "boom and bust" that had dogged the American economy since 1819. Yet, though historically the pattern was familiar— business failure, unemployment, social dislocation, and widespread human suffering—the American dilemma at the beginning of the thirties, as Adolf Berle pointed out, was unique in the economic history of the world: "We had warehouses bursting with foodstuffs of all kinds. We had a manufacturing plant second to none, with a more than ample supply of trained workmen, a technical staff of unchallenged

[*]Thomas Nixon Carver, *What Capitalism Is and What It Does.* See page 177.

efficiency. Every desire for goods or gadgets, for services or scenery, could be satisfied. And yet the great machine was slowly coming to a dead center. In the face of supply, men went hungry; in the face of unexampled possibilities for luxury, life was rapidly slipping toward squalor. The law of supply and demand, which theoretically means that when there is a want business promptly supplies it, had been hit below the belt by the more accurate law that business will supply only an effective demand. In business language, it doesn't matter what the customer wants, but what he can pay for." Since men were hungry in the presence of unsalable surpluses, it was clear that the country had not suffered a calamity of nature but a breakdown in the management of its wealth. Candid observers, who only a few years before had praised businessmen for their daring, were now forced to revise their opinions and to conclude with Lippmann that the development of the American economy had been "gravely perverted."[3]

Since the beginning of the twentieth century, the material welfare of the country had come to depend more and more upon the full use and free run of technique. Any defect or hindrance in technical management, any intrusion of non-technical considerations, any failure or obstruction at any point unavoidably resulted, as Veblen forecast in 1921, in "a disproportionate set-back to the balanced whole" and brought "a disproportionate burden of privation" on all those people whose fortunes were in any way linked to the technological economy. As later economic research confirmed, Veblen's analysis of the origins of depression in a technological society was largely borne out by events.[4]

By the 1920's, the phenomenal gain in technological efficiency made it theoretically possible for industry to turn out more and more goods, cheaper and faster, for more people. But actually, instead of passing on these savings to workers in the form of higher wages (factory productivity rose 55%, hourly wages 2%) or to consumers in the form of lower prices (consumer prices declined only 3%),

During the depression when bleak villages of shacks and packing-boxes known ironically as "Hoovervilles" sprang up on vacant lots and on the outskirts of cities, troubled America began to question an economic system which provided fortunes for a few and left millions without the basic comforts of life.

business kept the profits or expended them in a way which tended to enlarge savings and productive capacity without increasing or spreading purchasing power. The immediate effect of such business practices was to aggravate the unequal distribution of income, already accentuated by the drastic drop in farm income, by concentrating income in the upper groups—in 1929 the top 5 percent claimed 33.5 percent of the national income. Dividends went up 64 percent, and profits, interest, and rent, which went largely to upper-income groups, increased 45 percent; whereas the real annual wages of workers in industry and agriculture—

upon whom national purchasing power chiefly depended—rose a mere 10.9 percent. In relation to increased productivity, this was too low to buy the goods and services industry was able to produce at the prices business demanded. The end result of the prevailing business policy of taking the last cent of profit was a chronic maladjustment between production and consumption which so unbalanced the economy in favor of the businessman as to destroy his own market and bring on a national economic catastrophe.[5]

With business leadership apparently indifferent to the urgent needs of the country, Americans now asked whether it was any longer practicable to leave control of the economic system solely in the hands of businessmen. If the businessmen who ruled America in the twenties were responsible for the biggest boom in history, said the *New Republic*, "then it follows that they are also personally responsible for the world's biggest depression." Technologically, the nation had already solved the problem of production—the industrial system was able to produce more than enough to go around—but businessmen striving for their own personal gain had erected a dam between production and distribution with the paradoxical result, as Elmer Davis noted in *Harper's*, that people were "starving to death because there is too much food and freezing to death because there is too much coal." Those who did not view the depression as an inevitable, inherent aspect of the economy traced the cause of failure to the traditional attitude of the businessman who looked upon the economic system as a glorified gaming table whereby the American people were—if lucky—fed, sheltered, and clothed. Business, John Dewey pointed out, was essentially irrational, "a gamble in uncertainties," but the production and distribution of goods were not themselves business. "In business they became cards in a game in which all trumps are in possession of capital." After all, asked Stuart Chase, a popular writer on economic problems, what was an economic system for?° Was it merely a channel for personal aggrandizement or was it to provide the means, without excessive waste or loss, whereby those who lived under it might obtain the basic comforts of life in quantities as dependable and as adequate as natural resources and the state of technology permitted? The time had come, in his opinion, when Americans must recognize that the economic system was not a private hunting preserve but an integral part of the social order.[6]

## II

Social control of business was blocked by an almost sacrosanct belief in individualism. From the beginning of the nation, and even before, Americans had thought in terms of the individual, had distrusted government, had celebrated the virtues of an uncontrolled and unregulated economic system. No idea was more deeply ingrained, or diligently cultivated, in the minds of the people than the idea that the greatness of the nation, its prosperity and progress, was inextricably bound up with the efforts of those enterprising individuals who were shrewd enough to recognize economic opportunity and strong enough to take it. Since the individual was held to be the sole source of progress, Americans had traditionally shied from any scheme for improving society based upon collective action.

The twenties had witnessed a revival of individualism, and from 1921 to 1933 it was unquestioningly the reigning social philosophy. With President Harding it was probably instinct, with Coolidge a righteous faith, but the more thoughtful Herbert Hoover expounded his own semi-philosophical version of individualism or classical liberalism in which economic liberty was identified with absence of government action.† Blind to the fact that his own spe-

---

°Stuart Chase, *What Is an Economic System For?* See page 183.
†Herbert Hoover, *Economic Individualism.* See page 188.

cial interpretation of liberty was historically conditioned and was a product of the attack against economic monopolies created and sanctioned by the mercantilist policies of eighteenth-century monarchies, Hoover put forward his ideas as immutable truths good at all times and places. Though aware that liberty was a result of the "unending battle against economic domination," he looked at the twentieth century from the viewpoint of the eighteenth, narrowly conceiving government as the only serious enemy of liberty, and more or less overlooked the growing threat of economic domination by large corporations. While he called for regulation to prevent legal monopoly, he believed government should aim chiefly at stimulating and liberating economic forces, not at restraining or diverting them. Ironically Hoover, the staunch individualist, as Secretary of Commerce under Harding and Coolidge and later as President, encouraged the concentration of economic power by pushing trade associations in industry and advocating government sanction of business combination. Thus, wittingly or unwittingly, he reintroduced into government the mercantilist policy of favoritism and support to certain vested interests, against which early nineteenth-century liberals had so strenuously fought.[7]

Hoover's economic philosophy, however, proved to be a more accurate reflection of faith than of fact. His absolute belief obscured the fact that, whatever merits the creed may have had in the past, individualism was no longer applicable in the twenties to an economy in which the most powerful individuals were huge corporations, not persons at all (except by legal courtesy). At the end of the decade, Professors Adolf A. Berle and Gardiner C. Means of Columbia disclosed that nearly two-thirds of the industrial wealth of the country had changed from individual to corporate ownership. Not only had the continuing tendency of business to combine into large corporations significantly altered the picture of economic life as painted by Adam Smith, but Professors Berle and Means found that most of the accepted

concepts of individualism—private property, private enterprise, individual initiative, competition—were no longer
valid in a predominantly corporate economy.°

Their research further revealed that the dominant creed
of individualism had played into the hands of privileged
groups by serving as a kind of apologetics for the existing
economic regime. While touting the virtues of individualism,
business-minded Republican administrations had followed a
neomercantilist policy of non-regulation and cooperation
which had permitted big business to merge and combine
without hindrance from government. Investigation by Professor Means showed that by 1930 the combined assets of the
200 largest non-banking corporations (.07 percent of American corporations) amounted to nearly half of all corporate
wealth in the United States. The dominant position of the
large corporation was further emphasized by the fact that
these same 200 giants received at least 43.2 percent of all
corporate income (corporations with profits of more than
$1 million accounted for 80% of all corporate profits in
1929) and controlled roughly 22 percent of the total wealth
of the nation. These huge corporations, which were growing
much faster than the smaller companies, had come to
dominate most major industries—if not all industry in the
United States. Whether or not economic control was actually
vested in the 64 big businessmen who were picked out in
1930 as the real "rulers" of the country, there was little
doubt that the basic premise of individualism—equal
opportunity—was, in the economic realm, only a polite
fiction.[8]

If, as Hoover asserted, a social system could only be
judged by its results—whether it brought permanent and
continuous progress—then clearly events of 1929 and after
decreed that individualism was no longer a practicable
system of social management. Despite good intentions and

°Adolf A. Berle, Jr., and Gardiner C. Means, *Economic Organization*. See page
193.

valiant effort, President Hoover was never able to reconcile his brand of individualism with the social responsibility demanded of him. Part of his difficulty was due to the assumption that the economic crisis was temporary and would work itself out, but the chief obstacle was his firm belief that government intervention was a denial of American principles, a lack of confidence in the self-reliant individual. In 1930 he told Congress: "Economic depression can not be cured by legislative action or executive pronouncement. Economic wounds must be healed by the action of the cells of the economic body—the producers and consumers themselves." Accordingly the President resorted to moral suasion to prevent unemployment and loss of wages, which proved ineffective because business disregarded its pledge to maintain wages and jobs, desperately trying to cut them faster than prices fell. With the problem of relief, it was a similar story. Federal relief, Hoover informed broke and jobless Americans, would destroy "character" and strike at "the roots of self-government." Instead, amid growing destitution, he called upon local government and private charity to relieve the distress of millions of citizens, but the program broke down before it got underway because the states did almost nothing, and local governments soon ran out of money. By 1932, 100 cities had no relief appropriations at all. New Orleans refused new applicants; Dallas and Houston gave no relief to Mexican and Negro families. In face of mass unemployment and widespread hunger, President Hoover held doggedly to his faith, blocking a Congressional bill which would have provided direct relief and vast public works.

Finally, after private actions and individual decisions had failed to cure the depression, the President decided reluctantly upon direct intervention in the economic system, making federal funds available for public works, industry, and agriculture. A major fault of the Hoover program, however, was that his remedies applied largely to the top of the economy—financial institutions and business corporations—rather than the bottom where the need was most desperate. For example, Hoover approved loans to private capitalists for purposes of profit but, at the same time, forbade the federal government either to give or lend a dollar to an unemployed man so that he might keep himself and his family alive. Yet, in proposing the federal government interfere with economic forces and take measures to counter the depression, President Hoover by his standards acted boldly, and he went as far as his faith would allow. [9]

# III

In last analysis Hoover's failure to come to grips with the problems of depression was due to his inability to invoke the collective powers of government on behalf of the masses. This diffidence on his part stemmed from an elitist distrust of democracy and a genuine fear of the state. His view was that "the mass does not think but only feels." Acts and ideas that led to progress came from the individual, not from the crowd which had no mind of its own. "The crowd is credulous, it destroys, it consumes, it hates, and it dreams—but it never builds." It followed, then, that "popular desires are no criteria to the real need," and the task of constructive leadership was to firmly resist the clamor of the mob. Civilizations fell, Hoover believed, because great masses of men became impregnated with wrong ideas and wrong social philosophies—the most dangerous of which, in his opinion, was the Socialist delusion that government could produce economic equality by political action. Though troubled by the great abuses the depression had exposed in the economic system, the President, like his conservative business supporters, had an even more acute dread of "a regimented economy dictated by government through bureaucracy." He therefore determinedly opposed the centralization of relief in the federal government on grounds that it would concentrate power in the federal

government by the erection of a huge political bureaucracy and that relief would itself become an instrument
of patronage and the means for creation of a totalitarian
state.[10]

While national planning, to an assertive individualist such
as President Hoover, was "national regimentation," to
socially minded thinkers such as Lewis Mumford and John
Dewey it was more than an emergency measure, it was an
inevitable consequence of the advance of technology. Invincible technological trends, declared Dewey, made the
social control of economic forces necessary if the goals of
democracy were to be realized. Those who shouted "regi-

---

In summer of 1932, some 20,000 homeless, penniless veterans
descended upon Washington to lobby for passage of a veteran's
bonus bill. After the bill failed in the Senate, President Hoover
called out the U.S. Army to drive them from the capital at
bayonet point.

Wide World Photos

mentation" had failed to see that effective liberty was a
function of the social conditions existing at any time. As
favored beneficiaries of the economic regime, they were
blind to the fact that private control of the new forces of
production operated in the same way as unchecked political
power, imposing harsh regimentation upon millions of their
fellow Americans. "Brain-truster" Rexford Tugwell also believed the role of the New Deal was to free the country
from private economic regimentation. Big business had
created a "supertrust" outside our political forms which
threatened to swamp the state in the backwash of its progress. Hence the choice facing the American people in the
thirties, as Tugwell saw it, was that either the government would supervise the businessmen, or the businessmen
would supervise the government as they had done in the
1920's.[11]

If the state could organize for war, why—asked the
theorists—could it not organize for peace and plenty? If it
could mobilize against a foreign enemy, why not against
enemies close at hand—hunger, poverty, and unemployment?
If planning was necessary for the nation to exert its maximum military power, then, it was argued, national planning
was necessary for maximum social power. Wars, in the
past, had frequently helped to break the economic deadlock
of depression because people gladly gave to government
in wartime power and money for military purposes that
they would not allow it to use or spend in peacetime for
constructive aid to themselves. But, as the economist Paul
H. Douglas put it, since going to war to get out of depression was like burning one's house down to roast pigs, there
was a strong argument for national planning as an economic
equivalent for war.[12]

Such "collectivist measures" were repudiated by Walter
Lippmann, who saw them as an American manifestation of
the worldwide trend toward totalitarianism. While admitting that planning was necessary and feasible under war
conditions, he argued that peacetime planning was in-

While New Deal measures against the depression were decried as "national regimentation," the Civilian Conservation Corps rescued many young Americans from meaningless lives of poverty and despair and made them useful citizens.

---

compatible with democracy.° Although twenty-five years before in his *Preface to Politics* Lippmann had held that disorder and misery could be overcome only by the organized forces of government, he reversed his position in the thirties. Everywhere he observed men who called themselves Communists, Socialists, Fascists, Nazis, and even "liberals" unanimously holding that only through the power

---

°Walter Lippmann, *The Servile State*. See page 203.

of the state could men be made happy. Instead, Lippmann now believed that, by a kind of tragic irony, all attempts to rationalize society under the auspices of the state must lead inevitably to an intolerable choice between liberty and security.[13]

However, as breadlines lengthened and Hoovervilles proliferated, the mood of the country became more rebellious. Rumors of revolution were widespread during the last months of the Hoover administration, and many feared the muttering retreat of the Bonus Army might be the spark to set off a bloody conflagration. *Harper's*, a normally unexcitable magazine, played up the possibilities of revolution at great length, asking on one occasion: "What is the American with the revolutionary birthright thinking about these days? His own country and the world are now in the midst of a vast economic upheaval. The system of production and distribution have been badly jammed, and some of the parts will never again be of any use. . . . The word revolution is heard at every hand; we seem to face revolutions of all sorts and kinds." In 1931, the Secret Service had attracted front-page attention by "uncovering" an alleged Communist plot to seize Washington, and the dean of the Harvard School of Business warned that capitalism was skirting a revolution that might change the whole future of Western civilization. These and other scare stories prompted the *Nation* to note forebodingly that the apprehensions of those in charge showed businessmen clearly realized the justifiable threat to their control of social arrangements. Yet, despite all the talk of revolution, except for a few riots, there was never any concerted attempt to overthrow the established order. Those who suffered most—the masses of jobless and hungry Americans—were curiously inert, "awaiting nothing more drastic than the return of prosperity."[14]

In the end, as Thurman Arnold observed, there was no uprising of the downtrodden, only panic on the part of the well-to-do. After the industrial situation had gotten

beyond their control, the business leadership simply fled
from responsibility. By their timorous abdication, which had
been predicted by Veblen in 1921, the businessmen confessed their inability any longer to take care of the country's material welfare. Trapped in its own dogma, the business community was unable to propose or even to reconcile
itself to bold and drastic remedies. Businessmen, *Harper's*
observed, were too frightened: "frightened at what the
present situation might lead to and frightened still more
at the thought of trying any different policies than those
which have prevailed in the past." Instead of defending
capitalism by a positive leadership which accepted social
responsibility and met the real needs of the majority of
people, the laggard business directorate fought a series of
rearguard engagements to maintain its privileges. Faced
with new problems for which their methods and ways of
thinking were completely inadequate, business leaders
found that they were unable to exorcise the specter of depression by invoking the old catchwords, and they retreated
in disorder and terror. "Business, which nobody dared to
frighten," marveled the radio commentator Elmer Davis,
"is afraid at last of its own shadow."[15]

When business failed as a governing force, a government
based upon a tradition of inaction and non-interference
was compelled to rush in and fill the vacuum. By popular
mandate the incoming Roosevelt administration was called
upon to rescue the ailing economy and to correct by governmental action the shortcomings of the old economic order.
Since the chief fault of the old order had been a failure
in technical management—"private planning" wholly out
of social control had brought national economic ruin—the
problems business passed to government were ultimately to
be resolved only by technical means. As President Franklin D. Roosevelt told American voters, in order to achieve
the full employment of industry and manpower and to
bring about an equitable and sufficient supply of goods and
services to the people at large, it was necessary to add to

the traditional political role of government a new economic role and to extend the positive powers of government into economic affairs.° "We see things now that we could not see along the way. The tools of government which we had in 1933 are outmoded. We have had to forge new tools for a new role of government operating in a democracy—a role of new responsibility for new needs and increased responsibility for old needs long neglected." The new role of "progressive government" was to create and maintain a balance between the various elements within the economy: "What we seek is balance in our economic system—balance between agriculture and industry, and balance between the wage earner, the employer, and the consumer." To carry out this interventionist role, the positive program of government under the New Deal involved the regulation of private enterprise, economic planning, governmental ownership and operation of commercial and industrial enterprises, and the extension of economic aid and services to individuals and private groups.[16]

The revolutionary expansion of the powers of government under the New Deal provoked resistance and criticism from Right and Left—from those who had wealth and power and those who had neither but claimed possession of the formula for the future. The movement of the Right was composed of prosperous businessmen and lawyers, was elitist and capitalistic in outlook, favored monopolistic business, and inclined toward state capitalism or Fascism. The movement of the Left was made up of Marxist writers and intellectuals, was studiously proletarian in view, attacked capitalistic institutions, and tended logically toward state socialism or Communism. Though at opposite ends of the political spectrum, these two rival minority groups had common origins and ends. Both were radical collectivist movements born in rebellion against the free market; both in extreme and desperate form ended in totalitarianism;

°Franklin D. Roosevelt, *The Welfare State*. See page 210.

both distrusted democratic liberalism and bitterly assailed the New Deal, each purportedly seeing behind it the deceitful machinations of the other. On the Right, the American Liberty League, speaking for corporate wealth and all those fearful of encroachment on vested rights, protested unbridled government and denounced the New Deal as "socialistic"; on the Left, dogmatic Marxists of the Socialist and Communist parties rejected the "Roosevelt Revolution" as a capitalist counter-revolution exploiting democracy for the purposes of "social Fascism."[17]

## IV

As things turned out, however, the New Deal yielded neither to socialism nor totalitarianism, but evolved what Robert Heilbroner has called "a new form of *guided* capitalism." Rather than a radical revision of capitalism, the New Deal followed a policy of economic interventionism based upon government responsibility for the economic security and prosperity of the whole society. Despite business protests of "regimentation," the New Deal never moved as far toward collectivism as its critics feared. President Roosevelt, said Secretary of Labor Frances Perkins, "always resisted the frequent suggestion of the Government's taking over railroads, mines, etc., on the ground that it was unnecessary and would be a clumsy way to get the service needed." While recognizing that the economy had slowed down and the forces within it were no longer in equilibrium, Roosevelt refused to concede to the Marxists that the mechanism had permanently broken down. Instead of taking over and running everything, he proposed only to repair it and make it run again. "We took the middle road," said the President in 1936. "We used the facilities and resources available only to Government, to permit individual enterprise to resume its normal functions in a socially sound competitive order." Though condemned by men of wealth as a traitor to his class, Roosevelt through the New Deal may have checked the power of capitalism, but as Socialists bitterly complained, he did not kill capitalism.[18]

Innovation, not revolution, was the trade-mark of the New Deal. A politics of expediency in the sense that it sought pragmatic, not ideological answers, the New Deal searched for acceptable solutions to problems rather than imposing preconceived solutions. As Tugwell stressed at the time, its method was democratic experimentalism. It looked forward to "no antiseptic utopia and no socialistic paradise," but to "a changing system in which free American human beings can live their changing lives." Rarely did New Deal measures or New Dealers as a group represent a clear-cut ideological preference. "Total planners and piecemeal planners, budget-balancers and deficit spenders, trust-regulators and trust-busters, protectionists and free-traders, 'sound money' proponents and inflationists," wrote Heinz Eulau, "all vied with each other under the hospitable tent that was the New Deal." Yet, despite its ideological elusiveness, nearly all measures sponsored by Roosevelt—emergency relief, farm aid, social security, conservation, banking and securities reform, fair labor standards—were in the mainstream of American democratic tradition and involved strengthening the state not at the expense of society but for the benefit of society. It is noteworthy, for example, that the most "socialistic" undertaking of the New Deal, the Tennessee Valley Authority, caused private enterprise to flourish in an area where previously it had barely existed—after 1933 the rate of growth of private industry was greater in the Tennessee Valley than in the rest of the nation.[19]

At bottom the chief difference and underlying conflict between the New Deal and its Republican predecessors was not, as Hoover insisted, between two philosophies of government—for, after all, Hoover and Roosevelt were both capitalists rather than socialists, both democrats rather than totalitarians—but, as more accurately described by Roosevelt, between two theories of prosperity. Where Hoover associated the good of all with the prosperity of a chosen group—the businessmen of the country—and directed national policy primarily for their benefit, Roosevelt regarded public power as an instrument for the benefit of all the nation. While Hoover provided aid at the top of the economy calculated to "trickle down" from the producers to the mass of people, Roosevelt gave help at both top and bottom, and widened the scope of government to include direct aid to farmers being starved off their lands and to workers shut out of idle factories. For the first time, under the New Deal, the federal government underwrote the economic security of the farmer, as had been done for the businessman and industrialist since the 1860's, and offered organized labor the kind of governmental encouragement and cooperation that in the past had been the exclusive prerogative of organized business.

As a consequence, under New Deal auspices, not only was there a marked rise in farm income and prices, but organized labor made phenomenal gains. With government and the courts now guaranteeing the right of labor "to organize and bargain collectively," there was a rush to join unions. In 1935, John L. Lewis formed the Committee for Industrial Organization which, on being expelled from the A. F. of L., became a rival specializing in industrial unions. Hundreds of thousands of unskilled workers for whom there had been no place in old-fashioned craft unions flocked to join the C.I.O., whose membership in two years jumped to four million. Under the ruthless, dynamic leadership of the beetle-browed Lewis, the C.I.O. moved into industries which hitherto had successfully resisted unionization, especially steel and autos. Faced with widespread "sit down" strikes, United States Steel capitulated. General Motors resisted, only to surrender after a terrific struggle. Although subsequent strikes against "Little Steel" failed, there was no doubt that organized labor under the New Deal won a legitimate position in the economy as a "countervailing force" to the organized power of big business.[20]

In recognizing the interdependence of agriculture, industry, business and labor, and of the welfare of all, the New Deal employed mercantilist principles and methods advocated by Alexander Hamilton in 1791. By its bold approach to the problems of depression, Eugene Golob suggested, it "revived the mercantilist's willingness to experiment and his lack of fear of innovation" and, at the same time, directed to popular ends the Hamiltonian concept that government was to interest itself directly in the welfare of the citizenry. Under the New Deal, the narrow neomercantilist policy of the Hoover administration was democratized and greatly broadened in scope, and the eighteenth-century concern with money and fiscal management applied with renewed vigor. But private property was never seriously threatened, and private enterprise, though regulated more carefully, remained still the basic characteristic of the economy. So one may conclude with Golob: "If there was a 'Roosevelt revolution,' with the one possible exception of its hastening of the inevitable recognition of labor's place in society, it was only in the minds of those who had lost touch with the past. If the New Deal was 'radical,' it was so only in the sense that it constituted a radical return to the conservative tradition of the mercantilists." Historic confirmation of the triumph of neomercantilism was the moving of the economic capital of the United States from New York City to Washington, D.C., by passage of the Employment Act of 1946, which officially recognized that it was "the continuing policy and responsibility of the Federal Government . . . to promote maximum employment, production, and purchasing power."[21]

But, along with many far-reaching social and economic reforms, the New Deal made many mistakes and fell short of many liberal hopes, especially in the area of economic planning. Although labor had been granted a long overdue bill of rights, the importance of the consumer-worker whose economic function of mass consumption had grown more and more vital as technology increased the complexity and velocity of mass production had been generally overlooked; and no serious attempt had been made to adjust wages, not to a dwindling sum of toil, but to the growing total of consumption. A timid beginning had been made toward social security, but health was omitted, and provisions against the great hazards of unemployment and old age were mean and niggardly. The initial effect of New Deal economic policies had been to inaugurate four years of steady and rapid

---

On Memorial Day 1937, a peaceful crowd of C.I.O. sympathizers, including women and children, demonstrating before the non-union Republic Steel plant in Chicago were fired upon by police, and in the subsequent massacre ten demonstrators were killed and more than seventy-five injured.

Wide World Photos

recovery—industrial production in this period doubled and real income increased more than fifty percent, both regaining the 1929 peak—but hasty and ill-advised fiscal and monetary policies brought recovery to a halt in 1937. Roosevelt's deficiencies as an economist were in the opinion of Robert Heilbroner as striking as his triumphs as a politician. In many cases, as Thurman Arnold, a former New Dealer, complained, "measures were improvised and hurled at symptoms" without thorough diagnosis. Often where vigorous and decisive action was called for, the Roosevelt administration settled for halfway measures, especially when it came to deficit spending. For all the cry against government spending, the sums laid out by the New Deal for social welfare and public works were pitifully meager, far too small to "prime the pump" of a great economy. As a result, by 1939, although conditions had vastly improved, there were still 9.5 million Americans, about 17 percent of the labor force, without work.[22]

At last resort, it was primarily the demands of approaching war, not New Deal policy, which increased government spending and led to full production and employment. Ironically, the war expanded civilian consumption fifty percent. While the New Deal had created technical devices for governing the economy, it not only had not learned how to use them effectively but found it ideologically impossible to put them to full use because of the still prevailing popular distrust of compensatory government spending in times of peace. With the coming of World War II, however, the nation moved rapidly, and without undue sentimental shock, into a planned prosperity which was based upon huge government expenditures for arms and which necessitated tight controls over production and distribution, wages and prices, profits, rents, and consumer spending. What democracy and humanitarianism had been unable to accomplish in the name of a better life, patriotism and militarism easily achieved when the goal was mass slaughter.

# Readings:

# Collapse of the Old Order

## Thomas Nixon Carver (1865-1961)

*A respected orthodox economist, he was profes-
sor of economics at Oberlin College from 1894
to 1900, then at Harvard until his retirement in
1937. He specialized in the sociological aspects
of economics, taking the point of view that the
full development of the capitalistic system would
not be reached until practically everyone has become a capitalist.*

# WHAT CAPITALISM IS AND WHAT IT DOES

Whatever may be said against capitalism it has at least
abolished famine in every country where it has been permitted to develop freely. That is more than can be said of
any noncapitalistic system that ever existed. The worst
that can be said against the capitalistic system is that it
has not yet abolished inequality of wealth. Those inequal-

From *The Present Economic Revolution in the United States* (Boston: Little,
Brown & Co., 1925), pp. 209-12, 215-21. Copyright Thomas Nixon Carver;
reprinted by permission of Mrs. Ruth Ripley Carver.

ities which still persist, however, are not essential to the capitalistic system. In fact, where capitalism is given a chance to develop freely, unhampered by social and political obstacles, it tends to eliminate its own inequalities and secure not only great abundance for everybody, but to distribute the best things of life more evenly than any other system has ever succeeded in doing.

In spite of all the inequalities which persist under capitalism the masses of the people are better off under it than they have ever been under any other system. In fact, they are better fed, clothed, housed, and supplied with the adornments and embellishments of life than any but the rulers and a few hereditary aristocrats in any noncapitalistic country. . . .

It is an observed fact that laborers seldom migrate from a capitalistic to a noncapitalistic country, unless lured by free land or undeveloped mines, forests, or other natural resources. When these natural resources are once occupied and no longer free, the migration turns toward those places where capital has accumulated in largest quantities. That is where they find the best jobs, the highest wages, and the best living conditions. . . . Either the laborers are very unwise in doing this or there is a sound reason why they should do so.

These reasons are perfectly clear to anyone who understands what capitalism really is. The difficulty is that the word capitalism has been pronounced with such a wry face by so many persons. This has caused many of us to feel that it is necessarily bad. Those who feel that way about it have never really tried to understand it, but have tried, rather, to find new epithets to apply to it.

One difficulty in the way of a proper understanding of capitalism is the tendency to judge it by its superficial or temporary aspects rather than by its fundamental and permanent aspects. Strictly speaking, capitalism is not a system at all. It is merely a fact that grows out of the suppression of violence. Wherever violence is repressed, capital comes automatically into existence. Where violence is repressed, the man who has made a thing, or found it before anyone else has gained possession of it, cannot be dispossessed without his consent. No government can repress violence without automatically creating property as a result. Of course, this is only the beginning of our present system of property. This germ that is created by the mere repression of violence has been cultivated and developed by many other acts of government. Rightful possession has to be defined; what constitutes valid possession, a valid transfer, a valid contract, and many other questions of like character, have to be determined by government through its courts before any modern system of property is complete. Nevertheless, property would exist, in a simple and undeveloped form, even if government did nothing in the world except repress all violence. . . .

The so-called system of private property, therefore, is not a system in itself; it is a natural and unavoidable result of the repression of violence. . . .

The safety which comes from the repression of violence not only encourages accumulation but also invention. In fact, mechanical inventions and accumulations of capital go together like the two blades of a pair of scissors. Neither is of much use without the other. Where there are no mechanical inventors, no matter how many savers or accumulators there are, such accumulations of wealth as are possible must largely be in the form of hoards of money, jewels and other consumers' goods rather than of producers' goods. Where there are no savers and accumulators, there is no one who is willing to invest labor or money in expensive machines. No matter how many inventive geniuses there may be, productive inventions will not be used. If conditions are so unsafe as to discourage savings and accumulations, goods whose uses extend over the distant future are not likely to be accumulated at all because everyone is uncertain as to whether he will get the use of them or not. Mechanical inventions, especially of the larger and more productive sort, can seldom yield an immediate product sufficient to pay the cost. They must be kept for a long time before they will pay for themselves. In short, they are among the forms of accumulation which depend most closely upon safe conditions. No one will invest money or labor in such things unless he has confidence that they will not be taken away from him without his consent. . . .

The vast accumulation of machines and other expensive forms of capital that results from the permanent suppression of violence is very impressive. It seems to be one of the outstanding features of the present economic situation. It is not surprising, therefore, that a great deal of attention should be concentrated upon it, nor that they who concentrate their attention upon it should sometimes fail to see the underlying fact which produced it. The great tree is more impressive to the casual passer-by than the conditions which permitted it to grow.

These accumulations of powerful mechanisms, however, do not constitute the real capitalistic system. They are merely the visible manifestations of it. The real system was created when possession was protected by the suppression of violence. Wherever that fact exists, the outward and visible manifestations of it, such as the accumulation of wealth in durable forms and the development of powerful engines of production, will come into existence. These things will not go out of existence until possession is no longer protected. . . .

The existence of fraud or deception may still remain a factor unless the same power that defends the possessor against violence also defends him against fraud. When both fraud and violence are effectively repressed, industry and foresight, or general productive power, become the chief factors in prosperity. Differences in prosperity are based largely upon differences in the power to produce and in the foresight that leads to accumulation.

Even this situation is not free from danger. They who have, for any reason, failed to accumulate may envy those

who have succeeded. Others may sympathize with the envious ones and invent apologies and excuses for them. If
this envy grows strong enough, it is very likely to lead to
acts of violence either by individuals or classes. Class war
is especially dangerous and destructive of civilization. So
long as the government succeeds in repressing violence,
possessors remain safe in their possession. When, for any reason, the government fails to repress violence, possession
ceases to be property. Possessions must then be defended
by the prowess of their possessors or else the possessors
will lose them to those who have the power to take by
force what they want.

Sometimes the very engine, namely, government, that
began by repressing violence becomes itself the engine of
violence. Instead of defending the possessors, it uses its
superior power to dispossess them. There is always danger
of this if those who have not accumulated anything grow
envious enough and numerous enough to gain control of
the government. They may then use it as a means of taking accumulations away from those who accumulated them.
The wealth thus taken away from its accumulators may
then be disposed of in two ways. One is to give it to the
nonaccumulators, the other is for the government to hold
it and give the income derived from it to all without regard to the degree of foresight exercised by different individuals. Under these conditions, the foreseeing and the
thoughtless fare alike. Foresight would not be rewarded at
all because the individual would be given no opportunity
to exercise it, or to accumulate the results of his foresight.
If he tried to exercise it he would be dispossessed of his
accumulations by the government. The very power which
we now rely upon to protect us against being dispossessed
without our consent would then be perverted to the performance of that which it was designed to repress.

It was pointed out earlier that a highly capitalistic country . . . always attracts laborers from noncapitalistic countries. They come because wages and other conditions are

better than they were in their noncapitalistic homes. These good wages and good living conditions which attract immigrants also encourage the multiplication of thoughtless and thriftless people at home. There is, therefore, a strong probability that a considerable propertyless class will develop. It may become so large as to be dangerous. If it should be able to outvote the class of savers and accumulators, it may gain control of the government and use it as an engine for the dispossession of those who have managed to accumulate. The safety of modern civilization requires that these nonaccumulating classes shall be kept few in number.

The full development of the so-called capitalistic system will not be reached until practically everyone has become a capitalist, that is, an owner or part owner of some of the instruments of production called capital. The suppression of violence took power out of the hands of those who were willing and able to prosper by the use of violence. This made it possible for those who were too gentle or too weak physically to profit by violence to prosper by means of their industry and foresight. When everyone takes advantage of this opportunity, the full benefits of the suppression of violence will be realized. All real progress in the past has aimed in this direction, and all real progress in the future must lie in the same direction. No forcible leveling of the industrious and the idle is progressive; it is retrogressive. Any forcible leveling of the thrifty and the thriftless, of the forethoughtful and the nonforethoughtful, is equally retrogressive.

The crisis of civilization is reached whenever civilized people face this question. When the nonaccumulators refuse to respect the laws for the repression of violence, and begin to take by violence what others have peacefully accumulated, conditions are bad enough. In so far as they succeed in defying the efforts of the government to preserve law and order, to that extent must civilization decline. Conditions are much worse, however, when the nonaccumulators, instead of resisting the government, become numerous enough to gain control of it and unscrupulous enough to use it as the means of violence, that is, as the agency for the forcible dispossession of the peaceful accumulators. This is vastly more destructive of civilization than merely resisting government.

## Stuart Chase (1888-    )

*Born into an old New England family, he graduated* cum laude *from Harvard in 1910 and entered his father's accounting firm. His interest in social problems began the day he picked up Henry George's* Progress and Poverty. *In the 1920's, under the influence of Thorstein Veblen, he joined the staff of the Technical Alliance (nucleus of a later and more famous organization called Technocracy) and in 1927 helped found Consumers' Research. Although he has written many books, a single theme runs through them all, namely the impact of the machine on human beings.*

## WHAT IS AN ECONOMIC SYSTEM FOR?

John Maynard Keynes tells us that in one hundred years there will be no economic problem. He is probably right. We have already largely solved the problem of production, in the sense that the nations of America and Western Europe are equipped to produce more than enough to go around. In a few years Russia will undoubtedly join them. We have left the economy of scarcity behind and entered

From *A New Deal* (New York: The Macmillan Co., 1932), pp. 1–5, 21–3. Copyright Stuart Chase; reprinted by permission of the author.

the economy of abundance—though very few of us realize this, and most of our thinking is still in terms of scarcity economics, a cultural lag which we shall presently discuss. A billion and a half horses of mechanical energy, added to the time-honored stock of man and animal power, have at last put us in the position where, if we care to concentrate our energy, we can raise more food than we can eat, build more houses than we can inhabit, fabricate more clothing than we can wear out. Only by wasting and even deliberate destruction—such as the burning of cotton, corn, and coffee—can we dispose of the present output under the prevailing price system.

Distribution, the other wing of the economic problem, is *not* solved, as the present depression bears eloquent testimony. We can pile up the goods in the warehouse with an efficiency hitherto unknown to homo sapiens, but there they stick. We cannot get them out in sufficient volume either to keep the productive plant functioning steadily, and thus economically, or to keep the general population adequately fed, sheltered, and clothed. At times—as in America from 1922 to 1929—the flow, while far below capacity, leaving many millions on the ragged edge, is relatively better. At other times—as in 1921, and from 1930 to the present date—it is totally inadequate. Warehouses bulge and children cry for food.

That we have solved the main outlines of production—the inflow—does not help us much. Unless distribution—the outflow—can be directed, the misery which springs from economic causes will tend to continue unabated. Though we have entered the economy of abundance, its practical effects must be confined to certain classes in certain periods called "prosperity," unless the dam which impounds the warehoused products can be channeled. Strangely enough the dam, stubborn as it is, is made of paper. Goods do not flow out because there is insufficient purchasing power available to call them forth. Gradually students of economics are being forced to the conclusion—and this depression has helped to force them—that a dependable supply of purchasing power provides one basic answer to the riddle of distribution.

Why is purchasing power inadequate, why do we Western peoples fail to gain the full benefits of an economy of abundance; why must we go through such scarifying periods of mental panic and physical deprivation as the present? How can they be avoided? . . .

Certainly one fundamental cause of the failure of distribution is the prevailing attitude towards the methods whereby we are, if lucky, fed, sheltered and clothed. What is an economic system for? By and large it is regarded either as a means to achieve power and prestige, or as an amusing game to be played, the counters being those same pieces of paper which form purchasing power. Says John Dewey:

> The psychology and morale of business are based on trading in insecurity. They are criticised by serious moralists as if the animating spirit were that of acquisition. The accusations do not reach the mark. . . . It is the excitement of the game which counts. . . . We hunt the dollar, but hunting is hunting, not dollars.

The element of gambling enters into even the soberest and most orthodox of financial calculations. Profit is the reward of *risk*, the classical economists tell us. When the market is not rigged in advance, this is often true. Risk means something not sure, upon which one takes a chance, in short, a game.

It is assumed, in a left-handed way, that in accumulating the power, or in playing the game, we contrive somehow to grease the wheels of industry and serve a social purpose. Occasionally such is indeed the case, but normally this reasoning is pure rationalization. What man, starting in business, asks himself with any care whether the work he proposes to do will strengthen or weaken the economic system; whether it will serve a social function; whether it

will increase or decrease the evil effects of the business
cycle; whether it will choke or expand the flow of purchasing power? Such questions are normally undreamed of, and
are displaced by others: is there money in the venture?
or, is there fun in it? . . .

The cardinal questions simply are not asked. Hardly anybody bothers to inquire what an economic system is for.
Certain rules and procedures have grown up. These are
taken for granted, and within their limits, those responsible
for directing economic activity, primarily the business man
and the banker, attempt to satisfy their egos and appetites,
and to play their games. This would be all very well if
there were a divine providence looking after the system,
insuring, while men sought to amuse themselves, an automatic and dependable output of goods. But providence, we
ought by now to realize, displays not the slightest interest
in steering a mechanism men neglect.

Out of the human need for nourishment, a mechanism
has been established, simple among handicraft peoples, ex-
ceedingly complicated among peoples of the machine age.
In broad outline it may be compared to the human body,
where the cooperation of millions of cells is essential to
the efficient functioning which means health and life. When
a group of cells refuses to cooperate, becomes unduly
imbued with what might be called anatomical rugged individualism, we have a cancer and, in the end, death.
Persistent irritations are often responsible for cancers. For-
tunately the body has an automatic nervous system which
normally keeps the cells in order with little or no conscious
control. The economic body has no such biological protection; it lies defenseless against abuse. . . .

What is an economic system for? We return to the original point. Is it . . . primarily to be manipulated for some
individual's profit, power or amusement? This brings us to
a very important consideration, one frequently overlooked
by critics of the established order. It is not the profit which
the fortune hunter actually takes which makes the bulk of

the trouble; it is *the waste and maladjustment he creates in trying to take it.* For every success there are scores of failures, and most of the failures are responsible for at least as much dislocation as the successes. In an economy of abundance, properly organized, we could probably stand the cash drain on purchasing power caused by the profiteers and absentee owners. What no system can bear indefinitely is the continual roweling of its vitals by those who are trying to get rich. It makes little difference whether they succeed or fail; the operation is disastrous in either case. If we took all the income away from the wealthy and distributed it to the rest of the population, the standard of living of the latter would be increased, according to Professor Bowley, only some ten percent. But if we could eliminate the gyrations of those who are trying to become wealthy, we could abolish poverty and double the standard of living, virtually over night.

The defenders of the existing system roll their eyes to heaven at the thought of limiting these gyrations—with qualifications, perhaps, in respect to the more outré forms of racketeering and graft; but speculation they defend as providing some mystical variety of balance wheel. The pursuit of individual profit, they insist, is the force which keeps the mechanism going; progress, civilization itself, would collapse without it. . . . [This] is nonsense. Such activities throttle genuine progress.

Well, what *is* an economic system for? It is to provide a means, without excessive waste and loss, whereby those who live under it may eat. It has a function, and the function is to provide food, shelter, clothing and comforts in as dependable and adequate quantities as natural resources and the state of the technical arts permit, just as the function of human physiology is to supply every cell with enough oxygen and nutriment. When used as a channel for personal aggrandizement, a system's function and meaning collapse. It becomes an industrial whirlpool, throwing out a certain amount of goods and services as a byproduct, but susceptible to frightful stoppages, reverse twists, and even complete draining out. We have come in 1932 perilously close to the last.

From the functional point of view, economic activity takes on an entirely new meaning. It becomes at once more serious and less omnipotent. Order, discipline, the consciousness of definite social aim are needed to insure a dependable flow of goods from the earth to the ultimate consumer, but when that discipline—and it is largely one of engineering— is established, economic activity, with its four to six hours of work a day, becomes, if not a minor, at least a subordinate consideration. More important will be the problem of how to live; how to use fruitfully one's leisure time; how to improve the biological stock; how to educate; how to love and marry without the emotional miseries which now beset us; how to develop the arts; how to get the most out of life. These are the real problems of a civilized people who have yoked a billion of mechanical horse power. To go on stumbling through economic pits and mires, under a sky recurrently black with the horror of insecurity and even starvation, is tragic and needless waste.

# Herbert Hoover (1874-1964)

*Thirty-first President of the United States, he worked his way through Stanford University, and then engaged in mining operations abroad, first in Australia, then in China, Africa, Central and South America, and Russia. Between the Boxer Rebellion (1900) and World War I he built a $6 million fortune as an international consulting engineer. Because he left the country in the days of McKinley Republicanism not to return until the Harding administration, he entirely missed the Progressive period with its campaigns for political and social reform which,* *if experienced, might have tempered his inflexible individualism.*

# ECONOMIC INDIVIDUALISM

That high and increasing standards of living and comfort should be the first of considerations in public mind and in government needs no apology. We have long since realized that the basis of an advancing civilization must be a high and growing standard of living for all the people, not for a single class; that education, food, clothing, housing, and the spreading use of what we so often term non-essentials, are the real fertilizers of the soil from which spring the finer flowers of life. The economic development of the past fifty years has lifted the general standard of comfort far beyond the dreams of our forefathers. The only road to further advance in the standard of living is by greater invention, greater elimination of waste, greater production and better distribution of commodities and services, for by increasing their ratio to our numbers and dividing them justly we each will have more of them.

The superlative value of individualism through its impulse to production, its stimulation to invention, has, so far as I know, never been denied. Criticism of it has lain in its wastes but more importantly in its failures of equitable sharing of the product. In our country these contentions are mainly over the division to each of his share of the comforts and luxuries, for none of us is either hungry or cold or without a place to lay his head—and we have much besides. In less than four decades we have added electric lights, plumbing, telephones, gramophones, automobiles, and what not in wide diffusion to our standards of living.

From *American Individualism* (Garden City: Doubleday, Page & Co., 1922), pp. 32–40, 44–5. Reprinted by permission of Mr. Frank E. Mason.

Each in turn began as a luxury, each in turn has become so commonplace that seventy or eighty per cent of our people participate in them.

To all practical souls there is little use in quarreling over the share of each of us until we have something to divide. So long as we maintain our individualism we will have increasing quantities to share and we shall have time and leisure and taxes with which to fight out proper sharing of the "surplus." The income tax returns show that this surplus is a minor part of our total production after taxes are paid. Some of this "surplus" must be set aside for rewards to saving for stimulation of proper effort to skill, to leadership and invention—therefore the dispute is in reality over much less than the total of such "surplus." While there should be no minimizing of a certain fringe of injustices in sharing the results of production or in the wasteful use made by some of their share, yet there is vastly wider field for gains to all of us through cheapening the costs of production and distribution through the eliminating of their wastes, from increasing the volume of product by each and every one doing his utmost, than will ever come to us even if we can think out a method of abstract justice in sharing which did not stifle production of the total product.

It is a certainty we are confronted with a population in such numbers as can only exist by production attuned to a pitch in which the slightest reduction of the impulse to produce will at once create misery and want. If we throttle the fundamental impulses of man our production will decay. The world in this hour is witnessing the most overshadowing tragedy of ten centuries in the heart-breaking life-and-death struggle with starvation by a nation with a hundred and fifty millions of people. In Russia under the new tyranny a group, in pursuit of social theories, have destroyed the primary self-interest impulse of the individual to production. . . .

But those are utterly wrong who say that individualism

has as its only end the acquisition and preservation of private property—the selfish snatching and hoarding of the common product. Our American individualism, indeed, is only in part an economic creed. It aims to provide opportunity for self-expression, not merely economically, but spiritually as well. Private property is not a fetish in America. The crushing of the liquor trade without a cent of compensation, with scarcely even a discussion of it, does not bear out the notion that we give property rights any headway over human rights. Our development of individualism shows an increasing tendency to regard right of property not as an object in itself, but in the light of a useful and necessary instrument in stimulation of initiative to the individual; not only stimulation to him that he may gain personal comfort, security in life, protection to his family, but also because individual accumulation and ownership is a basis of selection to leadership in administration of the tools of industry and commerce. It is where dominant private property is assembled in the hands of the groups who control the state that the individual begins to feel capital as an oppressor. Our American demand for equality of opportunity is a constant militant check upon capital becoming a thing to be feared. Out of fear we sometimes even go too far and stifle the reproductive use of capital by crushing the initiative that makes for its creation. . . .

The domination by arbitrary individual ownership is disappearing because the works of today are steadily growing more and more beyond the resources of any one individual, and steadily taxation will reduce relatively excessive individual accumulations. The number of persons in partnership through division of ownership among many stockholders is steadily increasing—thus 100,000 to 200,000 partners in a single concern are not uncommon. The overwhelmingly largest portion of our mobile capital is that of our banks, insurance companies, building and loan associations, and the vast majority of all this is the aggregated small savings of our people. Thus large capital is steadily becoming more and more a mobilization of the savings of the small holder—the actual people themselves—and its administration becomes at once more sensitive to the moral opinions of the people in order to attract their support. The directors and managers of large concerns, themselves employees of these great groups of individual stockholders, or policy holders, reflect a spirit of community responsibility. . . .

Today business organization is moving strongly toward cooperation. There are in the cooperative great hopes that we can even gain in individuality, equality of opportunity, and an enlarged field for initiative, and at the same time reduce many of the great wastes of over-reckless competition in production and distribution. Those who either congratulate themselves or those who fear that cooperation is an advance toward socialism need neither rejoice or worry. Cooperation in its current economic sense represents the initiative of self-interest blended with a sense of service, for nobody belongs to a cooperative who is not striving to sell his products or services for more or striving to buy from others for less or striving to make his income more secure. Their members are furnishing the capital for extension of their activities just as effectively as if they did it in corporate form and they are simply transferring the profit principle from joint return to individual return. Their only success lies where they eliminate waste either in production or distribution—and they can do neither if they destroy individual initiative. Indeed this phase of development of our individualism promises to become the dominant note of its 20th Century expansion. But it will thrive only in so far as it can construct leadership and a sense of service, and so long as it preserves the initiative and safeguards the individuality of its members.

# Adolf A. Berle, Jr. (1895-      )

*Lawyer, teacher, diplomat, writer, and corpora-
tion expert, he was one of President Roosevelt's
brain trusters. An apprentice and friend of
Louis D. Brandeis, he refused to carry on
Brandeis' famous battle against the curse of
bigness in business, contending that it was a
"liberal stereotype" rather than a rational appraisal of the facts. Big business, in his view,
was one of the major forces steadily and almost
unintentionally transforming American life—
and doing this, he maintained, with less agony,
less noise, and less waste than was the case in
any other twentieth-century revolution.*

# Gardiner C. Means (1896-      )

*An influential economist with a doctorate from
Harvard, he was, like Berle, associated with the
New Deal in an advisory capacity. From 1933 to
1935 he served as economic adviser to the Secretary of Agriculture and then with the National
Resources Planning Board until the end of the
decade. Significantly, the statistics on corporate
concentration quoted by President Roosevelt in
the Commonwealth Club address of 1932 were
drawn from research done by Means while at
Columbia.*

# ECONOMIC ORGANIZATION

Underlying the thinking of economists, lawyers and business

men during the last century and a half has been the picture of economic life so skillfully painted by Adam Smith. Within his treatise on the "Wealth of Nations" are contained the fundamental concepts which run through most modern thought. Though adjustments in his picture have been made by later writers to account for new conditions, the whole has been painted in the colors which he supplied. Private property, private enterprise, individual initiative, the profit motive, wealth, competition,—these are the concepts which he employed in describing the economy of his time and by means of which he sought to show that the pecuniary self-interest of each individual, if given free play, would lead to the optimum satisfaction of human wants. Most writers of the Nineteenth Century built on these logical foundations, and current economic literature is, in large measure, cast in such terms.

Yet these terms have ceased to be accurate, and therefore tend to mislead in describing modern enterprise as carried on by the great corporations. Though both the terms and the concepts remain, they are inapplicable to a dominant area in American economic organization. New terms, connoting changed relationships, become necessary. . . .

### Private Property

To Adam Smith and to his followers, private property was a unity involving possession. He assumed that ownership and control were combined. Today, in the modern corporation, this unity has been broken. *Passive property,*—specifically, shares of stock or bonds,—gives its possessors an interest in an enterprise but gives them practically no control over it, and involves no responsibility. *Active property,*—plant, good will, organization, and so forth which make up the actual enterprise,—is controlled by individuals who, almost invariably, have only minor ownership interests in it. In terms of relationships, the present situation can be described as including:—(1) "passive property," consisting of a set of relationships between an individual and an enterprise, involving rights of the individual toward the enterprise but almost no effective powers over it; and (2) "active property," consisting of a set of relationships under which an individual or set of individuals hold powers over an enterprise but have almost no duties in respect to it which can be effectively enforced. When active and passive property relationships attach to the same individual or group, we have private property as conceived by the older economists. When they attach to different individuals, private property in the instruments of production disappears. Private property in the share of stock still continues, since the owner possesses the share and has power to dispose of it, but his share of stock is only a token representing a bundle of ill-protected rights and expectations. It is the possession of this token which can be transferred, a transfer which has little if any influence on the instruments of production. Whether possession of active property,—power of control over an enterprise, apart from ownership,—will ever be looked upon as private property which can belong to and be disposed of by its possessor is a problem of the future, and no prediction can be made with respect to it. Whatever the answer, it is clear that in dealing with the modern corporation we are not dealing with the old type of private property. Our description of modern economy, in so far as it deals with the quasi-public corporation, must be in terms of the two forms of property, active and passive, which for the most part lie in different hands.

### Wealth

In a similar way, the concept "wealth" has been changed and divided. To Adam Smith, wealth was composed of tangible things,—wheat and land and buildings, ships and merchandise,—and for most people wealth is still thought of in physical terms. Yet in connection with the modern corporation, two essentially different types of wealth exist. To the holder of passive property, the stockholder, wealth consists, not of tangible goods,—factories, railroad stations, machinery,—but of a bundle of expectations which have a market value and which, if held, may bring him income and, if sold in the market, may give him power to obtain some other form of wealth. To the possessor of active property,—the "control"—wealth means a great enterprise which he dominates, an enterprise whose value is for the most part composed of the organized relationship of tangible properties, the existence of a functioning organization of workers and the existence of a functioning body of consumers. Instead of having control over a body of tangible wealth with an easily ascertainable market value, the group in control of a large modern corporation is astride an organism which has little value except as it continues to function, and for which there is no ready market. Thus, side by side, these two forms of wealth exist:—on the one hand passive wealth,—liquid, impersonal and involving no responsibility, passing from hand to hand and constantly appraised in the market place; and on the other hand, active wealth,—great, functioning organisms dependent for their lives on their security holders, their workers and consumers, but most of all on their mainspring,—"control." The two forms of wealth are not different aspects of the same thing, but are essentially and functionally distinct.

### Private Enterprise

Again, to Adam Smith, private enterprise meant an individual or a few partners actively engaged and relying in large part on their own labor or their immediate direction. Today we have tens and hundreds of thousands of owners, of workers and of consumers combined in single enterprises. These great associations are so different from the small, privately owned enterprises of the past as to make the concept of private enterprise an ineffective instrument of analysis. It must be replaced with the concept of corporate enterprise, enterprise which is the organized activity of vast bodies of individuals, ·workers, consumers and suppliers of capital, under the leadership of the dictators of industry, "control."

## Individual Initiative

As private enterprise disappears with increasing size, so also does individual initiative. The idea that an army operates on the basis of "rugged individualism" would be ludicrous. Equally so is the same idea with respect to the modern corporation. Group activity, the coordinating of the different steps in production, the extreme division of labor in large scale enterprise necessarily imply not individualism but cooperation and the acceptance of authority almost to the point of autocracy. Only to the extent that any worker seeks advancement within an organization is there room for individual initiative,—an initiative which can be exercised only within the narrow range of function he is called on to perform. At the very pinnacle of the hierarchy of organization in a great corporation, there alone, can individual initiative have a measure of free play. Yet even there a limit is set by the willingness and ability of subordinates to carry out the will of their superiors. In modern industry, individual liberty is necessarily curbed.

## The Profit Motive

Even the motivation of individual activity has changed its aspect. For Adam Smith and his followers, it was possible to abstract one motive, the desire for personal profit, from all the motives driving men to action and to make this the key to man's economic activity. They could conclude that, where true private enterprise existed, personal profit was an effective and socially beneficent motivating force. Yet we have already seen how the profit motive has become distorted in the modern corporation. To the extent that profits induce the risking of capital by investors, they play their customary role. But if the courts, following the traditional logic of property, seek to insure that all profits reach or be held for the security owners, they prevent profits from reaching the very group of men whose action is most important to the efficient conduct of enterprise. Only as profits are diverted into the pockets of control do they, in a measure, perform their second function.

Nor is it clear that even if surplus profits were held out as an incentive to control they would be as effective an instrument as the logic of profits assumes. Presumably the motivating influence of any such huge surplus profits as a modern corporation might be made to produce would be subject to diminishing returns. Certainly it is doubtful if the prospect of a second million dollars of income (and the surplus profits might often amount to much larger sums) would induce activity equal to that induced by the prospect of the first million or even the first hundred thousand. Profits in such terms bear little relation to those envisaged by earlier writers.

Just what motives are effective today, in so far as control is concerned, must be a matter of conjecture. But it is probable that more could be learned regarding them by studying the motives of an Alexander the Great, seeking new worlds to conquer, than by considering the motives of a petty tradesman of the days of Adam Smith.

### Competition

Finally, when Adam Smith championed competition as the great regulator of industry, he had in mind units so small that fixed capital and overhead costs played a role so insignificant that costs were in large measure determinate and so numerous that no single unit held an important position in the market. Today competition in markets dominated by a few great enterprises has come to be more often either cut-throat and destructive or so inactive as to make monopoly or duopoly conditions prevail. Competition between a small number of units each involving an organization so complex that costs have become indeterminate does not satisfy the condition assumed by earlier economists, nor does it appear likely to be as effective a regulator of industry and of profits as they had assumed.

In each of the situations to which these fundamental concepts refer, the Modern Corporation has wrought such a change as to make the concepts inapplicable.° New concepts must be forged and a new picture of economic relationships created. . . .

Most fundamental to the new picture of economic life must be a new concept of business enterprise as concentrated in the corporate organization. In some measure a concept is already emerging. Over a decade ago, Walter Rathenau wrote concerning the German counterpart of our great corporation:

"No one is a permanent owner. The composition of the thousandfold complex which functions as lord of the undertaking is in a state of flux. . . . This condition of things signifies that ownership has been depersonalized. . . . The depersonalization of ownership simultaneously implies the objectification of the thing owned. The claims to ownership are subdivided in such a fashion, and are so mobile, that the enterprise assumes an independent life, as if it belonged to no one; it takes an objective existence, such as in earlier days was embodied only in state and church, in a municipal corporation, in the life of a guild or a religious order. . . . The depersonalization of ownership, the objectification of enterprise, the detachment of property from the possessor, leads to a point where the enterprise becomes transformed into an institution which resembles the state in character." †

The institution here envisaged calls for analysis, not in

°It is frequently suggested that economic activity has become vastly more complex under modern conditions. Yet it is strange that the concentration of the bulk of industry into a few large units has not simplified rather than complicated the economic process. It is worth suggesting that the apparent complexity may arise in part from the effort to analyze the process in terms of concepts which no longer apply.

†"Von Kommenden Dingen," Berlin, 1918, trans. by E. & C. Paul ("In Days to Come"), London, 1921, pp. 120–1.

terms of business enterprise but in terms of social organization. On the one hand, it involves a concentration of power
in the economic field comparable to the concentration of
religious power in the mediaeval church or of political
power in the national state. On the other hand, it involves
the interrelation of a wide diversity of economic interests,—
those of the "owners" who supply capital, those of the
workers who "create," those of the consumers who give
value to the products of enterprise, and above all those of
the control who wield power.

Such a great concentration of power and such a diversity of interest raise the long-fought issue of power and its
regulation—of interest and its protection. A constant warfare has existed between the individuals wielding power, in
whatever form, and the subjects of that power. Just as there
is a continuous desire for power, so also there is a continuous desire to make that power the servant of the bulk of
the individuals it affects. The long struggles for the reform
of the Catholic Church and for the development of constitutional law in the states are phases of this phenomenon.
Absolute power is useful in building the organization. More
slow, but equally sure is the development of social pressure demanding that the power shall be used for the benefit of all concerned. This pressure, constant in ecclesiastical
and political history, is already making its appearance in
many guises in the economic field.

Observable throughout the world, and in varying degrees
of intensity, is this insistence that power in economic organization shall be subjected to the same tests of public
benefit which have been applied in their turn to power
otherwise located. In its most extreme aspect this is exhibited in the communist movement, which in its purest
form is an insistence that *all* of the powers and privileges of
property, shall be used only in the common interest. In
less extreme forms of socialist dogma, transfer of economic
powers to the state for public service is demanded. In the

strictly capitalist countries, and particularly in time of depression, demands are constantly put forward that the men controlling the great economic organisms be made to accept responsibility for the well-being of those who are subject to the organization, whether workers, investors, or consumers. In a sense the difference in all of these demands lies only in degree. . . .

. . . Neither the claims of ownership nor those of control can stand against the paramount interests of the community. The present claims of both contending parties now in the field have been weakened by the developments described. It remains only for the claims of the community to be put forward with clarity and force. Rigid enforcement of property rights as a temporary protection against plundering by control would not stand in the way of the modification of these rights in the interest of other groups. When a convincing system of community obligations is worked out and is generally accepted, in that moment the passive property right of today must yield before the larger interests of society. Should the corporate leaders, for example, set forth a program comprising fair wages, security to employees, reasonable service to their public, and stabilization of business, all of which would divert a portion of the profits from the owners of passive property, and should the community generally accept such a scheme as a logical and human solution of industrial difficulties, the interests of passive property owners would have to give way. Courts would almost of necessity be forced to recognize the result, justifying it by whatever of the many legal theories they might choose. It is conceivable,—indeed it seems almost essential if the corporate system is to survive,—that the "control" of the great corporations should develop into a purely neutral technocracy, balancing a variety of claims by various groups in the community and assigning to each a portion of the income stream on the basis of public policy rather than private cupidity.

✧     ✧     ✧     ✧     ✧     ✧     ✧     ✧     ✧

In still larger view, the modern corporation may be regarded not simply as one form of social organization but potentially (if not yet actually) as the dominant institution of the modern world. In every age, the major concentration of power has been based upon the dominant interest of that age. The strong man has, in his time, striven to be cardinal or pope, prince or cabinet minister, bank president or partner in the House of Morgan. During the Middle Ages, the Church, exercising spiritual power, dominated Europe and gave to it a unity at a time when both political and economic power were diffused. With the rise of the modern state, political power, concentrated into a few large units, challenged the spiritual interest as the strongest bond of human society. Out of the long struggle between church and state which followed, the state emerged victorious; nationalist politics superseded religion as the basis of the major unifying organization of the western world. Economic power still remained diffused.

The rise of the modern corporation has brought a concentration of economic power which can compete on equal terms with the modern state—economic power versus political power, each strong in its own field. The state seeks in some aspects to regulate the corporation, while the corporation, steadily becoming more powerful, makes every effort to avoid such regulation. Where its own interests are concerned, it even attempts to dominate the state. The future may see the economic organism, now typified by the corporation, not only on an equal plane with the state, but possibly even superseding it as the dominant form of social organization. The law of corporations, accordingly, might well be considered as a potential constitutional law for the new economic state, while business practice is increasingly assuming the aspect of economic statesmanship.

# Walter Lippmann (1889–       )

*A well-known political essayist and newspaper columnist, he was reportedly one of the most brilliant undergraduates ever to attend Harvard. There he came under the influence of the philosophers George Santayana and William James, but neither affected him as did the visiting British Socialist Graham Wallas, who taught him to accept the fact that man often acts irrationally and to recognize the importance of looking at politics from that skeptical point of view. After racing through college in three years, he began in 1910 as an investigator for Lincoln Steffens, then served as an editor of the* New Republic *from 1914 to 1919. Afterward he went to the newspapers and wrote a syndicated column for the* Herald-Tribune *from 1931 to its demise in 1966. From a youthful liberal with distinctly leftist tendencies, he became in his late forties a conservative, shocking his old associates in 1936 by openly declaring himself a Republican.*

# THE SERVILE STATE

Although all the known examples of collectivism have had their origin in war or have as their objective the preparation for war, it is widely believed that a collectivist order could be organized for peace and for plenty. "It is nonsense," says Mr. George Soule, "to say that there is any physical impossibility of doing for peace purposes the sort of thing we actually did for war purposes." If the state can organize for war, it is asked, why can it not organize for peace and plenty? If it can mobilize against a foreign en-

From *The Good Society* (Boston: Little, Brown & Co., 1937), pp. 91, 93, 101–5, 385–7. Reprinted by permission of the author.

emy, why not against poverty, squalor, and the hideous social
evils that attend them?

It is plain enough that a dictated collectivism is necessary
if a nation is to exert its maximum military power: very
evidently its capital and labor must not be wasted on the
making of luxuries; it can tolerate no effective dissent, nor
admit that men have any right to the pursuit of private happiness. No one can dispute that. The waging of war must
be authoritarian and collectivist. The question we must now
consider is whether a system which is essential to the conduct of war can be adapted to the civilian ideal of peace
and plenty. Can this form of organization, historically associated with military purposes and necessities, be used for
the general improvement of men's condition? . . .

A call to arms is specific and everyone understands it. The
cry that the enemy is at the gates, even the cry that beyond
the deserts and mountains of Africa lies the promised land,
needs little explaining. This is a very different thing from
blowing the bugles and summoning the people to the abundant life to be achieved by "capacity operation of its plant,
on the balanced load principle." Anyone can imagine an
enemy and hate him; but to talk about an abundant life is
merely to begin an interminable argument. This is the reason, based on deep psychological compulsion, why the socialist propaganda has always relied more upon an appeal
to class war than upon the vision of a socialist society, why
the effective leaders from Marx to Lenin have always derided as "unscientific" and "utopian" any detailed concern
with the nature of a socialist society. Their intuition has
surely been sound. For it is the war spirit that most readily
imposes unanimity for collective action among masses of
men. When men are at peace, they have an incorrigible
tendency, if one likes collectivism, a noble tendency if one
dislikes it, to become individuals. . . .

The primary factor which makes civilian planning incalculable is the freedom of the people to spend their income.
Planning is theoretically possible only if consumption is

rationed. For a plan of production *is* a plan of consumption. If the authority is to decide what shall be produced, it has already decided what shall be consumed. In military planning that is precisely what takes place: the authorities decide what the army shall consume and what of the national product shall be left for the civilians. No economy can, therefore, be planned for civilians unless there is such scarcity that the necessities of existence can be rationed. As productivity rises above the subsistence level, free spending becomes possible. A planned production to meet a free demand is a contradiction in terms and as meaningless as a square circle.

It follows, too, that a plan of production is incompatible with voluntary labor, with freedom to choose an occupation. A plan of production is not only a plan of consumption, but a plan of how long, at what, and where the people shall work. By no possible manipulation of wage rates could the planners attract to the various jobs precisely the right number of workers. Under voluntary labor, particularly with consumption rationed and standardized, the unpleasant jobs would be avoided and the good jobs overcrowded. Therefore the inevitable and necessary complement of the rationing of consumption is the conscription of labor, either by overt act of law or by driving workers into the undesirable jobs by offering them starvation as the alternative. This is, of course, exactly what happens in a thoroughly militarized state.

The conscription of labor and the rationing of consumption are not to be regarded as transitional or as accidental devices in a planned economy. They are the very substance of it. To make a five-year plan of what a whole nation shall produce is to determine how it shall labor and what it shall receive. It can receive only what the plan provides. It can obtain what the plan provides only by doing the work which the plan calls for. It must do that work or the plan is a failure; it must accept what the plan yields in the way of goods or it must do without.

All this is perfectly understood in an army or in war time when a whole nation is in arms. The civilian planner cannot avoid the rationing and the conscription, for they are the very essence of his proposal. There is no escape. If the people are free to reject the rations, the plan is frustrated; if they are free to work less or at different occupations than those prescribed, the plan cannot be executed. Therefore their labor and their standards of living have to be dictated by the planning board or by some sovereign power superior to the board. In a militarized society that sovereign power is the general staff.

But who, in a civilian society, is to decide what is to be the specific content of the abundant life? It cannot be the people deciding by referendum or through a majority of their elected representatives. For if the sovereign power to pick the plan is in the people, the power to amend it is there also at all times. Now a plan subject to change from month to month or even from year to year is not a plan; if the decision has been taken to make ten million cars at $500 and one million suburban houses at $3000, the people cannot change their minds a year later, scrap the machinery to make the cars, abandon the houses when they are partly built, and decide to produce instead skyscraper apartment houses and underground railroads.

There is, in short, no way by which the objectives of a planned economy can be made to depend upon popular decision. They must be imposed by an oligarchy of some sort,° and that oligarchy must, if the plan is to be carried through, be irresponsible in matters of policy. Individual oligarchs might, of course, be held accountable for breaches of the law just as generals can be court-martialed. But their policy can no more be made a matter of continuous accountability to the voters than the strategic arrangements of the generals can be determined by the rank and file. The planning board

---

°Which may, of course, let the people ratify the plan once and irrevocably by plebiscite, as in the German and Italian plebiscites.

or their superiors have to determine what the life and labor of the people shall be.

Not only is it impossible for the people to control the plan, but, what is more, the planners must control the people. They must be despots who tolerate no effective challenge to their authority. Therefore civilian planning is compelled to presuppose that somehow the despots who climb to power will be benevolent—that is to say, will know and desire the supreme good of their subjects. This is the implicit premise of all the books which recommend the establishment of a planned economy in a civilian society. They paint an entrancing vision of what a benevolent despotism could do. They ask—never very clearly, to be sure—that somehow the people should surrender the planning of their existence to "engineers," "experts," and "technologists," to leaders, saviors, heroes. This is the political premise of the whole collectivist philosophy: that the dictators will be patriotic or class-conscious, whichever term seems the more eulogistic to the orator. It is the premise, too, of the whole philosophy of regulation by the state, currently regarded as progressivism. Though it is disguised by the illusion that a bureaucracy accountable to a majority of voters, and susceptible to the pressure of organized minorities, is not exercising compulsion, it is evident that the more varied and comprehensive the regulation becomes, the more the state becomes a despotic power as against the individual. For the fragment of control over the government which he exercises through his vote is in no effective sense proportionate to the authority exercised over him by the government.

Benevolent despots might indeed be found. On the other hand they might not be. They may appear at one time; they may not appear at another. The people, unless they choose to face the machine guns on the barricades, can take no steps to see to it that benevolent despots are selected and the malevolent cashiered. They cannot select their despots. The despots must select themselves, and, no matter whether they are good or bad, they will continue in office as long as they can suppress rebellion and escape assassination.

Thus, by a kind of tragic irony, the search for security and a rational society, if it seeks salvation through political authority, ends in the most irrational form of government imaginable—in the dictatorship of casual oligarchs, who have no hereditary title, no constitutional origin or responsibility, who cannot be replaced except by violence. The reformers who are staking their hopes on good despots, because they are so eager to plan the future, leave unplanned that on which all their hopes depend. Because a planned society must be one in which the people obey their rulers, there can be no plan to find the planners: the selection of the despots who are to make society so rational and so secure has to be left to the insecurity of irrational chance. . . .

[Aristotle's] argument that "some persons are slaves, other are freemen by appointment of nature," is the ultimate doctrine upon which every apologist of oppression must rely in order to make the law of the jungle take on the guise of rationality to civilized men. No doubt it seems like a long jump from Aristotle's apology for chattel slavery to the collectivists in democratic countries who dream of a rationally administered economy. But what conception of men as personalities does Mr. Stuart Chase, for example, have when he tells us that "a working dictatorship over industry is indicated, if the plant is to be efficiently operated" . . . that "the industrial discipline must be accepted—all of it—or it must be renounced" because "technological imperative is impersonal, amoral, and non-ethical"? I know that Mr. Chase is a civilized man. So was Aristotle. Are not Mr. Chase's regimented citizens mere "living instruments" of his glorified technicians? And as such, because they are less than men, are material to be fabricated by his engineers, have they not been stripped of their defenses against oppression? Have not the technicians who are to be their masters been relieved of all restraint? If the technological imperatives of his technocrats are so impersonal, so amoral, and so non-ethical, then how can they ever be challenged? Against these imperatives there are no human rights, not even the right of revolution.

Of the many rationalizations of tyranny the subtlest is that which teaches the individual that he is a cog in a corporate machine or a cell in a collective organism. Men have learned to defend themselves against personal sovereigns, against the doctrine that as slaves they belong to their lord, as subjects to their king. But in the presence of the anonymous master, the super-organism of the collectivists, they do not so easily discern its inhuman pretensions and brutalizing dominion.

For the demand that men be subordinated and submerged in the mass is easily mistaken for the ideal of a fellowship of free individuals in which the human personality realizes some of its noblest possibilities. It is not always easy to distinguish between the patriotism of the collectivist who sacrifices the individual and the patriotism of free men who sacrifice themselves voluntarily; or to distinguish between social obligation which is the respect of persons for the legal and equitable rights of others and social discipline which means that men's lives are to be planned and administered by their superiors. The counterfeit resembles the real thing just enough to be deeply confusing. Thus many cannot even distinguish between the plebiscites by which dictators ratify their supremacy and the elections by which free men choose their public servants, between the acquiescence which the dictators obtain when individuals are cowed, corrupted, and without recourse, and the consent of self-governing societies.

But the distinctions, though often obscured, are radical. In the social discipline of all collectivists the inviolability of men is somewhere denied. Men are not fully persons. They are things to be used for purposes which others, be they Aristotle or Mr. Stuart Chase, deem desirable. They are conscripts under commanders; in Mr. Hilaire Belloc's penetrating phrase, they are subjects of the Servile State. On the other hand, in the discipline of a free society, it is the inviolability of all individuals which determines the social obligations of each individual, of the official no less than the citizen. They are citizens who are consulted and consent. And their consent has meaning because they are protected in the right to withhold consent. The lives of such individuals cannot be administered. In their transactions justice can be dispensed, and that justice has its criterion and its sanction in the fact that they are inviolable individuals dealing wih other inviolable individuals.

So it is here, on the nature of man, between those who would respect him as an autonomous person and those who would degrade him to a living instrument, that the issue is joined. From these opposing conceptions are bred radically different attitudes towards the whole of human experience, in all the realms of action and of feeling, from the greatest to the smallest.

# Franklin D. Roosevelt (1882–1945)

*Thirty-second President of the United States, he came from an old and aristocratic New York family but, as Eric Goldman said, throughout his life showed "an upperdog concern for the underdog." He revealed in this campaign speech delivered at the Commonwealth Club in San Francisco in 1932 not only his concern that every man should have a right to life and a comfortable living but also a daringly new economic and social philosophy which contrasted sharply with Hoover's hollow assurances that the foundations of the economy were still sound. The speech, which expressed the essence of the New Deal creed, had been written by Adolf A. Berle with some help from Rexford Tugwell, and re-*

*portedly Roosevelt never saw the speech until*
*he opened it on the lectern. But, while dependent*
*on his advisers for ideas, the decisions were al-*
*ways his own.*

# THE WELFARE STATE

I want to speak not of politics but of Government. I want
to speak not of parties, but of universal principles. They
are not political, except in that larger sense in which a
great American once expressed a definition of politics, that
nothing in all of human life is foreign to the science of
politics. . . .

The issue of Government has always been whether individual men and women will have to serve some system of
Government or economics, or whether a system of Government and economics exists to serve individual men and
women. This question has persistently dominated the discussion of Government for many generations. On questions
relating to these things men have differed, and for time
immemorial it is probable that honest men will continue
to differ.

The final word belongs to no man; yet we can still believe in change and in progress. Democracy . . . is a quest,
a never-ending seeking for better things, and in the seeking
for these things and the striving for them, there are many
roads to follow. But, if we map the course of these roads,
we find that there are only two general directions. . . .

After the [American] Revolution . . . there were those
who, because they had seen the confusion which attended
the years of war for American independence, surrendered
to the belief that popular Government was essentially dangerous and essentially unworkable. They were honest people,

my friends, and we cannot deny that their experience had warranted some measure of fear. The most brilliant, honest and able exponent of this point of view was Hamilton. He was too impatient of slow-moving methods. Fundamentally he believed that the safety of the republic lay in the autocratic strength of its Government, that the destiny of individuals was to serve that Government, and that fundamentally a great and strong group of central institutions, guided by a small group of able and public spirited citizens, could best direct all Government.

But Mr. Jefferson, in the summer of 1776, after drafting the Declaration of Independence turned his mind to the same problem and took a different view. He did not deceive himself with outward forms. Government to him was a means to an end, not an end in itself; it might be either a refuge and a help or a threat and a danger, depending on the circumstances. We find him carefully analyzing the society for which he was to organize a Government. "We have no paupers. The great mass of our population is of laborers, our rich who cannot live without labor, either manual or professional, being few and of moderate wealth. Most of the laboring class possess property, cultivate their own lands, have families and from the demand for their labor, are enabled to exact from the rich and the competent such prices as enable them to feed abundantly, clothe above mere decency, to labor moderately and raise their families."

These people, he considered, had two sets of rights, those of "personal competency" and those involved in acquiring and possessing property. By "personal competency" he meant the right of free thinking, freedom of forming and expressing opinions, and freedom of personal living, each man according to his own lights. To insure the first set of rights, a Government must so order its functions as not to interfere with the individual. But even Jefferson realized that the exercise of the property rights might so interfere with the rights of the individual that the Government, without whose assistance the property rights could not exist, must intervene, not to destroy individualism, but to protect it.

You are familiar with the great political duel which followed; and how Hamilton and his friends, building toward a dominant centralized power, were at length defeated in the great election of 1800, by Mr. Jefferson's party. Out of that duel came the two parties, Republican and Democratic, as we know them today.

So began, in American political life, the new day, the day of the individual against the system, the day in which individualism was made the great watchword of American life. The happiest of economic conditions made that day long and splendid. On the Western frontier, land was substantially free. No one, who did not shirk the task of earning a living, was entirely without opportunity to do so. Depressions could, and did, come and go; but they could not alter the fundamental fact that most of the people lived partly by selling their labor and partly by extracting their livelihood from the soil, so that starvation and dislocation were practically impossible. At the very worst there was always the possibility of climbing into a covered wagon and moving west where the untilled prairies afforded a haven for men to whom the East did not provide a place. So great were our natural resources that we could offer this relief not only to our own people, but to the distressed of all the world; we could invite immigration from Europe, and welcome it with open arms. Traditionally, when a depression came a new section of land was opened in the West; and even our temporary misfortune served our manifest destiny.

It was in the middle of the nineteenth century that a new force was released and a new dream created. The force was what is called the industrial revolution, the advance of steam and machinery and the rise of the forerunners of the modern industrial plant. The dream was the dream of an economic machine, able to raise the standard of living for everyone; to bring luxury within the reach of the humblest; to annihilate distance by steam power and later by electricity, and to release everyone from the drudgery of the heaviest manual toil. It was to be expected that this would necessarily affect Government. Heretofore, Government had merely been called upon to produce conditions within which people could live happily, labor peacefully, and rest secure. Now it was called upon to aid in the consummation of this new dream. There was, however, a shadow over the dream. To be made real, it required use of the talents of men of tremendous will and tremendous ambition, since by no other force could the problems of financing and engineering and new developments be brought to a consummation.

So manifest were the advantages of the machine age, however, that the United States fearlessly, cheerfully, and, I think, rightly, accepted the bitter with the sweet. It was thought that no price was too high to pay for the advantages which we could draw from a finished industrial system. The history of the last half century is accordingly in large measure a history of a group of financial Titans, whose methods were not scrutinized with too much care, and who were honored in proportion as they produced the results, irrespective of the means they used. The financiers who pushed the railroads to the Pacific were always ruthless, often wasteful, and frequently corrupt; but they did build railroads, and we have them today. It has been estimated that the American investor paid for the American railway system more than three times over in the process; but despite this fact the net advantage was to the United States. As long as we had free land; as long as population was growing by leaps and bounds; as long as our industrial plants were insufficient to supply our own needs, society chose to give the ambitious man free play and unlimited reward provided only that he produced the economic plant so much desired.

During this period of expansion, there was equal opportunity for all and the business of Government was not to interfere but to assist in the development of industry. This was done at the request of business men themselves. The tariff was originally imposed for the purpose of "fostering our infant industry," a phrase I think the older among you will remember as a political issue not so long ago. The railroads were subsidized, sometimes by grants of money, oftener by grants of land; some of the most valuable oil lands in the United States were granted to assist the financing of the railroad which pushed through the Southwest. A nascent merchant marine was assisted by grants of money, or by mail subsidies, so that our steam shipping might ply the seven seas. Some of my friends tell me that they do not want the Government in business. With this I agree; but I wonder whether they realize the implications of the past. For while it has been American doctrine that the Government must not go into business in competition with private enterprises, still it has been traditional, particularly in Republican administrations, for business urgently to ask the Government to put at private disposal all kinds of Government assistance. The same man who tells you that he does not want to see the Government interfere in business—and he means it, and has plenty of good reasons for saying so—is the first to go to Washington and ask the Government for a prohibitory tariff on his product. When things get just bad enough, as they did two years ago, he will go with equal speed to the United States Government and ask for a loan; and the Reconstruction Finance Corporation is the outcome of it. Each group has sought protection from the Government for its own special interests, without realizing that the function of Government must be to favor no small group at the expense of its duty to protect the rights of personal freedom and of private property of all its citizens. . . .

A glance at the situation today only too clearly indicates that equality of opportunity as we have known it no longer exists. Our industrial plant is built; the problem just now is whether under existing conditions it is not overbuilt. Our last frontier has long since been reached, and there is practically no more free land. More than half of our people do not live on the farms or on lands and cannot derive a living by cultivating their own property. There is no safety valve in the form of a Western prairie to which those thrown out of work by the Eastern economic machines can go for a new start. We are not able to invite the immigration from Europe to share our endless plenty. We are now providing a drab living for our own people. . . .

Just as freedom to farm has ceased, so also the opportunity in business has narrowed. It still is true that men can start small enterprises, trusting to native shrewdness and ability to keep abreast of competitors; but area after area has been preempted altogether by the great corporations, and even in the fields which still have no great concerns, the small man starts under a handicap. The unfeeling statistics of the past three decades show that the independent business man is running a losing race. Perhaps he is forced to the wall; perhaps he cannot command credit; perhaps he is "squeezed out," in Mr. Wilson's words, by highly organized corporate competitors, as your corner grocery man can tell you. Recently a careful study was made of the concentration of business in the United States. It showed that our economic life was dominated by some six hundred odd corporations who controlled two-thirds of American industry. Ten million small business men divided the other third. More striking still, it appeared that if the process of concentration goes on at the same rate, at the end of another century we shall have all American industry controlled by a dozen corporations, and run by perhaps a hundred men. Put plainly, we are steering a steady course toward economic oligarchy, if we are not there already.

Clearly, all this calls for a re-appraisal of values. A mere builder of more industrial plants, a creator of more railroad systems, an organizer of more corporations, is as likely to be a danger as a help. The day of the great promoter or the financial Titan, to whom we granted anything if only he would build, or develop, is over. Our task now is not discovery or exploitation of natural resources, or necessarily producing more goods. It is the soberer, less dramatic business of administering resources and plants already in hand, of seeking to reestablish foreign markets for our surplus production, of meeting the problem of underconsumption, of adjusting production to consumption, of distributing wealth and products more equitably, of adapting existing economic organizations to the service of the people. The day of enlightened administration has come.

Just as in older times the central Government was first a haven of refuge, and then a threat, so now in a closer economic system the central and ambitious financial unit is no longer a servant of national desire, but a danger. I would draw the parallel one step farther. We did not think because national Government had become a threat in the 18th century that therefore we should abandon the principle of national Government. Nor today should we abandon the principle of strong economic units called corporations, merely because their power is susceptible of easy abuse. In other times we dealt with the problem of an unduly ambitious central Government by modifying it gradually into a constitutional democratic Government. So today we are modifying and controlling our economic units.

As I see it, the task of Government in its relation to business is to assist the development of an economic declaration of rights, an economic constitutional order. This is the common task of statesman and business man. It is the minimum requirement of a more permanently safe order of things.

Happily, the times indicate that to create such an order not only is the proper policy of Government, but it is the only line of safety for our economic structures as well. We know, now, that these economic units cannot exist unless prosperity is uniform, that is, unless purchasing power is well distributed throughout every group in the Nation. That is why even the most selfish of corporations for its own interest would be glad to see wages restored and unemployment ended and to bring the Western farmer back to his accustomed level of prosperity and to assure a permanent safety to both groups. That is why some enlightened industries themselves endeavor to limit the freedom of action of each man and business group within the industry in the common interest of all; why business men everywhere are asking a form of organization which will bring the scheme of things into balance, even though it may in some measure qualify the freedom of action of individual units within the business.

The exposition need not further be elaborated. It is brief and incomplete, but you will be able to expand it in terms of your own business or occupation without difficulty. I think everyone who has actually entered the economic struggle—which means everyone who was not born to safe wealth—knows in his own experience and his own life that we have now to apply the earlier concepts of American Government to the conditions of today.

The Declaration of Independence discusses the problem of Government in terms of a contract. Government is a relation of give and take, a contract, perforce, if we would follow the thinking out of which it grew. Under such a contract rulers were accorded power, and the people consented to that power on consideration that they be accorded certain rights. The task of statesmanship has always been the re-definition of these rights in terms of a changing and growing social order. New conditions impose new requirements upon Government and those who conduct Government. . . .

I feel that we are coming to a view through the drift of our legislation and our public thinking in the past quarter century that private economic power is, to enlarge an old phrase, a public trust as well. I hold that continued enjoyment of that power by any individual or group must depend upon the fulfillment of that trust. The men who have reached the summit of American business life know this best; happily, many of these urge the binding quality of this greater social contract.

The terms of that contract are as old as the Republic, and as new as the new economic order.

Every man has a right to life; and this means that he has also a right to make a comfortable living. He may by sloth or crime decline to exercise that right; but it may not be denied him. We have no actual famine or dearth; our industrial and agricultural mechanism can produce enough and to spare. Our Government formal and informal, political and economic, owes to everyone an avenue to possess himself of a portion of that plenty sufficient for his needs, through his own work.

Every man has a right to his own property; which means a right to be assured, to the fullest extent attainable, in the safety of his savings. By no other means can men carry the burdens of those parts of life which, in the nature of things, afford no chance of labor; childhood, sickness, old age. In all thought of property, this right is paramount; all other property rights must yield to it. If, in accord with this principle, we must restrict the operations of the specu-lator, the manipulator, even the financier, I believe we must accept the restriction as needful, not to hamper individualism but to protect it.

These two requirements must be satisfied, in the main, by the individuals who claim and hold control of the great industrial and financial combinations which dominate so large a part of our industrial life. They have undertaken to be, not business men, but princes of property. I am not prepared to say that the system which produces them is wrong. I am very clear that they must fearlessly and com-petently assume the responsibility which goes with the power. So many enlightened business men know this that the statement would be little more than a platitude, were it not for an added implication.

This implication is, briefly, that the responsible heads of finance and industry instead of acting each for himself, must work together to achieve the common end. They must, where necessary, sacrifice this or that private advantage; and in reciprocal self-denial must seek a general advantage. It is here that formal Government—political Government, if you choose—comes in. Whenever in the pursuit of this objective the lone wolf, the unethical competitor, the reckless promoter, the Ishmael or Insull whose hand is against every man's, declines to join in achieving an end recognized as being for the public welfare, and threatens to drag the industry back to a state of anarchy, the Government may properly be asked to apply restraint. Likewise, should the group ever use its collective power contrary to the public welfare, the Government must be swift to enter and protect the public interest.

The Government should assume the function of economic regulation only as a last resort, to be tried only when private initiative, inspired by high responsibility, with such assistance and balance as Government can give, has finally failed. As yet there has been no final failure, because there has been no attempt; and I decline to assume that this Nation is unable to meet the situation.

The final term of the high contract was for liberty and the pursuit of happiness. We have learned a great deal of both in the past century. We know that individual liberty and individual happiness mean nothing unless both are ordered in the sense that one man's meat is not another man's poison. We know that the old "rights of personal competency," the right to read, to think, to speak, to choose and live a mode of life, must be respected at all hazards. We know that liberty to do anything which deprives others of those elemental rights is outside the protection of any compact; and that Government in this regard is the maintenance of a balance, within which every individual may have a place if he will take it; in which every individual may find safety if he wishes it; in which every individual may attain such power as his ability permits, consistent with his assuming the accompanying responsibility.

CHAPTER FOUR

# The Materialistic Faith

## I

As business reached a higher level of sophistication in the 1920's, the aspirations of the American cult of success also changed. There was the same ingenuous love of money, and money still defined success, but the day was past when simple country boys could become the sole owners of large enterprises. For, as Irvin G. Wyllie noted, "With chances for success controlled by the corporations and by the widows and orphans who owned them, the trick now was to rise into the managerial elite." While Andrew Carnegie could become his own boss, the most a bright young man in the twenties might aspire to was to become the hired manager of a great industrial organization. Likewise, with the advance of technology, the uneducated, practical man was in less demand than the professionally trained executive who not only understood something of engineering or chemistry but who was also versed in business administration, salesmanship, and public relations. Business, in short, was becoming a profession, and to fill the great demand for scientific business training most of the large universities opened business schools. "These roaring mills of the new learning," the *American Mercury* reported, offered a wide field of study. "Thus, Cornell lists Hotel Supervision, and Syracuse bills Hotel Management, Store

Management, and Practical Table Service. Columbia offers Bond Salesmanship, the New York Money Market, and the Business of the Theatre. Southern California reveals the mysteries of Apartment House Management, Traffic Management, and Real Estate Advertising, with special highly scientific lectures on Billboards, Trips to Property, Golf Links, Country Clubs, and Model Homes." Besides its famous Oil Executives' Course, New York University was said to have also had on draft a course on Hosiery and Underwear for the training of buyers and executives. For good or bad, the effect of this academic enterprise upon higher education was to suggest that learning was a merchandisable commodity and that business instruction was to take precedence over scholarship as the goal of university training because it was allegedly more useful.[1]

The intrusion of businesslike ideals, aims, and methods into the temples of learning reflected the ruling interest of American society. "Of course," the President of the United States told American editors, "the accumulation of wealth cannot be justified as the chief end of existence. But we are compelled to recognize it as a means to wellnigh every desirable achievement." Beyond doubt the ruling interest in the twenties was pecuniary gain. And training for business, Veblen observed, stood to this ruling interest of the modern community "in a relation analogous to that in which theology . . . stood to the ruling interest in those earlier times when the salvation of men's souls was the prime object of solicitude." The business school had a place in the modern university similar to that of the divinity school in nineteenth-century America. Both schools were equally extraneous to that "intellectual enterprise" which was ostensibly the function of the university, but while the divinity school belonged to the old order and was losing out, the "seminary of business" belonged to the new order and was gaining ground. Plainly, for most Americans, the primacy among man's interests was passing from religion to business.[2]

Indicative of the new priorities, the most popular religious ideas in the twenties were those which sustained the dominant business values. Not only were religious spokesmen generally complaisant to the business point of view, but some gave divine sanction to the materialistic creed by suggesting that "it pays to pray." The Reverend Shailer Mathews, dean of the Divinity School of the University of Chicago and a former president of the Federal Council of Churches of Christ in America, when asked "Could a man make more money if now and then he prayed about his business?" replied, "I think so—if he is honest and serious." The Swedish Immanuel Congregational Church in New York, according to the *American Mercury,* recognized the supremacy of the business over the spiritual appeal by offering to all who contributed one hundred dollars to its building fund "an engraved certificate of investment in preferred capital stock in the Kingdom of God." And a church billboard in the same city issued the persuasive call: "Come to Church. Christian Worship Increases Your Efficiency. Christian F. Reisner, Pastor."[3]

Under the gospel of Service, a pragmatic variation of the Christian principle of brotherly love, a new American religion was created on the material plane. Instead of trafficking in divinely beneficial intangibles, it was based upon faith in the miracles of the existent commercial order and promises, not of divine glory, but of human ease. On these grounds, business was acclaimed "the sanest religion" by a popular journalist, Edward Earle Purinton.* According to this businesslike creed, the office or factory was the temple, work was worship, and salvation was success. "For the true believer, its commandment was Service, its sacrament the weekly lunches of fellowship at Kiwanis or Rotary, its ritual the collective chanting of cheerful songs," and its high priests the advertising men who with unflagging devotion publicized American business as the fount from

*Edward Earle Purinton, *The New American Religion.* See page 238.

which all blessings flow. It was hardly coincidence that the
most popular religious book of the twenties and the non-
fiction best-seller for 1925 and 1926 was Bruce Barton's
*The Man Nobody Knows*. An advertising executive, Barton
propagandized the faith by portraying Jesus as a "great
advertiser" and "the founder of modern business." This
simple "boy from a country village" had succeeded because
he used "the principles of modern salesmanship." "He
would be a national advertiser today." Jesus, the book revealed, was not only "the most popular dinner guest in
Jerusalem" but a great executive. "He picked up twelve
men from the bottom ranks of business and forged them
into an organization that conquered the world." That the
same principles of salesmanship should be found good and
profitable for business and religion did not seem in the least
profane to Barton, but rather to show how truly daily business carried on the business of the Lord. For as Barton
wrote, "All work is worship, all useful service prayer." In
this connection Veblen wryly noted that the Godfearing
businessmen who administered the nation's affairs appeared
to realize this congruity between sacred and secular salesmanship "so much so that they have on due consideration
found that investment in commercial advertising is rightfully exempt from the income tax, very much as the assets
and revenues of the churches are tax-exempt. The one line
of publicity, it appears, is intrinsic to the good of man,
as the other is essential to the continued Glory of God."[4]
Americans had come at last to openly worship a great
machine for making money, but to put it so bluntly would
have made believers uncomfortable. So, as in medieval days
when faith was thought better than reason, the actual
functioning of the economic system like the ways of God
was something to be accepted but never openly questioned.
As Edmund Wilson affirmed at the time, "The newspapers
will not deal with this subject; even the philosophers try
to get around it; and if you bring it into a conversation,
you are guilty of an act of bad taste comparable to joking

In American mythology the predominant figure was the businessman. All virtues were ascribed to him. He was, at the same time, a hard-boiled trader, a scholar, a patron of the arts, a thrifty housewife, a philanthropist, a statesman, a patriot, and a sentimental protector of widows and orphans.

---

about Scripture in the presence of a devout old lady."[5] Instead, Americans preferred to deal with symbols and myths that transformed the ugly facts of economic life into ideal aspirations. In dollar theology selfishness became service, profit the means of individual redemption, and success the reward of virtue. Thus, the virtuous man was a free individual who sought salvation by accumulating money. By extending this sacred symbolism to the corporation—treating great industrial organizations as inviolable persons before the law—business theologians, judges and lawyers, established taboos which made any attempt to regulate huge corporations appear as a profane attack upon the religion of capitalism. The effect of this twentieth-century version of the doctrine of the two swords, observed Thurman Arnold, a Yale professor of law, was to place the spiritual realm of business beyond the temporal jurisdiction of government; and thus when, as during the depression, necessity demanded government intervention, dogma denied it, hampering effective action at every turn.°

# II

If most Americans had come to worship at the shrine of business, there were still a few heretics who were not ready to accept business values as the standard of civilization. Though the businessman might live in a palace, ride in the most luxurious limousines, and fill his mansion with old masters and the costliest manuscripts, so long as he cared more for material things than intellectual and spiritual values, he was—from their point of view—not civilized but what the Greeks properly called a "barbarian." Under such circumstances, the businessman was "merely a purveyor and not a creator of the real values of a civilization." Civilizations rest fundamentally upon ideas, and in the United States where the dominant idea was profit the owner of a cigar-store chain, said James Truslow Adams, was "infinitely more valuable to humanity than a Keats"—even though from every past civilization the only things which remained of value to humanity were "the creative works of those who were not businessmen." But while Adams seriously questioned whether a great civilization could be built upon the philosophy of profit, Sinclair Lewis in his popular novels *Main Street* (1920) and *Babbitt* (1922) lampooned the American businessman as a clumsy, well-meaning "boob" trapped in sleazy middle-class philistinism. With vitriolic pen Lewis caricatured George F. Babbitt, a hustling, successful, all-American barbarian, to whom Keats was just another one

°Thurman Arnold, *The Theology of Capitalism.* See page 242.

of those "shabby bums living in attics and feeding on booze and sphagetti" and who had no use for "a lot of moth-eaten, mildewed, out-of-date, old, European dumps" that "aren't producing anything but bootblacks and scenery and booze, that haven't got one bathroom per hundred people!" Through the hapless Babbitt who congratulated himself on belonging to the new generation of Standardized Americans—"fellows with hair on their chests and smiles in their eyes and adding machines in their offices"—Lewis satirized "that clean fighting determination to win Success" that had produced in America "punchful prosperity," paved streets, bathrooms, vacuum cleaners, and all the other signs of civilization—minus the civilization.[6]

Certainly in a technically advanced nation such as America there was a strong temptation to regard the products and paraphernalia of technology as synonymous with civilization. Because of machines the average American in the 1920's enjoyed more power, more comforts, more amusements, and more leisure than any people had ever known. Airplanes and automobiles broke down barriers of space and gave him mastery over time; movies and radios extended his sensory powers and opened distant worlds once beyond sight and sound. New inventions and improved technology enabled American factories to provide him with a never-ending flow of automobiles, radios, refrigerators, telephones, typewriters, adding machines, rayon stockings, and countless other gadgets for his pleasure and convenience at popular prices. The constant endeavor of business was to get him to fill up his life with things—things that could be made and sold—and through advertising to foster the belief that there was a close relation between his well-being and the number of bathtubs, automobiles, and similar machine-made products that he might possess. Nor was the average American hard to convince, for the unprecedented abundance of goods was to him visible evidence of progress. And when he reflected further that the machine promised not only to lift the burden of poverty but also to emancipate him from a lifetime of drudgery, it was easy for him to believe in the beneficence of the machine.

Intellectuals, for the most part, were not so readily disposed to accept the machine as the paragon of progress. To these dissenters, the compulsive urge to produce and sell, to mechanize life—even when the results of mechanization were plainly disastrous—was destructive of human values. In America, said Edmund Wilson, "life had become a stampede to produce and sell all sorts of commodities— the question was not whether people really needed or wanted these things but whether by any means they could be induced to buy them." For himself, he was unable to accept an ideal of happiness based solely on the possession of things, nor recognize as valid a conception of civilization that "glorifies the United States as an inexhaustible market." Such a society functioned admirably in the large production of cheap automobiles, dollar watches, and safety razors. But the trouble was, according to Sinclair Lewis, "it is not satisfied until the entire world also admits that the end and joyous purpose of living is to ride in flivvers, to make advertising-pictures of dollar watches, and in the twilight to sit talking not of love and courage but of the convenience of safety razors." Such "purposeless materialism" —the American tendency not to satisfy the physical and aesthetic needs of living but to multiply indefinitely the physical accessories of life—was deplored by Ralph Borsodi as a misuse of the machine and a tragic waste of human energy. From his viewpoint happiness was dependent not upon producing as much as possible but as little as was "compatible with the enjoyment of the superior life."[7]

But these few voices of protest were drowned in the crash and clatter of the assembly line, for the majority of Americans appeared to be in thorough agreement with Henry Ford, world champion of mass production, that man's happiness was dependent upon an unending increase of machines and goods. Though the famed mechanical and industrial genius repeatedly insisted that machines were but means to an end and criticized Americans for being too wrapped up in the things they were doing and not enough concerned with the reasons why they did them, Ford nevertheless dismissed as "mushy sentimentalism" the notion that man might be happier producing less. "The purpose of a factory is to produce, and it ill serves the community in general unless it does produce to the utmost of its capacity." Ford proclaimed machinery "The New Messiah," and declared it was accomplishing in the world what man had failed to do by preaching, propaganda, or the written word. Agreeing with the Detroit manufacturer, Glenn Frank, president of the University of Wisconsin, praised the machine as "one of humanity's most promising instruments of emancipation."* Taking his cue from Henry Ford's statement, "Hard labor is for machines, not for men," Frank claimed to find the germ of a new civilization hidden in that simple sentence, the first line of a new Magna Carta for mankind. "There are a hundred unwritten Iliads in it. There is the birthright of a new Shakespeare in it. It is the charter of new art galleries. It foreshadows a new birth of education. There is unreleased music in it. It is a sort of secular 'Let There Be Light' for a new kind of world."[8]

By the thirties Americans had become much less enthusiastic about the machine-made millennium. The decline of this absolute faith resulted from a number of causes. The development and multiplication of highly destructive machines of war, without an accompanying development of higher social purposes, had served in many people's minds only to magnify the possibilities of depravity and barbarism. The airplane, instead of merely speeding up travel and intercourse between countries, had intensified their fear of each other. As an instrument of war, in combination with the latest advancements in explosives and poison gas, it promised "a ruthlessness of extermination that man has here-

---

*Glenn Frank, *Our Machine Civilization*. See page 247.

tofore not been able to apply to either bugs or rats." In mechanizing swiftly and heedlessly, men had failed to assimilate the machine and to coordinate it with human capacities and human needs. The automobile, for instance, which in 1924 was hailed as "the very acme of human aspiration," had soon proven to be a most lethal weapon—a mechanized killer that slaughtered more Americans on streets and highways than had been slain on the nation's battlefields. Finally, as the depression made so painfully clear to millions of Americans, the machine had not been

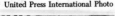

The automobile, instead of speeding up travel, created monumental traffic-jams, and the rising tide of traffic fatalities made it painfully clear, as the *New York Times* remarked, that these fuming monsters had not yet been brought "within the restraints of a decent civilization."

United Press International Photo

integrated into society. Instead of adjusting the use and rhythm of the machine to fit the actual needs of the community, the human gains of mechanization had been largely forfeited to the demands of private profit. Under the industrial regimen of the machine, man had been treated as a waste product and regarded like Mr. Zero in Elmer Rice's play *The Adding Machine* as nothing more than a slave to a contraption of steel and iron. It was these symptoms of social danger and cultural decay, according to Lewis Mumford, that had weakened the absolute faith in the machine. As a result, the absolute validity of the machine had become a conditioned validity.[9] While Mumford was hopeful of both man's destiny and that of the machine, he believed it imperative that the human question must always outweigh the question of profit or mechanical feasibility. It was his further conviction that once the objective of industry was diverted from profit-making, private aggrandizement, crude exploitation, the economy would function on a broader and more intelligently socialized basis. As social life became more mature, the nature and function of the mechanical environment would change, and the machine would fall into its proper place of servant, not master.°

# III

If quantitatively the American achievement was impressive, qualitatively it was openly challenged. It was, said Ezra Pound, "admirable as far as it goes. . . . But where does this get us? For everything above comfortable brute existence there is a vacuum." For himself, Pound—along with some of the best of American poets and novelists—had sought a more congenial atmosphere for the development of his creative talents by joining the postwar exodus to Europe. But, at home, indictment of America's spiritual emptiness was sustained by a few sturdy novelists, poets, and by a small but persevering group of academic critics known as Humanists who believed that with commercialism "laying its great greasy paw upon everything," there was no place in this country for "the true artist," no chance for development of the "inner life." "What must one think of a country," asked Irving Babbitt of Harvard, who with Paul Elmer More led the movement, "whose most popular orator is W. J. Bryan, whose favorite actor is Charlie Chaplin, whose most widely read novelist is Harold Bell Wright, whose best-known evangelist is Billy Sunday, and whose representative journalist is William Randolph Hearst?" What one must think of such a country, said Babbitt, was that it not only lacked "true" standards but suffered also from an inversion of what few standards it had. The end result of American materialism, in his opinion, was "a huge mass of standardized mediocrity."[10]

Taking issue with this bleak view, the philosopher George Santayana expressed his admiration for the materialistic

°Lewis Mumford, *The Diminution of the Machine*. See page 254.

"get up and go" of modern America and his distaste for the gloomy pundits whose oracular "humanism" was to him mere egotism or moralism.* As a hard, non-humanistic materialist of the Ionian school, he was able to stand aloof from both sides in America, criticizing the one for trying to "apply" culture to this raw vital energy and looking rather benevolently upon the primitivism of the other which he believed held promise of a new intellect and spirit. The distinctive quality of Americanism he admired was its ability to combine "unity in work with liberty of spirit," and he declared "that art, etc., has a better soil in the ferocious 100% America than in the Intelligentsia of New York. It is veneer, rouge, aestheticism, art museums, new theatres, etc., that make America impotent. The good things are football, kindness, and jazz bands."[11]

In America after 1932, however, when everything seemed to be breaking down at once, that "moral materialism" upon which Santayana had hopefully smiled appeared impotent in the face of disaster. It was, Alfred Kazin remarked, a "material failure which could not be understood in material terms alone." This economic disaster "was so manifestly something more" that to bewildered Americans it seemed that the very bottom had dropped out of things. The foundation of capitalism had been materialism, and when it failed to "deliver the goods," its social support crumbled, for its promise and ideology no longer had any meaning. Looking into the apparently bottomless pit of depression, intellectuals were already writing the obituary of capitalism. "If one cannot yet call capitalism dead," wrote Lewis Mumford in *Common Sense*, "it is only because no body can be treated as dead so long as the worms are actively crawling around in it. Attacks on capitalism are like wasting ammunition on a creature that has fatally poisoned itself. All our efforts should be concentrated, not in listening to the gasps and groans of this dying creature

*George Santayana, *The Genteel Tradition at Bay*. See page 262.

and in pointing reproachful fingers at it: our efforts should go into the task of creating a new order."[12]

In contrast to the dreary spectacle of a failing capitalism, the Soviet Union during the early thirties appeared to be a boom country. The difference between the two lands was to the American novelist Theodore Dreiser "fantastic." Here, on the one hand, was America, a scene of "poverty, frustration, and defeat of the many"; on the other, "that great, sound and by now successful experiment, the Soviet Union with all it has achieved in merging into one colossal entity the intellect and the naturally creative impulses and inventive vigors of all its immense population, and the using of those for the development as well as the permanent comfort of that population." The well-publicized achievements of the U.S.S.R. had an especial appeal for jobless workers who heard there was no unemployment in Russia and for American intellectuals who were "trying to escape from a feeling of isolation and ineffectuality." Dispatriated intellectuals, whether of fact or fancy—most of the "literary exiles" of the decade before returned home in the thirties—found in Communism a faith and an acceptance denied them under the capitalist system. As Malcolm Cowley, a repatriate and "fellow-traveler," confirmed, they were not as much interested in Marx as a philosopher or economist as "a prophet calling for a day of judgment and new heaven on earth." To writers and artists who had never liked the "Big Business system" and "always resented its crowding out of everything they cared about," these were exhilarating years. "One couldn't help being exhilarated at the sudden unexpected collapse of that stupid gigantic fraud," wrote Edmund Wilson. "It gave us a new sense of freedom; and it gave us a new sense of power to find ourselves carrying on while the bankers for a change were taking a beating." Beguiled by the "essential oneness" of Marx's vision of a "whole cultural revolution," the American intelligentsia piously embraced a new religion of materialism. Under the magic spell of Marxism, the thirties became an

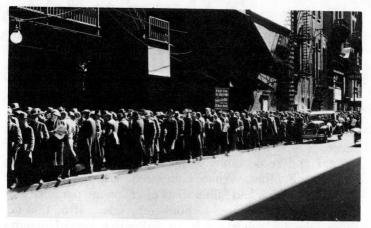

In the gloomy days of depression, as breadlines lengthened on city streets, everything seemed to be breaking down at once. With the world gone awry, poverty and frustration made new converts for Communism.

---

"Age of Faith," and in Daniel Aaron's words, it "turned college professors into union leaders, philosophers into politicians, novelists into agitators, poets into public speakers."[13]

Although in its purely materialistic and economic aspects Communism merely claimed to be in the long run a superior technical instrument for obtaining the same materialistic benefits as capitalism, its considerable appeal lay, as John Maynard Keynes noted, in "a combination of two things which Europeans have kept for some centuries in different compartments of the soul—religion and business. We are shocked because the religion is new, and contemptuous because the business, being subordinated to the religion instead of the other way round, is highly inefficient." Like other successful religions, Russian Communism exalted the common man and made him everything. Here was nothing new. But, Keynes pointed out, Communism—"though absolutely, defiantly non-supernatural"—was a new religion in the sense that it involved a revolution in ways of thinking and feeling about money. Unlike American Capitalism with "its habitual appeal to the Money Motive in nine-tenths of the activities of life," Russian Communism proposed to construct a framework of society in which materialistic motives, while not forsaken, should have a lesser importance, in which social approbation should be differently accorded, and where money-making, which previously was normal and respectable, should be no longer either the one or the other. When compared with an irreligious capitalism which had fallen short of economic paradise, the new religion was bound to hold tremendous attraction for those who had always felt an antipathy toward money-making and who normally, as a matter of course, placed moral above material advantage.[14]

The theory of the class struggle thus became for infatuated intellectuals the key to understanding the ultimate social reality that the Communists alone had been able to penetrate. When these Americans were converted to Communism in the 1930's, the one basic article of faith, they discovered, was the revolutionary nature of the proletariat and the counter-revolutionary nature of the middle class: "The proletariat was the revolutionary hero, the middle class the reformist villain. The proletariat was the guarantee of the ultimate goal, the middle class the corrupting influence of immediate demands. The proletariat was dedicated to the class struggle, the middle class to class collaboration." In *The Decline of American Capitalism* (1934) Lewis Corey, who as Louis C. Fraina had broken with the Communist party in 1922 but remained a Marxist, explained in rigidly orthodox terms that the mass of Americans exploited by "bankers' capitalism" had been thrust downward so that the few might live in ease and luxury. Though even in prosperity the working class, the driving force of the industrial system, had been victimized and tormented by the antagonisms and repressions of capitalism, their fate in depression was unbearable. For the inevitable collapse of capitalism had turned the American dream of well-being into a nightmare.* So, aroused intellectuals, embarrassed by their middle-class origins and synthetic social consciousness, belatedly aligned themselves with the "proletariat" and went forth to battle, in speech and on paper, for a workers' dictatorship.[15]

*Lewis Corey, *Decline of American Capitalism.* See page 267.

# Readings:

# The Materialistic Faith

## Edward Earle Purinton (1878–    )

*A popular writer and business publicist, he
specialized in self-help articles written in the
Horatio Alger spirit. Among his publications, for
example, were such titles as* How to Be Happy
*(1909),* Efficient Living *(1915), and* Personal
Efficiency in Business *(1919).*

# THE NEW AMERICAN RELIGION

Among the nations of the earth today America stands for
one idea: *Business*. National opprobrium? National opportunity. For in this fact lies, potentially, the salvation of
the world.

Thru business, properly conceived, managed and conducted, the human race is finally to be redeemed. How and
why a man works foretells what he will do, think, have,
give and be. And real salvation is in doing, thinking, having, giving and being—not in sermonizing and theorizing.

I shall base the facts of this article on the personal tours
and minute examinations I have recently made of twelve
of the world's largest business plants: U. S. Steel Corpora-

From "Big Ideas from Big Business," *Independent,* April 16, 1921, pp. 375–6.

tion, International Harvester Company, Swift & Company, E. I. du Pont de Nemours & Company, National City Bank, National Cash Register Company, Western Electric Company, Sears, Roebuck & Company, H. J. Heinz Company, Peabody Coal Company, Statler Hotels, Wanamaker Stores.

These organizations are typical, foremost representatives of the commercial group of interests loosely termed "Big Business." A close view of these corporations would reveal to any trained, unprejudiced observer a new conception of modern business activities. Let me draw a few general conclusions regarding the best type of business house and business man.

What is the finest game? Business. The soundest science? Business. The truest art? Business. The fullest education? Business. The fairest opportunity? Business. The cleanest philanthropy? Business. The sanest religion? Business.

You may not agree. That is because you judge business by the crude, mean, stupid, false imitation of business that happens to be located near you.

The finest game is business. The rewards are for everybody, and all can win. There are no favorites—Providence always crowns the career of the man who is worthy. And in this game there is no "luck"—you have the fun of taking chances but the sobriety of guaranteeing certainties. The speed and size of your winnings are for you alone to determine; you needn't wait for the other fellow in the game—it is always your move. And your slogan is not "Down the Other Fellow!" but rather "Beat Your Own Record!" or "Do It Better Today!" or "Make Every Job a Masterpiece!" The great sportsmen of the world are the great business men.

The soundest science is business. All investigation is reduced to action, and by action proved or disproved. The idealistic motive animates the materialistic method. Hearts as well as minds are open to the truth. Capital is furnished for the researches of "pure science"; yet pure science is not regarded pure until practical. Competent scientists are suitably rewarded—as they are not in the scientific schools.

The truest art is business. The art is so fine, so exquisite, that you do not think of it as art. Language, color, form, line, music, drama, discovery, adventure—all the components of art must be used in business to make it of superior character.

The fullest education is business. A proper blend of study, work and life is essential to advancement. The whole man is educated. Human nature itself is the open book that all business men study; and the mastery of a page of this educates you more than the memorizing of a dusty tome from a library shelf. In the school of business, moreover, you teach yourself and learn most from your own mistakes. What you learn here you live out, the only real test.

The fairest opportunity is business. You can find more, better, quicker chances to get ahead in a large business house than anywhere else on earth. The biographies of champion business men show how they climbed, and how you can climb. Recognition of better work, of keener and quicker thought, of deeper and finer feeling, is gladly offered by the men higher up, with early promotion the rule for the man who justifies it. There is, and can be, no such thing as buried talent in a modern business organization.

The cleanest philanthropy is business. By "clean" philanthropy I mean that devoid of graft, inefficiency and professionalism, also of condolence, hysterics and paternalism. Nearly everything that goes by the name of Charity was born a triplet, the other two members of the trio being Frailty and Cruelty. Not so in the welfare departments of leading corporations. Savings and loan funds; pension and insurance provisions; health precautions, instructions and safeguards; medical attention and hospital care; libraries, lectures and classes; musical, athletic and social features of all kinds; recreational facilities and financial opportunities—these types of "charitable institutions" for employees add to the worker's self-respect, self-knowledge and self-improvement, by making him an active partner in the welfare program, a producer of benefits for his employer and associates quite as much as a recipient of bounty from the company. I wish every "charity" organization would send its officials to school to the heads of the welfare departments of the big corporations; the charity would mostly be transformed into capability, and the minimum of irreducible charity left would not be called by that name.

The sanest religion is business. Any relationship that forces a man to follow the Golden Rule rightfully belongs amid the ceremonials of the church. A great business enterprise includes and presupposes this relationship. I have seen more Christianity to the square inch as a regular part of the office equipment of famous corporation presidents than may ordinarily be found on Sunday in a verbalized but not vitalized church congregation. A man is not wholly religious until he is better on week-days than he is on Sunday. The only ripened fruits of creeds are deeds. You can fool your preacher with a sickly sprout or a wormy semblance of character, but you can't fool your employer. I would make every business house a consultation bureau for the guidance of the church whose members were employees of the house.

I am aware that some of the preceding statements will be challenged by many readers. I should not myself have made them, or believed them, twenty years ago, when I was a pitiful specimen of a callow youth and cocksure professional man combined. A thoro knowledge of business has implanted a deep respect for business and real business men.

The future work of the business man is to teach the teacher, preach to the preacher, admonish the parent, advise the doctor, justify the lawyer, superintend the statesman, fructify the farmer, stabilize the banker, harness the dreamer, and reform the reformer. Do all these needy persons wish to have these many kind things done to them by the business man? Alas, no. They rather look down upon him, or askance at him, regarding him as a mental and social inferior—unless he has money or fame enough to tilt their glance upward. . . .

*The biggest thing about a big success is the price.* It takes a big man to pay the price. You can measure in advance the size of your success by how much you are willing to pay for it. I do not refer to money. I refer to the time, thought, energy, economy, purpose, devotion, study, sacrifice, patience, care, that a man must give to his life work before he can make it amount to anything.

The business world is full of born crusaders. Many of the leaders would be called martyrs if they weren't rich. The founders of the vast corporations have been, so far as I know them, fired with zeal that is supposed to belong only to missionaries.

Of all the uncompromising, untiring, unsparing idealists in the world today, none surpass the founders and heads of the business institutions that have made character the cornerstone. The costliest thing on earth is idealism.

# Thurman W. Arnold (1891–        )

*After growing up in the Wild West (Wyoming), he was educated at Princeton and Harvard Law School. Appointed Professor of Law at Yale in 1930, he joined the revolt against the narrowness of the traditional legal curriculum. His attempt to study legal institutions from the point of view of public psychology led to his first two books—*The Symbols of Government *and* The Folklore of Capitalism. *The latter led to his appointment by President Roosevelt in 1938 as Assistant Attorney General in charge of the Anti-trust Division. While he had earlier dis-*

*paraged the anti-trust laws, he became known
as the nation's "number one trust-buster," filing
more than two hundred suits in five years.*

# THE THEOLOGY OF CAPITALISM

In the United States the mythology used to be very simple.
The predominant figure was the American Businessman.
Warriors were respected, but they had a distinctly minor
place. The National Government had to imitate the American Businessman. Whenever it failed, people became
alarmed. A businessman balances his budget. Hence the unbalanced budget which was actually pulling us out of the depression was the source of greater alarm than administrative
failures which were actually much more dangerous. The
American Businessman bosses his employees. Hence the encouragement of the C.I.O. was thought to be the forerunner
of a revolution, in spite of the fact that never had industrial
unrest been followed with less actual disorder.

The creed of the American Businessman was celebrated in
our institutions of learning. Since the American Scholar was
a minor divinity, some of his characteristics had to be assumed by the great industrial organization. Therefore colleges were endowed to prove that the predominant divinity
was supported by reason and scholarship. All the Christian
virtues were also ascribed to him—for the selfishness of
business was an enlightened selfishness which resulted in the
long run in unselfish conduct if it were only let alone.

The American Businessman was independent of his fellows. No individual could rule him. Hence the "rule of law
above men" was symbolized by the Constitution. This meant
that the American Businessman was an individual who was
free from the control of any other individual and owed allegiance only to the Constitution. However, he was the only

From *The Folklore of Capitalism* (New Haven: Yale University Press, 1937),
pp. 35–6, 185–90. Reprinted by permission of the publisher.

individual entitled to this kind of freedom. His employees were subject to the arbitrary control of this divinity. Their only freedom consisted in the supposed opportunity of laborers to become American businessmen themselves.

It is this mythology, operating long after the American Businessman has disappeared as an independent individual, which gives the great industrial organization an established place in our temporal government. Every demand on these great industrial structures is referred to the conception of the American Businessman as a standard.

Thus pension systems for great corporations are all right provided businessmen inaugurate them. Economic coercion is permitted provided these heroes accomplish it. Boondoggling of every kind is subject to no criticism if businessmen finance it. Charity and welfare work, provided they are used to portray businessmen in their softer and more sentimental moods, are lovely things. When undertaken by the Government, they are necessary evils because such activity impairs the dignity and prestige of our great national ideal type. The businessman is the only divinity supposed to conduct such affairs. Therefore one never hears a community chest spoken of as a necessary evil as the dole is. Private charity even in times when it is an obvious failure is supposed to be more efficient than government relief.

In this mythology are found the psychological motives for the decisions of courts, for the timidity of humanitarian action, for the worship of states rights and for the proof by scholars that the only sound way of thinking about government is a fiscal way of thinking. Move Communism or any other kind of creed into this country, keep the present national hierarchy of tutelary divinities, and one would soon find that the dialecticians and priests were ingenious enough to make communistic principles march the same way as the old ones. So long as the American Businessman maintains his present place in this mythological hierarchy, no practical inconvenience is too great to be sacrificed to do him honor— every humanitarian impulse which goes counter to the popular conception of how the businessman should act is soft and effeminate. . . .

One of the essential and central notions which give our industrial feudalism logical symmetry is the personification of great industrial enterprise. The ideal that a great corporation is endowed with the rights and prerogatives of a free individual is as essential to the acceptance of corporate rule in temporal affairs as was the ideal of the divine right of kings in an earlier day. Its exemplification, as in the case of all vital ideals, has been accomplished by ceremony. Since it has been a central ideal in our industrial government, our judicial institutions have been particularly concerned with its celebration. Courts, under the mantle of the Constitution, have made a living thing out of this fiction. Men have come to believe that their own future liberties and dignity are tied up in the freedom of great industrial organizations from restraint, in much the same way that they thought their salvation in the future was dependent on their reverence and support of great ecclesiastical organizations in the Middle Ages. This ideal explains so many of our social habits, rituals, and institutions that it is necessary to examine it in some detail.

The origin of this way of thinking about organization is the result of a pioneer civilization in which the prevailing ideal was that of the freedom and dignity of the individual engaged in the accumulation of wealth. The independence of the free man from central authority was the slogan for which men fought and died. The free man was a trader, who got ahead by accumulating money. . . . There was nothing in that philosophy which justified far-flung industrial empires. Indeed, the great organization in which most men were employees, and a few at the top were dictators, was a contradiction of that philosophy. The great organization came in as a result of mechanical techniques which specialized the work of production so that men could not operate by themselves. Nothing could stop the progress of such organization, and therefore in order to tolerate it,

men had to pretend that corporations were individuals.
When faced with the fact that they were not individuals,
they did not seek to control, but denounced and tried to
break them up into smaller organizations. Those who did
not choose to dissent, however, sought refuge in transferring
the symbolism of the individual to the great industrial armies
in which they were soldiers. . . .

It was this identification of great organizations with the
dignities, freedom, and general ethics of the individual
trader which relieved our federation of industrial empires
from the hampering restrictions of theology which always
prevent experiment. Men cheerfully accept the fact that
some individuals are good and others bad. Therefore, since
great industrial organizations were regarded as individuals,
it was not expected that all of them would be good. Corporations could therefore violate any of the established
taboos without creating any alarm about the "system" itself. Since individuals are supposed to do better if let alone,
this symbolism freed industrial enterprise from regulation
in the interest of furthering any current morality. The
*laissez faire* religion, based on a conception of a society
composed of competing individuals, was transferred automatically to industrial organizations with nation-wide power
and dictatorial forms of government.

This mythology gave the Government at Washington only
a minor part to play in social organization. It created the
illusion that we were living under a pioneer economy composed of self-sufficient men who were trading with each
other. In that atmosphere the notion of Thomas Jefferson,
that the best government was the one which interfered the
least with individual activity, hampered any control of our
industrial government by our political government. We were
slower, therefore, in adopting the measures of control of industrial organization than a country like England. The Government at Washington gradually changed into what was
essentially a spiritual government whose every action was

designed to reconcile the conflict between myth and reality which men felt when a creed of individualism was applied to a highly organized industrial world. Government in Washington was supposed to act so as to instil "confidence" in great business organizations. The Supreme Court of the United States, because it could express better than any other institution the myth of the corporate personality, was able to hamper Federal powers to an extent which foreigners, not realizing the emotional power of the myth, could not understand. This court invented most of the ceremonies which kept the myth alive and preached about them in a most dramatic setting. It dressed huge corporations in the clothes of simple farmers and merchants and thus made attempts to regulate them appear as attacks on liberty and the home. So long as men instinctively thought of these great organizations as individuals, the emotional analogies of home and freedom and all the other trappings of "rugged individualism" became their most potent protection.

# Glenn Frank (1887–1940)

*Editor, publicist, and university president, he began his career as a protégé of the socially minded Boston merchant Edward A. Filene. Later he became editor of* Century *magazine, which provided him with a forum for his liberal ideas. In 1925 he was appointed president of the University of Wisconsin. While there his most talked-about undertaking was the Experimental College, headed by Alexander Meiklejohn, which sought to find some workable departure from the traditional methods of higher education. But the experiment, besides being expensive, had little faculty support and was abandoned.*

# OUR MACHINE CIVILIZATION

Must we smash our machines in order to save our souls?
The social mystics of the slower-paced Orient are sure that
we must. Every energy of the frail body and flaming spirit
of Mahatma Gandhi is invested in the attempt to convince
the Western world that it must emancipate itself from the
machine if it is to avert the downfall of its civilization.
To him, the application of machine power to production
meant the entrance of the serpent into the Eden of a
handicraft world. To this wistful ascetic of India, the
spinning-wheel is a symbol of salvation for our machine
civilization.

To Gandhi and his kind, machine civilization must always mean the centralization of production in great industrial cities where congestion breeds its ugly offspring; a
narcotic monotony of factory routine that turns masters of
tools into servants of machines; a mass production that puts
quantity above quality; a standardization of processes and
products that will not stop until it has ironed out the mind
and manners and morals of mankind into a sterile sameness,
the death alike of the inventive skill and the independent
spirit of the worker; an overspeeding that will leave mankind spiritually out of breath; and a subtle conspiracy
against beauty that will end by making ugliness and utility
interchangeable terms.

The business man of the Western world might dismiss
all this as but the natural reaction of the mystical East if
it came alone from Mahatma Gandhi, seated at his spinning-
wheel, clothed only in his loin-cloth, and his longing for a
premachine economy. But Gandhi and his fellow rebels
against the machine are winning converts in the West.

These Western converts to the social mysticism of the

From "Shall We Scrap Our Machines and Go Back to the Spinning-Wheel?"
*The Magazine of Business*, LII (Oct., 1927), 411–3, 424, 426, 428.

East are what the late Walter Rathenau, distinguished head of the *Allgemeine Deutsche Elektrische Gesellschaft,* called "the Shepherds of Arcady." Herr Rathenau was at once a social prophet and a successful profit-maker, seer, and business man in one. He had little patience and less confidence to give to men who, face to face with the admitted materialism and muddling of our machine civilization, had no remedy to offer save a cowardly retreat into some Arcadian simplicity of life which is possible only to a select few of the saints and seers. Herr Rathenau was willing to let these Shepherds of Arcady run away from the challenge of our machine civilization if they chose, but he preferred to buckle down to the practical task of wresting health and happiness and security and serenity from our machine civilization for the vast masses of men and women who cannot and will not run away from modern society to the haven of some private paradise.

Mahatma Gandhi is not more keenly aware of the perils of machine civilization than Herr Rathenau was; but Herr Rathenau was more keenly aware of the promise of machine civilization than Mahatma Gandhi is. Gandhi thinks mankind must emancipate itself from the machine; Rathenau thought mankind must emancipate itself through the machine. . . .

I am willing to grant to Mahatma Gandhi and his Western converts that to date our machine civilization has much to its discredit. It has too often subjected men to the new and more terrible drudgery of soul-killing speed of work. Its savings have not always been put to work for the improvement of its service. It has sometimes been guilty of the short-sighted business policy of paying its men the least they would stand for and charging its customers the most they would stand for. It has built and crowded into hideously ugly industrial centers. It has often forgotten beauty and frowned upon quality. It has often produced for sale rather than for use. And so on to the end of an indictment I shall not undertake to contradict.

But—and this is the nub of the matter—these are sins of a pioneer period. We must remember that our machine civilization is a mere fledgling among the social schemes of history. These sins will, in time, disappear from our machine civilization. In fact, they are disappearing more rapidly than appears to the side-line onlooker. And they are disappearing, not because business men have received a sudden baptism of brotherly love, but simply because it is becoming daily more evident that such sins are bad business.

And as a result of all this—if I may put it bluntly—I think that the masses have more to hope for from great engineers, great inventors, and great captains of industry than from the social reformers who woo them with their panaceas. The greatest social progress of the next 50 years is likely to come as a by-product of technical progress. Our most potent revolutionists are the really far-sighted manufacturers. . . .

My hopes respecting the future of our machine civilization rest neither upon outside reformers nor upon any internal reform of the human nature of business men, which, I suspect, has not materially changed since the American Indians passed their wampum from hand to hand.

I believe that the steady advance of technical progress, plus the increasingly intelligent effort of business men to find the soundest and most profitable forms of organization, processes of production, and methods of distribution will, without any "hifalutin" declaration of unselfish social purpose, correct the existing evils of our machine civilization and produce a social and business order the normal functioning of which will in itself be the highest social service.

Let me condescend to details and suggest some of the ways in which I think our machine civilization is correcting its more obvious shortcomings—the correction coming as an incidental by-product of technical progress and of business men's search for the soundest and most profitable ways of doing business. I can, of course, do little more than report a few tendencies by way of illustration.

First of all, there are technical and economic forces, making for an extensive decentralization of American industry, which bid fair to correct most of the evils of centralization and congestion against which muck-rakers and mystics have been railing for a generation. It is only a question of time until American industry will stop the complete manufacture and assembly of all the parts of complicated machines in great industrial centers. The parts will be manufactured in factories located at the source of the raw materials used in their manufacture.

For a time great industrial centers will persist as points at which the parts, manufactured elsewhere, are assembled and from which they are shipped to local markets. Ultimately the great congested industrial centers will disappear even as points of assembly, for in the end we shall ship parts to the very doorways of local markets for assembly.

This revolutionary industrial change—and the equally revolutionary social effects that will follow—will come, not because of any Utopian reformer's crusade, but as the result of technical progress in the field of superpower. Heretofore we have had to build our factories at the sources of motive power. The production of steel has stuck close by the coal mines of Pennsylvania. The production of flour has pitched its tent near the waterfalls of Minneapolis. And so on. Heretofore the flour industry has had to operate near the waterfalls, not near the wheat fields. Heretofore the iron industry has had to operate near the coal mines, not near the iron mines. All this will be changed as we perfect a nation-wide interlocking power system.

The critics of our machine civilization have assumed that we could not have mass production without centralization, and so they have said that we could not remedy the evils of centralization without renouncing mass production. They knew that we would not renounce mass production, so they have pronounced the evils of centralization as incurable. But now the outlook is that we shall ultimately find it possible to carry on mass production more profitably in a decentralized than in a centralized industry. When this is achieved many of the ugly social problems that have followed in the wake of industrial centralization will automatically disappear. . . .

Then, too, I am not sure that standardization of production processes, with all the factory routine that it implies, is the unmixed evil its critics assert. I realize the deadening effect that the monotonous repetition of a single specialized movement has upon the worker. It is true that, by and large, the man who makes one forty-secondth part of a watch is likely to become one forty-secondth of a watchmaker.

Standardized machine production does not make for creative craftsmanship in the worker. But it is not every worker who is a suppressed artist champing at the bit to "create." The brutal truth is that there is a vast amount of mediocrity in the human breed. And standardized machine production has given mediocrity its first chance to make a better living than the ancient artist-craftsman made. The mediocre workman, thanks to machine production, today has a cottage and a car; in a handicraft world he would be living in a hovel and walking.

And in the machine civilization of the next 50 years, I doubt that the craftsman blessed with the creative urge will be so badly off. The further development of mass production will give him two inestimable boons—leisure and means.

The outstanding fact of mass production and mass distribution is that its effective administration enables the manufacturer to do four apparently contradictory things at one and the same time—raise wages, lower prices, shorten hours, and increase total profits. And the first three mean leisure and means for the workman whose spirit is bigger than the set task he does in the factory. . . .

Even the most creative craftsman must face the necessity of living in a machine civilization. It is gratifying, therefore, to know that our machine civilization, in the normal perfection of its processes, is making for shorter hours and

higher pay, thus staking out in the lives of the rank and
file of workers larger and larger areas of leisure in which
they may laugh and love and adventure among things of
the mind and the spirit. When machine civilization has produced this leisure and means it will remain for the worker
to prove that he has it in him to make as intelligent use of
his opportunity for a broad and free life as the peasant
and craftsman of other days made of a similar opportunity.

So much for the problem of standardization and the individual. What about the effect of standardization upon our
civilization in general? I have broken my lance innumerable
times in fights against the standardization of the American
mind. But there has been a vast amount of sheer silliness
spent upon a wholesale condemnation of all standardization.

A certain amount of standardization is necessary to the
effective living of our lives. If we did not standardize
and render more or less automatic the processes of shaving, dressing, and eating, we should have to spend most
of our time in the bathroom and in the dining-room. I
know men who do most of their creative business and professional planning while they are shaving and dressing.
These processes have become so automatic that their energies are free for bigger things.

The same thing can be true of a civilization. The vast
processes of production of necessities can become so standardized and automatic that the major energies of a people
can be freed for bigger things. . . .

And, finally, our machine civilization is escaping from
its earlier enslavement to ugliness. Machine industry is
finding that beauty is not the foe but the friend of utility.
Machine production is coming out of its gawky age. It is
no longer enough that an automobile shall run well. It must
also look well. And it is significant, I think, that the $600
car is aspiring to beauty of form and color as well as the
$6,000 car. Machine industry has committed high crimes
against beauty, but one look at the exquisitely beautiful
period cabinet of a 1927 talking-machine shows that some-

thing revolutionary has happened since the days of the first talking-machine with its hideously ugly horn jutting out into the room like a steamer funnel. . . .

And the beauty born of a machine age promises to have greater social significance than the beauty born of the pre-machine age. The machine industry of the future promises to bring to the common man everywhere prosperity in the wages he receives and beauty in the things he sees and touches and handles day by day. This will be something new under the sun. . . .

Modern industry is leading to a time when men will bring the same beauty to the manufacturing of commodities that medieval religion brought to the building of cathedrals. And it will no longer be the case of beautiful cathedrals looking down upon sordid serfdoms. The new beauty of the machine age will be a democratized beauty. . . .

All in all, I prefer to take my stand with the Rathenaus rather than with the Gandhis, for it seems to me that our machine civilization is carrying about in its own process-es the cures of all the evils that have afflicted it in its adolescence.

# Lewis Mumford (1895–          )

*At the age of twelve, he built his first radio set and was soon writing short articles for popular technical magazines. Though he later attended City College and the New School for Social Research in New York, admittedly the most important influence in his life was Patrick Geddes, the Scottish biologist and civic planner, whose writings first turned his attention to social ecology, the interplay between man and his environment. Putting this theme to work, he published in 1934 a study of technics and civilization in which, among other things, he*

*pointed out that all the critical instruments of
modern technology had existed in other cultures,
but what was new was the fact that these
technical functions had been projected and
embodied in organized forms which dominated
every aspect of modern existence.*

# THE DIMINUTION
# OF THE MACHINE

Most of the current fantasies of the future, which have
been suggested by the triumph of the machine, are based
upon the notion that our mechanical environment will become more pervasive and oppressive. Within the past
generation, this belief seemed justified: Mr. H. G. Wells's
earlier tales of The War of the Worlds and When the
Sleeper Wakes, predicted horrors, great and little, from
gigantic aerial combats to the blatant advertisement of
salvation by go-getting Protestant churches—horrors that
were realized almost before the words had left his mouth.

The belief in the greater dominance of mechanism has
been reenforced by a vulgar error in statistical interpretation: the belief that curves generated by a past historic
complex will continue without modification into the future.
Not merely do the people who hold these views imply that
society is immune to qualitative changes: they imply that
it exhibits uniform direction, uniform motion, and even
uniform acceleration—a fact which holds only for simple
events in society and for very minor spans of time. The
fact is that social predictions that are based upon past
experience are always retrospective: they do not touch the
real future. That such predictions have a way of justifying

themselves from time to time is due to another fact: namely that in what Professor John Dewey calls judgments of practice the hypothesis itself becomes one of the determining elements in the working out of events: to the extent that it is seized and acted upon it weights events in its favor. The doctrine of mechanical progress doubtless had such a rôle in the nineteenth century.

What reason is there to believe that the machine will continue to multiply indefinitely at the rate that characterized the past, and that it will take over even more territory than it has already conquered? While the inertia of society is great, the facts of the matter lend themselves to a different interpretation. The rate of growth in all the older branches of machine production has in fact been going down steadily: Mr. Bassett Jones even holds that this is generally true of all industry since 1910. In those departments of mechanical industry that were well-established by 1870, like the railroad and the textile mill, this slowing down applies likewise to the critical inventions. Have not the conditions that forced and speeded the earlier growth— namely, the territorial expansion of Western Civilization and the tremendous increase in population—been diminishing since that point?

Certain machines, moreover, have already reached the limit of their development: certain areas of scientific investigation are already completed. The printing press, for example, reached a high pitch of perfection within a century after its invention: a whole succession of later inventions, from the rotary press to the linotype and monotype machines, while they have increased the pace of production, have not improved the original product: the finest page that can be produced today is no finer than the work of the sixteenth-century printers. The water turbine is now ninety per cent efficient; we cannot, on any count, add more than ten per cent to its efficiency. Telephone transmission is practically perfect, even over long distances; the best the engineers can now do is to multiply the capacity of the wires and to extend the inter-linkages. Distant speech and vision cannot be transmitted faster than they are transmitted today by electricity: what gains we can make are in cheapness and ubiquity. In short: there are bounds to mechanical progress within the nature of the physical world itself. It is only by ignoring these limiting conditions that a belief in the automatic and inevitable and limitless expansion of the machine can be retained.

And apart from any wavering of interest in the machine, a general increase in verified knowledge in other departments than the physical sciences already threatens a large curtailment of mechanical practices and instruments. It is not a mystic withdrawal from the practical concerns of the world that challenges the machine so much as a more comprehensive knowledge of phenomena to which our mechanic contrivances were only partial and ineffective responses. Just as, within the domain of engineering itself, there has been a growing tendency toward refinement and efficiency through a nicer inter-relation of parts, so in the environment at large the province of the machine has begun to shrink. When we think and act in terms of an organic whole, rather than in terms of abstractions, when we are concerned with life in its full manifestation, rather than with the fragment of it that seeks physical domination and that projects itself in purely mechanical systems, we will no longer require from the machine alone what we should demand through a many-sided adjustment of every other aspect of life. A finer knowledge of physiology reduces the number of drugs and nostrums in which the physician places confidence: it also decreases the number and scope of surgical operations—those exquisite triumphs of machine-technics!—so that although refinements in technique have increased the number of potential operations that can be resorted to, competent physicians are tempted to exhaust the resources of nature before utilizing a mechanical short-cut. In general, the classic methods of Hippocrates have begun to displace, with a new certitude of conviction, both

the silly potions prescribed in Molière's Imaginary Invalid
and the barbarous intervention of Mr. Surgeon Cuticle.
Similarly, a sounder notion of the human body has relegated
to the scrapheap most of the weight-lifting apparatus of
late Victorian gymnastics. The habit of doing without hats
and petticoats and corsets has, in the past decade, thrown
whole industries into limbo: a similar fate, through the
more decent attitude toward the naked human body,
threatens the bathing suit industry. Finally, with a great
part of the utilities, like railroads, power lines, docks, port
facilities, automobiles, concrete roads which we constructed
so busily during the last hundred years, we are now on a
basis where repair and replacement are all that is required.
As our production becomes more rationalized, and as
population shifts and regroups in better relationship to industry and recreation, new communities designed to the
human scale are being constructed. This movement which
has been taking place in Europe during the last generation is a result of pioneering work done over a century
from Robert Owen to Ebenezer Howard. As these new communities are built up the need for the extravagant mechanical devices like subways, which were built in response
to the disorganization and speculative chaos of the megalop-
olis, will disappear.

In a word, *as social life becomes mature, the social unemployment of machines will become as marked as the
present technological unemployment of men.* Just as the
ingenious and complicated mechanisms for inflicting death
used by armies and navies are marks of international anarchy and painful collective psychoses, so are many of our
present machines the reflexes of poverty, ignorance, disorder. The machine, so far from being a sign in our present
civilization of human power and order, is often an indication of ineptitude and social paralysis. Any appreciable
improvement in education and culture will reduce the
amount of machinery devoted to multiplying the spurious
mechanical substitutes for knowledge and experience

now provided through the channels of the motion picture, the tabloid newspaper, the radio, and the printed book. So, too, any appreciable improvement in the physical apparatus of life, through better nutrition, more healthful housing, sounder forms of recreation, greater opportunities for the natural enjoyments of life, will decrease the part played by mechanical apparatus in salvaging wrecked bodies and broken minds. Any appreciable gain in personal harmony and balance will be recorded in a decreased demand for compensatory goods and services. The passive dependence upon the machine that has characterized such large sections of the Western World in the past was in reality an abdication of life. Once we cultivate the arts of life directly, the proportion occupied by mechanical routine and by mechanical instruments will again diminish.

Our mechanical civilization, contrary to the assumption of those who worship its external power the better to conceal their own feeling of impotence, is not an absolute. All its mechanisms are dependent upon human aims and desires: many of them flourish in direct proportion to our failure to achieve rational social cooperation and integrated personalities. Hence we do not have to renounce the machine completely and go back to handicraft in order to abolish a good deal of useless machinery and burdensome routine: we merely have to use imagination and intelligence and social discipline in our traffic with the machine itself. In the last century or two of social disruption, we were tempted by an excess of faith in the machine to do everything by means of it. We were like a child left alone with a paint brush who applies it impartially to unpainted wood, to varnished furniture, to the tablecloth, to his toys, and to his own face. When, with increased knowledge and judgment, we discover that some of these uses are inappropriate, that others are redundant, that others are inefficient substitutes for a more vital adjustment, we will contract the machine to those areas in which it serves directly as an instrument of human purpose. The last, it is plain, is a large area: but it is probably smaller than that now occupied by the machine. One of the uses of this period of indiscriminate mechanical experiment was to disclose unsuspected points of weakness in society itself. Like an old-fashioned menial, the arrogance of the machine grew in proportion to its master's feebleness and folly. With a change in ideals from material conquest, wealth, and power to life, culture, and expression, the machine like the menial with a new and more confident master, will fall back into its proper place: our servant, not our tyrant.

Quantitatively, then, we shall probably be less concerned with production in future than we were forced to be during the period of rapid expansion that lies behind us. So, too, we shall probably use fewer mechanical instruments than we do at present, although we shall have a far greater range to select from, and shall have more skillfully designed, more finely calibrated, more economical and reliable contrivances than we now possess. The machines of the future, if our present technics continue, will surpass those in use at present as the Parthenon surpassed a neolithic wood-hut: the transformation will be both toward durability and to refinement of forms. The dissociation of production from the acquisitive life will favor technical conservatism on a high level rather than a flashy experimentalism on a low level.

But this change will be accompanied by a qualitative change in interest, too: in general a change from mechanical interest to vital psychic and social interests. This potential change in interest is generally ignored in predictions about the future of the machine. Yet once its importance is grasped it plainly alters every purely quantitative prediction that is based upon the assumption that the interests which for three centuries have operated chiefly within a mechanical framework will continue to remain forever within that framework. On the contrary, proceeding under the surface in the work of poets and painters and biological scientists, in a Goethe, a Whitman, a von Mueller, a Darwin, a Bernard, there has been a steady shift in attention from the mechanical to the vital and the social: more and more, adventure and exhilarating effort will lie here, rather than within the already partly exhausted field of the machine.

Such a shift will change the incidence of the machine and profoundly alter its relative position in the whole complex of human thought and activity. Shaw, in his Back to Methuselah, put such a change in a remote future; and risky though prophecy of this nature be, it seems to me that it is probably already insidiously at work. That such a movement could not take place, certainly not in science and its technical applications, without a long preparation in the inorganic realm is now farily obvious: it was the relative simplicity of the original mechanical abstractions that enabled us to develop the technique and the confidence to approach more complicated phenomena. But while this movement toward the organic owes a heavy debt to the machine, it will not leave its parent in undisputed possession of the field. In the very act of enlarging its dominion over human thought and practice, the machine has proved to a great degree self-eliminating: its perfection involves in some degree its disappearance—as a communal water-system, once built, involves less daily attention and less expense on annual replacements than would a hundred thousand domestic wells and pumps. This fact is fortunate for the race. It will do away with the necessity, which Samuel Butler satirically pictured in Erewhon, for forcefully extirpating the dangerous troglodytes of the earlier mechanical age. The old machines will in part die out, as the great saurians died out, to be replaced by smaller, faster, brainier, and more adaptable organisms, adapted not to the mine, the battlefield and the factory, but to the positive environment of life.

# George Santayana (1863–1952)

*While the better part of his life was spent in
the United States, and his books were written in
the English language, he never relinquished his
Spanish nationality. From the Boston Latin
School he went to Harvard and then after two
years in Berlin taught philosophy there from
1889 to 1912. Afterward he lived the rest of his
life in Europe. Though he never had any illusions about the world's being rationally guided
or true to any ideals, he thought it possible to
live nobly in this world only if one lived in
another world ideally.*

# THE GENTEEL TRADITION AT BAY

Twenty years ago the genteel tradition in America seemed
ready to melt gracefully into the active mind of the country. There were few misgivings about the perfect health
and the all-embracing genius of the nation: only go full
speed ahead and everything worth doing would ultimately
get done. The churches and universities might have some
pre-American stock-in-trade, but there was nothing stubborn or recalcitrant about them; they were happy to bask
in the golden sunshine of plutocracy; and there was a
feeling abroad—which I think reasonable—that wherever
the organisation of a living thing is materially perfected,
there an appropriate moral and intellectual life will arise
spontaneously. But the gestation of a native culture is
necessarily long, and the new birth may seem ugly to an

---

Reprinted with the permission of Charles Scribner's Sons from *The Genteel
Tradition at Bay*, pp. 3–6, 16, 17–23, by George Santayana. Copyright 1931
by Charles Scribner's Sons; renewal copyright © 1959 Old Colony Trust Company. British rights by permission of Constable & Co., Ltd.

eye accustomed to some other form of excellence. Will the new life ever be as beautiful as the old? Certain too tender or too learned minds may refuse to credit it. Old Harvard men will remember the sweet sadness of Professor Norton. He would tell his classes, shaking his head with a slight sigh, that the Greeks did not play football. In America there had been no French cathedrals, no Venetian school of painting, no Shakespeare, and even no gentlemen, but only gentlemanly citizens. The classes laughed, because that recital of home truths seemed to miss the humour of them. It was jolly to have changed all that; and the heartiness of the contrary current of life in everybody rendered those murmurs useless and a little ridiculous. In them the genteel tradition seemed to be breathing its last. Now, however, the worm has turned. We see it raising its head more admonishingly than ever, darting murderous glances at its enemies, and protesting that it is not genteel or antiquated at all, but orthodox and immortal. Its principles, it declares, are classical, and its true name is Humanism.

The humanists of the Renaissance were lovers of Greek and of good Latin, scornful of all that was crabbed, technical, or fanatical: they were pleasantly learned men, free from any kind of austerity, who, without quarrelling with Christian dogma, treated it humanly, and partly by tolerance and partly by ridicule hoped to neutralise all its metaphysical and moral rigour. Even when orthodoxy was reaffirmed in the seventeenth century and established all our genteel traditions, some humanistic leaven was mixed in: among Protestants there remained a learned unrest and the rationalistic criticism of tradition: among Catholics a classical eloquence draping everything in large and seemly folds, so that nothing trivial, barbaric, or ugly should offend the cultivated eye. But apart from such influences cast upon orthodoxy, the humanists continued their own labours. Their sympathy with mankind was not really universal, since it stopped short at enthusiasm, at sacrifice, at all high passion or belief; but they loved the more physical and comic aspects of life everywhere and all curious knowledge, especially when it could be turned against prevalent prejudices or abuses. They believed in the sufficient natural goodness of mankind, a goodness humanised by frank sensuality and a wink at all amiable vices; their truly ardent morality was all negative, and flashed out in their hatred of cruelty and oppression and in their scorn of imposture. This is still the temper of revolutionaries everywhere, and of philosophers of the extreme Left. These, I should say, are more truly heirs to the humanists than the merely academic people who still read, or pretend to read, the classics, and who would like to go on thrashing little boys into writing Latin verses. . . .

Why not frankly rejoice in the benefits, so new and extraordinary, which our state of society affords? We may not possess those admirable things which Professor Norton pined for, but at least (besides football) haven't we Einstein and Freud, Proust and Paul Valéry, Lenin and Mussolini? For my part, though a lover of antiquity, I should certainly congratulate myself on living among the moderns, if the moderns were only modern enough, and dared to face nature with an unprejudiced mind and a clear purpose. . . .

So far, then, the gist of modern history would seem to be this: a many-sided insurrection of the unregenerate natural man, with all his physical powers and affinities, against the regimen of Christendom. He has convinced himself that his physical life is not as his ghostly mentors asserted, a life of sin; and why should it be a life of misery? Society has gradually become a rather glorious, if troubled, organisation of matter, and of man for material achievements. Even our greatest troubles, such as the late war, seem only to accelerate the scientific bridling of matter: troubles do not cease, but surgery and aviation make remarkable progress. Big Business itself is not without its grave worries: wasted production, turbulent labour, rival bosses, and an inherited form of government, by organised parties and elections, which was based on revolutionary maxims, and has become irrelevant to the true work of the modern world if not disastrous for it. Spiritual distress, too, cannot be banished by spiritual anarchy; in obscure privacy and in the sordid tragedies of doubt and of love, it is perhaps more desperate than ever. We live in an age of suicides. Yet this spiritual distress may be disregarded, like bad dreams, so long as it remains isolated and does not organise any industrial revolt or any fresh total discouragement and mystic withdrawal, such as ushered in the triumph of Christianity. For the present, Big Business continues to generate the sort of intelligence and loyalty which it requires: it favours the most startling triumphs of mind in abstract science and mechanical art, without any philosophic commitments regarding their ultimate truth or value. Indeed, mechanical art and abstract science are other forms of Big Business, and congruous parts of it. They, too, are instinctive undertakings, in which ambition, co-operation, and rivalry keep the snowball rolling and getting bigger and bigger. Some day attention will be attracted elsewhere, and the whole vain thing will melt away unheeded. But while the game lasts and absorbs all a man's faculties, its rules become the guides of his life. In the long run, obedience to them is incompatible with anarchy, even in the single mind. Either the private anarchy will ruin public order, or the public order will cure private anarchy.

The latter, on the whole, has happened in the United States, and may be expected to become more and more characteristic of the nation. There, according to one of the new humanists, "The accepted vision of a good life is to make a lot of money by fair means; to spend it generously; to be friendly; to move fast; to die with one's boots on." This sturdy ideal has come to prevail naturally, despite the preachers and professors of sundry finer moralities; it includes virtue and it includes happiness, at least in the

ancient and virile sense of these words. We are invited to
share an industrious, cordial, sporting existence, self-imposed
and self-rewarding. There is plenty of room, in the margin
and in the pauses of such a life, for the intellectual tastes
which anyone may choose to cultivate; people may associate
in doing so; there will be clubs, churches, and colleges by
the thousand; and the adaptable spirit of Protestantism may
be relied upon to lend a pious and philosophical sanction
to any instinct that may deeply move the national mind.
Why should anyone be dissatisfied? Is it not enough that
millionaires splendidly endow libraries and museums, that
the democracy loves them, and that even the Bolsheviks
prize the relics of Christian civilisation when laid out in
that funereal documentary form? Is it not enough that the
field lies open for any young professor in love with his
subject to pursue it hopefully and ecstatically, until perhaps
it begins to grow stale, the face of it all cracked and
wrinkled with little acrid controversies and perverse problems? And when not pressed so far, is it not enough that the
same studies should supply a pleasant postscript to business, a congenial hobby or night-cap for ripe rich elderly
people? May not the ardent humanist still cry (and not
in the wilderness): Let us be well-balanced, let us be cultivated, let us be high-minded; let us control ourselves,
as if we were wild; let us chasten ourselves, as if we had
passions; let us learn the names and dates of all famous
persons; let us travel and see all the pictures that are
starred in Baedeker; let us establish still more complete
museums at home, and sometimes visit them in order to
show them to strangers; let us build still more immense
libraries, containing all known books, good, bad, and indifferent, and let us occasionally write reviews of some of
them, so that the public, at least by hearsay, may learn
which are which.

Why be dissatisfied? . . . Big Business is an amiable
monster, far kindlier and more innocent than anything
Machiavelli could have anticipated, and no less lavish in

its patronage of experiment, invention, and finery than
Bacon could have desired. The discontent of the American
humanists would be unintelligible if they were really
humanists in the old sense; if they represented in some
measure the soul of that young oak, bursting the limits
of Christendom. Can it be that they represent rather the
shattered urn, or some one of its fragments? The leaders,
indeed, though hardly their followers, might pass for rather censorious minds, designed by nature to be the pillars
of some priestly orthodoxy; and their effort, not as yet
very successful, seems to be to place their judgments upon
a philosophical basis. After all, we may actually be witnessing the demise of the genteel tradition, though by a death
more noble and glorious than some of us had looked for.
Instead of expiring of fatigue, or evaporating into a faint
odour of learning and sentiment hanging about Big Business, this tradition, in dying, may be mounting again to its
divine source.

# Lewis Corey [Louis C. Fraina] (1894–1953)

> *A self-taught intellectual and Marxist economist,
> he was born in Italy and grew up in the poverty
> and filth of New York's East Side. At the age
> when other boys were struggling through high
> school, he was already a full-fledged revolution-
> ary, delivering radical speeches on street corners
> for De Leon's Socialist Labor party. After the
> Russian Revolution of 1917, he became director
> of the American Bolshevik Bureau of Informa-
> tion, and when the Communist Party of America
> was formed in 1919, he served as a member of
> the Central Executive Committee and as editor
> of the official party organ,* The Communist.

*Then, in 1922, after a strange series of accusations, exonerations, and counter-accusations, he was repudiated by the party, although he still considered himself an orthodox Marxist.*

# DECLINE
# OF AMERICAN CAPITALISM

Underlying the class-ideological crisis created by the decline of capitalism is a crisis of faith in the old order. More concretely, it is a crisis of the constituent ideals which animate the faith. The ideals of the American dream—the trinity of liberty, opportunity, and progress—were becoming, long before the crisis of the capitalist system, increasingly restricted in scope and unrealizable in practice. They lingered on primarily as a cultural lag: for ideals may persist and affect social action after the material conditions of their origin are no more. Now the breakdown of the ideals is startlingly revealed by the decline of capitalism. The faith of the million-masses begins to crumble.

The stubborn cultural lag identified with the ideals of the American dream is proof of their former vigor and measurable reality. They were, it is true, ideals forged in the fires of the bourgeois revolution in Europe, but they acquired greater scope and realization in the American scene because of the frontier and the absence of feudal hangovers, resulting in more favorable social-economic relations for the practice of liberty, opportunity, and progress. The American dream assumed definite shape and flourished most vigorously in the 1820's–50's. An enormous mass of settlers was absorbed by the frontier, creating an agrarian democracy whose independence and rebellious spirit strongly colored American life. Industry developed

From *The Decline of American Capitalism* (New York: Covici-Friede, 1934), pp. 517–9, 525–6, 535–8.

rapidly, and it was in the small-scale stage which made it "open to all the talents." Restrictions on the right of labor to organize were overthrown. Remnants of semi-feudal tenure in the colonial land system were destroyed. The older aristocracy was breaking down, the new not yet entrenched in power. Free public education was enacted into law, and it measurably included higher learning. The ideals of the American revolution and of Jeffersonian democracy seemed wholly realizable. . . .

[But] developments after the Civil War constantly restricted the reality of the American dream: its ideals disintegrated, were limited in practice, or assumed a different character. Most of the libertarian spirit evaporated. Independence was increasingly replaced by insecurity. Class lines began to harden and government to usurp more repressive powers. Individualism was submerged, except for the freedom granted to capitalist buccaneers, as a constantly greater proportion of the population became direct employees or general dependents of large-scale corporate industry dominated by the financial oligarchy. Opportunity for the mass was more and more limited to survival or slightly improving one's lot within the new institutional setup. The dream became primarily a faith in mere material progress; its old cultural promise was destroyed. But the dream was still vigorous and profoundly affected American life, mainly because of cultural lag, partly because there was still progress in many directions and capitalism, by and large, still "delivered the goods."

The American dream lingers on, for the lag is stubborn. But it now experiences a crisis more serious than any in the past. For former crises did not shatter the dream; they merely destroyed some of its ideals, increasingly limited the realization of others, and gave still others new, if vulgar and unsatisfactory, forms of expression. Material progress and reform helped to sustain the dream's cultural lag; but these very forces (the one ending in monopoly capitalism and imperialism, the other making them acceptable to the mass of the people) prepared the conditions of the decline of capitalism, which turns the American dream into a nightmare. . . .

Mass well-being has become the most important ideal of the American dream for the workers, because of their occupational inflexibility resulting from constantly more rigid class stratification. The ideal was not, however, of bourgeois origin; it was created primarily by the upthrust of the masses and the ideology of the labor movement arising out of the conditions of capitalist development. Bourgeois revolutions called the masses to action but suppressed them after the conquest of power, disregarding their well-being. The industrial revolution was accompanied by increasing mass misery; improvement of the workers' lot in the epoch of capitalist upswing was offset by increasing misery in newly developing industrial nations and in colonial lands. Yet capitalism, by and large, raised considerably the level of mass well-being as a by-product of economic expansion and necessity and in response to the struggles of labor. Not as much, of course, as among other classes; not as much as was possible in view of the immensely augmented productive forces of society. There were recurrent depressions when mass well-being was submerged, and periods of prosperity when the workers did not share in the gains of material progress or saw their relative share decreased. Nor was poverty abolished, although its abolition has been possible these many, many years. But the tendency was upward, if slowly, interruptedly, agonizingly, and there was always the hope of better things to come. Now the hope is killed by the decline of capitalism and its crisis of the system, by mass disemployment, lower wages, and lower standards of living.

The shattering of the ideal of continuously greater mass well-being is of the utmost significance, as the great mass of workers have increasingly interpreted the American dream in terms of improvement on the job. Now jobs become scarce and working conditions worse. Mass well-being is replaced with mass misery, the ideal of the abolition of poverty with a new and wholly unnecessary poverty. Capitalism returns to the epoch of increasing misery. . . .

The bourgeoisie wrought the idea of progress, a concept of the utmost creative significance. It arose out of the struggle waged by the new bourgeois class against feudalism on all fronts: economic, political, cultural. Social relations had to become different, to change, to *move*. But not mere motion: it was a concept of development, of continuous upward movement to new objectives. As the bourgeois revolution thrust its ideals beyond immediate class objectives, so the idea of progress soared beyond its class-economic origins. It released the forces of the human will, created a new approach to the world, made man feel himself capable of mastering his fate.

Faith in progress was particularly vital in the American dream. It was invigorated by a new world taking shape in the wilderness, by an almost complete shattering of the fetters of the past, by an extraordinary economic development and its progressive accompaniments. The ideal arising out of these conditions is thus expressed by Dr. Charles A. Beard:

"Underlying all is a belief that the lot of mankind can be continuously improved by research, invention, and taking thought. This is the philosophy of progress. . . . All legislation, all community action, all individual effort are founded on the assumption that evils can be corrected, problems solved, the ills of life minimized and its blessings multiplied by rational methods, intelligently applied. Essentially by this faith is American civilization justified."

This ideal was always limited and distorted in practice. It is now, in its bourgeois form, a mere pitiable echo of what has been and a tragic ignoring of what might be. For Dr. Beard speaks (in 1932!) as if the ideal was now in action: but what a mockery of progress, of the rational and intelligent, is the social-economic breakdown created by the crisis of the capitalist system! Dr. Beard speaks as if

capitalism is identified with progress everlasting: but capitalism, limiting progress even in the epoch of upswing, now in
its decline openly revolts against progress and all its works,
because they undermine the existing order.

The revolt against progress originates in the movement
of economic forces. . . . Production and realization of surplus value move downward because of the increasingly
higher composition of capital and mass disemployment.
The productivity of labor creates an abundance which
presses upon contracting markets and endangers profit. In-
dustrialization of new regions is either completed or prevented by the contradictions of monopoly capitalism.
Capitalism is undermined by the very productive forces it
called into being. The formerly relative self-destructive
character of capitalist production now becomes absolute.
It resorts to limitation of output on a mass scale: repression
of the productive forces of society. Out of decline and
decay arises the capitalist revolt against economic progress.

The revolt against economic progress becomes an ideological revolt. Progress means the continuous upward movement of society. But capitalism is not eternal; it is not
immune to the law of social succession. Basing himself on
the idea of progress and its manifestations in the dialectical
movement of capitalist production, Marx saw the relations
of a new social order developing within the shell of the
old. Capitalism created collective or social forms of production, the objective basis of socialism. The capitalist
bourgeoisie moved and had its being by creating the industrial proletariat, the objective carrier of socialism. As
this dialectical movement appeared more clearly, threatening the old order, the bourgeois idea of progress began to
change. Where formerly it included the revolutionary
transformation of an old social order by the new, progress
was now limited to mere change and pedestrian reform
within the existing order. Among small but important intellectual groups a whole philosophy arose embodying a reaction against progress: limiting, scoffing, rejecting, mobiliz-

ing all the resources of the human mind to prove that progress was a delusion and a snare. Now the philosophy opposed to progress is seized upon by the capitalist class. For capitalism has outlived its historical utility. It is in the epoch of decline and decay. Progress is now realizable only in a form which endangers capitalist rule, by socialism releasing the creative social-economic forces of society, by the revolutionary struggle for power of the proletariat and its allies. Hence capitalism reacts against progress on all fronts: economic, political, cultural. Progress now again means the necessity of revolutionary change.

State capitalism clings to progress in words. But where is it in practice? The real job of state capitalism is to prop up the old order, to make it more resistant to progress, or socialism. State capitalism merely tries to "freeze" the breakdown and decay of capitalist decline. This eventually manifests itself in the fascist repudiation of the idea of progress. Fascism fuses into a system all the old reactionary ideas opposed to progress and deliberately moves backward to revival of a mixture of Cæsarism and medievalism, which was emphatically rejected by the revolutionary bourgeoisie. Reaction becomes a faith and retrogression its works.

New and finer fulfillments? They are doomed by capitalist decline and decay. New and finer fulfillments of progress are potential only in the revolutionary struggle for power, for socialism and communism.

Thus capitalism is driven to revolt against progress and all the other ideals of the American dream and of the bourgeois revolution. Now, in ideological form, the forces which sustained capitalism turn into their opposites and become its antagonists. For the ideals, seizing upon great masses, are an historical force. The masses believe in them and want them realized, having measurably identified them with their own mixed, groping, yet definitely plebeian aspirations. Cultural lag is identified with the bourgeois form of the ideals, with faith in the possibility of their realization in the existing order. As capitalist decline increasingly limits their already incomplete realization and moves toward their destruction, including destruction of the concrete democratic rights of the workers, the ideals become dangerous, for it is impressed upon the masses that they are realizable only in new forms and in a new social order.

This is the crisis of the American dream, underlying the class-ideological crisis created by the decline of capitalism. The crisis prepares the subjective conditions of fundamental social change. For the objective clash between the old and the new order must become a conscious class struggle, which transforms the quantity of accumulated social-economic changes into the quality of revolutionary action for the new social order. A class, in this case the proletariat, cannot become revolutionary and perform its historic task, cannot carry on the struggle for power, until it has broken the ideological fetters of the old order: it must replace the old faith with its own consciousness and ideals, and make the new world they express acceptable to the other exploited elements of society.

# CHAPTER FIVE

# Liberalism and Democracy

## I

In a society which placed such disproportionate emphasis on the production of material goods there was little room for liberal intellectuals. Business success was by common consent regarded as conclusive evidence of ability, intelligence, and wisdom, even in matters having no relation to economic affairs. "Give out the news that one has just made a killing in the stock market, or robbed some confiding widow of her dower, or swindled the government in some patriotic enterprise," gibed Mencken, "and at once one will discover that one's shabbiness is a charming eccentricity, and one's judgment of wines worth hearing, and one's political hallucinations worthy of attention." On the other hand, the "long-haired gentry" who called themselves "liberals" and "radicals" and "non-partisan" and "intelligentsia" and—"God only knows how many other trick names"—were looked down upon as fault-finders and knockers. As George F. Babbitt told the annual Get-Together Fest of the Zenith Real Estate Board, the ideal of American manhood and culture was not "a lot of cranks sitting around chewing the rag about their Rights and their Wrongs,

but a God-fearing, hustling, successful two-fisted Regular
Guy" ready to sell efficiency and to whoop it up for national
prosperity and whose answer to his critics was a "square-
toed boot that'll teach the grouches and smart alecks to
respect the He-man and get out and root for Uncle Samuel,
U.S.A.!" In such a hostile atmosphere where the good life
was calculated in dollars and cents, the dissident intellectual
unable to find comfort in the flivver, the telephone, the
radio, the movies, and the funnies was an outsider who
either fled to Europe with Ernest Hemingway and F. Scott
Fitzgerald or stayed to scoff with those modern disciples
of Diogenes, Sinclair Lewis and Henry L. Mencken. To
the normal American Babbitt, his critics were freaks who
deliberately disliked their neighbors because they were comfortable and contented, and though stung by their ridicule,
he took comfort in his more practical role. As a commercial rimester put it:

> Babbitts—though we jeer and flout them—
> We could never do without them.
> Artists all—we would be beggars
> Were it not for Butter 'n' Eggers.
>
> For though Art is very swell, it
> Hardly pays unless you sell it.
> And the artist—ain't it funny?—
> Like the Babbitt, values money.
>
> Also rather likes to grab it
> From the much-enduring Babbitt.
> Babbitts great and Babbitts small
> Speaking frankly "Aren't we all?"°

The modern-day Diogenes gained a great reputation jeer-

---

°Berton Braley, "Babbitt Ballads," *Nation's Business*, XVI (Jan., 1928), 29. Reprinted by permission of the publisher, The Chamber of Commerce of the
United States.

ing at useful citizens, said *Nation's Business,* but for all
his talk how much time and money did he give to charity
and to the upbuilding of his community?[1]

In contrast to the exuberant materialism of Babbitt and
his associates, the liberals appeared on the verge of exhaustion. Tired radicals who had gone through the "disillu-
sionizing" process of war seemed to be victims of what
John Dewey described as the "post-war mind." "With the
let up of war, with the issue determined, the tension re-
laxes, and the immediate present regains with added force
its command. Not the arduous labor of reconstruction but
enjoyment of the present, of the gains to be snatched from
using the opportunities of pleasure and profit in things as
they are, captures the mind."[2] Just as the fierce outburst
of materialistic money-making that followed in the immediate wake of the war was due in part to a release from the
unnatural strain of war, so the post-war relaxation of liberal endeavor can be explained as a natural human response.
When the stress of war was removed, the crusading zeal,
the spiritual exhilaration it generated could no longer be
sustained. Liberals who earlier had dreamed of remaking
the world turned at the end of the war with a sigh of relief to the homelier and less exciting satisfactions of peace.
To men in such a mood, the dull, commonplace virtues of
the American businessman no longer seemed contemptuous.
For all his foolishness, his smug faith in comfort and service, Babbitt was not wholly bad. Those who like Walter
Weyl had worn themselves out in the cause of humanity
now appreciated Babbitt's simple joy in the conveniences
of his life and his home. Reform and revolution, Weyl discovered as he grew older, were not everything, and if one
could find satisfaction in the "little busy-nesses" of everyday
experience, the good life was in way of being achieved.*

Others, however, took a less sanguine view of the de-

---

*Walter Weyl, *Tired Radicals.* See page 290.

cline of liberalism. While personally Weyl might attribute loss of the liberal fighting spirit to the mellowing of age, Floyd Dell, who also belonged to the pre-war generation, contended that the liberal movement had simply reached the point of bankruptcy. When its few tangible social achievements were matched against the enormous obligations incurred in the name of peace and reform, there remained an overwhelming deficit which few men had the courage to face. Because of this defeatist psychosis, Dell concluded, the liberals had fallen into a numbed state of "intellectual shell-shock." As a result, said Vernon Louis Parrington, middle-aged liberals, "whose hair is growing thin and the lines of whose figures are no longer what they were," found themselves "in the unhappy predicament of being treated as mourners at their own funerals." But, insisted Parrington, they were celebrating the wrong funeral —he and his generation were not yet authentic corpses. It was the faith of America that was dead, and Babbitt, "an empty soul," was symbol of that common emptiness.

For a hundred and fifty years America had sustained its hopes on the rich nourishment provided by the Enlightenment. "Faith in the excellence of man, in the law of progress, in the ultimate reign of justice, in the conquest of nature, in the finality and sufficiency of democracy, faith in short in the excellence of life, was the great driving force in those earlier, simpler days." But this "noble dream" had been slowly dissipated by an encompassing materialism in which "faith in machinery came to supersede faith in man." And now, in the twenties, Parrington lamented, America had fallen so low that "our faith in justice, progress, the potentialities of human nature, the excellence of democracy, is stricken with pernicious anemia, and even faith in the machine is dying." By 1925 liberalism had grown so infirm and politically impotent that Glenn Frank, editor and President of the University of Wisconsin, reported that he found very few "realistically minded liberals" who retained any confidence in the "practical possibilities of office-holding liberalism." With the conservatives firmly in power, the future looked dark for liberalism.[3]

Then, unexpectedly, with the coming of the depression and the election of Roosevelt, the liberals were catapulted into power. Though the Democratic party was a working coalition of liberals, conservatives, and machine politicians, President Franklin Roosevelt declared at the outset that his party was to be "the party of militant liberalism," and in the years immediately after 1933 the liberal outlook prevailed. While undeniably there was a pragmatic and opportunistic streak in New Deal liberalism, it was nevertheless consistent in its view that government should help the people "to gain a larger social justice." As Richard Hofstadter has noted, "Where Progressivism had capitalized on a growing sense of the ugliness under the successful surface of American life, the New Deal flourished on a sense of the human warmth and the technological potentialities that could be found under the surface of its inequities and its post-depression poverty." But like Progressivism, the liberalism of the thirties was a reaffirmation of faith in America. Just as Herbert Croly warned the nation at the beginning of the century that the fulfillment of the American national promise demanded a hard and inextinguishable faith, so Henry A. Wallace, Secretary of Agriculture and Vice-President under Roosevelt, reminded his countrymen in 1934 that the reforms of the New Deal would never succeed unless they were inspired in their hearts by "a larger vision than the hard-driving profit motives of the past."* Yet, frank and realistic, Wallace agreed with Croly that faith was no substitute for good works. Good intentions were not enough—there must be set up such social machinery as would give the human heart opportunity for translating its aspirations into practical action.[4]

*Henry A. Wallace, *The New Frontier*. See page 295.

Through innovation the New Deal searched for acceptable solutions to problems rather than imposing preconceived solutions. Its most "socialistic" undertaking, the Tennessee Valley Authority, caused private enterprise to flourish in an area where previously it had barely existed.

## II

Though the New Deal reaffirmed democratic principles, back in the 1920's democracy had come under slashing attack. In the cynicism that followed the war, wrote Parrington, "the democratic liberalism of 1917 was thrown away like an empty whiskey-flask." Clever young men and beardless philosophers who had recently discovered Nietzsche began to poke fun at democracy. Their leader was the irreverent Henry L. Mencken, who defined democracy as "that system of government under which the people, having sixty million native-born adult whites to choose from, including thousands who are handsome and many who are wise, pick out a Coolidge to be head of the state." A recent convert to behaviorism, Mencken had discovered that psychology had some amusing comments to make on politics. From army intelligence tests he had picked up the concept of the moron which he used as a bludgeon to flay democracy.° Flippantly defining democracy as "booboc-racy," he suggested that the mob—the raw material of democracy—was composed in the main of "men and women who have not got beyond the ideas and emotions of child-hood, hovers, in mental age, around the time of puberty, and chiefly below it." According to Mencken, the minds of these permanent adolescents could not grasp even the simplest abstractions; their so-called thinking was "purely a bio-chemical process exactly comparable to what goes on in a barrel of cider." Since all their thought was on the level of a few primitive appetites and emotions, it was a sheer impossibility to educate them, and therefore they could only be governed by playing upon their fears and prejudices.[5]

For all his flippancy and sarcasm, Mencken's was a serious indictment of democracy. If the masses were never to rise above sex appeals and belly needs, then there was not much hope for a democratic society. Certainly the belief that the majority of the people were unable to think for themselves found support in higher military and business circles. A U.S. Army *Training Manual* issued in 1928 defined democracy as "a government of the masses. Authority derived through mass meeting or any other forms of 'direct' expression. Results in mobocracy. Attitude toward property is communistic—negating property rights. Attitude toward law is that the will of the majority shall regulate, whether

°Henry L. Mencken, *Democratic Man*. See page 302.

In the thirties there were some who thought the answer to America's problems was a fascist dictatorship. Disillusionment with democracy and admiration for Hitler and his methods led to formation of the German-American Bund with its swastikas and Nazi salutes.

it be based upon deliberation or governed by passion, prejudice, and impulse, without restraint or regard to consequences. Results in demagogism, license, agitation, discontent, anarchy." In similar vein, the members of the National Association of Manufacturers were informed that the "working masses" constituted "a great class below" their employers. Left alone, the masses instinctively held to "right principles," but at the same time they were "unwittingly susceptible" to the demogogic appeals of agitators and "professional uplifters." From the viewpoint of its critics, the great problem in a democracy was the real and ever-present danger of the irresponsible masses dominating the "thinking people." As evidence of the perils of mass power, businessmen were asked to consider the mob's irrational demands: "Hear the chorused voice of the multitude screaming for an increase of compensation in direct proportion to a reduction in hours of labor. Listen to the strange philosophies of the living-wage, the check-off system, the minimum wage, government controlled children, the closed union shop, and the socialistic redistributions of wealth." In their deep antipathy for democracy, business spokesmen initially hailed the Fascist coup in Italy as "the most creditable development in human history," and Mussolini was praised as a "fine type of business executive." Some hoped the "same sound philosophy" was developing in America.[6]

Such disparagements of democracy did not go unchallenged. Nor were the majority of Americans convinced, for as Charles A. Beard pointed out, nothing was easier than the game of attacking democracy by citing scandalous incidents, absurd episodes, and the idiotic antics of some elected persons. It merely turned against democracy the weapons once employed against monarchy—the scurrilous reporting of authentic cases of imbecility, murder, poison, arson, adultery, bastardy, corruption, drunkenness, useless wars, and other examples of royal misconduct. Although eighteenth-century republican agitators thought they had made an unanswerable argument for their cause, in the end, said the historian, it produced nothing more important than amusement. If the United States were composed as Mencken asserted almost exclusively of beings without courage, ability, aspiration, or honor, then, reasoned Edmund Wilson, they could never have settled the West nor even made "the effort necessary to sustain a single street of shops," much less establish a great nation. Likewise dissenting, G. K. Chesterton, the British writer, accused the elitists and Menckenites of persecuting the common man and contended their anti-democracy was "as much stuffed with cant as their democracy." It was easy to weary of democracy and to cry out for an intellectual aristocracy. But, said Chesterton, "the trouble is that every intellectual aristocracy seems to have been utterly unintellectual." Although it was the fad to say that most modern blunders were due to the common man, it was his opinion that the most appalling had in fact been due to the uncommon man. For example, Adam

Smith, whom he cited as an uncommon man, advanced a theological theory that Providence had so made the world that men might be happy through their selfishness, a doctrine held sacred by the business elite of the twenties. But "the common man soon found out just how happy—in the slums where they left him and in the slump to which they led him."[7]

Most of those who argued against democracy in theory did so from their dislike of it in practice. They condemned democracy because it was too democratic. Since the practice was precisely what the theory intended, those critics were not arguing logically, but merely expressing a prejudice. For a long time, at least since the beginning of the national existence, America had been trying to improve the condition of the masses. Over the years the nation had been steadily gaining on this ideal, but "instead of celebrating the victory, the fastidious withdraw their skirts, anxious housewives deplore the passing of 'the good, old-fashioned servant,' and uneasy employers complain of the increase of wages and the standard of living." So argued Professor Ralph Barton Perry of Harvard, who found that while democracy had not been an unqualified success, neither had it proved a complete failure.[*] In his opinion the charge of failure was due in part to unrealistic expectations of success. Democracy had been expected to work miracles almost automatically. But as the depression taught, democracy was dependent on knowledge and wisdom beyond all other forms of government. Democracy, as the jurist Felix Frankfurter explained, "seeks to prevail" when the complexities of modern industrial life "make a demand upon knowledge and understanding never made before, and when the forces inimical to the play of reason have power and subtlety unknown in the past." Those who were filled with doleful forebodings about democracy not only overlooked the fact that the most brilliant civilization in recorded his-

[*]Ralph Barton Perry, *The Alleged Failure of Democracy*. See page 308.

tory was a civilization born under a pure democracy at Athens, but in their desire for an easy way out proposed to go back and begin over again, modeling modern American institutions on those ancient forms which their revolutionary ancestors had denounced as tyrannical. Yet, as was becoming increasingly apparent in the thirties, the Fascist governments of Mussolini and Hitler had not discovered any panaceas for the perplexing problems of modern industrial life, but had only "created out of disorder by terror of disorder" a brutal government of gangs. If the real test of any government was "what does it do for the average man?"—then compared to these reactionary tyrannies with their militarism, violence, and regimentation, democracy in America was a stupendous success.[8]

## III

The reactionary and materialistic temper of the twenties made all progressive and liberal programs seem sentimental, inept, and rather hopelessly out of touch with things. "The decadent religion of Liberalism" was denounced by the Right for having no "standards," and dismissed by the Left as a "flabby relativism" based upon a want of conviction. "It was useless," conceded the disillusioned muckraker Lincoln Steffens, "to fight for the right under our system; petty reforms in politics, wars without victories, just peace, were impossible." In the vanguard of liberal reform in prewar days, Steffens had written countless exposures of the shame of the cities, states, and corporate business between 1900 and 1910—as he said, "narrating rather bitterly the defeated struggles of heroic leaders to reform politics and government." If, after the war and the peace, he had forsaken the heroic course of the old muckraking days and had lost his "illusion about democracy as the road to democracy," Steffens proved a notable exception to the general rule that old reformers became "tired radicals." For he cast aside his liberalism only to embrace Communism. After

viewing the Russian Revolution at first hand, he came to
the conclusion that the Communists would "win out" and
"save the world." Despairing of the "good" people and
evolutionary reform, Steffens abandoned his role of "sentimental rebel" to become a prophet of revolution. He conveyed his vision in an historical parable called *Moses in
Red* (1926) which treated the revolt of Israel under Moses
as the classic pattern of revolution.* Since he himself had
been corrupted by "the easy life of the old culture," Steffens felt obliged to admire the revolution from a distance.
But, like Moses, he pointed the way to the Promised Land.
By the beginning of the thirties, as a home-grown radical,
he had become something of a hero; and when his *Autobiography* appeared in 1931, it was accepted as "almost a
textbook of revolution" and doubtless helped persuade
many idealistic young Americans to take a pro-Communist
position.[9]

Among these fighting young Communists, being a Socialist—like being a liberal—meant the person was "not really
thinking" in realistic terms of the class struggle. In seeking
"a New Deal for the world," they believed fervently in
the power of historical forces to move the mass of mankind
inexorably toward the glorious world of pure Communism.
As sectarian ideologues, they were rigidly committed to the
Soviet Union, the Communist Party, and the Marxist dox-
ology. To them "human aims seemed more important than
national goals," and they "talked more about the hope for
an ideal society than the benefits of the existing one." The
movement proved a haven for intellectuals who preferred
theories to facts, and much time was wasted in "endless
meetings" and "passionate speeches" about such unreal
subjects as the "culture of the working class." Yet, as Howard Zinn has said, it is all too easy to be witty at their
expense. "The stage whispering, the posturing, the dogma,
the in-fighting; the Talmudic debates among Trotskyists,

*Lincoln Steffens, *Why I Am a Leninist.* See page 315.

Communists, Lovestonites, old Wobblies; the hypocrisy, the self-righteousness" appear ridiculous today. But when measured against the evils which the Left faced in the 1930's: "the hungry children, the evicted families shivering in the streets, the men standing in long lines for a day's work, the Negroes lynched in the South and jammed into filthy ghettos in the North" and "overseas, the Japanese butchering China, Mussolini's tanks rumbling toward Ethiopian farmers carrying spears, German warplanes bombing Barcelona, Hitler beginning the deadly roundup of the Jews"—then these young Quixotes appear more realistic, for they at least took a stand against the crimes, here and abroad, and joined the fight against Fascism before it became respectable.[10]

Most important for American intellectuals was the indisputable fact that the Communists had assumed the leadership in the world struggle against international Fascism. A month after Hitler seized power in Germany, the *Daily Worker* called for "A United Front to Fight Fascism," and shortly afterward the *New Masses* published a manifesto against the Nazis. Hatred of Fascism, in the opinion of Daniel Aaron, brought many American writers and intellectuals into the Communist orbit who otherwise might never have had anything to do with the movement. The high point of anti-Fascist sentiment in the thirties was the Spanish Civil War in which the Loyalist cause was enthusiastically accepted by an overwhelming majority of the American intelligentsia as the cause of humanity against the brutish powers of darkness.[11]

Although a considerable number of American writers and intellectuals turned Left in the thirties, not all were caught by the Marxist dialectic. Some, derisively dubbed "fellow travelers," merely sympathized with Communism and adopted a pro-Soviet attitude; others, more independent, joined John Dewey in the call for a new radical party. A perennial liberal, Dewey in 1934 believed a second American Revolution loomed ahead. While it might not be *the* Revolution to the disciples of Marx, at the same time Dewey insisted there was to be "no truckling to capitalism." What Dewey actually proposed was, in the words of Norman Thomas, "an intellectualized version of a watered-down socialism," but it was never Communism. For Communism held no fascination for Dewey.° As early as 1928, reporting on a trip to the Soviet Union in the *New Republic*, he pronounced the Revolution "a great success" but wrote off Communism as "a frost."[12]

The first rift between American intellectuals and Communism opened at the time of the Moscow trials of 1936–38, during which Stalin methodically purged thousands of so-called "enemies of the people." They were deeply shocked to discover that Leninism was, after all, "the faith of a persecuting and propagating minority of fanatics led by hypocrites" and Stalin a Mahomet, not a Debs. According to Irving Howe and Lewis Coser, the mass treason trials "marked a major step in the collapse of morale among radical American intellectuals," for it was sensed by everyone involved that the moral fate of radicalism was at stake. The Leftist intellectual world was ripped into bitter factions. The anti-Stalinists sponsored a "Commission of Inquiry" headed by John Dewey which cross-examined Leon Trotsky in Mexico City and concluded that Soviet charges of counter-revolution were false. Party leaders, while pretending all was well in the "workers' fatherland," viciously denounced "renegade" intellectuals and summarily excommunicated doubting fellow travelers. But the final break, "the moment of truth," came in the summer of 1939 when Stalin signed a non-aggression pact with Hitler. For Lewis Corey, author of *The Decline of American Capitalism* and the leading Marxist economist in the country, the shock was so great that it not only cooled his Communist sympathies but destroyed his belief in Marxism itself. Since the flirtation of a great many American writers and

°John Dewey, *Why I Am Not a Communist.* See page 327.

intellectuals with the Communist party had been built upon anti-Fascism, when the Soviet Union deserted the fight against Fascism, they became disenchanted once and for all—for them, Marxism had proved a failure and the mission of the proletariat a delusion.[13]

The epitaph, however, was written, not by a disillusioned American intellectual of the thirties, but by an unknown expatriate in Paris in 1928: "Russia . . . I think . . . will become a sort of fat, complaisant, second-rate United States. It is rapidly adopting the American economic vision because the revolution cleared a way for it. When the country becomes properly Americanized, say in fifty years, it will be producing hordes and hordes of Russian Harold Bell Wrights and Edgar Guests, while the one time Dostoievskys will have become merely classical legends, like Shakespeare in England today. . . . The country will become industrialized, radioized, movieized, and standardized, the huge population of illiterate peasants will be taught how to read advertisements, newspapers, and bibles, the country will placidly settle down to the preoccupation of money grubbing."[14]

# Readings:

# Liberalism and Democracy

## Walter Weyl (1873-1919)

*A veteran Progressive, he gained a national reputation with the publication in 1912 of* **The New Democracy.** *One of the really significant books of the day, it called for a liberal, non-utopian program of democratic reform which would emphasize social rather than private ethics, common rather than individual responsibility. As one of the founding editors of the* **New Republic,** *he was slow to catch the war fever, but the appeal of the Wilson formula of "peace without victory" finally won him over. Though the war always taxed his conscience, the peace brought complete disillusionment, and he retreated from politics and reform to private life and personal consolations.*

## TIRED RADICALS

I once knew a revolutionist who thought that he loved

Humanity but for whom Humanity was merely a club with which to break the shins of the people he hated. He hated all who were comfortable and all who conformed. He hated the people he opposed and he hated those who opposed his opponents in a manner different from his. Zeal for the cause was his excuse for hating, but really he was in love with hate and not with any cause.

The war came, and this vibrant, humorless man, this neurotic idealist who was almost a genius, found a wider vent for his emotion. His hatred, without changing its character, changed its incidence. He learned to hate Germans, Bolshevists, and radicals. He completed the full circle and soon was consorting most incongruously with those whom he had formerly attacked. Today nothing is left of his radicalism or his always leaky consistency; nothing is left but his hatred. At times he hates himself. He would always hate himself could he find no one else to hate. He is becoming half-reactionary, half-cynical. He will end— But who knows how anyone will end?

Radicalism loses little in the defection of this unconsciously sadistical agitator, for despite his stormy eloquence he was always less embarrassing to his enemies than his friends. His case, however, suggests an inherent weakness in radical movements, an inevitable mortality among radicals, traceable to wars and other calamities, but due chiefly to the manner in which radicals are recruited and the kind of men they are.

There are two large, but not sharply defined groups of radicals: radicals by environment and radicals by temperament. The first are usually the slower and surer-footed because their course is controlled by the rut in which they live; the latter are quicker, more violent, more uncompromising, less realistic, because their radicalism springs from within. They would be rebels in Paradise and reformers in the Garden of Eden. They do not depend on environment for their passion but on their own psychological disequilibrium, their unsatisfied emotions, their agonizing perceptions of the gulf between their ideals and a world that is always out of joint. These men hate all dogmas and conventions that press down on them and they possess the gift of rebellion. But many of them are ill-grounded in their beliefs, for they have chosen a philosophy to suit their nerves, as one chooses a wall-paper. Give them a war or some other excitement and their emotion is deflected, and their radical ideas "cease upon the midnight without pain."

There are epochs in history when humanity becomes tired and emotions age quicker than usual, and radicals disappear. In the last centuries of the Western Roman Empire, discouraged reformers retired within themselves. Our own Civil War depleted the store of our emotion and for a generation put an end to American idealism. So, also, the aborted Russian Revolution of 1905, which destroyed Russian radicalism for a decade, or at least drove it underground. In such periods of reaction men who might have been rebels become saints or debauchés, depending on temperament and circumstances. At times this day of reaction is brief, a flicker of darkness, a thin black line in a brilliant spectrum. In all these periods, long or short, radicalism declines and radicals fall away.

At worst, however, it is not a unique calamity, for even in good times age deals harshly with radicals. Adolescence is the true day for revolt, the day when obscure forces, as mysterious as growth, push us, trembling, out of our narrow lives into the wide throbbing life beyond self. But one cannot forever remain adolescent and long before a man's arteries begin to harden, he sees things more as his father and grandfather saw them. Once he becomes an ancestor he imbibes respect for ancestors and for what they thought. As young radicals grow older they marry pleasant wives, beget interesting children, and begin to build homes in the country, and their zeal cools. Life, they now think, is more than reform or revolution. There are the lilies of the field, as sweet to radicals as to conservatives, and as softly beautiful as in the days of Solomon's glory. Life is old and tenaciously conservative, and so is Nature—the stars, the sea, the mountains—and so is Society; and what we are trying to do is only what futile generations long dead and rotted also tried to do. What is the use of these endless efforts to budge the immovable Earth? What use even to look ahead? You "wished to know the secrets of the future"? So Sylvestre Bonnard apostrophizes the perverse beauty, Leuconöé, dead these nineteen hundred years. "That future is now the past, and we know it well. Of a truth you were foolish to worry yourself about so small a matter."

After all, thinks the tired radical, each of us is bounded by his own tight skin, and his life is wrapped up in his own sensations. If I must have a world revolution to amuse me so much the worse; he is happier who can dig his garden and be content. Why fret? Let God in His own appointed time reform the world that He has been rash enough to create.

Such is the course from radical thought and action, from intense preoccupation with the affairs of humanity, to self—self-culture, self-indulgence. Those who return to self after wandering through a wilderness of altruism, acquire anew something of the child's fresh relish for simple experiences. They find all sorts of important little busy-nesses and discover in the small world all the absorbing interests in miniature that they abandoned in the great world. The wearied Charles the Fifth, abdicating as Holy Roman Emperor, takes up life again in a pleasant little garden in Estremadura. The deposed statesman who is sent to jail recovers his interest in life from a solitary blade of grass forcing its way up between the flagstones of the prison yard. So the tired radical in his smaller way applies his grand passion for Universal Housekeeping to a microscopic farm, and he who aspired to overturn Society (that obese, ponderous and torpid Society that hates to be overturned) ends by fighting in a dull

Board of Directors of a village library for the inclusion of certain books. To what little uses do we descend and how gratefully!

If I were the United States of America I would give a few acres, an agreeable wife, two or three docile children and a sufficient tale of kine and swine to every discouraged radical, replenishing him suitably like Job after his trials. I would make him sovereign over these acres and leave him there and forget him. I would not let him loose on the path which he had tired of treading. For progress is halted by these tired radicals who do not know that they have ceased to be radicals. They turn into pillars of salt. There they stand, aging every moment as though aging were all they had to do. Unconsciously they become sensible, glacially sensible. They become expert in the science of Impossibles; they know better than anyone else why everything is impossible because have they not failed in everything? Oh, how preternaturally practical they become! How they grow enamored of the Indifferent because better than the Bad, and of the Bad because better than the Worse! How they decline into feeble, dwarfed enthusiasms, the pale ghosts of their former ambitions! But let their decline be smooth and their transition easy. Let them tranquilly convince themselves that "every nation has the government it deserves," that "progress comes by good will alone," that the world will better itself or that it is past bettering, and let them accept all the other sedative aphorisms that end gently in a quietistic philosophy. Let them even grow into clever reactionaries, or after shedding all ideals, become absorbed in business, practical politics or pleasure, retaining only an ironical, half-regretful pity for their callow days of radicalism. Let them go peacefully into the great monastery of Effortlessness, where things are left to God or Inevitable Social Evolution, and whence strife and conflict and zeal are banished.

There is no use crying over those who are graduated out of Radicalism, for the young trees grow where the old trees die. In truth it is the growth of the young that kills the old. The aging, tiring radical, who has unwittingly given hostages to Society and knows what butcher's bills and baker's bills and the wife's dress and the children's shoes cost and what a steady job means, and who has learned in the course of the years what slow monotonous things revolutions are, is also discouraged by the radical fledglings who being younger and more ignorant are also more untrammeled, vehement and appealing than he. After all, radicalism is a young man's job and only a few older guides are needed, men who preserve an even balance between imagination and judgment, between enthusiasm and experience, and who though old are young. Every radical movement is a relay race in which a fresh runner seizes the torch from the hand of him who lags. It is better that the tired radicals who have run their course should drop out of the race. Let us therefore not berate them and let us beware of charging them with inconsistency, for they are consistent with the way of life and the law of growth. Let us rather give thanks to them and wish them Godspeed for the youngest of us in time may go their way.

# Henry A. Wallace (1888-1965)

*An Iowa farmer and one of the most controversial figures of American politics, he took to Washington his own vision of the promised land, a determination to slay whatever dragons stood in his way, and an intense hunger for social justice. As Secretary of Agriculture under Roosevelt, he introduced many programs which eventually became firm elements of modern farm and foreign policy—output controls, price supports, easyterm sales on surpluses to needy countries, and so on. Although he was Roosevelt's running mate in*

*1940, he broke with the administration over the
Cold War. Deserted by the New Dealers, he
continued to argue for friendliness toward
Russia, first as an editor of the* New Republic,
*then as the unsuccessful Presidential candidate
of the Progressive party in 1948.*

# THE NEW FRONTIER

When those forty thousand undisciplined slaves, the Children of Israel, left Egypt, it was possible for them to reach their promised land within a few months. But they were not fit to march a straight course, enter and take possession. The older men and women among them thought of everything in terms of the fleshpots of Egypt. Before the promised land could be attained it was necessary for the younger generation, hardened by travels in the wilderness, to come to maturity.

We have been forced away from the fleshpots. When our stock market crashed in 1929 it was plain that we would have to abandon them. We, too, know something about a new land and how it may be reached, but we are not yet fit to go in and take possession. Too many of us would like one last round with those fleshpots and golden calves. It may be that many of our younger people have been sufficiently hardened by suffering in our economic wilderness. But all will have to come to a more effective maturity before the new land can be fully possessed. Advance guards sent out to estimate the cost of the march tell us that there are giants in the way.

I am sometimes accused of undue idealism; but I know very well that it will not do to hope too much of the generation of which I am a part. It is simply impossible for us to let go overnight of the habits and beliefs of a life-

From *New Frontiers* (New York: Reynal & Hitchcock, 1934), pp. 269–77. Reprinted by permission of Mrs. Ila B. Wallace, Executrix.

time. Younger people, if they will, can easily accomplish changes which seem impossible to older people.

Unfortunately, many of the oncoming generation now in our schools, or idling in our homes, are handicapped by an inheritance of past concepts, bitterly complicated by the present stalemate. They are stirred into potentially menacing forms of protest by the fact that the present world does not seem to want their services. If misled by demagogues and half-baked educators, they may be inclined to assume more and more that the world owes them not only a living but a limousine. Their restlessness and present disillusionment can be fatal or infinitely constructive, depending upon which side they wake up on.

After all, we middle-aged, middle-course, people have some hard thinking and many hard jobs to do, before we can reasonably expect to arouse our young to hope for an enduring democracy. Talk alone will not lead them to consolidate the position we now strive to hold, and push forward to something better.

The Children of Israel's problems did not come to an end after they had crossed the borders, or even after they had taken possession of their promised land. Their real troubles as a people had then only begun. They had put behind them a vague, nomadic wandering, but they still had to adapt themselves in some measure to the commercial features of the Canaanite civilization. Their old frontier was gone. They had to work on new frontiers. These problems, in many respects strikingly modern, provoked the strife and turmoil which resulted in the tremendous literature of the prophets and the historical records contained in Chronicles and Kings. Amos, that farmer prophet of the hill country of Judah, first raised in dramatic form the problem of social justice, fair treatment of debtors, and balanced prices.

Physically, and in other ways also, the basic structure of our land of yesterday had been torn to pieces. By the raw pioneer rules of first stakes we have encamped as migrants and have taken greedily and unevenly of its wealth. A few of us, in consequence, have much more than we can comfortably or decently spend or handle; yet most of us have too little for comfort, decency and hope of a general progress. . . .

The old frontier was real. There were Indians and fear of foreign conquest. People in the older Colonies or States had to stand together against actual perils on the edge of a new civilization.

Their determination to stand together was continually renewed by romantic tales of many unknown kinds of wealth out on the frontier, of precious metals, and fertile valleys, although as a matter of fact, the old frontier was all too often a place of ragged, barbed-wire fences, dusty roads, unpainted shacks. Nevertheless, the hopes and fears that existed in the old frontier furnished a unity to our national life. For a hundred and fifty years we felt it was manifest destiny to push onward, until the Pacific Coast was reached, until all the fertile lands between had been plowed and bound together by railroads and paved highways.

The obvious physical task to which we set ourselves has been accomplished; and in so doing, we have destroyed in large measure the thing which gave us hope and unity as a people.

We now demand a new unity, a new hope. There are many spiritual and mental frontiers yet to be conquered, but they lead in many different directions and our hearts have not yet fully warmed to any one of them. They do not point in an obvious single direction as did that downright physical challenge which, for so many generations, existed on the Western edge of our life. Now we have come to the time when we must search our souls and the relationship of our souls and bodies to those of other human beings.

Can we build up a unified, national cultural life, unique, outstanding, one that will reinforce the cultural life of the entire world? Can we leave something that contributes toward giving life meaning, joy and beauty for generations to come?

During the sixteenth, seventeenth, eighteenth and nineteenth centuries, ideas took possession of our fathers and grandfathers which made them resolute hard workers, men of iron, equally good as Indian fighters, pioneer farmers, and captains of industry. They suffered and forged ahead in the world, believing that there was something prophetically worthy in all they did. Progress Westward, land-ward, and wealth-ward was their continual urge. They exploited not only natural resources but the generations which came after. We glorify these men, grabbers and exploiters that they were, and marvel at their conquests. But they did not know how to live with each other and they did not know how to teach the American nation to live with other nations.

The keynote of the new frontier is cooperation just as that of the old frontier was individualistic competition. The mechanism of progress of the new frontier is social invention, whereas that of the old frontier was mechanical invention and the competitive seizure of opportunities for wealth. Power and wealth were worshiped in the old days. Beauty and justice and joy of spirit must be worshiped in the new.

Many of the most lively, intimate expressions of spirit spring from the joyous, continuous contact of human beings with a particular locality. They feel the age-long spirit of this valley or that hill each with its trees and rocks and special tricks of weather, as the seasons unfold in their endless charm. If life can be made secure in each community and if the rewards of the different communities are distributed justly, there will flower in every community not only those who attain joy in daily, productive work well done; but also those who paint and sing and tell stories with the flavor peculiar to their own valley, well-loved hill, or broad prairie. And so we think of cooperative communities not merely in a competent commercial sense but also from the standpoint of people who are helping unfold each other's lives in terms of the physical locality and tradition of which they are a part.

In this way, every community can become something distinctly precious in its own right. Children will not try to escape as they grow up. They will look ahead to the possibility of enriching the traditions of their ancestors. They will feel it is a privilege to learn to live with the soil and the neighbors of their fathers. Such communities will be strung like many-colored beads on the thread of the nation and the varied strings of beads will be the glory of the world.

The pettiness of small communities will disappear as their economic disadvantages disappear. The people of small communities, rid of the pettiness which grows of economic fear, will be free to realize that community success may be truly measured only in terms of contribution to a spirit of world unity, even though political and economic ties may be very loose.

In the old days, we could not trust ourselves with joy and beauty because they ran counter to our competitive search for wealth and power. Men of the old days, whether Protestant or Catholic, accepted implicitly the discipline of the Protestant Ethic (see Weber's *The Protestant Ethic and the Spirit of Capitalism*). The men of the new day must have their social discipline comparable in its power with that of the inner drive toward the hard-working, competitive frugality of the old frontier. People may actually work harder than they did on the old frontier, but their motive will be different. They may make and use more mechanical inventions. They may do more to increase the wealth-producing power of the race.

But their efforts will, of necessity, be continually moved by the spirit of cooperative achievement. They will devise ways in which the monetary mechanism can be modified to distribute the rewards of labor more uniformly. They will work with disinterested spirit to modify the governmental and political machinery so that there is a balanced relationship between prices, an even flow of employment, and a far-wider possibility of social justice and social charity.

So enlisted, men may rightfully feel that they are serving a function as high as that of any minister of the Gospel. They will not be Socialists, Communists or Fascists, but plain men trying to gain by democratic methods the professed objectives of the Communists, Socialists and Fascists: security, peace, and the good life for all.

In their efforts they will not allow their work to be divided or embittered by the dogma or prejudice of any narrow, superficially logical, political or religious sect.

Some will seek for the fountains of an abundant life in renewed artistic, religious, and scientific inspiration. They will not, I trust, accept the animal view of human nature, put forth by the biologists and the economists of the 19th century. Of necessity, they will recognize competitive individualists and competitive nations and deal with them, as the anachronisms they are, treating them kindly, firmly, and carefully.

But the new frontiersman will be continually seeking for his fellows those satisfactions which are mutually enriching. The nature of these satisfactions can only be faintly shadowed now. They exist in a land as strange and far as was America in 1491. In this land of ageless desire we are all striving newcomers. It is not a mushy, sentimental frontier, but one of hard realities, requiring individual and social discipline beyond that of the old frontiers. It lies within us and all about us. A great seer of the human heart who lived nineteen hundred years ago called it the Kingdom of Heaven. He knew that the tiny spark of divine spirit found in each individual could be fanned into an all-consuming flame, an intense passion for fair play, man to man, and man to woman, in the little time that we are here. In the Sermon on the Mount, He spoke of the rules of the Kingdom of Heaven.

The land beyond the new frontier will be conquered by the continuous social inventions of men whose hearts are free from bitterness, prejudice, hatred, greed and fear; by men whose hearts are aflame with the extraordinary beauty of the scientific, artistic and spiritual wealth now before us, if only we reach out confidently, together.

# Henry L. Mencken (1880–1956)

*A lifelong newspaperman, he was temperamentally a "censor-baiting" subversive individualist and fundamentally a sentimental middle-class German-American who loved music, beer, and cigars. From 1906 on he wrote for the Baltimore* Sun *but held several "left-hand jobs," becoming in 1914 an editor of the* Smart Set *and from 1924 to 1933 serving as editor of the* American Mercury. *Hiding "a conservative's taste under a firebrand's vocabulary," he exerted a tremendous influence over the literary-minded youth of the 1910's and early 1920's.*

## DEMOCRATIC MAN

Democracy came into the Western World to the tune of sweet, soft music. There was, at the start, no harsh bawling from below; there was only a dulcet twittering from above. Democratic man thus began as an ideal being, full of ineffable virtues and romantic wrongs—in brief, as Rous-

From *Notes on Democracy,* by H. L. Mencken, pp. 3–11, 15–7. Copyright 1926 by Alfred A. Knopf, Inc., and renewed 1954 by H. L. Mencken. Reprinted by permission of the publisher.

seau's noble savage in smock and jerkin, brought out of the
tropical wilds to shame the lords and masters of the civilized lands. The fact continues to have important consequences to this day. It remains impossible, as it was in the
Eighteenth Century, to separate the democratic idea from
the theory that there is a mystical merit, an esoteric and
ineradicable rectitude, in the man at the bottom of the
scale—that inferiority, by some strange magic, becomes a
sort of superiority—nay, the superiority of superiorities.
Everywhere on earth, save where the enlightenment of
the modern age is confessedly in transient eclipse, the
movement is toward the completer and more enamoured
enfranchisement of the lower orders. Down there, one
hears, lies a deep, illimitable reservoir of righteousness and
wisdom, unpolluted by the corruption of privilege. What
baffles statesmen is to be solved by the people, instantly
and by a sort of seraphic intuition. Their yearnings are
pure; they alone are capable of a perfect patriotism; in
them is the only hope of peace and happiness on this
lugubrious ball. The cure for the evils of democracy is
more democracy!

This notion, as I hint, originated in the poetic fancy of
gentlemen on the upper levels—sentimentalists who, observing to their distress that the ass was over-laden, proposed
to reform transport by putting him into the cart. A stale
Christian bilge ran through their veins, though many of
them, as it happened, toyed with what is now called Mod-
ernism. They were the direct ancestors of the more sac-
charine Liberals of to-day, who yet mouth their tattered
phrases and dream their preposterous dreams. I can find
no record that these phrases, in the beginning, made much
impression upon the actual objects of their rhetoric. Early
democratic man seems to have given little thought to the
democratic ideal, and less veneration. What he wanted
was something concrete and highly materialistic—more to
eat, less work, higher wages, lower taxes. He had no apparent belief in the acroamatic virtue of his own class,

and certainly none in its capacity to rule. His aim was not
to exterminate the baron, but simply to bring the baron
back to a proper discharge of baronial business. When,
by the wild shooting that naturally accompanies all mob
movements, the former end was accidentally accomplished,
and men out of the mob began to take on baronial airs,
the mob itself quickly showed its opinion of them by butchering them deliberately and in earnest. Once the pikes
were out, indeed, it was a great deal more dangerous to
be a tribune of the people than to be an ornament of
the old order. The more copiously the blood gushed, the
nearer that old order came to resurrection. The Paris
proletariat, having been misled into killing its King in
1793, devoted the next two years to killing those who had
misled it, and by the middle of 1796 it had another King
in fact, and in three years more he was King *de jure*, with
an attendant herd of barons, counts, marquises and dukes,
some of them new but most of them old, to guard, sym-
bolize and execute his sovereignty. And he and they were
immensely popular—so popular that half France leaped
to suicide that their glory might blind the world.

Meanwhile, of course, there had been a certain seeping
down of democratic theory from the metaphysicians to
the mob—obscured by the uproar, but still going on. Rhetoric, like a stealthy plague, was doing its immemorial work.
Where men were confronted by the harsh, exigent realities of battle and pillage, as they were everywhere on the
Continent, it got into their veins only slowly, but where
they had time to listen to oratory, as in England and, above
all, in America, it fetched them more quickly. Eventually,
as the world grew exhausted and the wars passed, it began to make its effects felt everywhere. Democratic man,
contemplating himself, was suddenly warmed by the spectacle. His condition had plainly improved. Once a slave,
he was now only a serf. Once condemned to silence, he
was now free to criticize his masters, and even to flout
them, and the ordinances of God with them. As he gained

skill and fluency at that sombre and fascinating art, he
began to heave in wonder at his own merit. He was not
only, it appeared, free to praise and damn, challenge and
remonstrate: he was also gifted with a peculiar rectitude
of thought and will, and a high talent for ideas, particularly on the political plane. So his wishes, in his mind,
began to take on the dignity of legal rights, and after a
while, of intrinsic and natural rights, and by the same
token the wishes of his masters sank to the level of mere
ignominious lusts. By 1828 in America and by 1848 in
Europe the doctrine had arisen that all moral excellence,
and with it all pure and unfettered sagacity, resided in
the inferior four-fifths of mankind. In 1867 a philosopher
out of the gutter pushed that doctrine to its logical conclusion. He taught that the superior minority had no virtues
at all, and hence no rights at all—that the world belonged
exclusively and absolutely to those who hewed its wood
and drew its water. In less than half a century he had more
followers in the world, open and covert, than any other
sophist since the age of the Apostles.

Since then, to be sure, there has been a considerable
recession from that extreme position. The dictatorship of
the proletariat, tried here and there, has turned out to
be—if I may venture a prejudiced judgment—somewhat
impracticable. Even the most advanced Liberals, observing the thing in being, have been moved to cough sadly
behind their hands. But it would certainly be going beyond
the facts to say that the underlying democratic dogma has
been abandoned, or even appreciably overhauled. To the
contrary, it is now more prosperous than ever before. The
late war was fought on its name, and it was embraced
with loud hosannas by all the defeated nations. Everywhere in Christendom it is now official, save in a few be-
nighted lands where God is temporarily asleep. Everywhere
its fundamental axioms are accepted: (a) that the great
masses of men have an inalienable right, born of the very
nature of things, to govern themselves, and (b) that they

are competent to do it. Are they occasionally detected in gross and lamentable imbecilities? Then it is only because they are misinformed by those who would exploit them: the remedy is more education. Are they, at times, seen to be a trifle naughty, even swinish? Then it is only a natural reaction against the oppressions they suffer: the remedy is to deliver them. The central aim of all the Christian governments of to-day, in theory if not in fact, is to further their liberation, to augment their power, to drive ever larger and larger pipes into the great reservoir of their natural wisdom. That government is called good which responds most quickly and accurately to their desires and ideas. That is called bad which conditions their omnipotence and puts a question mark after their omniscience.

So much for the theory. It seems to me, and I shall here contend, that all the known facts lie flatly against it—that there is actually no more evidence for the wisdom of the inferior man, nor for his virtue, than there is for the notion that Friday is an unlucky day. There was, perhaps, some excuse for believing in these phantasms in the days when they were first heard of in the world, for it was then difficult to put them to the test, and what cannot be tried and disproved has always had a lascivious lure for illogical man. But now we know a great deal more about the content and character of the human mind than we used to know, both on high levels and on low levels, and what we have learned has pretty well disposed of the old belief in its congenital intuitions and inherent benevolences. It is, we discover, a function, at least mainly, of purely physical and chemical phenomena, and its development and operation are subject to precisely the same natural laws which govern the development and operation, say, of the human nose or lungs. There are minds which start out with a superior equipment, and proceed to high and arduous deeds; there are minds which never get any further than a sort of insensate sweating, like that of a kidney. We not only observe such differences; we also begin to chart them with more or less accuracy. Of one mind we may say with some confidence that it shows an extraordinary capacity for function and development—that its possessor, exposed to a suitable process of training, may be trusted to acquire the largest body of knowledge and the highest skill at ratiocination to which *Homo sapiens* is adapted. Of another we may say with the same confidence that its abilities are sharply limited—that no conceivable training can move it beyond a certain point. In other words, men differ inside their heads as they differ outside. There are men who are naturally intelligent and can learn, and there are men who are naturally stupid and cannot. . . .

The concept of arrested development has caused an upheaval in psychology, and reduced the arduous introspections of the old-time psychologists to a series of ingenious but unimportant fancies. Men are *not* alike, and very little can be learned about the mental processes of a congressman, an ice-wagon driver or a cinema actor by studying the mental processes of a genuinely superior man. The difference is not only qualitative; it is also, in important ways, quantitative. One thus sees the world as a vast field of greased poles, flying gaudy and seductive flags. Up each a human soul goes shinning, painfully and with many a slip. Some climb eventually to the high levels; a few scale the dizziest heights. But the great majority never get very far from the ground. There they struggle for a while, and then give it up. The effort is too much for them; it doesn't seem to be worth its agonies. Golf is easier; so is joining Rotary; so is Fundamentalism; so is osteopathy; so is Americanism.

In an aristocratic society government is a function of those who have got relatively far up the poles, either by their own prowess or by starting from the shoulders of their fathers—which is to say, either by God's grace or by God's grace. In a democratic society it is the function of all, and hence mainly of those who have got only a few spans from the ground. Their eyes, to be sure, are still thrown toward the stars. They contemplate, now bitterly, now admiringly, the backsides of those who are above them. They are bitter when they sense anything rationally describable as actual superiority; they admire when what they see is fraud. Bitterness and admiration, interacting, form a complex of prejudices which tends to cast itself into more or less stable forms. Fresh delusions, of course, enter into it from time to time, usually on waves of frantic emotion, but it keeps its main outlines. This complex of prejudices is what is known, under democracy, as public opinion. It is the glory of democratic states.

# Ralph Barton Perry (1876-1957)

*After graduate study at Harvard, where he was a pupil and close friend of William James, he taught briefly at Williams and Smith, then returned to Harvard in 1902 to teach philosophy and remained there until his retirement. An outstanding authority on James, his own philosophic system was a sort of extension of pragmatism called neo-realism. In the thirties, he was a vigorous spokesman against Fascism.*

# THE ALLEGED FAILURE OF DEMOCRACY

The rejection of democracy is nowadays regarded as evidence of superior wisdom. Although it is still customary, for political purposes, to pay it lip service, "between friends," or in the judgment of the hard-boiled fact-finder, it is often supposed to be an exploded myth—a practical

From "The Alleged Failure of Democracy," *The Yale Review*, XXIV (Spring, 1934), 37, 40, 49–51. Reprinted by permission of *The Yale Review*.

failure as well as a theoretical fallacy. Opinion has been veering so swiftly in this direction that while a few years ago the defense of democracy would have been condemned as hackneyed and banal, one who undertakes it now is suspected of seeking notoriety. . . .

We are here concerned primarily with the charge that democracy has broken down—that, owing to human nature and the complexities of life, it has proved a failure. In replying to this form of attack I would not for a moment argue, or seem to argue, that democracy has been an unqualified success. That it has in some measure failed is indisputable, and this partial failure has been, no doubt, in some measure due to the complacent assumption of success. Sound criticism, however, will know how to pass beyond complacency or rhetorical eulogy without leaping to the other and equally futile extreme of reckless despair.

The adverse judgment which the present age is disposed to pronounce on the success of democracy has, in the first place, to be qualified by the reflection that all human institutions are failures as judged by standards of perfection. They all leave room for improvement. There is what may be called a constant of failure in all great enterprises, arising out of the complexity of the problem, the weaknesses of mankind, and the weight of the obstacles to be overcome. Marriage is a failure, agriculture and industry are failures, religion is a failure, education is a failure. Government, being peculiarly difficult, is perhaps the greatest failure of all. But it would be equally true to say that government is a remarkable achievement. It all depends upon the height of your expectation; and if it be legitimate to remark how badly it is done, it is equally legitimate and sometimes more wholesome to wonder that it should be done at all. From time to time some particular institution becomes the symbol of human failure in general, and has to bear the brunt of human discontent. There are signs that economic institutions are taking their turn as such a symbol and that the sins of government may soon be deemed less scandalous.

In fairness, then, we should admit this constant of human failure, and at the same time eliminate it from the specific bill of indictment brought against democracy. Besides this ordinary failure, to be seen in every phase of human development, there is also an extraordinary failure peculiar to the times in which we live. It seems safe to predict that when the curve of human fortunes is charted by the historians of the future, it will show a pronounced dip between 1914 and some year later than 1934. Here again, we are likely to charge the whole account against some single factor such as democracy on which attention happens at the moment to be focussed. But nobody, so far as I know, has proved that democracy was responsible for the Great War, or for the economic prostration and lowered morale which have followed it; for the price of raw materials, or technological unemployment, or economic nationalism, or bank failures, or the increase of divorce, or the decline of religion and the arts. The fact is that with few exceptions everything has worked badly since 1914; and it is just as unnatural and unreasonable to hold a particular political institution wholly responsible for this as it is to charge every evil against the political party that happens to be in power. Thus so much of the failure of democracy as is shared by other institutions, whether it be the normal failure which attends all human affairs or the abnormal failure of this particular historic crisis, should be discounted. Let us now examine the evidence.

First, precisely what is it that is supposed to have failed? The answer is that it is *political democracy*. Social democracy has not failed, for the good and sufficient reason that it has never had the chance. The point is this. Political democracy is a form of government designed to produce a desirable social result. According to Aristotle the state exists for the sake of "the good life," and all parties to the discussion would doubtless agree upon the truth of that saying. Most proponents of political democracy believe that the good life, or desirable social result, which the state should promote, is an individualistic, free, and, in some sense, equalitarian society. The name we usually give to this standard is social democracy. It is not this which has failed, for social democracy is itself the ideal. By what shall it be judged a failure? To say that it has failed would be like saying that justice, goodness, or happiness has failed. The fact is that critics of democracy have not, as a rule, distinguished between democracy as a political means and democracy as a social end. Making the charitable assumption that they know what they mean, they probably mean that political democracy has failed to provide that minimum of security and order which conditions *any* form of the good life, including social democracy. Is this charge well-founded? Or, if it be conceded that mankind has recently suffered from insecurity and disorder, is this the fault of political democracy?

There is here, I think, at least that degree of reasonable doubt which is supposed to justify acquittal. Writing about the Great War in 1929, Professor G. G. Benjamin put the question, "What, then, do the source materials, the memoirs and monographs produced since the armistice, prove?" The third of the five summary conclusions with which he answers his question is, that "the failure of Germany was the failure of absolute power." I do not see how anbody who reads the history of Europe during the years immediately preceding the war can fail to be impressed by the stupidity and feebleness of the three great military monarchies, Germany, Russia, Austria. It is to be observed, furthermore, that these three governments were swept away by the war, and that the three nations which emerged victorious and are now the most powerful, England, France, and the United States, are all political democracies.

If we examine the charge more closely, we find that what is supposed to have failed is not political democracy in general, but only parliamentary government of a specific kind. Political democracy has a good many more tricks in its bag. There is, for example, representative government in the old-fashioned sense intended by the framers of the Federal

Constitution. There are alternative electoral and party methods, alternative forms of the legislative body, and of its relation to the executive. I am not qualified to propose a remedy, but I do not for a moment believe that therapeutic invention is exhausted or that institutional development is at a standstill. The failures of political democracy, even if they be granted, would suggest not that democracy in general be abandoned but that in respect of certain specific mechanisms it be varied and improved.

It is true that outside of England, France, and the United States there has been a very general abandonment or rejection of democratic institutions. The general trend towards political democracy that was so clearly marked in the last century has lately been checked or diverted. The most notable governments that have arisen since the war, Communistic Russia, Fascist Italy, and Nazi Germany, are blatant dictatorships. Turkey, Yugoslavia, Poland, Hungary, and Austria are dictatorships in substance, if not in form. Japan is in the throes of political reaction. The facts are indisputable. How shall they be interpreted? I submit that they are the effects of emergency rather than of constructive development.

In times of stress or national calamity, when heroic measures are necessary, when swift, remedial action is important at all costs—in times of civil war, actual or threatening, and in times of panic or desperation—in such times political procedure must be temporarily altered. A demand arises for unified and authoritative control. Liberty of action must give way for the term of the emergency to discipline, and discussion to obedience. There is nothing new in this. It happens in every country in event of war, in every community in case of flood or earthquake, in every family in case of accident or illness, in every individual in moments of crisis. There is then a temporary stripping for action and a massing of energies where the danger threatens, with sacrifice, abridgment, paralysis elsewhere. There are, in other words, peculiar modes of organization and control which are required for emergencies. But it would be a grave mistake to define our norms and ideals by such requirements. An emergency is by definition something out of the ordinary, requiring extraordinary measures. Their use is to keep one alive until the better life can be resumed. When one's leg is broken one puts it in a plaster cast, but one does not therefore conclude that freely moving limbs are a failure and should be permanently abolished. The ultimate purpose of the rigid cast is to restore the usual freedom of movement. . . .

The rejection of democracy as a practical failure implies a willingness to accept some alternative. What are the alternatives to democracy? There should be a law compelling every destructive critic to provide an alternative. The alternatives to political democracy have been tried, and it was because they had been tried unsuccessfully that political evolution up to 1914 moved in the direction of democracy. Jefferson remarked in his First Inaugural Address: "Sometimes it is said that man cannot be trusted with the government of himself. Can he, then, be trusted with the government of others? Or have we found angels in the forms of kings to govern him? Let history answer this question." I, for one, if I should withdraw my support from democracy, should not know where to find any other political investment that I would not distrust more, unless, as seems unlikely, an Almighty, All-wise, and All-benevolent God could be induced to assume the government himself.

It is a curious thing that those who turn in their thoughts from democracy to dictatorship forget that dictatorship consists to a large extent in the evils of a democracy without its merits. If anyone who is weary of democracy were asked to name its most intolerable abuse, he would no doubt name the demagogue. But, as Plato pointed out a good many years ago, the tyrant is essentially a great

demagogue, who is so artful and unscrupulous in his demagoguery that he drives out all the little demagogues and
monopolizes the business for himself.

An editorial writer in "The Manchester Guardian" recently recalled Bismarck's saying that "any fool can govern
by martial or semi-martial law. . . ." "It is a mistake," the
writer continued, "to suppose that a dictatorship brings the
able men to the top. The exact opposite is true—it eliminates
the courageous, the critical, the intelligent. . . . No pre-
mier in any European democracy has so many catch-phrases
as Mussolini or Pilsudski [and he might have added, Hit-
ler] to call forth popular applause so blind and hysterical."

There is no commoner form of sentimentalism than that
with which we color those forms of government under
which we are not obliged to live. The man who longs for a
dictatorship usually imagines that *he* is the dictator, or at
any rate that he is the dictator's best friend and most trusted
counsellor. He thinks of the system as a means of getting
done, promptly and thoroughly, what he himself believes
ought to be done. But the fact is that for most people most
of the time dictatorship consists not in dictating but in
being dictated to; not in getting done what one thinks ought
to be done, but in being compelled to submit helplessly to
what one thinks ought not to be done. It is true that we
are living in an age when non-democratic forms of government are being revived and modernized. But instead of
weakening our allegiance to democratic institutions this
should rather confirm our faith by presenting the odious alternatives in their stark reality.

Any government has in the last analysis to be justified by
the quality of the life which it promotes. A political democracy claims to secure more than that bare minimum of security and order which may be rightly demanded of any
social system. Those who adhere to it as a political creed
commonly do so because of an equalitarian social ideal.

This ideal means that a man should have his chance to
rise as high in attainment as his energy and natural capacity

will carry him. It is not implied that attainment shall be equal. There is only one way by which this could be brought about—by penalizing superiority and so reducing life to the level of the least competent. The ideal of social democracy implies a spirit that is rarer and more generous—a magnanimity which will respect genuine superiority wherever it appears, and prefer a pyramid of excellence to a plane of mediocrity. It will recognize the unalterable inequalities of endowment, and the inevitable inequalities of attainment; and will encourage eminence for the enrichment of the common life.

But the cult of social democracy is not satisfied with a vicarious equality, a merely theoretical equality of rights, or an unattainable equality of aspiration. In the common human faculties and the common human lot it discovers actual equalities. It focusses attention on these equalities, and from them it proposes to form the essential bond between man and man, believing that a society founded on mutual respect is the fundamental condition of the best life. Political democracy is both a means to this social end and one of its chief embodiments.

# Lincoln Steffens (1866-1936)

*After graduation from the University of California in 1889, he spent three years studying at Berlin, Heidelberg, Leipzig, and the Sorbonne. During the nineties as a police reporter and later city editor of the New York Evening Post, he met Theodore Roosevelt and Jacob Riis and first became interested in social questions. One of the greatest muckrakers, he was considered an enfant terrible who shocked people because he asked forthright questions and came to candid conclusions. Contradictory and paradoxical by nature, he liked people, including "honest crooks" and*

*"good bad capitalists." In his last years he was
subjected to constant persecution because of his
Communist affiliations.*

# WHY I AM A LENINIST

Revolutions, like wars, are social-economic explosions due
to human (political) interference with natural (and, therefore, divine) laws and forces which make for the gradual
growth or constant change called evolution.

"I believe in evolution, not revolution," says the righteous
citizen. So would the revolutionist prefer evolution, if he
had his choice. Nobody likes revolutions; they are violent,
messy, stormlike affairs which are almost impossible to
manage and direct. The revolutionist would rather work
out his reforms in the comparative quietude of evolution.
But that is quite impossible. The "evolutionist" won't permit it. The "evolutionist" works always for revolution, not
knowingly, of course. He does not do anything knowingly.
But the fact that he unwittingly uses the methods of violence he deplores only exasperates the honest reformer who
would willingly go slow if only he were allowed to go.
The "evolutionist" will not go at all. There is a definition
of a pessimist as a man who has just met an optimist. In
that spirit, revolutionists are reformers who have been up
against the righteous political evolutionists. For evolution,
if it means anything in political economy, is a process of
reformation of old laws, customs and institutions to make
them conform to the social, economic, and psychological
changes that are occurring all the time. When society
passes, however unintentionally, from hand-labor to machinery, man-made laws, constitutions and customs must
be altered and should be allowed to change consciously
and easily. It is this that the conservative blocks. He does
not know it because, being righteous, he has to believe

---

From *Moses in Red* (Philadelphia: Dorrance & Co., 1926), pp. 18–28, 33–9.

that he is for reform in general; he merely happens to find himself (and his interest) against each and every particular reform that strikes at the root of his old "rights" and privileges. What he cannot see is that the effect in general of his resistance in particular is to incite the maddened revolutionists and the mad revolution.

A revolution is a natural phenomenon, as natural and as understandable as a flood, a fire or a war, a financial depression, an epidemic of disease or a pimple on the nose. It has its causes and its natural history. And it should be preventable, therefore, but not by prayer and not by force. God obeys His own laws. Arresting revolutionists does not arrest the revolution any more than prohibition stops drinking. Force only puts off the red day as a warlike peace treaty carries on the process of war. The prayerful but impious pacifists, who do not seek the causes of war but would only forbid the arming of nations, should bring up their boys to be, not soldiers, perhaps—soldiers get killed—but officers. Pacifists rank with the evolutionists who fight the revolutionists with police force; they both are, like Pharaoh in the story of Moses, fellow-conspirators for the explosion which must break through all merely righteous conservatism —lest the people perish, as the Egyptians did, and the Greeks and the Romans, leaving only their names behind. The modern Egyptians, the modern Greeks, and the Italians in Rome today, are fit survivors of their "moral culture," which is ours. But, then, there is another culture growing up amongst us, a culture that tells us how to avoid the fate of the ancients.

The scientific culture that is coming in spite of the opposition of the righteous, teaches us that what we have to do to prevent revolutions, wars and all our so-called evils, is to study the forces involved in them, trace their workings back to their original, continuing misuse, correct that and so deal scientifically with causes. We followed this method when we examined the lightning and turned its terrors into electric light and power. We discovered then that what we had dreaded as an evil was good. And whenever we have looked reverently (scientifically) into a "bad" thing, we have found it made up of "good" elements. It is the pious belief of the high priests of science that there is no evil; that all the forces and all the laws of nature are good, *i.e.*, beneficent of God and blessings to man, if he will but learn to understand and use them. Legislators should be or they should consult, not lawyers, but biologists, chemists and economists. Lawyers study and live upon man-made laws. The scientists alone look for and learn the laws of God. Not the priests any more, and not yet the historians and political critics; they take the moral point of view, talk in the terms of superstition, and judge men and events by their standards of right and wrong. According to science, which is the only living religion in the world today, all nature is a book of revelations, every laboratory experiment is a worship and every natural phenomenon—whether it be a chemical reaction or a poem, a war or a revolution—is a sign of the hand, the voice and the knowledge of God, and as such to be respected; and so described.

The Bible sets an example. The Old Testament story of the revolt and the exodus of Israel is the history of a revolution, and it has the hand of God acting and His voice speaking all through it; literally. Jehovah is a character; He is the leading person in the plot of that great drama. The theologians dispute whether to read it literally or symbolically, but that makes no essential difference. The story rings true in the way that the New Testament gospels of Jesus ring true. The narrative follows the course of a typical revolution. Let Jehovah personify and speak for Nature; think of Moses as the uncompromising Bolshevik; Aaron as the more political Menshevik; take Pharaoh as the ruler who stands for the Right (the conservative "evolutionist"), and the Children of Israel as the people—any people; read the Books of Moses thus and they will appear as a revolutionary classic. Anyone that has gone through a revolution will recognize, not only the *dramatis personæ* of the story, but the regular stages of its progress, the typical individual and mob psychology, the tragic disappointments and excesses, and the comic criticisms and excuses of every such crisis in the affairs of men.

It seems necessary, however, to go through a revolution to see this. It was for me. . . .

When the World War broke in 1914, I was in Europe, preparing to muckrake England, France, Germany and Italy. I had gone far enough in my secret investigations to see that the same system of corruption which reigned in all American cities, states and business corporations, dominated Europe, too. There was some law at work, parallels of identical forces which made the social problem one and the same problem everywhere. The only difference between the United States and Europe was that due to time. The process of corruption was farther advanced abroad than at home, and old Italy was deeper in it than France, which was as much farther gone than England as France is older in experience and culture than England. Germany was the least corrupted, the nearest to the United States—the best of the big "bad" world governments I had studied, because it is the youngest. All of them, however, were so corrupt that—according to my theory—they could not be saved by reforms. Nothing but the revolution could adjust them to the economic changes that had occurred in our civilization and the strain of the war would precipitate THE revolution. I did not, therefore, go to the front. I went to the rear. I decided to make a study of revolutions. I took a boat and went to Mexico because there was a revolution there. On a theory again.

If one corrupted city was like every other city, if all states were alike and all countries—all governments in one and the same process of corruption; if one reform movement, whether in New York, San Francisco or Jerusalem was typical of all reforms, then, I reasoned, one revolution would furnish me with the key to all revolutions. The Mexican revolution would prepare me for the European revolution. And, that a human mind has to be thus prepared by experience to see straight, was illustrated the moment I landed at Vera Cruz. I met there a committee of socialists, sent from Italy, France and Spain to report whether the Mexican revolution was a "true" revolution, worthy of the sympathy and support of the Latin revolutionists of Europe. They had made their investigation and were about to sail for home to report against the Mexican revolt. Why?

It was not according to Marx! It had occurred, not in a highly capitalized country, but in a backward country with an undeveloped industrial system among an unorganized, illiterate people who knew nothing of socialism and little of labor unions. It had no clearly defined Socialist purposes; it was all mixed up: politics, economics, civil wars and graft; it was guilty of all sorts of cruel excesses, worse than the evils a revolution was intended to correct.

I went on through the Mexican revolution, most of the time on the inside among the leaders, and I found that all the counts of that Socialist Committee were true; and more beside, many more. From Mexico I went off to Russia when the revolution occurred there, and I have been following it ever since, that and the other revolutionary movements in Europe. I cannot say whether the Mexican or even the Russian revolution is a true Marxian revolution, because I do not know any more what is meant by that phrase. My own theory of "the" revolution and most of the written theories suffered in the revolutions I saw very much as the governments did that they exploded under. Theory was blown all to pieces. But I did what Marx did, when, after writing at length about "the" revolution, he witnessed the Paris Commune. He altered his theory to conform to the facts; I acted upon the same pious scientific principle that, whenever an actual experience in nature runs counter to our expectations, it is probable that Nature is right and that our theory was wrong.

Regardless, then, of theory, mine, Marx's and everybody

else's; regardful only of the facts, I say with assurance that the Mexican and the Russian revolutions revolved in their courses as like as two stars.

There is in that statement, if true, a basis for a science of revolution; there is in it an implication that revolutions are governed by some natural (economic-psychological-social) laws which make them alike and, therefore, understandable and perhaps manageable, if not avoidable. Having seen this parallel of two revolutions, I went back and read again the classic accounts of the other great historical revolutions and I found that they were, in all essentials, like the Russian and the Mexican revolutions. The laws held; whatever they are, the natural laws of revolution were always obeyed and they were not recognized by the historians, critics and statesmen only because they knew but one revolution or none. When I knew New York alone, I could only see and write that Boss Croker was to blame for the corruption. It was not till I knew St. Louis and saw there another boss with another name, but the same backers, methods and effects as Croker in New York, that I could describe the Boss as an institution and the boss system as a natural development out of the conditions common to all cities at a certain stage of growth under our universal culture.

When I had seen two revolutions and had understood several more, I looked around for some classic revolutions which everybody was familiar with. An incident recalled the Books of Moses. I took up the Bible and I reread once more the story of the Exodus of the Children of Israel, and lo and behold, there it was: The Revolution. I knew (in my bones) now, that that famous old story was a true report of an historical event. No doubt about it. The original tellers of the tale may have twisted it in the telling; that happens in a revolution always. . . .

Making every allowance for errors, priestcraft and politics in the Books of Moses, however, I hold to my thesis that they give an essentially true account of a typical revolution and that they are therefore worth studying as such. We have to make a science of sociology and we cannot do that so long as we look upon some social events with horror. The mind of man shies at revolutions, wars and other disasters in history, especially in the news of the day. We behave like a cab-horse that I saw meet the first automobile in New York. The new vehicle was coming swiftly towards him. He saw it suddenly when it was close upon him. The poor beast stopped in his tracks and, from terror or amazement, collapsed. His hind legs sprawled from under him and he actually sat down, his mouth open, his eyes and his ears fixed upon that new and unknown apparition. All Europe and North America sat down on their haunches before the Russian revolution; they haven't stood up to it yet. Able observers have gone into Russia to investigate it, as the Labor Socialists went into Mexico, and most of them have come out and reported that the Russian revolution was not according to Marx, or not up to their own expectations of a revolution. This is one of the incidents common to all revolutions: the outside world does not like them. People see only the excesses of it, and these they exaggerate. Moses had his experience with the investigators. The committee of chiefs he sent to spy out the Land of Promise came back with a majority report that the country was full of giants and that it would take hard fighting and long labor to make of it the heaven on earth that they had dreamed of. They preferred to go back to Egypt and servitude, and the people were with the pessimists. Jehovah, who, like Nature, was offering them not a heaven on earth but only an opportunity to make one, saw their uselessness and commanded them to wander off into the wilderness and die. Only their children, brought up in liberty, should inherit the land and liberty. . . .

"What we need," said Lenin to me in 1919, "is a revision of all our theories in the light of the war, the peace and this and the other revolutions. I can't undertake it. I can't even change my own ideas very much. When you are in action you cannot stop to theorize; it is difficult even to think. I have to live in the country to think clear. But if there were scientific men outside, in America, England—Europe—they could look on and they could study, think and tell us. We need criticism. The captains in all crises really need the counsel of wise, thoughtful, sympathetic observers safely, quietly out of the storm center. But there is no such criticism; there are no such critics. All we get is the ignorant horror at the signs of our distress, the height of the waves, the discipline of the crew and the number of poor devils washed overboard. That is no help. We feel all this, more than our critics do. What we want to know is how to get through the difficulties to an objective, which is the aim of all men who have a purpose in life. We differ about the route; we agree on the port— all of us."

The horrors of a revolution are never singular; they are the ever-recurring symptoms and signs of the natural phenomenon they accompany—always. This one can see by observing that they occur regularly in all revolutions, some of them in all social crises. There are killings and terrors, loot and destruction, in a war or a strike. The side or the leaders blamed for them do not always wish for and command them. They also deplore them. When I asked Lenin officially about the terror, he whirled on me fiercely.

"Who wants to ask us about our killings?" he demanded.

"Paris," I said, meaning, as he well understood, the Peace Conference.

"Do you mean to tell me that those men who have just generaled the slaughter of seventeen millions of men in a purposeless war are concerned over the few thousands that have been killed in a revolution which has a conscious aim—to get out of the necessity of war and—and armed peace?"

He stood a moment facing me with his blazing eyes, then quieting down, he said:

"But never mind, do not deny the terror. Don't minimize any of the evils of a revolution. They occur. They must be counted upon. If we have to have a revolution, we have to pay the price of it."

That is the point. The evils of revolution happen in a revolution. They have to be studied, therefore; not merely shied at, but examined and then, perhaps, when they are understood scientifically, they can be avoided or used. Take a few of them, for example: the "excesses" that shocked not only the public opinion of the world, but the theoretical minds of the scientists and even of some revolutionists. Take the dictatorship, democracy, the terror, and "liberty."

Both the Mexican and the Russian revolutions ran straight to a dictatorship. Looking back in history it appears that all other revolutions took on the form of an autocracy. Moses was the chief, the absolute ruler of the Exodus. But so do all great social crises develop into dictatorships. The Jews, the Russians and the Mexicans had lived under that form of government; it was the arrangement they were accustomed to. It might be peculiar to them to return to it. But during the World War all the modern governments changed from their old "democratic" to the autocratic form. Great Britain made Lloyd George a dictator, France ended up with Clemenceau as the absolute ruler, and the United States, for all its fixed representative form and hard and fast Constitution, let President Wilson be king. Having seen this happen, it would seem that the scientific observer might infer, not that the Russian dictatorship was bad and that therefore the Russian revolution was to be condemned, but that our theories, our wishes for democracy, had led us astray in our thinking. We might, if we had used our eyes and our memories, have been helped to a revision of our opinions, which is always good—progressive, evolutionary—and so have reached a tentative statement of some such general law as this:

*In revolutions, in wars and in all such disorganizing,*

*fear-spreading crises in human affairs, nations tend to return to the first, the simplest, and perhaps the best form of government: a dictatorship.*

For, after all, the original form of government is that of the chief and the tribe, seen in the gang organizations of savages, boys, criminals, politicians, financiers and morons. American cities, despite their carefully drawn charters for representative democracies, all had the boss and his gang as actual rulers. And, after the war, when the crisis of revolution approached Italy, Mussolini saw the empty throne of fear, leaped into it like the brave man he was, and found himself welcomed by enough of organized society to hold him in his dictatorship.

A dictatorship, then, is neither red nor white, good nor bad—it is a natural development out of a situation in which a people is so frightened that it huddles back into the herd state. Knowing this, as Lenin did before the Russian revolution, he could anticipate it, "seize power" and have the chance he sought to try to direct a revolution toward the achievement of economic democracy. Whether he succeeded or not, he was at any rate a wiser leader than the Mexican Madera, a liberal, who had democratic theories which made him hate his dictatorship and purposely share his power with the leading good citizens who, finally, had him murdered. Lenin was a more scientific historian than the liberals of Europe and a better revolutionist than those revolutionists, who, believing that the objective of a revolution is democracy and liberty, expected it to be free and popular from the beginning, and turned against it because it started off, like all revolutions, to go through the regular stages and forms of the revolutionary process.

Liberty and democracy may not be the objectives of a revolution, but even if they are, it is apparent in history and in the news of our day, that neither of these two human desires can be set up by the will of man or the law of a land. The United States, England—most civilized governments give Constitutional guarantees of free speech, free press, free assemblage. These free laws do not stand up under the pressure of war, panic or fear of a revolution.

This is a disappointment to liberals; all disillusionment is bitter. But there is a principle of disillusionment, too. My experience is that whenever I am losing an illusion, I need but make a study of the facts and the forces that are destroying it; these will provide me with another—illusion, no doubt. But that way lies progress. When I examined the causes and the advantages of a dictatorship, I lost my illusion about democracy as the road to democracy, but by watching the Russian people give up their power, with a sigh of relief, to Lenin; and by watching him, the dictator, introduce necessary economic changes so complicated and subtle that no people can understand (and vote for) them— I could see that a dictatorship may be able to deal with the causes of evil more easily and scientifically than a representative legislature can.

So with democracy. The Russian people did rule for the first six months of the Russian revolution, and they enacted idealistic laws. But nothing happened, nothing was done. The laws were not executed. It's a long story, but as I witnessed that first democratic phase of the revolution, I was convinced that political democracy simply cannot exist until after economic democracy has been set up and got to going well. Democracy and a free people are effects, not causes; ends, not beginnings.

And so, third: it was hard to see liberty go at the end of the first six months and tyranny come. But the sight of the abuse of the free press, free speech and free assemblage was so obviously a menace to a people which had to decide upon some one course and, for better or worse, unite upon it, that one was reconciled when the mob itself turned itself and its liberties out and chose to follow the leader. Taking that experience, and that of all the peoples in the war, I would offer (to liberals especially) this very liberal statement of a natural law of freedom:

*Liberty is a state of freedom which, related in some way*

*to the state of the public mind, increases in some ratio
with the general sense of security and decreases in some
similar ratio with the general sense of danger—regardless of
man-made laws and soul-felt idealism.*

Under this natural law freedom will be the last achievement of man. Liberty will arrive after a free, unprivileged
system of economics has been laid as a basis of a society,
which has lived on it long enough to have no fear of
tyranny or abuse. In other words: liberty, democracy, justice
—all our universally desired human ideals are conditions
subject to some natural (economic-psychological) laws
which we must understand and conform to before we can
establish them, as ends.

# John Dewey (1859-1952)

*Son of a small-town storekeeper in Vermont, he
received his Ph.D. in 1884 at Johns Hopkins
and in 1904 went to Columbia, where he taught
philosophy long past the usual retirement age.
Father of the Progressive School movement, a
leader in the fight for civil and academic freedom, he was in the 1930's the chief living exponent of Pragmatism. Anything but the retiring
professor, he participated actively in the rough-
and-tumble of politics and at the age of seventy
became chairman of the League for Independent
Political Action.*

# WHY I AM NOT A COMMUNIST

I begin by emphasizing the fact that I write with reference
to being a Communist in the Western world, especially

From *The Modern Monthly*, VIII (April, 1934).

here and now in the United States, and a Communist after the pattern set in the U.S.S.R.

1. *Such* Communism rests upon an almost entire neglect of the specific historical backgrounds and traditions which have operated to shape the patterns of thought and action in America. The autocratic background of the Russian Church and State, the fact that every progressive movement in Russia had its origin in some foreign source and has been imposed from above upon the Russian people, explain much about the form Communism has taken in that country. It is therefore nothing short of fantastic to transfer the ideology of Russian Communism to a country which is so profoundly different in its economic, political, and cultural history. Were this fact acknowledged by Communists and reflected in their daily activities and general program, were it admitted that many of the practical and theoretical features of Russian Communism (like belief in the plenary and verbal inspiration of Marx, the implicit or explicit domination of the Communist party in every field of culture, the ruthless extermination of minority opinion in its own ranks, the verbal glorification of the mass and the actual cult of the infallibility of leadership) are due to local causes, the character of Communism in other countries might undergo a radical change. But it is extremely unlikely that this will take place. For official Communism has made the practical traits of the dictatorship *of* the proletariat and *over* the proletariat, the suppression of the civil liberties of all non-proletarian elements as well as of dissenting proletarian minorities, integral parts of the standard Communist faith and dogma. It has imposed and not argued the theory of dialectic materialism (which in the U.S.S.R. itself has to undergo frequent restatement in accordance with the exigencies of party factional controversy) upon all its followers. Its cultural philosophy, which has many commendable features, is vitiated by the absurd attempt to make a single and uniform entity out of the "proletariat."

2. Particularly unacceptable to me in the ideology of

official Communism is its monistic and one-way philosophy of history. This is akin to the point made above. The thesis that all societies must exhibit a uniform, even if uneven, social development from primitive communism to slavery, from slavery to feudalism, from feudalism to capitalism, and from capitalism to socialism, and that the transition from capitalism to socialism must be achieved by the same way in all countries, can be accepted only by those who are either ignorant of history or who are so steeped in dogma that they cannot look at a fact without changing it to suit their special purposes. From this monistic philosophy of history, there follows a uniform political practice and a uniform theory of revolutionary strategy and tactics. But where differences in historic background, national psychology, religious profession and practice are taken into account —and they must be considered in every scientific theory— there will be corresponding differences in political methods, differences that may extend to general policies as well as to the strategy of their execution. For example, as far as the historic experience of America is concerned, two things among many others are overlooked by official Communists whose philosophy has been projected on the basis of special European conditions. We in the United States have no background of a dominant and overshadowing feudalism. Our troubles flow from the oppressive exercise of power by financial over-lords and from the failure to introduce new forms of *democratic* control in industry and government consonant with the shift from individual to corporate economy. It is a possibility overlooked by official Communists that important social changes in the direction of democratization of industry may be accomplished by groups working *with* the working-class although, strictly speaking, not *of* them. The other point ignored by the Communists is our deeply-rooted belief in the importance of individuality, a belief that is almost absent in the Oriental world from which Russia has drawn so much. Not to see that this attitude, so engrained in our habitual ways of thought and action, demands a very different set of policies and methods from those embodied in official Communism, verges to my mind on political insanity.

3. While I recognize the existence of class-conflicts as one of the fundamental facts of social life to-day, I am profoundly skeptical of class war as *the* means by which such conflicts can be eliminated and genuine social advance made. And yet this is a basic point in Communist theory and is more and more identified with the meaning of dialectic materialism as applied to the social process. Historically speaking, it may have been necessary for Russia in order to achieve peace for her war-weary soldiers, and land for her hungry peasants, to convert incipient class-war into open civil war culminating in the so-called dictatorship of the proletariat. But nonetheless Fascism in Germany and Italy cannot be understood except with reference to the lesson those countries learned from the U.S.S.R. How Communism can continue to advocate the kind of economic change it desires by means of civil war, armed insurrection and iron dictatorship in face of what has happened in Italy and Germany I cannot at all understand. Reliable observers have contended that the communist ideology of dictatorship and violence together with the belief that the communist party was the foreign arm of a foreign power constituted one of the factors which aided the growth of Fascism in Germany. I am firmly convinced that imminent civil war, or even the overt threat of such a war, in any western nation, will bring Fascism with its terrible engines of repression to power. Communism, then, with its doctrine of the necessity of the forcible overthrow of the state by armed insurrection, with its doctrine of the dictatorship of the proletariat, with its threats to exclude all other classes from civil rights, to smash their political parties, and to deprive them of the rights of freedom of speech, press and assembly—which Communists *now* claim for themselves under capitalism—Communism is itself, an unwitting, but nonetheless, powerful factor in bringing about Fascism.

As an unalterable opponent of Fascism in every form, I cannot be a Communist.

4. It is not irrelevant to add that one of the reasons I am not a Communist is that the emotional tone and methods of discussion and dispute which seem to accompany Communism at present are extremely repugnant to me. Fair-play, elementary honesty in the representation of facts and especially of the opinions of others, are something more than "bourgeois virtues." They are traits that have been won only after long struggle. They are not deep-seated in human nature even now—witness the methods that brought Hilterism to power. The systematic, persistent and seemingly intentional disregard of these things by Communist spokesmen in speech and press, the hysteria of their denunciations, their attempts at character assassination of their opponents, their misrepresentation of the views of the "liberals" to whom they also appeal for aid in their defense campaigns, their policy of "rule or ruin" in their so-called united front activities, their apparent conviction that what they take to be the end justifies the use of *any* means if only those means promise to be successful—all these, in my judgment, are fatal to the very end which official Communists profess to have at heart. And if I read the temper of the American people aright, especially so in this country.

5. A revolution effected solely or chiefly by violence can in a modernized society like our own result only in chaos. Not only would civilization be destroyed but the things necessary for bare life. There are some, I am sure, now holding and preaching Communism who would be the first to react against it, if in this country Communism were much more than a weak protest or an avocation of literary men. Few communists are really aware of the far-reaching implications of the doctrine that civil war is the *only* method by which revolutionary economic and political changes can be brought about. A comparatively simple social structure, such as that which Russia had, may be able to recover

from the effects of violent, internal disturbance. And Russia, it must be remembered, had the weakest middle class of any major nation. Were a large scale revolution to break out in highly industrialized America, where the middle class is stronger, more militant and better prepared than anywhere else in the world, it would either be abortive, drowned in a blood bath, or if it were victorious, would win only a Pyrrhic victory. The two sides would destroy the country and each other. For this reason, too, I am not a Communist.

I have been considering the position, as I understand it, of the orthodox and official Communism. I cannot blind myself, however, to the perceptible difference between communism with a small $c$, and Communism, official Communism, spelt with a capital letter.

# CHAPTER SIX

# The Modern Ethic

## I

At the beginning of the twenties the forces of prudery and restraint appeared victorious in their effort to keep America free, white, pure, Protestant, and sober. Their repressive legions swarmed over the land—the Ku Klux Klan to keep America white and Nordic, 100% Americans to censor school books (they began by excluding Bolshevist ideas and ended by banning Voltaire's *Candide*), fundamentalist ministers to wage holy war on evolution, prohibition agents to trap unwary drinkers, Will Hays to keep movies pure and beautiful, plus assorted Puritans and "blue-noses" eager to battle with sex, Sunday ball games, the devil, and Sigmund Freud. But at this very time there erupted a revolt of flaming youth that shook the hearthstones in respectable homes across the nation.

Although rebellious tendencies had been detected among the young intelligentsia shortly before the war, as Henry F. May has shown, they had never been widespread nor attracted a sizeable following. It was still, the *Nation* remarked at the time, only a revolt, not a revolution. Not until after the war did the "fluttering tastes of the half-baked intellectuals" infect most of the younger generation and capture the nation's youth (and some of the old) by storm. The "innocent rebellion" of 1912–17 had never at-

The "flapper" was a symbol of the revolt of flaming youth in the 1920's. As modern as the Charleston and the one-piece bathing suit, she discarded surplus clothes and surplus manners with the same enthusiasm she devoted to acquiring gin and cigarettes.

"Do you think the flapper is passing out?"
He—Well, I've had lots of them pass out on me.

Culver Pictures, Inc., from *Judge*, December 29, 1923

tained popular proportions, but the new revolt was decidedly different in temper and tone. Where the earlier rebellion had been somewhat furtive, even modest, the revolution of the twenties was open and shameless. It was, as John Flynn said, doubtless the most violent revolution against established manners and ideas of morality and religion this country had ever seen. "The flapper, the flivver, Freud, and gin ran wild over the land."[1]

Most revealing was the radically changed role of the young woman. Where the "emancipated" young woman of the previous decade had taken the lead in attempting to wipe out prostitution, abolish the saloon, and trying in general to raise the social standards of men to her own, the "flapper"—the free-wheeling female of the twenties—ran serious competition to the prostitute. She invaded the saloon not with raised axe but with lifted elbow, and she tried her best to beat the man on his own level. Though it is true Mencken had described the "flapper" as early as 1915, bringing the word into public use, his flapper had been an eccentric; in the 1920's she became a convention. She was, moreover, a different girl from her mother. Mother's skirt had "just reached her very trim and pretty ankles" and her newly coiled hair "exposed the ravishing whiteness of her neck," but daughter wore her hair in a short bob and her skimpy dress soared above the knees, revealing her rolled stockings and at times a fleeting glimpse of white thighs. Rather than Christabel Pankhurst and Omar Khayyam, she read Freud and F. Scott Fitzgerald and worried not about the evils of white slavery but the comparative merits of contraceptives. Discreetly sipping wine by candlelight was not for her; she smoked cigarettes and drank in public and got "blotto" on bathtub gin, preferring to take her booze like a man from a hip-flask or with one foot on the brass rail in a basement speakeasy. Instead of the romantic violin and the exotic tango, she chose the skittish saxophone and the boisterous Charleston; and after midnight, instead of returning to a garret in Greenwich Village to talk until dawn of Strindberg, Ibsen, Shaw, and Wells, she drove off in an automobile for a "petting party" down some dark side-street or country lane while her mother lay awake and worried. To be sure, not all "nice" girls behaved as she did, but there were enough of them who did to make the younger generation a topic of anxious discussion from coast to coast.[2]

Behind the flagrant change in manners was an even more radical change in morals. As with all great social revolutions, it was cumulative rather than catastrophic, compound rather than simple in origins. Beyond doubt, the war played a part, shaking many young people loose from settled moorings and deranging moral and religious values. But while war accelerated change, it was only a catalyst, not the major determining force. The old culture had collapsed not because of the war but because the war, combined with various scientific and intellectual developments, brought to light its inadequacies.

It was a "botched" civilization, and no one saw it more clearly than the young. His generation had emerged from the war, said F. Scott Fitzgerald, "to find all Gods dead, all wars fought, all faiths in man shaken." For the younger generation, the "war to end war" had turned out to be a

"cockeyed lunatic asylum," destroying all the ideals and
principles they most believed in. War, as one of its victims
concluded in John Dos Passos' novel *1919*, was "a dirty
goldbrick game put over by governments and politicians
for their own selfish interests" and "crooked from A to Z."
In a world "knocked to pieces," all deceptions were out.
If "these wild young people" shocked their elders who
could not see what all the concern was about, if they
were harsh, reckless, and sometimes wicked, it was because
—as one of them explained—the break-up of things was no
time for "little tin-pot ideals."° If they were mocking
and irreverent and took established institutions very lightly,
it was because the civilization they inherited was, in the
words of Ezra Pound, "an old bitch, gone in the teeth."[3]

Irritation at things as they were and disgust at the continual frustrations and aridities of American life led those
young people who could not escape to seek fresh values.
They could accept neither the war nor the Puritanical reaction that followed. Yet it was not Puritanism so much as
complacency that they fought. As Carol, the youthful heroine
of *Main Street*, made clear, it was the savorless quality of
the traditional pattern of life that the more intelligent
young people revolted against. They deplored the "un-
imaginatively standardized background," the "sluggishness
of speech and manners," the "rigid ruling of the spirit by
the desire to appear respectable." To the young such a
life was "the contentment of the quiet dead, who are
scornful of the living for their restless walking." It was
"negation canonized as the one positive virtue." It was
"the prohibition of happiness," "slavery self-sought and
self-defended." It was "dullness made God." Yet, said
Randolph Bourne, defending the young rebels, these mal-
contents were not barbarians and had no intention of being
cultural vandals, but simply sought the vital and the sin-

---

°John F. Carter, *These Wild Young People*. See page 353.

The most celebrated institution of the Jazz Age was the "speakeasy." In 1929, there were 32,000 speakeasies in New York City, double the number of saloons in the old days. Drunkenness, as F. Scott Fitzgerald said, became a mark "of the superior status of those who are able to afford the indulgence."

cere everywhere. "All they want is a new orientation of
the spirit that shall be modern," an orientation to accompany that scientific and technical apparatus which the war
accelerated and which was fast coming to dominate civilization. "So they are likely to go ahead beating their heads
at the wall until they are either bloody or light appears."[4]

Most of them found that "new orientation of the spirit"
through the popularized ideas of Sigmund Freud. In a time
of growing skepticism about civilization and morality,
Freud taught the primacy of natural desire, seeming to
uphold the world of nature against the hypocrisies and
cruelties of the world of man. The sexual urge was the
primordial force of man's nature, the fundamental drive
of life, and civilization was built upon the heroic sacrifice of man's desire. While Freud recognized that civilization required the repression or sublimation of sexuality, he
also warned that the continuous sacrifice of nature that
was demanded by civilization held great peril for the individual. "Experience teaches us that for most people there
is a limit beyond which their constitution cannot comply
with the demands of civilization. All who wish to be more
noble-minded than their constitution allows fall victims to
neurosis; they would have been more healthy if it could
have been possible for them to be less good."[5]

Early in 1922, Harold Stearns diagnosed the ills of
American society in just such Freudian terms. The intellectual life in America was sour and sterile because it had
"lost its earthy roots, its sensuous fulness." Scorning its
biological history and emotional setting, the American intellect had failed to reach its own proper dignity and effec-
tiveness because it made an "ascetic divorce between the
passions and the intellect, the emotions and the reason,"
where instead it should have tried to function "in some
kind of rational relationship with the more clamorous instincts of the body."[6]

Far from counseling license, however, Freud was a man
whose ideal was to control passion by reason and who, in

his own attitude toward sex, lived up to the Victorian sexual morality. Yet always implicit in his writing about the conflict between the natural urges of man and the conventions of society was the question whether "civilized" morality was worth the price. Though insisting sexual satisfaction was not in itself a universal remedy for the ills of civilization, his conclusion in *Civilization and Its Discontents* was that "our so-called civilization itself is to blame for a great part of our misery, and we should be happier if we were to give it up and go back to primitive conditions."[7]

The explicit primitivism of Freud appealed greatly to culturally jaded Americans who seized upon the idea that surrender to impulse was the scientific way to individual fulfillment, satisfaction, and happiness. Whether Freud intended it or not, Freudianism as popularly interpreted in the United States in the 1920's meant unrestrained sexuality. Not only was it regarded as healthful and expedient to get rid of one's "repressions," but to throttle the instincts on outdated moral grounds was to arouse suspicions that one was inhibited or neurotic and, among the more sophisticated, to invite social condemnation. The wide and pervasive obsession with sex which infected the older as well as the younger generation excited considerable indignation among the clergy and other righteous citizens of the republic. Cried a leading churchman, "The morale of the whole country has been lowered, minds have been polluted, tongues loosened from their decent reticencies, youth perverted, marriages dissolved, by this vicious theory flaunting itself under the name of Science. The psychoanalyst interprets everything in terms of sex." And, as he rightly lamented, so did a good many Americans.[8]

The new view of sex was applauded by George Jean Nathan on behalf of the *avant garde* in the *American Mercury*, of which he was co-editor. "It used to be thought pretty generally that sex was a grim, serious and ominous business, to be entered into only by those duly joined in holy wedlock or by those lost souls already in thrall to the devil. Sex was synonymous with danger, tragedy, woe, or at its best, with legalized baby carriages. This view of sex has gone out of style with such other contemporary delusions as French altruism, the making of the world safe for democracy and the evil of Bolshevist government." Though Nathan did not dispute that "back in the cow pastures of the Republic" the old view of sex still prevailed, he argued that "wherever lights are brighter" and "wherever a band, however bad, plays on Saturday nights, there you will find a change in the old order." The change in approach to the sex question, Nathan explained, had not been an arbitrary one but was based upon "a thoroughly clear and intelligent view of sex." In the past sex had been overrated. Through an "idiotic conspiracy" the world had been made to accept it as something of paramount consequence in the life of man. Yet the reflective man had long known that, as a matter of fact, sex was a relatively trivial and inconsequential event and of considerably less importance in life than his tobacco or his *Schnapps*. "Sex is, purely and simply, the diversion of man, a pastime for his leisure hours and, as such, on the same plane with his other pleasures. The civilized man," said Nathan, "knows little difference between his bottle of vintage champagne, his Corona Corona, his seat at the 'Follies' and the gratification of his sex impulse." Sex was "simply something always amusing and sometimes beautiful" and to be taken no more seriously than a symphony concert.[9]

Freudianism and Sex became a big business in America. Exploiting the sexually repressed, advertisements in the illustrated magazines sold pretty girls along with the product, conveying the impression that the curvaceous bathing-beauty went with the car or suggesting that to smoke a certain brand of cigarettes was the next thing to an orgasm with a dazzlingly better-than-life flapper or gigolo. "Chiropractors of the subconscious," as Nathan called them, began to flourish in every community that boasted a brick railroad station and a gilt movie parlor. The public craze for analysis, a conscience-stricken physician confessed in the *New Republic,* had permitted him to double, then triple his fees. As the demand was greater than the supply of trained analysts, the lucrative market was soon invaded by hucksters and shysters whose only qualifications were a secondhand couch, a straggly beard, and an *ersatz* German accent. In polite society, parlor Bolshevists made way for parlor analysts who found the Freudian slip a sure conversational gambit as well as a superior technique for seduction. In the greedy hands of popularizers such as Harvey O'Higgins, American history was rewritten in Freudian terms, and great figures of the past, the free man and the exceptional man, were converted into Freudian cases.[10]

Freudian psychoanalysis invaded almost every conceivable field of American thought and conduct. Anthropology, sociology, religion, penology, jurisprudence, pedagogy, medicine, art, and literature all succumbed in some degree to the blandishments of the Viennese sage. At the same time, there was no question that in the twenties Freudianism degenerated into a fad. "If there is anything you do not understand in human life," wrote Sherwood Anderson in *Dark Laughter,* "consult the works of Dr. Freud." And Americans did, for in the long list of books published on this subject before 1928 there were not only *Psychology and Common Life, Psychology and Sex Life, Psychology and Business Efficiency,* but also *Psychology of Golf, Psychology of Murder, Psychology of Package Labels.* A "great wave of mind culture" swept the United States, and Freudianism, which in its inception was a clinical method for carefully trained psychiatrists, became a sophisticated, fashionable jargon for debunking American life. The *New York Times Magazine,* for example, carried an erudite article explaining the enormous popularity of the then current song "Yes, We Have No Bananas" in terms of a national inferiority complex. In its popularized version, at least, one must agree with Aldous Huxley that Freudianism was in a class with phrenology, physiognomy, animal magnetism, and other pseudo-scientific fads of bygone years.[11]

Sex had been the great scientific discovery of the century, and, as Nathan said, could be more easily handled than relativity and was equally profound. The accepted panacea for every ill during the middle twenties, popular Freudianism was in full retreat by the early thirties. After the depression failed to yield to psychoanalysis, people began to poke fun at "sexology," and popular acceptance of such books as the facetious symposium *Whither, Whither or After Sex What?* and James Thurber's and E. B. White's droll *Is Sex Necessary?* confirmed the change in temper. So complete was the reaction against Freudianism that the *Atlantic* in 1934 could publish a serious article called "The Rise and Fall of Psychology." Its downfall had come about, the author explained, because in the modern mind science was a form of magic, and the magic of Freud had failed: "Psychoanalysis, for all its theories, has performed no miracles. It has renamed our emotions 'complexes' and our habits 'conditioned reflexes,' but it has neither changed our habits nor rid us of our emotions. We are the same blundering folk that we were twelve years ago, and far less sure of ourselves."[12]

By 1926, according to F. Scott Fitzgerald, the universal preoccupation with sex had become a nuisance. Sex, as the title of one of his books *All the Sad Young Men* suggested, had not proved the master-key to happiness. Uninhibited young men and women, world-weary at twenty-two, had rediscovered the Victorian truism that love and sex were not identical. Fitzgerald himself, who epitomized the Jazz Age both in his life and writings, suffered a nervous breakdown in the thirties, and his once gay young wife ended life tragically in a sanitarium for the mentally ill. Like his sad young men, Fitzgerald learned to his discomfiture that spiritual distress cannot be banished by

spiritual anarchy.° "What most distinguishes the generation who have approached maturity since the *débâcle* at
the end of the war," wrote Walter Lippmann in 1929, "is
not their rebellion against the religion and the moral code
of their parents, but their disillusionment with their own
rebellion."[13]

# II

The dilemma of the younger generation was a consequence of their having inherited worn and broken ideals
which failed to meet the practical test of daily life. Not
only had the soldiers and statesmen left things in a terrible
muddle, but the preachers and philosophers in trying to
explain the ugliness and chaos of life made things seem
only more hopelessly chaotic and unintelligible. However,
when in their frantic search for a serviceable plan of existence to replace the shabby old generalities they turned
to the scientists, they seemed to find a very different state
of affairs.

The scientific activities of man, unlike his other intellectual activities, apparently had not suffered shell-shock.
Life to the scientist, so it seemed, was not chaos at all
but a realm in whose apparent disorder he found a definite kind of order. For instance, out of those very aspects
of human life that had in the past seemed a hopeless jangle
of contradictions, the science of psychology had created
"an intelligible and practically demonstrable theoretic
unity." By what he claimed to find in the seemingly
chaotic jumble of the "unconscious," the psychologist was
enabled to correlate and explain all sorts of bewildering
and painful discrepancies in human conduct, previously
inexplicable. "Our mortification and our painful disillusionment on account of the uncivilized behavior of our

°F. Scott Fitzgerald, *Echoes of the Jazz Age.* See page 359.

fellow-citizens of the world during this war," Freud explained, "were unjustified. They were based on an illusion which had to give way. In reality our fellow-citizens have not sunk so low as we feared, because they had never risen so high as we believed. . . . The demands we make . . . should be far more modest." But of even greater import than a scientific explanation of disenchantment was the promise of Freudian science to undertake therapeutically the task of bringing harmony, order, and happiness into inharmonious, disorderly, and futile lives.[14]

In a world of uncertainties and half-certainties, science seemed to promise modern man a practical guide to a universe freed from the superstition of religion and the perplexity of philosophy. Although scientists warned of the dangers of oversimplification and deplored the public's habit of accepting the findings of science with too much reverence, a great many people—in their desperate desire to escape the discomfort of bewilderment—found in science "a plausible substitute for the simplicity of the Sunday sermon, an interpretation of reality at once convincing and easy to grasp." With the result, as Frederick J. Hoffman has described it, that "the genuinely popular religion in America in the 1920's was the religion of practical consequences—in short, science as it was known through its results, multiplied by efficient industrial means, and distributed over the extensive reaches of a democratic population."[15]

The apotheosis of science created a need for a modern scientific ethic which would bring human ethics into "active partnership with human science." Such was the contention of the distinguished mathematician and philosopher, Alfred North Whitehead of Harvard, who asserted that the business of philosophy was to fuse religion and science into one rational scheme of thought. In *Science and the Modern World* (1925) he began to construct a system of ideas which would "bring the aesthetic, moral, and religious interests into relation with those concepts of the world which have their origin in natural science." In his view modern science had imposed on the human mind the necessity for wandering. Its progressive thought and its progressive technology made the transition through time, from generation to generation, a true spiritual adventure. While he admitted modern science was destructive of faith in God as "an all-powerful arbitrary tyrant," Whitehead believed science was contributing to the development of religion by freeing it from the bonds of outdated imagery and thus helping to reveal its own genuine message.° It was his profound belief that once religion adopted the progressive spirit of science, it would regain its old power.[16]

Because science was popularly acclaimed as a new revelation, it attracted cults which "attached themselves to scientific hypotheses as fortune-tellers to a circus." These cults were an attempt to fit the working theories of science to the common man's desire for salvation, but sooner or later they ran into difficulty. For the great obstacle in the way of the conversion of modern science into a popular faith, as Lippmann saw, lay precisely in its "rejection of the belief, which is at the heart of all popular religions, that the forces which move the stars and atoms are contingent upon the preferences of the human heart." Where the science of Aristotle and the medieval scholars had been a truly popular science in the sense that they read into the cause and goal of the universe the experience and needs of ordinary men, the radical novelty of modern science, as Whitehead observed, was the fact that "scientific theory is outrunning common sense." Rather than providing an explanation of reality in terms of human desire and sense-experience, modern science disinterestedly describes the universe as a series of highly abstract relationships. Once this fact was perceived, science became useless to the unscientific man as an ethical or religious account of human destiny.[17]

° Alfred North Whitehead, *Religion and Science*. See page 370.

For the ordinary man in the twenties science proved a false messiah, and the disillusion with Freudianism was indicative of a larger disillusionment with modern science as a pseudo-religion. Popular Freudianism, as popular Darwinism earlier, had served to break down traditional moral and religious barriers by dissolving the age-old distinction between man and nature and had attempted to bring man back to nature, not only by teaching that man, like every other animal, was in reality in bondage to natural forces, but also by inferring that human virtues were biologic vices. In practice, however, the Freudian analysis with its deterministic emphasis on naturalism and primitivism had shown serious limitations, proving in many cases to be the disease it purported to cure. For as the painful experience of the Jazz Age had confirmed, the means of nature did not necessarily lead to human ends. On the contrary, as Fitzgerald's sad young men belatedly perceived, somewhere along the line a choice had to be made between an essentially animal existence or a life oriented toward human, as opposed to natural, values.[18]

It was here that Joseph Wood Krutch located the source of modern man's discontent. A young intellectual writing just before the depression, Krutch took an opposite view to Whitehead's, contending that science had proven progressively destructive of all ethical and human values. The universe revealed by science was one in which the human spirit could not find a comfortable home, because that spirit flourished only in a world where human values were of supreme importance. Men needed to believe, argued Krutch, that right and wrong were real, that love was more than a biological function, that the human brain was capable of reason rather than merely of rationalization, and that it had the power to will and choose instead of being compelled merely to react in the fashion predetermined by its conditioning. Since science had seemingly exposed those beliefs as delusions, Krutch concluded that man must either surrender his humanity by adjusting to the natural world or live some kind of tragic existence in a universe alien to the deepest needs of his nature.°

# III

Not all Americans succumbed to scientism and the Freudian demonology. The worth, the dignity, the soul of man also had champions in the twenties, but their unfashionable counsel of spiritual discipline and social cooperation ran counter to the dominant ideas of the time: scientific naturalism and economic individualism. The Protestant clergy generally deplored the reduction of theology to psychology, the majority being in agreement with Harry Emerson Fosdick that "What the Freudians call religion Jesus of Nazareth called sin." But perhaps the most resolute champion of the spiritual and altruistic side of human nature was Harry F. Ward, a clergyman and teacher of Christian ethics as well as an aggressive leader of the newly formed American Civil Liberties Union. To Ward the most hopeful fact of the immediate postwar era was that humanity was becoming conscious of itself as an organic unity and was seeking to come together as a whole. Though a man of utopian vision, Ward was well aware that the new social order would not come about by wishing and praying; and though a social evolutionist with strong Marxist sympathies, he never saw it simply as a project in social engineering. What was called for, in his opinion, was no mere tinkering with the machinery of society but a tremendous upheaval—a revolution in social ethics founded upon a conscious choice of the highest, most difficult end for human life. Social progress, Ward insisted, demanded a vital change in approach to the human personality. Hence he rejected the vulgar appeal of materialism, because he regarded man as vastly more than a goods-producing and goods-consuming creature. Neither did he yield to the prev-

°Joseph Wood Krutch, *Disillusion with the Laboratory*. See page 377.

A Suggestion for Our Cathedral Builders

Proposed Design for a Memorial Window to Moral Turpitude

Culver Pictures, Inc., from *Life*, March 11, 1926, p. 17

In the twenties a few brave Protestant ministers tried to revive the "social gospel"— the union of religion and social action—but their optimistic program of social redemption found little support in a money-minded society.

alent urge to find a mechanistic explanation for everything, nor resort to the heuristic fictions of the unconscious, the libido, id, and ego, for he believed any new social order must reckon with the immortal spark within man that refused to be satisfied with animal pleasures and creature comforts and that ever pursued the impossible. It was this spiritual aspect of human nature, rather than the instinctual, which must be freed and given expression and development in all social or economic arrangements. Once the supremacy of personality was established, Ward expected social progress to follow almost automatically.° For in his view the social order was not a framework external to humanity but was composed of humanity itself, and if the individuals composing society mastered their egoistic im-

°Harry F. Ward, *A New Social Order*. See page 384.

pulses and chose the promotion of the common welfare of humanity as the end of life, the new order would come into being.[19]

Viewing the world in 1932 during the darkest days of depression, Reinhold Niebuhr—unlike Ward—saw little hope for either the social gospel or its optimistic program of social redemption. Not only had human intelligence seemingly abdicated in face of social disaster, but the old brutal forces of economic and military coercion were everywhere in ascendancy. A Protestant minister and theologian, Niebuhr had been actively involved in the industrial and interracial difficulties of Detroit, and from his experience there had reached a conclusion similar to that of Krutch—that between technology and science, man was caught in a depersonalized society building up in a depersonalized universe. Although he conceded that social gospelists such as Ward realistically appraised the contemporary social situation, recognizing that modern civilization threatened man with reduction to machine-life, in Niebuhr's view they persistently erred in their romantic overestimate of human virtue and moral capacity. But what Niebuhr found lacking most among these modern religious idealists was an understanding of the profound difference between the moral and social behavior of individuals and of social groups.[20]

For Niebuhr the contradiction between the individual conscience and that of the group was dramatized by World War I: the moral man in 1916 was the protestant, the man of individual conscience; immoral society, the nation at war. The war convinced Niebuhr that, contrary to the social gospel, religion could be effective only if it resisted the embraces of civilization. The inferior morality of groups he explained by the fact that the collective egoism, compounded of the egoistic impulses of individuals, was harder to control and its cumulative impact when united in common impulse was more violent and exaggerated than when expressed separately. Though individuals might achieve a degree of reason and sympathy which would enable them to see and understand the interests of others as vividly as they understood their own and a moral goodwill which would prompt them to uphold the rights of others as vigorously as they upheld their own, such an ideal was beyond the capacity of society as a whole. Since the immorality of society might be mitigated but never overcome, the relations between groups must therefore always be political rather than ethical, that is, they will in the end be determined by power.

But, Niebuhr cautioned, this inevitable conflict between the individual and society should not make for moral cynicism but rather for a more realistic approach to the problem of social ethics. The hope of an ethical civilization rested not upon the possibility of making power completely ethical but upon the possibility of creating enough intelligence and conscience among the holders of power to make a gradual equalization of power possible. If society were to be morally regenerated, men of goodwill must combine the "wisdom of serpents" with the "guilelessness of doves."°

Niebuhr's refutation of unpolitical social idealism exposed the vast gulf between the ethical views of the 1920's and the 1930's. Just as the comfortable and uncritical materialism of the earlier decade easily overrode the crabbed moralism that strained to keep an expansive society within the narrow confines of Prohibition and Fundamentalism, so the practical political ethic of the thirties by its awareness of man's willfulness and self-interest sharply contradicted the sentimental and superficial notions current to the twenties that the individual could save himself and society simply by following his animal instincts or by responding to his Christian reflexes. It would be an oversimplification to attribute this radical reorientation entirely to economic factors, but they nevertheless played a major role. For the depression forced Americans to radically revise their ideas and painfully readjust their values. Prosperity, as Frederick

°Reinhold Niebuhr, *Moral Man and Immoral Society.* See page 394.

Lewis Allen observed, had been more than an economic
condition—it was also a state of mind. "There was hardly
a man or woman in the country whose attitude toward
life had not been affected by it in some degree and was
not now affected by the sudden and brutal shattering of
hope." Certainly the most conspicuous evidence of the
change in intellectual climate was the change in charisma.[21]

If Freud was the oracle of the Jazz Age, Marx was the
culture-god of the depression year. Each, in a sense, was
exalted by the *zeitgeist* of the times. In the comfortable
twenties, food, clothes, and warmth were accepted as instruments, and the most eager attention was directed, not
toward attaining them, but toward the gratifications of
status and emotional well-being which men are able to
pursue when necessities are granted. So complacent men
spurned Christian asceticism for the intemperate ethic of
Freudianism which, because it was a purely subjective
system of morality based upon self-indulgence of the individual's instincts and material aims, was better suited to
the profligate temper of the twenties. But the depression-
ridden thirties brought a fundamentally different atmosphere. Food, clothes, and warmth were in short supply, and
now instead of being considered as means to an end became
ends in themselves. In a world beset with the more urgent
problems of work and hunger, the psychoanalytic couch lost
its magic. The whole machinery of sexual symbolism, the
exciting quest for phallic images and dream equivalents of
fornication, now seemed so fantastic as to be quite un-
believable—especially when compared to Marx's realistic
insight that, not sexual hunger, but a more basic hunger
for material satisfactions was the driving force in life.
Acting upon the Marxist assumption that the only malad-
justments from which men suffer are social, the comrades
of depression threw out psychological individualism to
embrace a social ethic based upon an objective evaluation
of the collective material needs of mankind. But, ironically,
bemused by the belief that in a perfect economy all men

will be perfectly happy, the true-believers of the thirties refused to remember what the sad young men of the twenties had learned—though Fitzgerald reminded them—that physical well-being is no guarantee of felicity.

As ethical formulas for the Good Society, both Freudianism and Marxism turned out to be egregious failures. Because of their single-minded insistence on strictly and abstractly doctrinal approaches to the problems of the individual or society, they failed to translate even their valid discoveries and criticisms into social practice. Both betrayed a lack of social responsibility. In face of capitalistic greed and injustice, the Marxists begged the question of social reform by claiming the thirties was a time of "intellectual preparation" for revolution, not of radical social change. So, likewise, the Freudians who, having discovered the pathological effect of sexual repression on the human spirit, failed to follow through by either ridding society of its neuroses or providing a brave new morality to replace the "hush-hush ethics" of an ascetic Christianity. What prevailed in the end was the old pragmatic alliance between humanistic democracy and materialistic capitalism, the two disparate faiths once again reunited by war.

# Readings:

# The Modern Ethic

## John F. Carter, Jr. (1897–      )

*Son of an Episcopal clergyman and a member
of the class of 1920, he was at Yale with Stephen
Vincent Benét, Thornton Wilder, and Archibald
MacLeish. A serious infection in childhood left
him with bad eyes and a leaky heart, so he
learned to write, as he said, in self-defense. A
foreign correspondent and then a political
journalist, he wrote a brilliant, well-informed,
syndicated pro-New Deal column, "We, the
People," under the pseudonym Jay Franklin.*

## THESE WILD YOUNG PEOPLE

For some months past the pages of our more conservative
magazines have been crowded with pessimistic descriptions
of the younger generation, as seen by their elders and, no
doubt, their betters. Hardly a week goes by that I do not
read some indignant treatise depicting our extravagance,
the corruption of our manners, the futility of our existence,

John F. Carter, Jr., "'These Wild Young People' by One of Them," *Atlantic
Monthly*, CXXVI (Sept., 1920), 301–4. Reprinted by permission of the *Atlantic
Monthly*.

poured out in stiff, scared, shocked sentences before a sympathetic and horrified audience of fathers, mothers, and maiden aunts—but particularly maiden aunts.

In the May issue of the *Atlantic Monthly* appeared an article entitled "Polite Society," by a certain Mr. Grundy, the husband of a very old friend of my family. In kindly manner he

> Mentioned our virtues, it is true,
> But dwelt upon our vices, too.

"Chivalry and Modesty are dead. Modesty died first," quoth he, but expressed the pious hope that all might yet be well if the oldsters would but be content to "wait and see." His article is one of the best-tempered and most gentlemanly of this long series of Jeremiads against "these wild young people." It is significant that it should be anonymous. In reading it, I could not help but be drawn to Mr. Grundy personally, but was forced to the conclusion that he, like everyone else who is writing about my generation, has very little idea of what he is talking about. . . .

I would like to say a few things about my generation.

In the first place, I would like to observe that the older generation had certainly pretty well ruined this world before passing it on to us. They give us this Thing, knocked to pieces, leaky, red-hot, threatening to blow up; and then they are surprised that we don't accept it with the same attitude of pretty, decorous enthusiasm with which they received it, 'way back in the eighteen-nineties, nicely painted, smoothly running, practically fool-proof. "So simple that a child can run it!" But the child couldn't steer it. He hit every possible telegraph-pole, some of them twice, and ended with a head-on collision for which *we* shall have to pay the fines and damages. Now, with loving pride, they turn over their wreck to us; and, since we are not properly overwhelmed with loving gratitude, shake their heads and sigh, "Dear! dear! We were so much better-mannered than these wild young people. But then we had the advantages of a good, strict, old-fashioned bringing-up!" How intensely *human* these oldsters are, after all, and how fallible! How they always blame us for not following precisely in their eminently correct footsteps!

Then again there is the matter of outlook. When these sentimental old world-wreckers were young, the world was such a different place—at least, so I gather from H. G. Wells's picture of the nineties, in *Joan and Peter*. Life for them was bright and pleasant. Like all normal youngsters, they had their little tin-pot ideals, their sweet little visions, their naïve enthusiasms, their nice little sets of beliefs. Christianity had emerged from the blow dealt by Darwin, emerged rather in the shape of social dogma. Man was a noble and perfectible creature. Women were angels (whom they smugly sweated in their industries and prostituted in their slums). Right was downing might. The nobility and the divine mission of the race were factors that led our fathers to work wholeheartedly for a millennium, which they caught a glimpse of just around the turn of the century. Why, there were Hague Tribunals! International peace was at last assured, and according to current reports, never officially denied, the American delegates held out for the use of poison gas in warfare, just as the men of that generation were later to ruin Wilson's great ideal of a league of nations, on the ground that such a scheme was an invasion of American rights. But still, everything, masked by ingrained hypocrisy and prudishness, seemed simple, beautiful, inevitable.

Now my generation is disillusioned, and, I think, to a certain extent, brutalized, by the cataclysm which *their* complacent folly engendered. The acceleration of life for us has been so great that into the last few years have been crowded the experiences and the ideas of a normal lifetime. We have in our unregenerate youth learned the practicality and the cynicism that is safe only in unregenerate old age. We have been forced to become realists overnight, instead of idealists, as was our birthright. We have seen man at his lowest, woman at her lightest, in the terrible moral chaos of Europe. We have been forced to question, and in many cases to discard, the religion of our fathers. We have seen hideous peculation, greed, anger, hatred, malice, and all uncharitableness, unmasked and rampant and unashamed. We have been forced to live in an atmosphere of "tomorrow we die," and so, naturally, we drank and were merry. We have seen the rottenness and shortcomings of all governments, even the best and most stable. We have seen entire social systems overthrown, and our own called in question. In short, we have seen the inherent beastliness of the human race revealed in an infernal apocalypse.

It is the older generation who forced us to see all this, which has left us with social and political institutions staggering blind in the fierce white light that, for us, should beat only about the enthroned ideal. And now, through the soft-headed folly of these painfully shocked Grundys, we have that devastating wisdom which is safe only for the burned-out embers of grizzled, cautious old men. We may be fire, but it was they who made us play with gunpowder. And now they are surprised that a great many of us, because they have taken away our apple-cheeked ideals, are seriously considering whether or no *their* game be worth *our* candle.

But, in justice to my generation, I think that I must admit that most of us have realized that, whether or no it be worth while, we must all play the game, as long as we are in it. And I think that much of the hectic quality of our life is due to that fact and to that alone. We are faced with staggering problems and are forced to solve them, while the previous incumbents are permitted a graceful and untroubled death. All my friends are working and working hard. Most of the girls I know are working. In one way or another, often unconsciously, the great burden put upon us is being borne, and borne gallantly, by that immodest, unchivalrous set of ne'er-do-wells, so delightfully portrayed by Mr. Grundy and the amazing young Fitzgerald. A keen interest in political and social problems, and a determination to face the facts of life, ugly or beautiful, characterizes us, as it certainly did not characterize our fathers. We won't shut our eyes to the truths we have learned. We have faced so many unpleasant things already, —and faced them pretty well,—that it is natural that we should keep it up.

Now I think that this is the aspect of our generation that annoys the uncritical and deceives the unsuspecting oldsters who are now met in judgment upon us: our devastating and brutal frankness. And this is the quality in which we really differ from our predecessors. We are frank with each other, frank, or pretty nearly so, with our elders, frank in the way we feel toward life and this badly damaged world. It may be a disquieting and misleading habit, but is it a bad one? We find some few things in the world that we like, and a whole lot that we don't, and we are not afraid to say so or to give our reasons. In earlier generations this was not the case. The young men yearned to be glittering generalities, the young women to act like shy, sweet, innocent fawns—toward one another. And now, when grown up, they have come to believe that they actually were figures of pristine excellence, knightly chivalry, adorable modesty, and impeccable propriety. But I really doubt if they were so. Statistics relating to, let us say, the immorality of college students in the eighteen-eighties would not compare favorably with those of the present. However, now, as they look back on it, they see their youth through a mist of muslin, flannels, tennis, bicycles, Tennyson, Browning, and the Blue Danube waltz. The other things, the ugly things that we know about and talk about, must also have been there. But our elders didn't care or didn't dare to consider them, and now they are forgotten. We talk about them unabashed, and not neces-

sarily with Presbyterian disapproval, and so they jump to
the conclusion that we are thoroughly bad, and keep pes-
tering us to make us good.

The trouble with them is that they can't seem to realize
that we are busy, that what pleasure we snatch must be
incidental and feverishly hurried. We have to make the
most of our time. We actually haven't got so much time
for the noble procrastinations of modesty or for the elaborate rigmarole of chivalry, and little patience for the lovely
formulas of an ineffective faith. Let them die for a while!
They did not seem to serve the world too well in its black
hour. If they are inherently good they will come back,
vital and untarnished. But just now we have a lot of work,
"old time is still a-flying," and we must gather rose-buds
while we may.

Oh! I know that we are a pretty bad lot, but has not
that been true of every preceding generation? At least we
have the courage to act accordingly. Our music is distinctly barbaric, our girls are distinctly *not* a mixture of
arbutus and barbed-wire. We drink when we can and what
we can, we gamble, we are extravagant—but we work, and
that's about all that we can be expected to do; for, after
all, we have just discovered that we are all still very near
to the Stone Age. The Grundys shake their heads. They'll
*make* us be good. Prohibition is put through to stop our
drinking, and hasn't stopped it. Bryan has plans to curtail
our philanderings, and he won't do any good. A Draconian
code is being hastily formulated at Washington and elsewhere, to prevent us from, by any chance, making any
alteration in this present divinely constituted arrangement
of things. The oldsters stand dramatically with fingers and
toes and noses pressed against the bursting dykes. Let
them! They won't do any good. They can shackle us down,
and still expect us to repair their blunders, if they wish.
But we shall not trouble ourselves very much about them
any more. Why should we? What have they done? They
have made us work as they never had to work in all their

padded lives—but we'll have our cakes and ale for a' that.

For now we know our way about. We're not babes in the wood, hunting for great, big, red strawberries, and confidently expecting the Robin Red-Breasts to cover us up with pretty leaves if we don't find them. We're men and women, long before our time, in the flower of our full-blooded youth. We have brought back into civil life some of the recklessness and ability that we were taught by war. We are also quite fatalistic in our outlook on the tepid perils of tame living. All may yet crash to the ground for aught that we can do about it. Terrible mistakes will be made, but *we* shall at least make them intelligently and insist, if we are to receive the strictures of the future, on doing pretty much as we choose now.

Oh! I suppose that it's too bad that we aren't humble, starry-eyed, shy, respectful innocents, standing reverently at their side for instructions, playing pretty little games, in which they no longer believe, except for us. But we aren't, and the best thing the oldsters can do about it is to go into their respective backyards and dig for worms, great big pink ones—for the Grundy tribe are now just about as important as they are, and they will doubtless make company more congenial and docile than "these wild young people," the men and women of my generation.

# F. Scott Fitzgerald (1896–1940)

*From a prosperous midwestern family, he went to Princeton where for four years he "wasted his time scribbling." His first novel,* This Side of Paradise *(1920), at once established him as the spokesman of his generation in the Jazz Age. After a gay and precocious beginning—youth, charm, money, celebrity—he "cracked up" in early middle-age and spent his last years in Hollywood almost forgotten.*

# ECHOES OF THE JAZZ AGE

November, 1931

It is too soon to write about the Jazz Age with perspective, and without being suspected of premature arteriosclerosis. Many people still succumb to violent retching when they happen upon any of its characteristic words—words which have since yielded in vividness to the coinages of the underworld. It is as dead as were the Yellow Nineties in 1902. Yet the present writer already looks back to it with nostalgia. It bore him up, flattered him and gave him more money than he had dreamed of, simply for telling people that he felt as they did, that something had to be done with all the nervous energy stored up and unexpended in the War.

The ten-year period that, as if reluctant to die outmoded in its bed, leaped to a spectacular death in October, 1929, began about the time of the May Day riots in 1919. When the police rode down the demobilized country boys gaping at the orators in Madison Square, it was the sort of measure bound to alienate the more intelligent young men from the prevailing order. We didn't remember anything about the Bill of Rights until Mencken began plugging it, but we did know that such tyranny belonged in the jittery little countries of South Europe. If goose-livered business men had this effect on the government, then maybe we had gone to war for J. P. Morgan's loans after all. But, because we were tired of Great Causes, there was no more than a short outbreak of moral indignation, typified by Dos Passos' *Three Soldiers*. Presently we began to have slices of the national cake and our idealism only flared up when the newspapers made melodrama out of such stories as Harding and the Ohio Gang or Sacco and Vanzetti. The events of 1919 left us cynical rather than revolutionary, in spite of the fact that now we are all rummaging around in our trunks wondering where in hell we left the liberty cap—"I know I *had* it"—and the moujik blouse. It was characteristic of the Jazz Age that it had no interest in politics at all.

It was an age of miracles, it was an age of art, it was an age of excess, and it was an age of satire. A Stuffed Shirt, squirming to blackmail in a lifelike way, sat upon the throne of the United States; a stylish young man hurried over to represent to us the throne of England. A world of girls yearned for the young Englishman; the old American groaned in his sleep as he waited to be poisoned by his wife, upon the advice of the female Rasputin who then made the ultimate decision in our national affairs. But such matters apart, we had things our way at last. With Americans ordering suits by the gross in London, the Bond Street tailors perforce agreed to moderate their cut to the American long-waisted figure and loose-fitting taste, something subtle passed to America, the style of man. During the Renaissance, Francis the First looked to Florence to trim his leg. Seventeenth-century England aped the court of France, and fifty years ago the German Guards officer bought his civilian clothes in London. Gentlemen's clothes —symbol of "the power that man must hold and that passes from race to race."

We were the most powerful nation. Who could tell us any longer what was fashionable and what was fun? Isolated during the European War, we had begun combing the unknown South and West for folkways and pastimes, and there were more ready to hand.

The first social revelation created a sensation out of all proportion to its novelty. As far back as 1915 the unchaperoned young people of the smaller cities had discovered the mobile privacy of that automobile given to young Bill at sixteen to make him "self-reliant." At first petting was a desperate adventure even under such favorable conditions, but presently confidences were exchanged and the old commandment broke down. As early as 1917 there were references to such sweet and casual dalliance in any number of the *Yale Record* or the *Princeton Tiger*.

But petting in its more audacious manifestations was confined to the wealthier classes—among other people the old standard prevailed until after the War, and a kiss meant that a proposal was expected, as young officers in strange cities sometimes discovered to their dismay. Only in 1920 did the veil finally fall—the Jazz Age was in flower.

Scarcely had the staider citizens of the republic caught their breaths when the wildest of all generations, the generation which had been adolescent during the confusion of the War, brusquely shouldered my contemporaries out of the way and danced into the limelight. This was the generation whose girls dramatized themselves as flappers, the generation that corrupted its elders and eventually overreached itself less through lack of morals than through lack of taste. May one offer in exhibit the year 1922! That was the peak of the younger generation, for though the Jazz Age continued, it became less and less an affair of youth.

The sequel was like a children's party taken over by the elders, leaving the children puzzled and rather neglected and rather taken aback. By 1923 their elders, tired of watching the carnival with ill-concealed envy, had discovered that young liquor will take the place of young blood, and with a whoop the orgy began. The younger generation was starred no longer.

A whole race going hedonistic, deciding on pleasure. The precocious intimacies of the younger generation would have come about with or without prohibition—they were implicit in the attempt to adapt English customs to American conditions. (Our South, for example, is tropical and early maturing—it has never been part of the wisdom of France and Spain to let young girls go unchaperoned at sixteen and seventeen.) But the general decision to be amused that began with the cocktail parties of 1921 had more complicated origins.

The word jazz in its progress toward respectability has meant first sex, then dancing, then music. It is associated with a state of nervous stimulation, not unlike that of big cities behind the lines of a war. To many English the War still goes on because all the forces that menace them are still active—Wherefore eat, drink and be merry, for tomorrow we die. But different causes had now brought about a corresponding state in America—though there were entire classes (people over fifty, for example) who spent a whole decade denying its existence even when its puckish face peered into the family circle. Never did they dream that they had contributed to it. The honest citizens of every class, who believed in a strict public morality and were powerful enough to enforce the necessary legislation, did not know that they would necessarily be served by criminals and quacks, and do not really believe it today. Rich righteousness had always been able to buy honest and intelligent servants to free the slaves or the Cubans, so when this attempt collapsed our elders stood firm with all the stubbornness of people involved in a weak case, preserving their righteousness and losing their children. Silver-haired women and men with fine old faces, people who never did a consciously dishonest thing in their lives, still assure each other in the apartment hotels of New York and Boston and Washington that "there's a whole generation growing up that will never know the taste of liquor." Meanwhile their granddaughters pass the well-thumbed copy of *Lady Chatterley's Lover* around the boarding-school and, if they get about at all, know the taste of gin or corn at sixteen. But the generation who reached maturity between 1875 and 1895 continue to believe what they want to believe.

Even the intervening generations were incredulous. In 1920 Heywood Broun announced that all this hubbub was nonsense, that young men didn't kiss but told anyhow. But very shortly people over twenty-five came in for an intensive education. Let me trace some of the revelations vouchsafed them by reference to a dozen works written for various types of mentality during the decade. We begin with the suggestion that Don Juan leads an interesting life (*Jurgen*, 1919); then we learn that there's a lot of sex around if we only knew it (*Winesburg, Ohio*, 1920), that adolescents lead very amorous lives (*This Side of Paradise*, 1920), that there are a lot of neglected Anglo-Saxon words (*Ulysses*, 1921), that older people don't always resist sudden temptations (*Cytherea*, 1922), that girls are sometimes seduced without being ruined (*Flaming Youth*, 1922), that even rape often turns out well (*The Sheik*, 1922), that glamorous English ladies are often promiscuous (*The Green Hat*, 1924), that in fact they devote most of their time to it (*The Vortex*, 1926), that it's a damn good thing too (*Lady Chatterley's Lover*, 1928), and finally that there are abnormal variations (*The Well of Loneliness*, 1928, and *Sodom and Gomorrah*, 1929).

In my opinion the erotic element in these works, even *The Sheik* written for children in the key of *Peter Rabbit*, did not one particle of harm. Everything they described, and much more, was familiar in our contemporary life. The majority of the theses were honest and elucidating— their effect was to restore some dignity to the male as opposed to the he-man in American life. ("And what is a 'He-man'?" demanded Gertrude Stein one day. "Isn't it a large enough order to fill out to the dimensions of all that 'a man' has meant in the past? A '*He*-man'!") The married woman can now discover whether she is being cheated, or whether sex is just something to be endured, and her compensation should be to establish a tyranny of the spirit, as her mother may have hinted. Perhaps many women found that love was meant to be fun. Anyhow the objectors lost their tawdry little case, which is one reason why our literature is now the most living in the world.

Contrary to popular opinion, the movies of the Jazz Age had no effect upon its morals. The social attitude of the producers was timid, behind the times and banal—for example, no picture mirrored even faintly the younger generation until 1923, when magazines had already been started to celebrate it and it had long ceased to be news. There were a few feeble splutters and then Clara Bow in *Flaming Youth;* promptly the Hollywood hacks ran the theme into its cinematographic grave. Throughout the Jazz Age the movies got no farther than Mrs. Jiggs, keeping up with its most blatant superficialities. This was no doubt due to the censorship as well as to innate conditions in the industry. In any case, the Jazz Age now raced along under its own power, served by great filling stations full of money.

The people over thirty, the people all the way up to fifty, had joined the dance. We graybeards (to tread down F. P. A.) remember the uproar when in 1912 grandmothers of forty tossed away their crutches and took lessons in the Tango and the Castle-Walk. A dozen years later a woman might pack the Green Hat with her other affairs as she set off for Europe or New York, but Savonarola was too busy flogging dead horses in Augean stables of his own creation to notice. Society, even in small cities, now dined in separate chambers, and the sober table learned about the gay table only from hearsay. There were very few people left at the sober table. One of its former glories, the less sought-after girls who had become resigned to sublimating a probable celibacy, came across Freud and Jung in seeking their intellectual recompense and came tearing back into the fray.

By 1926 the universal preoccupation with sex had become a nuisance. (I remember a perfectly mated, contented young mother asking my wife's advice about "having an affair right away," though she had no one especially in mind, "because don't you think it's sort of undignified when you get much over thirty?") For a while bootleg Negro records with their phallic euphemisms made every-thing suggestive, and simultaneously came a wave of erotic plays—young girls from finishing-schools packed the galleries to hear about the romance of being a Lesbian and George Jean Nathan protested. Then one young producer lost his head entirely, drank a beauty's alcoholic bath-water and went to the penitentiary. Somehow his pathetic attempt at romance belongs to the Jazz Age, while his contemporary in prison, Ruth Snyder, had to be hoisted into it by the tabloids—she was, as *The Daily News* hinted deliciously to gourmets, about "to cook, *and sizzle, AND FRY!*" in the electric chair.

The gay elements of society had divided into two main streams, one flowing toward Palm Beach and Deauville, and the other, much smaller, toward the summer Riviera. One could get away with more on the summer Riviera, and whatever happened seemed to have something to do with art. From 1926 to 1929, the great years of the Cap d'Antibes, this corner of France was dominated by a group quite distinct from that American society which is dominated by Europeans. Pretty much of anything went at Antibes— by 1929, at the most gorgeous paradise for swimmers on the Mediterranean no one swam any more, save for a short hang-over dip at noon. There was a picturesque graduation of steep rocks over the sea and somebody's valet and an occasional English girl used to dive from them, but the Americans were content to discuss each other in the bar. This was indicative of something that was taking place in the homeland—Americans were getting soft. There were signs everywhere: we still won the Olympic games but with champions whose names had few vowels in them—teams composed, like the fighting Irish combination of Notre Dame, of fresh overseas blood. Once the French became really interested, the Davis Cup gravitated automatically to their intensity in competition. The vacant lots of the

Middle-Western cities were built up now—except for a short period in school, we were not turning out to be an athletic people like the British, after all. The hare and the tortoise. Of course if we wanted to we could be in a minute; we still had all those reserves of ancestral vitality, but one day in 1926 we looked down and found we had flabby arms and a fat pot and couldn't say boop-boop-a-doop to a Sicilian. Shades of Van Bibber!—no utopian ideal, God knows. Even golf, once considered an effeminate game, had seemed very strenuous of late—an emasculated form appeared and proved just right.

By 1927 a wide-spread neurosis began to be evident, faintly signalled, like a nervous beating of the feet, by the popularity of cross-word puzzles. I remember a fellow expatriate opening a letter from a mutual friend of ours, urging him to come home and be revitalized by the hardy, bracing qualities of the native soil. It was a strong letter and it affected us both deeply, until we noticed that it was headed from a nerve sanitarium in Pennsylvania.

By this time contemporaries of mine had begun to disappear into the dark maw of violence. A classmate killed his wife and himself on Long Island, another tumbled "accidently" from a skyscraper in Philadelphia, another purposely from a skyscraper in New York. One was killed in a speak-easy in Chicago; another was beaten to death in a speak-easy in New York and crawled home to the Princeton Club to die; still another had his skull crushed by a maniac's axe in an insane asylum where he was confined. These are not catastrophes that I went out of my way to look for—these were my friends; moreover, these things happened not during the depression but during the boom.

In the spring of '27, something bright and alien flashed across the sky. A young Minnesotan who seemed to have had nothing to do with his generation did a heroic thing, and for a moment people set down their glasses in country clubs and speakeasies and thought of their old best dreams.

Maybe there was a way out by flying, maybe our restless blood could find frontiers in the illimitable air. But by that time we were all pretty well committed; and the Jazz Age continued; we would all have one more.

Nevertheless, Americans were wandering ever more widely—friends seemed eternally bound for Russia, Persia, Abyssinia and Central Africa. And by 1928 Paris had grown suffocating. With each new shipment of Americans spewed up by the boom the quality fell off, until toward the end there was something sinister about the crazy boatloads. They were no longer the simple pa and ma and son and daughter, infinitely superior in their qualities of kindness and curiosity to the corresponding class in Europe, but fantastic neanderthals who believed something, something vague, that you remembered from a very cheap novel. I remember an Italian on a steamer who promenaded the deck in an American Reserve Officer's uniform picking quarrels in broken English with Americans who criticised their own institutions in the bar. I remember a fat Jewess, inlaid with diamonds, who sat behind us at the Russian ballet and said as the curtain rose, "Thad's luffly, dey ought to baint a bicture of it." This was low comedy, but it was evident that money and power were falling into the hands of people in comparison with whom the leader of a village Soviet would be a gold-mine of judgment and culture. There were citizens travelling in luxury in 1928 and 1929 who, in the distortion of their new condition, had the human value of Pekinese, bivalves, cretins, goats. I remember the Judge from some New York district who had taken his daughter to see the Bayeux Tapestries and made a scene in the papers advocating their segregation because one scene was immoral. But in those days life was like the race in *Alice in Wonderland*, there was a prize for every one.

The Jazz Age had had a wild youth and a heady middle age. There was the phase of the necking parties, the Leopold-Loeb murder (I remember the time my wife was

arrested on Queensborough Bridge on the suspicion of being
the "Bob-haired Bandit") and the John Held Clothes. In
the second phase such phenomena as sex and murder became more mature, if much more conventional. Middle
age must be served and pajamas came to the beach to
save fat thighs and flabby calves from competition with
the one-piece bathing-suit. Finally skirts came down and
everything was concealed. Everybody was at scratch now.
Let's go—

But it was not to be. Somebody had blundered and the
most expensive orgy in history was over.

It ended two years ago,° because the utter confidence
which was its essential prop received an enormous jolt,
and it didn't take long for the flimsy structure to settle
earthward. And after two years the Jazz Age seems as
far away as the days before the War. It was borrowed time
anyhow—the whole upper tenth of a nation living with the
insouciance of grand ducs and the casualness of chorus
girls. But moralizing is easy now and it was pleasant to be
in one's twenties in such a certain and unworried time.
Even when you were broke you didn't worry about money,
because it was in such profusion around you. Toward the
end one had a struggle to pay one's share; it was almost
a favor to accept hospitality that required any travelling.
Charm, notoriety, mere good manners, weighed more than
money as a social asset. This was rather splendid, but
things were getting thinner and thinner as the eternal
necessary human values tried to spread over all that expansion. Writers were geniuses on the strength of one
respectable book or play; just as during the War officers of
four months' experience commanded hundreds of men, so
there were now many little fish lording it over great big
bowls. In the theatrical world extravagant productions were
carried by a few second-rate stars, and so on up the scale
into politics, where it was difficult to interest good men in

° 1929

positions of the highest importance and responsibility, importance and responsibility far exceeding that of business executives but which paid only five or six thousand a year.

Now once more the belt is tight and we summon the proper expression of horror as we look back at our wasted youth. Sometimes, though, there is a ghostly rumble among the drums, an asthmatic whisper in the trombones that swings me back into the early twenties when we drank wood alcohol and every day in every way grew better and better, and there was a first abortive shortening of the skirts, and girls all looked alike in sweater dresses, and people you didn't want to know said "Yes, we have no bananas," and it seemed only a question of a few years before the older people would step aside and let the world be run by those who saw things as they were—and it all seems rosy and romantic to us who were young then, because we will never feel quite so intensely about our surroundings any more.

# Alfred North Whitehead (1861–1947)

*An Englishman and one of the leading mathematical theorists of the day, he went in 1924 to Harvard, where he was a professor of philosophy until his retirement in 1937. Primarily a mathematical philosopher using symbols as means of expression, he was also fundamentally a religious man, having an almost mystical attitude toward science. To him the discoveries of modern science supplied a basis for regenerative philosophy, but he protested against taking scientific abstractions out of their setting and treating them as if they were antecedent existences defining "reality."*

# RELIGION AND SCIENCE

The difficulty in approaching the question of the relations between Religion and Science is, that its elucidation requires that we have in our minds some clear idea of what we mean by either of the terms, "religion" and "science." Also I wish to speak in the most general way possible, and to keep in the background any comparison of particular creeds, scientific or religious. We have got to understand the type of connection which exists between the two spheres, and then to draw some definite conclusions respecting the existing situation which at present confronts the world.

The *conflict* between religion and science is what naturally occurs to our minds when we think of this subject. It seems as though, during the last half-century, the results of science and the beliefs of religion had come into a position of frank disagreement, from which there can be no escape, except by abandoning either the clear teaching of science, or the clear teaching of religion. This conclusion has been urged by controversialists on either side. Not by all controversialists, of course, but by those trenchant intellects which every controversy calls out into the open.

The distress of sensitive minds, and the zeal for truth, and the sense of the importance of the issues, must command our sincerest sympathy. When we consider what religion is for mankind, and what science is, it is no exaggeration to say that the future course of history depends upon the decision of this generation as to the relations between them. We have here the two strongest general forces (apart from the mere impulse of the various senses) which influence men, and they seem to be set one against the other—the force of our religious intuitions, and the force of our impulse to accurate observation and logical deduction.

A great English statesman once advised his countrymen to use large-scale maps, as a preservative against alarms, panics, and general misunderstanding of the true relations between nations. In the same way in dealing with the clash between permanent elements of human nature, it is well to map our history on a large scale, and to disengage ourselves from our immediate absorption in the present conflicts. When we do this, we immediately discover two great facts. In the first place, there has always been a conflict between religion and science; and in the second place, both religion and science have always been in a state of continual development. In the early days of Christianity, there was a general belief among Christians that the world was coming to an end in the lifetime of people then living. We make only indirect inferences as to how far this belief was authoritatively proclaimed; but it is certain that it was widely held, and that it formed an impressive part of the popular religious doctrine. The belief proved itself to be mistaken, and Christian doctrine adjusted itself to the change. Again in the early Church individual theologians very confidently deduced from the Bible opinions concerning the nature of the physical universe. In the year A.D. 535, a monk named Cosmas wrote a book which he entitled, *Christian Topography*. . . . In this book, basing himself upon the direct meaning of Biblical texts as construed by him in a literal fashion, he denied the existence of the antipodes, and asserted that the world is a flat parallelogram whose length is double its breadth.

In the seventeenth century the doctrine of the motion of the earth was condemned by a Catholic tribunal. A hundred years ago the extension of time demanded by geological science distressed religious people, Protestant and Catholic. And today the doctrine of evolution is an equal stumbling-block. These are only a few instances illustrating a general fact.

But all our ideas will be in a wrong perspective if we think that this recurring perplexity was confined to contradictions between religion and science; and that in these controversies religion was always wrong, and that science was always right. The true facts of the case are very much more complex, and refuse to be summarised in these simple terms. . . .

Science is even more changeable than theology. No man of science could subscribe without qualification to Galileo's beliefs, or to Newton's beliefs, or to all his own scientific beliefs of ten years ago.

In both regions of thought, additions, distinctions, and modifications have been introduced. So that now, even when the same assertion is made today as was made a thousand, or fifteen hundred years ago, it is made subject to limitations or expansions of meaning, which were not contemplated at the earlier epoch. We are told by logicians that a proposition must be either true or false, and that there is no middle term. But in practice, we may know that a proposition expresses an important truth, but that it is subject to limitations and qualifications which at present remain undiscovered. It is a general feature of our knowledge, that we are insistently aware of important truths; and yet that the only formulations of these truths which we are able to make presuppose a general standpoint of conceptions which may have to be modified. . . .

I will give you [an] example taken from the state of modern physical science. Since the time of Newton and Huyghens in the seventeenth century there have been two theories as to the physical nature of light. Newton's theory was that a beam of light consists of a stream of very minute particles, or corpuscles, and that we have the sensation of light when these corpuscles strike the retinas of our eyes. Huyghens' theory was that light consists of very minute waves of trembling in an all-pervading ether, and that these waves are travelling along a beam of light. The two theories are contradictory. In the eighteenth century Newton's theory was believed, in the nineteenth century Huyghens' theory was believed. Today there is one large group of phenomena which can be explained only on the wave theory, and another large group which can be explained only on the corpuscular theory. Scientists have to leave it at that, and wait for the future, in the hope of attaining some wider vision which reconciles both.

We should apply these same principles to the questions in which there is a variance between science and religion. We would believe nothing in either sphere of thought which does not appear to us to be certified by solid reasons based upon the critical research either of ourselves or of competent authorities. But granting that we have honestly taken this precaution, a clash between the two on points of detail where they overlap should not lead us hastily to abandon doctrines for which we have solid evidence. It may be that we are more interested in one set of doctrines than in the other. But, if we have any sense of perspective and of the history of thought, we shall wait and refrain from mutual anathemas.

We should wait: but we should not wait passively, or in despair. The clash is a sign that there are wider truths and finer perspectives within which a reconciliation of a deeper religion and a more subtle science will be found.

In one sense, therefore, the conflict between science and religion is a slight matter which has been unduly emphasised. A mere logical contradiction cannot in itself point to more than the necessity of some readjustments, possibly of a very minor character on both sides. Remember the widely different aspects of events which are dealt with in science and in religion respectively. Science is concerned with the general conditions which are observed to regulate physical phenomena; whereas religion is wholly wrapped up in the contemplation of moral and aesthetic values. On the one side there is the law of gravitation, and on the other the contemplation of the beauty of holiness. What one side sees, the other misses; and vice versa.

Consider, for example, the lives of John Wesley and of Saint Francis of Assisi. For physical science you have in these lives merely ordinary examples of the operation of the principles of physiological chemistry, and of the dynamics of nervous reactions: for religion you have lives of the most profound significance in the history of the world. Can you be surprised that, in the absence of a perfect and complete phrasing of the principles of science and of the principles of religion which apply to these specific cases, the accounts of these lives from these divergent standpoints should involve discrepancies? It would be a miracle if it were not so.

It would, however, be missing the point to think that we need not trouble ourselves about the conflict between science and religion. In an intellectual age there can be no active interest which puts aside all hope of a vision of the harmony of truth. To acquiesce in discrepancy is destructive of candour, and of moral cleanliness. It belongs to the self-respect of intellect to pursue every tangle of thought to its final unravelment. If you check that impulse, you will get no religion and no science from an awakened thoughtfulness. The important question is, In what spirit are we going to face the issue? There we come to something absolutely vital.

A clash of doctrines is not a disaster—it is an opportunity. . . .

In formal logic, a contradiction is the signal of a defeat: but in the evolution of real knowledge it marks the first step in progress towards a victory. This is one great reason for the utmost toleration of variety of opinion. Once and forever, this duty of toleration has been summed up in the words, "Let both grow together until the harvest." The failure of Christians to act up to this precept, of the highest authority, is one of the curiosities of religious history. . . .

For over two centuries religion has been on the defensive, and on a weak defensive. The period has been one of un-

precedented intellectual progress. In this way a series of
novel situations have been produced for thought. Each such
occasion has found the religious thinkers unprepared. Something, which has been proclaimed to be vital, has finally,
after struggle, distress, and anathema, been modified and
otherwise interpreted. The next generation of religious
apologists then congratulates the religious world on the
deeper insight which has been gained. The result of the
continued repetition of this undignified retreat, during
many generations, has at last almost entirely destroyed
the intellectual authority of religious thinkers. Consider
this contrast: when Darwin or Einstein proclaim theories
which modify our ideas, it is a triumph for science. We do
not go about saying that there is another defeat for science, because its old ideas have been abandoned. We know
that another step of scientific insight has been gained.

Religion will not regain its old power until it can face
change in the same spirit as does science. Its principles
may be eternal, but the expression of those principles
requires continual development. This evolution of religion
is in the main a disengagement of its own proper ideas
from the adventitious notions which have crept into it by
reason of the expression of its own ideas in terms of the
imaginative picture of the world entertained in previous
ages. Such a release of religion from the bonds of imperfect
science is all to the good. It stresses its own genuine message. The great point to be kept in mind is that normally
an advance in science will show that statements of various
religious beliefs require some sort of modification. It may
be that they have to be expanded or explained, or indeed
entirely restated. If the religion is a sound expression of
truth, this modification will only exhibit more adequately
the exact point which is of importance. This process is a
gain. In so far, therefore, as any religion has any contact with
physical facts, it is to be expected that the point of view of
those facts must be continually modified as scientific knowledge advances. In this way, the exact relevance of these

facts for religious thought will grow more and more clear. The progress of science must result in the unceasing codification of religious thought, to the great advantage of religion.

# Joseph Wood Krutch (1893–　　)

*Drama critic of the* Nation *from 1924 to 1950 and formerly professor of English at Columbia, he has generally taken a pessimistic view of life, literature, and Western civilization as a whole. Though his "gallant despair" has mellowed somewhat during the years, and he no longer believes that the mechanistic, materialistic, and deterministic findings of science have to be accepted as a fact, he still foresees only two rather dismal choices before man. Either he embraces the creed of atheistical existentialism, which is the tragic solution proposed in* The Modern Temper, *or he turns optimistically to social psychology for the creation of a Robot Utopia, "whose well-adjusted citizens will have comfortably forgotten that their forefathers believed themselves to be Men."*

# DISILLUSION WITH THE LABORATORY

We went to science in search of light, not merely upon the nature of matter, but upon the nature of man as well, and though that which we have received may be light of a sort, it is not adapted to our eyes and is not anything by which we can see. Since thought began we have groped in the

dark among shadowy shapes, doubtfully aware of land-
marks looming uncertainly here and there—of moral principles, human values, aims, and ideals. We hoped for an
illumination in which they would at last stand clearly and
unmistakably forth, but instead they appear even less certain and less substantial than before—mere fancies and illusions generated by nerve actions that seem terribly remote
from anything we can care about or based upon relativities
that accident can shift. We had been assured that many
troublesome shadows would flee away, that superstitious
fears, irrational repugnances, and all manner of bad dreams
would disappear. And so in truth very many have. But we
never supposed that most of the things we cherished
would prove equally unsubstantial, that all the aims we
thought we vaguely perceived, all the values we pursued,
and all the principles we clung to were but similar shadows, and that either the light of science is somehow deceptive or the universe, emotionally and spiritually, a vast
emptiness.

Hopes are disappointed in strange and unexpected ways.
When first we embrace them we fear, if we fear at all,
some miscarriage in the details of our plan. We are anxious
lest we should not be able to go where we hope to go,
acquire what we hope to own, or gain the distinction we
hope to win. But it is not thus that we are most frequently
or most bitterly disappointed. We accomplish the journeys,
assume the possessions, and receive the distinctions, but
they are not what we thought them, and in the midst of
success it is failure that we taste. It is not the expected
thing but the effect that is lost, the advantages of possession
or the joys of achievement which fail to materialize, in
spite of the fact that it was never at that point that we
feared a failure. And so it has been with modern science.
It has marched from triumph to triumph, winning each
specific victory more completely and more expeditiously
than even its most enthusiastic prophet predicted, but those

specific victories do not bear the fruits expected. Less follows than once seemed inevitable and we are disillusioned with success.

Your scientist, impatient and a little scornful of the speculations, dreams, and fancies which have occupied the man ignorant of the laboratory and its marvels, is inclined to feel sure of his superiority when he insists that it is with *realities* that he deals; but it may be that by that statement he is destroying himself, since the contact of the human mind with reality is so slight that two thousand years of epistemology have not been able to decide exactly what the nexus is, and it is easier to argue that our consciousness exists in utter isolation than to prove that it is actually aware of the external phenomena by which it is surrounded. Nor need we, in order to demonstrate this fact, confine ourselves to the consideration of such intangible things as those which have just been discussed, since the physical world of which we are aware through the senses is almost equally remote from that which the laboratory reveals.

The table before which we sit may be, as the scientist maintains, composed of dancing atoms, but it does not reveal itself to us as anything of the kind, and it is not with dancing atoms but a solid and motionless object that we live. So remote is this "real" table—and most of the other "realities" with which science deals—that it cannot be discussed in terms which have any human value, and though it may receive our purely intellectual credence it cannot be woven into the pattern of life as it is led, in contradistinction to life as we attempt to think about it. Vibrations in the ether are so totally unlike, let us say, the color purple that the gulf between them cannot be bridged, and they are, to all intents and purposes, not one but two separate things of which the second and less "real" must be the most significant for us. And just as the sensation which has led us to attribute an objective reality to a nonexistent thing which we call "purple" is

more important for human life than the conception of vibrations of a certain frequency, so too the belief in God,
however ill founded, has been more important in the life
of man than the germ theory of decay, however true the
latter may be.

We may, if we like, speak in consequence, as certain
mystics love to do, of the different levels or orders of
truth. We may adopt what is essentially a Platonistic trick
of thought and insist upon postulating the existence of external realities which correspond to the needs and modes of
human feeling and which, so we may insist, have their
being in some part of the universe unreachable by science.
But to do so is to make an unwarrantable assumption and to
be guilty of the metaphysical fallacy of failing to distinguish between a truth of feeling and that other sort of
truth which is described as a "truth of correspondence,"
and it is better perhaps, at least for those of us who have
grown up in an age of scientific thought, to steer clear of
such confusions and to rest content with the admission that,
though the universe with which science deals is the real
universe, yet we do not and cannot have any but fleeting
and imperfect contacts with it; that the most important
part of our lives—our sensations, emotions, desires, and aspirations—takes place in a universe of illusions which science can attenuate or destroy, but which it is powerless
to enrich.

But once we have made that admission we must guard
ourselves against the assumption, hastily embraced by those
who make the admission too gladly, that we have thereby
liberated ourselves from all bondage to mere fact and
freed the human spirit so that it may develop in its own
way. The human world is not completely detached and
autonomous. Since mind can function only through body,
the one world is interpenetrated by the other. The two
clash from time to time, and when they do so it is always
the solider which must prevail, so that we dare not attempt
to deny its existence. The world which our minds have

created to meet our desires and our needs exists precariously and on sufferance; it is shadowy and insubstantial for the very reason that there is nothing outside itself to correspond with it, and hence it must always be fragile and imperfect.

Science, to be sure, has sometimes imagined a wholly scientific man of the future, and the more thoroughgoing sort of scientist has sometimes predicted that the time would come when the world of the human mind would be precisely the world of the laboratory and nothing more. Conceiving a daily life far more thoroughly mechanized than that of today—of a society that sped through the air at incredible speed, that took its nourishment in the form of concentrated pellets, and generated its children from selected seeds in an annealed glass womb—he has imagined a man possessed of a soul fit for such surroundings. To him the needs and emotions referred to in this essay as distinctly human are merely troublesome anachronisms destined to pass away when we have accustomed ourselves more completely to things as they are, and it is our business to get rid of them as rapidly as possible in order to hasten the coming of the happy being to whom the roar of wheels will be the sweetest melody and a laboratory the only tabernacle for which he feels any need.

But it must be remembered that before such a creature could come into being changes more fundamental than are sometimes imagined would have to take place, since, even if we confine our attention to his physical surroundings only, he would have to be one who lived no longer, as all of us do, in the world of appearances, but one for whom vibrations were more real than colors because the spectroscope and the interferometer were more natural than the eye. For him the table in its most intimate aspect would have to be a swarm of dancing atoms, and not only all the art but all the thought and feeling of past humanity alien nonsense. We could understand him no more than we now understand the ant on the one hand or the dynamo on the other, and he would feel no kinship with us. And hence, though we may admit the possibility that the future belongs to him, we cannot feel any delight in it or make its possessor any concern of ours. It is to our humanity that we cling, because it is the thing which we recognize as ourselves, and if it is lost, then all that counts for us is lost with it.

What we have come to realize, then, is that the scientific optimism of which Huxley may be taken as a typical exponent was merely a new variety of faith, resting upon certain premises which are no more unassailable than those which have supported other vanished religions of the past. It has as its central dogma the assumption that truths (of correspondence) were necessarily useful, and that the human spirit flowered best in the midst of realities clearly perceived. After the manner of all religions, it instinctively refrained from any criticism of this essential dogma, and it was left to us in an age troubled by a new agnosticism to perceive how far this first article of the scientific creed is from being self-evidently true. Experience has taught us that the method of the laboratory has its limitation and that the accumulation of scientific data is not, in the case of all subjects, useful. We have learned how certain truths—intimate revelations concerning the origin and mechanism of our deepest impulses—can stagger our souls, and how a clear perception of our lonely isolation in the midst of a universe which knows nothing of us and our aspirations paralyzes our will. We are aware, too, of the fact that art and ethics have not flowered anew in the light, that we have not won a newer and more joyous acceptance of the universe, and we have come to realize that the more we learn of the laws of that universe—in which we constitute a strange incongruity—the less we shall feel at home in it.

Each new revelation fascinates us. We would not, even if we dared, remain ignorant of anything which we can learn, but with each new revelation we perceive so much the more clearly that half—perhaps the most important half—of all we are and desire to be can find no comfort or support in such knowledge, that it is useless to seek for correspondences between our inner world and the outer one when we know that no such correspondences exist. Many of the things which we value most have a relation to external nature no more intimate than the relation of purple to vibrations of the ether, and the existence of such a relation can never be to us more than an academic fact. We are disillusioned with the laboratory, not because we have lost faith in the power of those findings but because we have lost faith in the power of those findings to help us as generally as we had once hoped they might help. . . .

Nor is there any reason why we should fail to realize the fact that the acceptance of such despair as must inevitably be ours does not, after all, involve a misery so acute as that which many have been compelled to endure. Terror can be blacker than that and so can the extremes of physical want and pain. The most human human being has still more of the animal than of anything else and no love of rhetoric should betray one into seeming to deny that he who has escaped animal pain has escaped much. Despair of the sort which has here been described is a luxury in the sense that it is possible only to those who have much that many people do without, and philosophical pessimism, dry as it may leave the soul, is more easily endured than hunger or cold.

Leaving the future to those who have faith in it, we may survey our world and, if we bear in mind the facts just stated, we may permit ourselves to exclaim, a little rhetorically perhaps,

> Hail, horrors, hail,
> Infernal world! and thou profoundest hell,
> Receive thy new possessor.

If Humanism and Nature are fundamentally antithetical, if the human virtues have a definite limit set to their development, and if they may be cultivated only by a process which renders us progressively unfit to fulfill our biological duties,

then we may at least permit ourselves a certain defiant satisfaction when we realize that we have made our choice
and that we are resolved to abide by the consequences.
Some small part of the tragic fallacy may be said indeed to
be still valid for us, for if we cannot feel ourselves great
as Shakespeare did, if we no longer believe in either our
infinite capacities or our importance to the universe, we
know at least that we have discovered the trick which has
been played upon us and that whatever else we may be we
are no longer dupes.

Rejuvenation may be offered to us at a certain price.
Nature, issuing her last warning, may bid us embrace
some new illusion before it is too late and accord ourselves once more with her. But we prefer rather to fail in
our own way than to succeed in hers. Our human world may
have no existence outside of our own desires, but those
are more imperious than anything else we know, and we will
cling to our own lost cause, choosing always rather to know
than to be. Doubtless fresh people have still a long way
to go with Nature before they are compelled to realize
that they too have come to the parting of the ways, but
though we may wish them well we do not envy them. If
death for us and our kind is the inevitable result of our
stubbornness then we can only say, "So be it." Ours is a
lost cause and there is no place for us in the natural universe, but we are not, for all that, sorry to be human. We
should rather die as men than live as animals.

# Harry F. Ward (1873-        )

*An ordained minister, he was regarded as the
"stormy petrel of Methodism." From his "stock-
yards" church in Chicago he served as executive
secretary of the Methodist Federation for Social
Service, and the later shift of Federation per-*

*spective from a prewar emphasis upon social
service and reform to an outright opposition to
capitalism was his doing. Although he deplored
class conflict and espoused the social gospel as
a means of avoiding it, as head of the American
Civil Liberties Union in the twenties he defended
the political rights of Communist leaders. Unable
to surrender his idealism as had many other disappointed Progressives, he embraced the utopian
vision of Marxism. Yet, despite his seemingly uncompromising anti-capitalistic position, his social views in the end rested upon
a pure abstract revivalism.*

# A NEW SOCIAL ORDER

So far in our industrial society, efficiency has been interpreted too exclusively in terms of wealth production, and
the danger is that it will be so interpreted. To offset this
is the fact that many educators and social workers are
strenuously endeavoring to give social efficiency its real
content, to take it far beyond the field of wealth production into the wider ranges of human living. They are facing the question of the end of human living in order that
the means of life may be truly determined. They are asking
not only in what respects, but for what purpose, is humanity
to be efficient.

That, of course, is one of the old questions of philosophy,
both for individual and social living; but as the world
life becomes organized in such a way that humanity can
in fellowship choose its ends and work toward them, this
question of philosophy becomes a very practical issue for
the common people. The question of what the social organization is driving at is, after all, a very concrete question. Here is a scientific, mechanical age trying its best to

From *The New Social Order* (New York: The Macmillan Company, 1922), pp.
131–2, 135–8, 146–9, 151–3. Reprinted by permission of the author.

get its machinery adapted to certain immediate ends with the utmost possible perfection, without any general vision of the final end of human endeavor. So that after all the toil and struggle of social organization, the spirit of humanity remains unsatisfied and often defeated. In the most advanced communities there is still much cynicism and not a little despondency. . . .

Unless this state of affairs can be changed, history moves on to its supreme tragedy: the development of all the resources of knowledge and all the powers of civilization and their application to no other than material needs and sensuous enjoyments on the part of the majority of the people. Either humanity must find a higher goal than that for its energy, or perish, either from the diseases developed by the indulgence of its appetites or from the conflicts incident to such a mode of life. . . .

If, to the average person who does not know much about science or history or philosophy, the question is put, "What is the most valuable thing in the universe for you?" in what terms will the answer be likely to come? Will it not be in terms of personality? If it happens to be a particularly self-centered person it may possibly be in terms of their own existence, but for the ordinary run of persons it will be some other person or persons who hold for them the supreme values of life by ties of kinship or the choice of a supreme affection; some other person or persons for whom they are perfectly willing at any time to lose their own life. On the train quite constantly I see traveling men pull out their watches and in a big majority of cases there is a photograph of a person or a family group on the inside of the case, and that picture is their answer to the question of supreme values. As life enlarges its interests and associations the estimate of value in terms of personality is made in group forms; men value the family more than themselves, the state more than their family, and humanity above the state, because these groupings are really an enlargement of personality, with the power to increase its values.

If the question of supreme values is put to human institutions, the answer comes also in terms of personality. Ask the state and the school and the church what they are trying to do, and they will tell you they are trying to develop people; their end is to produce a certain type of individual and a certain kind of associated living. One of the greatest words of philosophy is that no human being must ever be treated as a means, but always as an end. The greatest teacher of religion asks, "What shall it profit a man if he gain the whole world and lose his own soul,"— that is, destroy his own personality? He declares: "I am come that they may have life; and that they may have it more abundantly."

Without the key of the meaning and value of personality, the universe is an insoluble riddle and man sinks into despair. With that key in his possession, he becomes, if need be, independent of the physical universe. For the development of personality in time and space, of course, he depends upon the environment of nature; but if he so will, he can defy the world, he can blow it to pieces about his head and with his body smashed to fragments go out into the future in a supreme assertion of himself.

It does not lie within our present purpose to define personality, but simply to point out that the new order must recognize and attempt to realize its supreme worth and value. It must be said, however, that personality is increasingly defined in social terms, its values are discovered and realized in fellowship. We shall be able to add a great deal to what the philosophers have told us about personality by experimentally discovering in social action what personality may become. If there is a greater sense of the dignity and worth of the common run of people today than there was a thousand years ago, it is due to the fact that improvements in social organization have developed and actually realized greater values in the common run of people. Thus the process of social development continually defines and enlarges the nature of personality. It becomes increasingly clear that the meaning and end of individual life and of social living is reciprocal and inter-dependent; that each feeds upon, enlarges and completes the other. The more the individual values the community, the more he contributes to it, and thereby enlarges his own life; the higher the community regards its constituent members, the more it provides for their development, the stronger and richer is its own life.

It follows, therefore, that the new order must seek for its chosen end and goal the development of personality. The things of the spirit and not material goods must be the ultimate and supreme object of its endeavor. This is not simply idealism, not merely a question of imagining, wishing and choosing a high goal; it is also a question of understanding the trend and direction of the evolutionary social process, of accepting and working with it. The social order is not spiritualized by injecting something into it, but rather by discovering what are its inherent spiritual values and then consciously developing them. This is the process of ethical and spiritual development for the individual. As he comes to consciousness he chooses certain values, he embraces certain ends; thus his understanding of life becomes moral and his actions religious. . . .

Institutions ought to be reverenced in so far as they serve to develop persons, and so make for the progress of society. They have a right to loyalty in the proportion to which they do these things. But the test must always be the extent to which they serve the life of all the people and not simply the degree to which they benefit those who belong to them. We ought not to wait to criticise our institutions until they begin to limit us, we ought to criticise them whenever it appears to us that they are in any degree limiting the development of personality anywhere. In other words, our institutions must be always a means and not ever an end; and they must always be a means to the general good, not merely to the good of a few. If they are the means to develop the social whole, they will then be an instrument for the development of the personality of those who compose them, giving these persons their proper social expression and function. The principle is this then, that men must serve institutions only in order that institutions may serve men. Personality must ever maintain itself supreme over the machinery it has created, lest in these latter days, imagining itself free from all false gods, it may unknowingly bind itself once again in utter bondage to the work of its own hands.

If institutions are to be tested by what they do to persons, if they exist for people and not people for them, then a state that permits a privileged few to live off the people is like some great Minotaur devouring their lives, it is a state against which the people must rebel. The state does that when it is the organization of a military autocracy; it equally does it when it is the organization of an economic autocracy. This generation has concluded that the autocratic state, demanding the sacrifice of the people, putting itself beyond morals and above God, is an outrageous blasphemy against human personality. But what about the tyranny of a majority in the democratic state? Should it repress and coerce dissenters? May not that too, become such a repression of personality as to be a violation of the individual and therefore an offense against the common good? If there is one thing above any other which the English people have contributed to the progress of humanity, it is their tradition of respect and reverence for individual rights, for the sacredness of persons, even of the meanest and lowest. It is the tradition of the English state that their voice may be heard, their rights and liberties protected. But that tradition is in danger, in the development of democracy. It is in danger in the increase of our social organization. The spirit of democracy may be threatened by mere bureaucratic routine. The state may become such a great cumbersome machine that persons are tied to the wheels, even ground up in it. The democratic state, even under the development of economic democracy, may become nothing but bureaucratic industrialism in which, in rigidly ordered routine, the people go through their monotonous lives. The problem is to make cooperation increase freedom. It is the province of democracy to enlarge personality. This is accomplished only when the people voluntarily give their best endeavor to the collective life. Such a condition is not yet even approximately approached in our industrial civilization. The test for the church and for educational organization, just as much as for industry, is whether it is leading the people into a larger life through its machinery or merely driving them into a lock step treadmill of routine. If the other social institutions are to fully promote personality, it is necessary for the institutions of education and religion to show the way. Those who operate them must see that they are given a continuous opportunity for the expression and development of their personality, that they do not become mere routine workers going through the same mechanical operations day after day like those who attend an automatic machine in a factory. They must see to it that these institutions reverence human life as a whole and that all their operations tend to develop human life as a whole. The meaning and value of church and state and school can be seen and measured in the last and lowest child within the sphere of their influence. By what they do to it; by whether they leave it neglected and dirty, weak and uneducated, or whether they give it care and protection and continuous unfolding, do they stand judged. This is the final test.

The urgent consideration for an industrial civilization is that personality must not be sacrificed to property, for in an industrial order, property becomes the major interest and increasingly determines the character and course of all the associations and institutions of life. In these days personality has to assert itself most of all in the conflict with property.

Our forefathers fought against institutions, both church and state, and well they fought for human freedom. Our fight is mainly against property, but not against property for its own sake, only in so far as it limits personality. The task before us is to establish the supremacy of personality in a civilization that is largely given over to materialism. The present order is a machine order and has produced a mechanistic mode of thought which has overlooked some of the essential factors and problems of life. The nineteenth century has been called the wonderful century because of its discoveries and inventions, but it left us the same social evils that troubled Babylon and Nineveh. Because it centered human energy upon the production and acquisition of material wealth, because, as Bertrand Russell has pointed out, it enlarged the possessive at the expense of the creative instinct, it raised in more crucial form than ever the old question of the choice between God and Mammon. With all its gains in knowledge, its social organization predominantly expressed a philosophy of life which has no outlook and no outreach beyond the things of time and space. It failed to organize civilization around the infinite, measureless possibilities of human life.

The question which man has to face today is whether in his great industrial civilization, he has made first a machine to enslave him and then a God to devour him. The plain fact that property enslaves people is every day to be seen. It enslaves both those who have it and those who have it not, and it is an open question which of them are more thrown into bondage by the increased concentration of property ownership. Property is today the goal of the strong and its possession is the sign of power. In the old order, property in land went to the strong in arms; in the modern order, property in capital goes to the strong of brain. On the one hand are many wage slaves, and the phrase is not rhetorical, held in bondage to the institution of property; on the other hand the owners of that property are also bound in chains, almost as strong, to the things which they own. The struggle for "these things," land in the old order and capital in the new, is not for property's sake, but for the sake of the domination over others that property gives. The miser is a rare bird, the capitalist a numerous species. The acquisitive instinct becomes socially dangerous as it is allied with and strengthens the instinct for dominance, which finally becomes a more consuming God than the passion to hoard. Man becomes a predatory being, not for the sake of gorging upon the possessions of others, nor to wantonly destroy them, but in order to exert control over others. Competitive industrialism is a struggle for power just as was militarism and is therefore likely to renew that ancient evil. . . .

There is another ideal of civilization which never got expression in wide organizations; it is contained in the teachings of the Hebrew law, the prophets and Jesus. Their ideal was to form a community life in which human rights were set above property rights, and property was made subordinate to the development of personality. The day has now come for the widespread organization of that scale of values. Mankind is about to value the creator of social values above the possessor, and to organize that valuation into social arrangements. The principles which the Hebrews have taken with them all over the earth, which the Christian teaching in its true form has still further developed, are sooner or later going to get a world-wide expression. . . .

The western world is about to make important changes in the institution of human property in order to secure a larger measure of freedom for all the people. The changes must go deeper than a wider distribution of income and a democratic control of the sources of income, both of which are needed for the enlargement of personality. They must rest upon the social control of the acquisitive instinct, for the failure to control this instinct, and not any external system or class is the real cause of the subordination of the people to property interests. What is needed is a true conception of the relation of property to personality. It is perfectly possible, in emancipating the working class in one form from the institution of property to enslave them to it in another, as the property class is now enslaved. From the bondage of improper production they may pass to the bondage of improper consumption. Mankind has yet to learn how to make property the servant and not the master of life. The beginning of the lesson is the fundamental principle that things are to be sought not for their own sake, not for self-gratification and power over others, but for common use and service. The problem of controlling the acquisitive instinct is to be solved by devising those measures which shall express the principle: "property for use and not for power." When production is organized for this purpose, and distribution democratically controlled to this end, then property in its creation will express personality and in its possession will develop personality, both individually and socially. Not until we accept this principle of common use and service, with whatever modifications are necessary to protect individuality, do things become the means to the development of personality. An economic order exists to produce wealth not for wealth's sake, but for the upbuilding of the people. To that end, and in whatever forms will best promote it, wealth production and wealth ownership and distribution must be socialized; they must be carried on for the common good. When they are carried on for the individual good their effect is always to break down and finally overthrow the standard of the supremacy of personality. But when they are safeguarded by common control for the common purpose, society comes to value creation above acquisition, the economic machinery is adjusted to produce life, and goods only as they increase life. Then the increase of personality becomes the supreme objective of social organization while property falls into its proper place as the base upon which man stands to derive from it the nourishment for his spiritual development.

# Reinhold Niebuhr (1892–        )

*Born in a little backwoods town in Missouri, he
became perhaps the most intellectually sophisticated of American theologians. Ordained a
Lutheran minister in 1915, he started out in
Detroit where his Socialist views and reformist
zeal made him unpopular with employers.
Between 1919 and 1938 his experience led him to
reject almost all the liberal theological views
with which he had begun. In his opinion
modern liberals had been led astray by a too
optimistic interpretation of human nature and,
for this reason, had been unable to cope with
their immediate problems, much less with
ultimate religious problems. Advocating a return
to basic Christian orthodoxy, he contended that
religion, in order to survive, must extricate itself
from the prejudices and illusions of a sinking
culture.*

## MORAL MAN
## AND IMMORAL SOCIETY

Though human society has roots which lie deeper in history than the beginning of human life, men have made
comparatively but little progress in solving the problem of
their aggregate existence. Each century originates a new
complexity and each new generation faces a new vexation
in it. For all the centuries of experience, men have not
yet learned how to live together without compounding their

Reprinted with the permission of Charles Scribner's Sons from pages 1–7, 8–9,
and 79–81 of *Moral Man and Immoral Society* by Reinhold Niebuhr. Copyright
1932 Charles Scribner's Sons; renewal copyright © 1960 Reinhold Niebuhr. British
rights by permission of SCM Press, Ltd.

vices and covering each other "with mud and with blood." The society in which each man lives is at once the basis for, and the nemesis of, that fulness of life which each man seeks. However much human ingenuity may increase the treasures which nature provides for the satisfaction of human needs, they can never be sufficient to satisfy all human wants; for man, unlike other creatures, is gifted and cursed with an imagination which extends his appetites beyond the requirements of subsistence. Human society will never escape the problem of the equitable distribution of the physical and cultural goods which provide for the preservation and fulfillment of human life.

Unfortunately the conquest of nature, and the consequent increase in nature's beneficences to man, have not eased, but rather accentuated, the problem of justice. The same technology, which drew the fangs of nature's enmity of man, also created a society in which the intensity and extent of social cohesion has been greatly increased, and in which power is so unevenly distributed, that justice has become a more difficult achievement. Perhaps it is man's sorry fate, suffering from ills which have their source in the inadequacies of both nature and human society, that the tools by which he eliminates the former should become the means of increasing the latter. That, at least, has been his fate up to the present hour; and it may be that there will be no salvation for the human spirit from the more and more painful burdens of social injustice until the ominous tendency in human history has resulted in perfect tragedy.

Human nature is not wanting in certain endowments for the solution of the problem of human society. Man is endowed by nature with organic relations to his fellow-men; and natural impulse prompts him to consider the needs of others even when they compete with his own. With the higher mammals man shares concern for his offspring; and the long infancy of the child created the basis for an organic social group in the earliest period of human history.

Gradually intelligence, imagination, and the necessities of social conflict increased the size of this group. Natural impulse was refined and extended until a less obvious type of consanguinity than an immediate family relationship could be made the basis of social solidarity. Since those early days the units of human co-operation have constantly grown in size, and the areas of significant relationships between the units have likewise increased. Nevertheless conflict between the national units remains as a permanent rather than a passing characteristic of their relations to each other; and each national unit finds it increasingly difficult to maintain either peace or justice within its common life.

While it is possible for intelligence to increase the range of benevolent impulse, and thus prompt a human being to consider the needs and rights of other than those to whom he is bound by organic and physical relationship, there are definite limits in the capacity of ordinary mortals which makes it impossible for them to grant to others what they claim for themselves. Though educators ever since the eighteenth century have given themselves to the fond illusion that justice through voluntary co-operation waited only upon a more universal or a more adequate educational enterprise, there is good reason to believe that the sentiments of benevolence and social goodwill will never be so pure or powerful, and the rational capacity to consider the rights and needs of others in fair competition with our own will never be so fully developed as to create the possibility for the anarchistic millennium which is the social utopia, either explicit or implicit, of all intellectual or religious moralists.

All social co-operation on a larger scale than the most intimate social group requires a measure of coercion. While no state can maintain its unity purely by coercion neither can it preserve itself without coercion. Where the factor of mutual consent is strongly developed, and where standardised and approximately fair methods of adjudicating and resolving conflicting interests within an organised group

have been established, the coercive factor in social life is
frequently covert, and becomes apparent only in moments
of crisis and in the group's policy toward recalcitrant individuals. Yet it is never absent. Divergence of interest,
based upon geographic and functional differences within a
society, is bound to create different social philosophies and
political attitudes which goodwill and intelligence may
partly, but never completely, harmonise. Ultimately, unity
within an organised social group, or within a federation of
such groups, is created by the ability of a dominant group
to impose its will. Politics will, to the end of history, be
an area where conscience and power meet, where the
ethical and coercive factors of human life will interpene-
trate and work out their tentative and uneasy compromises.
The democratic method of resolving social conflict, which
some romanticists hail as a triumph of the ethical over the
coercive factor, is really much more coercive than at first
seems apparent. The majority has its way, not because the
minority believes that the majority is right (few minorities
are willing to grant the majority the moral prestige of such
a concession), but because the votes of the majority are a
symbol of its social strength. Whenever a minority believes
that it has some strategic advantage which outweighs the
power of numbers, and whenever it is sufficiently intent
upon its ends, or desperate enough about its position in
society, it refuses to accept the dictates of the majority.
Military and economic overlords and revolutionary zealots
have been traditionally contemptuous of the will of majori-
ties. Recently Trotsky advised the German communists not
to be dismayed by the greater voting strength of the fascists
since in the inevitable revolution the power of industrial
workers, in charge of the nation's industrial process, would
be found much more significant than the social power of
clerks and other petty bourgeoisie who comprised the fascist movement.

There are, no doubt, rational and ethical factors in the
democratic process. Contending social forces presumably

use the forum rather than the battleground to arbitrate their differences in the democratic method, and thus differences are resolved by moral suasion and a rational adjustment of rights to rights. If political issues were really abstract questions of social policy upon which unbiased citizens were asked to commit themselves, the business of voting and the debate which precedes the election might actually be regarded as an educational programme in which a social group discovers its common mind. But the fact is that political opinions are inevitably rooted in economic interests of some kind or other, and only comparatively few citizens can view a problem of social policy without regard to their interest. Conflicting interests therefore can never be completely resolved; and minorities will yield only because the majority has come into control of the police power of the state and may, if the occasion arises, augment that power by its own military strength. Should a minority regard its own strength, whether economic or martial, as strong enough to challenge the power of the majority, it may attempt to wrest control of the state apparatus from the majority, as in the case of the fascist movement in Italy. Sometimes it will resort to armed conflict, even if the prospects of victory are none too bright, as in the instance of the American Civil War, in which the Southern planting interests, outvoted by a combination of Eastern industrialists and Western agrarians, resolved to protect their peculiar interests and privileges by a forceful dissolution of the national union. The coercive factor is, in other words, always present in politics. If economic interests do not conflict too sharply, if the spirit of accommodation partially resolves them, and if the democratic process has achieved moral prestige and historic dignity, the coercive factor in politics may become too covert to be visible to the casual observer. Nevertheless, only a romanticist of the purest water could maintain that a national group ever arrives at a "common mind" or becomes conscious of a "general will" without the use of either force or the threat of force. This is particularly true of nations, but it is also true, though in a slighter degree, of other social groups. Even religious communities, if they are sufficiently large, and if they deal with issues regarded as vital by their members, resort to coercion to preserve their unity. Religious organisations have usually availed themselves of a covert type of coercion (excommunication and the interdict) or they have called upon the police power of the state.

The limitations of the human mind and imagination, the inability of human beings to transcend their own interests sufficiently to envisage the interests of their fellowmen as clearly as they do their own makes force an inevitable part of the process of social cohesion. But the same force which guarantees peace also makes for injustice. "Power," said Henry Adams, "is poison"; and it is a poison which blinds the eyes of moral insight and lames the will of moral purpose. The individual or the group which organises any society, however social its intentions or pretensions, arrogates an inordinate portion of social privilege to itself. . . . Any kind of significant social power develops social inequality. Even if history is viewed from other than equalitarian perspectives, and it is granted that differentials in economic rewards are morally justified and socially useful, it is impossible to justify the degree of inequality which complex societies inevitably create by the increased centralisation of power which develops with more elaborate civilisations. The literature of all ages is filled with rational and moral justifications of these inequalities, but most of them are specious. If superior abilities and services to society deserve special rewards it may be regarded as axiomatic that the rewards are always higher than the services warrant. No impartial society determines the rewards. The men of power who control society grant these perquisites to themselves. Whenever special ability is not associated with power, as in the case of the modern professional man, his excess of income over the average is ridiculously low in comparison with that of the economic overlords, who are the real centres of power in an industrial society. Most rational and social justifications of unequal privilege are clearly afterthoughts. The facts are created by the disproportion of power which exists in a given social system. The justifications are usually dictated by the desire of the men of power to hide the nakedness of their greed, and by the inclination of society itself to veil the brutal facts of human life from itself. This is a rather pathetic but understandable inclination; since the facts of man's collective life easily rob the average individual of confidence in the human enterprise. The inevitable hypocrisy, which is associated with all of the collective activities of the human race, springs chiefly from this source: that individuals have a moral code which makes the actions of collective man an outrage to their conscience. They therefore invent romantic and moral interpretations of the real facts, preferring to obscure rather than reveal the true character of their collective behavior. Sometimes they are as anxious to offer moral justifications for the brutalities from which they suffer as for those which they commit. The fact that the hypocrisy of man's group behavior . . . expresses itself not only in terms of self-justification but in terms of moral justification of human behavior in general, symbolises one of the tragedies of the human spirit: its inability to conform its collective life to its individual ideals. As individuals, men believe that they ought to love and serve each other and establish justice between each other. As racial, economic and national groups they take for themselves, whatever their power can command. . . .

The evolutionary optimism of the eighteenth and nineteenth century, and the sentimentalisation of the moral and social problem in romanticism, have affected religious idealism with particular force in America, because they suited the mood of a youthful and vigorous people, youth usually being oblivious of the brutality which is the inevitable concomitant of vitality. Furthermore the expanding economy of America obscured the cruelties of the class struggle in our economic life, and the comparative isolation of a continent made the brutalities of international conflict less obvious. Thus we developed a type of religious idealism, which is saturated with sentimentality. In spite of the disillusionment of the World War, the average liberal Protestant Christian is still convinced that the kingdom of God is gradually approaching, that the League of Nations is its partial fulfillment and the Kellogg Pact its covenant, that the wealthy will be persuaded by the church to dedicate their power and privilege to the common good and that they are doing so in increasing numbers, that the conversion of individuals is the only safe method of solving the social problem, and that such ethical weaknesses as religion still betrays are due to its theological obscurantism which will be sloughed off by the progress of enlightenment.

It might be added that when the cruelties of economic and political life are thus obscured, and when the inertia, which every effort toward social justice must meet in any society, however religious or enlightened, remains unrecognised, there is always a note of hypocrisy, as well as sentimentality, in the total view. Those who benefit from social injustice are naturally less capable of understanding its real character then those who suffer from it. They will attribute ethical qualities to social life, if only the slightest gesture of philanthropy hides social injustice. If the disinherited treat these gestures with cynicism and interpret unconscious sentimentality as conscious hypocrisy, the privileged will be properly outraged and offended by the moral perversity of the recipients of their beneficences. Since liberal Protestantism is, on the whole, the religion of the privileged classes of Western civilization, it is not surprising that its espousal of the ideal of love, in a civilisation reeking with social injustice, should be cynically judged and convicted of hypocrisy by those in whom bitter social experiences destroy the sentimentalities and illusions of the comfortable.

Religion, in short, faces many perils to the right and to

the left in becoming an instrument and inspiration of social
justice. Every genuine passion for social justice will always
contain a religious element within it. Religion will always
leaven the idea of justice with the ideal of love. It will
prevent the idea of justice, which is a politico-ethical ideal,
from becoming a purely political one, with the ethical element washed out. The ethical ideal which threatens to become too purely religious must save the ethical ideal which
is in peril of becoming too political. Furthermore there must
always be a religious element in the hope of a just society.
Without the ultrarational hopes and passions of religion no
society will ever have the courage to conquer despair and
attempt the impossible; for the vision of a just society is an
impossible one, which can be approximated only by those
who do not regard it as impossible. The truest visions of religion are illusions, which may be partially realised by being resolutely believed. For what religion believes to be true
is not wholly true but ought to be true; and may become
true if its truth is not doubted.

Yet the full force of religious faith will never be available for the building of a just society, because its highest
visions are those which proceed from the insights of a sensitive individual conscience. If they are realised at all, they
will be realised in intimate religious communities, in which
individual ideals achieve social realisation but do not conquer society. To the sensitive spirit, society must always
remain something of the jungle, which indeed it is, something of the world of nature, which might be brought a
little nearer the kingdom of God, if only the sensitive spirit
could learn, how to use the forces of nature to defeat nature, how to use force in order to establish justice. Knowing
the peril of corruption in this strategy, the religious spirit
recoils. If that fear can be overcome religious ideals may
yet achieve social and political significance.

# War and the
# American Dream

## I

War has been traditionally the nemesis of American liberalism. Just as depression has proved to be the periodic foe of American conservatism, so throughout our history, as Richard Hofstadter remarked, "war has written the last scene to some drama begun by the popular side of the party struggle." Twice in the first half of the twentieth century the liberal dream of a better American future was dispelled by the shock and violence of war. The coming of war in 1917 put an end to the Progressive movement, and in 1941 it was war that finally liquidated the New Deal and checked the course of liberal reform.

Yet, at the same time, modern liberals have shown a curiously ambivalent attitude toward war. At the beginning of the century, when the National Association of Manufacturers and leading financial journals were denouncing Theodore Roosevelt's big navy policy, the Progressives, with few dissenters, either supported or went along with the imperialist policies of "Dollar Diplomacy." Two years after war began in Europe, the conservative business community—with the notable exception of big business, whose influence was thrown on the side of unneutrality and war—was still exhibiting timidity and voicing qualms, but the Progressive party was already committed to the defense of national honor, preparedness, and Americanism. By 1916, wrote William Leuchtenburg, "imperialism and militarism had replaced the old liberal formulas of protest, and within a year the party was dead." Likewise, Wilsonian liberals, who with their leader had been "too proud to fight," soon enlisted en masse and turned their sneers on the "snobbish neutrality, colossal conceit, crooked thinking," and "dazed sensibilities" of those few liberals who still opposed United States entry into the war. What is more, the war was justified before the American people, as Hofstadter said, "in the Progressive rhetoric and on Progressive terms."[1]

When war clouds threatened again in the 1930's, the liberals were once more in the vanguard. With the outbreak of civil war in Spain, it was the liberals—John Dewey, I. F. Stone, Lewis Mumford, Max Lerner, Malcolm Cowley, and hundreds of others—who first abandoned isolationism and demanded an end to neutrality. Later, when war spread to the whole of Europe, it was those same liberals who earlier, with a most knowing air, had applauded Senator Nye's investigation of the munitions traffic with its sensational revelations of the huge profits made by "the merchants of death" who now reversed themselves and called loudly for war. Archibald MacLeish, whose sarcastic account of the cynical machinations of the munition dealers in *Fortune* (March, 1934) won praise from the *New Republic* as an impassioned plea for peace, turned about in 1940 and excoriated fellow intellectuals for their failure to defend either themselves or the world by which they lived. Similarly, the *New Republic*, which had viciously denounced armament makers as "buzzards" and "hucksters of death" creating wars to sell guns, also had a change of heart and demanded an immediate declaration of war by the United States. As in 1917 it was the liberal leader President Wilson who guided the nation into war, so in the thirties President Roosevelt led the way. While ex-President Hoover spoke out resolutely against war, Roosevelt brought the country ever closer to conflict: in 1937 proposing a "quarantine" of aggressors; in 1939 persuading Congress to repeal the arms embargo; in 1940 giving Britain fifty overage destroyers in exchange for overseas bases; in 1941 gaining Lend-Lease for the Allies, ordering the U.S. Navy to "shoot-on-sight," and then finally, after the debacle at Pearl Harbor, obtaining war.[2]

Strangely enough, American business in these years stood at the forefront of the peace movement. Although it was standard left-wing doctrine and almost a settled folk-belief of the American people in the thirties that wars were fomented by business, public-opinion polls taken in 1939 showed business executives to be more opposed to war than the general public. While President Roosevelt's "moral embargo" against aggressors met with chilly reception from the oil companies of the United States, which insisted on "business as usual," most of the business community accepted its validity. *Business Week* conceded that the embargo represented the desires of the American people, and the *Wall Street Journal* concluded that such a high price was not too much to ask for war immunity. Business response to the President's provocative "quarantine speech" was likewise strongly anti-war. The *Magazine of Wall Street* pretty well summed it up by saying, "It would take more than the Orient appears to offer us in economic advantages to induce the United States to risk war." Even when prospects of a German victory appeared imminent in the spring of 1940 and there was a pronounced swing away from isolationism, *Nation's Business*—a diehard isolationist journal claiming to speak for 700,000 members of the U.S. Chamber of Commerce—fought the Lend-Lease Bill tooth and nail.

But, if business arrived at the same sentiments of isolationism which many other Americans felt at this time, it was for different reasons. The difference was, as Roland

Stromberg pointed out, that while for a good many Americans the issue was a moral one, businessmen generally looked upon war as an economic proposition and calculated the risks and gains of war as a commercial transaction. The existing economic order tended to favor peace because "The intricate organization of modern economic life, the huge investments, the international investments of capital, the desire of large enterprises for market stability—all these made the disruptions of war more and more to be feared. Modern business functioned as a part of an intricate, world-wide economic organization into which war was apt to throw a damaging monkey wrench."[3]

Rather paradoxically, in view of its anti-war sentiments, American business in the twenties had favored rearmament and encouraged "defense" spending. In 1929, the President could declare that the United States had the largest military budget of any nation in the world. By 1930 expenditures of the government on strictly military activities were 197 percent greater than in 1917 at the beginning of World War I. Nor did the depression curtail military spending under the business administration of Herbert Hoover. In the first year of depression $2,800,000,000 was spent for military purposes while millions of needy Americans went hungry. As the economic disaster deepened, the federal government in 1933 was still paying out 119 percent of its total budgetary receipts on the war system. There seems little doubt, moreover, that business interests were behind heavy military spending. In 1929 and 1930, for example, a Senate investigation revealed that an "expert" on naval matters had been hired by three large American shipbuilding concerns to wreck the Geneva Disarmament Conference in 1927. Again, in 1934, the Senate Munitions Investigating Committee, under the leadership of Senator Nye, disclosed that munitions interests through the use of propaganda, bribes, and lobbying had played an important role in the ever-mounting expenditures for defense. In short, the old contention that "business breeds war" appeared justified to the extent that business, though stopping short of war, nevertheless promoted war by its hankering for the easy subsidized profits of military preparedness.[4]

Along with their fear of economic disruption, businessmen (and especially industrialists) favored staying out of war because they were afraid of wartime regimentation by an administration they regarded as unfriendly. To many the war scare seemed a sinister plot hatched by politicians to destroy free enterprise. "There is only one small group with a hope of profit in war," *Iron Age* contended in 1939. "And that is the vociferous group that looks to war as the golden opportunity to do away with the profit system and the Constitution at one fell swoop." Others worried about who would be the wartime President and how he would employ his tremendous executive powers. The president of the American Iron and Steel Institute claimed that if war came, "as certain as night follows the day, while we were fighting to crush dictatorship abroad, we would be extending one at home." According to Stromberg, the pages of business and industrial journals were filled with horrific predictions of the dreadful dictatorship war would bring.[5]

Business fears for the profit system, however, proved groundless. What business called "the totalitarian plan of nationalizing industry, conscripting the wealth and labor of all, and suppressing the normal incentives of management and industry in favor of the authority and control of government officials" did not materialize. When President Roosevelt chose the leading men of industry for his Defense Advisory Commission and began to organize national defense on a cooperative rather than a coercive basis, the great bugaboo of dictatorship was laid to rest. In fact, as Stromberg put it, "once businessmen were at the helm of the defense commission, their attitude toward government control underwent a remarkable change. It was not long before a good portion of business was demanding more centralization. The suspicion is aroused that business had never been afraid of state control as such, but only of the people who might be wielding that control."

After Pearl Harbor, the New Deal was quickly dismantled. Some major agencies of the depression years were disbanded even before the Japanese attack. The Civilian Conservation Corps was the first to go, because boys of eighteen were urgently needed by the armed forces. The Works Progress Administration was also given an "honorable discharge" by President Roosevelt. With full employment in booming war industries, there was no present need for work relief. Housing, public health, recreational facilities, maternity care, day nurseries for the children of working mothers, loans and advice for small farmers, camps for migratory workers, crop control were all either abandoned for want of appropriations or carried on in a timid and ineffectual fashion in order to escape the attention of conservative hatchetmen. For businessmen, now back in the saddle, had begun to complain bitterly about continuing large non-defense spending, contending that "national defense and the New Deal will not mix."

High on the casualty list were a great many New Dealers or plain liberals who lost their government posts when their peacetime agencies were killed or crippled after 1941. Some resigned in protest, others were forced to resign, were transferred to unimportant positions, or were suddenly dismissed. Most important wartime agencies were turned over to conservatives—often conservative Republicans—or to "practical" men borrowed from business. While not exactly a counterrevolutionary purge, there was no doubt the New Dealers were losing out, and a new crowd was preparing to take over. "What has happened in Washington since Pearl Harbor," said Malcolm Cowley, writing for the *New Republic* in 1943, "is the defeat of a whole class of people who went to work for the government, not in the expectation of becoming rich or powerful—though some of them learned to love power—and not in the hope of building up estates that would provide safe incomes for their children, but simply because they wanted to have fruitful careers and get things done." With the coming of war, the liberals who had hoped to be the architects and engineers of the better American future found themselves powerless, as in 1917 their expectations submerged in the national enterprise of war.[6]

Once again the businessman came out on top. Just as the first World War had created huge profits for industry, so World War II greatly enhanced the wealth and power of American business. Between 1940 and the end of war, nearly 200 billion dollars of war contracts were given to private enterprise. No less than two-thirds of this went to the top one hundred corporations—in fact, almost one-third went to the first ten. General Motors alone received $13,813,000,000 in prime contracts, not to mention its share of the nearly $2,000,000,000 spent by the government for research and development. War-built production facilities increased the nation's peacetime manufacturing plant by better than 60 percent, and roughly two-thirds of this twenty-six-billion-dollar plant expansion was provided by American taxpayers under tax terms that were extremely favorable to industry. If there was irony in the fact that "by means of a war it strenuously resisted, administered by a man it regarded as its inveterate enemy, American business gained new profits and prestige," the greater irony was that by means of a war it loyally supported and led by a man whom it trusted, American liberalism marched to defeat.[7]

## II

No liberal worthy of the name thought of the better American future in terms of war. The liberal dream was of a world at peace, in the words of President Roosevelt, "a world founded on freedom of speech, freedom of worship, freedom from want, and freedom from fear." Liberals supported the President because they believed he wanted to achieve a new moral order for America and for the world. In their dislike of war, American liberals were as one, but they were less unanimous in agreeing upon the exact point at which America should resort to arms.

For those who supported war, civilization was at stake. Hating war, they were able to overcome their dislike of brutality and their aversion to force only by the conviction that America could not keep her soul if she stood idly by and watched the world rot. While not unforgetful of the "great betrayal of 1919," they rejected the notion so popular in the twenties that "war settles nothing." On the contrary, they argued that war settled what it was intended to settle. It settled who was to have charge of the immediate future, whether the world was to be run by dictators and militarists or by free men and their duly elected leaders. Although they realistically conceded that the war-won opportunity might be thrown away or illicitly diverted, the moral of the story, contended Herbert Agar, was "not that all wars are useless, but that peace is a struggle as exigent as war."[8]

Defense of national freedom and resistance to armed aggression might be sufficient cause for going to war, but it was not, in the opinion of more skeptical liberals, a sufficient answer to the question, what would follow victory? They recalled Wilson's wartime dictum: "Force, Force to the utmost, Force without stint or limit . . . the righteous and triumphant Force which shall make Right the law of the world, and cast every selfish dominion down in the dust . . ." and they reminded fledgling crusaders for democracy that Force did not cast down selfishness and was used only to make the dominion of might more secure. "And even the Germans," said one, driving the point home, "after we had traveled three thousand miles and spent thirty billions to introduce them to our American democracy, were openly critical of the way we did it."

To Lewis Mumford's ardent cry that the overwhelming

duty of the moment was "Prepare for battle!" Robert
Hutchins calmly replied that America was not ready for
war. Speaking not in a military sense, he meant that this
country was morally and intellectually unprepared to carry
out the holy mission to which the President called them:
"A missionary, even a missionary to the cannibals, must
have clear and defensible convictions. And if his plan is
to eat some of the cannibals in order to persuade the others
to espouse the true faith, his convictions must be very
clear and very defensible indeed. It is surely not too much
to ask of such a missionary that his own life and works reflect the virtues which he seeks to compel others to adopt.
If we stay out of war, we may perhaps some day understand and practice freedom of speech, freedom of worship,
freedom from want, and freedom from fear. We may even
be able to comprehend and support justice, democracy, the
moral order, and the supremacy of human rights. Today we
have barely begun to grasp the meaning of the words."
If Americans did not understand and believe in what they
were defending, concluded Hutchins, they might still win,
but the victory would be as fruitless as the last.[9]

But it was not only the futility of war that distressed
some liberals; there was also a fear that democracy, in seeking to resist totalitarianism by arms, must itself become
totalitarian. This was the view of W. H. Chamberlin, who
asserted that war was a shortcut to fascism. "There has
been one object lesson in this connection that should not
be forgotten. When did America most resemble a fascist
state? . . . It was when we were engaged in our crusade
to make the world safe for democracy." As he pointed out
in 1940, the ugly combination of profiteering and intellectual
repression so characteristic of America during the first
World War was once again raising its head. It was perhaps accidental but highly significant that the same issue of
the *New York Times* that published President Butler's warning to all Columbia professors to accept his views or get
out also published on its financial page the following note:

"A long war would be bullish for securities; and traders now apparently expect just such a state of affairs." Likewise, the bumbling activities of the Dies Committee, which had been authorized by Congress in 1938 to investigate all un-American groups, suggested that the country might be on the edge of another Red hunt. Although the Committee lost considerable credence when it implied that Shirley Temple was a subversive, it was not deterred from its scalp-hunting expeditions against New Dealers. Certainly such witch-hunting would have been unthinkable in the early days of the New Deal, when the scapegoat had been the "economic royalist," but there were clear indications of change in the political atmosphere of wartime Washington. As Malcolm Cowley remarked, "When a dollar-a-year man tells you late at night that maybe Hitler had the right idea—'But get me straight, we've got to lick him first'—and when an army officer says, 'We'll have to kick out all those long-hairs and set up a business government. Just wait till the boys get home'—at such moments you reflect unhappily that the United States Government is a vast machine that could be used for other purposes besides national defense and furthering the common welfare."[10]

Experience had shown, said Alan Valentine, president of the University of Rochester, that war and the American Bill of Rights were mutually contradictory. "It follows [then] that men who wish to think freely must strive to maintain a peaceful, secure society, for without it their influence wanes. It follows too that intellectuals should oppose the emotionalism which submerges rational thinking. The price that intellectuals pay in times of war is so high that the support of war is rarely, if ever, in their interests. No matter who wins, they are the losers." And the worst of it, concurred Oswald Garrison Villard, publisher and long-time editor of the *Nation,* was that all that civilization had painfully achieved must be sent into cold storage until war was over. "It leads our statesmen to believe that they fulfill their duty to their country and to humanity if they

just see to it that we have armaments enough to satisfy
the generals. It relieves them of any sense that they must
find a way out of this human wilderness. . . . It deprives
them of a compelling urge to build a new state of society.
. . . It enables them to repeat the banal idiocy that there
is now no time to think about anything else except destroying Hitler." Whether Hitler won or lost the war, Villard
believed the average American must resign himself to the
United States becoming a militaristic state.[11]

If nationalism was essentially capitalism's alternative to
social revolution, as D. W. Brogan, a well-known British
student of American affairs, maintained, then there were
grounds for viewing with suspicion every increase in military preparedness as a fascist defense for capitalist civilization. The Roosevelt administration had already established
for itself the record of making the most extensive preparations for war ever made by a peacetime government in the
United States. And as the popular news analyst Elmer Davis
commented in 1938, if the Industrial Mobilization Plan
worked out by the War and Navy departments were put
into force, "it would be ridiculous to pretend that we were
fighting for democracy; for this is Fascism in spirit, if not
in form and structure." Not only would this plan make
war our biggest industry and our greatest public-works project, but it would make America's industrial leaders "preferred stockholders in the nation at war." As things turned
out, his predictions proved quite accurate. The regimentation planned for wartime, however innocently initiated,
drifted as in the last war toward a wartime dictatorship
of big business. Not only did big business get the lion's
share of war orders and profits, but as a result of placing
most of the prime contracts in the hands of a few giant
corporations, economic concentration in the postwar era
was substantially higher and hence the power of big business greater than before the war.

Davis's conclusion that "this war dictatorship would be
turned into a plutocratic class dictatorship which could

hardly be thrown off by peaceful means" seemed far-fetched at the time, but later events appeared to justify his concern. As Eliot Janeway confirmed in his study of economic mobilization in World War II, along with a large armament industry, "the momentum of victory left behind it an unprecedented problem of Governmental organization—the Department of Defense. In the structure of big government, it is the Department of Defense which sets the limits of foreign policy and determines the course of the economy, not least by setting the tax rate." These wartime developments coupled with the postwar menace of Soviet imperialism furnished the ingredients as well as the provocation for maintaining a permanent warfare state. It was this conjunction of an immense military establishment and a large arms industry that led to President Eisenhower's warning to the American people on January 17, 1961, of the danger to their liberties and democratic processes by the "acquisition of unwarranted influence, whether sought or unsought, by the military-industrial complex. The potential for the disastrous rise of misplaced power," said the outgoing President, "exists and will persist."[12]

# III

War revealed both the strengths and weaknesses of liberalism. The same lofty idealism that inspired the liberal to join in the universal fight against the powers of evil and destruction blinded him to the great risk to democracy at home; and the incurable optimism which enabled him to perceive the hopeful possibilities of intelligence as a means of social action led him to underestimate the disruptive influence of economic and class interests in the social struggle.

In the struggle for dominion between the conservative businessman and the liberal politician which began after 1929, the issue was not collectivism—for, as Tugwell observed, that was already an established fact—but rather what was to be the future character of the emerging collectivism. "Was it to be something like fascism's corporative state, frankly owned and operated by business; or would it be a collectivized state with industry and finance subordinated to a culture planned for and wanted by the people?" Except for the practical question of who was to be in control, no one—surely not the big businessman—quarreled with the liberal's insistence on the necessity of avoiding drift into chaos and the corresponding necessity of an intelligent direction of social change. But when it came to the crucial matter of how that control was to be established and maintained, the big businessman and the liberal reformer, in theory at least, parted company. More pessimistic in outlook, the businessman tended to rely upon coercion and force as the means of social control, while the liberal built his hopes on intelligence as an alternative method of directing social change and, by so doing, betrayed a constitutional weakness in the liberal approach to politics. Committed to the use of intelligence, the liberal not only overlooked the extent to which force, rather than intelligence, was built into the procedures of the existing social system—normally as economic and legal coercion, in times of crisis as overt violence—but he also failed to realize the lengths, licit or illicit, to which the dominant economic class would go in its struggle to keep and extend the gains it had amassed at the expense of genuine social order, liberty, and democracy. Further, by falsely assuming—as many liberals did—that the method of intelligence already ruled, the liberal was totally unprepared for the capture of the collectivist apparatus of the New Deal by the dominant economic interests and its wartime conversion into a powerful and profitable instrument of violence and social control.[13]

Ironically, it was the fascination of the New Dealers with the methods of wartime collectivism that made the takeover so easy. As William Leuchtenburg has shown, the lesson the first World War had taught—that the federal govern-

ment could organize the nation's resources in a planned
economy—was not forgotten; and when the depression came,
the liberals turned almost instinctively to what Rexford
Tugwell called the "great experiment in control of production, control of price, and control of consumption" as
a design for recovery. While the liberal remembered the
war as a time when intellectuals had exercised unprecedented power over the economy and the feasibility of
a planned society had been brilliantly demonstrated, it
was hardly the "war socialism" he thought it to be. Although intellectuals did wield some power, important
agencies such as the War Industries Board had, after all,
been run chiefly by business executives. "If they [business-
men] learned anything from the war," wrote Leuchtenburg,
"it was not the virtues of [democratic] collectivism, but
. . . how to achieve massive government intervention without making any permanent alteration in the power of corporations." Had the New Deal liberals been perhaps less
idealistic and more critical, they might also have perceived
that "the immediate consequence of the war was not a
New Jerusalem of the planners but the Whiggery of Herbert Hoover as Secretary of Commerce."[14]

If the misreading of the war experience seemed to cor-
roborate Reinhold Niebuhr's criticism of liberalism as being too optimistic in its interpretation of human nature and
society, there was no doubt that with the approach of war
the liberal faced a real dilemma. On the one hand, he
stood the risk of sacrificing democratic institutions to a
system which incarnated war as the ultimate good; on the
other, he could hardly refuse to defend democracy because
it would cease to be democracy if he defended it. To say
then as Lewis Mumford did that the liberal, continually
hoping for the best, was unprepared to face the worst, was
not quite fair. For unlike the practical-minded businessman
who did not act as if justice mattered, as if truth mattered,
as if right mattered, as if humanity as a whole were any
concern of his—the liberal by creed was intensely dedicated

to truth, right, justice, and humanity. Like every sane person, he knew it was "a greater thing to build a city than bombard it, to plough a field than to trample it, to serve mankind than to conquer it." He was aware, too, of how insecurely we had been living, "how grudging, poor, mean, careless has been what we call civilization." And yet, knowing this, once the armies got loose, he was ready to fight for all that was to him valuable in civilization.

His gravest mistake—and that of the Progressives before him—was his failure to apprehend the devastating impact of war on democratic values and to take appropriate measures to protect those values. For he should have realized that war, once started, would sweep everything before it, seize all loyalties, and subjugate all intelligence. Infatuated by the analogue between war and depression, he had naïvely adopted, with few alterations, a collectivist system designed for the exercise of maximum force and autocratic power. Imputing superior intelligence and moral purpose to the New Deal, he embarked upon a program of economic nationalism using the authoritarian machinery of forcible regimentation. Though carried out in the name of democracy, with democratic intent and more often than not with democratic consequences, the New Deal was, in method, usually more coercive than persuasive. The overly centralized administrative system, thoughtlessly borrowed from the past, was essentially statist and provided no democratic safeguards strong enough to check a drift toward fascism. The truth of the matter was, in their concern to get results, the New Dealers abandoned democracy for totalitarianism.

Yet, the failure of liberalism was, in the end, the failure of American society. The hot crisis the New Dealers were called upon to handle had been mounting toward the boiling point for decades and was the cumulative product of years of error, selfishness, irresponsibility, and stupidity on the part of the American people. For it was they, not the liberals, who first abandoned democracy. Throughout our

history the great peaceful adventure of democracy has
never been able to excite the imagination of the American
people as has war. For every thousand people who shuddered at the horrors of the battlefield, only a handful felt
the horror of the slum. For the thousands who cheered
the efficient machinery of war, only a few recognized the
wasteful bedlam of peace.

The irony of the American dream, as the *New Republic*
pointed out in 1914 and again in 1939, is that "War is the
one activity that men really plan for passionately on a national scale, the only organization that is thoroughly conceived. Men prepare themselves for campaigns they may
never wage, but for peace, even when they meet the most
acute social crisis, they will not prepare themselves. They
set their armies on a hair-trigger of preparation. They leave

---

The Price of Prosperity.

their diplomacy archaic. . . . They turn men into military automatons, stamp upon every personal feeling for what they call national defense; they are too timid to discipline business. They spend years learning to make war; they do not learn to govern themselves. They ask men to die for their country; they think it a stupid strain to give time to living for it." Americans were never ready to spend on the enterprises of peace what they gladly spent on the devastations of war, but, loyal to long-standing tradition, they devoutly denied that the brain that invented the gun, organized armies, and conceived superb engines of destruction could understand the first principles governing the production and use of wealth or create a civilization free from hunger, fear, and war.[15]

After all, the crisis America faced in the thirties had not been a crisis of poverty, but a crisis of abundance. As the famed British economist John Maynard Keynes pointed out, it was not the harshness and niggardliness of nature which oppressed us, "but our own incompetence and wrongheadedness which hinder us from making use of the bountifulness of inventive science and cause us to be overwhelmed by its generous fruits."[16] Because it has always been ideologically impossible for any American government—except under war conditions—to plan or to organize on a scale necessary to meet the needs of the nation, the American people had to wait ten bitter years for war to end the depression. And although war provided a means of escape from immediate economic problems, in retribution it exacted a terrible cost, throwing away the wealth and treasure of generations to come in an orgy of profits and tragic waste, drenching earth and sea with the blood of millions of young Americans, and seriously—perhaps fatally—compromising the future of democracy.

# NOTES

## Prologue: The Businessman and the Politician

1  *Nation's Business,* XIV (July, 1926), 120; XIII (Nov., 1925), 52; *Literary Digest,* Dec. 11, 1926, p. 20.

2  H. L. Mencken, "The Last Round," Oct. 4, 1920, reprinted in *A Carnival of Buncombe* (New York: Vintage, 1960), p. 28.

3  *American Industries,* XXVI (Dec., 1925), 40; *Nation's Business,* XIII (Nov., 1925), 54.

4  Cleona Lewis, *America's Stake in International Investments* (Washington: Brookings Institution, 1938), p. 352.

5  Quoted in *Literary Digest,* Dec. 5, 1925, pp. 5–7.

6  E. S. Martin, "Shall Business Run the World?" *Harper's,* CL (Feb., 1925), 379, 381, and *Life* as quoted in James Warren Prothro, *Dollar Decade: Business Ideas in the 1920's* (Baton Rouge: Louisiana State University Press, 1954), pp. 94–5. I am heavily indebted to Mr. Prothro for the businessman's view of the politician and politics.

7  George E. Roberts, "Things to Tell Your Men: X—Price, The Basis of Industry," *Nation's Business,* XIII (Jan., 1925), 54; "The Nation's Business Through Editorial Eyes,"

*American Industries,* XXV (May, 1925), 21; cited in Prothro, *Dollar Decade* pp. 94–5.

8  *Nation's Business,* XVIII (Feb., 1930), 223; *ibid.,* IX (Feb., 1921), 12; *American Industries,* XXV (Oct., 1924), 7; Prothro, *Dollar Decade,* pp. 30–2.

9  Charles N. Fay, *Business in Politics: Suggestions for Leaders in American Business* (Cambridge: Cosmos Press, 1926), p. 18; Prothro, *Dollar Decade* pp. 147–8, 189–92, 197–200.

10  "What Young America Is Thinking: Why Youth Scoffs at Politics," *World's Work,* LIV (Aug., 1927), 446; *Independent,* Sept. 18, 1926, p. 313; *Nation,* CXVIII (Feb., 1927), 220; *Literary Digest,* July 14, 1923, p. 64.

11  Quoted in *Literary Digest,* Nov. 16, 1929, p. 65; *Proceedings,* N.A.M. (1924), 112.

12  Quoted in Prothro, *Dollar Decade,* p. 138.

13  *Proceedings,* N.A.M. (1920), p. 240.

14  Warren G. Harding, "Business Sense in Government," *Nation's Business,* VIII (Nov., 1920), 13–4; Coolidge quoted in William Allen White, *A Puritan in Babylon: The*

421

*Story of Calvin Coolidge* (New York: Macmillan, 1938), p. 253.

15 Quoted in Arthur Schlesinger, Jr., *The Crisis of the Old Order* (Boston: Houghton Mifflin, 1957), p. 61.

16 *Nation's Business*, XIII (May, 1930), 29; Herbert Hoover, *The New Day: Campaign Speeches of Herbert Hoover, 1928* (Stanford: Stanford Univ. Press, 1928), pp. 12–6; *Nation*, July 31, 1929, p. 112; *New Republic*, Dec. 11, 1929, p. 56.

17 Hoover, *New Day*, p. 214.

18 Coolidge quoted in Irving Bernstein, *The Lean Years* (Boston: Houghton Mifflin, 1960), p. 254; also see pp. 247–63.

19 *Report and Recommendations of the California State Unemployment Commission* (Sacramento: State Printing Office, 1932), pp. 145–6.

20 W. S. Myers and W. H. Newton, eds., *The State Papers and Other Public Writings of Herbert Hoover* (Garden City, N.Y.: Doubleday, Doran, 1934), I, 470, 496; *New Yorker*, Feb. 27, 1932, p. 10.

21 Louise V. Armstrong, *We Too Are the People* (Boston: Little, Brown, 1938), p. 10.

22 *Washington Star*, July 29, 1932, quoted in Bernstein, *Lean Years*, p. 454.

23 Alfred Kazin, *On Native Grounds* (New York: Harcourt, Brace & World, 1942), pp. 363–4; Bernstein, *Lean Years*, p. 294.

24 John Kenneth Galbraith, *The Great Crash, 1929* (Boston: Houghton Mifflin, 1961), p. 183; Ferdinand Pecora, *Wall Street Under Oath* (New York: Simon & Schuster, 1939), p. 283; N. R. Danielson, "From Insull to Injury," *Atlantic*, CLI

(April, 1933), 497–508.

25 Mellon quoted in Frederick Lewis Allen, *Since Yesterday* (New York: Bantam, 1961), p. 57; *Proceedings*, N.A.M. (1930), pp. 12–5; Prothro, *Dollar Decade*, p. 221.

26 "Vanished Prestige of Our Business Leaders, *Christian Century*, XLIX (June, 1931), 693–4; "Can Capitalism Be Trusted?" *ibid.*, 1301–3; O. G. Villard, "Failure of Big Business," *Nation*, May 25, 1932, p. 586; "Business on the Defensive," *ibid.*, May 13, 1931, p. 520; "Businessmen Are Bewildered," *American Mercury*, XXXIII (Sept., 1934), 69–76; John Moody, "Eclipse of the Superman," *Commonweal*, Aug. 10, 1932, p. 366; J. George Frederick, "Babbitt Cracks," *Scribner's*, XC (July, 1931), 46–9.

27 *New York Times*, Aug. 31, 1930, II, 1:1; May 10, 1931, III, 1:3; Oct. 4, 1931, II, 7:6; Sept. 18, 1931, 40:1; Jan. 17, 1933, 10:2; Apr. 14, 1933, 32:2; Oct. 21, 1933, 20:4.

28 H. Hart, "Changing Opinions About Business Prosperity: A Consensus of Magazine Opinion in the United States, 1929–32," *American Journal of Sociology*, XXXVIII (Mar., 1933), 686–7; F. R. Fairchild, "Government Saves Us From Depression," *Yale Review*, XXI (June, 1932), 661; Hoover, *State Papers*, I, 137, 184; *Business Week*, May 17, 1933, p. 3; W. M. Kiplinger, "Why Businessmen Fear Washington," *Scribner's*, XLVI (Oct., 1934), 207; Thurman Arnold, "The Crash—and What It Meant," in Isabel Leighton, ed., *The Aspirin Age* (New York: Simon & Schuster, 1949), pp. 223–4.

## *Chapter One: Back to Normalcy*

1 William Allen White, *The Autobiography of William Allen White* (New York: Macmillan, 1946), p. 496; *Bulletin of the U.S. Bureau of*

*Labor Statistics,* CCCLVII (May, 1924), 466; George Soule, *Prosperity Decade* (New York: Rinehart, 1947), p. 188.

2 Frank Cobb, "The Press and Public Opinion," *New Republic,* Dec. 31, 1919, p. 144; the best account is Robert K. Murray, *Red Scare, A Study of National Hysteria, 1919–1920* (New York: McGraw-Hill, 1964).

3 Meno Lovenstein, *American Opinion of Soviet Russia* (Washington: American Council on Public Affairs, 1941), pp. 9–16, 33, 50. See also *Bolshevik Propaganda,* Hearings before a Sub-committee of the Committee on the Judiciary (Washington: Govt. Printing Office, 1919).

4 *New York Times,* May 2, 1920, pp. 1–2; Murray, *Red Scare,* pp. 239–62; Zechariah Chafee, Jr., Felix Frankfurter, Roscoe Pound, *et al., Report Upon the Illegal Practices of the United States Department of Justice* (Washington: National Popular Govt. League, 1920), pp. 1–8.

5 George E. Mowry, "The First World War and American Democracy," in J. D. Clarkson & T. C. Cochran, eds., *War As a Social Institution* (New York: Columbia Univ. Press, 1941), p. 177.

6 *Hearings on the Ku Klux Klan,* House Rules Committee, 67 Cong., 1 sess. (1921); New York *American,* Sept. 13–22, 1921; *Literary Digest,* Aug. 27, 1921, pp. 12–3; Robert L. Duffus, "Ku Klux Klan in the Middle West," *World's Work,* XLVI (July, 1923), 30–40; R. A. Patton, "Ku Klux Reign of Terror," *Current History,* XXVIII (April, 1928), 51–5.

7 Amy Jacques Garvey, ed., *The Philosophy and Opinions of Marcus Garvey* (New York: Universal Publg. House, 1923), pp. 11, 18, 36; Gunnar Myrdal, *An American Dilemma* (New York: Harper, 1944), p. 749; W. E.

Burghardt DuBois, *Black Reconstruction in America* (New York: Harcourt, Brace, 1935), p. 703.

8 Walter Lippmann, *Men of Destiny* (New York: Macmillan, 1927), p. 28.

9 *The World's Most Famous Court Trial: Tennessee Evolution Case,* A complete stenographic report (Cincinnati: National Book Co., 1925), pp. 74–5, 77, 299, 338; J. W. Krutch, "Darrow vs. Bryan," *Nation,* July 29, 1925, pp. 136–7; H. L. Mencken, editorial, *American Mercury,* Oct., 1925, pp. 158–60; "A Country Trick—and a City Blunder," *Outlook,* Jan. 26, 1927, p. 108; "Tennessee vs. Civilization," *New Republic,* July 22, 1925, p. 221; Lippmann, *Men of Destiny,* p. 30.

10 White, *Autobiography,* p. 597; Alvin Johnson, "Why Will They Vote for Harding?" *New Republic,* July 28, 1920, p. 255.

11 Samuel Hopkins Adams, *Incredible Era: The Life and Times of Warren Gamaliel Harding* (Boston: Houghton Mifflin, 1939), p. 188; Lippmann, *Men of Destiny,* p. 107; Mencken, "The Last Round," Oct. 4, 1920, *Carnival of Buncombe,* pp. 25–6.

12 "Harding: Turning Back the Hands of Time," *Nation,* June 19, 1920, p. 816; *New Republic,* July 28, 1920, pp. 254–6; "The McKinley Qualities of Warren G. Harding," *Literary Digest,* Mar. 20, 1920, p. 55; F. M. Davenport, "Conservative America in Convention Assembled," *Outlook,* June 23, 1920, p. 375; Warren G. Harding, "Less Government in Business and More Business in Government," *World's Work,* XLI (Nov., 1920), 25–7.

13 "Eugene V. Debs, A 'Presidential Impossibility,' " *Literary Digest,* May 22, 1920, p. 53; Wilson in a speech of Sept. 5, 1919, quoted in Joseph P. Tumulty, *Woodrow Wilson as I Know Him* (Garden City:

Doubleday, Page, 1922), p. 505.

14 Harry Elmer Barnes, "Drool Method in History," *American Mercury*, I (Dec., 1924), 31–8; *Outlook*, May 26, 1920, p. 143; *Literary Digest*, Oct. 23, 1920, pp. 57–8; "European Impressions of Debs as a Presidential Candidate," *Current Opinion*, LXIX (July, 1920), 24–6; Ray Ginger, *Eugene V. Debs: A*

*Biography* (New York: Collier, 1962), pp. 424–5.

15 Herbert Croly, "The Eclipse of Progressivism," *New Republic*, Oct. 27, 1920, p. 210.

16 Will Hays quoted by Mark Sullivan, "One Year of President Harding," *World's Work*, XLIII (Nov., 1921), 27.

## Chapter Two: Dollar Democracy

1 Calvin Coolidge, "Enemies of the Republic: Are the 'Reds' Stalking Our College Women?" *Delineator*, XCVII (June, 1921), 4–5, 66–7; White, *Puritan in Babylon*, p. 166.

2 Lippmann, *Men of Destiny*, pp. 12–3; White, *Puritan in Babylon*, pp. 278–88, 351.

3 *Proceedings*, N.A.M. (1920), 11, 112; "Meeting on Open Shop," *ibid.* (1923); *Nation's Business*, XI (Oct., 1923), 26; *Literary Digest*, Jan. 2, 1923, pp. 18–9; "Who Is Behind the Open Shop Campaign?" *New Republic*, Jan. 26, 1921, pp. 259–62.

4 Savel Zimand, *The Open Shop Drive* (New York: Bureau of Industrial Research, 1921), p. 6, *et seq.*; *New York Times*, April 19, 1921, 9:2, 16:3; A. G. Taylor, *Labor Policies of the National Association of Manufacturers* (Urbana: Univ. of Illinois Press, 1928), p. 163.

5 "The 'Law' and Labor," *New Republic*, Jan. 26, 1921, pp. 245–8; William H. Leiserson, *Right and Wrong in Labor Relations* (Berkeley: Univ. of Calif. Press, 1938), pp. 24–7; *American Steel Foundries v. Tri-City Central Trades Council*, 257 U.S. 184, 209 (1921).

6 Bernstein, *Lean Years*, pp. 190–243.

7 Leo Wolman, *Ebb and Flow in*

*Trade Unionism* (New York: Nat'l. Bureau of Economic Research, 1936), *passim*; H. L. Mencken, *Prejudices: Fifth Series* (New York: Knopf, 1926), p. 274.

8 "Report of Earnings of Bituminous Mine Workers" (Oct. 3, 1923), *Annals of the American Academy*, CXI (Jan., 1924), 5–6; "Living Conditions Among Coal Mine Workers of the United States," *ibid.*, 12–23; also *passim* 1–344; "Are Miners People?" *New Republic*, July 4, 1923, p. 139.

9 "A Rockefeller Hits Labor Abuses," *Literary Digest*, Nov. 11, 1922, pp. 9–10; "The Worker's Right to a Living Wage," *ibid.*, p. 7; *Daily News* quoted in Bernstein, *Lean Years*, pp. 130–1.

10 Soule, *Prosperity Decade*, pp. 77, 99, 124, 229–51; *Literary Digest*, Dec. 24, 1921, p. 10; Arthur Capper, *The Agricultural Bloc* (New York: Harcourt, Brace, 1922), p. 9 *et seq.*

11 *New Republic*, June 18, 1924, pp. 88–90; *New York Times*, July 6, 1924, p. 1.

12 Croly, "Eclipse of Progressivism," pp. 210–6; Kenneth C. MacKay, *The Progressive Movement of 1924* (New York: Columbia Univ. Press, 1947), p. 21; *World's Work*, XLIII (Dec., 1921), 164; *Baltimore Sun* quoted in Theodore Saloutos & John Hicks, *Agricultural Discontent in the Mid-*

dle West 1900–1939 (Madison: Univ. of Wisconsin Press, 1951), pp. 367, 562.

13  "A Business Administration," *Nation*, Feb. 27, 1924, p. 220; Allen, *Only Yesterday*, p. 109; Bruce Bliven, "Ohio Gang," *New Republic*, May 7–June 4, 1924, pp. 276–7, 305–8, 334–6, 9–11, 40–2; W. E. Dodd, "Political Corruption and the Public 50 Years Ago and Today," *ibid.*, June 11, 1924, pp. 63–4.

14  Calvin Coolidge, *The Price of Freedom, Speeches and Addresses by Calvin Coolidge* (New York: Scribner's, 1924), pp. 334, 346; White, *Puritan in Babylon*, p. 396; *Nation's Business*, XIII (June, 1925), 15; MacKay, *Progressive Movement*, pp. 162–74.

15  Hugh Keenleyside, "The American Political Revolution of 1924," *Current History*, XXI (Mar., 1925), 833–40; Lippmann, *Men of Destiny*, pp. 23–5.

16  Robert L. Duffus, "Mr. Coolidge's Utopia," *New Republic*, May 7, 1924, p. 288; Coolidge, *Price of Freedom*, pp. 236–8.

17  Julius H. Barnes, *The Genius of American Business* (Garden City: Doubleday, Page, 1924), pp. 4–7; "Business Declares Its Principles," *Nation's Business*, IX (June, 1921), 48–50. For an elaboration of the business viewpoint see Prothro, *Dollar Decade*, pp. 79–95, 157–74.

18  Maurice Leven, *et al.*, *America's Capacity to Consume* (Washington: Brookings Institution, 1934), pp. 93–6, 147–238; Simon Kuznets, *National Income and Its Composition, 1919–1938* (New York: Nat'l. Bureau of Economic Research, 1941), I, 216–7.

19  Bernstein, *Lean Years*, pp. 144–89; "American Workingman," *Fortune*, IV (Aug., 1931), 54, 131; Kuznets, *National Income*, 332–3, 352–3.

20  R. H. Tawney, "The Churches and Social Ethics," *New Republic*, May 21, 1924, pp. 332–3; George Soule, "Why Isn't the Worker Satisfied?" *Survey*, Sept. 15, 1924, p. 635; John A. Fitch, *The Causes of Industrial Unrest* (New York: Harper, 1924).

## Chapter Three: Collapse of the Old Order

1  Harry Jerome, *Mechanization in Industry* (New York: Nat'l. Bureau of Economic Research, 1934), *passim;* *Historical Statistics of the United States* (Washington: Bureau of the Census, 1949), pp. 71–2; Bernstein, *Lean Years*, pp. 53–4; John Moody, "The New Era in Wall Street," *Atlantic*, CXLII (Aug., 1928), 255–62.

2  Steffens to Jo Davidson, Feb. 18, 1929, *Letters of Lincoln Steffens* (New York: Harcourt, Brace, 1938), II, 830; Lippmann, *Men of Destiny*, p. 26; Thomas Nixon Carver, *The Present Economic Revolution in the United States* (Boston: Little, Brown, 1926), pp. 239–40.

3  A. A. Berle, Jr., "A High Road for Business," *Scribner's*, CXLIII (June, 1933), 325; Walter Lippmann, "A Reckoning," *Yale Review*, XXI (June, 1932), 659.

4  Thorstein Veblen, *The Engineers and the Price System* (1921) reprinted in *The Portable Veblen* (New York: Viking, 1960), p. 440.

5  G. Burck & C. E. Silberman, "What Caused the Great Depression," *Fortune*, LI (Feb., 1955), 96–7, 206; Edwin G. Nourse, *et al.*, *The Distribution of Income in Relation to*

*Economic Progress* (Washington: Brookings Institution, 1936), I, 3–13, 415–29; II, 93–6; IV, 1–46, 142–54; Paul H. Douglas, *Real Wages in the United States, 1890–1926* (Boston: Houghton Mifflin, 1930), p. 391; Kuznets, *National Income*, pp. 332–3, 352–3.

6  *New Republic*, July 6, 1932, p. 193; Elmer Davis, "Can Business Manage Itself?" *Harper's*, CLXII (Mar., 1931), 387; John Dewey, "The Collapse of a Romance," *New Republic*, April 27, 1932, p. 293; Stuart Chase, *A New Deal* (New York: Macmillan, 1932), pp. 22–3.

7  Herbert Hoover, *American Individualism* (Garden City: Doubleday, Page, 1922), pp. 8–9, 19, 55; *Challenge to Liberty* (New York: Scribner's, 1934), pp. 145, 203–4.

8  This was a conservative picture, for it must be remembered that the influence of any one of these large companies extended beyond the assets under its direct control. Adolf A. Berle, Jr., & Gardiner C. Means, *The Modern Corporation and Private Property* (New York: Macmillan, 1932), pp. 18–46; *Literary Digest*, Sept. 6, 1930, p. 7; Burck & Silberman, "What Caused the Great Depression," p. 206.

9  Hoover, *American Individualism*, p. 56; Walter Lippmann, "The Peculiar Weakness of Mr. Hoover," *Harper's*, CLXI (June, 1930), 1–7; Allan Nevins, "President Hoover's Record," *Current History*, XXXVI (July, 1932), 385–94; *Cong. Record*, 71 Cong. 3 sess., 74: 407–8; Hoover, *State Papers*, I, 470, 496; William E. Leuchtenburg, *The Perils of Prosperity 1914–32* (Chicago: Univ. of Chicago Press, 1958), p. 253; H. G. Warren, *Herbert Hoover and the Great Depression* (New York: Oxford Univ. Press, 1959), *passim*.

10  Hoover, *American Individualism*,

pp. 24–5, 70; *Challenge to Liberty*, pp. 7, 57–9, 61, 70, 139; *The Memoirs of Herbert Hoover* (London: Hollis & Carter, 1953), I, 447–8.

11  Hoover, *Challenge to Liberty*, pp. 76–103; Lewis Mumford, *Technics and Civilization* (New York: Harcourt, Brace, 1934), pp. 395, 420; John Dewey, *Liberalism and Social Action* (New York: Putnam's, 1935, Capricorn edition, 1963), pp. 31–9; Rexford G. Tugwell, *The Battle for Democracy* (New York: Columbia Univ. Press, 1935), pp. 3–16, 193–207; "The Principle of Planning and the Institution of Laissez-Faire," *American Economic Review*, supplement, Mar., 1932, pp. 75–92; *The Industrial Discipline and the Governmental Arts* (New York: Columbia Univ. Press, 1933), p. 19.

12  George Soule, *A Planned Society* (New York: Macmillan, 1932), pp. 91, 187, 203, 310; Charles A. Beard, "A 'Five-Year Plan' for America," *Forum*, LXXXVI (July, 1931), 1–11; Paul H. Douglas, *Controlling Depressions* (New York: Norton, 1935), p. 84.

13  Walter Lippmann, *The Good Society* (Boston: Little, Brown, 1937), pp. x, 375. See also Albert Jay Nock, *Our Enemy the State* (New York: Morrow, 1935).

14  George R. Leighton, "And If the Revolution Comes . . . ?" *Harper's*, CLXIV (Mar., 1932), 466–7; *Literary Digest*, Aug. 13, 1932, pp. 16–7; *Nation*, May 13, 1931, p. 520; George Soule, "Are We Going to Have a Revolution?" *Harper's*, CLXV (Aug., 1932), 277.

15  Thurman W. Arnold, *The Symbols of Government* (New Haven: Yale Univ. Press, Harbinger edition, 1962), p. 106; Veblen, *Engineers and the Price System*, *Portable Veblen*, p. 445; *Harper's*, CLXIV (Mar., 1932), 466–9, 471–4; Davis, "Can

Business Manage Itself?" p. 387.

16 Franklin D. Roosevelt, *The Public Papers and Addresses of Franklin D. Roosevelt,* Samuel I. Rosenman, ed. (New York: Random House, 1938–50), III, 6, 9, 436.

17 For Rightist criticisms of the New Deal see *Documents,* American Liberty League, Washington, D.C., 1934; the best study is George Wolfskill, *The Revolt of the Conservatives* (Boston: Houghton Mifflin, 1962). For the Socialist view see Norman Thomas, *After the New Deal What?* (New York: Macmillan, 1936); for the Communist appraisal see the *Daily Worker,* 1933–35.

18 Robert L. Heilbroner, *The Making of Economic Society* (Englewood Cliffs, N.J.: Prentice-Hall, 1962), pp. 163–8; Frances Perkins, *The Roosevelt I Knew* (New York: Viking, 1946), p. 330; Roosevelt, *Public Papers,* V, 535.

19 Tugwell, *Battle for Democracy,*

p. 266; Heinz Eulau, "Neither Ideology nor Utopia: The New Deal in Retrospect," *Antioch Review,* XIX (Winter, 1959–60), 523–37; Mario Einaudi, *The Roosevelt Revolution* (New York: Harcourt, Brace, 1959), p. 179.

20 Under Section 7 (a) of the National Industrial Recovery Act (1933). When that Act was invalidated by the Supreme Court, Congress in 1935 passed the Wagner Act reasserting the right of collective bargaining.

21 Alexander Hamilton, *Report on Manufactures* (1791); Eugene O. Golob, *The "Isms"* (New York: Harper, 1954), pp. 143–4.

22 Gardiner C. Means, *The Corporate Revolution in America* (New York: Crowell-Collier, 1962), pp. 37–8; Heilbroner, *Making of Economic Society,* pp. 163–8; Arnold, "The Crash," p. 224.

## Chapter Four: The Materialistic Faith

1 Irvin G. Wylie, *The Self-Made Man in America* (New Brunswick; N.J.: Rutgers Univ. Press, 1954), pp. 168–70; A. J. Stone, "The Dawn of a New Science," *American Mercury,* Aug., 1928, p. 446.

2 Calvin Coolidge, "The Press Under a Free Government," address before the American Society of Newspaper Editors, Washington, Jan. 17, 1925, *Foundations of the Republic, Speeches and Addresses by Calvin Coolidge* (New York: Scribner's, 1926), p. 188; Thorstein Veblen, *The Higher Learning in America* (New York: Huebsch, 1918; Sagamore, 1957), pp. 149–50.

3 Coolidge, *Foundations of the Republic,* p. 320; Neil M. Clark, "Putting Religion to the Test," *American,*

CIX (June, 1930), 50–51; Allen, *Only Yesterday,* pp. 125–6.

4 Schlesinger, *Crisis of the Old Order,* p. 71; Bruce Barton, *The Man Nobody Knows* (Indianapolis: Bobbs-Merrill, 1924), introd. & pp. 104, 126, 162, 165, 180; Thorstein Veblen, *Absentee Ownership and Business Enterprise in Recent Times* (1923), *Portable Veblen,* p. 501.

5 Edmund Wilson, "Mr. and Mrs. X," *The American Earthquake* (Garden City, N.Y.: Doubleday, 1964), p. 436.

6 James Truslow Adams, *Our Business Civilization* (New York: Boni, 1929), pp. 9–31; Sinclair Lewis, *Babbitt* (New York: Harcourt Brace, 1922), pp. 182–4.

7 Wilson, *American Earthquake,*

p. 434; Sinclair Lewis, *Main Street* (New York: Grosset & Dunlap, 1922), p. 267; Ralph Borsodi, *This Ugly Civilization* (New York: Harper, 1929), p. 16.

8  Henry Ford, *My Life and Work* (London: Heinemann, 1922), pp. 2, 105–7, 274; "Machinery, The New Messiah," *Forum*, LXXIX (Mar., 1928), 363–4; Glenn Frank, "Shall We Scrap Our Machines and Go Back to the Spinning-Wheel?" *Magazine of Business*, LII (Oct., 1927), 412.

9  Lewis Mumford, *Technics and Civilization*, pp. 266, 412; Barnes, *Genius of American Business*, p. 14; Elmer Rice, *The Adding Machine* (1923), in *Seven Plays* (New York: Viking, 1950), p. 107.

10  Ezra Pound, "Where Is American Culture?" *Nation*, April 18, 1928, p. 443; Irving Babbitt, *Democracy and Leadership* (Boston: Houghton Mifflin, 1924), pp. 240–3.

11  Letter to Van Wyck Brooks, May 22, 1927, Daniel Cory, ed., *The Letters of George Santayana* (New York: Scribner's, 1955), pp. 225–6; George Santayana, "Americanism," in *The Idler and His Works* (New York: Braziller, 1957), p. 36; James C. Ballowe, "The Last Puritan and the Failure of American Culture," *American Quarterly*, XVIII (Summer, 1966), 123–35.

12  Kazin, *On Native Grounds*, p. 363; Lewis Mumford, "The Need for Concrete Goals," *Common Sense*, Oct., 1933, reprinted in *Challenge to the New Deal* (New York: Falcon, 1932), p. 225.

13  Theodore Dreiser, "Flies and Locusts," *Common Sense*, Dec., 1933, *Challenge to the New Deal*, p. 57; Malcolm Cowley, "1930's Age of Faith," *New York Times Book Review*, Dec. 13, 1964, p. 5; Granville Hicks, *Where We Came Out* (New York: Viking, 1954), p. 33; Wilson quoted in Hicks, p. 33; Lewis Corey, *The Decline of American Capitalism* (New York: Covici-Friede, 1934), p. 547; Daniel Aaron, *Writers on the Left* (New York: Harcourt, Brace & World, 1961), p. 367. Aaron offers the most intelligent and open-minded account of Communism and American intellectuals in the 1930's.

14  John Maynard Keynes, "Soviet Russia," *New Republic*, Oct. 28–Nov. 11, 1925, pp. 246–8, 301–3.

15  Theodore Draper, *The Roots of American Communism* (New York: Viking, 1957), pp. 28, 293–300. For samples of proletarian literature see Harvey Swados, *The American Writer and the Great Depression* (Indianapolis: Bobbs-Merrill, 1966) and Louis Filler, *The Anxious Years* (New York: Capricorn, 1964).

## Chapter Five: Liberalism and Democracy

1  H. L. Mencken, "To Him That Hath," *Smart Set*, May, 1920, pp. 33–4; Lewis, *Babbitt*, pp. 187–8; "Dare to Be a Babbitt," *Nation's Business*, XIII (June, 1925), 40.

2  John Dewey, "The Post-War Mind," *New Republic*, Dec. 7, 1918, p. 157.

3  Floyd Dell, *Intellectual Vagabondage* (New York: Doran, 1926), p. 260; Vernon Louis Parrington, *Main Currents in American Thought* (New York: Harcourt, Brace, 1927–1930), III, 368–9; Glenn Frank, "The Balance Sheet of Civilization," *Century*, CIX (Jan., 1925), 426–7;

Lincoln Steffens, "Bankrupt Liberalism," *New Republic*, Feb. 17, 1932, pp. 15–6.

4 Roosevelt, *Public Papers*, I, xiii; II, 5; Richard Hofstadter, *The Age of Reform* (New York: Vintage, 1955), p. 326; Herbert Croly, *The Promise of American Life* (New York: Capricorn, 1964), pp. 451–3; Henry A. Wallace, *Democracy Reborn* (New York: Reynal & Hitchcock, 1944), p. 73.

5 H. L. Mencken, *A Mencken Chrestomathy* (New York: Knopf, 1949), p. 623.

6 U.S. Army *Training Manual*, No. 200–25 (Washington: Gov't. Printing Office, 1928), p. 91; John E. Edgerton, "Annual Address of the President," *Proceedings*, N.A.M. (1929), 23; *ibid.* (1925), 10; *Nation's Business*, XII (July, 1924), 36, 38; *ibid.*, XV (Dec., 1927), 62; *Proceedings*, N.A.M. (1923), 289; Prothro, *Dollar Decade*, pp. 204–5.

7 Charles A. Beard, "Democracy Holds Its Ground," *Harper's*, CLVII (Nov., 1928), 680; Edmund Wilson, "Mencken's Democratic Man," *New Republic*, Dec. 15, 1926, pp. 110–1; G. K. Chesterton, "Persecuting the Common Man," *American Mercury*, XXXVII (Jan., 1936), 71.

8 Felix Frankfurter, "Democracy and the Expert," *Atlantic*, CXLVI (Nov., 1930), 650; Archibald MacLeish, *The Irresponsibles, A Declaration* (New York: Duell, Sloan & Pearce, 1940), pp. 15–6; William F. Borah, "Democracy Has Not Failed," *Fortnightly Review*, CXXX (Aug., 1928), 161.

9 Evans, "Klan's Fight for Americanism," p. 42; "Where Are the Pre-War Radicals?" *Survey*, Feb. 1, 1926, pp. 556–66; Lincoln Steffens, *The Autobiography of Lincoln Steffens* (New York: Harcourt,

Brace, 1931), p. 802; *Moses in Red* (Philadelphia: Dorrance, 1926), pp. 10–11; Granville Hicks, "Lincoln Steffens: He Covered the Future," *Commentary*, XIII (Feb., 1952), pp. 147–55; Aaron, *Writers on the Left*, pp. 126–30.

10 William Phillips, "What Happened in the 30's," *Commentary*, XXXIV (Sept., 1962), 204–6; Howard Zinn, "Emancipation from Dogma," *Nation*, April 4, 1966, p. 385.

11 *Daily Worker*, Mar. 5, 1933; *New Masses*, VIII (April, 1933), 3–13; Aaron, *Writers on the Left*, p. 156; also see *Writers Take Sides* (New York: League of American Writers, 1938) for a collection of statements by American writers on the Spanish Civil War. Of the 418 writers who gave their views, 410 strongly favored the Loyalists, 7 took no positive stand, and only one author, Gertrude Atherton, sided with Franco. The list included many prominent writers such as Ernest Hemingway, Thornton Wilder, Edgar Lee Masters, Fanny Hurst, Maxwell Anderson, John Steinbeck, etc.

12 John Dewey, "Imperative Need: A New Radical Party," *Common Sense*, Sept., 1933, *Challenge to the New Deal*, pp. 269–73; *Nation*, Dec. 14, 1932, p. 585; John Dewey, "Impressions of Soviet Russia," *New Republic*, Nov. 28, p. 41.

13 Keynes, "Soviet Russia," p. 246; Irving Howe and Lewis Coser, *The American Communist Party* (New York: Praeger, 1962), pp. 300–1; "Trotsky Appeal," *Literary Digest*, Mar. 20, 1937, p. 13; Hicks, *Where We Came Out*, pp. 70–9; Richard Crosman, ed., *The God That Failed* (New York: Harper, 1949), pp. 115–62, 196–228; Draper, *Roots of American Communism*, pp. 300–2; Lewis Corey, "Marxism Reconsidered," *Nation*, Feb. 17–Mar. 2,

1940, pp. 245–8; 272–5, 305–7.
14 From *transition* (Paris, 1928), pp.

100–1, reprinted in Aaron, *Writers on the Left*, p. 140.

## Chapter Six: The Modern Ethic

1   Henry F. May, *The End of American Innocence* (New York: Knopf, 1959), pp. 219–332; *Nation*, Sept. 4, 1913, p. 205; John Flynn, "American Revolution: 1933," *Scribner's*, LXLIV (July, 1933), p. 2.

2   Henry L. Mencken, "The Flapper," *Smart Set*, XLV (1915), 1–2; cf. Bruce Bliven, "Flapper Jane," *New Republic*, Sept. 9, 1925, pp. 65–7.

3   Fitzgerald quoted in Kazin, *On Native Grounds*, p. 193; John Dos Passos, *1919* (New York: Harcourt, Brace, 1932), p. 200; Ezra Pound, "Hugh Selwyn Mauberley," *Personae* (New York: New Directions, 1926), p. 191.

4   Lewis, *Main Street*, p. 265; Randolph Bourne, "Twilight of Idols," *The Seven Arts*, II (Oct., 1917), 700–2.

5   Sigmund Freud, *The Standard Edition of the Complete Psychological Works of Sigmund Freud* (London: Hogarth, 1953), IX, 193–204; XI, 223.

6   Harold Stearns, "The Intellectual Life," *Civilization in the United States* (New York: Harcourt, Brace, 1922), pp. 147–8.

7   Sigmund Freud, *Civilization and Its Discontents* (London: Hogarth, 1963), p. 23.

8   Viola Paradise, "The Sex Simplex," *Forum*, LXXIV (July, 1925), 108–11; David Seabury, "The Bogey of Sex," *Century*, CXIV (Sept., 1927), 528–31; *New York Times*, Oct. 2, 1925, p. 22; Aug. 7, 1925, p. 4; July 28, 1924, p. 1.

9   George Jean Nathan, "The New View of Sex," *American Mercury*, XI (April, 1926), 492–4.

10  George Jean Nathan, "Psycho-Osteopathy," *American Mercury*, XII (July, 1927), 369; "Confessions of an Ex-psychoanalyst," *New Republic*, Mar. 24, 1926, p. 139; Harvey O'Higgins, *The American Mind in Action* (New York: Harper, 1924).

11  Grace Adams, "The Rise and Fall of Psychology," *Atlantic*, CLIII (Jan., 1934), 84–6; Stephen Leacock, "Manual of the New Mentality," *Harper's*, CXLVIII (Mar., 1924), 471–80; G. K. Chesterton, "The Game of Psychoanalysis," *Century*, CVI (May, 1923), 34–43; Aldous Huxley, "Our Contemporary Hocus-Pocus," *Forum*, LXXIII (Mar., 1925), 313–20.

12  C. E. M. Joad, "Psychology in Retreat," *New Statesman and Nation*, IX (1935), 956; Adams, "Rise and Fall of Psychology," p. 92.

13  F. Scott Fitzgerald, *The Crack-Up* (New York: New Directions, 1945), pp. 13–22, 69–74 (originally written in 1931 and 1936); Walter Lippmann, *A Preface to Morals* (New York: Macmillan, 1929), p. 17.

14  Dell, *Intellectual Vagabondage*, pp. 235–61; Freud, *Works*, XIV, 385, 287.

15  Frederick J. Hoffman, *The Twenties: American Writing in the Postwar Decade* (New York: Viking, 1949), p. 272.

16  William Pepperell Montague, "The Promethean Challenge to Religion," *New Republic*, Aug. 6, 1924, p. 295; Herbert Croly, "Re-

generation," *ibid.,* June 9, 1920, pp. 40–7; Kirtley F. Mather, "The Scientist Bends the Knee," *ibid.,* Sept. 9, 1925, p. 73; Alfred North Whitehead, *Process and Reality* (New York: Macmillan, 1929), p. vi; Whitehead, *Science and the Modern World* (New York: Macmillan, 1925), p. 298.

17 Lippmann, *Preface to Morals,* pp. 125–7; Whitehead, *Science and the Modern World,* p. 166.

18 C. E. Ayres, *Science, the False Messiah* (Indianapolis: Bobbs-Merrill, 1927); Karl Menninger, "Pseudo-Analysis: Perils of Freudian Verbalism," *Outlook,* July 9, 1930, pp. 363–5; W. Beran Wolfe, "The Twilight of Psychoanalysis," *American Mercury,* XXXV (Aug., 1935), 385–94. For the effect of Freud on American writers see Frederick J. Hoffman, *Freudianism and the Literary Mind* (Baton Rouge, La.: Louisiana State Univ. Press, 1957).

19 Harry Emerson Fosdick, "Are Religious People Fooling Themselves?" *Harper's,* CLXI (June, 1930), 59–70; A. Clutton-Brock, "Evil and the New Faith," *Atlantic,* CXXXI (Mar., 1923), 298–308. For a thorough study of liberal theology and social reform in this period see Donald B. Meyer, *The Protestant Search for Political Realism, 1919–1941* (Berkeley: Univ. of California Press, 1960).

20 Reinhold Niebuhr, *Moral Man and Immoral Society* (New York: Scribner's, 1932), *passim.*

21 Allen, *Only Yesterday,* p. 242.

## Epilogue: War and the American Dream

1 Hofstadter, *Age of Reform,* pp. 272–5; H. C. Styrett, "The Business Press and American Neutrality, 1914–17," *Mississippi Valley Historical Review,* XXXII (Sept., 1945), 215–30; William E. Leuchtenburg, "Progressivism and Imperialism: The Progressive Movement and American Foreign Policy, 1898–1916," *ibid.,* XXXIX (Dec., 1952), 496; Randolph Bourne, "The War and the Intellectuals," *The Seven Arts,* II (June, 1917), 133–46.

2 John Dewey, "Aid for the Spanish Government," *Christian Century,* Mar. 3, 1937, pp. 14–24; I. F. Stone, "1937 Is Not 1914; Case Against Isolation," *Nation,* Nov. 6, 1937, pp. 495–7; Lewis Mumford, "Good Will Must Act," *Fight,* VI (Feb., 1939), 22–3, 26; Max Lerner, "Behind Hull's Embargo," *Nation,* May 28, 1938, pp. 607–10; Malcolm Cowley, "Abyssinia and Spain," *New Republic,* Feb., 16, 1938, pp. 50–1; Archibald MacLeish, "Arms and the Men," *Fortune,* Mar., 1934, pp. 53–7, 113–4, 116–7, 118, 120, 125–6; and "The Irresponsibles," *Nation,* May 18, 1940, pp. 618–23; "Hucksters of Death," *New Republic,* Mar. 7, 1934, pp. 88–9; "What Are We Waiting For: Declare War on the Axis," *ibid.,* Nov. 10, 1941, pp. 603–4.

3 For the business attitude toward war, I have relied heavily upon Roland N. Stromberg, "American Business and the Approach of War, 1935–1941," *Journal of Economic History,* XIII (Winter, 1953), 58–78. *Business Week,* Nov. 11, 1939, editorial; *ibid.,* Aug. 31, 1935, p. 32; *Wall Street Journal,* Oct. 31, Nov. 8, 1935; *Magazine of Wall Street,* Oct. 10, 1936, p. 750; *Nation's Business,*

Mar. & April, 1941, editorials; cited by Stromberg, "American Business and the Approach of War," pp. 63, 65–6, 67, 73–4, 61.

4  Merle Curti, *Peace or War* (New York; Norton, 1936), pp. 263–8.

5  *Iron Age*, June 1, 1939, p. 48; Stromberg, "American Business and the Approach of War," pp. 69, 74–5.

6  Stromberg, "American Business and the Approach of War," p. 75; Malcolm Cowley, "The End of the New Deal," *New Republic*, May 31, 1943, p. 731.

7  79th Cong., 2nd sess., Senate Document 206, *Economic Concentration and World War II* (Washington: Gov't. Printing Office, 1946), pp. 27, 29, 31, 37, 39, 51; Stromberg, "American Business and the Approach of War," p. 78.

8  Herbert Agar, "The War Is Worth Fighting!" *American Mercury*, LI (Dec., 1940), 404; Lewis Mumford, "Corruption of Liberalism," *New Republic*, April 29, 1940, pp. 568–73.

9  Rexford G. Tugwell, "Frightened Liberals," *New Republic*, April 26, 1939, pp. 328–9; H. Coggins, "Planning for a Better War," *Forum*, CII (Aug., 1939), 81; Mumford, "Corruption of Liberalism," p. 573; Robert Hutchins, "America and the War," a radio address given over a coast-to-coast network of the National Broadcasting Co. on Jan. 23, 1941.

10  W. H. Chamberlin, "War—Shortcut to Fascism," *American Mercury*, LI (Dec., 1940), 392, *Times* quoted, 395; Cowley, "End of the New Deal," p. 732.

11  Alan Valentine, "Intellectuals on Trial," convocation address, reprinted in *Vital Speeches*, Nov. 15, 1939, p. 78; O. G. Villard, "Death of Our Humanity," *Christian Century*, Nov. 19, 1941, p. 1441.

12  Denis W. Brogan, "Capitalism and War," *Harper's*, CLXXIII (July, 1963), 147; Elmer Davis, "We Lose the Next War," *ibid.*, CLXXVI (Mar., 1938), 345–6; Eliot Janeway, *The Struggle for Survival* (New Haven: Yale Univ. Press, 1951), p. 361; Eisenhower's speech reported in *New York Times*, Jan. 18, 1961, 22:4.

13  Tugwell, "The New Deal," p. 425.

14  Rexford G. Tugwell, "America's War-Time Socialism," *Nation*, April 6, 1927, p. 365; William E. Leuchtenburg, "The New Deal and the Analogue of War," *Change and Continuity in Twentieth-Century America*, John Braeman, *et al.*, eds. (New York: Harper, 1966), pp. 91, 106, 129.

15  "Force and Ideas," *New Republic*, Sept. 20, 1939, pp. 172–3.

16  John Maynard Keynes, "The World's Economic Outlook," *Atlantic*, CXLIX (May, 1932), 525.

| | | | | |
|---|---|---|---|---|
| | | | | |
| | | | | |
| | | | | |
| | | | | |
| | | | | |
| | | | | |
| | | | | |
| | | | | |
| | | | | |
| | | | | |
| | | | | |
| | | | | |
| | | | | |